# JOHN CARTER

# SOLDIER, BUSINESS TYCOON, POLITICIAN

# JOHN CARTER

## SOLDIER, BUSINESS TYCOON, POLITICIAN

Harry Hurst, Jr.

JOHN CARTER: SOLDIER, BUSINESS
TYCOON, POLITICIAN







This is a work of fiction. All the characters, organizations, and events portrayed in the novel are products of the author's imagination or are used fictitiously. Any references to persons, organizations, events or places are totally coincidental.

Printed in the United States of America.

ISBN    978-1-64552-037-5    (Paperback)
ISBN    978-1-64552-038-2    (Digital)

Lettra Press books may be ordered through booksellers or by contacting:

Lettra Press LLC
30 N Gould St. Suite 4753
Sheridan, WY 82801
1 307-200-3414 | info@lettrapress.com
www.lettrapress.com

*John Carter: Soldier, Business Tycoon, Politician*

**by Harry Hurst**
**Lettra Press**

To General John Carter, it's just like any other day: his 5 AM alarm went off, he made himself coffee, took his pills, and watched the morning news. He couldn't go for his morning run this particular day, but that isn't the only part of his morning that's sticking out. Just the day before, he was in his Tampa, Florida office at the Special Operations Center Command. A phone call from the Chief of Staff of the US Army has him in Washington DC less than 24 hours later. He is to meet the President in a few hours, for a reason he will be told of when he gets there.

Now in the Oval, and in front of four other higher-ranking generals, the President asks John to undertake his most crucial task yet: to go against all odds with a small team to find and destroy that one person responsible for the terrorism that his country is always in danger of. Having taken the oath at only 17, and having lived by it his entire life, his devotion to his country, family, and friends is shown as he accepts the challenge and becomes a political leader for the community he loves.

This novel by Harry Hurst, Jr. about a very dedicated middle-aged public servant being entrusted at this time of his life by the Commander-in-Chief of protecting and defending the nation is a gold mine of life lessons. It speaks both to those who have always been deemed responsible enough to handle the hardest errands, and to those who always thought themselves as not meant for the limelight. Regardless of one's experiences, the most common response to being endowed with a make or break duty is to stop and consider all visible and invisible angles and not just charge without spending appreciable amounts of time deciding things. This book helps one realize that grit and tenacity are admirable traits, but are not all that are needed to fully face challenges head-on. In this gripping work, we are taught that trust in oneself, and the desire for the greatest good, among others, are equally important qualities one must possess for a truly fulfilling endeavor.

# Part One

# CHAPTER 1

The alarm went off at 5 AM. John stopped the alarm and sat up in bed. He got out of bed and walked to the coffee pot and started the coffee. John then turned on the TV to the news and sat back down on the edge of the bed. He was hurting a little and he hated that. John reached for the pills he always took and swallowed two of them. The coffee was ready, and John got a cup and sat back down. He was again in Washington D.C. and in 4 hours he was to meet the President of the United State in the Oval Office. John had no idea why.

The day before, John had been in his office in Tampa, FL at the Special Operations Center Command. He received a telephone call from General Ledford, the Chief of Staff of the United States Army and was told to be in Washington at 9 AM the next day to see the President. The General had said "John you will be told why when you get here" and hung up. That had been less than twenty-four hours ago. John was now awake and ready for his morning routine. He would not be able to run this morning, but he did do to his normal push-ups, sit ups and stretching exercises. After his exercise, John shaved and then got into the shower. John always took a very hot shower for exactly three minutes, then cooled down the water to almost cold and stayed in that water for five minutes. John got out and looked at his reflection in the mirror. He thought "not bad for a guy in his fifties". John then got his dress uniform out and started the process of getting dressed. He loved the new material that the uniform was made of. It absolutely did not wrinkle, and John could pack it in a "jump bag" along with his boots and shirts and tie. John put on his pants, shirt, tie, and his Jump Boots. The boots were as highly shinned as Patent leather. The last thing John put on was his uniform coat. He had his hat in his hand. John looked into the mirror, and liked what he saw.

John was a very impressive officer. Hell, he was a 2 Star General Officer, Major General. He had so many awards and decorations he could barely get all of them on his left breast pocket. He had ten overseas bars on his right sleeve. The decorations started with the Combat Infantryman's Badge. John had that, and it had two stars above the bar, between the wreaths. He had been awarded that three times for three different wars. Then came the Congressional Medal of Honor (CMH). Then four Silver Star awards, then three Bronze Star awards, next three Purple Heart awards, and then numerous other decorations and various campaign ribbons. John was most proud of the Good Conduct Medal he had been awarded. Only enlisted personnel could receive that award and John had one and very few Officers had that award. To John it was a badge of honor. John approved of his appearance including his freshly cut hair. He had a very short crew cut, and had worn that hair style since he had been seventeen years old. The only time he had long hair was when he was required to do so for a mission. John had been in Special Operations since 1979. John turned slightly and checked the Ranger Tab on his left shoulder and the Special Operations patch. Then he turned the other direction and checked the combat patch. It was the patch of the 82nd Airborne Division. John wore that patch out of respect. That unit was his very first and the one he served with in Viet Nam. John could wear other combat patches be he always stayed with the 82nd. John was totally satisfied with his appearance. He left the room and went to the coffee shop and ordered breakfast.

The breakfast arrived, and John started to eat. John's mind drifted back over his life. John had been born in Houston Texas in 1953. His parents had a son, Ray that was six years older than John and a daughter, Linda that was three years older. The family lived in Houston and John's father had a very successful oil field and industrial supply business. It was one of the biggest supply companies in Texas in 1961. John remembered 1961 because that was when his parents died in a plane crash. John, Ray and Linda went to live with their grandparents in Hallettsville, Texas which is between Houston and San Antonio Texas. John's grandfather owned a twenty thousand acre working ranch. The ranch had cattle, but it also and most importantly had oil and natural gas. There were 1800 producing oil wells and 400 producing gas wells on the property. John's grandparents were billionaires and John, Ray and Linda were millionaires with what they had been left by their parents. The inheritance was available to each of them on their 21st birthday. John had inherited $38 million dollars when he turned twenty-one. The same amount went to his brother and sister.

John had a very hard time growing up and was a very unhappy child. He just stayed in trouble and really hated living in Hallettsville. Ray had done well. He graduated and went to the University of Texas. Ray got a BA Degree in Business then went to UT Law School and got a Law Degree. Ray worked with John's Grandfather running his business interests and the ranch. Linda had also done well, and she had attended Texas Tech University and graduated with a degree in accounting. Linda had met and fallen in love with a cowboy in her last year in college. John always called Miles a cowboy, but Miles' parents owned a forty-thousand-acre ranch in West Texas, outside of Midland, Texas. It too, had oil and gas. Linda had two children, a boy and a girl. Ray had gotten married to his high school sweetheart Donna, after they reunited, when Ray came back to Hallettsville, and they had a boy and a girl. John was single. John called the waiter and ordered some more coffee. When the coffee arrived, John drifted back into thought. John had finally graduated from high school and immediately enlisted in the US Army. He had been seventeen years old. John had gone to parachute "Jump School" training and been assigned to the 82nd Airborne Division at Ft. Bragg. In 1972 John went to Viet Nam. John had been in an infantry battalion and was in the recon platoon. After nine months in Viet Nam, John had the worse day of his life. John had been in combat over and over, but the fire fights had not lasted very long. He had already received one Silver Star award and one Bronze Star award and had received one Purple Heart award for a wound he had received. The wound was not very bad, and John had returned to his recon unit in two days. John was now a Sergeant and in charge of a six-man recon element. His recon unit had been attached to B Company of the 187th infantry battalion of the 82nd and the company was on a search and destroy mission in the highlands. The morning was typical of Viet Nam, hot and muggy as Hell. The company was approaching a hill and John was sent forward to recon the area with his unit of six men. John remembered well it was 9 AM. John and his unit saw what they thought were Viet Cong half way up the hill side dug in along a trail. John reported this back to the company commander. John was told to hold in place until the company arrived. As the company started up the hill all Hell broke loose. Artillery and mortar fire started coming in on the company. Then about 200 hundred North Vietnamese Regular Army soldiers attacked the company from two sides. John watched as the company took tremendous losses. It was then that John's recon unit got attacked. Three men in his unit died immediately and he along with the other two men were wounded. John was hit in the right side and he knew he had broken ribs. John attacked the eight enemy soldiers coming at his position and killed all of them. John then moved down the hill and attacked a machine gun position killing another six enemy. John continued to move toward the enemy soldiers from behind and killed another five before he was hit in the left leg just above the knee. John knew his leg was broken and he could not walk. John moved to a position of cover and using a machine gun he had retrieved from one of the dead infantrymen he fired on the oncoming enemy and killed another sixteen enemy. The enemy then stopped the attack. John had killed thirty-five enemy soldiers and there was no way of knowing how many he had wounded in the fire fight. John was taken down the hill and put on a Medevac Helicopter and sent to the hospital. After a month in the hospital John was sent back to the United States and was in Brooks Army Hospital in San Antonio, Texas for the next three months recovering. In 1974 John Carter was awarded the Congressional Medal of Honor. John was again promoted to the rank of Staff Sergeant and in 1975 he was honorably discharged from the United States Army. In 1975 John entered Texas A&M University and graduated in 1979 with a degree in Mechanical Engineering and a commission in the Regular Army as a Second Lieutenant. John was again back at Ft. Bragg. During his college time John had been allowed to attend Ranger School and received his Ranger Tab. He also attended Helicopter flight school during the summer of this junior and senior year and received his piolet wings. John was ready to go see the President and he was not feeling very good about it. John left the coffee shop and got into his staff car and headed for the White House. It was 8:15 AM.

# CHAPTER 2

ohn was admitted through the gate by the secret service uniformed guards and was directed to the north door of the White House. John arrived and exited the staff car. John walked into the White House and after showing his ID, was escorted to the Oval Office. John was asked to sit, and he did. After about fifteen minutes a lady opened the door and said "General the President will see you now. This way please." John got up and followed the lady into the Oval Office. The door shut behind him. John walked to the front of the desk and saluted the President. The President returned the salute and said "General, thank you for coming. May I call you John?"

John said "Of course, Mr. President."

The President said, "OK I believe you know these other officers so have a seat." John looked at the Generals sitting and yes, he knew all four of them. It was Ledford, Nathan, the commander of Special Operations and technically John's boss, Davis, the head of Army Intelligence and Watson, the Commander of Special Forces. John sat down. He was the lowest ranked General in the room. All the other Generals were four stars.

The President said "John we, the country, has a very big and unique problem. I have this problem and I think every American citizen has the problem. It is terrorists. The new wave of fighting is no longer Army against Army, but this terrorist threat we have everywhere in the world. There is only one man who controls all of this. He has the money to keep all the individual groups going, and the aim is to eventually have them all come together and rule the world.

I am not making this up, John. It is true. Now here is my problem. I do not fully trust the CIA, FBI, NSA and anyone else that is supposed to be doing all the work on finding him and bring him to justice. Hell, I do not want him brought to justice, I want him dead and all his organization wiped out. My problem with all the people I mentioned is that they cannot or will not keep things secret. There always is a leak to the media or someone and that I cannot have. John, I know your record. You have been in the military since you were seventeen years of age. Hell, you have won every award the country has to give and many of them more than once. You served in Viet Nam, Granada, Panama, Lebanon, Somalia, other parts of Africa, the Gulf War, Bosnia, various areas of South and Central America, and in Afghanistan and Iraq. I do not know of any one person that knows more about terrorists than you do John. That is why you are here." The President paused and waited. John did not say a word and after about a minute the President said "I need you to organize a special team. I mean a small team I do not know exactly how many people but as small as possible to find this person and kill him and destroy his organization completely. The task is daunting I know. I wish we could use our regular troops, but we cannot. Congress would go crazy. Our allies would also go crazy and the American people would probably want to tar and feather me. So, you have been chosen to do this thing. My question is, will you, do it?"

John sat for a good minute and then he said "Mr. President I will gladly take on this mission, however I am going to have to have only certain people I can use and trust. I am also going to have to have immediate contact with you 24/7 without going through all the normal bullshit staffers and aids. Then I am going to have to have one and I mean only one contact in the Pentagon who I can have do what I need done when I need it done. I realize this is asking a lot but, Mr. President, this is the only way it will get done. Also, as I see it, I will need other contacts. I need to feel I can get them no matter who they work for. Mr. President, if I have that I will do the job. I cannot and would not give you a time table but once we get moving on this thing I will be able to give your source updates, so you personally know what the progress is. I also want it clearly understood by the Generals here that I do not work for them and I do not mean any disrespect to them. I must have the ability to do what I do best, and I cannot be encumbered by any oversight by anyone other than you of course, Sir." There was silence in the room for a few minutes.

The President said "John you have what you want. I totally trust the men in this room and there is only one other person I trust. My brother Ted. He is running the business and is based in Houston, Texas. He and he alone will be your contact to me. I cannot trust anyone else to do this. Also, the men here will each give you one person they trust with their lives to be your contact to them if needed. You will be able to go direct in most cases because you are military, and military can, and dose talk to military. I am also promoting you to Lieutenant General, so you will now be wearing three stars. No one can know anything. I only have two years left in office, but I am going to talk to whoever comes into the office after me and explain the situation to them. I am sure they will continue to support this effort until it is finished. John, I personally thank you for taking this on. I could not have it done without you and I mean that. I know you will also keep things secret even in your family." The President then said, "Gentlemen thank you for this." Each officer rose and saluted and then left the Oval Office. Outside in the hallway, General Ledford said "We all need to meet in my office at 1800 (6 PM) tonight. Each officer said, "Yes Sir". The Generals including John left the White House and each got into a staff car and went their separate ways. They would have until 6 PM and it was just after 10 AM. John went directly back to the hotel.

John called room service and ordered six beers and a sandwich sent to his room. He had changed out of his dress uniform and was now in his Battle Dress Uniform (BDU) and feeling almost overwhelmed at the situation he was in. John opened a beer as soon as it arrived and laid out on the bed and sipped the beer and thought. John finished the beer opened another one and ate half of the club sandwich. He then took out his laptop computer and started to compile a list of the type personnel he would be needing. The list was longer than he had expected when he was finished, but John knew he was going to need these people to do the mission. John had listed Shooter's. Armorers. Piolets. Supply people. Mechanics. Weather expert. Intelligence people. Medical persons. Computer specialist (Hacker). Women. John was as ready as he could be for the meeting that afternoon. John then took a very good nap and at 3 PM he awoke and went down to the spa and pool. At 4:30 PM John returned to his room and dressed for the meeting. It had been decided that civilian attire would be worn because dinner was planned after the meeting and in Washington, that many General Officers together would always get media coverage. The media really did not know the Generals without seeing them in uniform. At 5 PM John went down to the lobby and then out to his staff car and headed for the Pentagon. John arrived and was allowed entrance and was at the Chief of Staff's office at 5:55 PM. John was immediately escorted into the Chief's office. John was the first General to arrive. John sat and waited. The other Generals were all there by 6:05 PM and the Chief of Staff came into his office at 6:10 PM. The meeting started.

Ledford started by saying "John how in the Hell do you figure on pulling this little deal off?"

John said "Well General, it is going to take one Hell of a lot of Intel work and a bunch of luck. I have made a list of the type of people I will need, and I have a good many names in mind for the slots. My one problem is that one of the people I must have is doing five years in Federal prison and I need him out today. Can we swing that little detail?"

Ledford said "John yes the President can do that. What is next on this list of yours?"

John said "I am going to raid Special Operations and Special Forces commands, but I am only taking a few people. I do Sir, need you to have LTC Sandy Martin transferred from Germany immediately and assigned to me. By the way, General how in the Hell are we going to have these people assigned?"

General Nathan, head of Special Operations said "John that is the easy part. They are all going to be assigned to me then I lend them to you but just not on paper."

John said "Good, Sir." The meeting went on for about another ninety minutes and John told the Generals he had decided to base the operation in Houston, Texas. They discussed the location and then said they agreed. The meeting was over and the men all went to dinner. During the dinner nothing was discussed about any part of the new operation. The men talked about the news and about what they were planning to do when they retired. They also talked about who was the best person in the Pentagon for a contact. They decided on one individual they all knew. June Pride! June had been at the Pentagon for over twenty-five years and was a civilian GS 12 level which is equal to a Colonel in the military. June ran the administration division of the Pentagon and was a person that never under any circumstances said a word to anyone. She had been cited for contempt of congress a few times over the years, but nothing ever came of it. It was decided she would be the go to in the Pentagon if John had a need to get someone on the line. The dinner finished, and each man said good bye and left. John went back to his hotel and relaxed for a while then went to bed. The next day he would go back to Tampa and clear out his office. Then he would clear his quarters and head to Houston. John was not looking forward to having to find a new place to live and all the crap that went with it. He was also going to have to change his banking and maybe his cell phone. He knew damn well he would have to get a new internet connection. John called his brother Ray and told him he was coming for a brief visit. Ray asked when and John said, "In two days if that is alright?" It was. The next morning John was back at Tampa at 11 AM and getting things done. John finished his office and went to his quarters. The military movers were scheduled for that afternoon and John waited for their arrival. The movers finished, and John drove to the hotel and got his room. The auto haulers would be there at 6 AM to pick up John's car and take it to Houston and store it until he was ready. John was leaving on a flight to Houston at 9 AM. Ray was sending a jet to pick John up at the airport and fly him to Hallettsville. John was happy to know he would probably get to see his sister as well and he was always glad to see his grandmother. John's grandfather had died three years before, and his grandmother was not in the best of health. John was glad he would have a few days.

# CHAPTER 3

John spent two days in Hallettsville and Linda came down to see him along with the children and Miles. John enjoyed the visit and he spent a lot of time with his grandmother. He returned to Houston and planned to spend the next few days finding an apartment and getting his belongings delivered. His car was delivered the morning he arrived from Hallettsville. John now started looking for an apartment and immediately ran into a major problem. Every apartment complex he went to required not only identification that could be verified but a total background and credit check. John saw the immediate red flag and he knew things had to be changed. John called Washington and had General Ledford call him back. In one hour, Ledford was on the phone and John explained the problem. Ledford told John to return to Washington the next day. John made the plane reservations and flew the next morning. John met with Ledford and General Davis the intelligence boss and they discussed the problem. John was told to return to Houston and in twenty-four hours he would be receiving a package delivered to him in Houston. John was to take a hotel and advise Washington where he would be staying. John returned to Houston and got a room at a hotel and waited. The next afternoon John had a knock on his hotel door. John opened the door and a man was standing there with a large manila envelope under his arm. The man said "General I am Dan Swift and I am a lawyer. May I come in?"

John said "Yes and shook Dan's hand. Dan and John sat, and John looked in the envelope and then said "Dan what the Hell is going on? And why did they send me a lawyer?"

Dan laughed and said "Sir, I am here to make you legal or at least to make it appear you are legal."

John said, "OK tell me about Dan Swift."

Dan said "I was a JAG attorney and left the military after six years and went to work for the Justice Department. I was then assigned to do legal work for the CIA. I have been doing that for the past six years. Now I am back at the Defense Department as a civilian and doing work for them. General Davis talked to me and asked if I was interested in a change and I said yes so here I am."

John said, "Dan do you have any idea what is going on?"

Dan said "No General. I was told if I was approved I would be informed. So here we sit."

John smiled and said "OK Dan, here is the deal and I know you have already been vetted or you would not be here. The only thing I can tell you is that if you tell anyone about this I will personally kill you and that is a promise."

Dan said "Understood." John then explained the situation to Dan and the problem John was having in renting anything.

Dan said, "I understand, and I can fix that in about two days."

John said "OK". Dan left and told John he would be getting back to him in two days. John started going through the envelope. It contained names, places, bank names, pictures and other information on the leader. The leader was code named "Solomon". John studied the information for the rest of the afternoon.

The next morning John received a phone call and was shocked to hear Don on the phone. Don Mc Cline had been the computer hacker John had requested to have released from federal prison. John told Don to get a plane and come to Houston and call John with his arrival time. John was liking the situation already. The President was a man of his word and John could get anything. John knew that was going to be the ticket to a successful mission. John received the call from

Don and he would arrive at 4 PM. John would pick him up. John had another call telling him that a bank account had been opened in his name at a particular bank and he was to draw money as needed for the immediate. John went to the bank and withdrew $5000. It worked as it was supposed to do. John arrived at the airport and met Don. John and Don had gone to college together and were good friends. Don had become a computer genius but had hacked the government computers in DC and was caught. John knew there was not a computer program in the world Don could not hack. That was why he needed Don. The men went back to John's hotel and Don got a room. John used his personal credit card for the room. John and Don went to the bar and had some drinks and talked. John did not say anything to Don about the mission and told him he would discuss things in the morning. Don was satisfied with that and really glad to be out of prison.

The next morning Don came to John's room and the men had about an hour talk. John explained the entire situation to Don and the men talked about how Don could help. After an hour or so John said "Don I will need a complete list of everything you are going to need as far as computers and all that stuff is concerned. I need it as soon as you can give it to me."

Don said, "I can do it now". Don took John's laptop and typed a detailed list of equipment and all the programs and things he would need. John e-mailed it to the special email account that had been set up. In less than three minutes John got an acknowledgement that his email had been received. He also got a delivery date of twety-four hours for the equipment to be in Houston. At 4 PM Dan knocked on John's door and when John opened it Dan came into the room pulling a suit case. John and Dan shook hands and Dan said "OK John here is everything you will need to open bank accounts, and get an apartment and an office location. I will go with you in the morning and we will get it done. Money will be transferred within one hour when we give the banking information."

John said, "OK and I want you to meet Don Mc Cline."

Dan said "Nice to meet you in person. I am the guy who got you out." Don and Dan shook hands and Don said "Thank you so much. Nice to meet you."

Dan said "Yes, it is nice to meet." John then listened as Dan explained the entire plan to him and to Don. Dan had set up a dummy corporation in Washington D.C that had been in business for ten years. John was the President and CEO. The corporation was called "Red Lion International Security Services, Inc." and was opening a new branch location in Houston, Texas. The corporation had a credit rating with Dunn and Bradstreet of AAA and had over $10 Million Dollars in the bank. John had a credit rating of 825 and his background was clear, and he also has a security clearance that would show up. Dan gave John a packet. John had a Texas driver's license and four credit cards that were $50,000 limited. His American Express was unlimited and platinum. Dan said that all other members of the team would have similar identification. Dan then told Don that Don would be creating the IDs as the members arrived and Dan showed Don were to get the necessary information from the computer site. John and Dan and Don went to the bar and then to dinner. John paid with his new American Express card.

The next day John and Dan went to the bank and opened two accounts. A personal one for John and a corporate one for Red Lion. John then went to four different banks and opened Red Lion accounts. Then John went to an apartment he liked and rented it. When John and Dan got back to the hotel, Don had already created his own new ID. The credit cards would be sent express mail that day and Don would have them in the morning. Don would then go rent an apartment but not in the same complex as John. John wanted the team to not live where he did. It was a security thing. No more than two members of the team could live in the same complex. That way no pattern could be established as to their movements.

The next morning John and Dan went to locate a place for the corporation to rent for a headquarters. John and Dan found the perfect location in Sugarland, Texas a suburb of Houston. The location was a warehouse complex that was only one year old. John and Dan looked it over and picked a perfect spot. The office part had eight individual offices and a large conference room. The hallway opened into the warehouse and John was leasing 50,000 square feet of space for warehouse and 20,000 square feet for the office part. The office and warehouse would be on the far end of the complex and there was a side gate that John made sure he would have control of. John signed the lease for a year with options to renew and paid the first year in advance. The owner was very happy and told John if there was anything needed please contact him immediately. John said he would and then John and Dan went $1/8^{th}$ of a mile to a private airport in Sugarland. The airport was big enough to land cargo jets and private jets. John rented three hangers one large and two medium size and again paid the lease for a year.

The next day John went to the utility companies and paid all required deposits. Dan rented him an apartment and Don also went to pay his utility deposits on the apartment he had rented. At noon John met Don and they went to the internet, phone, and TV Company and arranged service for the apartments and the office. Don told the company exactly what to install where and he also had a land line fax number installed at the office. John discussed the cell phone with the representative and John could get a plan for coverage anywhere in the world for everyone he wanted to put on it. John explained he would need about thirty phones and he would send his employees in over the next month or so to get the phone. The times were set for the installation and Don would be there to make sure things were done right at every location. Within three days everything was installed and working right. John had gotten the computer equipment delivered to the Red Lion office and now all he had to do was wait for the personnel to start arriving.

It took three weeks for everyone John had requested to arrive in Houston. As they arrived John met them and gave them an initial briefing on what he required them to do. Get an apartment, open bank accounts, making sure they were set up for direct deposit of funds from Red Lion, get new vehicles if required, buy civilian clothing, buy computers that Don would give them a list to use. Go get the cell phone set up for their own numbers, and learn as much as possible about the city. John also wanted each member to go immediately and have 6 passport photos taken using different dress for each photo. One in a suit and tie for men and the only female in a woman's business suit. The other photos were to be taken in a variety of clothing. These photos were to be delivered to the office immediately before anything else was done. John gave each one a packet with the new identity they would use for the banks and apartments. Once the apartments were rented and utility deposits were made the new address was to be given to the office, so the household goods could be delivered. John could see he was going to need clerical staff. He had not anticipated that requirement. John sent a message to the email drop and waited. In two hours he received a reply. Two civilian employees were going to be sent from the Pentagon in a week. They were both vetted at the highest levels and would handle all his needs. John was relieved. John could see the unit he was establishing getting bigger by the day. That was worrying him because the bigger the unit the more things could be leaked. John wanted to come up with a plan to make sure that did not happen.

A month had gone by since John had arrived in Houston and almost the entire unit was now in place. John had called for a meeting at 9 AM and wanted everyone to bring a notebook with them. Everyone was seated in the warehouse. John had rented chairs and two long tables for the event. John walked into the room and of course everyone stood at attention. John walked to the front of the room and said "Take your seats. This will be the very last time any of you will do that. We are now just a civilian company doing business. No military." The members understood. John then said "We are here to do one mission and one mission only! However, this is totally a volunteer assignment and after I finish if anyone wants to quit it is perfectly alright. Nothing will ever be placed in any records and you will be returned to your former units immediately. Now here is the only military thing I am going to say. I am a three star General and I have a bunch of power at my control. This mission is more than top secret it is so far beyond that it is funny. In the event any information about who we are or what we do, or anything ever get outside our circle the person who leaks the information will be found. Believe me they will be found. Then I personally will recommend to the President of the United States that that person be charged with High Treason against the United States and I will recommend immediate death. Do I make myself perfectly clear to you?"

Everyone said, "YES SIR".

John then said "Now here is our mission. There is one person in the world we have given him the code name "Solomon" who is furnishing 95% of all terror groups with money. He started in the Middle East and Africa because the tribal situation was already a hot bed. He has used the Muslim religion as his whipping boy so to speak and he has gotten these people all over the world to fight against the infidels, so he can say they are fighting a holy war. The man is evil, and his end game is to get as many of these radical groups fighting in as many places as he can. Then slowly he will consolidate all of them under his banner and control the whole world. No country or group of countries would be able to stop him. He would control 75 % of the oil, 80% of the food supply and God knows what other minerals and raw materials he would have. He would also get nuclear weapons from some of the countries that have them such as India and Pakistani and maybe even China depending on how bad it gets. So, the President has asked me to stop him by killing him and all his people in the command circle and to steal all of his money in every bank he uses. Nothing for a stepper, right? Well people that is our mission. As I said anyone can quit and it will not be held against you". John stayed in the front and watched as the members thought about what he had just told them. One man stood up and said "Sir, the way I understand it is that we are still in the Army on active duty and we will be paid according to our ranks, is that correct?"

John said "Yes that is exactly correct, except for this. As of the 1st of the month every soldier will be promoted one pay grade. You each will receive your standard Army pay with all benefits including housing and separate rations. These checks will be deposited in your accounts on the 1st and 15th of each month. They will be coming from Red Lion. On the 10th and 20th of each month a check will be deposited to your account for expenses, it will also come from Red Lion. The amount of that check will be determined as things progress, but I can tell you this it will be as much if not more as the amount of your pay check. The three, well actually four civilian's we have are special. The two ladies in our admin are the rank of GS-12 which is equal to a Colonel and the attorney is a SGS-2 equal to a Two Star General. The guy in the back with the beard down to his waist is a special case and he will be paid at a rate that we have determined." The operator sat down.

John said, "Now anyone want out?" No one moved. John said "Good. Now we will enjoy the rest of the day and get to know each other. We will be working together for as long as it takes".

John walked to the door of the warehouse and exited. He returned in a minute and lifted the large door and in came the caterers with food and drink. John had a complete bar set up in just a few minutes and a buffet set up in about 20 minutes. John said, "Ok now enjoy". Everyone started mingling around and talking with each other and drinking and eating. The group continued doing that for the next three hours.

# CHAPTER 4

The operation had been in place for a month. Supplies were being delivered daily to the warehouse. Don had gotten the satellite dishes and they had been installed on the roof of the warehouse. Red Lion now had capabilities to use US Government satellites and that was a great plus. It also gave John the ability to have live action feeds from anywhere in the world. The equipment was being stored in a section of the warehouse and all of the computers were now installed. The video surveillance cameras had been received and installed at Red Lion headquarters and at the airport covering the hangers. Complete security including badge entrance point had been installed. The basic headquarters was almost complete, and the warehouse section would be completed in a week. The aircraft were scheduled to arrive by the end of the month.

John was in his office looking at some reports about the different terrorist organizations throughout the world. It was looking like 6 major areas of concern would be the areas to concentrate all efforts for the initial work. John knew that was going to be a very long and hard process. John was buzzed by Nancy, his admin/receptionist and told he had visitors. John told her to have them come in and John walked toward the door to his office just as a very large black man entered and said, "General we are here to save your ass."

John immediately knew who it was, Jim Monroe. Monroe was 6 feet 6 inches tall and weighed 290 pounds and it was all muscle. He was a black man, but light skinned. John look at him and saw he was wearing a uniform with a Bridger General (1 Star) on his shoulder. John shook hands and had

Jim come into the office. Right behind Jim, was a short 5 feet 6-inch man, who weighed about 200 pounds. John knew right away who he was, Command Sergeant Major (CSM) Harry Hinds. John shook Harry's hand and had him come in as well. Both men sat, and John said, "What in the Hell are you two doing here?"

Jim said "Well, General we are here by order of the President to help you. I am your new second in command/Chief of Staff and the CSM is here to make damn sure things get done. I think his official title is CSM in Charge". Everyone laughed.

John said "I sure as Hell can use the help, but this whole deal was supposed to be kept small and totally covert. CSM I thought you were medically retired after the Afghan situation?"

Harry said, "Sir I was but the President called and asked me to come back to assist and of course I said yes."

John said, "And Jim, when did you get the star?"

Jim said, "One month to the day, Sir".

John said "I am just overwhelmed. I am now running a complete separate division of covert folks and we are almost ready to get going. This is going to be great. I think we need to do two things. First you guys need to get out of the military uniforms and secondly we need to go get some lunch and let me fill you in on how things work around here." All the men left the office and drove to the hotel where Jim and Harry were staying. Harry and Jim went up to their rooms and changed into civilian clothes. John had them get into his car when they came back down and they all went to lunch. During lunch, John explained to both new men all about how they would go about getting settled in Houston and what they would need to give the admin personnel. The lunch was over two hours and when John was finished both men were set to use the rest of the day and the next day to get things done. John dropped them back at their hotel and returned to the headquarters. He had a message from Washington waiting. His last member of the team, Lieutenant Colonel Tress Hunt would be arriving in three days. He had just returned from Iraq where he had been the assistant G-2 (Intelligence Officer) for the collation forces both operating in Iraq and in Afghanistan. John knew him well and had immediately requested him to lead all the intelligence for this mission. Tress was absolutely the best. John was looking forward to his arrival.

Two weeks had passed, and everyone was now in place. Tress had arrived and been briefed on what he had to do in Houston and was already planning and doing intelligence work. Jim was busy at getting the necessary things sorted out and making sure everything was ordered or had been received. Harry was doing his inspections and making sure everyone was doing their job. John was well pleased with the way things were working. John sat in his office and thought about Harry and Jim. Harry had been in Special Operations for about twenty-five years at least. His record was outstanding. Harry had been quite a soldier. He had six Silver Star medals, God knows how many Bronze Stars medals, five Purple Heart medals and he had been awarded the Congressional Medal of Honor. Harry had lost his left leg during the fight in which he received the CMH and then had been medically retired. The President, after being told by the Chief of Staff of the Army General Ledford to call Harry back for this mission, had personally called Harry and asked him to return to duty to help. Harry was delighted to be back in the thick of things. John was very glad to have him. John thought about Jim. Jim had been the Brigade Commander of the 75th Rangers and had been in the Rangers all most his entire career. Jim was a leader better than most John had ever encountered. Jim was also very damn smart and knew logistics better than anyone John had ever known. That was going to be vital to the success of the Red Lion operation and John was very pleased that Washington had recognized that.

John was now free to actually plan, and to study what had to be done and when it should be done. Tress knocked on John's door and John waved him in. Tress said "Sir, I have figured out where we need to hit as our first strike."

John said, "OK go on tell me who, where and why."

Tress said "The Who, is the Terrorist group operating in Thailand. The where is in Bangkok, and the why, is because they are right now the smallest and newest group that has come in to the picture. They have very limited leadership and even less name recognition. They have actually only done one act, bombing a night club, but the chatter says they are planning to do something big to make a statement."

John said, "Any idea when this statement is going to happen?"

Tress said "Sir, I think within the next month. That would make sense because of the annual celebrations in Thailand."

John said, "OK then plan what we need to do and let us go and do it, thanks." Tress said, "Yes Sir", and left. John was ready to start an operation. He would have the details in about twenty-four hours and then would sit with everyone and plan the actual operation. John could feel his body responding to the feelings of action. John loved the feeling and always had.

The next day John was told that Tress was ready for the initial briefing. John had Harry, Jim, the operators from "A" team, and Don all assemble in the planning room that had been created in a section of the warehouse. John walked into the room and took his seat. The other members of the team were already there. Tress started the briefing. "The group we are targeting is a small cell operating in Bangkok and is the newest of the terrorist elements to start to move beyond just small events. They are planning to stage a very large attack during the annual celebrations in Thailand. We have followed money from Switzerland that was placed into a bank account in Bangkok that they use. Don has tracked that part of the operation and he had the ability to take all the funds out of the account when we get ready. Now, we have identified the three major leaders of the group and in my opinion, without them, there will be no cell. I have given each of you the bio on the leaders. I feel the best way to eliminate this cell is to attack them directly at their headquarters which is just outside the capital. They have a farm type operation that is used for storing weapons, chemicals, and is where they usually do all the planning and prep work prior to the actual event. My suggestion is to use an assault at night and take out the entire area. The actual eliminating of the leadership would be a direct kill, then set explosive charges for the destruction of the entire farm and all buildings etc."

There was some discussion and then John said, "OK operators, how does this sound to you?"

The lead operator or unit leader, SGM Wayne Nelson, said "Sir, I see this as a simple action. We will need air support for our HALO jump and for extraction but everything else we can pre-position or bring with us. I think from seeing the aerial photos we will need about 200 pounds of C-4 and of course the primers and all of that. We will use our standard weapons silenced. We can actually use one of the vehicles there to evacuate to the pick-up point."

John said "OK then we go. Now Harry, you need to get with the Air Force and have our transportation laid on from Ellington. We will draw out ammo and explosives from Ft. Hood so have the supply people take a chopper there. You may want to ride along on this first deal. We have not tried it yet, but I am told we have the green light when we need it. Now Tress when do you suggest we do this thing?"

Tress said "Sir, I would say next Tuesday because that is the day before the celebrations start."

John said "Then it is a go for next Tuesday for the attack. I suggest the operators leave on Friday of the week before. Jim please set up whatever we need and let them know. Gentlemen, job well done. Thank you and Don pull the money on Tuesday so there is nothing left for anyone to get." John got up and left.

Everything went smoothly at Ft. Hood and Harry returned with all the ammo and explosives. The operators got things ready and double checked the parachutes and all the equipment then boarded a van and headed for Ellington AFB just outside Houston. A C-141 Star Lifter was waiting on the runway and the operators loaded the equipment and themselves on board and were wheels up at 9 PM on Friday. The operators would change into their jump suits in route. The flight would take about twenty-four hours with stops for fuel. The operations center at Red Lion was fully staffed and watching as the mission began. There was one change to the operation and John liked the change. The operators would drive to the commercial airport and take a commercial flight back to the US. The equipment, night vision, weapons and other things would be shipped under diplomatic seal from the airport to Houston on a commercial flight that Jim had arranged. The operators had a crate in their equipment and would put it together after the assault. They would then take it to the commercial shipping area of the airport and send it through customs and have it shipped to the US. Because the operators were carrying US Diplomatic Passports things would be good and no one would question a shipment marked Official. That was the plan and John hoped it would work.

At 8:45 PM Thailand time on Tuesday the operators jumped from the C-141 flying at 25,000 feet. The operators were on the ground and ready for the assault exactly at 9 PM. The team moved from one out building to another and cleared each building. The very last outbuilding was where the team found the bombs that had been made for the attack. Explosive charges were placed in each out building and the timers were set for one hour or 10:30 PM local time. As the team moved toward the main building one of the operators saw four men sitting on the steps in front. The team moved into a position and at the same instant fired and killed all four. The shots were never heard because of the silencers. The team then moved into a position and entered the building. There were six more men inside and all were instantly killed. The team searched the building and discovered some documents and maps and other items. These were placed in a bag and later would be loaded into the crate. The entire assault had taken less than twenty minutes from the first out building to the final search of the main building. Two operators assembled the crate and the others placed explosive charges in the main building. The team then moved the truck they had found to the front of the main building and after changing back into civilian clothes, loaded the crate and themselves into the truck and drove to the airport. The explosions went off as planned and the team could see the sky light up as they drove.

The airport was busy with people coming for the celebration. The team arrived at the commercial shipping section and unloaded the crate. The crate was sent through customs immediately and Nelson watched as it was loaded on a FEDEX Express plane. Then the team went to the gate and boarded the 11:45 PM flight to the US. They would have two stops, Philippines and Hawaii. They would change planes in Hawaii and have a direct flight to Houston. FEDEX was to deliver the crate to the Red Lion warehouse complex in two days. The mission was a complete success. Don came in and told John he had taken out $90 Million Dollars and had distributed it evenly to the four banks in Houston John had set up as holding accounts. Each bank was to hold money for 30 to ninety days then part of the money would be sent to Washington. The rest would be moved into the main operating account for Red Lion. John had an agreement that he would use half the funds recovered if he needed for the Red Lion operations and to pay expenses (Bonus) to the unit over and above their military pay. The President had approved so John was golden. John sent a classified message to the White

House that phase one was completed and successful. In one-hour John got a flash message saying, "Good Job, Thanks". John knew the President had been informed. John walked into the operations center and thanked everyone for a job well done. He then saw Harry and Jim and thanked them. John was very proud of the organization and how they had done the first mission. John knew this was the first of many and just hoped that they all would be as good.

# CHAPTER 5

The "A" team had returned, and the crate had arrived, and things were back to normal for John or pretty much. The "A" team was going to be off for a week and so were the armors and supply personnel. Don was working night and day on breaking bank security, but each bank was set up differently and so far, Don had not found one Trojan that would work on all of them. He was going to have to either create a separate Trojan for each or find the common thread. Don was as happy as John had ever seen anyone. A little marijuana, some wine and cheese and Don was in heaven. John just let him operate. Tress had a plan working for the people in Africa. There were three main groups that needed to be taken out and they were in three different parts of the continent. Tress estimated it would be at least a month before he could get a plan to present. John understood the problems and was studying a new problem that had just been sent by Washington. Pirates were high jacking commercial shipping along the coast of Somalia and demanding ransom from the shipping companies. Already 7 people had been killed in the high jacking operations. The US Navy was trying to assist but the area was huge and surface ships were almost of no use in trying to prevent the high jacking's. The source needed to be dealt with and that was on land in a foreign country and the US could not invade to stop the pirates. John informed Tress and he started gathering intelligence on the pirates. Somalia had been a trouble spot before and many US Army Rangers and Delta team members had been killed and wounded. It was also one of the targets on

Tress' terrorist list and to John's amazement Tress had already been planning an operation for Somalia.

Harry and Jim came into John's office and sat down. John said "OK CSM what is the problem?"

Harry said "General this situation is all fucked up with our training. We do not have a damn place to train our people or to sight our weapons or do a fucking thing we need to do, Sir".

John said "OK calm down Harry. What do we need? Can we use Ft. Hood for any of it?"

Harry said "Boss, I do not think we should use any military reservation for any of our stuff. We get enough strange looks at Hood when I had to pick up the ammo and explosives. Remember Soldiers are just like old women. The love to gossip." John broke out into a laugh and so did Jim.

Jim said "Sir, we do have a real problem. We need someplace we can jump, shoot and do house to house exercises. Things we will have to do for real and we do not have anywhere to do that."

John said "I understand. I will have to figure this one out. I also agree with you Harry. We do not need to be around anyone that may figure out what we are doing or even think they know what is going on. I worry about this place, but Houston is so big and growing so fast new business of all type is always springing up. Let me get back to you on this." The men nodded and left John's office. John sat back and thought about the problem. There was only one answer he could come up with and he was afraid he might have to get the President to approve that. John picked up the phone and call his brother Ray. Ray answered and after a minute or two John said "Ray I need you to come to Houston. Just you alone and I need you to bring a map of the whole property. Make damn sure it is marked with all the oil wells, gas wells and the pastures you are using for the cows. Also, any out buildings and shit like that."

Ray said, "OK John when do you need me to come?"

John said "As soon as you can. This is very important."

Ray said "I will be there in three hours. Can I land in Sugarland at that airport?"

John said, "Yes it can take your jet." Ray said, "See you in three, brother." John hung up and got ready for what he had to do.

Ray landed the Lear Jet as smoothly as it could land and taxied over to the hanger where John was standing. Ray got out of the plane carrying four large rolls of maps and hugged John. John said "Thanks for coming. I really need your help and not just me, the country needs you to help."

Ray said "God damn John you sound serious as Hell. What have you gotten yourself into this time?"

John said, "Get your ass in the car and I will show you wise guy." The men got into John's car and drove to Red Lion headquarters.

John and Ray were sitting in John's office when Harry, Jim and Tress came into the office. John introduced Ray to the men and then said, "OK Ray we need to borrow some of the family land for a few years."

Ray looked at John with a very puzzled look and said "OK explain that to me please. Borrow?"

John said, "Yes borrow or maybe lease." John then explained the problem he had about training and jumping and especially the shooting and house to house operational clearing of different type buildings and structures. John also told Ray that all of this had to be kept strictly secret no matter what. John along with Jim and Harry gave Ray a complete tour of Red Lion including the operations room and even so far as to show him Don's area where all the computer hacking took place. They were in the warehouse and Ray said "Damn John I would not believe this unless I saw it in person. Does anyone have any idea what Red Lion actually does?"

John said, "I sure as Hell hope not."

Ray said, "Well actually I do not know what you guys really do and I am happy with that."

John laughed and said "Ray my dear brother, you know more than you like to show. I know you are far from stupid and I also know you read the papers and watch the news every day. Let me put it to you this way. Sometimes people get into positions where the usual way of doing business is not available to them. We are the unusual way of doing business."

Ray said, "Alright what is your plan for our land, dear brother?"

John said, "Let's go into the operations room and lay out your maps." Everyone followed John into the operations room. John took the maps and laid them on the table. He looked at them and said "OK Ray show me a place about 200 acres of land we could use and be totally out of your way, so no oil or gas wells would be involved, and no cattle would be in the area. Also, some place that we could get equipment into to build things we need but not close to any major highway or roads that people travel."

Ray looked at the maps and studies them for a few minutes and said, "Here is what you need." Ray pointed to a spot on the far end of the ranch but still at least ½ of a mile from the property line. John looked at the spot and said "Perfect Ray. Now does it have anything under it like water?"

Ray said, "John how in the Hell would I know that?"

John said, "Well does not hurt to ask." The brothers smiled at each other and John said, "What do you guys think?", and pointed to Jim, Harry and Tress. Harry said, "It will be perfect I think but I would like to visually look it over".

Jim said, "I would also like to look at it with Tress and get his assessment of it for our use."

Ray said, "How about tomorrow?"

John said, "OK great we will be there".

Ray said "Alright, John I am heading back but I will see you in the morning. Land on the strip at the ranch or are you going to drive?"

John said, "We will probably come in a Black Hawk chopper."

Ray said "Good see everyone then and nice to meet all of you. John take care brother." Ray left and was driven back to the airport by one of the operators. John thanked everyone and went back to his office. He thought for a while and then decided to go have a drink. John had found a very nice little bar he liked and a young lady he liked that owned it. Houston was beginning to be a good place to live and work.

The next morning at 7 AM the Black Hawk lifted off and headed for Hallettsville and the ranch. The flight took a little over an hour and when the chopper landed, Ray was there with two vehicles to meet the group. Ray asked if they wanted to have coffee or breakfast before they went out and John said, "NO thanks we need to get after this."

Ray said, "OK we are on our way". Ray drove off the landing strip and followed a small road back to a paved road. He travelled down the paved road for almost thirty minutes then stopped. John's people got out of the vehicles and Ray explained about the road he was going to travel on. This would be the access road to the area and where the equipment would be brought in from. The group got back into the vehicles and started down the small road. Ray showed the land and pointed out some areas. The entire area would be very good for Red Lion. John was pleased, and Harry, Jim and Tress were excited about the prospects. Tress said "Sir, we could build about 10 different structures to train on in this area. I think it is perfect."

Harry said, "Sir we can build a range with target positions up to 2000 yards out."

Jim said, "Sir we can also use the acreage over to the west as a drop zone and we can actually build a small base here where we are standing."

John said, "I agree."

Ray said, "Is that all you need to see John?" John said only one more thing. Please drive to the end of the property."

Ray started driving as soon as everyone was back in the vehicles. The end of the property was just as John had remembered it. The property was divided by a river on the north side that ran the entire length of the 20,000 acers. John was glad no one had ever tried to divert the river. His would be very good for keeping people out of the area. The river would be one mile from the end of the 20-foot-high impact area of the firing range. The river would not interfere with the drop zone and in some ways, might become a good training tool. John told Ray they were through and Ray headed back to main house. When the group arrived at the main house Ray invited all of them to come in and have refreshments. John and Ray then went to Ray's office in the house and struck up a deal. John told Ray he wanted to lease three hundred acres, the extra would be a buffer, for $100 dollars an acre for the next five years and would pay the entire amount of the lease in advance. He also wanted written permission to build a firing range and to drill a water well and have utilities run to the property. He was also going to build a base building and training buildings. He would then secure the area with a fence so only one entrance would be used and that would be guarded 24/7. All of this would be in the name of Red Lion International Security Services. John would also give Ray a notarized paper stating that Ray and the ranch had no liability for anything that happened on the leased property and could not be sued for any reason and was held harmless. Ray told John to have the papers done and it was a deal. Ray got two beers and they both had a drink. Then John and Ray returned to the other men and then went back to the air strip and got on the Black Hawk and John and his group flew back to Houston.

John immediately called Dan and told him what legal papers would be needed. Dan said he could have everything ready the next day. John then called General Ledford and requested a meeting in Washington as soon as possible. John was told to be there in the Pentagon at 3 PM the next day. John got ready to present the idea and at 11 PM John had finished the proposal and had it printed and five copies made. John was ready to go home. The flight was scheduled for 8 AM the next morning and he had to be at Ellington AFB at 6 AM to get checked in and allowed on the plane. He was flying in an Air Force C-22, which was the military version of the Lear Jet. John was ready.

John landed in Washington at 11 AM and headed for his hotel. John got his room and went up and took a shower and lay down for a while. At 2 PM John got up dressed in a class "A" uniform and took a taxi to the Pentagon. John was permitted entry and escorted to the Army Chief of Staff's office. John was sent into the Chief's office immediately. After a few minutes of light discussion, Ledford said "OK John what is this all about?"

John said, "Sir I have a detailed plan I need approved by you or whoever needs to approve it so I can have a training center that we critically need".

Ledford said, "Show me." John took out his proposal and handed a copy to the Chief and then took out a map and lay it on the table. John then went over the complete proposal and he also explained why no military installation should be used. John also explained how John intended to finance the project using the money they had seized in Thailand. When John finished Ledford said "I am going to have to get this plan approved from higher up and you probably knew that. Did you get a room for tonight?"

John said, "Yes Sir I did".

Ledford said "Good then I will buy you dinner tonight at the Army and Navy club at 1900 hrs. (7PM).

John said, "I will see you then Sir, and thank you." John got up saluted and left the office. John had a staff car take him back to the Army and Navy club and John went to his room to rest. It was now 5 PM.

John was sitting in the bar when General Ledford arrived. The General came over and sat down and ordered a drink. John and Ledford talked about how things were working at Red Lion and then John said "Sir I need you to get me a meeting with the Commanding General of Ft. Hood. I need it as soon as possible and I need to make damn sure he understands to give me exactly what I need."

Ledford asked John to explain and John said "I need to get information on the range equipment he has and on some of the blueprints for ranges. I also want to get copies of his blueprints on his villages he has built for training".

Ledford said, "John that is a tall order without telling him why?"

John said "Sir, I know but it would save me about six months if I can get the stuff from him. Hell, they have already done all the work and I bet it took over two years for that to be approved."

Ledford said "Well I am the Chief of Staff so why not. He will know only that you are going to be building a special training center for Delta, how is that?"

John said, "Fine as long as General Nathan knows in front that it is a lie."

Ledford said "I will tell Wally do not worry about that. Now let's eat something I am starved". The two Generals went into the dining room and had dinner. After dinner John said good bye to Ledford and went to his room. Ledford said he would call John when he had an answer on the proposal. John was in bed and almost asleep when his phone rang it was midnight. John answered, and General Ledford said "John you have been approved at the highest level. It is a firm go. Good luck and your meeting at Hood is day after tomorrow at 11 AM. Wear your Class A and have everyone with you wear theirs."

John said, "Thank you Sir, very much." John hung up and went to sleep. The next morning John called the Air Force at 0600 (6AM) and had a C-22 set for a 9 AM flight back to Ellington.

John was back in Houston and called Jim and Harry into his office. John said "We got the go for our range and we are headed to Ft. Hood in the morning. Now gentlemen we wear our Class "A" uniforms. I will see you at Ellington at 6 AM. Bring any questions we need to have answered and make damn sure we do not forget anything. This is a one-shot deal and just follow my lead. I have no idea what lie the Chief of Staff told so we are playing everything by ear."

The plane landed at Ft. Hood and a staff car was waiting along with a police car. John and Jim got into the rear and Harry sat in the front and instantly the police car turned on the overhead lights and the siren and headed out the gate. John's staff car followed very closely behind. The ride was only about twenty minutes and the staff car pulled in front of post headquarters. The doors to the staff car were opened by three SGTs and all saluted. Everyone saluted Harry and John no matter their rank because of the CMH they wore. John and his group were escorted into the headquarters and went directly to the elevator and to the top floor. John got off the elevator and entered the main door marked Commanding General. Jim and Harry followed. The party was taken directly into the General's office and LTG Ben Wilson walked over to John, saluted him then saluted Harry and returned the salute Jim had given. Then Ben shook hands with all three men. John knew Ben Wilson and had for years. Ben had been the commanding general of the 4th Division when it went into Iraq. He had then been promoted to three stars and put in command of III Corps and Ft. Hood. He had been in that position for a year. Ben then introduced his second in command a Major General Evens and the head of the post engineering department a civilian and the head of contracting another civilian. Ben then ushered everyone into the conference room and had them sit down. Ben said, "OK John what can Ft. Hood do for you?"

John said, "I need some help and I hope Ledford explained things."

Ben said "Yes he did. He told me to give you every God damn thing you ask for and if you need anything in the future to make sure you had it. I have no idea what the Hell is going on and frankly I do not want to know. Ledford sounded like he would eat me for lunch if you had one problem and that is good enough for me."

John smiled and said "Ben it is not that scary. We have been tasked to come up with a special training facility and we need your help".

John turned to Harry and said "CSM tell the gentlemen what you need". Harry told then men what was needed, and the deputy said "CSM why don't you go with these two men to their offices and get exactly what you need. I will arrange a car. I will be back in a moment." The deputy left and Harry and Jim both got up and were ready to leave. The deputy came back and said "The car is waiting. Bill and Sam get everything they need and then come back here and do it fast." The two civilians nodded and headed toward the door. Harry and Jim followed. They both saluted Ben and the deputy and left. John and Ben and his deputy talked for a while about old times and about how Ft. Hood was doing. John was especially interested in the new Federal Police force. Ben explained that it was working very well, in fact better than having MPs on duty. John had some coffee and was waiting. Harry and Jim returned and had what they needed immediately. Plans and other information was going to be sent overnight that evening to Houston. Ben asked John why Houston and John said "Well that is where KBR is located, and they will be building the place, so Washington decided we needed to be there until everything was ready. Damn good TDY (Temporary Duty)."

Ben nodded and John thought" He does not believe one thing I am telling him, and I know it". The meeting was over, and everyone departed the Generals office and John, Jim and Harry got back into the staff car and were escorted back to the air filed and boarded the plane and went back to Houston. The next day Harry and Jim had everything they would need to start the ordering process. John called a friend he had made in Houston and asked him to meet John at Molly's bar that afternoon. Mike Allan said of course he would. John was to be there at 2 PM. John would also see the owner, Molly and that was a very good thing.

Mike was sitting at the bar when John walked into Molly's. John said hello to some of the people there and sat down beside Mike and told him hello. Molly asked John what he wanted, and John said, "I will have a beer." Molly got the beer John always drank and handed it to him and then said "I have missed you. Been busy?"

John said, "Yes very busy but when do you get out of here?"

Molly said, "I leave at 7 PM why?"

John said, "I would love to buy you dinner if you would allow me that honor."

Mike smiled, and Molly said, "John you just got a date".

John smiled and then he said, "Mike I need your help."

Mike said "John, how may I help you?"

John said, "You still know people at KBR, right?"

Mike said, "Hell yes I have only been gone for four years."

John said "Great. I need to get an appointment with the head of their construction division and I need it as soon as it can be done. I have a major project that needs to be done in record time."

Mike said, "Ok but tell me about it first then I will know where to send you and not waste time". John explained the project to Mike and of course did not tell him anything about the military other than to say Red Lion had been awarded a contract to train some of the troops doing special missions. Mike knew John only as the owner of Red Lion Security and that was exactly how John wanted it to be. John and Mike talked for a while and John was more impressed with Mike every time they talked. Mike had retired after 45 years with KBR. He had gone to work for them when it was Brown and Root Construction. Now Kellogg Brown and Root was the largest construction company in the world. Mike had been the Senior Vice President of Refinery Construction when he retired. Mike had traveled the world for KBR and spent most of his time in the Far East, Japan and much of his time in the Middle East. Mike was smart as a whip and still had a consulting business going. After he and John had talked for a while, Mike got his cell phone out and called KBR and asked to speak to a person. When the man came on the phone Mike said "George this is Mike. I need you to clear your schedule for tomorrow at 10 AM. I need you to meet a man I am bringing and then do his job. It is just that simple. Mike waited about 30 seconds and then said "Great, George we will see you tomorrow, 10 AM". Mike put his cell phone away and said "OK John see you say here at 9 AM then we can ride together to KBR. I got to go. Have fun tonight".

John said, "Thanks Mike I will be here tomorrow, and I am going to try to have fun." Mike left, and John had another beer and checked the clock. He had an hour and a half to wait. He was good with that. Molly came around the bar and sat down. Her night bartender was now there and gave Molly a drink. John said, "What would you like to eat tonight?"

Molly said, "I think I want a very good steak and maybe a shrimp cocktail."

John said, "I know a perfect place." Molly finished her drink and said "John would you mind following me to my place. I need to change and freshen up before I go anyplace with you."

John said "Not at all. You lead the way." John paid his tab and followed Molly out to her car and then followed her to her apartment. The apartment was only three blocks from John's.

Molly had John come in with her and gave him a beer. Then Molly excused herself and took a shower and fixed her makeup and put on a real dress. That took about thirty minutes and John had helped himself to another beer. While Molly was showering, John looked around her apartment. It was a one bedroom and Molly did not have it crowded with furniture. She had a glass top table and four chairs in the dining area. Another glass top table for a coffee table and a third glass top table she was using as a desk. The couch was leather as was the love seat that matched. John noticed that there were only a very few pictures in the apartment and none of family. Molly had some water color prints framed and that was it. Nothing fancy. Molly came out of the bedroom and she was fantastic looking. She had on a pale blue dress that was split up one side. The neckline was low and her shoes matched the dress. Molly had reddish hair, but it was not brassy. She had on blue ear rings and matching blue bracelets. Molly was 5 feet, 7 inches tall and weighed about 130 pounds. She had a very good figure and John guessed her breast size as 36 C or maybe D. Molly was 40 to 42 years old John figured. John really liked her and hoped that by chance things would work for him with her. John had never had any success with a relationship and he always believed it was his job. He had never found a woman he felt could handle what he did, and most of his life he had been in and out of everyplace he had been on missions. John knew he was going to not be able to tell Molly what he did, but maybe he could just live in the moment as the owner of Red Lion. Time would tell. Molly said, "I am ready and sorry for taking so long".

John said "That is not a problem and you look beautiful. Let's go eat." John and Molly left her apartment and walked to John's car and got in. John drove about two miles to Fleming's restaurant and the valet parked and went inside. John had called and made the reservation when Molly was showering. The dinner went very well and Molly told John about her life. John told her about his or at least told her part of the story. After dinner Molly and John walked over to the outdoor park area a block from the restaurant and sat for a while and talked about her business and John's business and about their lives in general. John was really enjoying the evening and Moly was as well. About 11 PM John drove Molly back to her apartment. Molly got out and John walked her to the door. Molly kissed John and thanked him for the evening and said, "We should do this again".

John said "I would really like that, Good night. John kissed her again and started to leave. Molly said, "John I want you to come in if you want to."

John said, "Molly you do not have to do that but yes I would very much like to come in." Molly smiled and opened her door. John and Molly went into the apartment and straight into the bedroom. The sex was totally fantastic, and John could not believe how he felt. Molly had told John she had the same feelings. This type of love making was something John had never had before with any woman. John for the first time in his life was thinking he just might have found someone he could really have a relationship with. The next morning, John was up and dressed and ready to leave at 6 AM. Molly woke up a little and asked John why he had to go?

John said, "I have to meet Mike and go to KBR this morning, so I must leave." Molly leaned up and John bent down, and they kissed. John stroked her hair and cheek and said "Molly you are fantastic. I will call you later. Do you work at the bar today?"

Molly said "Yes I have to open at 11 AM. I will wait for your call." John kissed her again and left. Molly went back to sleep until her alarm went off. She was dreaming about John.

John met Mike and the men got into John's car and drove to KBR. Mike told the security officer he was there to see George Masters and the guard showed Mike and John to the elevators and said "Sir, punch seven and when you get out of the elevator turn to the right and you will see the doors to the construction division. The receptionist will assist you from there." Mike thanked the guard and he and John went to the 7th floor. Mike and John walked into the construction division and Mike was immediately recognized by the receptionist. After they spoke for a minute or so, she led them into George's office. John was introduced, and the three men sat and Mike said "George we need KBR to build a bunch of stuff for John and we need it done extremely fast. John tell the man what you need".

John got out his plans and gave them to George and explained exactly what was required. John also told George where the location was and had to show him on a map of Texas exactly where Hallettsville was in relation to Houston and San Antonio. When John finished, George said "I will contact my estimators and we can have a bid to you by tomorrow. Now John speed is going to cost like Hell. Also, we will have to rent equipment from the area if they have it available or bring it from our Houston location. Then we have the cost of lodging all that to figure. I am guessing we are looking at around $20 Million Dollars just off the top of my head, but we will have the exact figures by tomorrow."

John said "I was figuring about that, so I think we are on the right page. Please call me as soon as you can get the numbers. We need to start immediately." George got up and Mike and John did too, and the men shook hands and John and Mike left. When Mike and John were back in the car, Mike said "Jesus, John that is one Hell of a lot of money you are talking about spending. I had no idea Red Lion was that big"?

John said "Mike we are not but we got this Army contract and it looks like we are about to become big. If things work well for us, we will be doing training for a good while."

Mike said, "I am happy for you, John".

John said, "Thanks". The car had just pulled into the parking lot of Molly's and John said, "How about a drink?"

Mike said, "I can always use a drink, my friend". John and Mike went into Molly's and had a drink. John saw Molly and the two exchanged a very knowing glance. John had only one drink then told Mike and Molly he had to go but he would try to get back in the evening. John left and went back to the office. It was 1 PM when he arrived.

<h1 style="text-align:center">CHAPTER 6</h1>

ress and Sandy came into John's office and Tress said, "Sir we have a solution for the pirates".

John said, "Sit and tell me what the two of you have come up with".

Tress and Sandy sat down, and Sandy said "Sir, the group is a splinter faction of al-Qaeda and operates from the coastal area. They have a base on shore and venture out into the ocean and strike targets that are anywhere from fifteen to thirty miles out to sea. The group uses small fast boats and these boats are equipped with RPGs and automatic weapons that the terrorists are armed with. The attacks are with the automatic weapons and are used as the group boards the vessels. The RPGs are used in the event the ship does not comply with the demands. Once the ship is under the control of the Terrorists, they ask for ransom or they threaten to blow up the ship. They usually have explosives with then when the board. Their base is the target for our operation".

John said, "OK what is your recommendation for an attack?" Tress said "We recommend a night attack when most of the terrorists will be in their base. Also, we recommend an attack on the boats they use to go out to attack the shipping. It will be very tricky because the terrorists have local support, so we may be looking at another very bad situation if we do not execute this raid perfectly. We will need one attack team and a covering team. The cover team should be large enough to immediately stop any threat to the attack team. We can either use another attack team to destroy the boats or use helicopters to do that job. Getting in and out will pose an additional problem for the teams and we will probably need to insert them by sea".

John said, "Well we have a lot of work to do on this one, do we not?"

Sandy said "Sir, maybe our best bet would be to try a very simple approach first. I have been thinking of taking out the actual leader of the pirate group and then see what happens. We could also take out the bank accounts if we can locate them."

John said "I like that approach and why not give me a scenario of that. Tress and Sandy get with Don and get him working on the money. Give him everything we can gather on the banking. Then get back to me with the leader recommendation. I would like to do it with only a very small amount of personnel." Tress and Sandy both said, "Yes Sir" and left John's office.

Don came in late in the afternoon and wanted to talk with John. John had him sit down and said, "OK Don what is on your mind?"

Don said, "John I want us to get a person that is going to be released from prison on Monday to come to work for us".

John said, "And just who is this person and why?"

Don said "Her name is Cindy Davis and she is probably as good a hacker as I am or maybe better. She is sure as Hell the most knowledgeable person I know about firewalls and all the things we need to find this "Solomon" guy".

John said, "And what makes you think she would be interested?"

Don said "Hell John she is a nerd and a hacker just like me and she sure as Hell needs a job. She has been in the system for three years."

John said" Ok Don here is what I will do. I will send two operators to pick her up just as she is released and bring her here. Then you, me, Harry, and Jim will talk to her and if she is willing and only if she is, we put her ass to work. Don, you will be totally responsible for her and trust this. If she fucks up you know the penalty."

Don said "I can live with that John and thanks. I will get all the info to Nancy about where, when, all of that and I will also get a message to her that she is going to be picked up."

John said, "Don I know better than to ask, but how in the Hell can you get a message to her?"

Don said, "She has internet access and we have a code." Don left the office. John sat back and thought "this is getting out of hand, but we sure as Hell need the help if Don says we do". John left the office and drove to Molly's and had a drink. Molly was already off and siting at the bar talking with a few of her regulars when John walked in. Molly said hello and John sat down and ordered a beer. In a few minutes, Molly sat down beside John and they talked for a while. Molly said she was going to get something to take home and asked John to come over. He readily agreed. Molly left, and John had another beer then left and went to Molly's apartment.

KBR called the next morning and gave John the price quotation, $21 Million Dollars. John told George to send the contract via messenger that day and then get a start date to John as soon as possible. George said he would. John called Ray and told him the deal was on. Ray was happy and said if they needed anything, let him know. John said he would call Ray with the official start date. John then called Harry and Jim and had them both come for a meeting. The two men were sitting in John's office and John said "We have the bid from KBR, $21 Million Dollars, and I need you guys to start coordination with them tomorrow. I will have George get you the people who you will be working with and I also want someone on the ground at least weekly to get a status. Harry, I guess you will be the range guy and Jim you will be working with the main building and the utilities part of this as I understand it."

Jim said "Yes, Sir that is how Harry and I have it broken down".

Harry said "Sir, I can actually stay out on site if I am needed."

John said "No we have too much going on here for the present. When things get further along you may want to do that or at least be there on certain days. Right now, I need you both to get with KBR and make damn sure they know exactly what is required".

Jim and Harry both said, "Yes Sir" and left. John called George and told him to get in touch with Jim and give Jim the names. George said he would do it right away. That afternoon, at 1 PM, the messenger arrived with the contract. John called Dan into his office and Dan went over the contract. Dan said, "John it is exactly what we asked for".

John said "OK". John signed all copies and handed them to Dan. Dan said "I will keep our copies for file and get this messengered back right now. Looks like we are on our way."

John said, "Yes we are, and I hope we know what we are doing". Both men laughed, and Dan left. Two hours later Don came to John's office and gave him two folders. One said Molly the other said Cindy. John picked up the Molly folder and opened it. Everything was there on Molly from the time she was born to now. John got up went to the refrigerator in his office, got a beer out and opened it and sat back down. John sipped the beer and read the file on Molly. When John finished the file, he placed it in his office safe. John was very glad everything in the file that Molly had told John was the exact truth. Molly had told John about 90% of her life. John had a very good feeling about that. The next file was on Cindy and John got another beer and read that file. When John finished, he knew exactly why Don wanted her. John did too.

John and Molly had been seeing each other every night that week and John asked on Thursday night if Molly could get away for the weekend. Molly said she could and what did John have in mind. John said he wanted to take her to Galveston for the weekend and wanted to drive down Friday afternoon. John planned to leave at 2 PM and come back Sunday evening. Molly was all for it and made the necessary plans. John was at Molly's apartment at 2 PM on Friday and Molly came out with her bag. John took it and placed it into the car and then helped Molly into the car. They headed for Galveston. When they arrived in Galveston Molly wondered why John just kept driving right thru the city. John was looking at his GPS and followed it straight to a very nice beach house that was located at the end of the island and almost sitting by itself. There was one other house about 100 yards from it at the very end of the beach and the other closest house was at least 200 yards from the house John pulled up in front of. Molly said "John what is going on? I thought we were going to be at a hotel or something?"

John said, "No my dear this is just you and me."

Molly said, "Oh you never cease to amaze me John." John and Molly got out of the car and John carried the bags into the house. John had gotten the house from a friend of Mike's and it was a beautiful place. John and Molly explored the whole house and found the sauna, hot tub, and the totally private beach. The beach had been fenced off with a 20-foot-high wooden fence. The only access was from the house or the Gulf of Mexico. John and Molly decided to have a drink and then go out for dinner. The next two and one-half days were fantastic and when Sunday afternoon came neither one of them wanted to go back to Houston. They both new they had to do so but they really did not want to leave. John packed up the car and Molly got in and John headed back to Houston. John stopped at Molly's apartment and helped her get her bag inside and then kissed her and went home. John was falling in love and he knew it and was scared to death.

Monday Cindy was met at the prison by two of the Red Lion operators. John had sent the two meanest people he could think of to pick her up. They had her get into the car and headed for the airport. They did not say a word. Cindy sat very quietly. At the airport, the operators showed identification showing they were US Marshalls and Cindy and the two operators boarded a plane for Houston. The plan landed and was met by a car. The operators had Cindy sit in the rear with one of them and the other sat in the passenger side in front. The car drove to the Red Lion headquarters and as soon as it arrived, the operators had Cindy get out and escorted her into the building. Don was waiting in the reception area. One of the operators had called when the plane landed in Houston. Don and Cindy hugged, and Don said, "God girl you look great".

Cindy said, "So do you but God damn Don who are these guys and what in the Hell are you into?" Don started to laugh and so did the operators. Cindy said "You bastard. I will get you back if it kills me. Now what the Hell is this all about?"

Don said, "You will know in about five minutes." John came out of his office and walked to the reception area. John said "Cindy nice to see you I am John Carter the boss. Please come into my office. Don join us". Cindy looked at John and then Don and followed John into the office. Cindy sat down, and Don sat beside her on the couch. John sat behind his desk. John watched Cindy look around the room and look at Don for a few moments then he said "Cindy I am John Carter as I told you. I am Lieutenant General John Carter United States Army and I am commander of this unit. The tall Black man you saw standing in the reception area is a General Officer as well and Jim is the second in command here. There are only five civilians that work here if you come on board. Everyone else is military. Mostly Army but there are a few Air Force people here as well. Now we do not use military rank and we do not wear uniforms very much. Let us say we are a very special unit of the military". John stopped and watched Cindy's reaction. She did not show any signs of panic or emotion. John said "Now I am going to tell you what we do and then I want you and Don to leave here and go somewhere private and discuss everything. When you have done that come back and tell me your answer." John then told Cindy exactly what the unit did including killing people and breaking into all computers in the world, including the US Government computers if necessary. Taking money from banks, using and making false identification, and the job she would be doing setting up firewalls for Red Lion computers and making sure everything was totally secure from any outside threat. John also explained that Cindy would be using all her computer skills to research people, things, locations, and number of other things, as required. John then said "And Cindy you will be responsible for the lives of our operators when they go on missions if your information is not correct. That is the most important thing you will ever do". John finished, and Cindy and she was shaking a little bit. John said "OK enough of this. I want you and Don to leave now and have Don tell you all about this place."

Cindy said "Sir, I will be very glad to do that." Don and Cindy left the office. John knew he was going to have a perfect team in his computer department. Cindy would take the job. John was confident of that.

Harry and Jim came in that afternoon and told John they had the first meeting with KBR and things would start in one week. John said "Alright, any problems?"

Harry said, "I do not think we will have any to worry about on my end."

Jim said "On my side, the only problems I see is the utility thing with the power company and maybe the water well. It depends on how deep we need to go. Other than that, we are good." John thanked them, and they left. John spent the rest of the day studying the temporary plan Tress and Sandy had given him. John was worried about which plan to use. His first instinct was to do a total assault on everything and everyone, but he also knew that might be very bad and cause the local civilians to come into the fight just as they had done before. The damn pirates were also giving the civilian population funds. This was how they operated so openly. Fear was another factor that the pirates used, and it worked. John had just finished reading the second plan for the fourth time when Nancy buzzed the phone and told him Don and Cindy were there to see him. John had Nancy have them come in. Don walked into the office and Cindy followed. John had them both sit and then he said, "Well are you on board, Cindy?"

She said "Sir, I am 100% on board and I thank you for giving me this chance. You have no idea how much I want to help in this war."

John said, "Welcome to Red Lion." John then said "Alright, Don first thing in the morning and I mean first fucking thing, get Cindy set up with Nancy and have her sign everything she needs to sign. Then you personally make sure she gets IDs and all the necessary stuff to rent a place, open a bank account all the stuff. If she needs a car and I am sure she will get with Jim and find out who we use and go get her a car. I also want you to help her get an apartment. Until then she can stay in a hotel."

Don said "I understand Sir. I will take care of it and she is staying with me for now. Is that alright?"

John said, "Yes of course". The two left, and John went out to the warehouse and walked around. John had opened a beer and was sipping on it and thinking.

The next month went by fast at Red Lion. KBR was working 7 days a week and making very good progress. Tress and Sandy had polished the plan for the pirates and were also working on a plan for the Philippines and the terrorist group there. John and Molly were spending a lot of time together and John had been talking to her about moving in with him. John knew if that did happen, he would have to tell her everything before the move and he worried about that. He had not been honest with her, but there were reasons. He hoped she would understand and accept the reasons. It was now November and John knew the holidays were coming and that he was going to have to tell Molly the truth. John knew Ray and Linda would expect him at the ranch for Thanksgiving and for Christmas. Linda might spend Christmas Day in Midland, but she would come the day after to Hallettsville to see John and her grandmother. Miles would make sure of that. John decided that on Saturday he would tell Molly the truth.

# CHAPTER 7

John had Molly come over to his apartment on Saturday afternoon. Molly was surprised that John had asked her, and she was excited. John had never asked her to come to his place, he always came to her apartment or they went some place. John picked Molly up and drove the short distance to his apartment. Molly was surprised that John lived so close to her and really liked the complex he lived in. She secretly wished she had moved there but she was alright where she lived, and the rent was probably a lot less than what John paid. John got Molly out of the car and walked her to his apartment. John opened the door and Molly walked in. Molly stopped and looked around. John had a large two-bedroom apartment with a large living room, a dining room, one half bath off the living room. A very large patio that opened off the living room by way of sliding glass doors, and a very large kitchen. The hallway went back to the bedrooms. One bedroom had a full bath across the hallway and the master bedroom had a complete bathroom off it. Molly looked as John gave the tour. John had a huge walk in closet in the master bed room and another huge walk in closet in the second bedroom. There was a closet off the dining room area and a very good large pantry off the kitchen. The kitchen had cabinets all over it. Molly thought "this is really big for just one single guy". John said, "Let me get you a drink and then we need to talk."

Molly said, "Ok get me a Fireball on the rocks if you have it."

John said, "Oh I got it." John got Molly's drink and he got a beer and they sat down on the couch. John said "Molly I am deeply in love with you and I have never been in love with anyone in my life. I am going to tell you things and no matter what, after we are finished talking if you stay or leave you cannot under any circumstances repeat anything I tell you to anyone. I mean anyone. Not your family or your best friend or your most trusted allies. This cannot leave this apartment. Do you understand that?"

Molly looked scared to death and said, "John I hear what you are saying and yes I understand but what the Fuck is going on?"

John said "Well, I am not exactly what I appear to be." John spent the next hour telling Molly exactly what and who he was and all about his life. He showed her his uniform and explained who each person in the pictures he had hanging in his bedroom and office was. Then John said "I also know everything about you and I know that may make you mad. It never was that I did not trust you and what you were telling me about your life, but I had to make sure you could be vetted if I was going to do more that screw you for a night every now and then. I damn sure wanted more so I had you vetted". Molly had walked around as John was explaining everything and was now on her third drink. She stood in the middle of the living room and looked at John and said, "Ok General I have one question for now".

John said "Ask".

Molly said, "Will you ever have to go and do what you told me you used to do again?"

John said "Maybe. That depends on a lot of things, but I am not an operator any more. I run the show." Molly slowly walked to John and said "Well General or Mr. Carter, President of Red Lion or whatever I love you and I understand exactly why you did what you did. Now from this minute on no more secrets between us. Is that a deal?"

John said "Yes, it is a deal". Molly then kissed John like he had never been kissed before and said, "Would you like to take me to bed?"

John said, "It would be an honor my Lady". Molly grabbed John's hand and led him to his bedroom and they both undressed and made love for the next few hours.

It was 6 PM when John and Molly got out of bed and went into the living room. John made drinks for them and then he announced he was cooking dinner. Molly said "Oh I also have a chef. Well that is just the icing on the cake. A lover, a Chef and who knows what else. Also, John, why do you always make the drinks? You know that is what I do for a living."

John said "Yes and that is why. I want you to relax and be waited on." Molly went over and kissed John and said "Oh My God. This is going to be one Hell of a ride."

John said "Yes, it is." John was letting the steaks marinate and was getting the salad out to warm just a little. The potatoes were in the oven and would be ready in an hour. The rest of the meal would only take ten minutes to prepare. Molly was sitting on the couch and had put on John's shirt. It was open, and she looked wonderful. John was wearing a pair of lounging pants and he came in and sat down with her. The TV was on and John was about to change the channel to music when a news bulletin came on. A special report came on talking about a US oil tanker that had been seized in the Indian Ocean off the coast of Somalia by pirates. John said, "Oh shit". Molly listened very carefully and said, "John this is bad, isn't it?"

John said, "Yes very bad." John got up and got another beer. He was standing in the kitchen when his cell phone rang. John went into the living room and answered. He listened for a minute or two then John said "Sir, we have a plan in place and can be executing in twelve hours. We will need major air support from Airlift Command and probably some tactical air as well but yes we can execute." John listened again and said, "Ok Sir, let me know". John hung the phone up and looked at Molly.

Molly said "If you need to go then go. I can stay here, or you can drop me at my place".

John said, "I have to wait till the President calls me back".

Molly said, "Oh Shit John you actually work for the President, don't you?"

John said, "Yes my dear that is what I told you, but I know it is hard to realize I meant directly for the President".

Molly said, "Sure as Hell is." John and Molly sat and sipped their drinks. John started cooking the steaks and started making the Cesar salad. Molly and John had dinner and an after-dinner drink. John was marveling at the way Molly was taking what she had learned and what was going on. John new she was the one for him. John's cell phone rang, and John said, "Carter here Sir". John listened for a moment and then said "Alright Mr. President. I will be waiting to get that call. I will be heading to the headquarters in about an hour. Yes sir." John hung up and said "I think we need to make love then we can go to work. You agree?" Molly got up and headed straight for the bed.

John and Molly were in John's office when the secure line rang. John picked it up and said "Carter". John listened and then said "Send me everything you have and make damn sure someone is standing by the fax and the phone. Yes, I will get back in about two hours." John hung up and said, "Molly this may take a while."

Molly said, "I am not going anywhere." John smiled and dialed the phone. When the party answered, John said "Harry call a red alert. Everyone at the office immediately. We have a problem". John sat down behind his desk and Molly sat in one of the chairs sand they waited. In about ten minutes John heard the fax machine in the outer office ring and then a transmission started. John got up and walked into the reception area and got the fax and came back to his desk and sat down. The fax was six pages long and John read it over twice. Then he said "Well the Navy is on the way, but it is going to take at least thirty-six hours for them to get there and the navigation markers on the tanker are turned off. It is like finding a needle in a hay stack. That is a very big ocean."

Molly said, "Well what now?"

John said, "We wait." In about ten minutes Harry came in the door. John introduced Molly and Harry said hello then went directly to his office. Within 1 hour the building was almost full of people. Tress and Sandy were in their offices and Don and Cindy arrived. They went directly to the computer room. John saw Jim come in and had him come into the office. John introduced Molly to Jim and then said "I am waiting for the President to call. Then we will know what the Hell we are going to do. Right now, we need to make damn sure we have everything we will need for Tress and Sandy's plan. Will you and Harry make that happen?"

Jim said, "You got it Sir" and left. Molly said "John I can go home because I had no idea this would happen. When you said you were going to the office, I thought it would be just you or maybe one other person. God this is something else."

John said "Ok Honey take my car and go to my place. I will be there as soon as I can". Molly got up and kissed John and went out to the car. John was already busy looking at the map of the area and studying Mogadishu where the pirates were based. This was the same city the US had problems with before. It was a very hostile area toward US personnel. John and his people were at the headquarters for four hours waiting on word from Washington. At 3 AM John got a call from Ledford. John was told everything was on hold because EXXON the owner of the tanker and the oil was going to pay the ransom demand on Monday. John understood and said "General I need to send something to you and I need it done if possible. With this information we want we just may be able to track the "Solomon" connection".

Ledford said "Send it secure to me as soon as you get it ready. I will have personnel monitoring until I get it John."

John said, "Thank you, Sir". John hung up and called for Don and Cindy to come into his office. When they were there, John said "OK I need you to tell me or write it out exactly what you want to track a money transfer from one US bank or maybe an overseas bank to the source it goes to."

Don and Cindy said, "We will have it to you in five minutes". Don and Cindy left. John called Harry and Jim and had them come to his office. John told them that the President wanted a hold until at least Monday on any action because EXXON was paying. John also told them that Don and Cindy were going to track the money and we would know what banks were involved. John said, "After you are satisfied we can go if called, send everyone back home but tell them they are on an hour recall". Jim and Harry acknowledged and left. Don and Cindy came in and handed John the information. John thanked them then sent the information over the secure fax to Ledford. John then had Harry take him home. John entered the apartment and Molly was sitting watching the news. John kissed her and went to the kitchen and grabbed a beer. He came in and sat down beside Molly and listened to the reporter talk about the ship. The news did not say anything new, so John turned on the music channel and looked at Molly. John said, "Well do you still want to be with me after seeing what I do?"

Molly pulled John over to her and kissed him and rubbed herself on him and then said, "John I love you and yes 1000 times over I want to be with you."

John said, "Well then we better start making plans for you to move."

Molly said, "I can do that, but not today, OK?" John smiled and nodded. John and Molly spent the rest of the day Sunday in and out of bed and lounging around John's apartment. John received a call on his cell that the information he had requested would be sent on Monday at 8 AM. John was ready to make a proposal to the President and to EXXON. John was going to try to get the President to make the proposal to EXXON. John and Molly went to sleep about midnight and John woke her at 5 AM and took her by her apartment on his way to the Red Lion headquarters.

# CHAPTER 8

John was busy typing his proposal into the computer when Don and Cindy came into his office. They were holding a piece of paper and seemed to be very excited. John had them sit and said, "What is so important that the two of you are here this early?"

Don said "John we believe it is not just one man that is doing all this, but we think it is a group of men. Like a special society or something like that. The numbers do not track and if it is just one guy he would have to be worth trillions and I mean a bunch of trillions".

John sat straight up in his chair. That made sense. No one had enough money available to fund all the networks without selling all their holdings and that would be a very big red flag, but with a few people all supplying funds it would be very easy to fund the terrorists. John said, "Ok what proof do we have?"

Cindy said "We have tracked money from about forty banks all over the world and the accounts are all different, but we have narrowed them down to six that are as I call it the base banks. John what these guys are doing is putting money in the base banks and then moving it by small transfers to other banks. Now we have located the base banks and we have tracked the money from one base bank to some of the as I call them out banks. The thing is that all six base banks send money to the same accounts in the out banks. I know it seems weird but when you draw it out you can see the lines."

John said "Guys that is great. Ok draw out a sample of the transfers for me. This is great."

Don and Cindy left. John continued to work on his proposal. The information John had received from

Washington outlined the demands and how the money was to be delivered. The ransom was for $30 Million Dollars and it was to be in US currency. The money was to be delivered to the tanker by helicopter and dropped on the deck. Then the pirates would leave the tanker and if anyone tried to stop them they would blow the tanker up. The Captain of the ship had confirmed the ship had been wired with C-4 explosive charges and it would in fact blow up, especially with carrying three million barrels of oil. Lloyds of London had the insurance policy on the vessel and contents, but EXXON could not afford to lose the cargo or the ship. The exchange was to be at noon, US east coast time, on Monday. It would be dark on the tanker but that was exactly what the pirates wanted. John had his plan done so he called Don and Cindy into his office. John said, "If these pirates put money into a bank locally in Somalia, a cash deposit could you guys know about it?"

Don said "If we knew the account yes, but otherwise we would have to wait until the daily tallies were done and then try to figure out where the money went. If it is large enough, it is easy, but if they spread it out that is almost impossible to track."

John said, "Ok can we find out what the tallies were in each bank in Somalia was on Saturday?"

Cindy said, "Yes but what if they used a bank in another country?"

John said "Well then they would have to transport $30 million Dollars out of the country and that much cash would probably cause major problems. Someone would take the chance. I think they will use a bank in Mogadishu but which one or how many is the question. See what you guys can come up with in the next hour or so for me." Don and Cindy left. John had Nancy go over the proposal when she arrived and make damn sure it had no typing errors. John then called the Chief of Staff and spoke to Ledford. John explained the plan and said he would forward a copy to Ledford, but he was also sending a copy directly to the President as requested. Ledford agreed. John then sent the plan to the secure fax number he had for the President. After the fax had been sent he called the President's chief of staff and alerted him to the fax. Then John waited for the call. John got the call at 8 AM and it was the President. John listened as the President spoke and then John said "Mr. President I believe we can not only recover the money but then we can eliminate the entire group of pirates once and for all. We will also eliminate any one who has worked against us as we go. All we need is your go."

The President said, "John you are a Go." The phone went dead and John sat back. It was now action time.

John called Jim and had him set up an action brief for the operator commanders, Harry, Tress and Sandy, the helicopter unit commander and Don and Cindy for 11 AM. Jim had everyone in the conference room when John walked in. John went to the big board and hit the button and a map of Somalia covered the board. John picked up the pointer and said "Ladies and Gentlemen this is our target. We have been cleared to go and we are now on the clock. We will do this in ten days. Here is the plan". John told the group that the Cobra helicopter gun ship would be flown to Galveston along with two of the Black Hawks. They would then be loaded on the deck of a containership. All the necessary equipment and ammunition and explosives will also be loaded on the ship. Six operators and one of the mechanics will then go to the port and will board the vessel and go with the ship. The choppers will be loaded, and the rotor blades would be placed in a container. The choppers will be wrapped for ocean voyage. All the equipment would be loaded into a container at Red Lion and then transported to Galveston and loaded on the ship. One, 5000-gallon fuel truck loaded with fuel for the choppers would be loaded as well. The container ship would leave Galveston in route to the Mediterranean

Ocean. Then the ship will port call in Italy. The balance of the operators will fly commercial to Italy two days prior to the docking of the container vessel. The piolets will also fly with the operators. All the Red Lion personnel will proceed to the port and board the container ship. The ship will then go thru the Suez Cannel and into the Arabian Sea and head to the coast of Somalia. The container ship will be carrying containers which will be empty to serve as camouflage for the choppers on the deck. The containers will be placed around the outside of the deck with the choppers and fuel truck inside the wall the containers will build and at night fall immediately before the attack the containers will be sent into the sea. The choppers will we ready to take off and the operators will be flown to the targets. The operators will be parachuted from 7000 feet and use a HALO jump to get to their targets. There are three vital targets. The operators will take out two of the targets the Cobra gunship will take out the other one. A four-man team will also be used on the target the Cobra will attack. After the attacks have been completed the operators will be picked up at an extraction point and flown back to the container ship. The ship will then proceed to South Africa. The container ship will dock, and all members of Red Lion will get off. The container ship will refuel and proceed back to Galveston. Once back in Galveston the choppers and fuel truck will be off loaded and returned to Red Lion Headquarters. The equipment use by the operators will be put back in the container and returned. Four members of the unit that did not go on the mission, will be in South Africa and they will board the containership and come back with it safeguarding the equipment. The mission operators and the piolets and mechanic will fly back on commercial flights to Houston. The coordination will be done, and the personnel flying will have prepaid tickets waiting. When John had finished the explanation of the plan he said "As you can see this is a very complicated mission and timing is everything. We have planned it down to damn near the second but as always things do not always go as planned. The operator leaders will be given updates as necessary by SAT phone so make damn sure everyone has enough batteries and keep the damn phones monitored from the time you people get on the vessel until you get off the damn thing. We have satellites that will allow us to watch as the mission goes along, and Washington will be seeing exactly what we see. I have 1000% faith in all of you people and I know we will get it done. Thank you." John left the room and went to his office. It was ten minutes until noon. John called Tress and Sandy and hade them turn on the communications set so they could watch the money drop. John, Jim and Harry joined Tress and Sandy in the Intel center and watched as the chopper dropped the bag onto the deck of the tanker. John had been told a tracking device was in the bag. It was very hard to see things. The ship had turned on the navigation lights and a spot light on the deck but as soon as the chopper made the drop, the spot light was off. John hoped the satellites could track the pirates when they left the tanker. John had studied the photos from the day before and he knew that there were four boats tied to the tanker. The boats were speed boats used by the pirates and the idea was to follow the boats via satellite back to their base. If that worked John would know exactly where the boats would be. That was the target the Cobra would attack. The screen went dark after a few minutes and John left the room. The men of Red Lion were very busy packing the equipment into the container that was sitting in the warehouse. The helicopters were scheduled to leave for Galveston at 6 PM and the operators going by ship would be on one of the Black Hawks. The mechanics would be flying in the other Black Hawk and all their tools and equipment would be with them. The fuel truck was at the dock waiting to be loaded. John wanted the ship completely loaded and underway by midnight.

At 3 PM Don and Cindy came to John's office and told him they could not track the deposits immediately but could probably see action in five to seven days. John said "Alright how about this. There are only four banks in the country, is that right?"

Don said "Yes".

John said "Can you people create a virus or whatever you call it to do two things. One wipe out every bank in the country and keep the money moving from one location to another for six days at least. In other words, keep it out in computer land so no one can find it? The second thing I would like is to be able to know what bank was used for the ransom money and could we get only that amount out of the bank while the other funds are out in space?"

Cindy said "John we think we can do exactly that. We will let you know in about an hour". They left John's office. John was really wanting to get everything moving but he knew timing was everything and he also knew his people would not move until they were sure everything had been checked and double-checked. That was why he had them and that was why they were the best. John was buzzed by Nancy. John's brother Ray was on the phone. John answered, and Ray said, "John we have a small problem here".

John said, "What is wrong, Ray?"

Ray said "The fucking Sheriff is asking a bunch of questions and he is really pissed off that his people are not being used as security here on the project. I cannot handle him and with all the KBR people here in town he knows something big is going on and he damn sure wants in on it."

John said "OK Ray two things. First, I am up to my ass in alligators today. Second and this is what I need you to do. Get with the Sheriff and tell him I want to buy him lunch tomorrow and discuss things with him. Where is the nicest place in that town of yours to have lunch?"

Ray said, "Hell we can use the country club, I am a member."

John said "OK then set it up for noon there. I will fly in at 11 AM and you and I along with Dan and Harry will do our thing."

Ray said, "I will get it done".

John said, "Thanks Ray". John hung up and called Harry to come into the office. He also had Dan come. He told Nancy to call the private contractor Red Lion used and schedule a Lear Jet to pick them up at the Sugarland airport at 9 AM in the morning and fly them to Hallettsville and back. When Dan and Harry arrived, John said "Ok we have a problem in Hallettsville we need to fix tomorrow. Dan get us a contract for security ready. Make it for two officers 24/7 payment to the officers $30 per hour and payment to the Sheriff's department $20 per hour. Harry call KBR and tell them we will assume the security for the project and give them an effective date of day after tomorrow. We are all going to Hallettsville the morning. Civilian clothes, suit and tie. We have wheels up from Sugarland at 0900." Both men nodded and left. John thought "Fucking Sheriff. Things never change. He is a greedy as the rest of the world". John was getting a little tired. He wanted to go see Molly, but he had to get the operation going and needed to be there. He would see her later that night, he hoped.

At 8 PM Harry came in and said "Sir, everything has gone to Galveston and in two hours the ship will be completely loaded and underway at 11 PM".

John said "Great, thanks see you in the morning".

Harry said, "Yes Sir". Harry left, and John headed for Molly's bar. He had called Molly earlier and told her he would be there sometime after 8 PM. She was going to wait for him at the bar. John arrived at Molly's bar and went in. He saw Molly sitting at the bar and he sat down beside her. She leaned over and kissed him and said, "Long day?" John said, "Yes it was and tomorrow will be longer probably".

Molly said, "Ok I am ready whenever you want to leave".

John said, "I will have a beer or maybe two then we can go is that OK?"

Molly said "Of course". John drank the first beer very fast then sipped on the second one for a while. John liked the atmosphere at Molly's and he liked just being there with her. Molly was moving around from table to table and from seat to seat at the bar talking to her customers. That is why she had such a great business. Everyone felt important and everyone really loved her. About 11 PM John and Molly left and went to John's apartment. They were both tired and went to bed almost as soon as they got home. John knew tomorrow would be another long day.

# CHAPTER 9

The Lear Jet touched down in Hallettsville at the ranch at 11 AM. Ray was waiting, and he had driven an SUV to pick John and his group up and take them to the country club. John greeted Ray and gave him a hug and Dan and Harry shook hands with Ray and then everyone was in the vehicle and Ray headed to the country club. John and Ray talked on the way about the ranch and the family. Harry and Dan looked over the countryside and then looked at the town as Ray drove through it. There were dozens of KBR vehicles parked around town and business at the local restaurants was great. Ray told them that the town was really liking the KBR people being here and it was fantastic for the economy. Ray pulled up to the front of the country club and everyone got out. Ray led the way and the men went into the bar and sat down. Ray had the waiter take orders for drinks and when the drinks arrived, Ray said "OK John what are you going to do with Sheriff Wilson?"

John said, "Hell Ray, we are going to hire him".

Ray looked at John and said "Oh My God. This is one for the books."

John said "Yes, it is a little strange, but we need him to stop digging and to be happy. I think we can do that."

Ray said, "I hope you can". The sheriff came into the bar and greeted Ray. John stood up and Ray introduced John and then the others. Wilson sat down and ordered a cup of coffee. John said, "Sheriff my brother tells me you have resources available to handle our security requirements, is that so?"

Wilson said, "Well John that depends on what the requirements are and of course what my people would make working on their off time."

John said, "I will let Dan explain what we propose."

Dan said "Sheriff we will need two officers 24/7 to protect the site. It would be of tremendous value to us if it was your deputies that were working as our security. We will pay the officers $30 per hour. We of course would want the Sheriff's department or you or whoever to handle all the scheduling of the officers, the payment to the officers, and all the paperwork that may be required. If the officers could possibly use their patrol vehicles that would be a real plus. For that service we will to pay the department or whoever you designate $20 per hour for every hour worked by your deputies. So, in reality we are paying $50 per hour security costs".

The Sheriff looked very pleased and said "I think that would be a workable situation for everyone. When should I tell my officers to plan on extra work?"

Dan said, "Harry when you want to start using the deputies?"

Harry said, "Sheriff would tomorrow morning at 7 AM be good for you and your men?"

Wilson said, "Yes that would be fine."

Dan said "Great. Sheriff I have a contract prepared and we need you to sign it just to make sure we both understand the fees and the requirements but especially so that if anyone should ask about why your deputies are there you have this document."

Wilson said "I will be very glad to sign and thanks for thinking about that. You know people they always try to find something to bring up." Dan handed Wilson a pen and he signed. Dan then signed, and Ray signed as a witness. Dan gave Wilson a copy and put the other copies back in his briefcase. Ray said, "Well let's go in and eat." Everyone got up and followed Ray into the dining room. During the lunch Wilson asked a lot of questions about the project and John answered all of them. When lunch was over, Wilson shook hands all around and took John's business card and left. Ray said "Brother, you are amazing. You just bought a County Sheriff for $20 per hour. God Almighty". Everyone at the table laughed. Lunch was over, and Ray took the men back to the airstrip and the plane lifted off for Houston. John and party arrived back in Sugarland at 3 PM and all the men went to the office for an update on the containership and any other information. Tress and Sandy had been able to track the money bag to the shore and had the location of exactly where the boats were anchored. Tress had requested some new satellite photos of the area and was waiting for the feed to come in. Don and Cindy were waiting to talk to John, so he had them come to his office.

Don and Cindy sat down, and Don said "Well John we have done it. We have installed two virus programs in the bank and no one will ever know. As soon as the programs are activated they destroy themselves, so no trace is left no matter how smart their computer guys are. Now how do you want to do this and when?"

John said "OK I want you to use the one that empties everything in every bank exactly as the attack begins. We will be watching from here via satellite so as soon as the first shots are fired, you guys wipe out the banks. Then after 24 hours, take the $30 Million Dollars and transfer it to one of our off-shore banks. I really do not give a damn if it is from the actual bank or not, but we need the $30 Million available to transfer when we are told. Then after another ten days, take the two banks we have identified as the one's used by our pirates and move all their money into the Red Lion accounts in the overseas banks. We must make sure no one can trace this. If we cannot identify the pirate's bank, then move all the money from all the banks into our accounts. Can we do that the way I have explained it?"

Cindy said, "Yes we can and there will be absolutely no trace that the money came from Somalia".

John said "OK then we wait until the attack is on. Thanks guys". Don and Cindy left the office. Tress called with a new update on the container ship. It was half way across the Atlantic. John thought" Damn it is making better time than we have anticipated".

For the next five days Red Lion was slow. Tress and Sandy were constantly updating any information they could get from the "chatter" they monitored. The terrorists were not saying anything that set off any "red flags" and there was nothing that Tress or Sandy could find showing if any attacks were being planned. The pirates were not doing anything, and no money had moved from any bank in Somalia as far as Don and Cindy could tell. Don and Cindy had seen some large amounts of deposits made in one bank over the five-day period, and when it was calculated it was a total of $30 Million Dollars. Don was sure he had the right bank. Don and Cindy were going to watch for another deposit and confirm. Cindy had also been working on her theory of more than one person being behind the funding. So far, she had located what she thought could be four locations and it was a total shock that two of the locations were in the United States. Cindy briefed John and John was taken by surprise. John thought "It makes good sense in a way that one or two people in the US would be doing this. After all, there were some very powerful men in the US and many of them hated the way the country was run and what it had become. This could be very logical". Now all John had to do was prove it.

The next morning, John was told the operators and piolets were now on the container ship and it was headed for the Suez Canal. The estimated arrival in the Arabian Sea was in three days. That was exactly on schedule. John had been told by Washington that the Navy had been ordered out of the Arabian Sea around the area of Somalia and would be deployed in the northern part of the Sea. That was how John had requested it be done. The entire area was open. John had sent a special message to the President and was waiting for a reply. That afternoon the reply came in and John called Don and Cindy into his office. John said "OK Here is where you are to send the $30 Million Dollars and gave them an account number and a routing number. Make damn sure no one can trace it back to the bank."

Don said, "You got it Boss" and Cindy and Don left. In ten minutes John was told the money had been transferred. John sent a flash message to Washington. In three minutes he received a message that simply said "Thanks". John knew the President had made huge points with EXXON and that was a good thing. John might have to use that sometime down the road.

The container ship had now made in the Arabian Sea, there was only two days left before the raid. John was sitting at his desk in Red Lion when Tress came running into his office. Sandy was right behind him and holding piece of paper. John said, "What is so important people?"

Tress said "Sir we just got word that the whole fucking bunch will be meeting in Mogadishu on the night we are going to attack. All the War Lords we want and the head of the pirates".

John said "Christ. Where did that come from?"

Sandy said "CIA and NIS have it or at least they just got it. They will fuck around with it for at least three days interpreting the language and all that shit and by the time they pass it on the meeting will be over. That is what they always do, Sir".

John said "Yes that is why we do not fuck with them. Now tell me about this."

Tress said "Sir, they are meeting in a villa about one Kilometer outside Mogadishu about where the pirates keep the boats. It will be heavily guarded of course, but I think we can take them all out with the assets we have, I can change a few things in the battle plan and the teams can adapt to the changes, so we have a very good chance to kill everyone in Somalia that we want to kill."

John said, "Tress and Sandy do it and get it to the teams now."

Tress said, "Yes Sir". Tress and Sandy rushed back to their office and made an adjustment to the plan and sent it to the teams. Tress got the confirmation the teams had received the message and were changing the attack accordingly. Tress told John.

The raid had been changed from a 3 AM time to midnight time. This would insure everyone would be at the location. History had shown that the meetings always went at midnight for some strange reason. Tress had been doing this for a long time and he knew his business. John was ready. It was now 11 PM and John and Jim were in John's office talking about the attack. Jim was worried about the parachute drop but neither man could figure a better method to get the operators on the ground close to the target. There was such a chance that the local people would sound an alarm. Jim said, "We have no support for those guys if the shit hits the fan, General".

John said "Jim I know that, and I wish we could use the Navy, but I just do not see how we can let them in on what we do. That would blow everything. You and I both know it would be all over the fucking news and then where would we be? In deep shit that is where". Tress called John and said it was time. John and Jim went into the operation center and sat and watched the live feed. The Black Hawks had lifter off and the Cobra was almost ready to depart. The jump was set for fifteen minutes from the time John sat down. John watched the screen and knew the President and others he allowed were doing the same thing. There was a secure line sitting on the table beside John's chair and it was direct to the President. Time ticked away and then the screen came to life. The first operator had just left the Black Hawk. The raid was on. John felt his stomach start to tighten and he noticed his hands were sweating. Jim was sitting next to John and was breathing hard. Harry was standing behind both John and Jim and John could hear his breathing and John knew how it felt. These men, had done this many, many times before, and not being there was harder than actually doing the mission. The tension was high in the room and John could only imagine what it was like in the Situation Room of the White House. The first team was now on the ground and the second team was just landing at the target closest to the boat docks and fuel tanks on the south end of the dock. The last team had just jumped, and the Black Hawks had gone back out over the water and were waiting.

# CHAPTER 10

The operators made their way toward the villa and noticed that few guards were outside. Nelson sent two of his team to silence the guards. Nelson watched as the men had their heads explode and fell where the stood. Nelson counted four down and started moving closer to the villa entrance. The second team was on the east side of the villa and ready to enter through the side entrance. That team had eliminated two guards and had also eliminated the two guards in the rear. Nelson gave the order and both teams charged into the villa.

The War Lords and the pirate leaders were seated at a large table in a room off to the left of the main entrance. Nelson and his team entered the room and immediately started firing at the individuals seated. Bullets ripped into the men and they were forced out of their chairs by the impact. The operators went one by one and insured all men were dead. The second team had gone upstairs and sounds of gunfire were coming from that area. In four minutes there was silence. Nelson checked with the second team leader and found one operator had been wounded but everyone else was alright. All the pirates upstairs had been killed. The second team came down and the wounded operator was initially treated and made ready for evacuation. His wound was to the left leg but was not very bad. He could walk with assistance. Nelson had both teams do another sweep of the villa and take the photographs of the dead men. They also used the fingerprint scanner and printed each of the dead men and took a DNA swab, and when Nelson was satisfied there were no more targets, so he told all operators to leave and go to the evacuation point. Nelson then called the Cobra and had the Cobra do a gun run and use his rockets on the villa. The Cobra gunship came in on the first pass and fired two rockets. The explosions were tremendous, and the villa was torn apart and in flames. The Cobra then made another pass and fired the 20 mm cannons into the burning structure. Nelson was satisfied the villa was destroyed. Nelson left to join the teams at the evacuation point.

While Nelson and the second team were attacking the villa, the third team of operators was attacking the boats and the docks. The operators attacked the building that the pirates used as a makeshift base and killed seven men in the initial attack. The operators set explosive charges on all the boats and on the fuel tanks and killed an additional four pirates that were around the boats. The team then moved to the evacuation point and set off the charges with the remote detonators. The entire dock and all the boats exploded. The fuel tanks exploded and sent burning fuel flying into the air catching the dock and surrounding buildings and some vehicles a blaze. One of the Black Hawk choppers came in and the operators were picked up and the Black Hawk was out over the ocean. The extraction took two minutes from the touch down by the chopper until it was over the ocean and climbing to 1500 feet. John and the White House had watched the entire raid on both the villa and the docks as they raid played out. Each operator had a camera on his helmet and these pictures were sent to the satellite then sent to the special feed system. There was also a satellite that had been overhead the entire time and was still sending pictures. John watched and saw the trouble coming. The local people were moving toward the evacuation point for the two teams. Nelson had the teams ready for pickup by the Black Hawks but a group of locals, all armed, were coming down the road that lead to the field that was being used to pick up the operators. John and Jim watched the crowd grow larger and larger in just minutes. Jim saw flashes coming from the crowd and said, "The bastards are firing on our people". John watched and saw three operators go down. The operators were out in the field and had very little cover.

John said, "What is the plan, Jim?"

Jim said, "We drop the barrel bombs and we do it now." Jim told Tress, who had the direct SAT phone communications with the Black Hawks, Cobra and Nelson to give the command and Tress did in a matter of seconds. John and the rest of the people in the operations center watched as both Black Hawk choppers made a run into the evacuation area. The choppers hovered for a few seconds only and John could see each chopper release a barrel bomb. The bombs had been created by Harry and the munition experts. Each bomb had 400 pounds of C-4 explosives packed into a plastic 55 Gallon barrel. The barrels were then filled with twenty-five pounds of white phosphorous and a remote detonator was placed to set off the explosives when triggered. Jim had wanted something just in case the operators needed to use it. Jim had been with the Rangers and had gone thru the mess years ago in Mogadishu and did not want a repeat of that situation. The bombs were dropped in front of the group of people coming into the evacuation zone. The Black Hawks then turned and landed and picked up the operators. John could see the gunfire coming from the civilian group that was trying to come into the evacuation area. As the Black Hawks lifted off the bombs exploded. Each barrel bomb was equal to a 500- pound aerial bomb and the explosions ripped the civilian gunmen apart. The blast created a crater in the road that was 20 feet wide and 10 feet deep. There was another crater that was 25 feet wide and 15 feet deep to the side of the first one. The Black Hawks were now over the sea and headed to the container ship. The Cobra then made a pass and used the cannons and machine guns on the people trying to shoot at the Black Hawks. The Cobra then headed out to the container ship. The area was total chaos, and people were running everywhere. John told Tress to get a report on the wounded as soon as he could. John then went to his office and waited for a call from Washington. It came within five minutes. When John picked up the phone he heard "Well done". Then the phone went dead. John hung up his phone and sat back. The raid had done exactly what it was supposed to do and more. Now John had to find out about his wounded operatives. The Physician's Assistant assigned to the unit and a paramedic had been on the container ship and an area had been set up for treating any wounded operators. John needed to know how bad the wounds were and then arrange for the wounded to get to a hospital. It took about thirty minutes before Tress was able to get any information on the wounded men. When Nelson was able to get the report from the PA, he sent it to Tress via SAT text. Tress brought the text into John's office and said "General, we have a total of six operators that received wounds. All but one was minor. We have one critical. He was hit in the neck and the PA is working on him now. The other operators have been worked on by our paramedic. The leg wound has been taken care of and Nelson thinks everyone except the neck wound can wait until the ship docks in South Africa. That is what the PA and the medic say according to Nelson".

John said "Thanks. Now can we find a place to use if we need to get the operator who is critical into a hospital?"

Tress said "Sir, Sandy is working that as we speak, I will keep you informed."

John said "Good". Tress left.

Don had received the photographs and the fingerprints. Cindy and Don were running them thru the recognition programs of the FBI and INTERPOL. Don had been able to hack the programs and make a complete copy of each program so Red Lion had the exact same programs each agency had. Don had also installed a Trojan that automatically updated Red Lion's programs when either the FBI or INTEROPL updated their programs. The DNA would be brought back by the operators and then sent to a holding lab and a profile would be made and added to the DNA Data base Don had also hacked. John was always amazed that Red Lion had exactly what the FBI and INTERPOL had, and no one knew a damn thing about them having that resource. Cindy came into John's office and said "Sir, we confirmed all the people there and we got the War Lords and the leaders of the pirates, but we have two unidentified people and these individuals do not come up in any data base. We do not know who they are only that they are Caucasian and were well dressed. One was in European clothing. The other was wearing American clothing. Both men look to be in their late 40's or early 50's. I would say they were there for the meeting but that is all we can get".

John said "OK we need to work on that. I need them identified if we possibly can. See what you can do and thanks". Cindy left the office.

Tress came to John's office and said "Sir, Nelson has just told me that the operator that was wounded the worse is stable. The PA did a temporary surgery and stop the bleeding, but we need to get him to a hospital. CSM Harry and I have already contacted some people we know in Kenya and they have arranged a doctor and hospital we can use. We will need cash of course, but the people on the ground say if we can fly our guy there he would be safe, and he could be taken care of".

John said, "OK how much do we need in cash?"

Tress said, "I think $100,000 would be more than enough".

John said "Get the bank coordinates and then tell Nelson to get a Black Hawk moving with our guy. I want the paramedic to go as well as two shooters for protection. Have the PA remain on the ship. When you get the coordinates give then to Nancy. Thanks, Tress."

Tress said, "Yes Sir" and left the office. Two hours later Tress informed John that the operator was in the Hospital in Kenya and doing very well. He would probably stay for three to five days. John was relieved. Jim came into the office and told John Don and Cindy had identified the American that was at the meeting. Jim said "John he was a lawyer and he works for Ben Gall, the billionaire that owns oil and gas interests and a lot of other businesses including some financial investment firms. This is not good. Could this idiot Gall be "Solomon"?"

John said "I do not know but Cindy had already said she thought this deal was a combination of more than one person. What the Hell are we into, Jim?"

Jim said, "I have no idea".

# CHAPTER 11

Six days had passed, and the container ship was in South Africa at port. The operators, the PA and the piolets were all on flights coming back to the US. Two operators and the mechanics had remained on the ship and would make the voyage back to Galveston with the container ship and the helicopters. The wounded operator and all the personnel that had been in Kenya were also taking a special medical flight back and should be in Houston in twenty-four hours. All the other operators, piolets, and the PA would also be landing in Houston in thirty hours. The container ship was due in port at Galveston in eight days. John was now completing the award recommendations and doing the last of the follow up work that he had to review and sign. John had recommended all operators, mechanics, and medical personnel on the raid for Bronze Star Medals. The piolets were also recommended for the Bronze Star Medal and Nelson had been recommended for the Silver Star Medal. Tress, and Sandy were also recommended for Bronze Star Medals along with the entire compliment of the ground support personnel at the Red Lion base. The wounded operators would receive the Purple Heart Award. John was sure these recommendations would be approved. Dan came into John's office and sat down. John said, "What is on your mind?"

Dan said, "John I believe Cindy is 100 % right about the "Solomon" thing. I did some research and I know who both civilians at the meeting are. I know we have an idea about the one working for Gall but the other one was from London and I have an idea he was working for Simmons the investment banker who is worth billions.".

John said, "Dan can we prove it?"

Dan said, "I do not know but this guy from London was in the firm that Simmons uses for all his legal work".

John said "Dan that is good. Make sure Tress and Sandy know and Don and Cindy. Have everyone dig up everything there is on these dead guys." Dan said "OK" and left the office.

The operators and all the Red Lion personal had arrived back in Houston and the container ship was five days out. John had spoken to all the personnel and told them how proud he was of them and what a great job they had done. They were given three days off as soon as they completed getting their paperwork done and handed into Nancy and her assistant. John was also going to take a day or two off and spend it with Molly. They had not been together since this action had begun and John was a little worried about how Molly was feeling about that fact. John left the office and drove to Molly's bar and went inside. Molly was behind the bar and immediately came around and hugged John and gave him a kiss. John returned the kiss then sat and ordered a beer. Mike and a few other people were there so John talked a little with them and then said, "Molly I am going to go to my apartment and clean up and then we can do something tonight if you would like".

Molly said "Yes, I would like, you know damn well I would like so I will see you about 7:30 PM".

John said "Great". John left and went to his apartment. He still had to get Molly moved but he planned to do that this week. Molly had a lot of her clothes already in John's apartment and all her makeup, and her personal stuff. There was not very much left to move so John figured it would be very quick and easy. Molly got to John's at 7:20 PM and had a drink then a shower and got ready to go out. John had decided they would go to Eddie V's and spend an evening sitting at the bar and listening to the Jazz music. Molly always loved that. John and Molly were listening to the music and talking about things. It was now time for John to make his move. John said

"Molly I love you and I want you to move into my apartment. How do you feel about that?"

Molly said "John I love you and yes I would like to move in with you. I have a lot of my things there already, but then I have my lease and all of that, so I would have to see what I could do about breaking the lease and all of that but Yes my darling I want to live with you".

John said "OK then tomorrow we start. I will take care of your lease problems and all you have to do is cancel the electric and the TV and Internet plus put in a change of address with the post office".

John and Molly looked at each other and then Molly said, "John this going to be one Hell of a ride, you know that don't you?"

John said, "Yes I do, and yes, it is". John and Molly left Eddie V's and went to John's apartment and made fantastic love for most of the remaining night. John was up at 5 AM as usual and Molly was sleeping very well. John checked his e-mail and then did his exercises. Molly woke up about 8 AM and they had coffee on the patio. The rest of the day John was arranging the movers and taking care of the least at Molly's apartment. The movers were schedule for the next morning at 8 AM. The next day John and Molly were at her apartment at 7 AM and watched as the moving team packed up the items and loaded the truck. John led the movers to his apartment and by 4 PM everything was unloaded, arranged in a temporary fashion and the movers were gone. John and Molly left and went to get a very quick dinner and a few drinks. The following day John helped Molly arrange the things she wanted to keep in the apartment and then had Harry bring a truck and some people and load the things Molly did not want and take them to the Red Lion warehouse and put them in storage. John and Molly were officially living together. John was very happy.

It was now the middle of November and the money Don had taken from all of Somalia was still floating from one bank to another and another and so on and would continue to do so until Don stopped that process. John had been watching the reports and he knew the world banking community was having a fit over the banks being whipped out. John was wanting some type of connection to the possible banks that had been used to fund the terrorists and the pirates, but so far Don and Cindy had nothing that could be used. John was ready to make a very bold move. John called Don and Cindy into his office and said "OK. Here is the plan. I want you guys to put half of the money we took back into the banks. There are six banks so put an equal amount into each bank. Set it up so it looks like a giant computer malfunction but then track every withdrawal made over the next week. If our guys do what I think and hope they will, we will have a good idea where they are putting the money. I believe our guys will withdraw all their funds and transfer them to a bank they use. How does that sound?"

Don and Cindy said, "Too easy, we can do that".

Then Don said, "What about the other half, it is over $300 Billion Dollars, Sir?" John said "I want you to evenly distribute it over our accounts. Put half of what we have into each of our accounts and the other half in one account we can transfer to Washington when I get the word". Don and Cindy nodded and left the office. John called June at the Pentagon and told her to get to Ledford and get him a bank account number and routing. That afternoon John received a secure fax with the numbers. Don transferred $155 Billion Dollars into the account. They money from Somalia was now in play and being tracked by Don and Cindy. In two days a transfer was made to a bank in Belize. John was now following one of the bank accounts used to fund worldwide terror activities. John sent a coded secure message to Washington, President's Eyes Only. The Red Lion operation was running as usual. Tress had a plan for the terrorists in the Philippines and John was ready to start that operation after the first of the year. Don and Cindy had been looking through banking records in the Philippines and had already discovered some transfers from the same bank in Belize. Don had the bank in Manila hacked and a Trojan in place. John was also ready to have Jim prepare a complete plan of assault. The group in the Philippines was larger and more military organized than any of the terrorist groups Red Lion had encountered before. Things would be very different, and Jim was a tactical genius. Jim told John a plan would be ready by January 5th and then John could decide on having it activated. John was alright with that. John got a phone call and he was to meet the President at his ranch in two days. The President had a ranch in central Texas and John would drive to the location. The ranch was just north of Austin about 250 miles from Houston. John was looking at a six-hour drive with traffic he would have to go through. John was ready and had no idea what the President wanted now.

The cover was a party, a Bar-B-Q, the President was holding on his ranch for some 200 invited guests both from the political party and many of the local people. Business leaders as well as actors, singers, and a variety of people would be attending, and John would not be noticed by the media. Some military members would be there as well as some of the President's Cabinet. All and all it was just a social event so John was going to take Molly along as a good indication it was just social. John had that detail approved so he told Molly to be ready to leave on Friday at noon. Molly was excited and of course had no idea what to bring as for as dresses or anything like that was concerned. John told her to bring about 4 different outfits from formal to country. John was going to bring a suit, some casual clothing and of course his dress uniform. John had a reservation in Austin for Friday night and the plan was to drive the rest of the way to the ranch Saturday morning and be there by 1 PM when the party started. John and Molly left Houston and arrived in Austin and got their room. John decided that they would stay inside the hotel and not go out, so they went to the bar and then to dinner in the restaurant at the hotel. The next morning John and Molly were up and on the road by 10 AM and arrived at the President's ranch at noon. John and Molly were screened by the Secret Service and allowed into the ranch. An aid showed them to a room that could be used to change their clothes in and told John to dress casual for the event. Molly and John got dressed, John had the bags taken out and placed back into his car and then John and Molly entered the main room. The President came over and shook hands with John and John introduced Molly to the President. John was told he would be summoned after a while, so he and Molly got a drink and mingled with the other guests. The party was very nice, and John and Molly stayed outside most of the time watching the fire pit and looking at the people. It was a nice day for November and the temperature was in the mid 50's. After an hour had passed John was directed to the President's office in the far end of the house. Molly stayed outside. John walked to the office and knocked. John was told to go into the office.

The President was sitting behind his desk and John walked to the front and saluted. The President said, "John please sit down we have some things to discuss." John sat in a chair looking at the President. The President said, "What the Hell is going on with you and Gall?"

John explained all he had learned and what Cindy had said about the situation as far as the money was concerned. John also told the President about the bank account in Belize and about the fact that Don and Cindy had linked that bank to banks in the Philippines that were being used by the terrorists there. Also about the Somalian banks and the money transfers.

When John had finished his explanation, the President said "I do not like this one God damn bit, John. I know Gall is very eccentric and he is radical as Hell about certain things, but Jesus Christ, sponsoring worldwide terrorists. Come on John".

John said "Mr. President, think about this Sir. The man wants to control everything in his industry is that, not right?"

The President said "Yes and he does not like the government telling him he can only own so much of a certain thing or it would be illegal. Yes, I give you that."

John said "Yes Sir, and what if he had three or four other people around the world that felt exactly like he does? And what if these men or women Hell we do not know yet, got the idea to disrupt the world by having terrorists build up large bases of support and then start to control countries or areas of land. Eventually they would control so much land and have so many people under their control no one could stop them. These leaders, would have to do exactly what the three or four people told them to do or they would be replaced. Sir, I know it sounds very crazy, but the more we look at this the more I am convinced we have just what I described to you. My people think so also".

The President sat very quiet for about three minutes and John was worried he might have gone too far. After another minute went by the President said "John I do not know if you are right, but it does make sense when a person stops and looks at what you said. If these people are doing this and I see no reason to doubt you, I can see exactly how they would want this. It would boil down to a small number of people owning the world and having the power to run it exactly the way they wanted it to run. That would endanger the way of life for everyone. John, I agree with you and now how in the Hell do we stop them?"

John said "Mr. President, we find out exactly who they are, where they are, and we eliminate them and their organization. We kill everyone connected to them from the top to the bottom and if possible, steal their money and possessions."

The President said "OK John you have your mission. Get it done and get it done as quickly as possible." John stood up, saluted and said, "Yes Sir." John left the office and returned to the party and found Molly. Molly could tell from John's face things had gone well. She stopped worrying and enjoyed the rest of the night. John and Molly left the ranch about 10 PM and drove back to Austin and the hotel. The next morning, they drove back to Houston. John explained the visit and everything else to Molly. Molly said "God, John these people are totally insane. Can you stop them?"

John said, "I sure as Hell am going to try".

# CHAPTER 12

KBR had informed Harry that the complex in Hallettsville would be completed in four days. John and Molly were planning to spend Thanksgiving in Hallettsville at the ranch, so John had Harry, Dan, Jim, and some other operators ready to meet him the day before Thanksgiving and inspect the new complex. John and Molly were going to drive up the day before the meeting with KBR and the rest of the Red Lion people would fly up the morning of the meeting. Things were getting very interesting with Don and Cindy tracking the funds. Don had now followed funds back to a bank in the US and it was one of the banks used by Gall. Hell, he owned the bank. Money had also been tracked to a bank in Switzerland that had as one of the major customers, a Sheik from Saudi Araba. John was positive he now had at least three people who were involved as "Solomon". John had told Don to keep digging and get as much information on these guys as possible. Cindy had also uncovered a line to an industrialist in Germany that could be connected. She was trying to find something to tie any one of them to him or maybe all three.

Ray and Donna were very happy to see John and were just as happy to meet Molly. John and Molly got settled into the guest room and then came down and had drinks with the family. John introduced Molly to his grandmother and Molly was accepted by her immediately. In fact, John's grandmother wanted Molly to sit right by her and visit. John just shook his head but did not say a word. He knew better. The night went well, and dinner was as always great. Donna was a fantastic cook and John always liked being there. Molly was accepted right away by everyone and she had a very good time. John and Molly sat in front of the fire and talked with Ray and Donna for a long time. Ray was glad the project was finished but he did say the town would miss the workers and the money they spent. John understood that part all too well. The Sheriff would still be providing security so that part was intact. John and Molly went to bed around 12 midnight.

John was up early the next morning and Ray got him some coffee and then drove John to the compound. The Red Lion people arrived about 8 AM and at 9 AM KBR arrived. John was ready to do his inspection. The inspection took 2 hours and Harry and Jim were very pleased. John was also pleased with the operation. Dan was with the KBR attorney and signed the acceptance documents and was handed the keys to the complex. The entire group went to the country club and had lunch. After lunch was done, KBR left, and the Red Lion people left and returned to Houston. John and Ray went back to the complex and spent the next few hours looking at everything. John and Ray returned to the ranch house and had drinks with Molly, Donna and John's grandmother then dinner. The next day was Thanksgiving and Molly had been helping Donna bake and prepare all day. Linda, Miles and their children were due to be at the ranch around 10 AM on Thanksgiving Day. The plane landed about 10 AM. John had ridden with Ray to go get Linda and everyone. Linda hugged John and John and Miles shook hands. The kids hugged John and Ray. Miles' parents were also on the plane and John and Ray greeted them. Everyone got into the SUV and Ray drove back to the house and all went inside. Linda, Miles and his parents met Molly and Molly got everyone a drink. Dinner was served at 2 PM and it was a feast. Donna had given her housekeeper the day off to be with her family, so it was Donna, Linda and Molly doing the serving and all the kitchen work. Donna had everything left after dinner until her housekeeper returned the next day to take care of things. The day was very pleasant, and everyone enjoyed being together. John and Molly went to bed last and were the first up the next morning. They headed back for Houston and Molly and he talked about his family and how much she had enjoyed being there.

During the first week of December, John had called a meeting of his main staff. John had decided that Red Lion would not plan any operations against any terrorist group for the time. John wanted all efforts on finding the people who ran this show and that were called "Solomon". There were three for certain that had to be looked at in detail and possibly more. Cindy always thought at least four and probably six due to the amount of money that was being spent. John was ready to believe her and wanted to get the names and locations of each of the six if possible. The war was still going on in Iraq and Afghanistan. John was watching the way troops and materials were being allocated and he did not understand why almost everything was now going into Iraq. Afghanistan was not being followed up on and John could see that the enemy was only waiting and regrouping. These tactics were totally wrong, but there was not a thing he could do about the situation. John realized that Red Lion would be having to re-fight many of the same battles in a few years. John got the intelligence daily briefs, the same brief that went to General Davis the commander of Army Intelligence. John would read the brief and if there was something Red Lion did not have he would pass it to Tress and Sandy. Otherwise John would put the brief into the burn bag for destruction. A week before Christmas John was reading the Intelligence Brief and he noticed a name. It was the name of a German industrialist that John had seen before. Hans Grubber. Grubber was a very wealthy German who had many industrial chemical operations in Germany and was also heavily into precious stones and into minerals. John passed the name Grubber to Tress, Sandy, Don and Cindy and had them start digging into everything they could find on the man. The next day, John got another name. Prince Allie of the United Arab Emeritus. The Prince was one of the Seven heads of the Emeritus and second in line if the current Prince died or quit. John also had everyone working on this name and doing everything to identify all there was to know about him.

Christmas was now two days away and almost all of Red Lion was on leave. The only people not leaving were a few operators and Harry. John was going to Ray's and Molly was looking forward to being there for Christmas. John had already gotten Molly's engagement ring and now he was ready for Christmas. John and Molly left the day before Christmas and drove to the ranch. The entire family including Miles' parents were there just like Thanksgiving. The tree was up and there were presents all over the place. Way too many to remain under the tree, so they were stacked on either side. Christmas morning was a riot. The kids were up and ready to get the presents open. John's Grandmother was sitting in her chair and Ray, Donna, Linda, Miles, John and Molly were all sitting around facing the tree. Miles' parents were sitting on the love seat facing John's Grandmother. The couch was loaded with presents. John was on his second or maybe third cup of coffee and watching the kids open their presents. Ray was playing Santa. After everyone had opened presents and shown off what they had received, John stood up and walked over to Molly. John reached into his pocket and pulled out a small box and handed it to Molly. Molly's eyes got wide and she said, "Oh John!" John then said, "Molly will you please marry me?"

Molly said, "Oh Yes I will John Yes I will". Everyone laughed at the way she had said it and then she opened the box. She took out the ring and John placed it on her finger. The ring was a four-carat white diamond solitaire mounted on a gold band. Molly jumped up and kissed John and held him. It was perfect, and John felt great. The day was off to a wonderful start. The dinner was again excellent and after dinner everyone sat around and had coffee and an after-dinner drink. Everyone wanted to know when the wedding was going to be and where. John said he and Moly would decide and let everyone know but probably not for a few months. John and Molly came back to Houston the day after Christmas and Molly was looking forward to telling her friends about the engagement and showing off the ring. John was glad he had made her happy. New Years was spent at Molly's. She always had a New Year's Party and this year many of the Red Lion people came. The crowd was very good, and the band was great. Molly had food catered in and of course at midnight Champagne was served to everyone. The party was a lot of fun and John and Molly got home about 5 AM on New Year's Day. Molly had to stay and closed and then run the money by the bank. Molly was smart because she had an off-duty Police Officer as her security and he followed her to the bank. Molly had always had that at nights when the bar closed and had never been robbed. To her the cost was well worth the fact that she could feel safe and so could her employees. John and Molly spent the entire day in bed. It was now 2007.

The year started off good for Red Lion. John had been approached by some people in Houston to furnish security for a project they had in Louisiana. John was going to have to quote them, but it had to be a very high rate. John had worried about the possibility of having someone hire Red Lion or try to hire them. John prepared a quote and of course it was about seven times as much as any other security firm quoted. John did like the people who had asked for the quote, but he explained to them that Red Lion did mainly international work and due to the nature of their contracts their people got paid a lot of money and Red Lion had to charge a large price. The people understood and remained friends with John and Molly. John was very relieved.

Red Lion was now doing training in the new complex and that was wonderful. The operators were getting better and better with their skills and everyone liked the complex. John was also getting members of Delta and Special Forces sent in for training by Department of Defense. Operators would be the instructors and the training lasted a week. John had arranged rooms at three of the local hotels and business was good for Hallettsville again. Ray liked that fact and was glad John was able to do it for the community. John was watching the training closely and was happy with the way the process was going. John received a secure message from the Chief of Staff on Tuesday. The message told John that ten new operators would be assigned to his unit and that eight Navy personnel would be arriving in ten days and would also be assigned to his unit. John had no idea why Navy personnel would be in his unit, so he sent a message back requesting an explanation. Two hours later John received a phone call on the secure line from Ledford. John was told the Navy personnel would be there to take over the operation of the container ship. John was also told the ship would be going to a shipyard facility, in New Orleans, for certain upgrades and would be unavailable for about ninety days. John was told he would receive a message within twenty-four hours about the new situation with the container ship. The operators and the Navy personnel arrived and were processed into Red Lion. John had received his message and now he understood about the Navy people. The container ship was to be re-fitted with a special engine, a lot of new computer equipment and special items such as a complete hospital emergency room, guns and missiles as well as a complete machine shop. The Navy people would be in-charge of the vessel. The exterior would remain the same and the guns and missiles would be mounted so that they could not be detected until barriers were removed. John liked the idea and informed Jim and Harry. The ship would be based in Galveston and John was to rent a pier space for it under the Red Lion company. John had Harry and Dan work that issue. Dan found a warehouse at the docks and a slip that Red Lion could rent and got the paperwork done and everything was set for the new arrivals. Harry was in-charge of the new operators, and would in process them.

# CHAPTER 13

The months had really gone by fast and it was now June. John was compiling a complete list of the men responsible for "Solomon" and would be ready to present his information to the President in a week. Don and Cindy had identified the last member of the "Solomon" group as a Chinese business billionaire by the name of Wang. This put five men in the circle. John believed that was the complete group for two reasons. The first was only a small group at the top could get along well enough to make the decisions and get things done. And secondly Don and Cindy could find no other relation from anyone to the money transfers. The background that Red Lion had been able to find on these men showed that they were totally power hungry and that they had a very great hate for any form of government that told them how to act. The key elements in forming a "New Society" and John could see how they would work together to control the entire world. The terrorists would become their army and enforce their will on everyone at a certain point in time. This was a real threat and John knew it had to be eliminated. Just how to do that was the question.

The container ship was now back and in port. John had gone to Galveston and met the Navy people and was given a complete tour and briefing on the new ship. Jim and Harry as well as Tress had been along. The ship was ready to be used and with the new engines the speed was tripled. The damn thing could go over 40 knots so John was told. The fuel tanks had been enlarged and now the ship could go almost around the world without re-fueling. The deck had been reinforced and was now set up to land up to eight helicopters on it. Also, a small vertical takeoff jet could be used off the deck. The hospital section was up to date with the latest equipment and the computers and satellite equipment were the newest and best the government had. John really liked the ship and he was very impressed with the Navy crew. The Captain was a young man in his late 40's named Anderson. John knew he was the best or he would not be assigned. The rest of the crew were also the best and had been hand-picked for the assignment. The Navy personnel would be living in Galveston. John was glad of that because Red Lion was getting big and no questions about what they did needed to be asked. The personnel on the ship would be just merchant seamen working for a specific company. It was a good cover. The warehouse at the pier was also a good thing because it had a drive through approach, so any trucks could be unloaded inside and away from people who might get curious. John sent Don and Cindy down to the warehouse to install all the computer equipment, the secure fax, phone, SAT phone, and the visual screens that would be needed. Harry also went along and did a security assessment.

Harry had a security company that Red Lion used. The company was owned by Wayne Hudson, a former Navy SEAL, who Harry had known for twenty years. Hudson had retired in 2005 and formed his security company in Houston, his hometown. Harry had Hudson supply security officers for Red Lion and for the airfield in Sugarland. The officers were vetted by Red Lion and the agreement was to pay the officers $30 per hour and Hudson would be paid $20 per hour for each officer. The officers were all armed and were sharp. Red Lion was the largest client Hudson had and Harry got exactly what he wanted when he wanted it. Hudson would be adding additional officers for the Galveston location. John was pleased with that arrangement and knew the money was not a problem. John had met with Hudson originally and John was impressed with the man. Hudson had a very good company and was not really interested in doing much more than Red Lion. He did have a few special clients, they were the bigger people in Houston and required personal protection for themselves and their family members. Hudson had 150 officers on his payroll and added more as was needed. All his people were sharp and worked well with each other. All of Hudson's vehicles were equipped with computers and SAT phone communications. Harry had Hudson immediately take charge of the security at Galveston.

John was still concerned on how Red Lion was going to be able to eliminate all the players in "Solomon". The two that would give the most problems were Wang and Prince Allie. Getting into China was almost impossible and killing the Prince would have to be sanctioned by the head of the Emeritus. John was going to have to have a lot of assistance from many agencies to pull this off unless he or his team could figure out some way to get all five together. The Intelligence was always very undependable, so Tress and Sandy had their hands full getting fact from fiction. Don and Cindy had the same problems with the computer tracking. These men could and did buy the very best and it made things very hard. Tress had learned that most of them had large security forces that were used to protect not only the individuals but their complexes. Without using a direct assault with the operators, which John knew was not a real option, John was unable to find a way in. He was going to have to tell the President that and John did not want to do that. John called Don and had him, and Tress come to his office. When the men arrived, John had them sit and then said "I need to know exactly what US holdings each one of the five has. I need to know the dollar value and everything we can find out about what they own and where everything is located. Break down any shell companies and anything that is in the way, so we know exactly and then can figure out a solution". Don and Tress understood and left John's office. The new search was now in full swing. John would wait until he had the information before he did anything about the President.

It took until the end of July for the team to actually find all the holdings. Tress and Sandy were also concerned with the "chatter" that was going on from the terrorist sources. Something was going to be done but there was not one hint of the location of an attack or the type of attack. Don and Cindy had been having real problems in breaking security firewalls on the "Solomon" leaders and Don was not sure it was going to happen. It seemed to him that the firewalls were being updated every twenty-four hours with new systems and even when Cindy and Don got a break-through, it only worked for a short amount of time. Then they had to start all over again. John could see the problems were getting larger. The terrorists were getting smarted. Tress did have a solid lead on what the world called "The Bomb Doctor". Al-Qaeda had one man who designed and produced bombs of all types for them. He was an absolute genius at doing it and had constructed bombs that had been used in England, Africa, Libya, and South America and in the Far East. He was currently in Yemen. Tress was working on his exact location. The US military had used drone aircraft to send rockets into suspected locations and try to kill the bomb maker, but so far, no success. His designs were being used in Iraq against our troops, on a daily basis, and the casualties were increasing. John was wanting to send in a team to eliminate this mad man. Yemen was a "so called" ally to the US but nothing was being done in the region of the country he was in. The al-Qaeda terrorists controlled about one quarter of the country and the Yemen armed forces would not even go into that region. No matter how the US tried to get them to attack the area, the Yemen Army refused to do it. John was ready to use his operators to do the job, but he needed the exact location. The last week of July Tress and Sandy found the location of the "Bomb Doctor". John had Tress and Sandy plan a raid.

John wanted it ready in 48 hours. John was sitting in the briefing room when Nelson, Jim, Harry, Tress, and Sandy came in and sat down. John said, "Tell me the plan".

Tress stood up and took the pointer and hit the button to illuminate the screen on the wall. A map of Yemen appeared with the location of the target outlined inside a box. Tress said "Sir, as you can see the target is about 50 kilometers inside the zone the Yemen Army will not go into. The compound is made up of three buildings. One we have identified as the living quarters, the second is the lab or what we think is the lab and the third is an unknown. It could be used as a living area for guards or a storage for supplies. The latest satellite pictures show a limited number of actual terrorists in the compound. We estimate no more than six not counting the target. There are women and probably children, but we have not gotten a good count. The plan is simple. We will use a small unit of operators, four and have them do a HALO jump into the compound. The time will be at 2 AM local time. They will then eliminate everyone in the compound. As soon as they have eliminated the target and gotten the picture, fingerprints and DNA from the target and others if necessary the team will set explosive charges and leave. If possible, the team will do a search of the lab and living area and the other building for any information that could be of help. The exit route will be directly down this road (Tress pointed the road out on the map) and as soon as they have crossed over the line that the Yemen troops will not cross, they will be met by members of the Yemen Army and taken to an air field here (Tress again pointed to the map) and put on a plane to Israel. After the team lands in Israel, they will board a US Air Force plane for the flight back to the US".

John said, "I see we will have to use regular Air Force units to get this done, is that going to be a problem?"

Tress said "Well General, not if you can coordinate it with Washington. I suggest we tell the Air Force that the team is

Delta so there will be no real questions. Delta is operating all over the area".

John said, "I like it but are we sure the Yemen guys will assist us?"

Tress said "Yes, I personally know the head of one of the special operations groups and that is who will meet our team and take them to the air field. He will also get us clearance for the Air Force plane to land there".

John said, "OK anyone have any questions?"

Jim said, "Who will we coordinate with at the Air Force level, Sir?"

John said "I will talk to Ledford and have him talk to the Air Force Chief. That should get us a flight." No other questions were raised, and Nelson was given the green light to conduct the raid with his team. The raid would be in 3 days, weather permitting. John got up as did the entire room and John went to his office and got on the secure line to Washington. The rest of the people went back to their offices. John made his call and waited for the return fax to come into the operations center. The fax arrived in thirty minutes and was given to John. A copy was given to Jim, Tress, and Harry. The planes would be there as requested. The first plane would be at Ellington AFB and ready to fly the day before the raid. A re-fuel was scheduled for the air, so the flight would go from Ellington directly to Yemen and the target. The operators would HALO jump from the original aircraft and the jump would be at 30,000 feet. That way no chance of detection. It would be on the same flight path as the commercial airlines used but only for three minutes. The pickup plane would be a C-22 Lear Jet. The final flight would be the C-141 again and would be the one that had originally flown the operators from Ellington. It would land in Israel after the jump and wait for the operators. Things had been cleared with the Israeli government. John had informed the President via special "Eyes Only" fax of the raid and the time.

Tress had the satellites ready to be in position and Jim had made sure SAT phone communications would be up and running. The operators arrived at Ellington AFB, boarded the C-141 and were airborne and eighteen hours later would be deployed over the target. Harry had checked to make sure the ammunition was civilian issue and not military. That was always the case because no one could trace the shell casings back to the US Government. The operators would use civilian weapons as they normally did. Only when major raids were scheduled, did the operators use military weapons and then it was only machine guns. John had insisted on that from the start of the operations.

John was again sitting in the operations room and Jim and Harry were standing behind him. Tress and Sandy were on the sat phone head sets and Don was sitting and controlling the computers that would be used to move the satellites into different positions. It was now twenty minutes before the drop. John was as always tense. It never went away and this time it seemed to be worse than usual. The operators would have no back-up and no medical help if things went wrong. Nothing could be done about that. The screen came to life and John saw the tail gate opening on the C-141. The next picture was of the operators exiting the aircraft and free falling. The helmet cameras gave a very good picture. John knew the President was watching just as closely as John was. The operators were now landing and approaching the building that was unknown as to what was in it. The operators had split up and only two entered the building. John could see with the night vision attachment on the cameras that there was only three men in the building and they were eliminated in seconds. John watched as Nelson and one of the operators took photos and prints and then got the DNA samples. The two then moved to the second building the lab. Again, when the team entered, only two terrorists were there. They were instantly eliminated. The operators left that building and staged to attack the main building that housed the living area. The operators went into the building and immediately eliminated four men. They worked their way into a room in the rear and saw the target in bed with a woman. Nelson moved to the side of the bed and eliminated the target. The woman started to attack Nelson and another operator eliminated her. The team then moved to the next room and found three women and four children asleep on the pallets on the floor. Nelson immediately tied the women with flex cuffs and had the children tied with flex cuffs. The women were then removed from the room and taken out side. The children were taken outside but separated from the women. One operator placed the children into a van that he had found and then he placed the women one by one into the van after they had been searched for weapons. The other members of the team were now searching all the buildings and placing papers, books, audio tapes, plans and almost everything they found into the jump bags they had brought with them. When the bags were filled, they were loaded into the van. Pictures, prints and DNA had been taken and gathered from all the terrorists, including the woman and then the team of three set the explosives. The team then got into the van and headed toward the meeting point. The entire raid took a little over thirty minutes. When the team was one mile from the compound Nelson set off the explosives. The entire compound exploded and was in flames. The fires lit up the night skies and could be seen for miles. The team arrived at the meeting point and the members of the Yemen special operations group lead the van to the air field. At the air field, Nelson and his men loaded the bags into the C-22 and handed the women and children over to the Yemen operators. The Red Lion team boarded the jet and were in route to Israel. John received a call on the special phone and again the message was the same "Well done". The phone went dead. In four hours John received a call from Nelson on the SAT phone and Nelson said, "We are onboard the C-141 and ETA Ellington is eighteen hours from now, Sir".

John said, "Well done and I will be glad to see you at home. Make sure your team has what they need. It should be on board."

Nelson said, "Yes Sir". John hung up the SAT phone and told everyone what a great job they had done. John then went home to see Molly. It was now 6 PM the next day. John had been at Red Lion for over twenty-four hours. He was ready for a cold beer and Molly.

The operators landed at Ellington and were met by Harry and Jim. All the bags were loaded into the van and the weapons were loaded as well along with the bags containing all the equipment. The van left for the Red Lion headquarters. The operators got into the SUV and they were also taken to the headquarters. Harry and Jim spoke to the Air Force piolets and crew and then drove to the headquarters. The bags with the material seized during the operation were taken to the warehouse and Tress and Sandy started going through the material. Everything was documented. Don and Cindy were running the photographs and the finger prints as well as the DNA. It was confirmed that the "Bomb Doctor" was dead. Then the surprise came. Don came into the office and said, "John from what we just ran, we have killed the "number-two-man" in al-Qaeda. It is a positive match. Facial recognition, prints, and DNA".

John said "I will be damned. He must have been on a visit or some damn thing, we got very lucky. Ok Don, get the report done right away and to me. I have to let Washington know".

Don said, "I will have it in about twenty minutes". Don went to his office and John called Tress and gave him the news. Tress was very excited. John had sent a message to Ledford and he recommended that Ledford have the Pentagon public relations/news secretary tell the American public in a news release live on all networks, the following: "Yemen, it has been confirmed that the "Bomb Doctor and the number-two-man in al-Qaeda have been killed in an explosion of a bomb factory deep inside Yemen. The explosion destroyed the factory and killed seven other terrorists along with the ones I just told you about. The confirmation of identification is positive. We are very glad this terrible threat has been eliminated". John watched the noon news and saw the special report. It was said just as he had written it out. John was now ready to concentrate on the "Solomon" group and taking them out once and for all.

# CHAPTER 14

O ctober was now here, and John was almost in position to go to Washington and talk to the President. Sara, one of the civilians that had been originally sent to the Red Lion base wanted a meeting. Sara was in-charge of the financial operation for Red Lion. John had not really taken the time to get to know Sara. She had been one of the people in the Pentagon on 9-11 and had been hurt. Her son had died in New York as one of the hundreds of firemen that died that day. Her other son had been killed in Iraq in 2005. Sara hated the terrorist and would do anything to stop them. John had Sara come into his office and sit down. John said "Sara, what is on your mind and how can I help?"

Sara said "Sir, we have far too much money and I am having trouble doing anything with it, so no one will know".

John said "That is a problem most of America wishes they had. Too much money. Ok how much are we talking about?"

Sara said, "Well over $1.3 Billion Dollars, Sir". John sat for a minute. The words would not come out. Finally, John said "$1.3 Billion Dollars. Is that after we have disbursed to Washington?"

Sara said, "Yes, it is Sir."

John said, "How in the Hell did we get all of that?"

Sara said "It seems like we are getting paid for every operator we have for training, then we get paid to train other operatives and then Don deposit's money into the banks from God knows where. I am just a little worried that someone will start asking a bunch of questions and I have no answers. We also get funding for the ship in Galveston and for our headquarters here. I can only do so much "creative accounting".

John said "Ok well then we need to look at some things. Do you have any ideas?"

Sara said "I think we need to open at least four new accounts off shore under different names. I mean not using Red Lion in any way. I could then move money around some and we could always get to it if we needed to do so".

John said "OK Sara get with Dan and do what you need to do. If I have to sign anything, let me know. Thanks for bringing this up."

Sara said, "You are welcome Sir, and thanks for trusting my judgment." Sara left John's office.

Tress and Sandy came into John's office and Don and Cindy followed. Tress said "Sir, would you call General Jim and CSM Harry and have them come in here?" John buzzed Nancy had had her get them in his office. In ten minutes the two men arrived and sat down. John said, "OK what is going on?"

Tress said, "General we know when and where the "Solomon" leaders are going to meet, and we can kill all of them at once".

John said, "Ok go on".

Tress said "The meeting is set for November the 4th and it is going to be on an island off the coast of Belize. They have rented a villa and all the intelligence and computer traffic tells us that it is a very high- level meeting to talk about us".

John said "I will be damned. They are that worried about us?"

Don said "Yes we have intercepted email and they are trying to find out who we are and how we can get into the banks and especially how we can kill off their leaders in all these locations. Gall is very worried that we may know the names of the group. Grubber and Simmons are worried about the money and the Chinese guy, Wang is concerned he will not be able to keep the terrorists in the Far East under control enough to keep things in turmoil. The terror groups are scared that they will be the next on the hit list. That is why the meeting is being called from what the emails say".

John said "Then we need to do this and do it right. Tress you and Sandy have a plan?"

Tress said "Yes but it is just in the infant stages. We will need at least a week to finish it and we also need to get a satellite over the villa at least three times before the 4th".

John said" Jim you and Harry work with these guys and get them everything they need. I will get with the President. He has no choice now if he really wants this stopped". Everyone left John's office and John called Washington and left word that he needed to see the boss. In an hour John had his meeting. It would be the next day at 6 PM Washington time in the White House. John had Nancy call the private aviation company and arrange a jet. John then left and went to see Molly at the bar.

John went into Molly's and sat at the bar. The place was not busy, and Molly came over and sat down beside John and kissed him. John said "Hi sweetheart. I am going to Washington in the morning and will be gone at least one day." Molly said, "Ok problems?"

John said, "No just need to get some clarification."

Molly said "Well then we need to do something special tonight. You will be away, so you will probably need some tender attention for your trip".

John laughed and said, "Of course I always need that". Molly smiled. John had a few beers and talked with some of his friends as they came into the bar. John liked being at Molly's and wished he could be honest with his friends about what he did. That was going to be a huge problem when he and Molly got married unless they just went to Vegas. John knew Molly wanted a wedding and probably a big one. John did too. Working it out was going to be the thing. That was one reason they had not planned the wedding and John knew Molly wanted to get married and soon. John was going to have to really work on that. John left and went to the apartment and started packing his bag for the trip. John had decided to wear a business suit to the White House. John would pack his dress military uniform of course because he never knew when he would need to have it on. Molly arrived about 7:30 PM and John got her a drink. They talked for a while and then John said, "OK Lady what do you want to eat tonight?"

Molly said, "I think I want to go to Eddie V's and eat sea food, is that alright with you?"

John said "Sure is. Tell me when you are ready".

Moly said, "Give me thirty minutes and we can go". John got another beer and turned on the TV to the news. The markets had dropped again. John knew things were getting very bad. In fact, things were almost critical. John and Molly had a very good dinner and were back home by 10 PM. John was ready for bed but not to sleep. Molly was more than ready, and they made love like there was no tomorrow. The next morning, John was up and on his way to the office by 7 AM. The jet would pick him up in Sugarland at 9 AM. Nancy had made his reservations at the Army and Navy Hotel. A car had been arranged to take John to the White House and would pick him up at 5 PM. John got on board the jet and headed for Washington D. C.

John arrived at the White House at 5:30 PM and was cleared for entrance. John went into the north door and was met by a staffer and escorted to the Oval Office waiting area. At 6 PM John was sent into the President. John walked into the Oval Office and saluted the President. John was told to sit, and he did so in a chair that was at the coffee table. The President sat in the other chair. John said, "Mr. President I need you to see this" and handed the President a folder that contained the workup on each of the five heads of "Solomon". The President studied the folder for a good ten minutes. Then the President said "John you are absolutely sure of this. No mistakes or anything like that?"

John said "Mr. President I am positive what you have is the exact truth. That is what is so bad."

The President said, "Yes it sure as Hell is."

John said, "Now Sir we can stop the whole bunch and totally destroy "Solomon". All I need is your GO! And it will be done".

The President said "Ok but I need you to be sure it can never be traced back to us in any way shape or form. John if it is the country will explode. People already do not trust the military and they do not trust me much anymore. If this were to get out the news media would go crazy and Congress would really be on fire. No one could survive that even the Congress. They are just too stupid to know it".

John said "Sir, Mr. President that is exactly why I am here, and I never let you know anything before things happen. The secure feeds are all that is ever shown you and that is in real time. You can always claim you had no knowledge of anything till it came on the screen".

The President said, "I know that, John that is why it is you and me here alone". Then President said "John do what you think is best for our country. That is all I can or will tell you. It has worked up to now, so I see no reason why it will not work again. But remember, we will still have a bunch of these fucking people around. They just will have no money or direction and that can be a very dangerous thing. You will then have to figure out how to stop them".

John said "Sir, that is already in the planning stage. We have identified 9 groups that are immediate threats and we can eliminate them even quicker after we get the leaders now". The President stood up and John jumped to his feet. The President said "John thank you for this and for coming to me before you actually put the plan in effect. I still have a hard time with Gall. I really thought he was one of the good guys".

John said "Not really Mr. President. In fact, my people think he started this bullshit". John then saluted the President and left the Oval Office. It was almost 7 PM. John had been in there an hour almost. John was ready to return to Houston. He used his cell phone and told the plane to be ready to fly in an hour. John went back to the hotel and checked out and had a car take him to the plane. At 8:30 PM the jet took off. John landed in Sugarland at midnight and drove home. He arrived at his apartment at 1 AM and Molly was up and waiting for him. She handed him a beer and they sat and talked about his trip. John told Molly what was about to happen, and she listened very closely. When John was finished, Molly said "John tell me honestly are you going to be there, I mean on the ground?"

John said "No my dearest, I see no need to get in the way. These guys are the best and I have absolute faith in them."

Molly said "Good."

John had everyone involved with this mission. He wanted all operators to be on the mission. A total of 30 were now assigned to Red Lion and they were broken down into six-man teams. John had five teams he knew were the best in the world and the overall commander was Nelson. Harry had already gotten ammunition bought and there were over 100,000 rounds available. The Cobra was fully stocked with eight rockets and all the 20mm cannon ammunition and machine gun ammunition it could carry. The Black Hawks had over 100,000 rounds of ammunition for the M-60 machine guns they had mounted for the door gunners to use. The container ship now had twelve medium range missiles that could be launched to target 200 miles away, with laser GPS guidance. John knew things were ready. John had spoken with the container ship's Captain and it would take two days at the most to travel from Galveston to Belize. The ship could be off the coast in no more than forty-eight hours. That was all John needed to know. Tress and Sandy had the plan. The satellite photos had proven very helpful. The villa was large and three stories high. It covered about five acers of ground including the pool and the garages. There was only one road leading to the villa and it backed up to the ocean. A cliff of some 100 feet went directly down to a small beach. There was an elevator that could take guests down to the private beach. The beach was not fenced, and entry could be made from either side. The beach was patrolled by a foot patrol and a dog when not in use and when people were on the beach a patrol was at either end stationary in a vehicle. From what the views showed, about forty armed personnel were the guards that would be on duty when the "Solomon" group met. Tress had counted the guards arriving each day during the two-week period before the meeting. There was an airstrip about a mile from the villa and Tress figured that was where the participants would arrive. The strip was not large enough for the planes to stay so they would land, off load the passengers and then depart. Tress was prepared to give the operators the plan.

All the operators and all the personnel from the Navy were at Red Lion headquarters. The piolets, mechanics, gunners, medics and ground personnel were also at the briefing. John had decided to use the warehouse as the briefing area and Don and Cindy had set up the screen and readied the computer for Tress and Sandy to use. The entire staff of Red Lion was waiting when John walked in. Everyone was standing at attention. John said, "Good morning, please take your seats". John watched as everyone sat and pulled out notebooks. John had always been a proponent of taking notes and asking questions. He was delighted his people were doing exactly that. John said a few things to the group and then turned the floor over to Tress. Tress had a map of Belize on the screen and described the island. Then he put up a picture of the villa and a floor plan and a complete map of the grounds on the screen. All three images were on the screen together.

Tress gave the brief. The container ship would be fifteen miles off shore and would remain there. It would be blacked out until the raid started. With the radar capabilities on the ship, there was no concern about other ocean traffic hitting the ship. The Black Hawk's would be launched each carrying a ten-man team of operators. The Cobra would be the last to launch and would be on station fifteen miles out, until the raid started. Black Hawk one would be the designated Medevac and would have two medics on board. The PA will remain on the container ship to be used in the emergency room if needed. The Black Hawks will do a low-level approach and land on the air strip. The operators will dismount and move to the villa and attack. At that time the Cobra will approach and cover the roadway leading into the villa from the town.

The operators will attack from the front, and both sides. Using night-vision they will have the total advantage of surprise and vision. Don and Cindy will disable the power to the villa and scramble all communications to and from the villa. All cell phones will be blocked. Additionally, Don and Cindy will scramble the police communications. Belize does not have an Army or Air Force. They rely on their police force and we must assume the "Solomon" group has already bought the police. The Cobra will only engage the police if all else fails. Try to disable the car if you can and maybe the cops will get the message. If not do what you do. The main job is to protect the operators and to not allow any reinforcements into the villa. Once the raid has given the all clear, the operators will do the necessary ground work of collection of any possible information, pictures, prints and DNA and then go to the air strip for pick up. In the event of wounded, immediately call Black Hawk one and request evacuation. The Black Hawks will be flying cover during the assault once the operators have breached the villa. This is going to be hot because we estimate at least 40 armed guards and we can figure them for mercenaries. Our advantage is that they fight for money and do not like to have the odds against them with air power and tactics. We will have both. Once the operators are picked up and in bound to the ship, the Cobra will do a missile and cannon attack on the villa. The object is to set the damn thing on fire and destroy everything inside. Tress finished the brief and asked for questions. There were a few but nothing very important. Everyone understood and was ready to go. Sandy had arranged the satellite for an over view during the mission and it would be sending video for an hour. John was not going to have Washington watch this attack. He could not chance the fact that this would put the President in the hot seat if things went wrong in anyway. It was one thing to kill known terrorists. It is a completely other thing to kill world business leaders even if they are sponsoring terror. The world would want a trial and that would take years plus no one would stop the flow of money. John was confident he could stop both the leaders and the flow of money. Don and Cindy were set to do that as soon as the raid started. The operators, and everyone except Tress, Sandy, Don, Cindy and the bosses would be on the container ship for travel to the raid. The ship was to depart on the night of the 1st. All the equipment would be loaded during the day to include the helicopters. This time the choppers would be covered with tarps not dismantled and the rotor blades placed into containers. After the briefing all personnel went to work and got things ready. The movement to Galveston was set for the next day.

The Red Lion personnel were now loading the ship at Galveston and loading their gear on board. The choppers had been flown down and the ship yard cranes were placing them on the deck of the ship. By 11 PM that night everything was loaded, and the ship was leaving the dock. John had gone to the port and watched as his unit got things ready and loaded. He had the latest on weather and the latest satellite pictures and gave them to Nelson. John and Jim and Harry stood and watched the container ship being pushed out into the channel by a tug boat. The vessel soon was over the horizon and on the way to Belize. John called back and spoke to Tress. The "Solomon" Group were also headed to Belize and would be in the villa by the 4th. John and Jim looked at each other and smiled. This time it was going to be their turn to stop this crap and they both were extremely proud. Harry was standing and watching the ocean. His thoughts were miles away from Galveston and Belize. John could really appreciate that and so could Jim. They had all seen way too much war and it never seemed to end. John and his friends got into the vehicle and started back to Houston and then to the headquarters. John was going to go home. It would be a couple of days before he would be able to be there after tomorrow morning. Molly at least fully understood. John was very glad he had her.

# CHAPTER 15

The SAT phones were working, and the communication checks were complete. The operators had boarded the Black Hawks and the Cobra was ready to take off as soon as the Black Hawks left. It was 1:30 AM and Don was ready to scramble the police computers. Cindy was ready to scramble the electric grid and the cell phones. The land lines were left alone because no one could respond in a timely manner anyway and John did not want to cut off the civilian population any more than necessary. It was now time to launch and Tress got the word that the birds were in the air. Don and Cindy went to work. Don scrambled the computers at the police department and then he shut down the cell phone communications. Cindy emptied the two bank accounts that had been identified as having the money funding the terror operations. The accounts had a total of $9.5 Billion Dollars in them and this money was sent to different banks used by Red Lion. Then Cindy set up a virus that would immediately transfer any money that was deposited into the accounts out.

The operators were on the ground and from the pictures the command center was getting, no guards had reacted to hearing the Black Hawks touch down and then leave. Tress had identified eight guards on the exterior of the villa. There were an additional two guards and a dog on the beach doing patrol. This information was passed to Nelson. John was watching the screen and could see the operators moving toward the villa. The villa was lit up with the flood lights and John could see the lights inside were on in the first and second floor. John was again very nervous but that was the way it always was. John never got used to sending men into harm's way and never would. Jim was watching the one building attached to the garage part of the villa. Jim had decided that was where the off-duty guards would be staying, and Nelson had planned to hit that building as soon as the guards were eliminated on the exterior. The operators had weapons with silencers and they were experts at being unseen when they moved on a target. John watched as the operators divided into four teams and prepared to assault the villa. The tension in the operations center was very high and no one said a word except Tress when he advised Nelson or the Black Hawks over the SAT net.

John watched as Nelson positioned operators to eliminate the four guards on the front of the villa and each of the guards on the sides of the villa. In almost the same exact instant the guards were shot and fell to the ground. The two guards that were on the road about 100 yards from the villa were also shot within one minute of the exterior guards going down. John was watching as a team of four operators entered the building attached to the garage. The helmet cameras gave a clear picture of the operators getting twelve guards immediately on the ground and then John saw the operators use flex ties to restrain the guards. The operators also used duct tape and taped the guard's mouth and eyes shut. The guards were left on the floor. John was glad that Nelson had not had them shot. There was no need to shoot them at that point. John wanted to be as humane as possible and if there was no actual threat to the operators then why kill them just to kill them. The next movement that was seen in the operations center was the operators moving into position for the actual assault on the inside of the villa. A team of ten operators led by Nelson was staged to enter the main doors. Another team of six operators was staged to enter the rear of the villa through the kitchen and another team of six operators was scheduled to enter the side entrance using the patio entrance. The other operators were set in over watch positions.

Nelson entered the main door and immediately eliminated four guards that were in the front room. The operators followed and rushed into the villa. The operators entered the kitchen at the same time as did the operators entering from the patio area. The operators took all the kitchen staff, four locals into custody and used flex ties to restrain them. Their mouths and eyes were tapped, and they were left on the floor of the kitchen. One guard had been killed in the kitchen as the operators entered. The operators then moved to the stair case and Nelson led them upstairs. There were guards sitting outside the room where the meeting was being held, and they were eliminated immediately. Then Nelson and six operators burst into the room. All the targets were sitting at the table and each was shot in the head. Nelson confirmed the kills and took photos and fingerprints. Another operator collected DNA samples. The operators had by now completely searched the villa and every room was cleared. A total of eight women were also taken into custody and Nelson reported back that these women were the prostitutes that had been hired for the weekend. The women were tied with flex ties and had their mouth and eyes taped. They were left in one of the bedrooms on the floor. The operators then made a complete search of the villa for any documents or other things that were available. Four computers were taken and all the cell phones from the targets were recovered. The operators then prepared to evacuate the villa. Tress had contacted the Cobra and called of the missile attack because of the civilian captives. It was decided that the villa would be left just as it was and when some of the locals got free which they would, they could report the incident to the police. John was good with that decision. John watched as the operators moved out of the villa and started for the air strip. The assault had gone off perfectly and had lasted only thirty minutes. The operators arrived at the air strip and were loaded into the Black Hawks and headed back to the container ship. In less than one hour from the time the Black Hawks lifted off they were back on the deck of the ship. The Cobra landed four minutes after the Black Hawks and it took about an hour to secure the choppers for the voyage and to get all the equipment and recovered items loaded below decks. The container ship was headed back to Galveston at 3 AM. John was relieved and over joyed with the raid and with the results. At 3 AM Don restored the cell and computers, so everything was back to normal operations. Tress and Sandy were monitoring the communications and the police were now just being notified of the situation at the villa. John was relieved that no local police had been involved. At 4 AM John went home. He was of course tired, but he felt good about everything. John had sent a message to Washington for the President before he left and was sure it would be delivered the first thing in the morning. John was also sure the news media would be immediately involved especially when the names of the targets were released by the Belize government.

Jim had decided to have the choppers fly off the container ship before it docked in Galveston. His reasoning was to insure no one could connect the container ship coming back with the cargo it left with. John had agreed, so Jim had Don and Cindy hack the FAA computer system and put a flight plan in place. The flight plan was dated two days earlier and was sitting in the FAA computer. When the choppers entered the air, they would be automatically given clearance to fly to Sugarland and land at the airport there. With the war ongoing, no one really questioned military movements and Jim had used a special operations code to file the plan. The choppers would fly off the ship when they were seventy-five miles from Galveston. The entire process would be over in about two hours, so no one would really question the flight. Jim also had the trucks waiting at the dock inside the warehouse to load all the equipment and ammunition and bring it back to the Red Lion headquarters. The operators would be picked up in vans and returned as soon as the equipment was loaded on the trucks. Nelson and the PA along with one of the armorers would be flown back by a rented chopper. Everyone should be back where they belonged within forty-eight hours.

John was just getting up and Molly turned on the TV, so they could see if the news was covering the raid. They were all over the area in Belize. The coverage was insane. No one had any idea of what had really happened and so the speculation was running ramped. Molly got John some coffee and then made a Bloody Mary for them. They sat and watched the news coverage for a while then John and Molly got dressed and went to get some food. John was waiting for a call from Washington and he wondered who would call first and what the questions would be. John and the President had agreed that John would deny any involvement in the operation and say his sources claimed it was a plot of terrorists and then say Red Lion was trying to find out who had done this thing. No matter what, John was to keep the US out of this in every way possible. John was concerned, but he was very glad the villa had not been set on fire and no missiles had been used. Only small arms were used and of course the casings had been totally civilian issue. Also, people had survived this raid and that had not happened before. The operators were always covered so no real descriptions could be given other than men in black clothes. The helicopters had not been seen and from what John's people could listen to, no mention of the helicopters had ever been given to the police. The police were convinced that the attack had been launched from the beach area. Nelson had planted enough evidence on the beach to make that idea very possible. John and Molly finished their food and went back to the apartment. John watched the stock market report and was surprised that the market had only fallen 400 points. John had figured it would be much more when the identity of the targets was released. The first call came from General Davis. John denied any connection to the event. Then he received calls from Ledford, and from General Nathan. John denied any connection once again to both officers. John knew he had just lied to his superior officers, but he knew the President would cover his ass in the event they ever found out the truth. John was good with that.

# CHAPTER 16

John and Molly went to the ranch again for Thanksgiving. John's grandmother was not doing well. She was after all ninety-two years old and had problems that came with age. The weekend or Thursday, Friday and Saturday were good, and John and Molly enjoyed being with everyone. John and Molly returned to Houston on Sunday and when they got back to the apartment, John had Molly sit down and then he said, "Molly I think it is time we planned a wedding, how about that?"

Molly said, "John you know I want to marry you, but how in the Hell are we going to do it and not let everyone know who you really are?"

John said "Well we are going to do it and when they find out they find out. I really do not care any longer about that. I know this thing is going to be a surprise to many of our friends here in Houston and to all your friends, but it is what it is".

Molly said "Ok I will start the process. Do you happen to have a date in mind or do we just pick one?"

John smiled and said "I was thinking about May. That is a very nice time of year".

Molly said, "And where do you want to have the wedding, my dear?"

John said, "In Washington of course".

Molly said "Oh My God. Ok let me figure out what the Hell I am going to do". John kissed her and just sat back and watched her expressions. The next month went by fast and Christmas was here and gone. John and Molly had gone to the ranch for Christmas and then spent New Year's at Molly's as usual.

It was now 2008 and it was an election year for the US. The President would not run again. He had done his eight years and new blood would be taking over. John had no idea who would win and that worried him. All this operation that had been set up was done at the direction of the current President and no one knew if the new guy would want it continued. Also, John knew that Ledford and probably most of the Generals now in positions would be retiring. The new President would replace Ledford and then the new Chief of Staff of the Army would probably replace the heads of each of the units John had been working with. That was the way it always worked. John realized that Red Lion might have only one year left in existence. John decided to set up some good raids during the final or possibly final year of the unit. John had Nancy prepare a staff meeting and he wanted every one of his top people ready to present plans of action. Nancy sent a message on email to the people John had told her to be there, advising them of the meeting and what John wanted them to bring to the meeting. The meeting was set for the next Friday at 10 AM.

The staff meeting started with John telling everyone that within the next year Red Lion would have to be very involved in eliminating as many terrorist groups as possible throughout the world. John also explained that the loss of the financial backers was already hurting many of these groups, but the larger organizations were actually growing, due to the total unrest in many parts of the world. Many people think the US is waging a War on the Muslims in every part of the world. This is a real problem and is contributing to recruiting. When John finished his opening remarks, he said "Ok now let me hear from each of you about what you think we should do".

Jim said "General we have basically four groups we can really attack. The rest of these smaller groups are by no means not important but logistically we would have a hard time if not an impossible time in destroying them. I feel if we can take out the four groups Tress has identified, we will reduce the smaller groups ability to wage war on anyone. No money or support no war!"

John said, "I agree with that".

Tress stood up and said "Sandy has identified the four groups and their main locations. We have two in the Middle-East in the Syria and Palestine areas. Then we have the major group still in Afghanistan, the Taliban. Al-Qaeda is not as potent as it was, but it is still very active and as long as Bin Laden is still on the loose, it will be a factor."

John said, "Ok how do we go about this?"

Tress said "General, we have to attack one group at a time and we have to study everything we can about them. Right now, the military is still fighting a war on two fronts and is not really interested in getting to the actual bottom of the problem. They are too busy trying to keep what they have and not allow the situation to fall apart again. Of course, Special Ops and Special Forces, both Rangers, Green Berets, and SEAL units are being used to try to track down and kill as many of the leaders as possible, but they are limited and cannot work the way we do. My recommendation is to concentrate on the targets we know we can eliminate quickly and with as little exposure as possible. I would recommend Red Lion first strike in Yemen again and totally take out all the al-Qaeda forces there. Then we proceed to Sudan/Chad and do the same with the rebels there. Once that has been done, we can then plan attacks in Palestine, but we will have to coordinate any action there with the Israelis. By leaving that area as last or next to last we will not have to show our hand to anyone before we must do business with Israel".

John sat back and said, "Anyone else have any ideas or suggestions?"

Nelson said "Sir, I think we can work with Delta and get a good idea of how this group in Yemen is actually doing business. They have been constantly moving around since Bin Laden has been in hiding and I think most of the senior leadership has already been killed or captured. It is the young new guys that we need to target. That is why we need to have some face to face with Delta. Can you make that happen, General?"

John said "Nelson I will see what I can do and that is a damn good idea. Anyone else?" No one said anything, so John said "Well here it is then. Tress and Sandy will start a plan on Yemen. I will see about getting Nelson a face to face with Delta and Don you and Cindy keep tracking the computer usage and especially try to find the money. We need a plan and we need to get it activated in sixty days". John rose and so did everyone else. John left the room and went to his office. The other members of the meeting talked a little then went to their individual offices. John called General Nathan and discussed having Nelson meet with the "smart guy" on Yemen. Nathan agreed to set it up and would get back to John. Nathan called back to John and told John the meeting would be on Monday at Ft. Bragg at the Delta compound. 8 AM was the time. John thanked Nathan and called Nelson and had him arrange to go to Ft. Bragg for the Monday meeting. Tress would also go along as well as Sandy. All the people going would be in military uniform while they were on post at Bragg.

The meeting at Ft. Bragg went well and Nelson and Tress and Sandy were able to get a tremendous amount of information. They also enjoyed visiting with members of Delta that they had known for years. The group returned to Houston on Tuesday and briefed John, Jim and Harry about the meeting. It was decided that a plan to attack the Yemen base for al-Qaeda would be put in motion and the attack would be scheduled for April. Don and Cindy had uncovered some computer messages sent from Pakistan and were sure they had originated from Bin Laden. Don had also located a bank that Bin Laden used and had an account number. Tress and Sandy went to work on the attack plan and used the information they had received at Bragg. Harry was busy getting the new weapons the operators would use ready and having the operators go to Hallettsville to get them sighted in and get familiar with the new systems. John was now convinced that within a few months all the main leadership of al-Qaeda would be destroyed. There would be no capture.

John and Molly were busy planning the wedding when John was not at Red Lion. Molly had almost totally stopped working at the bar, but did go in everyday and visit with her customers and friends. It was decided that Washington D.C. would be the perfect place to hold the event. John had arranged for the actual ceremony to be at the National Cathedral and the Bishop was going to do the ceremony. The wedding would be a formal military wedding and then the reception was going to be at the Congressional Country Club. John had been able to get permission to use the facility even though he was not a member. Ray had gotten one of the Texas Senators to arrange the use of the club. John just wondered what that had cost in the way of a campaign donation. It really did not matter because Ray was the best man, and everyone was so excited that John was finally going to be married, money was no object. Molly was going to have Linda, Donna, and three other friends of hers as Bridesmaids and her best friend, Carol was going to be her Maid of Honor. John was having Jim, Harry, Nelson, Tress, Miles as his Groomsmen. The guest list was large, and John had counted over 300 invitations so far. John had decided to use the Hilton hotel in D.C. and had reserved 200 rooms for the event. No rehearsal dinner was planned yet, so John and Molly set about doing that chore and chore it was. John was going to use members of the Red Lion unit eight of them, all operators, as the ushers for the wedding. Molly did not have any particular menu in mind, but wanted the dinner to be very nice and wanted a special place to hold it. John had decided on Malcom's Steak House and set things in motion. John was looking at a total of forty-five people at the rehearsal dinner and he knew the restaurant would be able to handle that with ease. The reception was another thing. Molly and John wanted a buffet with meat and sea food as well as other specialty items. The cake was of course traditional, and the groom's cake would be also. An open bar was also required, and the topper was the music. Molly had called Willie Nelson the country performer and he was going to play along with his entire band. It was his wedding present to her. They had been friends for many years. Molly had at one time, been a singer and that is where she and Willie had become friends. He was also arranging another band to play for the entire night before and after he performed. John was ready for this and he was looking forward to the entire experience. Invitations were going to be sent to all the members of the Joint Chiefs, about twenty General officers, over 100 members of Delta, Special Forces, Ranger, and SEAL units. Also, members of Congress, the Secretary of Defense, the Director of Homeland Security, the Secretary of the Veterans Administration and the President and Vice President of the United States. Molly had over 200 people in Houston and Las Vegas plus some in New York she was inviting. All of Red Lion was invited and also their dates, spouses or whoever. John was going to lease aircraft from Southwest Airlines to take anyone who wanted to go to D.C and bring them back. Ray was planning to have everyone including John's grandmother flown up on a private jet. By the time this wedding was over, no one would have any doubt who John was and that he was well respected. He had already decided that he was going to tell everyone from Houston and Vegas as well as New York that he had retired and then been asked to return to run Red Lion as a civilian contract firm, contracted to the US Government as well as to governments overseas. This had already been discussed and approved by

Washington so when the news media got into things the story was very sound, and with the war the way it was, it was very logical the government would contract out much of the training and security as possible. The military did not have the manpower available to do the job. John knew the news media would all over the wedding. During the next month and a half, the plans were made and finalized for the Yemen attack. This attack was going to be probably the largest operation Red Lion had ever done. There were four different locations that had to be neutralized. John was ready to finish al-Qaeda once and for all.

# CHAPTER 17

The raid on Yemen was now only one week away. John was in his office and Tress came in and asked to discuss some details with John. John had Tress sit and then said, "Do we have problems, Tress?"

Tress said, "No Sir, but I would like to see if we can get some special air support to use at the training camp, one of our targets."

John said, "OK what do you suggest we need in that arena?"

Tress said "We need heavy bombers to hit the damn camp right before our guys do. The camp is going to be the most dangerous target we have because of the amount of people there. All of them are nuts and of course they have weapons and are just itching to use them especially on anyone they think might be American. If we can have a targeted bomb run hit ten minutes before our guys jump we will have a total advantage on the ground. I realize it would be at night, but Hell General, our Air Force is great at night and no one would ever figure a parachute drop would follow the bomb run."

John said "That is a good idea. I will see what I can do to make that happen." Tress stood up and said, "Thank you, Sir". Tress left, and John made a call to Washington. This was going to be a hard sell but maybe someone would see the point.

John informed Tress that the Air Force was going to contact him and discuss exactly what he needed. Tress got the call and explained exactly what would be required and when. The coordinates were given to the Air Force and the times and dates were set. The bombers would drop 1000-pound bombs on the target and planes would fire missiles on the target ten minutes before the operators jumped. The operators would be doing HALO jumps from 30,000 feet. The bombers would make two passes at the target. Tress briefed John and Jim and had the operators jumping on that target, briefed on the situation. The Air Force would be dropping all operators and four C-141 aircraft would be used. Each individual target would be hit at the same time by the operators. The operators would also have escape vehicles dropped by parachute at given locations close to each target. These vehicles would be dropped as soon as the operators were on the ground. Communication was going to be vital for this operation. Each team of operators would be ten men strong. Two vehicles would be dropped at each location. Once the raids were finished, the operators would then drive back into the safe zones and would be picked up and transported out of Yemen. Coordination would be made with the Yemen government just as the first operators were on the ground. Trust was always an issue and John did not trust the military of Yemen or the government there. The final briefing was done, and all the operators and their equipment were taken to Ellington Air Force Base and loaded on to the C-141s for the trip over. The C-141s would land in Saudi Araba and the operators would split up on to four other C-141 aircraft. Saudi had agreed to Red Lion using one of their remote airfields for the mission. The C-141 from Ellington took off at 11 PM and was on the way. John was waiting at the office for the word and when it came he went home. Nothing was going to happen for the next thirty-six hours.

John was again in the operations center and the screen was showing four different views. Each target was displayed, and John watched as he observed movements at each target. It was now fifteen minutes before the operators would jump. The bombers were making the final approach to the training camp complex. John watched as the first bomber dropped the bomb load and saw the explosions. The camp was totally taken by surprise and people were running in all directions. John saw the second bomber drop bombs and saw the explosions. Then the planes with the rockets made their pass and John saw rockets hit targets all over the compound. John thought "how could anyone survive that". Jim and Harry were standing where they always did and watching as the last of the planes left the area. The operators were just landing and were only half of a mile from the camp. The other operators had also landed and were advancing toward their targets. John was watching every target switching from one to another. The operators were now attacking each target. John could not tell exactly what was happening because the helmet cameras were not sending clear pictures. Don said it was something to do with the atmosphere that was causing the problem. Tress was getting reports from each operator team leader and things were going well. The C-130 aircraft had delivered the vehicles for the operators and had landed at the designated coordinates to wait for the operators. The vehicles were Toyota pickup trucks and were identical to the trucks that were used by the civilian population of Yemen. They had been supplied by Delta which had captured these trucks a month before in Saudi. The Saudi government did not know that fact and John had made damn sure no one would advise them of it. Toyota trucks were used all over the Middle-East and no one looked twice at them.

The operators being led by Nelson were now attacking his target. He had the compound that was base for the new leaders or at least four of them. Sandy had discovered by watching the satellite footage of the targets, that no guards were present at night or even during the day unless something very special was going on. Al-Qaeda was so confident they had control over the entire area they did not put out guards for early warning. This mistake was very deadly to them. Nelson had gained entry to the main building and John could see the flashes of gunfire on the screen. John also saw Vance, the team leader of the operators attacking the second compound that housed five members of the new leadership. Again, flashes of gunfire could be seen on the screen. John watched the final target, the ammunition and bomb holding compound. He saw three al-Qaeda members shot and fall to the ground. Then he saw eight more al-Qaeda members get shot. John was now watching as he saw from the cameras on the operators that pictures were being taken, fingerprints and DNA being collected. John knew all resistance had been done away with. John watched as all the operators left each target. In fifteen minutes each target erupted in massive explosions. The explosions at the ammunition and bomb target were of course the largest and many secondary explosions were occurring. Tress said "Sir, all operators are now at the vehicles. We have two wounded but not very bad".

John said "Thanks". In less than an hour Tress was told the C-130 aircraft were airborne and all operators were accounted for and on board. The trucks had been left in the desert and would be taken by the local tribesmen as soon as the sun was up. John was waiting for the satellite to make a pass over each target for the final time. Tress was making sure the pictures were being recorded. Sandy was on the SAT phone with Nelson and when she got off, she turned to John and said, "Sir, we have a total body count of 137 plus twenty-eight women that were there. We got all the new leaders and four of the older ones from what Nelson says. The pictures will be coming to us in about thirty minutes as soon as they can all be down loaded. I will make sure Don and Cindy get them and start the programs for identification".

John said "Job well done people. Thank you". John then left the ops room and went into his office and sent a fax to the White House. John got an acknowledgement in less than two minutes. It simply said, "Great Job". John sat down and waited until the C-130 aircraft had landed back in Saudi. When the word came in that they were on the ground, John went home. He was very tired.

All the operators including the wounded arrived back in Houston at Ellington AFB thirty hours later. They were picked up and escorted back to the Red Lion headquarters. John met them and told them that they had done an outstanding job. He also thanked them for their work. John then drove to the hospital and visited with the operators that had been wounded, Jim and Harry went along. The wounded operators were in good condition and John was told they would be released in twenty-four hours. They were mainly being kept for observation. One had undergone surgery for his wound, but was recovering nicely. After the visit to the hospital, John and the others left and went to the air field and met with the piolets. John wanted to get some information from them about what they needed as far as weapons on the helicopters were concerned. John was not satisfied with the way his piolets were armed and wanted to talk to them about that. John, Jim and Harry met with Chief Warrant Officer-4, Miller who was the overall commander of the piolets assigned to Red Lion. John asked about the weapons and Miller said "Sir, we are fine with the Cobra. We have everything we need there. The Black Hawks are another issue. The only guns we have are the M-60 machine guns that are mounted on the doors. When we try to cover our guys, we can only shoot by flying parallel to the targets. That puts us in a very bad position because we create a very big target".

John said, "Ok what is the fix, Chief?"

Miller said "Sir, we would like to mount a Gatling-Gun, under the choppers. That will allow us to fire forward and the type of gun that can swivel up to 90 degrees left and right".

John said "I see. Ok we will get to work on that for you Chief. The CSM will handle that so stay in touch with him".

Miller said, "Thank you Sir and I will have the mechanics get with the CSM". John and the group left the air field and returned to the office. Harry went into his office and started making calls about the new guns. Jim and John sat in John's office and discussed the next operations and when they should happen. The economy was really in a mess and things were getting worse daily. John was still monitoring the news about the situation in Belize and no one had any real ideas who had done the killings. John and Jim discussed the idea of leaking some information about who may have done the shootings. Drug cartels were always good to blame in that part of the world. John and Jim decided to wait until things got slowed down and then see if it would be required. May was fast approaching and John wanted to do nothing if possible during the month of May. The entire Red Lion unit was going to be involved with the wedding, either in it physically or in attendance so John had informed Washington the unit would be on "stand down" until the first of June. So far Washington was alright with that. The rest of April and the first two weeks of May the Red Lion unit worked on replacing equipment, installing new GPs, Computers, the Gatling-Guns Harry had gotten, and new equipment on the Container ship. John had meetings with each division head and was very happy about how things were going. John also had a detailed meeting with Sara and got a very good idea exactly how much money Red Lion had hidden in off shore accounts. The figure was $8.8 Billion Dollars. John knew Red Lion had more than enough cash to do anything that was required. Sara had also arranged for the Red Lion special fund, as she referred to it, to pay the costs of the wedding and the honeymoon. Sara was going to use gifts of money as the way it could be covered and that was very legal. John and Molly would pay taxes on the money just as if they had earned it. The wedding was going to cost about $750,000 dollars by the time everything was finished and then the honeymoon would cost about $250,000. All in all, John was going to be spending about $1 Million Dollars. He personally had that type of money, so it would not be questioned. John was now ready to relax for a day or so and devote his energy to Molly and the wedding. Molly was ready for that.

John and Molly had everything done or at least as done as they could get it. The wedding was going to be at 6 PM on Saturday May 20th. Then the reception would be immediately following the wedding and with travel time, photographs and everything, John estimated everyone would arrive at the Congressional Country Club by 8 PM. The club was going to use tents for an outdoor reception. The tents would be joined together, and a bandstand/stage would be erected at one end of one of the tents. The buffet and bar would be in a different tent and seating for guests would be arranged so a dance floor could be directly in front of the bandstand/stage. The official receiving line would be in the same tent the bar was located at the front entrance. John had arranged limos for the wedding party and for Ray and John's grandmother. He also had arranged an overseas private jet to be ready for takeoff to Europe the morning after the wedding. The first night would be spent in Washington in a suite at the Hilton. The honeymoon would be a month long with stays in Paris, Heidelberg Germany, Italy both Rome and Venice, and then England. John as always would be able to be contacted by his cell phone or by a SAT phone that would be along with him. Molly was going to have Carol run the bar. Carol had moved to Houston about five years before after her husband had died. They had a very successful restaurant in Vegas for twenty years before his death. Carol and Molly had been friends for many years. Carol had gone to work for Molly when she arrived in Houston and was the second in charge. Molly was confident Carol would have no problems running Molly's Bar. Jim would be in command at Red Lion and John knew he was more than capable of that task. The clothes would be packed and sent via special air transport to be loaded on the overseas flight so when John and Molly left the hotel they would only have to take their personal items. The wedding dress, and John's uniforms would be picked up by a member of Red Lion and returned to Houston. John and Molly were confident everything was done. Molly had been receiving replies from the invitations and so far about 600 people were going to attend. The President, Vice-President, the Governor of Texas and both Texas Senators and six US Representatives from Texas were also coming. All the Joint Chiefs as well as the Secretary of Defense and the Secretary of the Army and the Secretary of Homeland Security were coming. John also had reviewed the RSVP list and he had seen many Army Officers he knew that had said they would attend. A group of 100 people from Houston had replied and they would be there. John and Molly sat back and sipped a drink and talked about what was about to happen. It was very hard to believe that so damn many "high powered" people would be at the wedding. For just a moment John and Molly both thought of just running to Vegas and getting it done. Then they both laughed, and John said "Not on your life my dear. We are going to show our ass on this one and I am damn glad we are." Molly smiled and said, "Me too".

On May the 5th John received a special express package from Washington. Nancy brought it into John's office and handed it to John. John opened the package and said "Oh My God, Nancy. Get everyone including the Galveston Navy people to be here at 6 PM today and no one can be absent. This is an order from me".

Nancy said, "Alright Sir."

John said "That includes you and Sara and all the civilian people, Dan, Don and Cindy. Everyone must be here."

Nancy said, "I understand, Sir". Nancy left and started making the calls.

At 6 PM the entire Red Lion unit was sitting in the warehouse and John walked into the room and stood at the front. Everyone rose, and John said, "At Ease and be seated".

John then took out paperwork from the package and said "Ladies and Gentlemen please listen very carefully to what I am about to tell you. By order of the President of the United States the following individuals have been promoted to the following ranks, effective 1 May 2008: John read the list of names. Each member of the unit had been promoted one pay grade. The civilian personnel, Nancy and Sara had been promoted to the rank of GM-15. Dan had been promoted to the rank of SGS-3. Don and Cindy had been given a 50% increase in their pay. Each one now made $300,000 dollars per year. The Naval promotions made the Captain, a Rear Admiral, and all other members of the Navy were now promoted one pay grade. The rest of the members of Red Lion had been advanced one pay grade and now all team leaders were Sergeant Majors. All other operators were Master Sergeants and all the ground crew had been promoted to either Master Sergeants or Sergeant First Class. The PA had been promoted to CW-4. Harry was of course as high as he could be. Jim had now been promoted to Lieutenant General (three stars) and John had been promoted to full General (four stars). John said, "I personally want to thank all of you for a job very well done". John then dismissed the unit. The time was then spent congratulating everyone and John watched as his unit celebrated the promotions. Jim came up to John and said "God John this is something. You are now a four star and I for God's sake am a three star".

John said "Yes Jim I never expected this. Guess the President likes what we do. And, now he will expect us to do more, I can count on that." Jim just laughed. Harry was smiling. John said, "What is so funny CSM?"

Harry said "Well General, I got a very nice pay raise today. I am now over 40 years in service and that means when I finally quit I get 150 % of my pay forever thanks to a Presidential Order. In the meantime, they must pay me a bonus each month. Not bad for an old fart". John just laughed.

# CHAPTER 18

I t was 1 PM and John had just stepped out of the shower. Today was the day. Molly had left the suite at noon along with Donna, Linda and Carol and was going to the beauty shop then to the church. John had been making sure his dress blue uniform was totally correct and he even had his sword ready. He had his white gloves packed along with the sword, shoes and socks in a travel bag. He would put his uniform and hat in another travel bag and all of that would go with him to the church at 4 PM. John sat for a moment and thought about the rehearsal dinner. The dinner had gone well, and John was very happy about that. The rehearsal at the church had also gone well and it seemed to John that things were moving exactly as planned. John got a beer from the mini-bar and sipped it as he watched TV. There had been almost no coverage of the wedding and John was thankful for that. Only one reporter had asked a question about why the President and Vice-President and so many other Washington dignitaries were going to a wedding of a General. The President had said "General Carter is an outstanding Officer, a Medal of Honor recipient and a close personal friend. I know him and his soon to be wife and The First Lady and I both like and admire them both very much". John was very glad that the President had not tried to side step the question because now the news media had nothing to dig into. It was out in the open and the media did not like that. They wanted a scandal. John finished his beer and put on his class "A" dress uniform for the ride to the church. He picked up his two travel bags, made damn sure he had the ring and went down stairs to meet the limo.

John was feeling some nerves and he was not liking that at all. Hell, he had nothing to worry about. Ray was there, and Ray looked fantastic. His tux was great. Ray and Miles were the only non-military members of the groomsmen. The rest of the groomsmen had on their dress blue uniforms with all awards and decorations and each had a sword and white gloves. John was as ready as he was going to be. Exactly at 6 PM, John led the groomsmen out of the side room and into the Cathedral and took his place to the right side of the Bishop. John looked out at the seats and was amazed to see the church almost full. The President and his wife and the Vice-President and his wife were sitting on the front row on the left side as John faced the seats. The rest of the politicians and Secretaries were sitting in the rows behind them. The military members were sitting on the right side as John faced the seats and were three rows back from the first row. John had reserved those rows for his family and for people Molly wanted to sit with John's family. Members of Red Lion were scattered throughout the seats and so were the friends from Houston. There were also many other military personnel scattered throughout the seating. The organ music began playing, and John watched as Donna started down the aisle. She was followed by Linda and the rest of the bridesmaids. Carol was the last before Molly.

Molly was standing just inside the doors that opened into the Cathedral. By her side stood a very small man in his late 60's wearing a tux and he was smiling almost more than John was. The man was Mr. Joseph Delasondro, Molly's very dear friend, from New York. He was going to give the bride away. Molly had explained to John who Joe was and John had met Joe once before. John really liked Joe and even with Joe's background of supposed being a Don in the New York Mafia, John had gotten him cleared by the FBI and everyone else to be at the wedding. Molly and Joe started down the aisle just as the organ started playing the Wedding March.

Everyone in the cathedral rose and turned to look at Molly. The ceremony went perfect and John was amazed it only took fifteen minutes from start to finish. John kissed Molly and started down the aisle hand in hand. The rest of the wedding party followed. All the wedding party waited in a side room until all the guests were outside the cathedral and then as the ushers raised their swords and made an arch, John and Molly left the cathedral and walked under the arch and got into a waiting limo. The limo pulled around the side of the cathedral and John and Molly got out and went back into the side door of the cathedral and the pictures were taken. It took about thirty minutes and then the limo with John and Molly inside headed for the Congressional Country Club. A police motorcycle escort led the way.

The reception was wonderful. John and Molly and the rest of the wedding party stood in the receiving line and greeted all the guests. The President and Vice-President came through the line and then to John's amazement sat at a reserved table and enjoyed the music and food and drink. The rest of the guests did the same. At 9 PM, Willie Nelson and his band took the stage and played for forty-five minutes. It was very exciting to have that many people enjoying everything. Immediately after Willie finished, the President and Vice-President departed, and John thanked them for attending. The rest of the guests dance and enjoyed the evening. John and Molly danced and had cut the cake just before Willie performed. John's grandmother had left right after Willie finished and was taken back to the hotel by her nurse. The reception ended around 1 AM. John and Molly had left to go to the hotel at midnight. The rest of the guests had stayed and most of the Red Lion people and of course Ray, Linda, Donna and Miles stayed on. Everyone finally left the club about 6 AM. The next day, John and Molly boarded the jet and left Washington at 9 AM in route to Paris France. Ray and the rest of John's family left that afternoon and returned to Hallettsville and then to Midland. The Red Lion group and the people who had flown up on the chartered jets left at 2 PM and headed back to Houston. Joe had gone back on an early flight that morning. All the clothing and other things had been picked up and were packed and sent back to Houston on the charter jet.

John and Molly were enjoying everything in Europe. Paris had been wonderful, and Moly had very much enjoyed Germany. Italy was only so-so for Molly and John was not impressed with Italy at all. John had been to Italy a few times and he never did like the country or the people. France was both of their favorites. They had gone all over Paris and had toured the Normandy battlefield and cemetery. They had also spent a day on the Rivera beaches in southern France. Molly wished she could have stayed longer there. John said, "Well we do not have to stay a week in England so why do we not come back here for a few days?" Molly agreed immediately. The England trip was cut to only two days. John decided to remain in southern France for an additional week when he checked in with Red Lion and found nothing critical was working. Tress had a plan in place for Chad and Sudan, but it was on hold for now. The US economy was now the talk of everyone. It was going into a depression and businesses were failing. These were very high-profile businesses. The housing market had gone bankrupt and millions of people were losing their homes. Things were bad and getting worse. John had a conference call with Ray and Miles and they had told John that all the stocks and other investments for them and John's grandmother were being converted and realigned. John was relieved with that and Ray and Miles assured John they would keep him advised on how things were progressing. Red Lion was staying very quiet for now. John and Molly were due to be back in Houston by the middle of July. Molly had also checked with Carol and the bar was doing well. Business was steady, but everyone was worried about the damn economy. John could not believe the President had let things get this bad. The elections were in November and that was four and ½ months away. Then the new President would not take office until the middle of January. That was a Hell of a long time for things to continue to be going bad. John was worried about how he was going to keep Red Lion functioning. He had the money to continue, but what would the new President say about how Red Lion operated and how they got the money they had. Only time would answer that. John and Molly enjoyed the rest of the honeymoon and on July 6th returned to Houston.

# CHAPTER 19

John had been back to work for a week and things were going along very slowly. Washington had decided to have Red Lion stay quiet and not to do any type of actions for a while. The main work being done was the economy and Washington had no answers. Just the same old crap. Republicans blaming the Democrats and Democrats blaming the Republicans. Nothing was being done to solve the problem. John was glad things had slowed down. He had spent two days getting Molly ID cards and all the stuff she needed. At least as a General, he did not have to wait in line. It just took time to travel to San Antonio which was the closest place to get it done. Molly was now all set, and she was also back at work at the bar. Nancy buzzed John and said "Sir, Washington on line one". John picked up the receiver and General Ledford said "John we need you here tonight. Get a flight and be here as soon as possible. We have big problems and the Boss needs to talk to you."

John said "Yes Sir. I will advise my flight time". John hung up and had Nancy call the private jet. John went home and packed. He stopped by the bar and told Molly where he was going and said he would call her later. John kissed Molly and drove back to Red Lion. His Jet would be there in one hour. John advised Jim and Harry and told them to have everyone on standby and able to be recalled until further notice. John then drove to the air field and waited for his jet. It landed in ten minutes after John arrived and he boarded and was airborne. ETA Washington four hours. John called Ledford and told him. Ledford would have a staff car waiting.

John arrived at the White House and was admitted. John was met and escorted to the situation room in the lower level. John had never actually been in that room, so he wondered why it was now being used for a conversation with him. John entered and saw all the Joint Chiefs sitting at the table and the Secretary of Homeland Security as well as the Director of the FBI and the Director of the CIA. John knew something bad was about to happen. John sat down and in five minutes, the President and Vice-President entered and took their seats. The President said, "Do we have anything new, Bob?"

The Director of the FBI said, "No Sir, just what we already have".

The President said, "OK Bob tell John what exactly happened I think he is the only one not up to speed". The FBI director told John that three days before a package had been delivered to the FBI headquarters in St Louis, Missouri and it contained a type written three-page letter, and a vile of a substance. The letter was a rambling demand to release a federal prisoner and to give a ransom of $1 Billion Dollars to a renegade rebel group. The letter went on to say that if the demands were not met by the 1st day of August, four cities would be attacked with the substance in the vial. The cities were Las Vegas, St. Louis, Houston, and Chicago. The letter said that the group was giving the sample to be tested so that the US Government would have proof that this was not a joke or a threat that was not real. Then the letter claimed that the rebel group had over 5000 followers in all 50 states. John listened and then said, "What was in the vile?"

Bob said "Ricin" and they claim to be able to produce it in an aerial substance. The letter also said that the rebels had a stock pile of over two tons of this stuff". John sat back and shook his head. The President then said, "John do you think a Delta force could do this job?"

John said "Mr. President I do not think we have the time for Delta or Special Forces and what about using troops on our own soil? Can we actually do that?"

The President said "Yes under these conditions, I can get approval from Congress or at least I can get the leaders to allow an Executive Order to be put in effect and they will not fight it. My question is still can they do the job in your opinion?"

John said, "Mr. President I have been away from that for quite a while, so I would think the Chiefs could better answer."

The President said, "Ok what about it guys?"

The Chairman of the Joint Chiefs said, "Mr. President we may be able to do it if we know where we need to go but with this as our only lead I have no idea if we can find this in the time we have left."

John said, "Mr. President what does the FBI and CIA have on this group?"

The director of the FBI, Bob said "We know exactly who these guys are, but we have no idea where they are located other than in southern Missouri and in Arkansas where the two states meet. We have some names and very few photos and a bunch of email traffic. The leader was convicted of weapons charges and sent to prison for 20 years. We really do not know who took over the leadership because after the arrest this group went very quiet. Only now have they re-surfaced and if this is as bad as I think they are going to kill millions of US citizens".

John said, "I fully understand."

The President said "Well alright. Thanks everyone. Keep working and keep me up to speed. John, I am sorry you had to make a trip for nothing, but you were the only guy I could think of, that knew Delta as well as you do". John watched the President very carefully and noticed him as he stood up. The President looked at John and barely nodded his head then he gave John a very dry smile. The President, Vice-President and the Secretary left the room. John sat and waited. After a few minutes of discussion between the Chiefs and the Directors everyone left and when John was outside, General Ledford said, "John I would like to see you for a moment to discuss some issues we have".

John said, "Of course General". And followed Ledford to the elevator and rode to the first floor with him. The other people go off on the first floor and left the White House. Ledford waited until they had departed and then got back into the elevator and along with John went to the second floor. The two Generals got out of the elevator and went directly into the Oval Office. The President and Vice-President were waiting for them.

John sat down at the direction of the President and waited. It took about two minutes before the President said anything. He was looking at a piece of paper he had removed from his desk. The President handed the paper to John and said, "Can your team stop this John?"

John looked at the paper and realized it was a detailed map of Missouri and Arkansas and it had four circles on the map. John said, "I have no idea Mr. President but we sure as Hell can try".

The President said "OK then General get your ass back home and start. I will have Bob send everything we have to you immediately and if there is anything you and your guys need let me know personally."

John said, "Mr. President does the Director know about Red Lion?"

The President said "Not exactly, but Bob is not a dummy and he knows full well someone is doing what you do. He just does not know it is you. We will keep it that way for now".

John said, "Yes Sir". John got up, saluted and left the Oval Office. John then called the plane and had them get ready to go to Texas. The staff car delivered John to the plane and as it was taking off, John called Jim and had Red Lion re-called. In six hours every member of Red Lion would be at the headquarters including the Admiral in charge of the Navy detachment. Anderson was going to be very useful with his knowledge of boats and waterways. John was glad he had been promoted and knew Andy as he was called, would have a few ideas. John landed in four hours and already Red Lion personnel were waiting in the warehouse briefing area. John went to his office and had a cold beer. This mission was going to be the hardest anyone had ever gotten into and the fact that it could not fail was even a heavier burden on John. John had sent an email address to the President that was one of the many that Red Lion used that could not be traced. Don had set up about 20 email accounts that were so protected no one in the world could follow the routing. John had also had Tress and Sandy get a detailed map of Missouri and Arkansas and load it into the projection screen in the warehouse briefing room. Nancy was going through personnel files of the Red Lion unit looking for anyone that had been born or had lived in Missouri or Arkansas at any time in their lives. John had initially briefed Jim and Harry on the situation and would give all the details in less than thirty minutes to the entire unit. John had also given Don and Cindy orders to hack the FBI computer system and look for the individual who was in Federal prison. John wanted everything the FBI had on this man, named Bales, even though the FBI was to send the complete file via email in an hour to the special email address John had sent to Washington. John also wanted Cindy to do a search of the CIA for the same name and any information they might have. Then John was going to search the ATF and probably the DEA. There was no time to ask and wait for days or weeks for the request to be approved by simple minded people. John left his office and walked toward the briefing area. The entire Red Lion unit was there including all the Navy personnel.

John walked into the room and said "Keep your seats and listen very carefully to me. We are now in the biggest mess we have ever been in and if we lose millions of Americans will die. We may have to kill as many as 5000 US Citizens to do the job". There was dead silence in the room. No one moved. The unit was barely breathing. John said, "There is a radical rebel group that has threatened to disburse "Ricin" over Houston, Chicago, Las Vegas and St. Louis. They say they have two tons of the stuff and have converted it so it can be sprayed. They also want $1 Billion Dollars and their leader released from federal prison. They want all of this by 1 August, so we have fifteen days to locate the people, locate the "Ricin" develop a plan to kill the fuckers and carry it out with no loss of civilian life. Nothing else will work so the President gave us the job". Again no one said a word or moved. John said "OK now this may sound very strange but anyone who has ever lived in Missouri or Arkansas stay after I dismiss you. We will also be going thru the records to see if by chance we have a record of you having any relatives in either of these states and you do not remember. I trust each one of you but Hell no one remembers where their relatives might have lived when they were very young. The background checks you have had for the clearance will say if you had or have any who were ever there. We need all we can possibly get on these people and how they live and think. Now as of this minute we have only one mission and that is to stop this bunch of fuck heads. Nothing else is important as of now. We commit every resource we have to this the mission. Is that clear?"

The entire unit said, "Yes Sir".

John said "Ok then get to work. Dismissed". The unit rose, and John walked to his office. He called Molly and talked to her for about twenty minutes explaining what was going on. She understood and told John to call her when he could or would be coming home. John said he would.

Don and Cindy had gotten a lot of information from the FBI files and some from the CIA files. The ATF had much more information on the radical rebels. Don had also been receiving the file from the FBI and for once it was very detailed and John thought it might be a complete file. That was a first, but then the President had given the director the order. Tress and Sandy had plotted the circles on the maps and had the nearest towns located. John met with nine personnel who had lived in Missouri or Arkansas. Each person listened as John explained exactly what he needed them to do. John said "I need you to write down as many names of people you can remember from the towns you lived in and give us the dates you lived there. Friends, high school students, the local people no matter the age. If you can remember the age it would help. Also think about people who were against the government in ways like talking about taxes, rights, anything anti-government. We also need to know if any of these people were big gun people and had any special guns they liked to show off. Then try to remember places you or your friends or Hell anyone liked to go camping or to just be out in the woods. Remember everything you can possibly remember about that time may be of use to us. Thanks. As soon as you finish get it to Tress and Sandy. Also have a copy made and give it to Cindy of the names only". The unit personnel got up and left John's office. John went into the intelligence room and Tress showed him the location of the nearest cities. In Missouri Tress pointed out the town of West Plains and just outside of it about twenty miles was a circle. A place named "Angel Ranch" was in the circle. The next town in Missouri was Waynesville. It was also located next to Ft. Leonard Wood an Army post. The place circled was Devil's Elbow about fifteen miles from Waynesville. Tress then showed John the Arkansas map. The first town was Hardy, and the circle was about eight miles out of Hardy and on a river. The name was Sims Resort. The last city on the Arkansas map was a town called Mt. Home. The circle was halfway between Mt. Home, Arkansas and Gainesville, Missouri and on the banks of a lake. There was no name on the circle. The lake was Bull Sholes. Tress also had some information on the highways and other roads that were the main ways to get into these areas. Water would be one way and John had Tress get with Anderson and show him the water ways. John was now ready to go home, and he decided nothing else could be done until the files had been completely gone over by his people. John left and headed for Molly's bar. He had called Molly on the way and she was expecting him. John arrived and went into the bar. He kissed Molly and said, "Hello to the customers." John sat down and had a cold beer. He was ready for that. After an hour and two more beers, John left and went to the apartment. Molly was going to be home in about thirty minutes. John went inside and took off his clothes and got into the shower. The water felt great and John was feeling all the aches and pains he had accumulated over the years. John felt something touch his back and he realized Molly had gotten into the shower with him. It was a nice thing and John and Molly enjoyed being together in the shower. After the shower, they both put on casual clothes and had a few drinks and ordered Chinese food to be delivered. It came, and they sat in the living room and ate and talked. John explained everything to Molly and she understood how very bad this was. Molly was very worried that Houston was on the hit list and so was John. They went to bed and made love and tried to forget about the rebels. It worked and they both went to sleep.

During the next week the unit had developed a plan to attack each location on the map they had received. The main problem was no one had any idea where the "Ricin" was or if it had been already sent to the cities named. John was thinking that prisoners would be required and that they needed to be taken soon. Don had been searching files of every agency that might have anything on the rebel group and one name kept coming up. Higgins. Don had no idea who or where Higgins was, but the name was in FBI, CIA, and ATF files and was always referenced to the rebel group. John wanted a location on this guy and he remembered one of the operators had listed a Higgins as a friend in high school. The operator had attended West Plains High school. John called Don and had him do a search for Higgins in West Plains and the surrounding areas. John also called the operator into his office and they discussed all about West Plains and the area around it. John asked if the operator remembered a place called "Angel Ranch" and the operator told John all about it. "Angel Ranch" was a resort or at least was a type of resort. Individuals bought memberships to the place and could use all the trails, camp grounds, rivers and all the recreation areas for free. They could also buy a permanent camping location or have a structure build on their part of the property. The place was remote and of course had all the nature aspects to it. That was the draw for people to come. John was convinced that was where the rebel group had its headquarters now. John asked the operator if he thought it possible for the operator to get into "Angel Ranch" and try to confirm that Higgins did have headquarters there. John also asked how hard it would be to capture Higgins and bring him back to Red Lion. The operator said "Sir, I can get into the place. I think it will be very easy to take Higgins unless he has a bunch of the militia types there. Then we will have bloodshed but so what".

John said, "Ok Master Sergeant, I will let you know when to leave for the Ozarks". The operator got up and said, "Yes Sir". Then he left John's office. John called Tress and Sandy and had them bring a map of the "Angel Ranch" area in and sit and discuss the operation John had in mind.

John explained his suggestion and Tress said "Sir that is a very good idea. We can have that done in about six hours. We can use Ft. Wood as our intake and exit base and we can use one of their Black Hawks as our transport. We will furnish the piolets and all we will have do get is the clearance to use one of their birds. Or we can fly our own bird up and use the airfield there to launch from. We are talking about 100 miles distance from Wood to the target. If we use our bird, we would have to refuel, and Little Rock AFB would be the spot. The distance is about 800 miles so that would be putting our bird at almost bingo fuel if we tried to go all the way. I would like to use our assets, but that call is yours, Sir".

John said, "Ok can you arrange for the bird to be fueled at Little Rock without a bunch of problems?"

Tress said "I cannot but Don sure as Hell can send a coded message to Little Rock AFB from Air Force Command to let it happen. They will never check it, they never do. As long as they are covered by the message they could care less".

John said "OK get the plan and call the Master Sergeant and find out who he wants to go along for the ride. Then alert our piolets and most of all tell Don what to send to Little Rock and exactly when". Tress and Sandy left the office. John called Jim and they talked about the mission. Jim was highly in favor of capturing Higgins and making him talk. Jim would handle that end of the mission as soon as he was back at Red Lion. John knew this was going to get very nasty and he really did not care. Time was running out. Tress had the plan set in three hours and the only unknown was where Higgins would be. Cindy had an idea about that and she presented it. She wanted to send an email to Higgins that would make him go to "Angel Ranch" at a certain time. If he was already there, he would respond that he was. If not, he sure would be there. Cindy was going to use an email address from one of the people who had been identified as a cell leader in Nevada. The message would tell Higgins that DEA and the Missouri Task Force was going to raid "Angel Ranch" on a certain date and at a certain hour. Of course, the date and time would be twenty-four hours from the time the email was sent. Cindy figured that Higgins would either respond that he was at "Angel Ranch" and could take care of things or that he would be there to take care of things. The response would dictate how the team would deploy and when. Everyone liked that idea and with SAT phones the team could be immediately alerted as soon as the message was received from Higgins. The Black Hawk could be on the ground at a very secluded area and immediately take off as required. The plan was now set. Six operators would be on the mission just in the event Higgins had men at the location. Again, it was eliminating all but Higgins or his second in command if that person could be singled out. The plan was to be initiated at 8 AM the next morning. The Black Hawk would fly to Little Rock AFB refuel and then proceed north to Missouri. A secure spot would be taken after the fly over and John was sure no one on the ground would even give a second thought to a military helicopter flying. They did so all the time back and forth for training. At 8 AM the Black Hawk took off from the air field in Sugarland with the six operators on board and the crew of three. The mission was on. Tress and Sandy were tracking every step. No satellite was available so only the cameras on the operators and the cameras in the Black Hawk were sending pictures back. John waited along with everyone else. Don had sent the message to Little Rock and the re-fuel was taken care of. Now only Cindy had to do her thing with Higgins. That would happen as soon as she got word the Black Hawk was on the ground in a secure area. The team had the location of Higgins place at "Angel Ranch" from hacking the computer at the main office of the resort. The location was listed in coordinates because if there was an emergency Air Evac from West Plains was called to fly the injured person to the hospital. The nearest ground ambulance was forty-five minutes ways. It worked out well for Red Lion and now they knew exactly what location the operators had to be taken to for the raid. Cindy had done an outstanding job on recovering that information. The word came in that the team was now on the ground in Missouri and waiting for Cindy to act. Cindy sent the email and in 3 minutes she had the answer. Higgins was at the "Angel Ranch" location along with 3 other members of the rebels and he would get ready to move everything. Now the question was, did he have the "Ricin" there? The word was passed to the team and they started the raid. It was now 11 PM.

# CHAPTER 20

The Black Hawk flew over "Angel Ranch" at 6500 feet and the operators jumped. An operator exited from each door one after the other so three men jumped from each side and did a free fall to 1200 feet. The landing area was only 100 yards from Higgin's building. All the operators were safely on the ground and the Black Hawk returned to the secure area and landed. It would wait until the signal came and then the chopper would go straight into the area and land and load everyone on board and depart. The operators moved toward the building and saw a truck being loaded with 55-gallon drums. The two men loading the truck never saw the operators and were immediately taken into custody and gaged with duct tape and immobilized with flex ties. Jerry, the operator who knew Huggins went into the building and fired a dart gun into Higgins. Higgins fell to the floor unconscious. The second man in the building tried to fire his weapon but was killed by another operator. The situation was over and in less than ten minutes the team had captured three men. Jerry then looked in the truck and then into one of the 55-Gallon drums. He had on a mask and protective gloves and he saw that the drum was filled with a white powder. Jerry immediately put the lid back in place. Jerry called on the SAT phone and Tress ran to get John. John was in his office and when Tress rushed in John said, "What is wrong?" and jumped to his feet.

Tress said "General we have a huge fucking problem. You need to come to Como immediately". John followed Tress and was also running. John got into the operation room and took the SAT phone and said, "This is Red Lion-6-actual go".

Jerry said, "We have ten each 55-gallon drums of what looks like "Ricin". They are loaded on a truck. We have three in custody and one enemy KIA. What is the order?"

John thought for a moment and then said "Operator one this is 6-actual. Remove the truck and drive it to a location away from people if possible. Then as soon as you have the truck away from the population get a GPS on the location and advise Red Lion. Have the prisoners picked up by Black Hawk-1 along with the other operators. Have the chopper follow the truck and land when the truck is in a secure location. Then advise Red Lion".

Operator-1 said, "Roger that".

John said "Ok we have a real time fucking problem. Stay with these guys and keep me and Jim up dated. Jim, I am going to call Washington. I will be in my office".

Jim said, "Yes Sir". John went to his office and placed an emergency call to Ledford. John told Ledford the situation and Ledford said for John to stay at the phone and he would be contacted. In five minutes the phone rang, and John said, "Carter here". The President said, "John you have the "Ricin"?"

John said "Mr. President we have ten each 55-gallon drums of it but I do not know exactly if that is all of it, not yet anyway. Our people have captured three of the rebels and one is now who we think is leading the group and the one who sent the demands. We have not had a chance to question him because of the "Ricin". Right now, I need to know what you want us to do with the stuff. We cannot drive it out or get it out by our chopper because we have no idea if it is stable or what. We need hazmat people and we need them now. Mr. President".

The President said "John stay by the phone. I will have the Secretary of Homeland call you. Just tell her what she needs to know, and I will handle her after we get this mess cleared up".

John said "Yes, Mr. President" and hung up the phone. In three minutes John's phone rang and again he answered, "Carter here" The woman on the other end of the line sounded sleepy but said "General this is the Secretary of Homeland the President said you have a situation. Tell me". John explained about the truck and what it had on it and how much of the suspected "Ricin" was there." The Secretary said, "Do you have a recommendation for the immediate, General?"

John said "Madam Secretary, I think we need to do the following: First call Ft. Leonard Wood and get a platoon of Military Police in helicopters in route to the truck. They can secure the area. Second: You need to get in touch with CDC or whoever handles this and get them in route here within the hour. They can sure as Hell move if they have to do so. If you have problems, get the President to call. And the third thing we need to do is have you call the Governor and have him send the State Police and the County Sheriff here as soon as they can get here to secure the truck until the MPs get on location. Make very sure that the Governor knows that the truck might have "Ricin" in it and that he explains that fact to Law Enforcement. This is a must. Madam Secretary. ".

The Secretary said "Ok General I will call CDC and the Governor. Will you please call Ft. Leonard Wood and military to military get the Commanding General to get the MPs on the way. I believe you do out rank him do you not?"

John said "Yes I do, and I will handle that. Thank you, Madam Secretary", John hung up and called back to General Ledford. John could not be the one making the call to Leonard Wood, but Ledford could. Ledford agreed to call immediately and get things rolling. There was still one major problem. John had men and a Black Hawk on the ground at the truck and they could not be there when the State Police or Sheriff arrived. John called Don and had him find the radio frequency for the State police and the Sheriff in Ozark county Missouri. Then Don was to monitor it and listen for the radio call to go out. As soon as the call was sent out Don would advise Tress and Tress would have the Black Hawk lift off and hover at 8000 feet until the law enforcement arrived. John told Tress to advise the operators to load and have the chopper take off as soon as Tress got the message about the radio dispatch. The chopper would hover at 8000 feet until the first law enforcement arrived at the truck. Going back to Little Rock was a no go so John was going to chance stopping at a civilian airport for fuel. He was thinking of Texarkana and he knew that with money no one would really question why the Black Hawk was there. It was a risk, but John did not want to try a military facility now with everything going on. God knows how many people were now in the loop about the "Ricin". John had Tress tell the Black Hawk. All operators and piolets had credit cards on them at all times, so there was never a problem if things were needed. Tress got the word from Don in about fifteen minutes that the State Police and the County Sheriff had just been dispatched to the truck. They did know what might be inside and they had been told to only secure the area until the military arrived. Tress informed the Black Hawk and it took off. In five minutes Tress was told law enforcement had just arrived at the truck. The operators, prisoners and crew were in route to Texarkana. ETA was one and one-half hours.

Red Lion headquarters was busy. Jim and Harry had set up a special area in the hanger at the air field to do the interrogations. The PA and one medic were standing by along with three operators. The Black Hawk arrived at the air field and landed in front of the hanger. The team and the prisoners were off the chopper and the prisoners were taken directly into the area that had been set up for the interrogations. All three rebels were put into individual rooms and tied to chairs and the blind folds, which had been placed on them at capture, were left in place. The operators then left and went with the Black Hawk to the hanger and unloaded the equipment. Everyone was then transported along with the equipment back to Red Lion headquarters for the de-briefing. Jim and Harry were now ready to start. The first person to be interrogated was Higgins. Jim and Harry were dressed in black fatigue uniforms and looked very scary. Jim walked up to Higgins and told him that he was going to be questioned and if he did not answer and give honest answers he would be severely hurt every time he gave a false answer or did not answer the questions. Jim also told Higgins that no matter what Jim was going to get the information wanted and it could be easy or hard, that was Higgins' choice. Jim removed the blind fold and started the questioning. Higgins at first refused to answer questions and started spouting a bunch of Rights he had and all of that and things about him being a patriot and as he was spouting off Jim tasted him with a stun gun. Higgins stopped talking and sat and shook all over. Jim again ask a question and again Higgins started to spout off with patriot sayings and Jim again tasted Higgins with the stun gun and this time Jim increased the voltage on the gun. Higgins' body leaped violently in the chair and blood trickled from his nose. Jim again ask a question and this time Higgins answered. Higgins was not nearly as macho as he thought and after three hours had given Jim the location of twenty more 55-Gallon drums. Higgins had also given the names of the heads of the rebel organizations in Houston, Las Vegas, Chicago, and St. Louis. Jim immediately got the names to Don and Cindy and a search was started. Higgins was finally given food and water and then he was locked in a very small cell (5 foot by 8 foot) that had been constructed. There were no windows or lights. Totally black inside the cell.

Harry had been interrogating the other prisoners while Jim was working on Higgins. Both men were scared and did not want to be hurt in any way, so Harry got answers without having to use much in the way of pain. He did use the stun gun on each one just to show them what it felt like and threatened to continue to use it if they lied. After an hour, Harry was satisfied he had learned all they had to tell. One of the operators had been writing down everything the men told Harry and Jim and that information was taken directly to Tress and Sandy. The two men were then placed in individual cells the same size as the cell use for Higgins. These cells were also totally dark.

Tress and Sandy had continued to work on the plans for raids on all the known locations of the rebel groups. The main threat that had to be immediately taken out was the Gainesville location. That was where the 20 drums were located. The main weapons holding area was at Devil's Elbow and the Hardy location was the manufacturing location for the aerial spray equipment. Higgins had told Jim that the plan was to use Higgins' trucking company units to transport barrels to each city and give them along with the spray equipment to the heads of each rebel group in the cities. Then the rebels would place the "Ricin" into the spray equipment and locate the sprayers so the most effective spray would take place. The sprayers were equipped with a timer, so they could be pre-set to turn on and start the spraying. The attack was planned for morning rush hour in each city because emergency responders would be slowed by traffic. Jim had also learned that no drums had been shipped and none of the spray equipment had been shipped. The plan was to have the spray equipment picked up at the Hardy location and taken to West Plains. The drums would be picked up at the Angel location after they had been delivered from the Gainesville location and all would be taken to West Plains to Higgins trucking company. Each over the road transport truck would then be loaded with drums for each city and the trucks would leave on a schedule that would have them in the designated cities when it was time to put the plan into action. John was amazed at the plan and how well it had been constructed. John now had a decision to make and he worried that by not telling the FBI he would be possibly violating a statute, but he knew the FBI would screw the deal up because they would want to capture everyone and bring them to trial. The

FBI always wanted the media headlines. John decided to not inform any one and do the job with Red Lion assets only. John had Anderson and Tress come to his office and when they arrived, John said "Ok we have water at three locations we need to attack. How can we best use that to our advantage?"

Anderson said, "Sir, we can use rubber boats but nothing bigger or we will be totally exposed. The sound of the motors will alert anyone, and we would have to get the boats to a location we could put the boats in the water from and that would be dangerous because people always look at boats they do not recognize".

Tress said, "Sir, we can use the rubber boats we can get immediately, but we will have to limit the operators to only four per boat, so we will need about ten boats. We can transport the boats in the SUV's we are going to use and inflate the boats when the operators get to their locations. We leave the boats after the raid, actually sink them, and we leave no trace".

John said, "OK Anderson work out the currents, depths all the Navy things and Tress continue on the raid planning". The men left John's office and John walked to Don and Cindy's computer area. Higgins was a problem because no one had heard from him in two days and John was afraid that would cause the rebels to start asking questions.

John sat down in Don and Cindy's computer area and said, "Could we use Higgins email account to communicate with the people he gave us?"

Don said, "Yes we should be able to do it".

Cindy said "The only problem would be if there was a code or something. So far I think they have been pretty open and we have identified all the code names for the "Ricin" and the cities so we can try".

Don said, "What do you have in mind, General?"

John said "We need to postpone the attack and the delivery for a week or maybe ten days, but we cannot let the rebels know anything is wrong. Now how do we do that?"

Cindy said "I will send a message to everyone that because of problems in West Plains, Higgins has to be out of touch with everyone for ten days. He was alerted that the FBI has a warrant for him to be questioned and they are actively searching for him in the West Plains and Springfield, Missouri areas". Cindy then said "Of course I will send it, so it looks like Higgins sent the email. This should buy us ten days or more. But we do need the FBI to show up in West Plains and tell the locals they are there to serve a warrant on Higgins. Without that his people might question him being out of the area".

John said, "I like that idea and I will have the FBI in West Plains tomorrow". John left and went back to his office and called Washington. He had to tell the President where he was so far and get him to have the FBI go to West Plains. John made the call and waited. It took much longer to get the return call. Almost three hours. John wondered if things elsewhere were going up in smoke also. The phone call came, and John explained to the President what was happening, what had been accomplished and what John needed. The President told John he would make sure the FBI was in West Plains at the local departments in the morning. John thanked the President and hung up. It was now time to go home and get a little rest. John needed to get his head clear and to relax a little. Molly was just the person to do that for him. Before John left Cindy came into his office and told John the Higgins message had been sent and replies had already been received. John had his ten days. John also had Jim arrange for Homeland Security to come and get Higgins and the other two and keep them totally out of sight and not to let anyone know they were prisoners. Jim had that arranged for a pickup at 11 PM. John was now out the door on his way home. The Red Lion headquarters was still working on plans and logistics.

# CHAPTER 21

The next day John was at the Red Lion office at 5 AM. He had gotten some sleep, but his mind was going 100 miles an hour, so he had decided to go to his office. John read the messages that had come in from Washington and was satisfied that the FBI would be in West Plains and that would solve that problem. The prisoners had been taken away by Homeland Security and were going to be sent to Gitmo for holding. They had been classified as domestic terrorists and would be held until a hearing was held. After that, they would probably be transferred to a US prison to await trial. The FBI and ATF had enough evidence on Higgins to convict him and probably by the time things were over if anyone was still alive they would also be charged. John wanted most of these rebels killed. That was the only way to send a message and John was ready to send a very strong message.

Tress arrived at 6 AM and was in John's office at 6:15 AM. Tress said "Sir, we have the plan finalized. We will attack all targets at the same time".

John said, "Alright I will get the people together and let us brief at 8 AM today".

Tress said "Fine, Sir". Tress left, and John called Jim and had him get everyone ready. Only the operators and Don and Cindy were going to be required for this briefing. At 8 AM everyone was in the briefing room and Tress started the brief. The operation was going to be an attack on all the locations that still were the threat. One team of eight operators would attack the Hardy area, one team of ten operators would attack the Gainesville area and one team of six operators would attack the Devil's Elbow area outside Waynesville. The operators would be driving north to Missouri and Arkansas in SUV's and carry all their equipment including the rubber boats. Only four operators would be in any one vehicle, so it was going to take two vehicles for Hardy, two vehicles for Waynesville, and three vehicles for Gainesville. Gainesville was the top priority target and again the State Police and Sheriff would have to be notified once the operators had the situation under control. John would be the one to notify the Homeland Security Secretary when the time came. The operators would destroy the spray equipment in Hardy and size the weapons at the Waynesville location. At that location a rental truck would be required, and the operators would rent it the day before the raid. The Lear Jet leased by the Red Lion company would be sent to the airport at Rolla, MO and would be waiting for the operators to bring the weapons so they could be loaded and returned to Red Lion Headquarters. The operators would drive back in their vehicles and the rental truck would be returned. In the event of wounded operators, they would be sent to the nearest local hospital and then transferred back to Houston as soon as possible. The site in Hardy would be totally destroyed, as well as the site in Waynesville. If possible the site in Gainesville would be left for the local officials to do what was necessary. All the "Ricin" would be again guarded by Military Police and the "Ricin" handled by the CDC. It would be an exact duplicate of the raid on "Angel Ranch" only the drums would not be moved from the site. The raids were scheduled for Saturday at 11 PM. Tress had picked that day and time because he believed more rebel members would probably be at the sites on a weekend. John agreed, and things were set. The operators would leave Red Lion the next morning and drive straight to their target areas. They would take hotel rooms and only leave the hotel in time to prepare their equipment before the raid. Given the locations, the longest drive would be the Waynesville location and that was going to be about fourteen hours. Each team would leave in staggered times so the possibility of attracting attention on the highway would be reduced. The SUV's were all different colors so that too would help with the deception. John said a few words then everyone was off to get ready. John went back to his office and looked at the information about the heads of the rebel groups in the different cities. They would be next to go and that would be twenty-four hours after the site attacks. Sandy had located all the names and Don and Cindy had traced all their computers and cell phones. two operators per man would be sent to eliminate these individuals. They were to be terminated.

The operators were now in their locations and the hours were counting down. So far, no problems had been detected by Higgins being out of contact and Cindy was monitoring the email at all times. It was Saturday morning and John had spoken to the Homeland Security Secretary on Friday and briefed her on the situation. The Secretary was going to be available by cell phone for John to call and again she would get the CDC and the Governor involved. John liked working with the Secretary because John trusted the woman and so far, John's trust had been rewarded. No media coverage of anything but what the locals had found and of course what the CDC had done. The official line was that a radical rebel group had tried to extort money and the release of their leader and with the help of many intelligence agencies, both federal and local law enforcement had been able to stop the threat and disband the rebel organization. Credit was given to the locals and John really liked that idea. The local departments were too busy claiming the spotlight to really look for John's people and that made things much better.

At exactly 11 AM all three targets were attacked by operators. Admiral Anderson had given each team a landing area that was within 200 yards of their target. The rubber boats had been exactly what was needed for the operators to gain complete surprise. Anderson had been able to gauge the currents and the depth of the water using Corps of Engineer charts and had done an outstanding job. John had decided that only if necessary would the operators kill the rebels at the locations. The plan was to capture as many as possible and leave them for the local authorities and the FBI to take into custody. Only if the rebels fired on the operators would they be killed. It was a risk, but John was worried about what repercussions would come if that many US citizens were killed.

The Hardy manufacturing plant was hit and there were eight rebels on site. The operators were forced to kill three when they fired on the operators and three rebels were wounded. The rebels were then placed in flex ties and blind folded and left on the ground about fifty yards away from the manufacturing building. Inside the building, a complete machine shop along with fifty spray devices were found by the operators. The operators placed thermite grenades on the manufacturing equipment and on the spray equipment as well as C-4 charges. Timers were set, and all weapons were left so they would be found by local law enforcement. The operators then re-boarded the rubber boats and left the area. The charges were set on timers for a forty-five-minute delay. The operators were back in the SUV, the rubber boats were sunk in the river and the SUVs were about one mile from the site when the explosions went off. The flames shot 200 feet into the air and the entire area was one huge fireball. All three buildings were burning. The operators drove directly out of the area and in twenty minutes they were headed toward the highway that would lead them back to Houston.

The raid on the Gainesville operation was more intense. The operators were immediately fired on by 4 rebels and had to return fire killing all four. The entrance into the building that stored the "Ricin" barrels was also a problem and again two rebels fired on the operators. They were also killed. The nine other rebels on site in another building were captured and tied with flex ties and blind folded. The building that was used for the laboratory that the "Ricin" was produced in was secured and the barrels of "Ricin" were also secured. A total of thirty barrels were found and an additional six barrels were found to be half full. The operators made certain all the rebels still alive were totally secured and after checking every area for any intelligence that might be of uses, Nelson, the lead operator, placed the SAT call to Red Lion. Tress took the call and immediately informed John that the site was secure. John called Washington and gave the Secretary of Homeland the word. The operators were already back in the rubber boats and almost back to the SUVs. They would also sink the boats and head towards the highway that lead to Houston. The operators had been able to retrieve some information on the rebel group and they had a list of names and locations of about forty locations throughout the US where the rebels operated from.

The raid on "Devil's Elbow was excellent. Only three rebels were on the site and the operators were able to capture them immediately. They were also tied with flex ties and blindfolded and placed about 50 yards away from the building that all the weapons were in. The operators moved the rental truck down the road into the site and loaded up weapons. A total of 300 weapons, and about 20,000 rounds of ammunition was seized. two boxes of hand grenades along with three cases of Claymore Mines were seized. Over 200 pounds of C-4 explosives were also seized. The rental truck was loaded and left for the airport in Rolla. The operators placed two charges in the main building and set the timer for forty-five minutes. The idea was to create and explosion and a fire that would destroy the building and immediately draw the attention of local law enforcement. Enough ammunition and some of the explosives were left at the scene to insure the local cops realized this was a storage area for the rebels. The

FBI would also be notified by Homeland Security and sent to all locations. The operators had also checked for intelligence information and had found some papers and a few maps. The operators were on the road headed to Rolla and the explosion had sent a fire ball about 100 feet into the air. The building was totally engulfed in flames. Three hours after the start of the raids, all operators were on the way to Houston. The cargo jet had been loaded and was in the air headed to the Sugarland airport. Tress and Sandy confirmed that the local sheriff departments in all three locations were now on seen along with the State Police at the Gainesville location. The FBI was also in route from Springfield and St. Louis Missouri as well as DEA and ATF. Hazmat had been sent from CDC. The Homeland Secretary had informed the President. John was very satisfied. The body count had been more than he wanted, but he knew the operators had only protected themselves. Nine rebels had been killed and law enforcement had the rest in custody. Homeland and the FBI were now going to question them and try to get answers.

Tress and Sandy had the next targets ready to be briefed. These were the leaders Red Lion had found that were in Houston, Chicago, Vegas, and St. Louis. John wanted them eliminated as soon as possible. The information on them had come from Higgins. These were the people who were going to carry out the "Ricin" attacks. Tress and Sandy had created a two-operator mission for each location. The plan was extremely simple. The operators would kill the leaders. Tress and Sandy had the home, work and other locations for each target. John wanted the operators to take out only the targets, no other people were to be hurt. With the elimination of the leaders, the rebel organizations in each city would be broken up. This was the plan. John wanted the hits done as soon as possible because he was sure word of the raids would be sent out by other members of the rebel group and he knew damn well the news media would be all over things. They were already reporting the situation in Gainesville and the discovery there. Tress had all the plane reservations made. John was listening to the briefing and watched the operators that had been given the assignment. They were taking notes and getting prepared to leave. John was very glad that all his operators could do any mission. Some were of course better than others, but all were excellent at their work. This mission would be done without the normal lead operators. Those operators were not back from the missions in Arkansas and Missouri. The weapons had been sent to locations overnight via UPS and would be waiting when the operators arrived in the three cities. All operators were scheduled to depart in the afternoon. John was hoping the targets would be eliminated within thirty-six hours. The Houston target would be the first to be taken out and that was to happen in three hours. John listened to the briefing and when it was done, John went to his office and checked the list one more time. John was convinced that after this mission there would be no more threat by the rebels.

The plane had landed and the ground personnel and some of the operators had unloaded the weapons and ammunition. The explosives and mines as well as the grenades were also unloaded and placed in a separate area. John went to inspect the weapons and was very surprised to find many M-16s that were US Army issue. These weapons would fire both semi and fully automatic. There were also six, M-60 machine guns. John knew these weapons could only have come from government stocks. Jim had already had all the serial numbers run and nothing had been reported stolen. Jim and John both wanted to know how in the Hell these rebels had gotten their hands on the weapons. This was a very serious situation and John needed to make damn sure it was followed up on in Washington. Jim had the serial numbers sent via special message to June at the Pentagon and she gave the information to the General in charge of the Criminal Investigation

Command. CID was now going to have to investigate this and do it immediately. John had sent a copy and a brief to Ledford. The real question now was, do with the rebels in the locations targeted? Do they have this type of weapon and if so where in the Hell are they stored? John had Tress and Sandy along with Don and Cindy working on that part of the puzzle. The operators from the raids in Missouri and Arkansas, were back and the information they brought from the locations was being analyzed by Tress and Sandy. This rebel organization was bigger than John or anyone realized. Two days had passed, and John was awaiting word from the operators that the hits on the three targets, that were the leaders in the target cities, had been carried out. It was early in the morning about 6 AM when Tress called John's cell phone. John answered, and Tress said "Sir, all targets are now eliminated".

John said, "Thank you". John was satisfied. The operators would be arriving back in Houston that afternoon. The hits had been individual and were conducted mainly as sniper shots. Only one had been up close, the one in Houston. The target had been taken out in a restaurant while eating lunch. One other man had also been shot. The shots to the targets were all head shots either by sniper or the Houston hit, up close. There was no doubt that the targets were killed, and the message was sent. The next step was to make damn sure the weapons locations were identified and taken out, but John was going to leave that to the AFT and CID. Red Lion was now going to stand down. August was about over, and John knew the next two months would be nothing but the Presidential race and everyone in Washington was about to change jobs. John decided that Red Lion would go on vacation for 30 days. John had Nancy type up a directive to all employees and send it out.

# CHAPTER 22

The time off had been good for the Red Lion unit. It was now November and the election were over. The new President-elect was a young man who the country had embraced wildly. He was a black man, the first to ever run much less be elected, as the President. His background was non-military and mainly political. He was from Chicago. John had no idea what was going to happen to Red Lion now. The economy was the worse it had been in over fifty years, and things were very bad in the United States. The wars were not getting any better. The US had been involved in fighting since 2002 and heavily involved since 2003 on two fronts. To John, nothing had been accomplished. More than 4000 service members had been killed and over 275,000 had been wounded. Many of the wounded had such severe wounds that the VA system was totally over loaded and in a very bad state. The wounded personnel could not be cared for and the country was having a very hard time dealing with that fact. Businesses were going broke and the banks were in very bad trouble. Many had gone under and so had some Wall Street brokerage firms. The government had bailed out two of the auto manufacturers and some other businesses. It was a real mess. John was thinking about the next step for Red Lion and he wanted to try to find out from Washington what the future might hold. Ledford had already submitted his retirement and it would be effective on January 1st, 2009. The other Generals, were also probably going to retire so the new administration would have a new bunch of positions to fill. The Cabinet, of course would all be different, so John would no longer have any pull with the Secretary of Homeland or

Defense or the Secretary of the Army. The CIA would get a new director and maybe the FBI. The ATF and DEA would get a new leader because they both fell under the Department of Justice. A new Attorney General was always appointed. John decided to have a staff meeting and discuss the events that were pending. John had Nancy set the meeting up for the following morning. John called Sara and had her come to his office. Sara came in and sat down. John said "Sara I need you to make me a detailed list of exactly what Red Lion actually owns as far as equipment, anything we own not lease. I also need to know exactly how much money Red Lion has and where it is. In other words which banks we have the money in that no one knows we have. The operating money we get from DOD make sure that is split out and any equipment they furnish is also split out. And could you get me a value of the DOD equipment after it is depreciated?"

Sara said "Yes Sir. When do you need this?"

John said "By 9 AM in the morning or sooner".

Sara said, "I can do that". Sara got up and left the office and John turned his attention to the report from the CID that had arrived that morning. It was twenty pages long. As John read the report he was very happy that the guns and ammunition had been resolved. CID, FBI, and Naval Investigative Services had all investigated and arrested ten members of the military. six Navy and four Army. The weapons and ammunition and everything, mines, grenades, you name it had been stolen from the shipments heading for the overseas war. The reason nothing had been reported was because the shipments had been taken as they arrived directly from the manufacturers. The paperwork had been changed and then the Navy people had put the items in a special holding area. The Army people had then picked up the items and taken them off the docks. The Army personnel had used the computers to change the amounts received from the manufacturers only on the shipping documents. The invoices going to DOD had remained the same, so they were paid. No one even questioned the shipments. It was a great plan. If Red Lion had not taken the weapons and other items no one would have ever realized the thefts. John finished the report and smiled. If anyone only knew how the information was obtained, all Hell would break loose.

The staff meeting was about to begin. Jim, Harry, Tress, Sandy, Anderson, Nelson, Don, Cindy, Nancy, Dan, and Sara were all sitting at the conference table. John walked in and said "No one get up. This is going to be very informal. I just want everyone to relax and listen very carefully then we will discuss things". John pressed the button and the white-board on the wall lit up. The first slide was the breakdown of the Red Lion unit. John said "As you all can see, we have the unit broken down into six major groups. I think this was a very good way to originally organize the unit, but now we may want to re-look at things. As we all know we will have a new President in less than ninety days. Officially he will take office on 20 Jan 2009 so after that all bets are off. I have no earthly idea what the man will do, and I do not think anyone does so far. That is why I have called this meeting. We may be totally out of business after the new guy takes over. We may still be in business but restricted. Now, I have an idea, but it has some risks, so I want all of you to think about things very carefully before you decide. Everyone at this table can retire from military and government service as of today if you so choose. Most of our operators and piolets can also retire. Andy, I do not know about your guys, but they should be just about ready to retire. As for the ones that are almost there, we can probably do something to get them assigned to a job that will take them to the retirement year. The reason I am bringing this up, is because if we get terminated as an active Army unit, we can go into business as a civilian contractor. We have already been approached by different countries and other businesses to do work for them, but so far, we have not been able to do it, because we are actually a DOD unit, paid for by the DOD and our people are paid by the military and given their benefits by the military. Conflict of interest. If we decided to go into business as a civilian company, Dan can get all the necessary paperwork done and we would then be a corporation. Everyone would be a stock holder that works for us. We would have a Board of Directors and all the things businesses have. Then we could work for anyone anytime anywhere. From what I have been told, we have over $5.9 Billion Dollars in assets and cash so that would be a great start. We could also buy what we have now from DOD for reduced prices or replace the equipment. All of that would depend on what we decide to do. Now here is the challenge I put to each of you. If we get terminated, do you want to retire and go it as a civilian corporation or just retire?" The table was silent. Each person looked at the others and then back at John. Dan said "Sir, what will our legal status be as a civilian company? What I mean is as far as our operations within the US. Will we be able to have the protections we now enjoy or at least some of them?"

John said, "Dan I have no idea!"

Jim said "Sir, if we do this civilian thing who exactly would we be working for and what would we be doing?"

John said "We would be a security force so to speak for people like KBR, and other contractors in the war zone and other places that have terrorist activities attacking their jobs. We would also be working for some countries that have problems both outside and inside their borders".

Harry said "How about the Hallettsville operation? Will we still be doing that and expanding it?"

John said "Yes that is one of our biggest assets and I think we can get a good contract with DOD for training their special operations people. Also, we can offer our expertise to Texas Law Enforcement and actually do their qualifications and other things". John then said "We have a lot of things to look at and right now I just want all of you to think about what you each would do. It boils down to either retire from the military and government service or go back to another assignment that DOD will pick for you. It is strictly your choice, and nothing is even in the works right now. I just wanted each of you to know what the situation is and let you think about it for a few months". On that note, John closed the staff meeting. There was a great deal of talk before anyone left the room. Everyone was talking to each other and John was glad. That was his intention. John left and went to his office. He had two messages from Washington waiting on his secure email. John read them and knew the time was now on for his first and maybe last meeting with the new President-elect. John was to be in Washington D.C. on December 20th. The President wanted to see him at 5 PM that day. John was also to bring a total listing of every operation Red Lion had done since it started.

John was looking over the information Sara had given him about Red Lion. $5.9 Billion Dollars was a great amount of money and John knew that over $3.5 Billion Dollars of that was cash. The container ship was worth $85 Million Dollars and there was about $60 Million Dollars in computer, GPS, SAT phones, and other specialized equipment that Red Lion owned. There was $5 Million Dollars in vehicles and another $200 Million Dollars in airplanes. The Hallettsville complex was worth $200 Million Dollars. John knew that DOD would sell all of the weapons, night vision gear, tools, and probably at least all of the Black Hawks if not the Cobra to Red Lion for a reduced price. John was thinking a deal of $120 Million Dollars would buy everything including the Cobra. John could probably get that done before the change of personnel went into effect. John called General Ledford and discussed the possibility with him on the secure line. Ledford said he would make it happen and get back to John with the how. John was now set. Either way, John wanted to control the critical things even if Red Lion was still an Army unit. John called Don into his office and said "Don I want you to order brand new, the most up to date, computer equipment we can possibly get. Order new everything and put it on the special rush purchase numbers we use. We need it here as soon as we can possibly get it. Make sure we have it for here, the airfield, Galveston and Hallettsville. Anything you can dream of that you and Cindy might want order it. Also get with Tress and Sandy and check on their Como needs as well".

Don said, "OK John you got it". Don went back and started a list. John knew now was the time to get everything Red Lion could possibly need. The next person was his medical PA. John told the medical section to do the same thing, order everything they could think of in the way of equipment and to triple the supplies of medical on hand. Then John called the armors and had them also order new guns for everyone plus new weapons systems for all the vehicles and helicopters. John was going to make the best of what might be a very bad situation and he was damn sure he would have the blessings of the Chief of Staff and probably the President.

John and Molly were sitting at home and John had gotten them a drink. John said, "Honey what would you think if I was to retire from the Army?"

Molly looked at John and said "Well, would you really be happy retired?"

John said, "I have this idea about Red Lion and what we could do with it".

Molly said, "OK tell me about it". John explained the entire situation to Molly and they had about three more drinks as he told her what he had in mind. When John finished, Molly said "I think it would work but you do realize you would be a civilian and that no matter what you think it will change what you have the power to do".

John said "I know that, and I think that I can deal with that fact. I will still have connections in DOD. A General always does. That is the way it works".

Molly said "I am good with whatever you want to do. Just let me know how I can help".

John said, "You know I will". Molly and John left the apartment and went to have dinner. John liked the fact that he would be moving into a new arena and that was exciting to him. He knew he would have a lot to learn, but Molly was there to help him become a civilian if need be. During dinner they talked about maybe buying a house if John retired. John was agreeable to buying a house if that was what Molly wanted to do. The apartment was nice, but John knew they did need more room and would sure as Hell need it if he was totally in business in the civilian world. He would then be able to entertain and so could Molly. No more deep, dark secrets or at least not as many.

The next weeks went fast. John and Molly went to Hallettsville again for Thanksgiving and were planning to go for Christmas as well. John was preparing his proposal for the new President and would have it with him on the trip to Washington. John had talked with most of the people at Red Lion and everyone was ready to retire and have Red Lion become a full civilian company. The breakdown of personnel showed that only 28 were not eligible to retire in January. John was going to get personnel both at the Army and the Navy to assign these people to special assignments until they reached the retirement mark. He could do that at his rank. Then as soon as they retired he would hire them to come to work. Both the civilian ladies would retire and go to work for Red Lion as would Dan. Don and Cindy were working for Red Lion now and were the only employees the company had. Dan was going to redo the paperwork making Red Lion a corporation not just a one owner company as soon as John told him to do so. Right now, John was the sole owner of Red Lion.

Don's computer and other electronic gear was now delivered. The weapons were also being delivered. The additional gear that had been ordered by the medical staff and everything else was also arriving. The operators and other personnel were busy putting everything into place or storing it. Anderson had ordered some new equipment for the container ship and it was being installed. John wanted Jim to accompany John to Washington for the meeting with the President-elect. Jim was a little reluctant, but he agreed to go. John had a very good reason. Jim was black, and so was the new President. John wanted this fact to be very clear to the new President. John had finished his proposal and gave Jim a copy to read and study. The proposal would be only given in the event John and Jim were told Red Lion was out. No one knew what was going to happen. No one really had a guess. That was upsetting to John. Normally someone had at least a guess. This time it was running in the dark. The plane was set to fly from Ellington AFB and would be an Air Force C-22 the same as the Lear jet. The takeoff time was at 11 AM on 20 Dec. John and Jim would stay at the Army and Navy Hotel. A staff car would pick them up and take them to the White House. The Generals would be wearing their Class "A" uniforms. John wanted to impress this new guy and with two General Officers as highly decorated as John and Jim it should work. The generals would wear class "B" uniforms on the plane. That was simple, shirt, pants, and windbreaker jacket. No decorations other than Jump Wings and CIB plus the General Officer Badge. General Stars on the shoulder boards, and on the "Cunt Cap".

The C-22 took off right on schedule and was headed to Washington. John and Jim talked about the proposal and about how things would be really different if they were no longer in the Army. Both men knew they would miss the Army. But under the circumstances they may have no choice. Neither man could go to another assignment. They both knew that. Neither man could ever go higher in the Army and they both knew that as well. John and Jim had been friends for many years and they understood one another. John knew it would be a fantastic team if Red Lion did become a corporation and completely civilian. The C-22 touched down at Andrew's AFB and the staff car took the Generals to the hotel. It was now 2 PM. The same car would pick them up and take them to the White House at 4:30 PM. John and Jim checked into the hotel and their bags were taken to their rooms. John and Jim went to the bar and had a drink. There were a few other officers in the bar but all and all it was very slow. John and Jim had two drinks then went up and got ready for the meeting.

# CHAPTER 23

John and Jim were waiting outside the Oval Office and exactly at 5 PM the President's secretary came out and said, "General Carter, the President will see you now". John and Jim went into the room and both Generals saluted the President. The President said "Gentlemen this is Leon Trill, the President Elect. The officers saluted Trill. Then the President said, "Please sit". The officers sat in the two chairs that had been arranged for them. The President and the President Elect sat in chairs across from the Generals. No one else was in the room. The President said "John I am glad you brought Jim along. Leon need to meet him as well as you. Do you have the list I ask for?" John reached into his inside pocket of his uniform and handed the President the list of targets Red Lion had done since it was formed. The President then handed it to The President Elect who looked over the list then placed it face up on the coffee table. The President then said "Leon, I am going to tell you exactly who these men are and exactly what they do for me and this country. In 2006, I signed an Executive Order, creating Red Lion. The order was so far past "Top Secret" it was not funny. I did it only so the men would be protected in the event things went badly. I knew that my order to them would be enough for them to do their job, but just in case it was needed the Executive Order was official. This order is in a very secure place and only 3 people know of it. Now what these men do is what we as the elected President of the United States cannot do or even order out armed forces to do. The CIA, FBI, NSA, NIS do not know what they do. In my administration only one of my people knows of their existence and that is only because we had a very bad situation come up where "Ricin" was involved and they had to have outside help to get the "Ricin" taken care of. There is one person or actually three people, who are military who know of these men and what they do. They have the ability to do things, no matter what, where, or when that no other organization on this earth can do. Their use is strictly my decision and mine alone. They do not deploy on any mission without my direct approval. General Carter has the right to call me anytime of the day or night and I will give you all that and show you how it works. Normally John, uses a person to contact me so I am not directly involved should something go wrong. It gives me deniability." The President Elect sat and studied the President and both the Generals.

After a minute he said, "Then what you are telling me is that you have your personal hit squad is that right?"

The President said, "I guess you could say that".

Then the President Elect turned and looked at John, and said "General where does this unit of yours base from?"

John said "Sir, we are located in Houston, Texas, well in a suburb of Houston, called Sugarland".

The President Elect said "Why?"

John said "Because we are not around any military facility except Ellington AFB and that is forty miles across Houston. It is also where NASA and all the space flight people come in and out of. That way no one in the military will even give us a second look".

The President Elect said "I understand. How do you get funded?"

Jim said "Sir, all our people are assigned on paper to Special Operations and the three civilians that we have are also assigned there. We have two other civilian employees and they are independent contractors to DOD. Our personnel are paid by their branch of service at their pay grades and of course paid rations and housing. The civilians are also paid according to their pay grades and the contractors are paid per the contract.

The other funding is put thru Special Operations, which includes equipment, fuel, ammunitions, rental of equipment and anything we need to staff our operation. It is tightly controlled by one of our civilian accountants. All purchase orders are placed with DOD contracting for major purchases and a cash fund that is again controlled by our accountant is used when necessary. We also have actual sources of income we use, and that money is sent back to the Treasury. We are audited annually by both DOD and by GAO".

The President Elect said, "I see that you have covered all your bases".

The President said "Leon we have done the right thing in today's world. Now it will be your call to keep this unit or not to keep it. I personally advise you to retain the unit as it is and use it when no one else can do the job. And believe me you will face that situation almost daily in this job".

The President Elect said "I want to think about this. I must know that what is being done is legal and that I do have the authority to do this without having Congress approve it. That is my worry and I realize you have been doing it Mr. President, but I need to run it by my people".

The President said "OK I can understand that. But remember the more people who know about this, the better the chance it will get out and you cannot live with that for a minute. It will destroy you before you even get started".

John said "Mr. President Elect, I understand your concerns and I do have an alternate proposal for you to look at. I can either leave it with you now, which I do not think is the best course of action or I would be more than glad to return and speak to you one on one after you have taken your oath. I would like to do that in February if you would permit me".

The President Elect said "General that would be an excellent idea. But in the meantime, I want you to continue just as you are. I am not the President yet and until then you do what The President says to do".

John and Jim rose and saluted both men and left the oval office. They had been in the room for over an hour. John and Jim returned to the Hotel and went straight into the bar and ordered a drink. It had been one Hell of a meeting. John and Jim discussed the meeting for the next two hours and had drinks. They decided to have dinner at the hotel and Jim called the Air Force base and arranged for the return flight to leave at 8 AM the next day. John and Jim went to their rooms and John called Molly and told her he would be home about noon the next day. Molly said she would be at Ellington to pick him up. John agreed and went to sleep. He was tired, but he felt good. In his mind, Red Lion was going to be a civilian corporation by February. He would also be retired with an effective date of 1 March 2009.

The C-22 landed at Ellington at 11:45 AM and John saw Molly's car parked and waiting. A Red Lion vehicle was parked next to Molly waiting for Jim. Both Generals deplaned and walked to the vehicles. Air Force personnel brought the bags and placed them in the vehicles, saluted and departed. John told Jim good bye and returned his salute and then got into the car with Molly. Molly drove out the gate and headed for the apartment. John was very glad to be back with Molly. The next day John and Molly drove to Hallettsville for the Christmas celebration. John was going to tell Ray about his decision. He had already told Molly and she was very happy. Linda and Miles and his parents along with their children were due to be there at 7 PM. John would tell everyone that night. His grandmother was not well, and John knew anytime she could be gone.

Everyone was sitting in the living room and having a drink and talking. John stood up and said, "I need to tell you something so please listen carefully". Everyone stopped and looked at John. John said "I am retiring from the Army. My effective date will be 1 March 2009. I am going to be a civilian for the first time since I was 17 years old". The entire family looked and finally Ray said "I will be God damned. You finally did it. Ok. Now what in the Hell are you going to do with him, Molly?" Everyone laughed and got up and hugged John. John walked over to his grandmother and bent down. She kissed him and patted his hand. John knew she understood. Christmas was very good, and everyone really enjoyed it. To John it seemed like the family enjoyed it more than usual. The next day John and Ray talked about what John had planned and how it would affect the compound on the ranch. John told Ray that the compound was still going to be used just like it had been only now probably much more. Ray was happy with that. It was about 1 PM and everyone was gathering around for lunch. John looked in the den and saw his grandmother slumped over in her chair. He rushed to her and immediately knew she was dead. John grabbed her and placed her on the floor and felt for a pulse. There was nothing. Ray was there as well and so was Miles. The girls were in the kitchen and then Linda saw what was happening. She screamed, and Donna and Molly rushed into the den. Donna called 911 but John knew it was too late for that. It took the ambulance about twenty minutes to arrive. A deputy car had gotten to the house about five minutes before the ambulance and the deputy was clearing a path into the den from the front door. The paramedics came in and checked. No sign of life. John told them to take his grandmother to the hospital and have her pronounced there. He did not want to wait until the coroner arrived. His grandmother was loaded into the ambulance and it took off. John and Molly got into John's car and followed the ambulance. Ray and Donna along with Linda and Miles followed John. The children stayed in the house with Miles' parents.

Everyone was gathered at the hospital and the ER doctor came out and said "I am sorry, but Mrs. Carter is gone. From what we can tell she had a massive heart attack and was dead instantly. She did not suffer as far as we can tell".

John said, "Thank you doctor". John turned to Ray and said, "Ray can you call the funeral home and have them come to get her?"

Ray said, "Yes John". John hugged Linda and then Molly hugged John. Miles said, "John is there anything I can do?"

John said "Miles, not at this time. Do you know about her will or is that Ray's department? We need to see if she had anything special in it about her funeral".

Miles said "Ray and I both have a copy, but the original is with her lawyer in Houston. I have his name and I will call him right away."

John said "Thanks". Ray came back and said the funeral home would be there in about thirty minutes. John walked into the ER room and had a few moments with his grandmother in private. Then when John came out Ray and Linda went into the room. The funeral home came and removed the body. John and Ray and Linda were to be there at the funeral home the next morning at 9 AM to make the arrangements. Everyone went back to the ranch. The rest of the evening and night the family talked and made plans for the service. It was now December 26th and John wanted to have the service on December 30th. Everyone was in agreement. The service would be at 10 AM in the Catholic Church in town and burial would be next to John's Grandfather at the ranch. Molly had called Nancy and told her, and she had alerted the Red Lion unit. Molly had also called Carol and told her. Carol was going to run the bar until Molly returned.

The service was very good, and the burial was done with grace and excellence by the funeral home. The church had been full and then many people came by the ranch to pay respects. It was a long day for everyone. John was tired, and he now had the extra problem of the will. Miles and Ray had showed John the will and it was straight forward. His grandmother was worth $900 Million Dollars not counting the ranch. The $900 Million was in cash and stocks. Miles and

Ray had made sure that when the economy went bad, they had moved her assets into oil and gas stocks and into gold. The will had everything split one third going to John. One third to Linda and one third going to Ray. The land would go to Ray in total and trust accounts had been set up years ago for the Great Grand Children. John was to receive $300 Million Dollars. Because he was on active duty he did not have to pay inheritance tax. That had been waived by a Congressional bill some twelve years ago. John would get the whole amount. The attorney had advised it would be the middle of January before the probate would be completed and he would advise everyone at that time. John wanted his money to be in cash, so he had to get with Linda and Ray and then figure out how it could be done. Miles was great at that part, so he came up with a plan. John would sell his stock and Gold shares to Linda and Ray and they would pay cash for the certificates. Because the price of Gold was up and down, a date was set for the price. The price paid would be on the 15th of January. Whatever the gold closing was then that is what John would receive. Everyone was happy with that. The stocks were handled the same way and the same date was used. John was not going to go through any of his Grandmother's things until much later. He really did not know of anything he wanted, but he would look at a later time. John and Molly left on the 31st and drove back to Houston. They went to Molly's bar for the New Year's celebration. John wanted to enjoy the night with Molly. He loved his Grandmother and knew he would miss her, but he also knew she had lived a long and full life. John was happy with that. Molly's was very busy, and John and Molly enjoyed the people and the time together. They went home and made love and went to sleep. New Year's Day they stayed in bed until noon and then went to have breakfast at Brenner's restaurant. It was a good day. John was still upset over the death of his grandmother, but it was a good day.

# CHAPTER 24

John was back at the Red Lion operations center on the 5th of January. He called a meeting with all his unit heads and advised them he would officially retire from the Army with his effective date being 1 March. They all agreed and for the next week they also put in their retirement papers. Dan was busy getting the corporation paperwork done and by February the 3rd Red Lion was officially a corporation with the power to issue 1 million shares of stock. John had also set up a Board of Directors and officers of the new company. John and Jim had started the purchase of equipment and the government had done exactly as both men had expected. They sold everything Red Lion had at a depreciated price including the Cobra Gunship. John had also bought the warehouse and the hangers at the airfield under the Red Lion name. Only sixteen personnel had to be transferred to jobs back in the military and the longest was for only twenty-four months until retirement. Now everyone was going to be a civilian as of 1 March. The ladies had retired from Civil Service and Dan had simply quit. Harry was going to be the person who ran the Hallettsville range and training for Red Lion and had moved there. He bought a house about two miles away from the compound. He had six instructors that would also be living in Hallettsville and they had also bought houses and were settling into the life there. John was now looking at the final part of the puzzle. He had to see the new President on the 22nd of February and then he would be ready. John had his proposal to the new President and was very certain it would be exactly what the man wanted. The old way was gone, and John knew that. All the main officers

John had worked with had retired and all the department heads and Cabinet officers had been replaced. Washington had changed and always did with a new President. John was ready. John met with Sara. She informed John that there was still almost $5 billion dollars sitting in a bank and it had never been transferred to the government or into Red Lion bank accounts. John told Sara to transfer the money into the Red Lion accounts right away. The transfer was made, and John was now in a position to have access to all the funding he would need initially. The Red Lion accounts had over $9.5 Billion Dollars in cash in them.

John needed a payroll and Human Resources person. Nancy had a recommendation and she contacted the lady and had her come for an interview. Nancy walked into John's office and introduced Barbara to John. Barbara was a very nice-looking woman in her 40's, and stood 5 feet 8 inches tall. She weighed about 150 pounds and wore a very nice brown business suit. John said hello and asked her to be seated. John said "We are looking for a person who can do our payroll and be our Human Resources person. We are a very unique corporation and we need someone who is totally able to conduct business and never tell a soul about what we do or what they see. Can you fit that bill, Barbara?"

Barbara looked at John and said "Sir, if I could not I would not be here and Nancy sure as Hell would not have asked me to come to apply. Now what do you want to know about me?"

John smiled and said "Everything you are willing to tell me. You may start whenever you like".

Barbara told John about her life and about her business experience. She had been married to a Captain in the US Army who had been killed in action in Iraq in 2004. She had a son and had been on her own since her husband's death. Her last position and the one she now had was in HR, for a firm in the oil industry. Barbara had been a payroll clerk for government finance, the Army for four years before moving into the Human Resources field. She had a degree from Texas Tech University and was now taking courses for a Master Degree. John liked what he heard and liked the woman. John said, "What do you make right now?"

Barbara said "I make $45,000 per year and have medical benefits for me and a plan for my son. I get the usual vacation, one week per year and most Holidays off".

John said "Ok that is what I needed to know. Now here is a question I want you to think long and very hard about before you give me an answer. We are in the business of killing people. We always call it something else, but basically, we kill people. Sometimes innocent people get hurt and even killed but our intention is to not hurt or kill anyone other than who we target. Now Barbara can you accept that, and can you live with that knowledge?"

Barbara said "It is my understanding that you are a four star General and that you will be retiring soon. Yes, General I can live with that fact. I realize that in the world we now live in, people need to be killed and our government sure as Hell will not do it. They send troops to do things but to actually do what needs to be done, they refuse. I know it will be bad at times, especially if we have losses in our company, but I can and would like very much to live with that and work for this company".

John said "Well I think you just got a job. Pleased to have you on board. Your starting salary will be $200,000 per year and you and your son will have fully paid for insurance. Now we work time off differently, so Nancy will explain that". John called and asked Nancy to come into his office, and said "Meet our new HR/Payroll department. Now you can relax".

Nancy said "Sir, if that was my only problem I would be Golden. It is the rest of this that gives me ulcers". Everyone laughed. Barbara thanked John and left with Nancy. Barbara would be coming to work in two weeks. The 1st of March.

The payroll was going to be a very large expense and John was working on what each position would be paid. He had broken down the company into divisions. There would be a management division which included John, Jim, and Harry. The IT and Intelligence Division would include Tress, Sandy, Don and Cindy and probably one or two new people. The Marine Division would be Anderson and about ten other personnel. Medical Division would be Leonard, the PA and four medics. John wanted a doctor also in that division and at least two Registered Nurses. Leonard had a doctor in mind and was now looking for nurses. The Aviation Division would include all the piolets and the mechanics. The Logistics Division included all the personnel that did the supply, armorers, vehicle mechanics, and general mechanics that mainly worked on the equipment at the Hallettsville location. The Instructors were also in that divisional breakdown. The Administration Division included Nancy, Sara, Dan, and Barbara. Then the Operations Division was totally made up of all the operators. Nelson would be the head of that Division. John now had the problem of figuring the salaries for each person. John was going to have a company that employed over 200 hundred people. It was going to be quite a challenge. John started his figures. Each division head would be paid $350,000 per year. Each operator would receive $150,000 per year as well as each piolet. The mechanics would receive $100,000 per year. The instructors would be paid $125,000 per year. The marine personnel would be paid $100,000 per year. The medical personnel would each be paid $125,000 per year which included the nurses. Leonard the PA would be paid $300,000 per year as division head until the doctor was on board. Once the doctor was hired, Leonard would no longer be the division head, but would receive the same pay. $400,000 would be reserved for the doctor. Nancy, Sara and Barbara would be paid $200,000 per year. Dan, Cindy and Don were going to receive special pay. Dan would receive

$400,000 Don and Cindy would each receive $375,000 per year. Sandy would receive $300,000 per year. The Division heads, Tress, Anderson, Harry, Jim, Nelson, and Jerry, chief piolet would receive $350,000 per year. John would draw $500,000 per year. The total payroll was $24 Million Dollars per year. John knew Red Lion was going to have to stay busy under contracts and getting very special clients to meet that requirement, but he also knew there was no other company in the world that could do what Red Lion did. John also wanted straight security personnel that would be deployed in areas for extended periods of time. In order to get the right people, the salaries had to be at least $120,000 per year. John was looking at another thirty personnel and another $3.6 Million Dollars. Other expenses would be at a minimum $20 Million Dollars per year. John would need to have a yearly income produced by Red Lion of $45 Million Dollars before any profit would be seen and probably closer to $50 Million Dollars. John was confident that could be done.

The next big thing was all the retirements and who would have a ceremony and where they would have it. John had requested a list and Nancy had just brought it to him. Over 80 % of the personnel retiring were having the ceremony at Ft. Bragg, North Carolina. John could understand that, because almost all his operators and many of his other people had come from units at Ft. Bragg originally. John was also going to have his there. Jim and about 10 other members were going to be at Ft. Benning with the Rangers. Anderson and his people were going to be in Newport, Virginia. John had recommended all retires receive the Legion of Merit as the retirement award and the Secretary of Defense had approved the award be given. The President had signed off before he left office. John had also been told he would also receive his third Legion of Merit award as his retirement award. Because of the number of people retiring on the 1st of March, Ft. Bragg wanted to hold the ceremony for everyone on that exact day.

The ceremony for the Ft. Benning people would also be on the 1st of March and all the Navy personnel would have their retirement on the 2nd of March. John approved of the decisions to do as many as possible at the same time. It would be longer in some ways, but no time for speeches and all that so John was happy. He was sorry he would miss Jim's ceremony, but that was the way it went all too often. No one can do both on the same day. John had everything ready for the ceremony, because he was presenting the awards to all the personnel at Ft. Bragg. His award would be presented by General Ledford in Washington prior to the actual ceremony. That was planned when John would be there to meet with the new President. The days were moving fast now, and John was ready to go to Washington. He would be meeting with the President at 10 AM the day after next. His ceremony would be at 3 PM the same afternoon at the Pentagon. Molly was coming along on this trip because of the ceremony and would stay at the hotel while John met with the President. Ledford wanted to have lunch with both John and Moly after the Presidential meeting so 12 noon was set as the time. Lunch would be at the Army and Navy Hotel where they were staying.

John and Molly were arriving in Washington and the staff car was waiting on the tarmac. The Air Force C-22 taxied up to the holding area and John and Molly got off and went to the car. The driver got their bags and after placing them in the trunk of the car, opened the doors and made sure John and Molly were inside. The driver then headed for the hotel. The doorman met the staff car and escorted John and Molly into the lobby. Bellmen had already gotten the bags and John signed the register and was taken along with Molly to the elevator then to his suite. It was now 7 PM and both Molly and John wanted a drink and something to eat. The flight had been a little bumpy due the weather being like it always was in February in Washington. John and Molly went down to the bar and ordered drinks. They sat for a few minutes and Molly said, "Honey are you going to miss all of this?"

John said "Of course I am but now is the time for us to do it, sweetheart. We cannot stay forever and actually I am looking forward to becoming a civilian and spend more time with you".

Molly leaned over and kissed John and said, "Thank you". The drinks were good and they both had another one before going to dinner. John's cell phone rang in the middle of dinner and he saw the caller. It was Jim. John answered and listened as Jim explained to John what was happening and what had happened. John said "OK tell them I will be back in two days and then we can meet. Make damn sure you tell them I am meeting with the President, so they will not think we are stalling".

Jim said he would handle the situation. John hung up and looked at Molly. John said "We just got a job as a civilian company and it sounds like it is going to be huge. Exxon has called, and the Chairman of the Board wants to meet with me as soon as possible. God only knows what is going on".

Molly said "Ok well we will handle it when we get this over with. I know you can do anything he wants so relax, and enjoy the night. You can always call Jim tomorrow before you see the President".

John smiled and said, "OK I will do just that my dear". John and Moly finished dinner and had a drink at the bar then went to the suite and to bed.

John was at the White House on time and again waiting in the area just outside the Oval Office. The door opened, and a man came out and said "General, the President is ready to meet with you". John got up and walked into the Oval Office and saluted the President. There were four other men in the office and John did not know any of them. The President said "General good to see you again. Let me introduce you. Gentlemen this is General John Carter". Then the President said "General this is Secretary Davis, Homeland Security, this is Secretary Phillips, Defense, this is my Chief of Staff, William Martin, and this is Director Evens, CIA. Please everyone, take a seat". John sat in a chair that faced the President's desk and was also tilted toward the couch where the Secretaries were sitting. The CIA Director and the Chief of Staff were sitting in chairs on the other side of John. The President said "General, John, I have studied what the former President and you had been doing and I am very aware of the tremendous good you have done the country. In fact, if I could give you another Congressional Medal I would because you damn sure deserve it. This last mission to eliminate the rebels on our own soil and our own people was nothing short of brilliant and you and your people saved hundreds of thousands of lives. We can never thank you enough. I also realize that you and your people have dismantled many terrorists and the major plots against the United States. But I am now the guy in charge and for many reasons I am not going to be able to have you continue as you are. I cannot sign an Executive Order and frankly my legal team says that if it had ever been questioned the former President did not have that authority. So be it. As of now you are to no longer operate as an independent unit of the military. I am truly sorry, John but it is what it is".

John said "Mr. President, we have already thought that was your answer and we do not blame you one bit. You are new, and you have more to lose than to gain by doing the order. Everyone in the media is watching for you to screw up and even the people in your own party are really watching to see if you will be the leader you need to be. Sir, I am not a political person, but I do understand your problems. It is for that reason I have a proposal to present to you and to these gentlemen as well. The only person missing that probably should be here is the FBI Director, but I am sure you can fill him in. May I proceed, Mr. President?"

The President said, "Please General tell me what you propose".

John said "As of 3 March 2009, Red Lion will be a civilian corporation. Actually, it is right now. At that time no military active duty or reserve personnel or any DOD personnel will be employed with the corporation. All employees will be retired or ex-military or civilians with no connection to the US Government. Red Lion has been approved under Chapter 22 of the VA as a 51% owned Veteran Corporation and because of that it automatically, by law, receives a 15% advantage in any government bids. Additionally, and again by law, the government must contract our class of company first before putting out a bid request to non-veteran company. Now here is my point, Mr. President. We do not need to have your or anyone in the government's approval to do what we do. We can run around the world and kill as many terrorists as we want so long as we do not get caught. But that would be stupid and the last thing we want to do. So now that we are who we are we would like a contract open end from the government to provide security and intelligence for and to the government. This contract would be a no-bid contract and would go through government contracting or anywhere you would like it to go. The main thing is that when Red Lion sends an invoice it is paid within five days orless and not questioned by a bunch of accounting people. Normally it can be paid out of special funds that everyone in this room knows exist. Red Lion will continue to do the things that no official government agency can do and not one person will know if and this is the big if, we only have one point of contact in your administration. More than that, Mr. President and you might as well call CNN". John watched the reaction on everyone's face including the President. There was silence for about two minutes.

Then the President said, "John is there anything else in this proposal of yours?"

John said "Yes Sir. Now I may seem to you and these other gentlemen that I am dictating terms, but nothing could be further from the truth. I have served this Country all my adult life and I know exactly how hard it is for the President to not get caught up in situations. I have the best people in the world, better than the NIS, NSA, anyone the government has. We will and do protect you Mr. President. That is our job. If you agree with this proposal and I sincerely hope you do, I would request three things happen. The first is that this is the very last time I or any of my people come to Washington. Second is that my people set up secure communications and are allowed to request certain satellite use and re-supply as well as being able to receive certain ammunitions we request from the military. We can work all of that out later. And the last request is that if we are to be on your team after you have decided, you personally give me a telephone call saying GO! I trust your word and that is all I will need to get everything in place. When you decide please send the contact person to Houston, so we can educate him or her on how things need to be done. This is the only way I know to keep you and your administration totally out of harm's way with the Congress, the media and our Allies".

The President said "General thank you for the proposal. I want to really study this and make sure everything is going to be legal. I will have an answer for you in forty-eight hours one way or the other. Again, thank you".

John rose, saluted the President and left the room. John was back at the hotel at 11:30 AM and went up and changed clothes into his Class "B" uniform for lunch. He would again put on his Class "A" dress uniform for the ceremony.

The lunch went well, and Ledford was in great spirits. John told Ledford and Molly about the meeting in the Oval Office and both laughed. Ledford said, "Damn John, I bet the President never thought he would be spoken to like that by one of his officers".

John said "Bet he did not either, but he damn sure got the point. Now we see if he has the guts to act. I think maybe he will because he really has no one that can do what we do, and he damn sure needs it done or he will have more trouble than he can handle". Lunch as over and Ledford said good bye until later and left. John and Molly had a drink and then went up to the room, so John could again get into his dress uniform. The staff car was waiting and delivered John and Molly to the Pentagon at 2:45 PM. They went to the office of the Joint Chiefs and into the conference room. It was crowded but John and Molly were taken directly to the front. At 3 PM exactly General Ledford stepped to the platform and a Captain called the room to attention. The young Captain read the orders awarding John his Legion of Merit. After the award was presented, the same Captain again read the orders for retirement. Then John was asked to say something, and he read a very short group of remarks. The entire ceremony was over in thirty minutes. John and Molly then went into a larger room where refreshments were served. After an hour of visiting with various people, many who John had served with or known and had come to say farewell, John and Molly departed the Pentagon and went back to the hotel and got ready to leave for Houston. The C-22 took off at 6 PM and headed back to Ellington AFB. John was now an official civilian or would be on the 1$^{st}$ of March.

# Part Two

# CHAPTER 25

J ohn had called Jim and they were to meet at 7 AM at the Red Lion office. John was already in his office when Jim arrived. Jim said, "Hell I thought you were coming back today so I told Exxon it would be tomorrow".

John said "I know so now we really impress them. What time does this guy get to work?"

Jim said, "Hell I have no idea, but I do have a number to call so you want to call him, or should I?"

John said "Jim make the call and tell him I came back early because of his problem. That should impress the Hell out of him. By the way what is his name?"

Jim said "Williams. He is the big boss".

John said, "Ok Williams, got it". Jim called and immediately Williams was on the line. Jim told him that John had gotten back early because of the Exxon problem and when would be a good time to meet?"

Williams said "Is 9 AM alright in my building?"

Jim said, "We will see you then". Jim hung up and said "9 AM his place". John smiled.

John and Jim entered the Exxon building and were directed to the executive elevators and then told to press the top button. They entered the elevator and pressed the button and were rushing toward the top in seconds. The elevator opened, and John and Jim got off and looked at the large glass doors. Above the doors was the sign Corporate Offices. John and Jim entered the doors and were met by a security officer. John identified himself and immediately he and Jim were led into an office to the right. The man behind the desk stood up and said "I am Bob Williams so glad you could come. John introduced himself and so did Jim. Williams offered coffee and in a minute the coffee arrived. Williams then called someone on the phone and in 3 minutes a man entered the office. John looked at the man and knew right away he was ex-military or ex-law enforcement. The man said "Hi, I am Will Pierce, the head of security for Exxon". John and Jim both stood up and shook hands with Will and introduced themselves. Everyone was sitting again, and Williams said "Gentlemen we have a major problem and I have asked you here to see if in the event we need your services, you would be interested in helping us. I remembered how well the situation with the pirates was handled by you John and the former President gave me your name. I hope that was alright?"

John said "Yes of course. What is the situation?"

Pierce said "We have a kidnapping in the Philippines and we have women and children as well as one of our top executives involved. It seems that our Vice President of Far East Operations, his wife and two children have been kidnapped and are being held somewhere in that country. We had an initial ransom demand of $200 Million Dollars which we totally said No to. We have been in contact with the Philippines authorities and the State Department but so far, we have had no luck in getting anything done. State is totally useless as always and the authorities there are just corrupt or stupid. The ransom was totally unrealistic. We have been told we have until the 15th of April to make the arrangements for the money to be sent, and then after that we will get instructions on where the people are. That is all we have, at point this time".

John looked at Jim and then he said "First of all will you pay the ransom if it is reduced to a smaller figure? In other words, what are you willing to pay to get these people back?"

Williams said "We do not know what they will take and then if we do pay, there are over 3000 of our employees scattered all over the Far East area. They would immediately be in danger if we pay at all. But we cannot let our people die either. The kidnappers are going to contact us in ten days. They do it by email that we cannot trace".

John said "Ok here is the deal with us. First, we will require a payment of $20 Million Dollars as a retainer. Then when the job is completed we will bill you for all our expenses and another $20 Million Dollars. If we do not get the people back, you will have the $20 Million returned and only pay our expenses. That is how we operate. If you decide on hiring us, we will be available after March 5th".

Williams said, "Ok I will take it to the Board and let you know when we decide".

John said "I can tell you one thing we will need at least thirty days to do this so get your ass moving if you want us. We can do a lot of preplanning so the sooner we sign a contract the quicker we can start. We will need everything you have on the family also". John and Jim stood up, shook hands with both men and left. On the ride back to Red Lion, Jim said "I liked the way you did that John. I really liked it. We may really have something here".

John said "I know we do. This is going to be our first real client. I cannot consider the things we have done as really clients even though we did bill the damn CIA". Both men laughed as they drove back to Red Lion headquarters.

John called Tress into his office and told him to get with Sandy and pull up everything Red Lion had on the Philippines and the terrorist groups that operated there. That was now the top priority for Red Lion and would be their total focus after the retirement ceremonies were finished. On the last day of February, the entire Red Lion organization was closed, and everyone was at one ceremony or the other. On March 4th everyone was back at work and now Red Lion was totally civilian. John had been able to get letters done for everyone showing their position and their pay. Barbara was now on board and handling all recruitments. John had already given her 30 positions to fill and he also wanted her to get an insurance provider to send in quotes. Nancy was busy getting all the files and the letterheads and business cards made and delivered as well as getting all the office supplies needed for all divisions. John had another major problem he had just discovered. He needed someone to estimate costs for operations and he did not have anyone on board that could do that. He had really winged it with Exxon, but he also knew he may have been short on his estimate and no all clients would have that much cash to spend. John and Jim talked at length about that situation and finally came up with a name they both were familiar with. The name was Kevin Smith. Kevin had been a Lieutenant Colonel in the Army the last time John or Jim had any dealings with him. He was a total asshole and was great at his job. He worked for the comptroller of the Army and did cost projections for everything the Army did. His goal was to show exactly what it cost the Army to operate and he did just that. Most of the time, he was ignored on things but now and again he was taken very seriously and that is when things got bad. No waste allowed. John and Jim decided he was just what they needed. John called Don and had him start the process of finding Kevin Smith. It took Don two hours to get the exact location of Kevin's house, his phone number and everything about the man including his total financial history. Kevin had retired in 2007 and was barely able to survive on his retirement. Kevin lived in Florida and was trying to do cost analysis for companies with his own company. He was drowning, and John wanted to get him on board. John decided to take Molly and go for a visit to Orlando. Nancy called the private jet company that Red Lion would now use and scheduled a pick up at the Sugarland air field for the next morning. Nancy also made reservations for John and Molly for the night in a very nice hotel. John called Molly and told her to be ready to travel the next day.

Molly was thrilled. John called Kevin and talked to him for a while. John told Kevin that John would be in Orlando the next day and would like to have dinner with him. Kevin was shocked but said he would have dinner. John told Kevin that John would call and tell Kevin the place and time the next day. John was very confident Kevin would be the newest Red Lion employee.

The flight to Orlando was good and only took two hours. Molly was ready to enjoy the time. John and Molly went to the hotel and checked in. The place was very nice, and Molly immediately went to the pool. It was in the high 80's and she loved the sun. John made reservations for dinner in the hotel dining room for 7 PM and reserved a table at the bar for 5 PM. Then he called Kevin and gave him the location and the time of 5 PM to meet in the bar. John finished and joined Molly at the pool. They spent most of the afternoon until 3 PM in and out of the pool and relaxing. John was wondering if he would hear from the President. Probably not for a while. Not until someone got way too crazy to be controlled. Then it would be a do it now deal, and John was determined that was not going to be the way it went.

Kevin came into the bar and John rose to greet him. They shook hands and John introduced Molly. Kevin sat down and ordered a drink, a Martini extra dry straight up. Molly glanced in John's direction and raised her eyebrow. John knew exactly what she was saying without even hearing it. John talked about the Army and old times for a while and asked Kevin how he liked Orlando. Kevin said, "I really hate it but from my research it was one of the best places to come to open my business".

John said, "Yes and how is that going?"

Kevin said "Truthfully it is not. I am not really good as a civilian, and especially in dealing with people. They just hate the truth and then they get mad at me for telling them they are screwed up".

John laughed and said, "Well Kevin as I remember you never did have any real tact with saying what you meant".

Kevin smiled and then said, "Tell me General what in the Hell are you doing here and why in the Hell am I having dinner with you and your wife?"

John said, "Because I want you to come to work for me that is why".

Kevin said "Me work for you. What would I do for you?"

John said "Kevin I need a cost estimator and you are the best one I have ever met. I need someone that will tell me exactly what things will cost if we do them and will not be nice about it when they tell me. Think you could do that for $150,000 per year?"

Kevin said "Oh My God. Yes, I can and when do I start?"

John said, "Well how long before you can be in Houston, Texas?"

Kevin said "I think I can be there in a week or less. I have to get the movers, and then figure out if I want to drive or sell the car and buy one there. I will probably drive, my car is only two years old, and it is paid for".

John said "OK then we have a deal. Great now let us go eat". Molly and John went into the dining room and Kevin followed. During dinner John told Kevin what Red Lion did and all about how everyone was either ex-military or ex-civil service. John also told Kevin that things were totally different because the corporation was not military and had its own guidelines. After dinner, Kevin said good night and thanked John and Molly. He would call John in two days to tell him exactly when He would be in Houston. John and Molly went back to the bar and got a drink and talked about Kevin. The next morning John and Molly flew back to Houston. On the flight back, Jim called and said Exxon was on and John had a call from the President on hold and Don was patching it into John's cell. The cell rang, and John said, "This is John Carter". The voice on the other end said "GO" and hung up. John said,

"Well we are now in business with the US Government, God help us".

Molly laughed and said "OK so what is new? Hell! John, you have always been in business with the Government". John nodded.

# CHAPTER 26

Jim had sent Tress to Exxon to get everything Exxon had from the kidnappers. Don had also gone to get the email and to hack the account that was being used. Both Red Lion team members were busy working on identifying the kidnappers. Sandy was listening to every conversation she could to also try to find the exact group. John had called Anderson and gotten a time for him to be off the coast of the Philippines. It would take 10 days to get there from Galveston if the weather cooperated. John had also called Jerry and had him start getting the Cobra and two Black Hawks ready to go to Galveston and be loaded into the special containers for the trip. Tress was now working on a plan for the rescue. Don had back tracked the email and had been able to link it to a group that was known to be in the far north part of the main island. Sandy had also identified conversations that gave her a good idea exactly where the hostages were being held. Cindy was busy hacking the computers used by everyone in that town by way of one router that was the only one available in that region. The group that was identified was a very bad group and had kidnapped before. Never this large but they had done business men and other people but only one at a time. John knew the children would be trouble for them to keep under control and that fact worried John. They could kill the children, and no one would know. Actually, they could kill everyone, but proof of life was what kept that from happening.

Exxon had been able to make a deal by sending $1 Million Dollars to a bank in Manila as good faith. The money was as John and Don expected routed through five banks before it stopped in one account. Don had put a trace on the wire movement and now Red Lion knew exactly where the money was. Nelson was now ready to send operators to the Philippines. He dispatched four operators and they flew out on a flight that would get them there in twenty-four hours. Their weapons were shipped via DHL and would arrive in twenty-four hours. Only hand guns were shipped but that was enough for what Nelson wanted. All of this had been done two days before Exxon wired the money so the operators were on the ground when the bank was identified. Cindy had now identified the owner of the bank account and pictures were sent via SAT phone to the operators on the ground. John was using a commercial satellite for his SAT phones, but it was working well. There was no satellite imaging, so headquarters could not get pictures like it had been able to do before. Now the operators had to send voice back to inform headquarters what was happening on the ground. The operators now had the photo of the man who owned the account in the bank. They watched and when the man entered one operator also entered the bank. The operator observed the man withdraw $400,000 dollars and place it in a brief case. When the man left the bank, all the operators followed the car he got into and watched as it made its way up a road into the hills behind the town. The town was called Longia. The operators watched from a distance as the car pulled into a gated road about two miles from the town. The gate was guarded by men in fatigue clothes and armed with AK-47 rifles. Once the car was inside the gate it was closed. The guards remained inside. The operators sent the coordinates back to Red Lion using the SAT phone. After an hour the operators left and returned to the town. The location of the money had been pinpointed. John, Jim, Tress and Sandy all felt the hostages were at that compound along with the money. Tress pulled maps off the military satellite he still had clearance to use. Typical, no one had bothered to cancel any clearances and probably would not for months. Tress was going to use what he had for as long as he could. The town was inland but only eight miles from the sea. It was a very small town and that was probably why the terrorists had used it. Tress gave the information to Anderson, so he could get the necessary charts. The ship was scheduled to depart at 5 PM that evening. The helicopters had been taken down the day before and were now loaded in the containers and the containers were being loaded on the ship. Four aircraft mechanics were also going to make the trip. The piolets would fly to Manila and then go onboard the ship at the dock. All the weapons necessary for the operators had been sent with the choppers. The operator's equipment was also on board. All the operators on the raid and two medical personnel would also fly to Manila and get on the vessel.

Tress had the attack planned. The operators already on the ground in Longia would serve as the covering force and make sure no assistance arrived at the compound when the actual attack took place. Because they had only hand guns, one of them would drive to Manila and pickup weapons and return to the town. Tress estimated the round trip would take about eight hours including loading time. The rest of the operators led by Nelson would be doing a HALO jump into the compound. It was very dangerous but at night and with the terrorists not expecting anything it was the best solution. The raid had to be swift and very brutal. All terrorists had to be eliminated instantly including and especially the ones inside the main house. Then four operators that would not be in the initial raid would locate and remove the hostages. They would be loaded onto a Black Hawk along with the operators and flown out to the container ship. The Black Hawk would then return and pick up other operators. The other operators would make sure no terrorists were left alive and recover money, papers and any computers and electronics on site. Once the operators had cleared the compound and were clear of the area, the Cobra gunship would then make a gun run on the compound and destroy it. The Cobra would be flying cover in the event it was needed to support the operators in the raid. The operators on the outside would enter and load on the last Black Hawk and return to the container ship. The ship would proceed to Manila and dock. The hostages would then be escorted by operators to the airport and board a private jet that Exxon would have waiting. The operators and piolets would also board commercial jets back to the US at different times and in small groups. The container ship would re-package the helicopters in the containers and head toward Galveston. That was the plan. Now all that was left was to put it into action.

John was worried about everything going according to schedule. There was a lot that depended on air lines being able to fly, the weather for the ship, then there was the problem of the compound. Tress had gotten some satellite photos of the compound during another pass he had directed, and the team had identified four buildings inside the fenced area. One was the main house and one looked like it could be a storage building that was very large and newly constructed. It was different from the other structures. There was a smaller building that connected to the main house by way of a covered walkway. John and Jim thought that was where the hostages would be held. The storage building worried John. It was large and probably was used for storage of weapons and explosives. If it exploded, major damage could be done, and the hostages might be hurt or killed. John made sure Nelson was informed of all this. All the planning was done, the ship was only one day away from Manila. The operators were in the air and would land in twelve hours. It was now just a waiting game. Don and Cindy were monitoring the email accounts and Exxon had no contact. The last contact was to arrange for the good faith money to be sent. The next contact would be to give all the accounts the rest of the ransom was to be sent to. That was to be in twelve days. The actual raid was set for one day from the time the ship left the dock in Manila.

John was waiting to be connected back to the person that had called from Washington and was in no mood for any type of bullshit. A voice came on the line and said "Good morning General, this is Martin Davis from the President's office. A lady by the name of Liz Miller will be visiting you at the request of the President in about two hours and the President asked if you could assist her. She is very interested in Military History and the President thinks you would be the right person to give her what she needs. Also, he sends his regards to Mrs. Carter and hoped the two of you might enjoy dinner with Ms. Miller. Do you understand, Sir?"

John said "Yes of course, and please tell the President thanks for his confidence in me. My wife and I would be very pleased to show Ms. Miller around and we have great restaurants her in Houston". John hung up and knew exactly what was happening. This Miller would be the liaison between John and the President. John thought "very smart Mr. President, very smart".

Liz Miller walked into the Red Lion headquarters and Nancy greeted her and had her sit down in the outer area. Nancy called John and told him the lady was there and asked where he wanted to meet her. John said, "Have her come into my office and get Jim, Tress, Dan and Don in here as soon as you can". John got up and met Liz at the door to his office and they shook hands. John motioned to a chair and Liz sat down. John said "Very nice to have you visit. We have some other people that should be here momentarily". In about 3 minutes everyone John had requested was in his office and John said "Gentlemen this is Liz Miller, from Washington. She is here to talk to us".

Liz said "General I"...John put his hand up and stopped Liz in mid-sentence.

John said "Liz we do not use military rank in this organization. Never. It is for everyone's protection and especially for yours and the President's. Please call me John".

Liz said "Well then, John I am here as you probably have already figured out because I am now the go-between for Red Lion and the President. Me alone. No one else should ever be contacted. I can arrange anything that is needed with any agency in the government".

John said "Very good, Liz. The President made a very wise choice with this. I understand from the news you are an advisor and actually do not work in the White House or anywhere in Washington for that matter".

Liz said "Yes that is exactly right. That is why the President picked me. No one ever cares about me and most people do not know I even exist. That is the way we will keep it". John and the others sat and listened to Liz and were all surprised at how much knowledge she had about Red Lion. Liz told them she had read everything John had given the President in his initial briefing and she had also read the proposal. Liz then said "Tress I have made sure you still have satellite clearance and will have for as long as it is necessary. Also, I feel Sandy should be given the same clearance so in the event you cannot order changes in the position she will be able to do so. What is your thought?" Tress said, "I agree and thank you".

John then said "OK Liz now you get your assignment from us. Don will take care of that and after you finish I would like to give you the nickel tour".

Liz said, "Don please lead the way". Liz and Don left and went to Don's office. Don gave Liz the e-mail she was to use and explained the password operation to her. He also showed her the secure fax and made sure she would have one at her home and at her place when she was in Washington. The e-mail system was something Don had invented. The user name was America all in capital letters. The password was the key. It would be LM (then the day of the month, then the number of the month). The password automatically changed every day. Liz wrote down the formula, so she could memorize it later than she would destroy the paper. Liz and Don finished, and Liz went back to John's office. John then took her on a complete tour of Red Lion including the air field area. John explained to Liz that the helicopters were now involved in a mission and so was the container ship and most of the operators, but, at a later time, she was more than welcome to visit and see everything. Liz said she would like to do that. It was now almost 2 PM and John asked Liz if she had a hotel or was she flying back that night. Liz said "I have a room at the Westin for tonight and I plan to fly back to California in the morning. I live at Berkley where I am a professor".

John said, "OK then would you honor me and my wife as our guest for dinner?"

Liz said "yes".

John said "Well I will take you for a drink and then to the hotel. We will pick you up at 7 PM and go to dinner".

Liz said, "OK lead the way". John walked to his car and Liz got in and John headed to Molly's Bar.

John and Liz went into the bar and Molly saw John. She walked over and kissed him and said, "Who is this John, my competition?"

John laughed and said "Molly meet Liz Miller. The President sent her, but we will keep that between us".

Molly said "Hello Liz welcome to my bar. What can I get you to drink?"

Liz said "I will have a Crown Royal with just a splash of water. Please". Molly went around the bar mixed the drink, got John's beer, made a drink for herself and came back to the table and sat down. Liz and Molly talked, and Liz told Molly all about herself or at least a lot about herself. John had gotten up and was talking with some of the men he knew at the bar and Mike walked in. John said, "Hi Mike, how is everything?" Mike said, "Great John in fact better now, I need to talk to you when you get a minute". John said, "Sure get a drink and we will go out on the deck". Mike got his drink and John got another beer and they stepped outside on the covered deck. Mike took a long drink out of his glass and said "John I have been asked by KBR to run a special project for them. I mean create it from top to bottom. It is in Iraq and is worth $50 Billion Dollars over 5 years. Now the nice part of the contract is that 50% of that is guaranteed finish or not. Now here is where I need you, John. I need a security force that can maintain our areas as a secure place for our workers both on the job sites and in the living areas. This will be a separate contract worth $15 Billion Dollars. Congress has already funded the money. You are the only firm that I know of that could do that mission".

John said "Good God Mike, Iraq. Shit the fucking war is still going on and the fucking people over there are crazy. What are you going to do?"

Mike said "We are going to re-build the country. We will build 2 new hospitals, God knows how many roads to repair or actually build, re-do the oil refineries, re-do the water plants and build eight more, build twenty new schools and that is just the start. It is so fucking big, I do not know how we will actually do it, but we have the contract and KBR will be starting in ninety days. Now I need you to tell me how many people you think we will need to secure all of that".

John said "Hell Mike you will need the 82$^{nd}$ Airborne, the 101$^{st}$ Airborne and about ten other infantry divisions, but we both know that will not happen, so I will have a man get with you and then we can have a better understanding of exactly what we are talking about. The guy is Kevin and he is fantastic at estimating costs and all of that. I will have him call tomorrow and set something up, OK?"

Mike said "Yes, time is running out".

John said, "I will have it done and thanks for the job". Mike and John walked back into the bar. John immediately called Kevin and told him to be at John's office at 6 AM. John took Liz to her hotel and told her he and Molly would pick her up at 7 PM. John then went home. Molly was already there and had just stepped out of the shower. John got into the shower and they both got a drink when John was finished. They talked about Liz and then John told Molly about the conversation he had with Mike. Molly said "Holy Shit John, $15 Billion. Do you have any idea how much money that really is?"

John said, "Oh yes my dear I surely do". John and Molly finished getting dressed and left to pick up Liz.

John had made reservations at Eddie V's and Liz and Molly were very glad. They both liked sea food and of course that was probably the best in Houston, so Molly thought. During dinner John received a call telling him that all the operators, piolets and medical personnel were on the ship and it was departing Manila in six hours. Information had also been learned about the compound and just as John had suspected, the hostages were being held in the building that joined the main building by the covered walkway. John knew things were about ready to explode in the Philippines. Exxon had the special jet standing by on the private section of the airport. Customs had been taken care of by Exxon. John had no idea what that cost but he really did not give a damn. All he was concerned with was it was done for the airport and for the docks. The dinner was fun, and John and Molly really liked Liz. They dropped her at her hotel and went home and to bed. John was going to be up at 4 AM. It was going to be one very long day or two. At 6 AM the next day Kevin and John met, and John explained the situation to Kevin about the KBR requirements. John gave Kevin Mike's phone number and Kevin said he would set up the meeting as soon as Mike could meet. Kevin left John's office and John was called by Tress. The operation was about to start. It was almost 11 PM in the Philippines. John went to the operations center and sat down.

# CHAPTER 27

The Black Hawks reported that the operators had jumped. Nelson was the lead operator to jump and would be the first on the ground. The operations center was watching the screen. Tress had once again used his code and had a satellite in position to send pictures to the center, but it would only be for twenty minutes then the satellite would be out of range for at least an hour and a half.

Nelson landed along with 4 other operators and immediately came under heavy gunfire. The terrorists were awake and alert and had been able to see the operators as they landed. The firing was intense, and two operators went down immediately. Other operators landed and attacked the main building. Nelson moved to a position at the side of the main building and using a grenade took out the machine gun that was being used on the operators. Other operators moved against the terrorists that were coming at them and killed nine instantly. Another operator was hit and went down. Nelson continued to fire at various targets as they appeared. The 4 operators assigned to the hostage rescue had made their way to the building attached to the main building. One guard was outside and trying to hide in a flower bed. An operator fired, and the shot hit the guard dead center of his head. The other operators then breached the building using flash-bang grenades. three guards were inside, and they were immediately killed. The hostages were on the floor and tied with ropes. The operators cut the ropes and removed the blind folds. The Vice President was in very bad condition. He had been severely beaten and tortured. His wife was also in bad condition. It looked like she had been raped. She was naked when the operators removed the blanket that had been put over her. There was blood on her arms and legs and she had open wounds on her face from being beaten. The children seemed to be in good condition but were dehydrated as were the others. The fighting was still raging in the compound and the operators could not move the hostages.

Nelson now was inside the main building and working his way up the stairway. He could hear gun fire coming from the room to his left and as he entered the room he saw one terrorists firing an AK-47. Nelson fired a short burst (3 Rounds) and the man fell to the floor. Nelson turned and saw another man coming toward him with a pistol in his hand and Nelson fired again hitting the man in the face and chest. The terrorist went down immediately. Nelson was still trying to locate the leader. Firing was coming from a room on the right side of the hallway. Nelson and two other operators approached the door to the room and saw six men firing at the compound yard from the windows. Nelson saw one of the men was wearing a fatigue shirt with 2 gold stars on the collar. Nelson knew he was the leader from the intelligence that had been supplied and from the way he was ordering the firing on certain targets. The operators charged into the room with their guns on full automatic and fired till none of the terrorists moved. All six men were on the floor covered in blood and dead. In another minute all firing stopped. Nelson returned to the outside and looked at the situation. He saw dead terrorists laying all over the ground and some hanging out of windows. Operators were giving first aid to wounded operators and Nelson saw one of his men covered with a poncho. Nelson got a very sick feeling and almost threw up. This was the first KIA of the Red Lion team. Nelson called the operations center on the SAT phone and made the report. five operators wounded, one KIA. There was dead silence in the operations center. John said, "Oh Fuck!"

The first Black Hawk landed and all the wounded plus the body of the dead operator were loaded and the chopper took off for the ship. The second Black Hawk landed about 30 seconds later and the hostages and the four operators were on board and the chopper took off and headed to the ship. Nelson had the operators search the entire compound and take any money, papers, maps, and anything else they might think would be useful. Some operators had entered the large building that looked as a storage facility of some kind. Inside they found three pickup trucks with machine guns mounted in the bed of the trucks, over 600 weapons of all types, then they found the explosives and ammunition. Nelson inspected the explosives and ammunition and after he had counted it he reported to headquarters, 200 pounds of C-4 explosives, over 500 blasting caps, over 40,000 rounds of assorted ammunition. John was listening and said "Tress have them destroy all of that and make damn sure it is totally gone. Do they have thermite grenades?"

Tress said, "Yes they do plus we have the Cobra on station".

John said "Ok have them blow the building with the weapons and ammo and explosives then have the Cobra make a rocket run just to be sure. Also have the Cobra attack the main building on the second run".

Tress said, "Yes Sir". Tress relayed the orders to Nelson and to the Cobra gunship.

The Black Hawks were now coming back into the compound to get the rest of the operators when the operators outside the gate on over watch radioed that 3 pickup trucks loaded with terrorists were coming up the road from the town. Nelson contacted the Cobra and had the gunship make a run against the trucks using the Gatlin Gun. The operators on over watch watched as the Cobra attacked. The lead truck was destroyed and ripped into pieces. The second truck took fire but was just stopped on the road. The terrorists were jumping off the truck and trying to hide in the woods along the road. The third truck stopped before it was hit and again the terrorists were taking cover in the woods. The Cobra was starting another pass and the over watch operator radioed the piolet the location of the terrorists. The Cobra came in following the road until the operator said stop. The Cobra was only fifty feet off the ground and stationary as it fired the Gatlin Gun into the wooded area. After 3 minutes of fire the Cobra lifted off and flew toward the compound. The operators on over watch went into the woods and worked their way to the location of the terrorists. The bodies were torn apart and laying everywhere. The operators counted thirty-seven bodies. Next the operators moved to the two pickup trucks and destroyed them using thermite grenades. After the trucks were destroyed the over watch operators went to the compound. The Black Hawks had taken all the operators back and would return for Nelson and the 4 operators that were left. Nelson made one last walk through the compound before he set off the charges to destroy the storage building. He would do that as he was leaving and was on the chopper. The Black Hawk was setting down as Nelson made a final look around the compound. He was satisfied so he got on the chopper and as it lifted off and was about 500 feet in the air Nelson pressed the detonator. The building exploded, and flames rushed 300 feet into the air. Secondary explosions were going off and Nelson watched as the entire building collapsed. The Black Hawk was now at 1200 feet and hovered as the Cobra Gunship made the first run with rockets on the main building. The rockets hit, and the building exploded. There was only burning rubble after the attack. The attack on the storage building produced the same effect. The rockets hit, and the entire area exploded. Nelson made the report to headquarters.

The container ship was very busy. One of the Black Hawks had been placed back into the container and was ready for the trip home. The second Black Hawk would be put away as soon as it landed, and the mechanics had taken off the rotor blades. The same would take place when the Cobra returned. The operators had loaded their equipment into the containers and had already put on the civilian clothes they would travel in on the planes. Below the ER section was extremely busy. There were five operators wounded and three were serious. The hostages had been given medical care when they first arrived and were now resting in another area of the ship. Andy had reported to headquarters that both the adults would need immediate hospital treatment as soon as the ship docked. This information had been given to Exxon. Exxon security would be taking over at the dock and would make sure the hostages got what was needed. A team of 20 Exxon security personnel were on standby waiting for the ship to dock.

John had Don send an emergency message to Liz to call on the secure telephone immediately. In ten minutes Liz was on the secure phone. John said, "Liz we lost an operator and we need State to clear everything in the Philippines, so we can bring his body home tomorrow on a commercial flight".

Liz said "John I am so sorry. I will take care of it".

John said, "Thank you". John hung up and Jim walked into his office. Jim said "We have the funeral home in Manila waiting at the dock and they will prepare the body for transport. Two operators have already volunteered to accompany the remains on the flight. The flight is scheduled for noon tomorrow and will land in Hawaii and then come directly to Houston. I have a funeral home here that will receive the body".

John said "Thanks Jim. This is our first and it really hurts. Plus, it also brings home what we are doing. The question is it worth it?"

Jim said "John you know damn well it is and I know what you are feeling. This is special and always will be. I suppose we will need a Wall".

John said "Yes I am afraid we will. Will you see to that please, Jim?"

Jim said, "Of course I will be honored". Jim left, and John sat for a few minutes in deep thought.

The operators were all back in Houston and so was the body of the dead operator. His family had been notified and they wanted his body to be delivered to a small town in Alabama. Red Lion made all the arrangements and had all expensed sent to the corporation. In addition, a check for $1 Million Dollars was issued to his next of kin, his mother. The service was held and of course almost 90% of the Red Lion Corporation attended. John had arranged a charter jet to take the Red Lion people to the service and bring them back. John presented the check to the operator's mother and told her how very sorry he was. It probably did little to stop her pain, but it was all that could be done. Jim had gotten the wall prepared and John and Jim put up the picture. The operator was Eugene "Gene" Johnson. He was 37 years old and had been a US Navy SEAL before coming to work for Red Lion. John stepped back and looked at the wall. He thought "this may be the first of many if we continue to do this work". John knew deep in his heart he would continue. He had to do so.

# CHAPTER 28

Red Lion had received the check from Exxon. $20 Million Dollars plus $8 Million Dollars for expenses. John was pleased but he also knew it had been a very hard fight and he was determined not to let that happen again if possible. Kevin had been working with Mike and had gotten all he needed so he was now ready to brief John. Kevin came into the office and John had him sit. John said, "Well what do we need Mr. Estimator?"

Kevin said, "A bunch of people, guns, trucks, Hell everything an Army division needs just about".

John said, "OK how many people are we looking at for just the guards?"

Kevin said "Mike and I think about 1000 would be a good start and it will probably grow to at least double that as the work goes along. Then we will need supply, cooks, medics, and mechanics for the vehicles and the equipment like computers, GPS, sat phones, all type of stuff. I recommend about 400 more people at least."

John said "Well get with Barbara and have her start recruitment. What do we start as far as pay is concerned?"

Kevin said "John I have an idea about that. I think we should offer the guards $120,000 yearly but here is the deal. They get paid monthly for six months then one month they get no pay then paid for six months again. The month they do not get paid, we fly them back to the States to where they want to go for a 29-day vacation. Now here is the hook. If we do that all their money is totally tax free because they have been out of the states for more than twelve months in a row as far as pay is concerned and that is all the IRS looks at. What do you think?"

John said "I love that idea. Make damn sure Barbara pitches that to everyone". Kevin left and got Barbara going on the recruitment process. Our best candidates would be soldiers just getting out of the service. Barbara was right on top of that and had a lot of connections in the VA and the Pentagon she could tap.

It was now starting into June and John was ready for some time alone with Molly. It had been a very rough year so far and things looked like they were going to be just as busy if not busier for the rest of the year. John and Molly decided to take a few days and go to the beach. John suggested they go to Corpus Christie and Molly said, "I have never been there so sure why not?" John made plans and they left on Monday morning and drove to Corpus. John had rented a beach house about three miles down the beach from the actual city limits and it was great. The rooms were large, and the best part was that the main room had all glass walls and opened onto a private beach that was only about twenty yards away. John had the real estate people completely stock the bar and the food with a list he had sent. The house came furnished with all the linens and cooking utensils as well as china and sliver wear. Nothing was required except your clothes. John and Molly arrived about 3 PM and went inside. Molly was very happy and immediately put on her swim suit and went out to the beach. John got his suit on and followed, after he made drinks for both of them. The entire atmosphere was very romantic, and Molly and John made the utmost of that. The days were good, and John and Molly went places and did things just for fun. They found a local bar and also found a few nice restaurants. They were interacting with many local people and it was nice to be just people nothing special. When asked they said they were retired and just having fun. No one even questioned that. The week was over and on Saturday

John and Molly returned to Houston. It was about 11 PM when they got home, and they were tired. It had been a great time, but it was more than either one of them had done in a long time. They had stayed out every night and gotten up early to enjoy the many things that were available to do. John and Molly had been in bed for about an hour when Molly's phone rang. She answered, and John heard her say "Yes this is Molly Carter". Then John heard Molly say "OH My God. How many are hurt and all of that?" Then John heard "Oh No. Yes, I am on my way I will be there in ten minutes". Molly leaped out of bed and was yelling "We have to get to the bar. There has been a robbery and shooting. People are wounded and maybe dead. Oh God John". John was on his feet and getting dressed. He grabbed Molly and held her for a minute and said "It will be alright. Let's get there and find out what is happening". John and Molly ran to John's car and he raced toward the bar.

The parking lot was full of Police cars and there were two ambulances. John and Molly got out and started toward the door. An Officer stopped them and after identifying them had them proceed. Inside it was a mess. There were still three people being treated for gunshot wounds. Then John saw two people that had cuts and wounds to their heads that were also being treated. Molly was looking for Carol and a detective said, "The lady Carol has been rushed to Memorial with a gunshot". Molly went limp. John grabbed Molly and had her sit down. John also looked in the corner and saw a sheet draped over a body. Someone had been killed. The bar was a mess. The register had been thrown on the floor and there was broken glass all over the place. The jukebox had been smashed where the money was put into it and the holder for the bills was laying on the floor. John went outside and saw many people he knew. John went to one of the men he knew was a lawyer and said, "Christ Gil what the fuck happened?"

Gil said "John these fucking black punks rushed into the bar and started shooting. Then they had everyone get on the floor and empty their pockets. Bobby tried to grab one of them and they shot him point blank. Then another one, shot Carol, just because she said there was no safe. Then two others started hitting people and shot a couple of them for no fucking reason. They are just animals. Animals, John".

John said "Ok Gil are you alright? Hurt or anything?"

Gil said, "No just my damn pride and the fact that I was too scared to do a fucking thing".

John said "Gil you did right. Hell, they would have killed you". John patted Gil on the shoulder and went to talk to the detectives. It was about three hours later when the police left. John had called and gotten the same security firm that did Red Lion security to send out officers to guard the bar. Molly had finished speaking with the detectives and had gotten a cab to the hospital to be with Carol. Carol had been shot in the side and was lucky. The bullet had not hit anything and had gone right through. She was going to be fine after a few days in the hospital. John got the names of all the other people that had been wounded and was ready to check on them. The detectives had no real leads and told John this was another robbery and shooting that would probably only be solved if someone turned in the suspects. John said "How about a reward? Dose that really work?"

The detective said "Well sometimes but we do not get very much on this type of robbery. Personally, I think people fear the suspects and feel they would turn on anyone who speaks to the police. It could also be gang related. We will give the Gang Detail our information as well as the robbery division and see if they can identify a pattern. That is about all I can promise you Sir".

John thanked the detective and as soon as the guards were on site and he had briefed them he drove to the hospital. John was mad. In fact, he was more than mad. John got to the hospital and went to Carol's room and sat with Molly until Carol woke up. Molly and John left the hospital and went home so Carol could rest. Molly was going back after a few hours. John was then going to the office. He was now on the attack and would sure as Hell find the people responsible for this and kill then. It was just that simple.

It was Sunday and John was in the office alone. He knew he should not take this on, but he also knew the police were never going to solve anything like this unless they just plain got lucky. Because someone had been killed it was of course more important but not really. Every day in Houston someone was killed. It was just life in a big city. John did know that because of the people who were at Molly's and their status the police were going to work double hard on this case. There were far too many top citizens involved plus Bobby was a very well-respected man. John's cell phone started ringing. He had four incoming calls at the same time. John looked and saw Tress, Jim, Nelson, and Nancy were calling. John answered Tress then the rest and had everyone hang up. John then placed a conference call back to them and when everyone was on line he said "OK Molly is fine or at least she was not there. We got back about thirty minutes before it happened. Carol was shot and some others. Bobby was killed, and many were pistol whipped. It was a gang of black guys and the police have no leads. Now how in the Hell did you people find out about it?"

Tress said "Hell Sir, it is all over the morning news. Pictures of the bar and everything". John looked at his watch. It was just now 7 AM. He had lost track of time. Jim said, "John we will come in if you want?"

John said "No not now. I must go back to see Carol and then try to get some information from the police. I think we should just hold until tomorrow. Do we have anything active at Red Lion other than KBR?"

Jim said "No not right now but Liz has sent an alert for us for possibly the end of the week. Something to do about Mexico. Hell, she is still having growing pains with the new President making up his damn mind when to act and when not to act".

John said "OK well thanks and I will keep everyone in the net. See all of you in the morning". John hung up and sat back. How in the Hell was he going to locate the guys responsible in a city of 5 million plus people? He had no idea. Don called, and John told him the story and the situation. Don said, "John did they steal cell phones?"

John said, "Yes they took everyone's phone".

Don said, "Can you get the numbers by chance?"

John said, "Hell I have no idea, but I know I can probably get a few, why?"

Don said "Well if they are really fucking dumb and I hope they are they will use them for a while until the company stops service and I can track the fucking phones. It usually takes about twenty-four hours before the company stops the service, and this is a weekend, so we may have more time. Just an idea".

John said "And a great one Don. I will see what I can do and call you if I get a number". Don hung up and John started trying to remember where people went other than Molly's. There was a bar called Westside that many used on occasion just to have a change. It opened at noon on Sunday, so John was going to be there.

It was 8 AM when John got to the hospital. Molly had called and told John she hand gone back so when John walked in he was surprised to find two Houston Police Detectives in the room. They had returned Carol's purse and were asking her some follow up questions now that she was able talk to them. John listened and watched as Carol described the night before. It was very hard on Carol and the detectives did their best to not press past a certain point. They finished, and John walked out into the hall with them. They told John that the IT people at the police were trying to track the cell phones but normally it was not possible because the providers stopped the service as soon as the phone was reported stolen and most people had already called. Bobby's phone was still in his pocket so that was out as far as a trace of any kind was concerned. John thanked the detectives and went back into the room and spoke to Carol. Carol was still medicated for pain, but she was doing very well. The doctors had been in just before the police and they were saying she might be released the next day. Molly had already made plans for Carol to come to the apartment. John had no objection. John said, "Carol do you have your phone by chance?"

Carol said "No they probably took it. It was on the bar where I always keep it and I bet the bastards got it."

John said, "Which company do you use?"

Carol said "AT& T".

John said, "OK thanks". John stayed for a while then he told Molly he was going to check on some things and would be back after a little while. She agreed and said she would be in the room so let her know. John kissed her and said he would. John left and when he was in his car he called Don and gave Don Carol's number and the provider. Don said "John, I will get on this right away." John thanked Don and drove to the Westside Bar.

John went in the bar and saw two people that had been at Molly's during the robbery. John went over to them and said hello then said, "Guys did you turn in your phone as being stolen yet?"

They said, "No we will do it tomorrow why?"

John said, "Can I please have your number and the carrier you use?" They both gave John the information. Then one asked "John what are you going to do with that information?"

John said "I have a contact that may be able to find the phone if these assholes use it. It is a real long shot but who knows. He likes to fuck with this type of thing, so I figure why not let him try? If he succeeds we tell the police". John thanked them and left. Again, he called Don and gave him the numbers and the carrier. John then went to Molly's bar and looked at the damages. He would get a contractor immediately and things should be fixed in about two days. John called Mike and spoke to him about a contractor. Mike said he knew one and would get him out Monday morning. Mike also said how sorry he was and that he was very glad Molly and Carol were going to be fine. John thanked Mike and hung up. John went back to the hospital and after an hour he told Molly she needed to leave and let Carol rest. Molly agreed and told Carol she would be back first thing in the morning. John and Molly left, and both drove home. It had been a very long day. John fixed a drink for them and they turned on the TV to the news. The shooting and robbery were all over the screen.

Monday morning Molly went to the hospital and John went to Red Lion. John arrived about 8 AM and went into his office. Nelson knocked on the door and John motioned him into the room. Nelson said "General, I am so sorry about Molly's. Now if we do a mission and I do not know we will but already I have volunteers. Actually, I have 159 volunteers".

John said, "Nelson we only have 100 operators so how in the Hell can we have 159?"

Nelson said "General, all the operators volunteered, and then all the mechanics, ground personnel and Hell sir even the medics. Everyone wants to go, and the piolets are pissed because they cannot fly over the city".

John laughed and said "Nelson thank you and tell the men I said thanks as well. I will let you know if we get anything we may want to act on. And one more thing, do you always have to call me General? I thought we had agreed not to do that".

Nelson said "Yes, General we did so I only do it when we are alone and probably always will Sir". John shook his head and Nelson left the office. Don came into John's office around 10 AM and said "I know exactly where Carol's phone is. I even have an address. I bet the other phones are there also and Cindy and I are monitoring them. All the bastards have to do is turn it on and we got their ass".

John said "Great work Don. I am calling Tress, Sandy, Jim and Nelson. We will probably have you come in also".

Don said, "Ok let me know". Don left, and John got everyone to come to his office right away.

Sandy, Tress, Jim and Nelson were in John's office. John said "Don has located Carol's phone and he thinks probably the other phones are there also. Now we need to get intelligence on these people and we need to do it the right way".

Nelson said, "I can put some people there and gather what we need, Sir".

Jim said, "OK Nelson but make damn sure they are one, the right color and two, they do not look military or like the police".

Nelson said "Sir, I have just the right people in mind. They are very far from military or police. Where do we go?"

John said, "Get with Don and he has the address".

Sandy said "I have done research on this and from what I can gather, these guys like to hit places on Friday and Saturday night about 11 PM or 2 AM depending. Usually they hit a bar and then go hit something like Denny's or IHOP where people are eating a late meal. They always take phones, because, they can sell them when the phones are turned off to go overseas. They get about $30 dollars per phone and more if the phones are high end. They wait until they get a couple of hundred then sell them and ship them out".

John said "Sandy that is great work. Should I ask where you got all of that information from?"

Sandy said, "The Houston police files, Sir".

John smiled and said "OK then Nelson get your guys on the ball and we only have 48 hours. Make then count".

Everyone left John's office. The rest of the day and the next day were routine for Red Lion. Kevin was ready to present KBR his price and Liz had not gotten back to them. Barbara had interviewed 50 people for the KBR job and Nelson had approved all of them. As soon as KBR signed the contract Dan had drawn up, the new operators would go to Hallettsville for two weeks. John had made that part of the agreement with the new hires and included it into the price Kevin quoted. John had the contractors working on Molly's and they would be finished by Friday and she could open again Saturday. Carol had been at John and Molly's for two days and was almost ready to go to her apartment. She had recovered well. John was very glad Carol had not been killed or hurt worse. That would have destroyed Molly. Molly would have always blamed herself because Carol was working. It had worked out very well.

Nelson came into John's office early Thursday morning along with the two operators that had been undercover. They looked like they really belonged in the part of town they had been in for two days. John greeted them and had everyone sit down. John called Tress, Sandy and Jim and had all of them come to his office. When everyone was there, John said "Ok these are our guys so let's hear what we have". The operators explained how the group worked and told about how the group met up at this one house, the one Don had given the address of. The operators felt this was a headquarters so to speak and the occupant was the leader of the ring. He was a big black man in his 30's and the rest of the people that had been coming and going were in their early 20's. Sandy and one operator had done a ground recon of the area. The house was located on a street in the 3$^{rd}$ Ward of Houston and sat in the middle of the block. Sandy had observed a U-Haul rental truck that people were using to move items out of a house across the street and three houses down the block from the target house. No one paid any attention to the truck and

Sandy and the operator had been in the area both during the day and at night. The street was only ¼ mile long and there were good escape routes to allow access to the freeway at one end of the target street. Sandy had a plan and after checking on traffic at the 11 PM hour, she was ready to present it to John, Jim and the operators. Nelson had picked 6 operators plus himself for the mission. Each operator would be using silenced weapons. Tress and Sandy had John, Jim, Nelson and the 6 operators as well as Don and Cindy in the briefing room and Sandy started. Sandy said "The best way to do this mission is in a rented U-Haul truck. The operators will be in the rear and one will drive. The truck should be parked in front of this house (Sandy pointed to the map of the street that showed each house) and the operators will go from there. The raid will be a two-entry point attack. The front door and the rear door are the points of entry. Sometimes there are people on the porch of the target house, but we only observed two and that was only for a short period of time. It does not appear that any actual lookout is being used, but I want everyone aware of that possibility. Once the raid is over, operators will board the truck and the truck will leave and take the freeway headed toward San Antonio. The truck will clear the Houston city limits and stop in Katy at the Buckeye's truck stop and the operators will unload and get into SUVs that will be pre-positioned. Then the U-Haul truck will be left in the parking lot. It will be returned on Monday. The U-Haul being left is strictly for a diversion in case anyone reports the truck to the police. The truck will be rented by an operator using our fake identification and paid for with a credit card that Don can track and delete. This is our recommendation". John liked the plan and so did everyone else. It was simple, quick and easy to do. Nelson said, "I will get things in motion we go tonight". Everyone left the briefing and John returned to his office to check the new message that had come in from Liz.

The U-Haul truck stopped in front of the house it was supposed to at 10:45 PM. Nelson was driving, and he had observed two young black men sitting on the front porch of the target house. The men had paid no attention to the truck. Nelson had parked the truck with the back away from the target house and he got out and slowly opened the rear. He told two operators to get out and work their way across the street and up to the target house. Their job was to eliminate the men on the porch. Two other operators would work their way to the rear and be ready to enter on command. The remaining two operators would work their way down the street and then across and be on the opposite side of the porch from the operators that would take out the men on the porch. Nelson would be across the street behind cover and would give the order to enter as soon as the porch was clear. All the operators had radio communications and ear pieces, so they would all hear the order. Red Lion headquarters would also be monitoring the radio and would hear the order. The operators also had on cameras so visual pictures would be sent to Red Lion during the entire operation. At exactly 11 PM Nelson gave the order to eliminate the men on the porch. Both men were instantly killed with one shot to each man's head. ten seconds later Nelson gave the order to enter. The operators entered the front door and engaged three men and two women in the front room eliminating all of them. Nelson had crossed the street in less than ten seconds and entered the house. A man in his thirties wearing only underwear came out of the bedroom on the right and Nelson shot him in the forehead just as the man entered the front room. Another operator went into the bedroom and eliminated the woman in the bed with one shot in her head. The operators that had entered the rear door into the kitchen had eliminated two women and two men who were in the kitchen. A search of the other bedroom was made, and ten large boxes filled with cell phones was discovered. Nelson searched the bedroom and discovered $20,000 in cash and a check book. He took the cash and the check book as was Red Lion policy. In less than ten minutes the operators were back in the U-Haul truck and it was headed toward the freeway. thirteen people had been eliminated and the cash and bank book had been seized. The U-Haul truck pulled into the parking lot of Buckeye's at 12:30 AM on Friday morning. The operators loaded into the SUV's and returned to the Red Lion headquarters. They arrived at 1:45 AM. Nelson brought the cash and check book into the operations room and handed the check book to Don. Nelson counted the cash again and handed it to Jim. Don immediately accessed the checking account and saw a balance of $75,000 dollars. Don moved the funds to one of the off-shore accounts and then kept the money moving from bank to bank for 48 hours. At 3 AM everyone was on the way to their houses and Red Lion was closed and being guarded by the normal security patrols. Don placed a call to 911 on a "burn" cell phone saying that possible shots had been fired at the target house and gave the address to 911 before he left. John and Jim listened to the police dispatch before they left and knew this was going to be one Hell of a mess for HPD. The next day the news coverage was tremendous. HPD had no leads but they were talking about the fact that it looked like the gang that had been committing robberies and possibly had done some of the murders. The team had left all guns in the house as well as the cell phones. The police would probably check the guns against the bullets that had been recovered from Bobby and the other victims of other shootings and then have a positive match and close the case. It really did not matter to John. John was satisfied with the results. He told Molly when he got home. She was very happy.

Jim had made some unusual connections since coming to Houston and one of them was the man who controlled most of the crime in the black community in Houston. Jim had met the man at a club Jim went to and they had become very good friends. Jim knew exactly who this man was because Don and Cindy had done a background check. Jim could careless because they were social friends only. The man's name was Red Sinclair and Jim called him and asked Red to meet Jim at the club for a drink.

Red was at the club when Jim arrived, and Jim went to the table and sat. Red said hello and Jim said "Red I need to explain some things to you so listen and listen very damn carefully to what I am going to tell you. You know me as a person who works for a security corporation. Well in a way you are right, but you do not have any real idea who I am or who I work for. The little mess that was done in your area was done at my direction and that should show you that I do not bullshit about things. Now here is the deal for you. First here is a list of places that are totally off limits to you and your gangs. Absolutely no one will do a fucking thing to any of the places on this list. Should something happen, and I do not give a flying fuck why I will hold you personally responsible and the penalty is instant death. No excuses will be used or accepted so it is your ass. I want to continue our friendship, but you have now been warned so you now know how things are".

Red sat and stared at Jim for a minute or so then he said "I had no idea and I do apologize for the situation. I will make sure this list is known to everyone in the area and if in fact some stupid fucker does anything I will guarantee you they will be dead in less than two hours from the time they fuck up. Is that acceptable to you Jim?"

Jim said, "I can live with that promise". The men finished their drinks and Jim left and headed home for the night. Red was still shaking a little and he and his Lieutenants talked about what they had gotten into and decided the list was golden and no one would even go around anyone on that list.

# CHAPTER 29

John had studied the message from Liz. John referred to it as "A warning order". That was what the military called messages that alerted units that something was about to happen. It had been four days since Liz had sent the message and at 10 AM John got another message. This one was simple. A package would arrive via courier at 2 PM. All the information John would need would be in the package.

Barbara had been able to hire another 200 personnel for the KBR requirement and now 250 men were at Hallettsville going through training. Harry had built a road that covered five miles, so he could train the new personnel on convoy escort duties and how to protect the convoy. Harry also had hired an ex-explosives and demolition man who had years of experience with IUDs. The IUDs were the biggest threat to everyone in Iraq. It had been a new type of weapon at first and had taken a great toll on US personnel. The insurgents used these devices well and finding them was a real challenge. Part of the training was to teach our people what to look for and how to react when they found a device. John was glad Harry had incorporated that into the training. The 250 men would be ready in two weeks and could then be deployed to the KBR facilities in Iraq. More would be needed but the contract stated Red Lion could provide personnel, over time, until the 2000 mark was met. Right now, 250 would be enough to start. KBR was only working in ten areas but would expand every month.

The courier arrived, and John was handed the package. He opened it and started reading. Liz was damn good at her job. She had a brief as the first pages and after John finished reading he knew exactly why Red Lion was being asked to do the mission. two months earlier two DEA agents and one ATF agent had been ambushed and brutally killed on a road, ten miles, south of Matamoros Mexico. Of course, the media covered the story in detail and Congress had gone crazy as they always do for about twenty-four hours. The State Department and other agencies had tried to work with the Mexican government, but nothing had been done. The drug cartel that operated from just outside Matamoros was responsible, but 75% of the Mexican police and 90% of the politicians were being paid off by the cartel so nothing was done. The President of the US had his hands tied because he could not use military troops on Mexican soil and DEA and AFT were also out. The CIA had gathered intelligence just as the FBI had done, but basically nothing could be done. The tourist's business in the border areas was also being hurt badly because the cartels were constantly having a war between one or the other drug cartels and innocent people were getting killed. Some tourists had even been kidnapped and held for ransom. The government knew the banks that the cartel used but even with the agreements that had been done after 9/11 things were still not very good. The President needed the cartel or cartels whipped out. That was the mission he gave to John and Red Lion. Now all John had to do was figure out how. John called Tress, Sandy, Jim, Nelson, Don and Cindy to a meeting in the conference room. John said "Ok gang we just got a very hot potato from the President. I have no fucking idea how we will pull this one off". John explained the situation to all of them and then went over the information that had been in the packet. After John finished, Tress said "Sir, we will have to do about two months of intelligence work before we can even start to make a plan. These people do not know a God damned thing about getting operators what they need. I suggest Sandy and I start on it with what we have but I will give Jim a list of what type of intelligence we will need. Maybe we can get some operators down there to gather up what we need. Hell Sir, what are they doing in D.C.?"

John said, "Damn if I know".

Jim said, "OK Tress get me everything you need as soon as you can, and Nelson and I will try to figure out who to send and how we can obtain the information for you".

Tress said, "I will Sir". The meeting was over, and everyone went back to work. Don had a copy of the banking that was thought to be the cartel's, so he and Cindy went to work on figuring out how to steal the money. Jim met with John and said "Sir, we need a fucking C-130. How in the Hell can we get one?"

John said, "Well let me call a certain lady and find out". John put in a call to Liz. In an hour Liz was on the line returning the call. John said "Liz we need a C-130 aircraft. Now we do not want to just borrow the plane we want to buy it. Can you make that happen?"

Liz said "John I have no idea but let me check around. I will call you back as soon as I have something". John thanked her and hung up.

During the next two weeks Red Lion worked on getting a plan for the cartel problem. Nelson had sent four operators to Mexico all were Mexican and some of them were familiar with the area around Matamoros. They had been sending reports back almost daily via SAT phone to Tress and Sandy about the things Tress had put on his list. Molly was open again, and Carol had totally recovered from her gun shot and was working again. The customers had many ideas about what had happened in the 3rd Ward but never asked Molly or John. Many of them would look at John when he was there and just smile. Mike was the only person who asked John straight out about the 3rd Ward and John simply said, "Looks like the robberies have stopped for a while, right Mike?"

Mike shook his head and then said "They really picked the wrong place when they came here. God Damn they were totally stupid. Hell, just looking at the people who come in here is enough to make a person stop and think".

John said "Oh they thought alright. They thought they would make a great score and of course never get caught. Guess they were wrong".

Mike smiled and said, "Well lessons learned".

The third week things started happening. Liz had sent a fax that gave John the information on the C-130. Red Lion could buy a plane from the government for $200,000 dollars. It would be a sealed bid but that was already taken care of, so all Red Lion had to do was submit a "Demand Bid" and in twenty-four hours they would own the plane. John had Sara handle that end. Barbara was now tasked to hire a complete C-130 crew, two piolets, one flight engineer, one navigator, one load master and two mechanics that worked on that type of aircraft. Jim was busy ordering the equipment necessary for the C-130 to be ready for use by Red Lion. Tress and Sandy had a plan of action and now had everything necessary to finish the plan in detail. Don had been able to isolate the cartel money in a bank in Belize and Cindy had created a worm program that she could insert to move the money when the time was right. Don told John that billions of dollars were in the account and it would be a total bankruptcy of the bank if it was moved. John passed that information on to Liz. The reply was quick and simply said "So what!" John knew this was going to cause real ripples with the Belize government and with the Mexican government, but that was the President's problem. John had enough of his own to worry about. In a week Barbara had hired all the personnel needed for the C-130. John had met them and was pleased. They were all ex-Air Force and the piolets had over 5000 hours in C-130 aircraft. The rest of the C-130 team had years of experience with the aircraft. It was a perfect fit for Red Lion. The plane was ready to be flown from Nevada to Texas and the C-130 team was sent to get it. The plane arrived back in Texas in two days and was painted so it did not look like a military plane. No markings were on the plane except the required registration numbers. Dan had already gotten the plane registered in the name of Red Lion.

Tress and Sandy were now ready to present the operation plan. The briefing room in the warehouse was full. All the operators, forty of them, the C-130 team, the chopper piolets, Andy and two of his crew, the medical personnel including the new doctor, John, Jim, Don, Cindy and Nancy were all ready for the presentation. A map of Mexico was already displayed on the screen. Tress and Sandy both were standing in front of the group. Tress said "We have developed the plan for the operation. It is going to be a large-scale operation and we have absolutely no permission to use Mexican air space or to be closer than twelve miles to the shore. Our target is a villa, six miles south of Matamoros on the ocean. It is heavily guarded and the people who guard it are very professional Mercenaries who work for the cartel and have for about five years. They have heavy weapons and are normally armed with M-16 or AK-47 rifles. They also use Issue sub machine guns and most of them have access to RPG rockets. There are at least 2ea 50-Cal machine guns on property and probably at least 4ea M-60 machine guns. And that ladies and Gentlemen is the good news".

Sandy took over and said "The local police and most of the Federal police are in the pocket of the cartel. There is no Army presence in the entire area. We have no real idea if other forces are close enough to aid if the villa is attacked but we will proceed as if they will have a reinforcing unit available. As far as we know the villa is occupied by the leader of the cartel and his family. There are servants that live on the grounds and we have identified one building that is used by the mercenaries as there living quarters. There is a large garage type building that the vehicles are kept in and a fuel location. The villa has its own underground fuel storage.

The communications are located on the roof of the main building and consists of four satellite dishes which are used for cell phone and computer. We estimate the opposing force at twenty plus a few four or six of the cartel that are always with the leader. twenty is the count of the mercenaries that are on the grounds. They patrol in shifts every four hours the shifts change. It is always the same number day or night. two people on the front gate, two people on the roof, one on each side to observe, two people on the beach access. That is the rotation. No dogs are used, and no outside areas are patrolled. There are cameras covering the entire area and from what we think these cameras are monitored 24/7. The main gates are remote controlled so vehicles going in and out must be let in and out by the control room. That room is located on the second floor on the west side front".

Tress then said "Now here is a kicker. DEA tells me that they have an informant inside the villa. That is how we know so damn much about how things work. The informant is a cook and she sent a drawing of the inside of the villa out last week". Tress said "Please look at the screen. As you can see the villa is three stories high and has twenty rooms. The main floor has the living room, dining room, kitchen, a recreation room, one office, bathrooms and a Sun room, an area open that goes to the patio and pool areas and the walk to the beach. The first floor also has one room that is used by the down stairs guards. The second floor has eight bedrooms plus the control room. The third floor has a large room that is used for the office and a larger room off the office that is used as a meeting room. This place is very well built and is not going to be destroyed without a lot of explosives. Copies of the floor plan are available along with copies of the exterior layout of buildings". Tress paused and let everyone look at the floor plan for a few minutes. Tress continued "Now here is the tricky part or at least one of the tricky parts. We have been authorized to use four brand new missiles that the Cobra can fire. These missiles are designed to destroy buildings on impact. We will pick them up at Ft. Hood. We will also pick up ammunition and Laws Rockets as well as grenades. We will use the US Marshall IDs we have for this and one truck covered and one SUV as a guard escort vehicle with four people. Now the most important part at Hood is to not answer any questions. The fort has or will be informed that we are on a special mission involving National Security and that should cover us, but if there is any problem at all, immediately pull back and inform Red Lion headquarters via SAT phone not cell phone. That is critical".

Sandy then resumed her part. "The initial group will be four operators that will do a HALO jump from the C-130. Once on the ground they will mark the drop zone for the second drop and after that they will proceed to the front gate and set the explosives to blow it open. Then they will remain hidden and observe until the main attack happens. The second drop will be thirty operators and will be a standard jump from 7500 feet. The drop zone is two miles south of the villa and is as flat as we can find. Once the operators are on the ground, they will divide into teams of ten and team one will proceed to the west side of the villa, team two will proceed to the east side of the villa and team three will proceed to the front gate area. When all teams are in place the Cobra will start the gun/rocket run. The first target will be the building housing the mercenaries. Then as soon as that target is hit the second target is the villa. Two runs and two missiles will be fired into the villa. The last run will be the garage area. One missile will be fired into that building. When the first rocket is fired, and the target is hit, the front gate will be blown. The teams will then proceed to the villa area and kill anyone there. The teams on both sides of the villa will blow the fence and attack the villa killing everything inside. Don and Cindy will try to cut the communications one minute before the Cobra attack and will have already cut the power about five minutes, so the cameras will be out. It should look like a computer problem so hopefully it will not alert the guards for at least five minutes. Once the raid has been completed, the operators will return to the drop zone and be picked up by the Black Hawks. The choppers will be in a holding pattern during the raid for assistance if needed or to evacuate wounded operators. They can land in the villa compound but with the explosions and fire we would prefer them to land outside the fence line. The entrance road will be the Medevac area if needed. Once the operators have been recovered, the Black Hawks will return to the container ship. The Cobra will stay on station in the event reinforcements try to come on the road. If they do appear the Cobra will do a gun run and eliminate them. Then when it is totally clear at the villa the Cobra will return to the ship. The container ship will immediately head for Corpus Christi and there will off load the operators who will be flown back to the headquarters via commercial airlines. Once the ship has discharged the operators and piolets it will return to Galveston".

John then rose and walked to the front. He said "Ok now we have the plan. We also have a date. It is 1 September. The leader always celebrates his birthday on that date and has a very large party at the villa. Many people are invited and all his cartel Lieutenants as well as his political friends are there. There will be many people who need to be eliminated, so we will do this job. I will warn everyone that there may be women and children there and if possible do not take them out if it is not necessary. But if there is a threat do it. I want everyone back in one piece. If there are questions or problems get with your individual unit leaders and get them resolved, we have about thirty days to get things right. Good luck and thank you". John left the room and the rest of the unit also left.

The next twenty-five days were very busy for the people at Red Lion. Equipment had been delivered and the trip to Ft. Hood had gone off without a problem. The container ship had gotten all the necessary supplies and all the operator equipment had been checked and double checked. The helicopters had been loaded into the containers at the base this time and then trucked to Galveston. John did not want to take a chance that someone might put things together. The C-130 had enough fuel to fly over and back from the Sugarland base, but John decided to ask Liz if he could use one of the abandoned military training fields outside Corpus Christi for the actual launch. He was granted permission, so a fuel truck was scheduled to be on site when the C-130 arrived and top off the tanks. It would also give the operators and crew a break. The plane was going to be on the ground six hours before it was needed in Mexico. Flight time was only two hours at the speed the plan would be flying. The container ship was leaving Galveston three days before it was to be off the coast just in case the weather was a problem and so the choppers could be out of the containers and ready. Don had been checking emails sent by the cartel and he now knew exactly what accounts would be the target accounts. Cindy was ready to activate the worm she had planted, and things were set. John had informed Liz that the operation was a go and would take place on the night of the 1st of September. Liz informed the President. The DEA had also informed their asset to not be at work on the 1st no matter what happened, and then decided to remove her all together four days before. John worried about that but could do nothing to stop it. Tress came in and said "Sir, that is not a problem because it is almost a week before we do anything, and they will not suspect anything if it does not happen the day she is gone. I think it will work to our favor. They will be on guard and then when nothing happens they will relax". John nodded but still was worried.

The C-130 was now fully loaded with the operators. Nelson was leading the raid as he usually did. John watched as the plane rolled down the runway and lifted into the air. The container ship was off the coast and would come to within twelve miles of land as soon as it got dark. Don was ready to stop the communications and Cindy had the power ready to be disrupted. Now it was wait time. That to John was always the hardest part. John knew it was still fifteen hours before the attack and he really wanted to get it over. John had ordered Chinese food for everyone at the headquarters and it had arrived. Nancy, Barbara and Sara had set it up in the warehouse area and Jim had gotten beer and drinks set up. The coffee would be made about 7 PM. Tress was monitoring the radio and SAT phone traffic and had it on the speaker that went throughout the building. It was actually very quiet. The C-130 was now on the ground and being topped off with fuel. The container ship was now almost fourteen miles from shore and the choppers were ready to depart as scheduled. John went out and got some food and a beer. Jim joined him and then Sandy and Tress came out. In about twenty minutes all the Red Lion personnel at the headquarters were sitting and eating. Kevin and Dan also came in and got some food. Kevin had never been around when a raid was in progress and he was amazed. He asked John if it was alright if he stayed and John said "Of course. Hell, this is what we do, and you are part of us so yes just do not get in the way".

Kevin said, "Oh I won't Sir and thanks". The hour was fast approaching and at 9 PM John, Jim and the others were sitting in the operations room watching the screen. Tress had once again redirected a satellite, so they had visual and they had the pictures on the operator cameras and in the Cobra and the Black Hawks.

# CHAPTER 30

The C-130 was now on the first run and John watched as the first of the operators jumped. Tress had discovered a problem as soon as he saw the satellite footage of the villa. Cars had been parked in a field on the north side outside the fence and a gate, which had not been on the drawings or detected in any photos, had been opened to let people use so they could go inside into the villa grounds. The gate was guarded by two mercenaries. The main gate was also open, and two mercenaries were guarding that as well. Tress immediately contacted Nelson on the SAT phone and told him about the gates. John was watching and trying to count the cars that were parked in the field and inside the villa walls. His best count was over 100. John thought "this is going to be a fucking blood bath of the highest order and nothing can be done about it now but call off the raid." John knew that was not an option because he could not get his people out without losing some and that was not going to happen. John now saw the second pass being made by the C-130 and watched as he saw the operators exit the aircraft. In ten minutes all operators were on the ground and moving toward their areas. Nelson had already told the original ground force to split and take out the guards. The operators had silencers on their hand guns, but the MP-5 weapons were not silenced. No real need after the Cobra attack. Tress and everyone watched as the operators took out the guards on the front gate and then the north gate. No movement was detected going toward either gate by people inside the compound.

The Cobra came in low and fired the first rocket. The rocket hit the building the mercenaries used as their sleeping area and it exploded into flames and pieces. The flames shot up 200 feet into the air. Then the Cobra immediately fired a rocket into the villa and it too exploded and started burning. The group at Red Lion could see people running from the villa and then the Cobra fired another rocket into the villa. The second explosion demolished the entire building and blew it apart. Fire was everywhere and some of the cars parked started burning. The operators moved into the villa court yard and then around the villa. John watched as the operators shot targets and continued to shoot anything that moved. By now the villa was totally in flames and no one could even get within 100 feet of it. John watched as the operators continued to shoot individual targets and then everything stopped. John saw no more targets and knew the operators had finished their job. John leaned forward and said, "Tress get the Cobra to do a complete gun sweep with the Gatlin Gun as soon as we are clear". Tress sent the message to the Cobra. John watched as the operators moved out of the villa area and back toward the drop zone. The Black Hawks came in and loaded the operators and were off in three minutes. The Cobra made the gun run and fired over 30,000 rounds into the entire compound area. Then the Cobra moved to the over watch position and waited for ten minutes before heading to the ship. While the raid was going on, Don and Cindy had activated the worm and all the money from the cartel was now moving from bank to bank to bank and would move like that for the next twenty days. At 1 AM Tress announced that all personnel were accounted for and the ship was thirty miles off the coast of Mexico headed for Corpus. John thanked everyone and went to his office. He sent a fax to Liz. It said "DONE". John went home. He was very tired. Molly was waiting for him when he came in and handed John a beer. John said, "It is done, and we lost no one". Molly kissed John and said "Fantastic".

Over the next week things were almost back to normal at Red Lion. The container ship had docked at Galveston and the containers holding the choppers and the one with the operator equipment had been off loaded and delivered to Red Lion. The operators and piolets had already returned, and Don and Cindy had been very busy on the internet making it look like the competing cartel was responsible for the attack. The idea was working and working well. The DEA and the Mexican drug enforcement had made raids along the border and had arrested over 400 people and seized over 20,000 pounds of drugs. The news media was going wild of course but were reporting that the competing cartel had done all the damage to gain total control. The official reports had 219 people killed and over thirty critically wounded. Many of the dead were Mexican government officials and local police or Federal police. The Mexican government was in no position to question who had done the raid and John knew that. Liz had called John on the secure line and she was so excited he had to calm her down. The President was very happy and wanted John to know how much he appreciated what Red Lion had done. John was pleased. Sara sent the invoice to the special address she had, and it was paid in less than two days. The bill was $45 Million Dollars. It was never questioned. John had made sure all the personnel involved in the raid including the ground operators and mechanics had a bonus. John paid them 50% of their yearly pay as that bonus and gave them seven days off. The replacement equipment had been ordered and most of it was arriving as the week closed. John was ready to have a quite weekend. On Friday Red Lion got three messages from foreign governments to arrange a meeting. Germany, Italy, and Holland wanted to meet to discuss some business. John smiled and thought "yes I am sure you do want to discuss some business with us. Ok we will meet". John headed home and took Molly out on the town for the night.

On Monday John called the contact in Germany and discussed their needs. He was on the phone for about an hour and decided he would go for a meeting. John told the contact to arrange a meeting with the right people and let Red Lion know in plenty of time. Then John called Italy and did the same thing. The call to Holland was very strange and John did not like it at all. John declined to meet and told the contact that Red Lion could not help now, which was a nice way of saying no. John and Jim had a meeting with Sara and discussed the financial position of Red Lion. As of October 1st, the corporation would have over $19 Billion Dollars available to use and would be worth about $21 Billion counting all the assets it owned not counting the "special" account. John and Jim could not believe the figures but knew they were right. John looked at Jim and said, "Hell not bad for some washed up Generals".

Jim laughed and said, "Who is washed up?" John started laughing and then both men headed to Molly's for some drinks and lunch.

Molly's was crowded and that was unusual for Monday. John saw a table and took it as Jim came in. Jim saw John and went to the table and sat down. Molly and Carol were both working so John waited and Molly finally could come over. She kissed John and then Jim and took the drink orders. There was a new girl doing the bartender work and John asked Molly about her when Molly brought the drinks. Molly said Carol had hired her when Molly was gone, and her name was Judy. Molly said everyone really liked her and she knew her business. John nodded, and Molly took off to serve another table. John and Jim talked about Red Lion and about the German and Italian deals. Jim was worried about Italy and he wanted to make sure John knew that Italy was terrible about paying bills. John said, "Well Jim you are going to be there, so it will be your call".

Jim said "What? I did not mean that I needed to be there I was just warning you".

John said "I know but I want you there. Hell, you know as much about what we do and what we can do as I do or probably more".

Jim said, "OK when do we go?"

John said, "They are going to set up the meeting and let us know". Then Jim asked about Holland and John told him what had happened and why. Jim agreed that Red Lion did not need to be involved. John and Jim had their third drink and then ordered lunch. Molly had sandwiches and some pizza that was bad, but people would buy it, so John ordered a sandwich and Jim did too. The crowd had thinned out and Carol and Molly came over and sat down. The four of them talked and John and Jim ate the food as they talked. Jim said, "Well Molly you ready to go to Europe?"

Molly said, "Yes of course, when?"

John said "We are going to Germany and Italy for some meetings, so we figured we would make it a vacation. A working vacation of course but not too much work".

Molly said, "Ok I need to know so I can get things here covered and all of that".

Carol said, "I will handle this place you just go and enjoy".

John said, "They are going to let us know, probably in a week or so".

Jim said "Well I have to go and do a few things. Nice to see you again Molly and Carol". Jim left, and Carol got up and went behind the bar and started doing her thing. Molly and John sat and talked about Europe. Molly was already excited.

On Wednesday Germany called and asked John to come on the next Thursday week for the meeting. The meeting would be in Heidelberg and it would be with the Head of the German Army and the Minister of Defense. John was very intrigued. John called Jim and told him. Jim said he was also going to bring a friend along if John did not mind.

John told him sure and then John had Nancy make the plane reservations and the hotel reservations. John then called Molly and told her to be ready to fly on Tuesday. Molly was ready to go then, but she told John Tuesday was fine.

Tress had a new project he and Sandy were looking at. The troops were going to be pulled out of Iraq starting in 2010, so the President had been telling the American people and Tress knew that a huge vacuum would be created immediately. Iraq had no standing Army and would never have an Army that could do a damn thing. The US had defeated the Army when it invaded and with all the sectarian mess in that country, no one could put together a government that would work. No matter what Washington said it was going to be a complete disaster and Tress knew Red Lion could help with training. Sandy spoke Arabic and had been in Iraq as an intelligence operator for the Army for three years. She knew how the people thought and how they acted. The US government was going to spend $500 Million Dollars on training the Army and they did not have a fucking clue what it would take. Also with the war still going on in Afghanistan the US Army did not have the manpower to train anyone much less the Iraq Army. Tress and Sandy met with John and told him what they had been thinking. John agreed and said "OK we are slow now so you two come up with a plan to train these people and put down everything you could possibly need to do it. Once you get it down give it to Kevin and have him cost it out for us. Then we will see where we are and probably take it to Washington". Tress and Sandy thanked John and left to start to work on the total plan. John liked the fact that his people were always looking for ways to make money for the corporation and in turn for them.

John called the Italian contact and asked for a meeting to be on the Monday after the German meeting on Thursday. John did not say he would be in Germany, but John had thought "why make two trips". The Italians agreed to the

Monday date and said it would be in Rome and that they would send the time and location via email. John now had Nancy make reservations in Venice and Rome for the four people. John was planning to leave Germany on Thursday night or afternoon after the meeting and take a train to Venice. Then on Sunday they would take a train to Rome. They would fly back on Tuesday from Rome. Nancy took care of everything. John informed Jim and Jim was excited. John then called Harry and asked some questions about how many people he could train at one time. How long training would last for special operations training and other questions. Harry said he would get the figures together and email John the answers the next day. John was alright with that. Kevin came into John's office and wanted to discuss the KBR deal. John said, "OK what is on your mind?"

Kevin said "John I think we need to re-look at the figures we submitted to KBR. I do not think we charged enough for the special operators they are now requesting for the oil refinery. It is only fifteen people, but we need to charge more because they are high risk personnel under the new situation in Iraq. We have no army support if they need it and the US Army is leaving so my thought is we need to increase the amount per man or have KBR put thirty people in place. Even then we should charge more for the damn refinery".

John said "Have you talked to Dan about this? We do have a contract so find out what we can do under our present contract. Then let me know and we will see what we can do. I agree with you about the refinery. It is a prime target".

Kevin said he would get with Dan and left. John now had a decision to make. If he had some business to do with Germany and or Italy did he have to tell Liz? That was a question he wanted to think about.

# CHAPTER 31

ohn had arranged for a limo to pick everyone up at Red Lion headquarters and take them to the airport. They were flying first class and would only have to go thru a small screening at the airport. John and all his people were still using Diplomatic Passports and that included Molly. Jim's friend would have no trouble because she would be with John and would be sent immediately thru customs wherever they were. John and Molly were standing in the parking lot and the driver had just loaded their bags into the limo. Jim drove up and parked. He opened the door and a very beautiful woman got out. Jim introduced her and said, "John and Molly meet Latoya Mitchell or actually Dr. Mitchell". John and Molly said hello and the driver loaded Jim and Latoya's bags into the limo. Everyone got in and off they went. Jim explained on the ride that he had first Latoya when she was a doctor on active duty in the Army. They had spent some time together, but she had gotten out and gone into civilian practice and they had lost contact with each other. Jim had seen her about six months ago at a restaurant in Houston and had spoken to her. It just started off where they had left it fifteen years before. Latoya was a beautiful black lady. She was almost 6 feet tall and weighed about 145 pounds. She had a golden colored skin and everything about her nails, hair, and make up was perfect. Latoya was from New Orleans and had gone to Tulane Medical School then did six years in the military. She was now a neurosurgeon and worked at Memorial Houston. John really liked her, and Molly really liked her and was very happy she was along. Jim said, "Latoya does not really know what I do now, so I always tell her I just do what John says to do".

John said "My ass that will be the day. Latoya Jim here is president of a multi-million-dollar company that does specialty security work all over the damn world. That my dear is why we are going to Europe. We must visit with some potential clients and see if they want us to work for them. Now have you ever been to Germany and Italy?"

Latoya said, "Germany yes, Italy no, so I am really looking forward to this".

John said, "I do not believe you will be disappointed".

Jim said, "No you will not". The limo had arrived at the airport and John and party got out and the driver had a porter get the bags and have them checked. Then the group went to the VIP Lounge and had a drink and were then taken thru special security screening and sent to another VIP lounge to await the flight. The hostess called them to board in about an hour and they got on the plane. The plane took off and the group was on the way and enjoying every minute of the trip.

The plane landed in Frankfurt Germany and the car was waiting for them. They were immediately sent through customs and on the way to Heidelberg in less than one hour. The hotel in Heidelberg was very nice and the suites were fantastic. The group had slept most of the trip so after a quick shower they met in the hotel bar. It was just past 8 PM. After a couple of drinks, they went to a restaurant the hotel concierge had suggested and had a wild game dinner. It was fantastic, and everyone enjoyed the food and atmosphere. After dinner they walked along the river for a while then returned to the hotel. John and Jim had a meeting at 10 AM the next day at the old US Army European Command Headquarters building.

The meeting was unique in two ways. The first was that John and Jim were meeting with the Head of the German Defense Ministry including the Chief of Staff of the German Army and second, that the Head of the Federal Police (Polizi) was also included in the meeting. John and Jim went through the usual introductions and sat down at a large table. The

German Defense Minister said, "Gentlemen we are here to find out if you would be willing to train 120 of our personnel in the exact tactics and way you train the operators that work for Red Lion?"

John said "Alright, now Sir, would you tell us who exactly we would be training and where you want this training to take place?"

The Chief of Staff said "We would like you to train fifty soldiers as operators. The additional ten soldiers would then be trained as instructors, so the Army would have you train a total of sixty".

The head of Polizi said "We would also like you to train fifty of our officers as operators and the additional ten as instructors."

The Minister then said "The training would take place at your facility in the United States. The reason for the training and qualifying of instructors is so we can then create a training facility here in Germany to train additional personnel. We would of course ask that you assist us in building that facility".

Jim said "We could of course train the personnel you are discussing and assist you with building a facility, but gentlemen it is going to be very expensive. You do realize that I presume?"

The Minister said "Of course, we expect you to make a profit and we can dedicate about $50 Million Dollars to the training and the assistance on our facility".

John said "Well, I can have you a total bid in a week and will have it sent to your office via fax. It will include the training time and we will bid it to include lodging and food for your people. Transportation can also be included if you wish, however we prefer you arrange that part to Houston. We can then get your people from Houston to our facility. If you choose, it could be a military flight that could land in San Antonio just coordinate that with our Military".

The Minister gave Jim the contact number for the bid to be sent and the meeting was ended. John and Jim said their good bye and left. In the car riding back to the hotel, Jim said "Well looks like we may become a training academy".

John said, "Yes it seems like that but Hell it is great money and we do not get shot at". Both men laughed. When John got to the hotel he called Kevin and gave him the instructions for the bid. John made sure Kevin understood that $50 Million Dollars was available, so Kevin was to make the bid in that range. Kevin understood and told John he would have the bid out in three days. The bid would be for $50 Million Dollars, with $15 Million of that amount being for Red Lion supervision and guidance in the construction. That afternoon, John, Molly, Jim and Latoya boarded a train and left for Venice.

The train was quite an experience for the group. John had gotten two sleeper compartments that connected, and the ride was going to take nine hours. The group spent most of their time in the club car and the dining car and only used the sleeper for a few hours, making love on the trip. When the train arrived in Venice, a car met the group and took them to the hotel. The next three days were spent going around Venice and having a great time. The train to Rome was also a good ride and even though the Italian train system was nothing like the German system, the group did enjoy the ride and saw quite a lot of the country as they traveled. In Rome they were met at the station and taken to their hotel. The hotel was nice, and that night John had arranged for a dinner in one of the best restaurants in Rome. The next day, the ladies would be taken on a sightseeing tour while John and Jim met with the Italian officials. The flight back to the states was scheduled for the morning following the meeting.

The meeting went well with the Italians. Jim was the lead on the meeting and after the Italians explained what they were needing, Jim said "Yes we can do that type of training, but it is very expensive, and we would need payment in advance of at least 50 % of the cost". John watched as the Minister and two other officials discussed that part and was surprised when they said, "Of course we expected to pay in advance, however we would require that all expensed are paid for our people by Red Lion and that we in turn then pay that along with the actual bill for services."

Jim said, "That is very satisfactory with us, Sir". The training was going to be almost identical to the German training, only no mention of building a training center was mentioned by the Italians. Jim explained that the cost would be about $35 Million Dollars including everything. The Italians wanted fifty people trained as operators only. Jim got the necessary information for Kevin to send a written bid and the meeting was over. John and Jim again said their good byes and left and went to the hotel. The girls were still on the sightseeing tour, so Jim and John went to the bar and had a few drinks and waited. Both men discussed the events of the trip and were very surprised about how the training was now becoming a major income producer for Red Lion. The Italians were sending only military personnel for training and that was about the only difference between them and the Germans. Of course, in Italy the military was used much more for situations than in Germany or of course the US. The police in Italy were mainly for investigations and minor things. The girls arrived back at the hotel and joined the men in the bar. Everyone decided to eat dinner at the hotel and enjoy the bar for a while before and after dinner. The next morning, the car delivered the four to the private section of the airport and they boarded the jet and returned to the United States. The trip had been a lot of fun for all, and the business looked very promising.

John was back, and things were moving along. Kevin had completed the bids for both the Germans and the Italians by the end of the week and had faxed them. On Monday the Germans had called to accept the bid and requested a contract be sent forward. Dan had the contract working. The Italians called on Wednesday and accepted the bid, so Dan was working that contract as well. KBR had been doing well and the operators there were showing no signs of having any real trouble. They had been involved with a few minor firefights, but mainly they had been doing basic convoy and guard duty. A new terrorist group had been making noise in Chad and Tress had been following all the chatter on this new group. Libya had been in a civil war for about two months and the leader was about out. The rebel group had gained a tremendous amount of support and was taking city after city. Sandy and Tress both had been monitoring that situation and John could see problems looming. Washington had been very quiet, but John had a feeling that was not going to last. December was now here, and John was ready for what 2010 would bring. The rest of the year was not very busy as far as operations for Red Lion. The contracts had been sent and signed and the training was to begin for the Germans in January. The Italians would begin in April. Libya had been overthrown by the rebels and the leader had been killed. That country was in a very bad civil fight over who would be the new leader. The United States was trying to figure out which side to back. The Chad situation was getting worse and Tress was predicting a complete mess in the coming year over there. The terrorists were now taking young girls as captives and demanding the Chad government pay ransom and release prisoners to get the girls released. There was also unrest in other African nations and more unrest in Mexico and South America involving drug cartels. John knew there was just too much money involved in the drugs and human smuggling to not have new cartels spring up. John had given Tress and Sandy instructions to monitor that well. Don and Cindy were also monitoring all email and any other internet traffic about the cartels and other areas of interest.

# CHAPTER 32

The first week of January the German personnel arrived in San Antonio and were picked up and driven to Hallettsville. All the personnel were put into motels two people to a room and the training was started. Harry had written a new training plan especially for this requirement and the instructors were very busy making sure all the students were trained to the highest standards. The training would be for two months. John had talked to Ray about the operation at Christmas and Ray had gotten the entire community behind having that many people for the two-month period. The estimated income to the area would be about $20 Million Dollars and that was a win fall for the city and the surrounding area. John was glad things could help the area and knew it would be a great asset to have the entire community on Red Lion's side.

The second week of January all Hell broke loose in Libya. The US Embassy was attacked, and the Ambassador and two other people were killed. The others were CIA operatives. The President and his advisors handled the situation very badly and the news media and Congress were all over the situation. It was very bad for the President and the Secretary of State. John had Tress and Sandy immediately try to find out who was responsible and where they were located in that country. It was very difficult to pin point the actual responsible parties because of all the lies the government was telling about what had happened. The first lie was that a demonstration had gotten out of hand and spilled over into the embassy. Then the next lie was that a small faction had attacked. Then the story went on and on. No one was believing a thing that the administration was saying about the situation. It was not looking good for the administration and John knew that the President was under real pressure to get things resolved quickly. Tress and Sandy had intercepted traffic about a Delta Team operation that was scheduled for the middle of February. The exact details were not available, but Tress was convinced that Delta would be trying to find and eliminate the people who had attacked the Embassy. John knew that was going to be a mistake if anything went wrong or if the media got any idea US forces were being used to kill not capture the people involved. The news media had reporters all over the area and of course these reporters would do anything to get a story even if it meant risking the lives of US military personnel. John had seen this happen for years from Viet Nam to the present. There was no control on the media. John was relieved when Tress and Sandy came into his office and said "Sir, we know exactly who is responsible for Libya and we know exactly where there are hiding in that country". John got all the details and after the briefing by Tress and Sandy, John sent a fax message to Liz. The next day Liz called John on the secure line and they discussed the situation in detail. The President wanted the Delta Team to capture the people responsible, so a trial could be held. He was looking for press and Liz was not able to convince him to change his mind. John told Liz that the capture would not work and that if the Delta Team was discovered being in Libya, the Congress would go crazy and even the American people would not accept US boots on the ground for this. Liz agreed but told John there was nothing that could be done right then. John understood, but had Tress and Sandy come up with a plan all the same.

The first US combat troops were leaving Iraq and on the way back to the US as February went on. 25,000 had been sent home and that was being covered by the entire press corps. The Delta Team operation was a complete disaster and two Delta Team members had been killed. The terrorists had known exactly when the      Team was going to attack and had been waiting for them. That little fact did not make the news, but John knew it had been a very bad thing for Delta. Liz called John one day after Tress had given John the news about Delta. Liz said the President wanted to know if Red Lion could and would try to eliminate the problem in Libya. John said, "No Red Lion would not". Liz thanked John and hung up.

The next few months went by fast for John. The Red Lion operation was still doing well, and a few clients had asked for a few things to be talked about. Mainly drug cartels and some terrorist activities in the Middle East countries were the main areas of concern. Tress and Sandy had done most of the initial interviews with the prospective clients and so far, the price was the hold up on getting contracts done. Everyone wanted the job done, but no one wanted to pay the price. John and Jim had discussed this before and they both agreed the prices would not be lowered. Washington was quite since the Libyan thing and John knew the President was having trouble with his policies. The economy was not doing as good as predicted. The Germans had come and gone, and the Italians were now in Hallettsville. Ray did not like the Italians and John knew why. They are very cheap, and they do not even try to learn English. John was very glad they would only be there one month. The Germans had now paid the invoice and the money was really building up at Red Lion. John and Sara had a meeting and Sara showed John how much the corporation had in cash. $525 Billion Dollars was the figure she used. John was surprised but very happy. He knew the corporation was making money and he also knew that all drug and terrorist money found was seized using Don and Cindy to hack the banks. John decided it was time to spread the wealth. John called Nancy into his office and dictated a memo for every employee of Red Lion. The memo said, "Effective July 1st, 2010 every employee will have a 25% increase in their individual annual salary". John had Nancy distribute the memo to every employee and made sure Sara put it in effect. John also had the memo set to be approved by the Board at the next meeting which was scheduled for the last week in June, 5 days later.

The Board meeting was at 10 AM and all members were present. John opened the meeting and gave an overview of how the corporation was doing. After he had finished the overview he turned the floor over to Jim and Jim went over the pending operations Red Lion was looking at doing and the new equipment that was needed. After Jim finished, John had Sara give the financial report. When Sara finished, John then brought up the new salary memo and the vote passed unanimously. Dan then said "Now that we have patted ourselves on the back, I have some very disturbing news I was given an hour before the meeting. It seems like we have a fucking reporter that has been doing research on Red Lion for over a year and he is now getting ready to do a full-blown story on us". The entire Board was silent. John said, "How in the Hell did this son-of-a bitch get information on us?"

Dan said, "John it is this new administration that is the only place it could be coming from".

John said, "Can we stop this guy short of killing him?"

Dan said "I really do not know. I just got word from a trusted friend and I have not had a chance to really find out much more".

John said "OK that is our only priority as of right now. Don, Cindy, Tress, Sandy, Hell everyone we need everything on this guy. I want to know where he lives, eats, sleeps shits, everything he does and has ever done and who he does it with and we need this NOW!"

Dan said "I have his name and social and his address plus he works for CBS. He is some hot shot field reporter that does all types of stories on how bad the government is and how they spend money and all that bleeding- heart crap. I will get all of that to everyone as soon as this meeting is over with".

John said "OK now we have a real enemy that we must stop. The bottom line is if he will not be reasonable he dies. It is just that simple. We have way too much to lose, and I will be damned if one snotty reporter is going to destroy us". John made a motion for adjournment and it was seconded and passed. The meeting broke up and Dan got everyone the information on Mr. Bob Stevens. Now Mr. Stevens was going to feel the wrath of Red Lion. Everyone went to work getting all the information available on Stevens. Dan could find out that Stevens was just starting to write his story and it was not going to be ready to air or really be a finished product until he could get an interview with Red Lion or at least try. He would need that for the TV Special he was doing. He also had some interviews he was trying to get with CIA, FBI, DOD and other parts of the government. Dan figured it would be at least four months before he could go on the air. That was what Red Lion needed to destroy this guy. John was as mad as he had been in a very long time. He blamed the White House for this and he even blamed Liz in a way. Washington could do nothing right and this new President was a prime example of that. John also knew that if the story ever got out even with no actual proof Red Lion was probably finished and that would not only hurt all the employees but would really hurt the country. John was not going to let that happen. Normally, John would never consider breaking the law, well by that, not doing what needed to be done to people who damn sure deserved what they got. Now John was considering just plain killing this Stevens and destroying his entire place and all his files in one blow. It might come down to just that. John hoped there was another solution.

# CHAPTER 33

In six hours from the end of the Board meeting Don and Cindy had a complete file on Stevens sitting on John's desk. John was reading it over and realized that there was absolutely nothing bad in this man's file. He had been a good student in high school and in college and had graduated from Columbia with a degree in Journalism. He had gone to work for CBS as a reporter covering the last part of Viet Nam then covered all the conflicts since. He had been awarded a Pulitzer Prize for a story about Bosnia and had been totally in favor of the Afghanistan invasion. It was Iraq that had changed his views on the government and especially on the former President and this President. Stevens hated both men because in his mind they had caused thousands of deaths and injuries both to US military personnel and innocent civilians. Stevens did not believe anything Washington said about anything and had now made it his life's mission to expose all the people in Washington as liars and cheats. CBS had allowed him total control over his broadcast and had even given him a prime-time spot on Sunday night. Stevens was 63 years old and not married. He had divorced about thirty years before and had three children. His children were now grown and in various businesses. They too had no records to use. John knew he was going to have to speak face to face with the President about this and damn quick. John placed a telephone call to Liz and waited. In two hours Liz called back. John explained to Liz what was happening, and she said "John you will need to speak to the President. I will set it up. When can you be in D.C.?"

John said "Liz I will not come there. We need to do it someplace else. Maybe some place where he would be, and I could be and then we arrange a meeting. We cannot chance having me in the White House especially now. What is his schedule for the next week?"

Liz said "I will have to check and find out. I think he is scheduled to vacation in a week in Mississippi on some damn island he has been given to use by one of the contributors. It will also be a fund raiser type event one night. He has an election in 2012 so he is already raising money. I will get back to you". John agreed and hung up. Liz called back to John in three hours and told him that the meeting was set for Saturday night in Biloxi at the Grand Hotel. That was where the fund raiser would be held, and John was to meet the President before the event in his suite. John would be brought into the suite by the Secret Service and no one would be on the President's hotel floor during that time including his staff or anyone other than Secret Service. Liz would not even be there. John agreed.

John and Molly had arrived in Biloxi on Friday and spent some time at one of the casinos and walking around the city. Biloxi was an old town and there was an Air Force base there. The President had flown to the base, but John had flown into New Orleans then rented a car and driven to Biloxi. Molly was extremely worried about the reporter and she did not want John to get into trouble by having him killed. John knew things would be very bad if in fact that had to be done, but then, John had a very good bunch of professionals that worked for him. It could be done in a way no one would question, especially at Steven's age. People died of heart attacks every day. John and Molly had dinner in a very nice seafood restaurant and then went to the hotel bar. Reporters were of course there, and John looked to see if Stevens was among them. He was not. John was relieved. No one noticed John and Molly and they sat and had a drink or two then went to the room. The next day, John and Molly slept in late then went down and had a late breakfast and did some gambling at the casino. About 5 PM they went to their suite and John changed clothes and got ready. He was to meet with the President at 6:30 PM.

John took the stairs to the President's floor as he was instructed to do. A Secret Service agent was in the stairwell at the doorway and showed John into the hallway. Another agent was waiting and took John directly into the President's suite. As John entered, the agent exited, and the President stood up and said "John, good to see you again". John saluted and said, "Mr. President it is always a pleasure, Sir". John and the President sat, and John said "Mr. President we have a major problem. I will explain". John told the President about Stevens and what he was going to do. John also told the President that intelligence showed that Stevens would do anything to bring down the President and his administration and had that for his actual agenda.

The President said, "John what do you suggest we do to stop this?"

John said "Sir, I do not know if we can without killing the man!"

The President look at John and then said, "So you are here to get my approval?"

John said "Mr. President if that is required then yes, but I am here to advise you of the situation and see if there is anything we can do to protect you other than killing him. My priority is to protect you, if possible, like it always has been".

The President said "John I know that and believe me I appreciate that about you. Now how do you think Stevens found out about Red Lion?"

John said "Mr. President I do not know without asking him and he probably would not tell me anyway. I believe it had to come from someone in your circle. I say that because I pay my people way too much money to have them chance

Red Lion going out of business. I also trust all of them and I just do not believe they would talk to a reporter or anyone about what we do".

The President said "John I know you are probably right, but I hate to think it was one of my people. I too trust them, but then again it is Washington and I sure as Hell do not pay them what you pay your people. Plus, here everyone is looking to make favors with someone". Then the President said, "Now how do we handle this guy?"

John said "Sir we are working on that and we have a few months well actually we have only one month but that is not a problem. I guess I just wanted you to know things may get a little tense and I need to know you will not ask any questions and neither will your people if something does happen. I know you cannot control everything, but try to make sure unless there is a reason no one opens an investigation".

The President said "John I will do my best. You do what you must do, and do not inform Liz or anyone in my administration about it. I trust Liz with my life but who knows what this guy has on anyone or how he gets his information. I just want you to be covered and I sure as Hell need to be covered".

John stood up and said "Mr. President, thank you for your time. It is always a pleasure. John saluted again and left the room. John went to the elevator and got into it and pressed the button for his floor. Now anyone could see him coming out of an elevator and never know where he had been. The roof was where the spa was located.

John went into his suite and Molly was waiting. She got John a beer and freshened her drink and John told her about the meeting. John finished, and Molly said, "Ok then you actually have a green light on this bastard, right?"

John said, "Yes if necessary I do have that". John changed into a sport shirt and some slacks and Molly and John went down to the hotel bar. The fund raiser event was being held in the ballroom and was scheduled for 8 PM. It was now 7 PM and people were streaming into the hotel. As John walked into the bar he saw Liz standing talking to some donors. She looked at John and he nodded. Liz knew things had gone well. John and Molly sat at the bar and ordered a drink. About 9 PM, John and Molly went across the street to the casino and played until midnight, then had a late dinner and returned to the hotel. They left at 7 AM the next morning, drove back to New Orleans and boarded the private jet. They arrived in Sugarland at 11 AM. Molly went to her bar and John went to the office. Now he needed to get a plan in motion to stop Stevens and he did not really care how that got done. He wanted to try one time to talk to the man but if that failed, he was going to have him eliminated.

Stevens lived in New York in an apartment on 44th street. The building had gone condo about five years earlier and he had bought his unit. The apartment was two-bedroom and he used one for his office. The apartment was on the 20th floor two floors from the roof. Don had gotten the floor plan from a contractor who had renovated the apartment two years before. The name of the contractor was on the city permit so Cindy had hacked the New York City records computer and come up with the name and business address of the contractor. Don had then hacked that computer and gotten the plans. Jim and Tress had devised a plan to bug Steven's apartment and knew it would be very easy to do. They would also search the apartment for a safe and get the IP off his computer. John approved the action and Tress had Nelson get the right operators and send them to New York.

The operators got to New York and watched Steven's apartment. They were set to enter his apartment and would need about two hours to do the job right. They picked the perfect time, when he was at CBS taping his segment of the show. The operators picked the lock and disabled the alarm in a matter of twenty seconds. They started the process.

One operator placed the cameras in six locations giving total coverage of each room of the apartment and sound. The cameras would transmit 24/7 to a receiver. Then the receiver would transmit to a secure web site that was monitored all the time by Red Lion and be recorded at the Red Lion headquarters. The second operator down loaded all the files from Steven's computer to a thumb drive. It took 2 thumb drives to down load everything. Then the operator up-loaded a special worm, that Don had created, into Steven's computer. The third operator was searching the apartment for anything of value to Red Lion. The operator would take pictures of any documents if they were found. After the cameras were set up, voice bugs were placed throughout the apartment. The video cameras could not be detected by a "bug sweeping" device and the voice bugs would only be activated when the sweep had been done. It really did not matter if a voice bug was detected but that would let Stevens know someone was doing something and John did not want that if it could be helped. After the apartment was finished, the operators went to the roof and set up the relays for sending the information from the cameras and voice bugs to another receiver they had placed on another building across the street from Stevens. The tests then went on with Don and Cindy monitoring the feeds. It was perfect. The operators then left the building and stayed in a hotel for the night. They would stay in New York for one night in case they had to go back to the apartment to correct something, then John had a private jet pick them up for the return flight to Houston. The apartment had been scanned by the "bug sweeper" and nothing had been detected. The device Stevens was using was not very high tech and Don figured he had bought it either on line or from a store in New York. The operators were contacted and told to go to the private terminal and get on the jet.

Don and Cindy had down loaded the information on Steven's computer and Tress and Sandy were going over everything and separating out anything that might be connected to Red Lion. Don and Cindy were also going over the information looking for any email addresses or other information they could use to track sources. The intelligence team and the computer team worked for over twenty-four hours without leaving Red Lion headquarters. When each team was satisfied they had been over everything that was available, the teams asked for a meeting with John and Jim. John and Jim were sitting in the briefing room and Tress started. "Sir, we have major problems and we know exactly where the leaks are. We have a leak in CIA, an analysis name George Hull is the bastard that has been feeding Stevens information and believe me Hull has really given him a bunch of things. The second leak is in the Pentagon in the records section. It is a Specialist Fourth Class, a fucking E-4 that has furnished Stevens the names of damn near everyone associated with Red Lion. At least everyone that was here before we became a civilian corporation. This little bastard also gave Stevens information on what the pay was for the personnel. Stevens also has information on Hallettsville and we think that came from the local Sheriff's department, we have not located it yet but from what we have read, that is about the only place it could have come from". John and Jim sat frozen for a minute or two.

Cindy said "Sir, I have hacked the bank accounts of Hull and of the E-4 May, and they have been receiving wire payments of $20,000 every two months for a year. The money is wired to off shore accounts and comes from an account in New York from Chase bank. The account in Chase has no actual name just a shell identifier that is being used so Chase must know the actual owned of the account. That is the law. The money is wired in denominations under $5000 due to the new change with the Patriot Act. The wires are set up to go out every 3rd day".

John said "This is very good work and I thank all of you for this. Now we must figure out our next move. Tress how ready is Stevens to run the piece on his TV show?"

Tress said "Sir, he is still writing the show and getting film on things. He so far, has not gotten any film on Red Lion headquarters, but he does have film of Hallettsville and he probably got that from the Sheriff's contact".

John said "Cindy please hack every bank account of the whole fucking Sheriff's department there. They will use the same bank and call Ray and find out which one that is. Tell him I asked you to call. Better yet check every bank in that area for an account for any name from the Sheriff's department".

Cindy said, "Yes Sir I will get on it now". Cindy left and went to her office. Don said "John we need to also do an email and cell phone search of all the deputies and all of the employees. I will start that but getting the numbers may take a while. I think I will start with the Sheriff's Department phone lines. I should be able to separate cell numbers that way".

John said, "Go for it". Don got up and left. John said "Ok now Sandy and Tress we need to find out how bad we have been exposed. Can we do that?"

Tress said "Yes Sir. I will work the CIA deal and Sandy can do the Pentagon thing. We should know by this afternoon". John and Jim thanked them again and left and went into John's office.

Jim sat down, and he was as mad as John had ever seen him. Jim said "That fucking little punk. God, I just want to pull his damn head off".

John said "I totally agree but we have to wait for a few days. Then we charge the fucker with High Treason. That my friend is the death penalty".

John and Jim discussed the situation and tried to figure out a way to stop the TV show from going on. Finally, Jim said "John what if we have the guy Stevens in for an interview?"

John said "What?"

Jim said "Hell he knows about Hallettsville and he damn sure knows about KBR and what we do for them, so why not have him in and tell him exactly what we do. We can talk about KBR and our security job with them, the Germans and Italians and even talk about our contract with the Army to train Special Ops guys. Hell, if we admit things he will be left in the cold as far as any dirt. We can always use the National Security and that before we retired everything is still classified. I am sure you can have Liz make that happen and classify everything we have ever done if it already is not".

John said "Jim that is a wonderful idea. Shit Stevens will at least have to change his whole story about a secret unit of the government operating. This may just be the thing to end this once and for all. Hell, we can even offer to let him do a book about us. All these assholes love to write books".

Jim said, "OK then I will start to work on that and on the interview". Jim left, and John sat and thought for a long time. In the end, Stevens would probably have to be eliminated, but this interview would serve to be a great cover and who would think after the interview Red Lion would do anything to Stevens.

# CHAPTER 34

Stevens had gladly accepted the invitation to come to Red Lion and do an interview. He had sent a list of questions he wanted to ask, and Dan had reviewed the list and marked out over half of the questions. John had also marked out some of the questions. Tress and Sandy had ordered twenty ten-foot tables and they had been arranged in a classroom type setting in the warehouse. The four 60-inch TV monitors were set up and chairs were arranged at each table. There was SAT phone equipment and night vision equipment sitting on a table as well as hand held GPS devices. The headquarters was ready. Offices had been designated as private and special electric entry locks had been installed. The airfield was also re-done to insure only the C-130 and two Black Hawk choppers were seen. The information from Stevens' computer did not say anything about the Galveston operation and John did not believe Stevens knew about the ship. Very few people knew about the container ship and no one knew about the oversized containers that were used to hide the choppers except Red Lion personnel. No one knew about the Cobra either and that chopper was now loaded in one of the containers. The four containers were sitting at the air field at the end of one of the taxi ways and were not marked with anything that referred to Red Lion. The one hanger that would be used in the interview was totally clean of everything but mechanical equipment and mechanic's tools. John had spoken to Harry and Hallettsville was also ready. The plan was to have Stevens and his crew come to Red Lion in the morning and do the interview. Then John and Jim would go along with Stevens and his crew to Hallettsville for the afternoon interview there. John was purposely making Stevens drive. It would take at least 2 and ½ hours and it was not an easy drive. Red Lion was as ready as it could be for this and John was hoping it would work.

John had scheduled the interview to start at 8 AM and he had given absolute instructions that if the crew and Stevens were not there at that time the interview would be called off. Stevens could not take that chance and John knew it so at 8 AM Stevens started by walking into the main doors of Red Lion. John met him at the reception area and after the usual pleasantries John led Stevens to John's office. John motioned to a chair and Stevens sat down. John sat in the chair across from Stevens and was ready. Stevens asked the first question. "Mr. Carter, I understand that you are a retired General, 4-Star General, and you started this company while you were still on active duty. Is that correct?"

John said "No it is not. Red Lion is a totally owned civilian corporation and is owned by Veterans or at least over 51% is owned by Veterans. By law we come under the VA Act for Veteran owned corporations". Stevens asked more questions and John answered some, but most were not answered John using the fact that the information was classified and involved National Security. Stevens asked, "What is the purpose of Red Lion?"

John said "Our purpose or as we like to say our Mission Statement, is to train special security personnel or operators for jobs required by our clients. We also train foreign personnel in special operations and we are lucky enough to have a contract with the US military to train some of their Special Operations personnel".

Stevens asked, "Do you as a company, ever send personnel to do covert operations at the request of the White House or any other branch of the US government?"

John said "No Mr. Stevens we do not. We only do what our contracts call for and so far, all we have is a training contract.

Now should we be given a contract for something other than training, I am sure we would look at it very carefully but as you know, what you suggest would be illegal so no we do not do any covert operations other than in training situations". The interview lasted about an hour and then John said "Let me show you our facilities. I think your viewers would appreciate what we can do for our country and their fighting men and women". John got up and Stevens followed. The camera men also followed. John led Stevens into the area that had been set up as a classroom. John explained about the training and introduced Tress and Sandy as the instructors on aerial photos, maps, movement, and other subjects. Then John introduced Cindy as the instructor on the computer equipment and the GPS units. After that was done John had Stevens go to the air field and there, John showed Stevens the C-130 and the Black Hawks and explained how they were used in Hallettsville. John also explained the reason the aircraft were in Sugarland and not in Hallettsville, was a matter of room to do mechanical work and to store the aircraft when not in use. The complete interview and walk through took until 11 AM. John then said "It is now time to go to the training facility in Hallettsville. Mr. Stevens if you would be so kind as to follow us in your vehicles we will now depart. The drive will take about two and 1/2 hours". John and Jim and Tress got into one of the vehicles Red Lion and had the driver head to Hallettsville. Stevens and his crew followed in three vehicles.

Hallettsville was ready for Stevens. Harry was primed and waiting to be asked questions. John introduced Harry and Stevens started asking his questions. Harry was answering while he had Stevens in a vehicle and was showing him the entire layout of the training operation. As luck had it, a group of Mexican Federal Police, thirty of them, were in training and Harry was able to show Stevens how the training was done. After the tour, Stevens turned to John and asked, "How many countries come here for your training?"

John said, "So far we have had personnel from Germany, Italy, and United Arab Emeritus, Saudi Araba, Mexico, and Canada".

Stevens was shown why the C-130 was needed and told about the airborne training that was done. The Black Hawks were also explained to Stevens and he was shown how they were used in training. At 5 PM the interview was completed, and Stevens thanked John, Jim, Tress and Harry. Stevens and his crew left and returned to Houston. John and everyone but Harry drove to the air strip and got on the jet that was waiting and returned to Sugarland. The vehicle was driven back by the driver the next day. When John and his group were back at Red Lion headquarters, John sat down and had a discussion with them about how they felt the interview went. The consensus was that the interview had gone well if Stevens was honest about using the footage he had shot and the questions he asked. Now the waiting game started. John asked Don if there was any way to get a copy of the actual program that would be run prior to it going out. Don said "John all I can do is try. Now how much can we pay for a bootleg copy?"

John said, "What is the going price?"

Don said "I do not know, but maybe Cindy knows some people who could get it for us. I will get her on it right away. I figure it will be a week before this is ready to go out, so we have a few days".

John said "Do what you can. We really need to know what this bastard is going to show". Everyone then left for the day.

On Thursday a week before Stevens was to have his show on TV about Red Lion, Cindy had gotten a copy of the entire show. It had cost $50,000 but it was worth every cent in John's opinion. The entire Board of Directors watched the tape and after it was over it was obvious that Stevens was out to destroy not only Red Lion but the President as well. The show was in two parts and the title was "The Story Behind the Story". The first part was Stevens showing the interview with Red Lion and the film of the facilities including Hallettsville. Then the second part was Stevens doing interviews with Hull and May, both men were in disguises to keep their identity secret. The interview was bad and then Stevens went on to say that Red Lion was just a cover for the President and had been a cover for the ex-President as well. Stevens had all type of financial figures about the costs of the facilities, the equipment, and the salaries that had been paid the personnel when they were in the military. He kept stressing that a big lie had been given the Congress and the American people and that the current President was using Red Lion for his own personal agenda and against his enemies not just enemies of the United States that were threatening the country. It was just sickening how this asshole had distorted the interview with the Red Lion personnel and especially with John. John was livid. John had a copy made and then arranged for a jet and one of his operators to fly to Washington and deliver the copy to the President. John made damn sure Liz had it set so only the President got the tape in person from the operator. The operator left at 11 AM and landed in D.C. at 3 PM. The tape was delivered to the President at 5 PM. At 11 PM John received a call on the secure line from the President. They discussed the situation and when the President told John he could not stop CBS from putting on the tape, John knew what had to be done. John told the President it would be handled and then both men hung up. John went home. Tomorrow would be the day to plan a murder.

The morning was fast and very busy for Red Lion. John was talking to damn near everyone about Stevens. Tress had been monitoring the camera feeds and Stevens was a very boring person. He had no life outside his work. Only two people had come to his apartment since the cameras were installed and they were both people who worked on his show. Stevens had been busy on the phone and had called May and Hull about 20 times since his return from Houston. From what Cindy could make out of only one end of the conversation, Stevens was re-checking the statements the men had made on camera and wanted to be very sure the same thing would be said at a Congressional hearing. Stevens was planning on forcing a hearing and there were enough Congressmen and Senators that would be scared enough of him to do anything he wanted. John met with Jim and Tress and listened as Tress explained the plan for Stevens' elimination. He would have a massive heart attack in his apartment at night and would be found later by probably one of his assistants. Tress figured it would be at least twelve to eighteen hours before Stevens would be missed if it was done on a Friday night. In fact, it could be Sunday about 3 PM before he would be missed. He usually arrived at the studio at 3 PM on Sunday to get ready for his 7 PM show. The show was live, but it contained a lot of tape coverage of interviews and other things. Sometimes, Stevens had live guests on and then only a small amount of tape was used. For the Red Lion story, Stevens was going to be the commentator so to speak. The plan called for operators to enter Stevens' apartment at night and give him a shot of Hydroclodien. This was a drug that instantly killed the person, but made the death look to a medical examiner exactly like a heart attack. There would be no trace of the drug in any blood or in the tissues. The operators would inject the needle into the mouth under the tongue. The drug worked within one minute of it being injected so the operators would be able to make sure Stevens fell against something that would make a large bruise on his head and would look as if he had fallen when he had the heart attack. The reason for this was to cover the bruise that would be on his forehead when they initially held him down to inject the Hydoclodien. As soon as Stevens was dead, the operators would insert a thumb drive that would wipe his computer clean of all records. Don was going to make sure the CBS computers were also wiped clean of any records that Stevens may have placed on them. Cindy was going to get the original tape for the show and all copies the same way she had gotten the bootleg copy. The cost would be about $250,000 but Cindy was confident her source would do it and then just disappear. Other tapes would also be taken so it would look like a robbery of the tapes for all the CBS shows, not just Stevens's show. The plan was good, and John knew things would work. Everyone would be so involved with Stevens' death they would forget about the show that was to be on in a week. John gave Tress the green light and the plan was in action. Nelson would be the team leader and three other operators would be on the mission. Tress arranged for a jet to arrive at the air field and take the operator team to New York on Friday morning. The operation would be Friday night.

The second part of Tress and Sandy's plan was even more daring, but John liked it a lot. Everyone knew that as soon as Stevens' death was made public, Hull and May would probably go underground. They would not believe Stevens had a heart attack because they had been giving him information and would think it was a conspiracy. Sandy knew exactly where both men lived and that they were always home early Saturday mornings between the hours of 2 AM and 8 AM. She also knew that they probably had information in their homes about not only Red Lion but many other things the government was doing, especially Hull if not May. The plan on them was very simple. Operators would go into their homes and eliminate them as quickly as possible. Then the residences would be set on fire with incendiary devices, so everything would be burned so badly, nothing could be recovered. Before the operators set the fire, they would down load the computer in each residence on to a thumb drive, and the operators would search the entire residence just in case these people were stupid enough to keep hard copies of anything. It was set for two four-man teams to go to Washington and conduct the operation. They would travel by chartered jet and return the same way. The time for the mission was set at 4 AM for both residences. John and Jim both approved of the second plan. John wanted each attack to take place at the same time, just in case one or all of them were communicating at that time of morning. All the operators were advised of the time. Both Jets were on the way to the respective cities. John and the rest of the Red Lion people could only wait and hope for the best at this point. John had also instructed Don and Cindy to clean out the bank accounts of Hull and May. Stevens was not going to be touched.

It was now 3:50 AM and all operators were in position at their locations. The operators were counting down the time as were the personnel at Red Lion. At 4 AM all three doors were opened, and the assaults were now on. Hull was lying in bed on his right side as the operator entered his bedroom. The operator moved to the side of the bed and fired one shot into Hull's left ear. The silencer made only a swishing noise and Hull was instantly killed. The operator checked to confirm and then the other operators went about the search and planting of the devices. Hull's computer was down loaded, and the information was put on the thumb drive. The devices were set for a twenty-minute delay, and the operators left the apartment and were back on the street and in their rental vehicle. They drove two blocks down the street and waited for the explosion. In twenty minutes the entire apartment exploded in flames. The operators drove back to the airport and returned the rental vehicle and then went to the private terminal to wait.

The operators at May's apartment were in and out in ten minutes. May had been in bed sleeping on his stomach and an operator had shot him in the base of his head. He too was dead. The other operators had searched the apartment and planted the devices. These devices were set with a fifteen-minute delay and the operators were again in the rental vehicle and waiting two blocks away from the apartment. The explosion at May's apartment was tremendous and blew out the windows across the street. Fire leaped into the air and out all sides of the apartment building. The operators drove to the airport and turned in the rental vehicle. When they entered the terminal the first group joined the second and all the operators got on the jet and headed back to Sugarland. The collateral damage was not going to be very bad other than loss of property. The devices were set to only destroy the apartments they had been placed in and only some smoke and water damage would be the result when the fire department got finished. It would look like a gas explosion had occurred.

New York was entirely different, and it took more time. When the operators had opened the door, the first operator silenced the alarm. This had to be done so no trace of a break in would be detected. Don had given the code to Nelson and he would re set the alarm in the on position when he left. Don would then remove any record of entry and re-set from the alarm company's computer. When the operators were inside Stevens' apartment they saw him in the kitchen. He did not hear them, so Nelson got directly behind Stevens and yelled. Stevens turned, and Nelson hit him in the forehead and knocked Stevens out. The operators then injected Stevens with the shot and in thirty seconds smashed Stevens' head into the corner of the kitchen table and let him fall to the floor. The blow by the table opened a six-inch cut across Stevens' forehead, exactly where Nelson had hit him. Nelson checked, and Stevens was dead. The operators then got busy removing the cameras, mics and all the devices they had put in originally. Nelson and the two operators searched the entire apartment. The computer was down loaded to a thumb drive and the worm Don had given Nelson was put into the computer. Nelson and the operators discovered a file cabinet in the bedroom closet and found over 200 audio tapes which they took. After very carefully making sure the apartment looked like it had before they entered everyone left and Nelson re-set the alarm. The other operator had been on the roof and recovered the equipment that had been placed there. The team then returned to the rental car and drove to the airport, turned in the car and boarded the jet. They were in the air and on the way to Sugarland at 8 AM. John was happy. Now this problem was solved. The only thing left was to get the original tape and Cindy was working that problem. She was going to get it delivered to her at 3 PM that afternoon. She would then pay the contact. John was tired, and he headed home to tell Molly. On Sunday Stevens' death was announced by CBS. He had died of a massive heart attack at his home over the weekend. He would be very much missed by his friends and the people at CBS. At 10 PM Sunday John got a text message from a secure source he knew well. The message said, "Thank You". John knew the President was relieved and happy.

# CHAPTER 35

John was pleased at the results of the last operations, but he still had a feeling Red Lion had missed something. There had to be another leak and it had to be in the White House. There was no other explanation for all the information Stevens had on Red Lion and all he had on what was happening when everyone was still on active duty. John had Tress, Sandy, Don and Cindy come to his office and he discussed the situation with them. They also felt there had to be another leak because Stevens had far too much information for just May and Hull to be his only sources. Tress knew Hull was an asshole, but he was not clever enough to add things up without having a road map. May was just a stupid little boy who wanted to be somebody and had access to records in both personnel and finance. The finance records showed nothing other than base pay and benefits that the Army was paying. The personnel records only showed that everyone was assigned to Special Operations Command and that alone was nothing unusual. No someone was the leak and John was worried that another reporter would be contacted. Stevens bank records did not reflect payments and the records from the CBS account were almost impossible to track without a name or account number that money went into. Hell, CBS had over 6000 payments each month out of that account and it was legal as Hell. John had everyone take another look at the things Red Lion had and review all the tapes and records for something they might have missed. Kevin wanted to see John, so the meeting was set for 10 AM.

Kevin came into John's office and said "Sir, I think I know who may have told about Red Lion".

John said, "Well go on Kevin, who?"

Kevin said "It may have been a guy named Martin. He worked in the comptroller's office and his job was to follow all the money that was never accounted for by normal channels. He also always was pals with Congressional aids from the House and the Senate. He would be the one to try to impress them with his knowledge. Hell, they were just using him, but he was too fucking dumb to realize that. Yes, he is my bet".

John said "OK Kevin I need you to get with Tress and tell him all you can about this Martin. Also talk to Don about him".

Kevin said, "Yes Sir right away". Kevin left John's office. John knew he was right about another leak and it could be more than one. Nancy buzzed John and told him Harry was on the line for him. John answered, and Harry said "Hey Sir, I have a guy here in my office that wants to talk about us doing training for SWAT teams throughout Texas. He is with the Texas Rangers and says he knows you".

John said, "Well put him on CSM".

The Ranger said, "Hello John this is CAPT James do you remember me?"

John said, "Hell yes I remember you Pete. How in the Hell are you?"

Pete said "Oh I am old and worn out but still hanging in. How about you General?"

John said "About the same. Now what can we do for the Texas Rangers?"

Pete said "John I need you to develop a program to train all the SWAT teams in the state under one and only one way to do business. The Governor has set aside $150 Million Dollars to get this done and you are the only guy I know that can do it".

John said, "Ok Pete we need to meet and figure this out".

Pete said, "I can be in Houston or Sugarland in three hours so what about 5 PM is that alright?"

John said, "I will see you then my friend". John hung up and waited for a few minutes then called Harry. John would have a jet pick Harry up in two hours and bring him to Sugarland. Harry was ready to come. John had Nancy call and get the jet in the air.

Harry arrived, and an operator picked him up and brought him to John's office. Harry walked into the office and sat down. John said, "Well looks like we have one Hell of a mission".

Harry said "Sir you can bank on that. Now what do we do?"

John said "Pete is on his way, so we will go to Molly's and have a few drinks then to dinner and find out what we will do. Do you need a room?"

Harry said, "Yes I think I will". John buzzed Nancy and told her to get Harry a room for the night. In an hour Pete walked into the reception and Nancy showed him to John's office. The three men talked for a while and then John said "Hell let's go get a drink. Pete, you want to follow us?"

Pete said "Sure". The men left and headed for Molly's bar. When John and his group walked into Molly's he saw Molly busy behind the bar fixing drinks. The bar was crowded, and John looked for a place to sit. There was a table all the way in the rear, so John headed for it and the men sat. Molly had seen John come in and she came over, kissed him and then kissed Harry and said, "God Harry what brought you off the farm?"

Harry reached out and patted her ass and said, "You did my darling."

Molly said, "Bullshit you are just a dirty old man and I love it". Everyone laughed. John introduced Pete and then Molly got the drink orders. The drinks came, and the men started talking about how things were and how much things had changed. Molly joined the table, and everyone talked and relaxed for a few hours. About 7 PM John decided that dinner was going to be a Fleming's, so he called and reserved a table. At 7:30 PM everyone left and headed to Fleming's. Harry rode with Pete and Molly dropped her car off at the apartment and rode with John. At dinner Pete explained what was required and that the Governor was wanting the training to begin by the first of January. John and Harry said that was alright and then John said "Pete I want you and Harry to sit and figure out exactly what you, not the fucking Governor, want us to do for these officers. Then we will get a firm training plan set up. Harry how many officers can we train at one time do you think?"

Harry said "John I would like to keep the classes small, no more than thirty at a time. That way we can do the stuff right and with that amount we can do it in thirty days from start to finish. We can do eleven classes a year, so we are looking at 360 officers a year. Now Pete how many officers do we need to train?"

Pete said "Harry and John we need to train about 600 officers to start. So, can we do fifty a month?"

Harry said, "Yes we will do that many."

Pete said "OK then I will come to see you the first of next week in Hallettsville and we can do the plan. Is that alright?"

Harry said, "Yes that will be good". The discussion was over, and the table then turned to other subjects and Molly then joined in. Harry had a room at Town and Country, so Pete took him and got a room. John and Molly left and went home. They had a drink and talked about the events of the day. Then they went to bed and made love. John was glad things were getting back to normal.

The year was really going fast, and John was ready to take a good break. November would mean Thanksgiving but this year he did not want to go to the ranch. Red Lion always closed for six days at Thanksgiving. John and Molly talked, and they decided to go to Florida for the holiday. Molly had a beach town she really liked, and John made reservations to lease a beach house for the week. John and Molly left Sugarland airport in a private jet and headed for Orlando, the only airport, close to the beach town of Redman Beach. The jet landed, and John had a rental car waiting. He and Molly drove for about an hour and arrived in Redman Beach. They went to the house and were very surprised at how nice it was. John liked the city immediately. The next few days John and Molly explored the entire area and looked at many houses and areas. On Friday, the day after Thanksgiving, John and Molly found a house. It was exactly what Molly wanted. The house had three bedrooms, three baths, a large kitchen, a huge den that opened onto a patio that was partly covered. The pool was small but enough for them and it had a hot tub built into the pool. The beach was only thirty yards from the house and it was private or could be. A fence could be built because the property extended all the way to the beach. There was a two-car garage built on to the house and the yard in front was nice but not big at all. The street the house sat on was a very quiet one and only had six houses on it. John called the real estate agent and found out the price, $230,000. Molly liked it and John met with the agent and issued a check to cover the cost. The closing would be in thirty days or less. John wanted it in less, so the agent set to work. The rest of the trip was spent having a great time and John looked the entire town over. There was a small airport for private planes and it was not big enough to handle a jet. John had an idea, but it would wait until he was an official resident. John and Molly left at the end of the week and drove back to Orlando. On the flight back to Sugarland, John told Molly to figure out exactly what she wanted to do with the house and let him know so he could get the contractor on the job at the first of the year. Molly was so happy she almost burst. When she got back to Houston and to the apartment, Molly and John talked about how much time they would really spend in Florida. John said, "I do not know exactly but I think at the rate things are going we can be there at least once a month". Molly said "OK then

I need to really talk to Carol about the bar. I think I may just let her take it over totally".

John said "Ok but why not do this. Let her run it and double her salary. You still actually own it, but it would be hers to run day to day and especially when we are gone. Hell. Let her make all the decisions. If it does not work out, then you can either take it back or sell the thing".

Molly said, "Yes that is exactly what I will do". When the jet landed, they went to Molly's and John had a drink while Carol and Molly talked.

John was back in the office and called Don in to talk to him about the Florida house. John told Don that John would need a complete office set up with all the secure email, fax, sat phone communications, TV for picture transmissions and anything else Don could think of. John wanted Don to order the equipment for delivery to the house during the second week of January. He would have Don install the items or have him hire the job done but be on site during the installation. Don understood and told John not to worry it would be taken care of it. John then called the air crew chief piolet and had him come in to see John. The piolet arrived, and John had him get a complete specification on the type runway that would be needed to land a heavy jets including landing lights. He also wanted the specifications on a hanger that would be large enough for the C-130 and the heavy jet. The piolet also told John he would have the information back to John in two days.

Molly called in the afternoon and told John she had everything ready for him. John said for her to fax it to the office. John received the fax and looked at what Molly wanted. It was just paint and drapes. There were a few renovations to the kitchen and to the master bathroom, but nothing major. She had decided to wait to buy the furniture after she got to the house and wanted to buy it locally if possible. John liked that idea and knew it would be good for the town and in turn good for Molly and John. John had Cindy get the name of the

Mayor of Redman Beach and his phone number. John then called Jim and had him come in for a chat. Jim came into John's office and sat down. John said "Jim I bought a house in Redman Beach, Florida and Molly and I are going to be staying there a good amount of time. I want you to start doing most of what I do for the corporation. Hell, you damn near run the thing now, but I think it is time you are making the decisions on things. I will still be involved and of course if I need to I will make the final decisions, but you are more than capable of running this monster we have created".

Jim sat for a good minute and then said "John I am shocked. I never thought you would not be right in the middle of everything, but yes I can do the job and thank you for the confidence in me".

John said "Hell Jim, we have been friends and been through way too much over the years. I trust you with everything and I know you can do the job. That is why I wanted you as my deputy when we were on active duty and that is why you are the President of this company right now. So as of January, you are the boss".

Jim said, "OK I guess I will need to get with Nancy and have her get me my own secretary or as you do my actual right arm".

John said "Yes I think that will be good, and I will talk to Nancy and see what she intends to do. I think she may want to continue to work in her position and she sure as Hell can handle what I will be needing so we will just talk to her. How about now?"

Jim said' "I think that would be good". John buzzed Nancy and had her come into his office. Nancy entered, and John had her sit. John explained the new situation to Nancy and discussed what he was planning to do. Jim also talked to her about his new functions.

When both John and Jim had finished, Nancy said "Well this is somewhat of a shock, but I see things like this. I will get Jim a secretary. I will train her and give her all the tools she will need to do the job and then Jim will get with her and the two of them will get just like I am with you John. I will also be in the same position as an Officer and a Board Member. Additionally, I will remain your secretary John and will continue to do exactly what I do for you and assist the others just as I always have. Is that alright with both of you?" John and Jim both agreed to what Nancy had said and were very happy she was still going to be in the mix.

Nancy then said, "OK now, when you are out of town, John do you want me to be here or what?"

John said "Nancy, I think you can schedule your time as you see fit. Do what the Hell you want and that will be nothing new. You have done that from the start". Everyone laughed, and Nancy got up and left. Jim and John continued to discuss the new situation for the next few hours.

Things were winding down in Iraq with the military. Most of the troops had been returned to the US and Washington was saying that by Christmas only 10,000 troops would be left in the country. Those troops would be support such as Military Police, Engineers, Medical and Supply/Logistics troops. All combat troops would be out. The new mission was to train the Iraq military and to support the re-building of the country. The new head of the government was in place and things were looking good for now. KBR was winding down on their projects and the number of Red Lion personnel was decreasing. John and Jim had discussed that, and it boiled down to letting about 400 people go. That was how it worked. The operators had been paid very well so hopefully they had saved some. They would all be kept on a list for re-hire if needed. The SWAT training was ready. Harry and Pete had the lesson plans and the instruction ready for the first class. It was scheduled for January. Nothing else was really on the table for now. The Middle East was still a complete mess and the fighting in Afghanistan was now the main-focus of the US military. Also, Syria was in a civil war and there had been problems in Egypt. The Palestine and Israel situations were becoming worse by the day. John decided to have a meeting with Sara and the accountant that Red Lion's books and John's personal accounts. John scheduled the meeting and Sara informed David, the accountant, of the time. David was bringing two of his people. John needed the meeting before he called a special Board meeting and John wanted to do that before Christmas. The finance meeting was scheduled for 9 AM the next morning. John made sure Jim was available and wanted him there.

The meeting with David was started exactly at 9 AM. John, Jim and Sara were sitting on one side of the table and David and his two accountants were on the other side. John said, "Well David how are we doing?"

David said "John you are doing extremely well and Red Lion will continue to do well as far as we can tell. I will have Willis give you the figures".

One of the accountants introduced himself as Willis Mann and said "Sir, presently Red Lion has a cash position of $400 Billion. The assets other than cash total $9 Billion Dollars. So, we are looking at a figure of $409 Billion Dollars for the corporation. Now the expense portion is high, but I have broken it down into four categories: Salaries will be $5 Billion per year including the overseas operators and the personnel Red Lion has on retainer. Then come the operating expenses which include fuel, utilities (included is Sugarland and Hallettsville), internet, phones, janitorial services, security services, aviation rental (Private Jets), property rental (Hallettsville), equipment rental (vehicles and other specialty equipment), lodging, operator expenses while on missions, replacement of equipment, maintenance of facilities, maintenance of aviation assets, maintenance of container ship, maintenance of vehicles and maintenance of all electronic equipment, accounting fees. This figure is

$1 Billion per year. Next is fees, licenses, special permits. The dock charges, and airport charges are included in this figure along with the security license and registrations for the aircraft and the ship. The figure is $2 Million Dollars per year. The last item is taxes and insurance. The figure for this is $300 Million Dollars per year. The total expense picture yearly for Red Lion is $ 6 Billion, 302 Million Dollars per year".

John said, "Ok now how much money do we make a year?"

The second accountant introduced himself as Terry and said "Sir, presently Red Lion has the following income: KBR $8 Billion per year. US Government training $70 Million per year. Training from all sources other than the government $10 Billion per year (revenue this year up to today), special operations revenue (up to today) $1 Billion Dollars. Total revenue for year up to date is $ 18 Billion, 70 Million Dollars".

David said "John we are looking at a profit for this year up to right now of $ 12 Billion, 268 Million Dollars. Not bad Sir". John and Jim looked at each other and smiled. John thanked David and the other accountants and Sara, David and the accountants said Good bye and left. John and Jim then discussed the expenses and the income. Things were going to change with KBR cutting back and with no guarantees Washington was going to use Red Lion. But if the missions cut back, the expenses would also cut back. Harry had the SWAT deal starting in January and hopefully Red Lion would be receiving some calls about the Middle-East. No matter there was plenty of money in cash reserves to fund the corporation for a year if nothing came in. Of the $400 Billion accounted for, there was also an additional $350 Billion that was in a special account that never was listed on the books of anyone. That was John's fund to do certain things that needed to be off the books. Jim knew about the fund, but only John would control it.

David was waiting for John at Molly's bar when John arrived. They had arranged a meeting there to discuss John's personal finances and his net worth picture. John and David were sitting at a back table that Molly had reserved for them and she came over and joined the table. David said "John and Molly I have figured out your position well, it is John's position, so here is the breakdown. I have a folder for you John that has all of this in it, but I will go over it now. You have a net worth as of right now of $1.9 Billion Dollars give or take a few million. Cash wise you have $1.2 Billion available to you immediately and another $550 Million in your off- shore accounts. That can be available in twelve hours. You have $200 Million Dollars in stock as of the opening of the market today. That is why I said $1.9 Billion more or less. The stocks of course move up and down but yours are very stable".

John said "OK David that is what I needed to know. Thanks". David said "You are welcome John. Molly how are you doing? And can I help you in anyway with your financial situations?"

Molly said "Yes David you can. I have an accounting firm to handle the daily stuff for Molly's but personally I have no real idea what I have. What do you need from me to figure it out?"

David said "I will need a lot of things and I want one of my people to get with you and do this right. I will have them contact you and set up a meeting if that is alright?"

Molly said, "Yes as soon as you can, please".

David said, "I will see to it today". John and David finished their drink and ordered a sandwich. Molly also had a drink and a salad. Carol was working, and she was having a great time. Molly decided to leave the business accounting where it was for now and have David only do her personal stuff. David agreed after John and Molly explained that Carol would be the actual manager and totally running the day to day operations. David liked the fact that Carol would not know that Molly had another accounting firm doing her personal work. Molly and John liked it also.

John had called the Board meeting, and everyone was present. John started by giving a brief status report on where Red Lion was as of the present time and what was projected for the coming year. Then he asked Sara as Chief Finance Officer and Treasurer to give the financial report which she did. The Board liked what they heard about the condition of the corporation. When Sara had finished her report, John said "Now here is the new situation. I am no longer going to be the Chief Executive Officer of Red Lion effective January 1st. I will remain Chairman of the Board and be an advisor to the CEO and President. The new CEO will be Jim. The new President will be Tress. Sandy will move into the position of Division Chief for the Intelligence Division. Everyone else will remain in their same positions. I have bought a house in Redman Beach, Florida and Molly and I will be spending time there. I have already asked Don to make sure I have everything I will need in the way of communications and video, so I will be able to talk with everyone on secure lines as well as on my cell phone. Nancy will still be my secretary and right-hand, so things should not change much. Jim knows his business just like all of you do. I think we will be slow as far as missions for the first few months and maybe the entire year, but we never know. Right now, we will continue to monitor situations worldwide and as always be ready to react when called". There was some discussion about how things were running and what was needed and topics like that for about thirty minutes then John called for a motion to adjourn and it was seconded and approved. The meeting was over.

The rest of the lead up to Christmas was good. John had again arranged the corporate Christmas party to be held and this year he had picked Lakeside Country Club as the location. John had joined Lakeside and really liked it. The party was a huge success, and everyone had a very good time. Bonus checks were handed out and again all the employees were very happy to be working for Red Lion. John and Molly had a jet chartered to fly them to Hallettsville for Christmas. John did not like driving as much as he had in the past and he wanted to be there quickly. Christmas was good, and John and Molly announced that they had bought the house in Florida at dinner Christmas day. The family was surprised but not unhappy. Miles and Linda were leaving for a trip to Europe in February and would be gone six weeks. John was happy they were going and asked Miles if he wanted an operator to be with them just in case because of the world situation. Miles turned down the offer but thanked John for the thought. Ray was going to think about running for State Representative in the 2012 election. John was surprised but then could see how Ray would like that. John and Molly pledged their support and offered to help in any way they could. Christmas was over and on the 27th John and Molly flew back to Houston. New Year's was going to be a blast at Molly's bar this year. The party was going to be bigger and hopefully better than ever. The New Year's event was wonderful. Jim and Latoya went with John and Molly and Don and Cindy joined then later in the evening. The party was a mixture of Houston at its best. There were people of all types there and everyone was enjoying themselves. The band was a real delight. Carol had found the band at one of the local places she went to with some of her men friends. Carol had many men friends but that was a story that could fill an entire book itself. The band played all types of music and did all night long. People danced and ate the food that had been catered in and drank a bunch of liquor. Carol had hired two off duty Houston Police Officers for security and that made everyone feel good. Gangs were still targeting bars and other places and Molly's had been hit once before. Of course, the word had spread about what happened if Molly's was a target, but it was better to not take the chance. Also hiring the off-duty police made very good relations for Molly's and the city. Jim had invited John, Molly, Don and Cindy over to his apartment after the New Year's party shut down for breakfast. Jim loved to fix breakfast and Latoya loved helping. The group all went and relaxed while Jim and Latoya prepared the food. Molly fixed drinks for everyone and then when the food was ready the group ate everything in sight. John and Molly got back home about 4 AM and went to bed. They made love and continued that until mid-morning. Then they slept until almost 9 PM. John was very much at peace with his life and so was Molly. They were going to Redman Beach in five days.

John got an email on the special email address on the 3rd of January. The same email had also gone to Jim and to Tress. Don had set it up that way, but the sender only knew that John had received the message. Red Lion was back in the hostage rescue business. This time it was in Africa, deepest Africa and not only Americans but British civilians had been taken. It was really a nasty situation. The terrorists that had taken the people wanted $500 Million Dollars US in twenty-four hours. John, Jim and Tress knew that would not happen so now all that was left was to get more time. John replied to the email and the exact information would be sent via secure fax in one hour. The time for Jim had come sooner than he or John had really expected.

# CHAPTER 36

The fax was received, and all twenty pages had come through. Jim and Tress asked John to join them in the briefing room and spread a map of Angola on the table. The fax said that one British doctor and three aid workers, two American and one British had been kidnapped from a clinic about two miles outside the town of Lobito in Angola. The clinic had been attacked by rebel forces and 128 people had been killed. The UN had been working on this problem for two weeks and had made absolutely no headway. The CIA had only one operative in Angola and the British MI-6 had only one so intelligence on the rebels was almost non-existent. The rebels had been fighting the government for over a year and so far, the Angolan government had made little progress in stopping them. The local people were supporting the rebels and again the government was not doing much for anyone. The fax had almost no information that Red Lion could use other than the rebels were vicious and would kill the captives if no money was sent. Tress and Jim studied the map and the surrounding territory and tried to figure out a location the rebels may be using. The area was not populated with any towns and as always no one had a fucking clue where the captives were. The good part of all of this was that only a few banks in the country could accept wire funds. Don and Cindy got busy hacking the banks computer systems. The capital was Luanda and it was the largest city in the country and had the banks that could be used. Don and Cindy had identified six possible banks that were able to do wire transactions. Don and Cindy were able to hack each one, but had no idea what to look for. They were in the systems of the banks but that was where they stopped.

Jim needed more information to even start on a plan. Tress could not get anything on his sources and Sandy could not find any "chatter" about the kidnapping. Anderson arrived and came into the briefing room. Jim briefed him and thanked him for getting there as quickly as he had. Anderson said "We can use the port at Luanda to dock and board the operatives and piolets. Container ships arrive and leave that port 24/7. It is the only real port the damn country has so we can work that angle". Tress left and when he returned, he said, "I had Don and Cindy try to hack into DOD and find some old records that were done back in 95' of that group. I personally did some Intel work there and if my notes are still with the report, we may get lucky".

Jim said "Well we sure as Hell need something other than what we have been given. John do you have any ideas?"

John said "I have been looking at this and if we do not get more from Washington, we cannot take the mission. No way to search the whole fucking country and we have no idea what we are really looking for".

Jim said "I think you need to get with Liz and let her know the problem. She only talks to you and we need to keep it that way for now".

John agreed and went to his office to get Liz on the secure phone.

John placed the call to Liz and had a return call in twenty minutes. John explained the problems and told Liz that Red Lion was going to have to have fourteen days to do the mission at a minimum. Liz told John she would pass on his concerns and be back as soon as she could. John thought about who he might know in the Special Operations community he could ask about Angola, but he knew that that was a very dangerous thing. People would always put things together and he did not need anyone knowing that Red Lion did missions like the ones they did for Washington. John was not sure this would be a go as it stood now. Liz called John back in an hour and told him he would be getting some additional information via fax in three hours. Also, the deadline was being re-negotiated by the UN and proof of life had to be verified by someone on the ground before any money could be exchanged. Liz told John the proof of life issue was a real gamble, but the rebels needed the money badly to continue their fight. In less than two hours ten more pages came over the fax. This time there was usable information. Tress and Jim went to work on the new information and Don had in fact gotten the report from the Army archives for Tress. The puzzle was coming together and now if the UN could do something right and get more time, things may work. That was the problem having the UN do anything right. John had no faith in the UN and had never seen them do a damn thing to help anyone in this situation.

The extra information from the report Tress had done years ago and the new fax information now gave Red Lion the name of the leader of the rebels. He was an ousted Colonel in the Angolan Army that had been kicked out three years before for brutality and was trying to over throw the current government. There were about 900 loyal followers under his control but with the money, he planned to get hundreds more. The base camp for his group moved constantly because the army tried, occasionally, to attack his camp and capture him. So far, he had stayed out of sight and only caused minor damage to some installations. Now however he had moved into the big time by taking international hostages. The village that was now his safe-haven was about fifty miles into the bush country and was very small. Tress and Jim were sure he had relatives there and that would be about right, so he had early warning if the army came to attack. Tress and Jim wanted our people on the ground if the UN got the meeting for proof of life. They both knew the rebels would not keep the hostages where the UN would meet to verify, and Jim wanted our people to be able to follow the hostages to the new holding location. Jim called Nelson and had him come to the briefing room. Jim told Nelson what was now happening and had Nelson get two operators ready to travel. The flights were a problem because it took over thirty-six hours to get there on a commercial flight. There was no direct flight into Luanda the capital, so many plane changes had to be made and hopefully seats were available. It would also be a problem if the mission became a Go. The crews, mechanics, armors and two medics, the PA, plus eleven operators would have to fly into the country and they could not fly at the same time. It would take at least three days to get everyone there. Then they would have to load on the container ship and spend one day getting everything ready for the mission. Jim was checking with the map to see what port would be best to dock in after the raid had been conducted. It was looking like Cape Town in South Africa was again going to be the best bet. Then the same protocol would be used as the last mission in Africa. The entire Red Lion team except for the ship's personnel would fly commercial back to the US. The hostages would be turned over to the South African government for return to the US and Brittan. Nelson came into the briefing room and told Jim and Tress that the operators were ready to leave as soon as the arrangements were made. Jim called Nancy and she made the plane reservations and got the travel money ready. The operators would not have weapons until they reached Angola, but the CIA operative would be instructed to provide two hand guns and set up a dead drop. Liz would handle that end. John got a fax from Liz stating the rebel leader had agreed to the UN demand and was giving an extended time of thirty days after the proof of life for the money. It was now going to be $750 Million US Dollars. Washington and London were not going to pay, but the President had convinced the Prime Minister of Brittan to keep the negotiations open. The President was betting on Red Lion but could not tell the PM yet. John hoped he never would. John gave Jim and Tress the fax and they had Nelson dispatch the operators to Angola. The UN meeting was in three days. The place picked was Lobito.

The two operators had landed and rented a vehicle. They were posing as geological engineers and had brought the SAT phones and some other equipment with them. Customs had cleared then and the CIA had done the dead drop and provided weapons. The operators then waited until the meeting was to take place. The UN team consisted of four people and of course as always drove a vehicle with UN makings all over it. The operators followed the UN vehicle to Lobito and then set up to wait and watch. The meeting was to take place in a small building just out of the town. The operators watched as the UN vehicle pulled up and stopped at the building. Two rebels came out and searched the UN team then led them back into the building. One of the Red Lion operators went down to the back of the building and saw a vehicle parked. He put a tracking device on the vehicle and return to his over watch position without being seen. The meeting was over in twenty minutes and the UN team left. The operators observed the building and in ten minutes after the UN had departed, the hostages were brought out and walked to the vehicle that had the tracking device on it. That vehicle was loaded and left heading out into the bush. The operators sent a SAT signal to Red Lion and the tracking device was activated and showed the vehicle moving into the bush area. The vehicle drove for 53 miles then stopped. The map showed a town of Kuito. The operators waited for an hour then followed the tracking device and went to the town. The town was very small but did have about thirty buildings and three were separated from the town about ¼ of a mile away. The tracking device showed that was the location of the vehicle. The operators drove past the buildings and photographed them then pulled into the town and asked about some areas north where oil had been discovered. The local people were not very cooperative but did send the operators out to an area. The pictures were sent by SAT phone and received at Red Lion. Tress and Jim started the plan. Jim called Anderson and told him it was a GO and the choppers would be there the next day. Jim then called the air division and had the Cobra and two Black Hawks loaded into the containers. The equipment for the operators was also being loaded along with the ammunition and explosives for the operators and the extra for the Black Hawks and Cobra. Jim had arranged for the trucks to pick the containers up at 4 AM and deliver them to the dock in Galveston.

The ship would take twelve days to reach Angola and then three more days would be needed before the raid could be done. That gave the team fifteen days before the actual raid would take place. The rebels had given an extension, so things should be alright if the hostages were not moved. The operators on the ground were told to maintain observation if possible and if there was a movement, advise Red Lion as soon as possible of the new location. The operators had GPS so Red Lion knew where they were always. The rest of the mission personnel were set to fly six days before the raid and two days before the ship docked. They would all be arriving during the day on three different flights. Tress and Sandy were monitoring traffic and so far, no problems with the Angolan Army had been detected. Don and Cindy were also tracking cell phone activity and it was busy. The rebels used cell phones to do most of their communicating. Sandy had been trying to interpret but was having trouble with the regional language. She could understand most of it, but the special phrases were her problem. She was getting enough to know the rebels were waiting for the money and she did find the name of the bank. Don had already hacked that bank and now all he needed was the account. On an off- chance Don looked for the name of the Colonel and sure as Hell he found an account under his name. The account had over $600,000 dollars, so Don knew it was the right account. Jim wanted Don to drain the account as soon as the hostages were free. Cindy was checking all the banks in the country for the name and using the account they had discovered to track all money in and out as to where the money had been sent if it was transferred. The information would be useful in the future.

John was at Molly's bar and he was talking to Molly about the mission. Molly said "John you need to stay here to make sure things go alright. I know you put Jim and Tress in charge and they will do fine, but what about Washington and all of that you need to be handling? Now we can go to Florida when this is over, and we will then be able to stay a lot longer and not have you under pressure".

John agreed and kissed Molly and said, "Thanks for understanding".

Molly smiled and said "Of course. I know what you do and how you do it so when the time is right we will go". John had another beer and walked around visiting with the people he knew. John saw Mike come in and walked over and said hello. Mike got a drink and then asked John if he could speak to him out on the patio. John followed, and the men sat down. Mike said "John we just received another contract and this one is in Kuwait. It looks like we are going to need about 100 of your people and the contract will take two years. I want to send you the requirement tomorrow if that is ok?".

John said "Yes Mike that would be fine. I will have Kevin work up a bid and get back to you. And my friend I have news. Molly and I have bought a beach house in Florida".

Mike said, "God damn John that is great, but are you going to move?"

John said "No we will be going there for a couple of weeks at a time, but I will still be at Red Lion. I have given Jim the CEO position and Tress is now the President. I am still Chairman and will be an advisor to them. I just will not be doing the day to day stuff anymore".

Mike said, "Well good luck but look at me when I tried to retire". John and Mike both laughed.

Word had come in from the operators on the ground in Angola that it looked like the hostages were not going to be moved. They also reported that normally there were fifty rebels in the town, always, and sometimes up to one hundred were there. The leader would have a meeting and then forty to sixty would leave. Jim and Tress did not like the odds but there was nothing they could do now. The Cobra was going to be damn busy as well as the door gunners on the Black Hawks. The raid was set to be done at night and with night vision Red Lion should have the advantage. Also, the element of surprise was in the operators favor. From the reports back from the operators on the ground, a landing area about one mile from the town would be the spot to drop the operators. They could then make their way into the area of the buildings and attack without being seen. The attack was set for 2 AM so only two guards would be out or at least that was the way it had been. The ground operators would take out the guards before the choppers came in so there would be no possibility of hearing them. Then the operators would go into the building housing the hostages and secure them. The Black Hawk operators were going to split into two groups and attack the remaining buildings. The Cobra and the Black Hawks would be about 5 miles out until the attack started. Then they would come over the area and serve as a covering force until all resistance was eliminated. The Black Hawks would then land and load the hostages and the operators and return to the ship. The Cobra would remain until all personnel were gone from the area and then return to the ship. Once the choppers were back on the ship, the choppers would be placed back into the containers and all the equipment would also be placed back into the containers. The ship would then travel to South Africa and put in to port. The hostages would be taken off and immediately turned over to the South African government.

The operators, air crews, mechanics and medical personnel and armors would then exit the ship and go to the airport and fly back to the US. That was the plan and now it was time to see how well it would work.

The Black Hawks had left the ship and the Cobra was leaving when the transmission was received at Red Lion headquarters. The raid was now in full gear. The ground operators moved swiftly and eliminated both guards in the front of the building holding the hostages, then they went inside and got the hostages ready to leave. The Black Hawks came down and the operators were off in less than thirty seconds. Nelson led the first team into the main building and immediately took out two rebels. Other operators were inside and took out four more rebels. Nelson had told the operators to not kill the women unless, absolutely necessary, and three women immediately ran out of the building screaming. Two women did grab AK-47 rifles and were instantly killed by the operators. Nelson went into the room in the rear and saw the Colonel and shoot him in the forehead. Other operators killed the three rebels in the room with the Colonel and the two women ran out as the other ones had done. Outside Rebels were firing at the operators and the Cobra made a pass firing the Gatlin Gun. Seven rebels were instantly killed. The second building was full of rebels and the operators that went inside faced heavy fire. Two operators were shot and went down. The operators retreated, and the Cobra made a run firing rockets into the building. The building exploded and was torn apart. The Cobra then made another run firing the 20MM cannons and then a final pass using the Gatlin Gun once again. On the right side of the building a group, fifteen rebels, came in from other buildings in the town and were shot by the operators. The Black Hawks came in and started covering fire. Then one Black Hawk landed, and the operators helped the hostages on the chopper. As soon as the hostages were on board the 6 operators got on and the chopper lifted off and then was the covering unit. The second Black Hawk landed and all the remaining operators, including the two wounded, boarded. The medic was on the second Black Hawk so that was why the wounded operators were loaded on that chopper and not on the first one. The medic immediately went to work on the wounded operators and the Black Hawks left for the ship. The Cobra made one final pass firing machine gun fire into all the buildings and then fired one rocket at a vehicle that was approaching from the town. The vehicle had rebels in the back of the bed and a machine gun mounted on the roof. The rocket hit the truck and it exploded and flew into pieces. The rebels were thrown out and killed immediately. The Cobra then headed for the ship. The entire raid was over in fifteen minutes from start to finish. The mission accomplished signal was sent to Red Lion.

The container ship reached port in South Africa in one day. It docked and re-fueled. The operators and other personnel got off and the wounded operators were immediately taken to the hospital. Nelson and three other operators took the hostages to the police station and left them. The hostages went in and told the story. Nelson and his men were almost back on the container ship when the hostages went into the station. Nelson had asked then to wait five minutes before going inside and they had. Nelson checked everything and then left with the rest of the operators and headed to the airport. Cabs had been waiting for them at the dock and they had changed into their civilian attire on the ship. In one hour the ship left the port on the way back to the US. The operators and others boarded their plane and took off. The plane would stop in Paris then come directly to the US. The mission had gone well. The wounded operators were in the hospital and one operator had remained to safeguard them. His report was encouraging. Both men were out of surgery and now resting. Condition was good. They would be there for about five days. A message had been sent to Washington as soon as the hostages had gotten on the Black Hawk. Now a follow up message was sent so Washington had the news before the Angolan government informed them. John congratulated Jim and Tress on the operation. John was very pleased. He knew the corporation was in good hands.

The next day the TV was going crazy. Reporters were all over the city of Luanda and were reporting the stupidest things about the rescue. The hostages had given statements that men in black had rescued them and taken them to an ocean liner then to the police station. Of course, no one believed them so now the investigation was on by the media. The US and Brittan gave a joint statement thanking the UN and the Angolan Army for the successful return of the hostages. Neither of the parties thanked had any idea why they were being thanked. John had told Jim and Tress he would take care of sending the invoice to Washington and had Sara send it that morning. The bill was for $80 Million Dollars and John was sure it would be paid as usual. It was in less than three hours.

# CHAPTER 37

Two weeks had passed, and the ship and the wounded operators were all back. Jim and Tress had gotten everything done on the after-action reports that were done after every mission. Lessons learned was a key to not making the same mistakes again and John demanded that. Before any operation the files were searched for any similar operations that had been done and studied. That way no slip up could occur. It had been a great way to do things and Jim and Tress wanted it continued. Each operator had been debriefed and had done a field report. The same was required of the aviation assets and the ship. The reports were then consolidated and placed in the computer. The supply personnel had already ordered the replacement equipment and ammunitions for the unit. They would go to Ft. Hood on Friday to pick up the special ammunitions required for the Cobra and the Black Hawk guns. Things were about back to normal. Kevin had received and bid the KBR Kuwait job and Dan had already prepared the contract for it. Nancy had an interview scheduled for Jim's secretary and she really thought he would like her.

Don had a piece of information he wanted John, Jim and Tress to see as soon as possible. They all met in John's office and Don walked in and said "Gentlemen I think I have found the true mole that gives us away. He is in the White House and his name is Bill Sanders. He was there when the last President was there, and he still has the same damn job. He is the computer repair man for the White House and can get into every damn thing they do". Everyone sat very still.

John said" Don, are you positive about this?"

Don said "Yes. Cindy and I have been going through all the emails from Stevens we recovered on his computer and this guy Sanders has emailed over 2000 times during the past four years. I have recovered most of the emails and they plainly tell the story of Red Lion, of you John, and of the special CIA account that is used to pay us. They also tell about the operations we have done for the Presidents and about the no-bid contracts we have. Hell, this guy has everything we do and has sent it to Stevens and God knows who else. We considered his banking, and he has an off-shore account in the Cayman Islands that has over $220 Million Dollars in it as of today. He damn sure did not make that working for the government and his local bank account always stays below $5000 each week. I would say this bastard has another account in the States but so far, we have not found it. Cindy is still looking".

John said "Well we need to know everything about this guy and we need to then make a very simple plan to eliminate him. We need to know who else he may have contacted about us. Also, can we track the incoming deposits into his Cayman account?"

Don said "We can do that, but I do not think we can track back to the original source. In other words, we can get the bank the money came from but not the account. That would be impossible!"

John said "Ok then get as much on this fucker as you can and get it to Tress and Sandy. Also get a copy to Jim and me. Thanks Don. This is great work". Don left and went back to his office. Jim and Tress sat and looked at John. John said "We have to stop this guy and recover everything we can. We also need to find out if he had other media involved and get the information back from them if he did. You guys need to develop a plan quickly and we need to get him stopped even before we have all the information on his other contacts. This looks like we may be in the torture business, but we have Hallettsville to use if we need to do so. Can we have something in 24 hours we can work with?"

Tress said "Yes we can. But, it may be messy".

Jim said "I really do not care we have to stop this guy and we need to do it now. John should we let Washington know?"

John said "Absolutely not! They would want to get involved because he is in the White House and they would of course have the FBI involved and that would take years to get anything done. Also, this guy might not have broken any laws, they could charge him under. No, we need to do this without anyone knowing. Just a bad accident. Hell, we will send flowers". Jim and Tress left and headed to do the planning.

The next twenty-four hours were very busy for Tress, Jim, Don and Cindy. Sandy was working on finding exactly what this Sanders guy did daily, and exactly what his route to and from work was including times he left to go to work and times he usually got home. Sandy had his vehicle information and address, so she had had Cindy hack the traffic cameras in the area Sanders lived and she had weeks of footage to go through. Sandy cut down the search time by only going back one week. She found a pattern immediately, so she was confident this asshole would be doing the same exact thing most of the time. The weekends were also looked at as to the travel showing on the traffic cameras. Sandy had Cindy ready to hack the cameras on Saturday morning, so Sandy could see live what was happening. Tress and Jim had a plan formed and it called for operators to grab Sanders and bring him to Hallettsville for interrogation. It was going to be impossible for anyone to get the information needed or to find out if the only source was Stevens without making Sanders tell. John had approved the idea and Harry had been informed that he needed to make a place to do the work. It was going to be bad with SWAT people all over the place, but Harry had something in mind, so Tress and Jim left that totally up to Harry.

Tress had Nelson and three other operators in his office when Jim and John walked in. Everyone stood, and John said, "OK good morning please sit". Tress started his briefing. Aerial photos taken thirty minutes before were displayed on one of the TV monitors. The photos showed Sander's house and the surrounding streets as well as the houses on either side of Sanders' house. Tress pointed to the house and said "Gentlemen, this is our target and it does have surveillance cameras and alarms, so we will have to eliminate them on entry, but we need to make damn sure they are functioning when you exit. The cameras do not have to be working, they will be scrambled to look like a malfunction, but the alarm must be re-set. Don and Cindy can then hack the alarm company and reset the computer to show no activation or that the alarm was off. Sanders has on dogs or cats, so we are clear on that front. The neighbors are pretty much elderly, so they will not be up late, and I believe that 2 AM is our best strike time. The police do patrol but we have a fix for that. Cindy will put in a call to draw the cops away from the area for at least thirty minutes so that is your window. Sanders lives only about thirty or forty minutes from the airport we will use so travel will be fine. The plan is to get inside and drug him, so you can then take him to the aircraft. We have a leased jet, the same crew we always use, so no questions will be asked. The jet will fly directly to Hallettsville and land. Once you get there Harry will direct everything. Now any questions?"

Nelson said "Ok what about the search of his house? Do we do it or just take his computer and hard drive and all of his equipment or what?"

Jim said "We will use the thumb drive down load then put in the virus Don will give you to whip the computer hard drive. Also, we need to do a search to find out if he as a safe or anything like that and to see what he may have there. If possible, we do not want to make it look like anything was touched or out of the ordinary. One of you will drive his car to the airport and put it in long term parking before you leave. Make damn sure the driver is covered as to his face as best he can be without raising suspicion. At that time of morning, no one is on duty so there should be no problems. The briefing was finished, and Nelson and his team left. Tress and Jim looked at John and Jim said, "Are we Ok on this Sir?"

John said "Yes perfect. If there are problems the operators know to eliminate Sanders in the event things go bad. Right?"

Tress said, "They will have that order before they depart, Sir".

John said "Fine". Jim had originally come up with the idea to use the same flight crew on the leased jets. The planes would be different, because the tail numbers could be traced if someone wanted to do so, but with as many jets coming and going it was not likely anyone would put it together if different planes were used. The flight crew was paid special above their salary from the company that Red Lion leased the planes from. Jim always made sure each member of the crew got an envelope containing $10,000 in cash for the flight. The crew would not jeopardize that for anything, so no one talked about what had happened on any flight.

Sandy had watched the traffic cameras on Saturday and now knew what Sanders did on his day off. He was truly a creature of habit. He left his house at 9 AM and drove only one mile to a shopping center and had coffee at a small café. That took about an hour. Then he was next seen driving to a park about one mile from his house. He parked and walked through the park for about thirty minutes then returned to his house. He was home by 11 AM. Sanders car was not seen again on the traffic cameras the entire day. Sandy told Tress the 2 AM time would be good. If someone missed Sanders, it would not be before 9:15 AM or so and then they would probably think he was working or something. He had not met up with anyone as far as Sandy could find out. Tress was satisfied so the mission was on for the next Saturday morning at 2 AM. Nelson was informed, and he and his team prepared.

The jet left Sugarland at noon on Thursday and arrived in Washington D.C. at the National Airport at 2 PM. The operators rented an SUV and drove to Arlington, VA and around the neighborhood where Sanders lived. They observed the house and took a few photos with the cell phone cameras. They rented a hotel and then at 1 AM Friday morning the operators went back to Sanders' house and observed the streets and the area for six blocks around the house. They drove so no one would be suspicious of the vehicle and after they were satisfied, returned to the hotel. They would check out the next day and go to an area to wait until 2 AM. They had decided on a spot that stayed open until 3 AM and was a western dance place for their waiting. The checkout would be at 3 PM on Friday so they could sleep until 2 PM. Nelson was a professional at all of this and so were his operators. Things were ready, and Tress and Jim were watching and waiting. Don and Cindy would empty the bank accounts both in Cayman and in the US bank at 9 AM on Saturday morning.

At exactly 2 AM on Saturday the operators disabled the cameras and the alarm and entered Sanders' house. They made their way down the hall to the bedroom and saw Sanders sleeping. Nelson had the injection ready and two operators grabbed Sanders and Nelson injected him with the drug that knocked him out. Sanders was then tied hand and foot with flex ties and his mouth was taped. The operators then searched the entire house. One computer was sitting in the bedroom and Nelson down loaded the information on that computer then put the worm in to wipe the entire hard drive. Another computer was discovered in the study and Nelson again down loaded that computer to a thumb drive and again put in the virus to wipe the hard drive. One operator found a laptop and Nelson decided to take that when they left. The operators continued to search and found nothing of value to lead Red Lion to any source Sanders may have been in contact with. Nelson and an operator then carried Sanders out to the SUV and one operator backed Sanders' car out of the garage and pulled out onto the street. The alarm was re-set and Cindy was notified. Cindy had sent the fake call for service to the police three minutes before the operators had entered the house, so no police vehicles were in the area. The operators then left with Sanders' car following and drove to the airport. Sanders' car was parked in long term parking and the operator was picked up and the entire team went to the private terminal. The operators drove into the hanger and loaded Sanders into the jet and loaded all their equipment back on board. One operator returned the SUV to the rental area and then boarded the jet. At 4 AM the jet was cleared for takeoff and was on the way to Hallettsville. The jet touched down in Hallettsville at the air strip of the ranch at 12 noon. Harry was there to meet the team and Sanders. Nelson told Harry that Sanders had been drugged so Harry knew what to do and how long it would take to have him come out of the drugged state. Nelson then left two operators with Harry and he and the other operator re-boarded the jet and flew back to Sugarland with the laptop computer and the thumb drives to give to Don. Harry, the operators and Sanders drove to a special building that had been constructed on the far side of the compound out of sight of any other buildings and put Sanders in a chair in the middle of the 10-foot by 10-foot cell, that had been especially built in the building. The room the cell was in had been set up with lights, speakers and other items that would be used to gain the necessary information from Sanders. Then the operators and Harry waited for Sanders to start to revive. It took about two hours for that to happen. Don had created a trail for Sanders using his credit cards and other items. The trail showed Sanders leaving Washington on a flight at 6 AM Saturday morning and going non-stop to Paris. Then another flight was shown leaving Paris the next day going to Turkey. Then another flight going to Moscow. The trail ended there. The passenger list showed Sanders as being on each flight and his credit cards showed that he had bought tickets. Now when he did not show up for work on Monday and finally when he was discovered missing the agencies would have a trail and that would put them into a frenzy. John liked that part of the plan the best. John knew that the CIA, NSA, NIS, and the military would be going nuts about a possible defector with the type knowledge he might have. When someone finally got into his computer it would be totally clean with no history of any activity and that would really show he was rogue.

Don had the laptop and was going through it. Cindy had the thumb drives and she was working that with all her skills. Most of the information on the thumb drive from the computer in the den/study was not of any value. The information on the computer in the bedroom was another story. It contained the files Sanders had created showing all the Red Lion operations, the agreements with the government, and some of the money payments that had been made. John was furious about the fact that some stupid bastard had recorded the money payments and did not use the cover that had been set up for that. He was also just as mad that the records of Red Lion had been placed on a computer that was in the White House. Both Presidents had been the same and they were so fucking dumb John wondered how in the Hell they could even think about running the country. The information would have put both men in federal prison not including all the Red Lion personnel. "God what next?" John thought. The computer experts at Red Lion were really having a hard time gaining access to Sanders files on many things. The files were protected with passwords that if tried more than two times would lock the files for at least thirty days before they could be opened. The only way around that was to re-program the clock and dates on the computer and that was taking a chance that it would lock the whole thing, so no one could ever get in. Don was trying everything he knew to figure out the passwords before he tried to open the accounts. Don told Tress and Jim about the problem and they called Harry and told him.

Harry had requested a copy of the file log be faxed to him and when he got it he looked at it very carefully. Most of the files were named with trick names and only a few were real files that a person could look at the name and know what it was about. Harry scanned the list into a computer and headed back to the building that Sanders was being held in. It was now time to get things started and started they would be. Harry and the two operators walked to the cell, opened the door and the operators went into the cell and untied Sanders from his chair and took off the blind fold and the tape from his mouth. They then pushed Sanders out of the cell and forced him into another room. The room was empty except for a table holding a computer and one chair. The operators told Sanders to sit and he did. Harry walked over to Sanders and had him face toward the middle of the room. Harry then stood about two feet in front of Sanders and said" Mr. Sanders I believe you realize who we are. Just to make it very clear to you we are the organization you have been selling information about for the past few years. Yes, we know about your Cayman account and others and yes, we know you gave information to Stevens on us. We also know that you have fourteen files that are password protected and set up to be locked for at least thirty days if the wrong password is tried. Now Mr. Sanders you have one chance and only one chance to survive this. I have placed the file names on the computer in this room. You will go to the side of each file using the computer and put in the password for that file and it will be right because we will try it and if it is wrong we will then be left with no choice but to torture you until you give us the right password. Now if you think you can play with us and not give us the right passwords before we lock the computer, remember we will hold you alive for the thirty-day period and then start again. You have no choice but to cooperate with us or the pain will be more than you can imagine, and we can keep it going and keep you alive for years or for as long as it will take. Now to make clear you understand, we will give you IV Injections, to give you fluids and nourishment so you will stay alive until we get what we want. Do you understand?"

Sanders nodded his head and started to speak. One of the operators hit him across the face and said "Shut up. You do not speak. You just work the computer". Sanders studied the operators and Harry. He waited for a minute and refused to work on the computer. Harry motioned to an operator and the operator put a stun gun to Sanders' neck and fired. The jolt shook Sanders and he fell backwards from the chair. The operators picked him up and put him back in the chair. Harry said "Now what is the password. Type it next to the file name, now!" Sanders hesitated again, and Harry looked at the biggest operator and said, "He needs more persuading I believe". The operator grabbed Sanders and threw him against a wall and then hit him about four times in the stomach. Sanders screamed in pain. The operator then put Sanders back in the chair and Harry said, "Now the passwords". Sanders still refused so Harry had the electric shock machine brought out. Sanders was tied to the chair by the big operator and the other operator clamped two electrodes to Sanders chest and two to his stomach. The machine was turned on and Harry pushed the button. The shock went into Sanders and he jumped in the chair. Harry hit the button once more and Sanders screamed in pain and jumped in the chair again. Harry stepped in front of Sanders and said, "Now we need the passwords". Sanders nodded. The operators released Sanders and he immediately started typing passwords to the side of each file. When he was finished, Harry placed the file in the save mode and then sent an email with the file attached to Don. Sanders was then taken back to the room with the cell and placed into the cell. The operators left the room and Sanders was all alone. The cameras showed Sanders sitting on the cell floor and not moving.

Don received the email from Harry and started trying the passwords that had been typed by Sanders. Every password worked and in three minutes all the files were open. Don studied the files and discovered only four files had anything to do with Red Lion. The Red Lion files were very complete and showed all the missions that had been given to the corporation. Another file showed the payments out of the special CIA account and exactly how much and where the money had been sent. Another file showed the listing of all the military personnel that had been originally assigned to Red Lion and the last file showed the purchases of equipment that had been made for the aircraft, weapons, operator equipment and showed the agreement that was in place with Ft. Hood for supply of ammunition. Don looked at the other files and discovered a file containing bank account numbers for five off shore banks and a complete list of payments made into that account. The payments were coded so additional information would be needed to break the code. Then Don hit a gold mine. There was a group of five files that had information on the past President and the current President. This was information of a very personal nature and was very damaging if it ever went public. The files included information on the sexual habits, the money received from various individuals and corporations that was sent directly to the private accounts of the men and listings of stock that had been set aside for each President when they left office and who the brokerage firm was that controlled these stocks. Don immediately called John, Jim and Tress and had all three come to the computer room. Don showed the group what he had. John told Don to make a copy on a disk and get it to John as soon as possible. Jim and Tress wondered what else Sanders knew or may have given to someone for money. The bank accounts were now a total of $630 Million Dollars and that meant Sanders had been selling information for a long time. Some of the file entries were dated six years back. Before Red Lion had even started. Don sent an email to Harry and told him that the codes were needed for the payments that had been received. Don also sent a list of the codes needed.

Harry got the email and went back to the building Sanders was in. Harry told Sanders what was needed, and Sanders quickly gave Harry the information about the codes. Then Harry turned on the recording devices and sat with Sanders and talked to him asking questions for over three hours. At the end of the discussion and talk Harry was convinced Sanders had told Harry everything Sanders knew. Harry called John on the SAT phone and told John and John said "OK CSM eliminate the problem". Harry walked back into the room where Sanders was and shot him in the center of the forehead. The body was loaded into the bed of a pickup truck and taken away. Harry would dispose of the body. The next morning a Black Hawk arrived for training and after the training was completed the operators that had been in D.C. boarded and the Black Hawk returned to Sugarland. The operators off loaded and went for a de-briefing and then home. The Sanders situation was closed for now. On Thursday Don had taken every cent out of all the bank accounts and had it in the special Red Lion accounts. Then Don had wiped clean the bank records. John had called Liz and wanted a meeting with the President and her as soon as it could be arranged. Liz called back and told John that if he would be in Washington on Sunday, the President could meet at 3 PM in the White House. John decided to take the chance and agreed. Nancy arranged a flight by private jet and a room at the Army Navy Hotel. John had also contacted the former President and wanted a meeting with him as well. That meeting was set for Houston Texas on Saturday at the Lakeside Country Club where the ex-President would be attending a fund raiser for the Republican Party. John was now ready to get every damn thing he wanted when he wanted it from both men.

# CHAPTER 38

ohn and Molly arrived at the Lakeside Country Club and went into the smaller ballroom. That was where the bar was set up and people were gathering and visiting. The main ball room was set for the fund-raising dinner and John was not staying for that. It would be a good cover being seen in the bar area and no one would notice if he and Molly were not at the dinner. Jim and Latoya had come with John and Molly and that was great because when John and Jim met with the Ex-President, no one would notice the women being alone. John and Jim circulated and talked with various people for about 30 minutes. A young man came up to John and Jim and said "Gentlemen would you both please come with me. The President is waiting for you". John and Jim followed the man into a private room that was down a hallway toward the end of the club house. The secret service agents knocked on the door and then allowed John and Jim entry. The ex-President was sitting in a chair and stood up as John and Jim entered. The ex-President said, "God damn John and Jim, nice to see you both but what the Hell is so fucking urgent you had me come to a special room?"

John said "Sir, we have a bunch of problems, well we did have and may still do but we are here to brief you". Everyone sat down, and John said "Mr. President there has been a major leak in the White House and it started when you were there and continued until about 5 days ago. It is now contained well eliminated but there may be problems for you and we wanted you to know firsthand".

The ex-President said, "OK go on and tell me what is going on".

John outlined the situation and told the ex-President about the files on him and his money, stocks, contributions into the special fund and the facts that he had created Red Lion and had authorized the payment out of special secret funds for services. John also explained that one reporter did have the story but that had been taken care of and that the leak had been from a contract worker hired by IBM and not part of the administration. John was upset about how much information had been put into files and that no one kept it classified as John had been promised. When John finished, the ex-President said, "Well John, do you think it will get out?"

John said, "We do not know for sure, but we have done everything we can to make sure it does not, Mr. President".

Jim said "Mr. President, there is no way to know if anyone else has copies but so far we do not think that they do or it sure as Hell would have come out before now. Most of the information this guy sold was about foreign relation things and of course covert operations and us. The stuff about you and all that I think he was saving for the last big payoff. It looks like that to us from what we can gather".

The ex-President said "Who are we talking about? Names John".

John said "Well the first one was Stevens with CBS, but he had the heart attack, so nothing went any further because his notes were never found. Then the second guy and the actual mole was a guy named Sanders and he was the contractor that worked in the IT section of the White House and no one ever replaced him when the administrations changed. He was not a White House employee, so he was just never looked at. He from all indications fled the country but trust us when we tell you he left all of his information before he fled".

The President look at John and Jim and then said, "I really do not want to know more about this do I?"

John said "No Mr. President you do not. Just want you to know there is a chance a very small chance that something may still be out there, but we are still working the situation. We have always protected you and we intend to continue to do that". John and Jim thanked the ex-President for seeing them and left the room. They had been with the man for damn near an hour. John and Jim found the ladies and the four of them left and went to dinner at Eddie V's and enjoyed it very much.

John and Molly were picked up at the airport in Sugarland by the jet and headed to Washington. It was 9 AM on Sunday. When they landed in Washington, John got a taxi to go to the hotel. He wanted to be very low key and certainly did not want a staff car or a car from the White House to meet the plane. John got checked into the room and took a quick shower and dressed in a fresh shirt, tie and suit. Molly was already headed for the spa and John went to the lobby and had a taxi called. John arrived at the White House and was passed through security and taken inside the south doors. Liz was waiting, and they took the elevator to the residence. John and Liz entered the residence and the President met them. The President was dressed in casual clothes and showed them into a sitting room and had them sit down. He offered John and Liz a drink and the attendant got the drinks and then left the room. The President said "John what is so damn important? I thought you did not want to come here anymore? Has something changed?"

John said, "Mr. President you and I have big problems, but I am afraid yours are the biggest". John explained in detail what had happened and about Stevens and Sanders. He also explained about the files and that some had, likely, been sold to the Republican National Committee. John stressed the fact that people in the administration had recorded many of the payments, missions, and special deals that the President and the government had with Red Lion and when it was all put together the entire picture was there. Sanders was the guy who had put it all together because he had access to every fucking computer in Washington and no one ever knew. The President sat unable to say anything for a few minutes. Liz was in total shock and only whimpered a little when John hit certain points during his talk. John waited until the President spoke.

The President said, "Then it is my understanding that this guy Sanders has been eliminated and so was Stevens?"

John said "Sir, Stevens died of a heart attack. He was with CBS and you probably saw it on TV. It seems like Sanders fled the country and may be in Moscow, or so the trail says".

The President then said, "But none of the files survived is that right, John?"

John said "None that will ever be seen. Red Lion has all the original files, so they are safe. Mr. President. But now here is your problem. The Republican's probably have the files Sanders did on your stock special deals, the special money that was contributed and put in the off-shore accounts and any special deals you ever did with anyone. Now I advise you and Liz to get the money out and put it somewhere no one can ever find it. I have people that can do that, but only if nothing else will work. That must be done instantly. The stocks are a Hell of a problem so again they need to be changed out of your name and something done with them and that needs to be done as soon as you can without raising any red flags. The rest of it is on you, Mr. President. We have covered you from the Red Lion end, but we have no idea what else is going on and should not know".

The President said, "I will see to this tonight. Now what about the leaks? Can they be stopped or is it just the way it is here?"

John said "Mr. President, I think that is just the way it is, but by not putting anything in writing or talking when the fucking recordings are on it will help. That is always the God Damn problem. People want to cover their ass, so they make damn sure they have a record and that is what bites you in the ass. The damn record".

The President said "Yes I know John and maybe we are all too cautious. Now is there anything you need from me right now?"

John said "Sir, I only want to continue to serve you and to do what we must to protect the country and you. I will let you know if we need more but right now with what we have in place we are golden". The President stood up and John and Liz did as well. John and the President shook hands and Liz said "I will show you out John. Mr. President I will be back as soon as I get John taken care of". The President nodded, and John and Liz left the residence. When Liz and John stepped out of the elevator, Liz said "John how bad is it for the President?"

John said "Liz if this really gets out he is finished and of course will not be reelected. Hell! He may face jail time if they want him bad enough in Congress. He has the Democrats in the Senate so that should cover him but who knows in Washington. Just get him covered and tell him to let us do most of the stuff he is always trying to negotiate. Hell, that never works and you and I both know it. Well I will see you and be talking to you. Thanks Liz". John went out the door and got into the waiting taxi and went back to the hotel. It was past 7 PM and he was hungry. Molly was waiting in the room, so John washed his face and they headed for the restaurant. John had decided on the Williamsburg Steak House for dinner. It was supposed to be the best in Washington D.C. Molly and John would see. The flight back was scheduled for 9 AM so they had plenty of time for dinner and anything else they wanted to do.

John was in his office at 6 AM on Tuesday and Jim and Tress were there with him. John briefed the men on the visits with both Presidents and said, "I believe we are going to be very busy, soon. The President is getting the picture that all this bullshit talk does not get the job done so I think he wants to use us more now that he fully understands that we cover his ass no matter what". Jim and Tress agreed.

Jim said "John you need to meet my new secretary. She is something else and where the Hell does Nancy and Barbara get these people?"

John said "I have no idea. Yes, get her now, Jim". Jim buzzed his phone and told his new secretary to come to John's office. In two minutes a tall mid-thirties woman walked into the office. Jim said, "John this is Pam, my secretary".

Pam said, "Sir nice to meet you".

John said "Yes nice to meet you. Now make sure your boss keeps his nose to the grind OK?" Everyone laughed. Pam left and went back to Jim's office. The contractors were due to make her an office next to Jim's.

John said, "OK Jim, tell me her story".

Jim said "She is 39 and a retired Sergeant First Class from the Army. She was in admin all her career and ran several school admin departments as well as serving as the admin NCOIC for General Hughes in Europe for six years while he was the Commander there. She knows her business and is very likable but efficient".

John said "Great".

# CHAPTER 39

Things were really going good at Red Lion, so John was ready to go to Florida. The plans were made, and Molly and John boarded the lease jet and took off at 9 Am for the new house. They landed in Orlando and rented a car and drove to the new town. Molly had seen a nice motel, so John and Molly got a room and then contacted the real estate agent and met with him to get the keys for the house. The paperwork had been done and Dan had taken care of all of it after John and Molly signed as required. John and Molly drove to the house and went inside. Dan had also had the utilities turned on so the only thing missing was furniture. John and Molly had decided to wait on the furniture until the contractors had completed the extra work they wanted so the next day they would meet with the contractor John had spoken with about 3 weeks earlier. John and Molly looked around the house and then left to go see the entire town again.

Redman Beach had a population of 25,000 and was a resort town primarily. The town was sectioned off with the beach and beach front bars and restaurants and the night clubs on one side of the town and on the other side was the area that the fishing boats used. The boats were for charter and took parties or individuals out for the day fishing in the Atlantic. The city hall, police and the main fire station were all located off main street about three miles inland from the beach area. Three more fire stations were spread out across the town. The hospital, 200 beds with Emergency Room and four clinics was located at the northern end of the city three miles from the beach. On the southern end of the city there was the country club and golf course. The golf course was open to the public, but the club was membership only. Two miles beyond the country club was the airport. The airport was small but there was plenty of land to expand it if necessary. Behind the hospital was the mall shopping and it was very nice. It contained about twenty stores with the anchor stores being Lowes and Macey's. There were three large grocery stores and numerous small businesses all over the town. The court house and legal center was five blocks behind the city hall and city government building and the Sheriff's department and Jail were located there. The town had four good first-class restaurants and two plate lunch type restaurants all located on main street. There was every type of fast food restaurant any one could think of and more than one of some of them. Liquor stores were located throughout the town and of course the car dealers were there. Two dealerships were located on the main highway south of town and the fairgrounds was also there. The place was very nice, and John and Molly liked it immediately. There were twenty motels located on the beach and on the highway on both ends of the town and one major truck stop was on the north end about two miles out of the city. The rest of Redman Beach was housing mainly single family but there were some very nice apartment buildings scattered over the city. Of course, there was the low-rent area but surprisingly that area was not as bad as other places. The city had good control. The police force was large, but John figured that was because of the tourist business. John and Molly's house was at the south end of the beach area and in a very nice division. The street only had six houses on it and dead ended so no thru traffic would be a problem. John and Molly were at the end of the street with on one on one side of them. After the drive around town John and Molly went to the beach area and walked around checking out the clubs and bars. They both liked the entire area and found a great bar to call home. The bar was named Ted's and the owner was a retired Navy SEAL. John was at home immediately.

The next day John and Molly met with the contractor and went over what they wanted done. The contractor was a local builder and he did have an architect that he used to draw plans so John made an appointment to have the contractor and architect meet at the house on Friday at 10 AM. John then called back to Red Lion and had Don and Cindy schedule a jet to Orlando and then told them to rent a car and drive to Redman Beach and be there Thursday about 5 PM. Don was also to bring the specifications he needed for the cameras, exterior lighting, computer hook ups, fax lines, and any other electrical items he would need to install. Cindy would get with the internet people in town and have what was needed installed when the contractor called. After John had finished with his call he and Molly drove to the bank and opened an account for her and two accounts for John. One was his personal account the other was a Red Lion account. The bank was given instructions to transfer $8 Million Dollars to John's and $4 Million Dollars to Molly's account. Then a transfer of $75 Million Dollars was to be made to the Red Lion account. John called his bank in Houston and had the transfers done via his phone call. In less than thirty minutes the Redman Beach bank had the money and the accounts were open. After the bank John and Molly went to the country club and became members there. Molly wanted to have lunch on the beach, so they went to a small little restaurant and had lunch and it was wonderful. John was liking the area better and better, and Molly was just in heaven.

The next morning, John was up and dressed in a suit and tie and left Molly sleeping. John drove to city hall and asked to speak to the Mayor. In about twenty minutes the Mayor's secretary showed John into the Mayor's office. John introduced himself and talked to the Mayor about the airport. The city owned the facility and it was not a money maker. It had originally been built by a man who had almost owned the whole town, but he had died, and he left the airport to the city in his will. The city did not have the money to expand or even modernize the facility, so it was just there. John found out that the area left to the city was 120 acers and the current airport only took up 44 acers of the land. Also, there was an additional 240 acers that was adjacent to the airport and was always for sale. John asked the Mayor if the city would be willing to sell the airport to Red Lion his company. The Mayor said, "I think we probably would, but it would be up to the city council to say yes or no and we would need to get a price figured out as to what we think it is worth".

John said "Mr. Mayor could you do that for me? I would love to meet with the city council and present my idea to them". The Mayor agreed to find out about the airport and to call John about the City Council meeting. Usually the meeting was the first Monday of the month unless something special was to be discussed. The Mayor would let John know when he could speak. John thanked the Mayor and left and returned to the motel and changed clothes. Molly was up and having coffee. John and Molly went to the beach area and had breakfast and then to Ted's and had a few drinks.

Don and Cindy had arrived, and John and Molly took them to Ted's bar then to dinner on the beach. Everyone enjoyed the entire night. The next morning everyone was up by 7 AM and Cindy wanted to be at the internet company at 8 AM sharp. The company serviced internet and cable, but Cindy did not know how good they would be for John's needs. John and Molly drove to the house and started look around again. The contractor and his architect arrived about 9:30 AM and Don and Cindy arrived about the same time. John told the contractor that he wanted two additions, one being an office and the other being an exercise room. Then the master bath needed to be totally re-done and a dressing area and two walk-in closets put into the area. John also wanted the kitchen totally redone. After John had said what he wanted the contractor said, "OK I will start with the bathroom area in the master bedroom". Molly and the contractor and the architect walked to the bathroom and Molly explained exactly what she wanted done. The contractor and the architect made notes. Everything was discussed including the plugs for the electricity. The outlet for a TV cable hookup and the lighting. The bath fixtures Molly would pick out the next day at the showroom the contractor used. Molly would also pick out the kitchen fixtures and any other plumbing items necessary. The contractor told Molly that he also needed her to go to the lighting showroom and pick out the fixtures she wanted for the rooms and other places. He was sending one of his office staff to meet her and make sure everything was written down. The same person would be at the plumbing place, so Molly decided to meet at the contractor's office and then go with his person. Next John showed the contractor and the architect exactly what he needed in the way of the office and made damn sure they had a built in safe set in a wall of concrete that was about waist high for the dials. John then had Don tell the two of them exactly what electrical and other requirements would be needed for plugs and other things. Cindy had the internet man with her and was explaining and showing him where to install everything he would be doing. The entire house was gone through to include the outside and the fence was discussed. When everyone was satisfied that they totally understood what was required, John said "I need a bid on this Monday and we need to start on Tuesday. I need it done in thirty days or sooner".

The contractor said "I will be able to guarantee it done by the first of April, but weather may be a problem if we do not get the new rooms done. We will do our best Mr. Carter".

John said "I know you will and I would like to make it a bonus contract if you would accept that. On or before the 1st of April and a 25% bonus will apply. After the 3rd of April a 1% penalty for every three days late will apply. Is that a fair offer?"

The contractor said, "Yes that is very fair, and I accept that willingly". Everyone left, and John and Molly took Don and Cindy to lunch and then they left and drove back to Orlando and got the jet back to Texas.

The next morning John drove Molly to the contractor's office and she met the lady that would take her around. Molly and the lady left, and John drove to the airport. John looked over what was there and looked at what would be needed for the airport to become a working facility and be able to land commercial jets as well as other planes. The runway was going to be the biggest expense and the taxi ways. Then a terminal was needed as well as fuel storage and pump areas. The airport had no navigation equipment or landing lights so actually John would have to build a complete airport. The cost would probably be well over $1 Billion Dollars when finished, but Hell Red Lion had that kind of money and John could see the need for a base of operations closer to the areas he figured they would be working in. He would see how it went with the city council. John then drove to the police station and looked over the situation. He liked the way the cars were maintained, and John saw that the station had satellite equipment installed on the roof. The Sheriff's department did also as John saw. Molly called on his cell and said she would be a while so why did John not go to the country club and look it over. She would have her escort drop her there. John agreed. Molly arrived at the country club and met John in the bar. Molly was excited and told John about everything she had done and about the paint, drapes, the new flooring and the rest of the things she had picked out. John was glad Molly had the chance to really get involved with the new house and now get exactly what she wanted. They stayed at the country club and had dinner. Then they went back to the hotel and went to bed. The next morning John and Molly drove back to Orlando and took the jet back to Texas.

# CHAPTER 40

John was looking over the new clients and the requirements that Red Lion was now going to have to fill. KBR now needed fifty new operators for their contracts in Kuwait and Jim had moved some of the operators that had been in Iraq to that job. The Malaysian government had contacted Red Lion about a problem they were having with terrorist kidnapping civilian workers from US and British companies working in the oil business there. Jim and Tress were working the details and Kevin was working the cost for services. Sandy had been studying the developing problems in Chad and monitoring the "chatter" from the intelligence communities. Chad was becoming an ever increasing, problem and the US was trying not to get drawn into the situation. The UN of course was useless in doing anything, so John knew the US would become involved in the long run. Washington had been very quiet, so John knew the President was in a very bad spot. The country did not want, or would they accept, additional US forces fighting on another front. The election was looming, and things were not going well for the President. He would start his campaign officially after the State of the Union message which was in January so then things would really get moving. That was over seven months away, but the media was of course always predicting things and normally they got everything wrong. Harry was on the phone and John answered. Harry said "Sir, I just received a call from Special Operations group in Tampa asking if Red Lion could do some specialized training for a special group. The details would be sent via secure fax in four hours to both Harry and to Red Lion headquarters". The project would require some construction, but Harry saw no real problem with that, but US Army Engineers would be used to do the work and Harry was worried about having Engineers on the compound.

John said, "I agree with that, can we offer local construction assets?"

Harry said, "Hell yes Sir. We have a group we use all the time to do work for us".

John said "Then that will be how we do it. Our local people or we do not take the job".

Harry said, "Roger that Sir". John wondered what this was all about and told Nancy to bring the fax to him as soon as it came in. Shell Oil had also contacted Red Lion about needing security on some of their projects and Jim and Tress were also working up what would be needed so Kevin could get a quote ready. Don and Cindy were still checking bank records of various people and making a chart of the accounts and the activities on each account. The fax arrived, and Nancy brought it to John. It was marked "TOP SECRET".

John read the fax and knew right away this was going to be something that was not ordinary and would require special security at the compound in Hallettsville. John called Harry and the two discussed the fax. The operation would be a seven-day training session for a very special group of special operations assets and would have to be done with the maximum security. John told Harry to find out what the cost of construction would be and get the local people to make damn sure they could do it in forty-eight hours or less. Then John called Jim and had him come in and they discussed how many of the Red Lion operators would be needed to secure the area for the duration of the training. Harry called John back and said he could get the building done in forty-eight hours or less for what was needed but would have to use wood, plywood, not bricks or stones. Jim had ten operators figured for the 24/7 security needed. John then had Kevin cost the project out and that afternoon Kevin handed John the figures. The cost would be $15 Million Dollars. John called Special Operations Command in Tampa and told them the costs. The purchase order was faxed in thirty minutes after John's phone call. The construction was to start the next day. The special operations assets would arrive in three days. Jim and Harry made the necessary preparations.

The construction was finished in a little over forty hours and Harry was ready to receive the assets. Jim had sent the Red Lion security operators to Hallettsville and they were in place. The special operations assets arrived, and it was SEAL Team 6. Harry knew this was something very big. The assets went to work. There were two Black Hawk helicopters that came along and would be landing in the Red Lion compound and would stay there during the training. The training would be at night most of the time so all training at Red Lion of the SWAT groups was changed to day hours only. The compound that had been built for the SEAL team was far away from the Red Lion facilities, but Harry did not want to take a chance on someone getting nosey. The SEALS went to work and trained long and hard hours. They went over the operation repeatedly, for four days. On the fifth day they did one run through and were satisfied. The SEALS left the next morning. Harry then made sure nothing was left that could identify the target and had the compound sealed. The operators from Red Lion returned to Sugarland and the training of SWAT resumed as usual.

John was now letting Jim and Tress do most of the work at Red Lion but as with any organization, some clients only wanted to speak directly with John about requirements. Chad was the hottest project on the table for Red Lion and it was going to be a Hell of a project to pull off. It would require almost all the assets the corporation had and would also require a lot of coordination with friendly countries in the area. John knew that would require Red Lion to use the State Department and CIA assets and as always, he did not like to be in that position. Too many things could go wrong with them involved. Tress had the intelligence on the area and there were about four war lords that had to be satisfied, to go into the area, and eliminate the terrorist operating there. The good thing was that from all Tress and Sandy could learn, the terrorists had a running fight with three of the War Lords and that was the opening Red Lion would use. Don and Cindy had gained information on the banking that the terrorist's cells were using to fund their operations, and where they placed the ransom money they received. The accounts also showed transactions from other locations in the Middle-East that supported the cells. Don had tracked much of the money back to Iran and to Saudi Arabia where private accounts were used. The Saudi government did not stop this flow of money and this had been a problem for years. John was told a plan to attack the Chad problem would be ready for a May execution. It was now the middle of March. John knew things would be tense until the plan was ready, approved and in progress.

The SEAL Team would be returning to the compound in April sometime around the 20th to do some additional training. Harry and Jim had everything ready, so things should go smoothly. John was ready to let things play out with the problems in Malaysia and in South American. All would require a major amount of planning to get anything done and right now Red Lion had its hands full with Chad and other smaller projects. The smaller projects were an ongoing thing for Red Lion. Operators were used by clients to secure VIP's on travel overseas and used to do specialty work in the US that was not published. Most of this work only required a team of three operators and was done in two to four days. The bills were always sent to the special fund account in Washington D.C. It was always sanctioned by the White House, so John was comfortable that no problems would arise. They never did. Dan had been working on John's idea about the airport in Redman Beach and was ready to discuss it with John. Dan and John went to Molly's bar for the meeting and discussion.

Dan and John sat down and had a drink then Dan said "John the answer to your question about buying the airport is NO! I advise you not to do that. There are many reasons, but here is the biggest one. FAA. They control all airport permits and everything to do with the damn things, so it would take you about four years to get all the necessary things together to actually open the field and run the airport".

John sat and then said, "OK what is the alternative?"

Dan said "You lease it from the city. They still own it and their permits are still good. Hell, all they would have to do is request an upgrade and that is automatic for a permit holder".

John said "Well, how would we do that legally Dan? I would have to do what exactly to lease the present area and what about the additional land?"

Dan said "First of all we find out if the city will go along with a lease. Then you buy the additional land and donate it to the city. The city will have to guarantee that the land will be used for the airport".

John and Dan discussed the situation and had lunch. They left and returned to the Red Lion headquarters. John called the real estate agent in Redman Beach and had him look at the land by the airport, and get a price. In three hours John got a return call from the agent. The price would be $700,000 for additional acers. John had the agent make the deal. John had also gotten a phone message from the Mayor of Redman Beach and John was scheduled to speak to the City Council on May the 2nd. John advised Dan and had Nancy make plans for the Jet and then a helicopter to take John and Molly to Redman Beach, during the first week of April. Dan would then be joining, them there on the 1st of May, to go with John to the council meeting. The house was to be ready during the first week of April and John and Molly wanted to be there to do the final inspection. Don would also be coming to set up all the equipment.

# CHAPTER 41

John and Molly arrived at the Orlando airport and the helicopter was waiting at the private terminal. The helicopter was a Sikorsky S-92 Executive model and had a crew of three, two piolets and one hostess. John and Molly boarded the helicopter and it took off heading for Redman Beach. The flight was 45 minutes. John was very impressed with the service and really liked the company. The company had 6 of the helicopters available and did a very good business around the Orlando area. The flight was perfect and when the helicopter touched down in Redman Beach a rental car was waiting for John at the airport. John and Molly drove to the hotel and checked in, then drove by the house. It was finished and look fantastic. John had contacted the real estate agent and would meet him at 2 PM to get the keys. John and Molly drove to the beach and went to Ted's bar for a drink and killed a little time before the meeting. People were friendly and welcomed John and Molly back to town. It was a great place and John and Molly both felt right at home.

John and Molly arrived at the house and met with the real estate agent. He showed them through the house and as they were looking at things the contractor arrived along with his female assistant. Everything was perfect, and John and Molly were pleased with the new house. Everyone then left and went to Ted's and celebrated. John also received the papers on the land purchase from the real estate agent. The next day John and Molly were up early and at the furniture store when it opened. They spend three hours buying furniture for the entire house and it was to be delivered and set up that afternoon. At 7 PM the last deliverymen left, and John and

Molly were now ready to spend the first night in the new house. Don was due to be there the next morning to get the computers, fax, video, and all the security working. Don arrived on schedule and spent about half the day getting the equipment up and running. John now had everything in the Redman Beach house he had at Red Lion headquarters. Don left that afternoon and went back to Orlando then on to Texas. The following morning, John and Molly went shopping for food and liquor. It was delivered that afternoon and John and Molly fixed a drink and sat on the patio and watched the sunset over the ocean. It was the start of a whole new life for them, and they were very ready.

John received an email every morning from Red Lion with a situation report he had made sure would continue when he was not physically in the office. The SITREP was normally sent out by Nancy after she compiled all the division reports and made a short synopsis covering the reports. John always read the SITREP before doing almost anything. John and Molly had been at Redman Beach for 3 weeks and things were running well at Red Lion. Presently the corporation was doing security work for KBR in Iraq, Kuwait, Saudi, and in Brazil in South America. The training was going well and starting in June, 4 corporations would be sending their personnel for a two-week course in personal protection for VIPs. Harry had designed the course and Jim had sold the idea to 4 of the biggest US corporations. Red Lion was paid $250,000 per company to do the training. John was looking over the operator report and saw that three operations were on-going. Two were in the Far-East and one was in Bolivia. The Bolivia operation was a rescue of a mining engineer who a small group had kidnapped over six months prior and now wanted $20 Million Dollars for his release. The company that had hired Red Lion was based in Dallas, Texas and wanted the man back. The Bolivian government had been of no use to the Mining Company and the US State Department had done nothing, so it was Red Lion's mission to get the man back. John had read the initial plan and it was sound, just as all of Tress and Sandy's were

John was called about 8 AM and briefed by Jim on the operation. John thanked Jim and said to tell everyone good job.

John and Molly had now seen what it would be like to have an operation going on and John not being at Red Lion headquarters. It was new to them and it was going to take some adjusting. John went back to bed for a few hours and Molly swam and then exercised for a while before taking a shower and getting dressed. John was up and showered and got dressed so they could go get some breakfast and have a drink or two at Ted's. It was now the middle of April and the next Red Lion project was the Chad situation. John also had the city council meeting in three weeks. John and Molly left Ted's at 4 PM and drove to the car dealership out on the highway. John liked the Mercedes as a personal car and so did Molly. They went into the dealership and ordered their cars. Molly got a Mercedes 2 door SEL Coup color, Red. John got the same car in Black. The dealership would have the vehicles ready with license plates and everything in two days. John purchased the vehicles in his and Molly's names.

Dan had just arrived, and John and Molly showed him the house. Dan was very happy for them and really liked the entire set up of the place. All three went to Ted's for a few drinks, then to dinner and then returned to the house. The council meeting was at 6 PM the next day. John and Dan drove to the airport in the morning and looked it over. They also looked over the additional land that had been bought. Dan had prepared a proposal for the city council and John took the afternoon to read and memorize it. Dan swam in the pool and then was dressed and ready about 4:30 PM. John was also ready, so the men drove to the city hall and prepared to speak to the council.

The council chamber was not very crowded with only about twenty people sitting and listening to the proceedings. After about thirty minutes, the Mayor introduced John and Dan and gave John the floor. The council was made up of one woman and three men. The Mayor would only vote to break a tie. John also saw that the city attorney, an attorney that had a private practice in town, the fire chief, the police chief and the county Sheriff were also present just as John had ask for. John rose and walked to the mic in the center of the council room and said "Lady and Gentlemen my name is John Carter and I am the Chairman of the Board of the Red Lion International Security Services, Inc. This is Mr. Dan Swift our corporate attorney. I am also probably the newest resident of Redman Beach. I would like to thank you for giving me and Dan this opportunity to address you and to furnish you with our proposal about the airport. I would also like to thank the police, fire and sheriff for being here tonight. Members of the council, you will now be given a copy of our proposal and Mr. City Attorney, police chief, fire chief and sheriff will be given a copy. Our plan is very forth coming and extremely simple, so I will not bore you with everything that is in the documents. Simply stated we as Red Lion would like to lease the current airport for a period of twenty years. We will build new runways, taxi ways, a new terminal, parking garage, upgrade the radar, computer system, communication systems, build hangers and other essential facilities to make the airport capable of receiving jet planes, short haul commercial planes and other aircraft. We have purchased additional acers that adjoin the present airport". John stopped and looked at the council and the other people sitting at the table. Everyone was looking at John and waiting. John continued speaking. "The best part is two-fold. One we will pay a yearly lease of $1 Million Dollars per year with an initial payment of $5 Million Dollars as our good faith and secondly the new land, and all but three buildings along with all equipment will become city property. The land will be donated to the city, just as the original airport was. The only buildings that will not be owned by the city will be three hangers built for Red Lion. Additionally, Red Lion will build and pay the cost to staff a fire station at the airport if the fire chief wants it. The police chief and Sheriff would also be asked to give their input as to the law enforcement requirements that have to now be included and advise Red Lion that cost. Members of the council, I do not think you could find a better proposal to allow the city to become an aviation facility of first class ability. Now the reason we do not ask to buy the airport is very simple. The city already has the FAA permits and can very quickly get upgrade permits issued by the FAA. Lastly, I would ask that each of you study the proposal and advise us as soon as possible of your decision. Again, thank you for your time". John turned and sat down next to Dan.

The Mayor said "Mr. Carter we would like to thank you for this proposal and I feel we can have a decision in principal within a few days. I will personally call you with our decision".

John and Dan got up and left the council chambers. John called Molly and had her be ready to go when they arrived. All three went to the country club for drinks and dinner. In about an hour most of the city council and the Mayor came into the club and had some drinks. They all came over to John's table and said hello and visited for a few minutes. John and Dan liked that, and Molly was happy things were going well for them in the new town. The next day Dan flew back to Texas and the day after John and Molly also flew back. Now all that was left was the Mayor's phone call. It came two days later, and the answer was yes. The deal was a go in principal. All that was needed now was the contracts, the plans and then the city could approve all the necessary permits. The police, sheriff and fire departments would be sending their requirements to Red Lion within the week via fax.

# CHAPTER 42

Chad was the hot project now at Red Lion. Washington had already informed John that it was a critical problem and US involvement could not be seen. The UN was making no progress like usual and the Chad government was not able to do anything about the terrorists. Tress and Sandy had studied the terrorists and knew this was going to be a very hard operation and without air power it was almost impossible. Tress and Jim had both asked John to assist with this mission.

Chad was land-locked so no way the container ship was an asset for Red Lion. Also, no neighboring country was friendly with the US except maybe Nigeria. John asked Don to get a list made up of all the US oil companies working in Nigeria and get it to him. Don had the list in about twenty minutes and one name stood out to John. Exxon. John placed a call to the chairman of the board of Exxon and spoke to him at length about what Exxon had as far as facilities in Nigeria. Then John said "I would like to meet face to face and discuss some business with you. Are you free tomorrow for lunch?" The Exxon Chairman said, "I am and would love to meet with you".

John said, "How about the Lakeside Country Club at 1 PM?"

The Exxon Chairman said, "See you there". John knew this might not work but it was really all Red Lion had going for it.

John met with Bob Williams, the Chairman of Exxon and the two men had lunch and discussed the situation in Chad. Bob had about 10 facilities in the country that were working but like everything in that part of the world, it was all 50/50 with the government and everything was always a problem to control. John said, "Bob could you use your connections to allow Red Lion to fly out of Nigeria and back without being hassled by the government?"

Bob said, "Well John all I could do is ask and see if they really care". That was good enough for John. Exxon owed Red Lion or at least John big favors for the pirates and for getting their people released and rescued from other areas. John was convinced Bob would do what he could. John went back to Red Lion and told Tress and Sandy to plan to use the ship. The raid would have to be delayed for at least fifteen days and could not be done now until the very end of May or the first of June. Everyone understood, and a new plan was formulated. The total assets of the aviation division were now going to be used. Israel was now going to be involved, but John knew that was no problem. The C-130 would land and fuel there and land with the hostages on the return trip. The container ship would be in port at Port Harcourt Nigeria which was the port used by Exxon to bring in their supplies. Then a field owned by Exxon would be used as a refuel and launch point. The C-130 would also use the same field as the launch point. Exxon had aviation fuel on site for their helicopters and fixed wing planes and some corporate jets that came and went. Intelligence had reported that forty-five hostages were being held and most of them were young girls. The terrorists were selling the women into slave trade to be used for sex. That was the way they were getting most of their funds to continue to fight the government of Chad. John had Tress prepare the plan working on the fact that permission was going to be granted for air space. The C-130 would not need permission when it flew over any of the countries on the way because it would be at an altitude of international flight status. The plans were being worked. The container ship would leave Galveston on the 8th of May with the chopper assets and all the equipment for the operators on it as well as the ammunition and explosives. The operators would fly commercial to Nigeria and then go by train the Exxon compound. There they would board the C-130 when it arrived and be ready to conduct the raid. The equipment would be off loaded from the cargo ship and transported overland to the Exxon compound. The piolets and flight crews plus the medics would also come by train to the port. The plan called for a HALO drop of twenty Red Lion operators and support by the Cobra and Black Hawks. The Black Hawks would then take any wounded operators back and some of the operators if required. The C-130 would land at the terrorist camp and the hostages would be loaded and then the C-130 would fly directly to Israel to deplane the hostages and the operators. The hostages would be turned over to the Israel government and the operators would fly back commercial on the first flights out to the US. The C-130 would refuel and start back to the US. One fuel stop would be arranged in Spain and then again in Charleston S.C. The C-130 would then return to Texas. The choppers would return to the container ship waiting off the coast of Nigeria and then the piolets and crew along with the medics and mechanics would be taken to a different port, Legos, and let off. All the personnel let off in Legos will fly commercial back to the US. Tress estimated the entire operation from start to finish would take twenty-five days. The actual raid to free the hostages would take one hour on the ground.

Three days had passed since John had met with Bob and at mid-morning John received a phone call from Bob. Bob said "John it is a go from the government, but they expect some type of payment as always. I would suggest about $5 Million Dollars. I will send you the banking coordinates we use for this type of thing".

John said "Bob I really appreciate this, and we can do the payment, however, if anything goes wrong on their end, we will not only take the money back, but the penalties will be extreme. Please pass that on for me".

Bob said "John I already explained that to the officials we deal with and they totally understand who they are dealing with. I will make damn sure they are reminded. Good luck my friend". John called Tress and told him the operation was a GO.

The container ship was loaded and left port and was in route to Nigeria. The operators were staged to fly out in six days. Arrangements had been made with all the governments for the things Red Lion would need and the C-130 crew was ready to fly in six days also. Things were moving along, and John was satisfied the operation was a good one and would succeed. Sunday was a slow day for John and Molly and they were relaxing at the apartment watching the late news when the President came on TV about 8 PM. John watched as the President announced that SEAL Team 6 had attacked a compound in Pakistan and the team had killed Bin Laden. It was positive. The President said the leader of al-Qaida was dead and his body had been removed by the SEALS. There had been no casualties on the American side, but one Black Hawk helicopter had been lost. The President said that there would be more in a news conference the next day. John sat for a moment and was surprised that the raid had been done and was successful. Then John knew why the SEALS had been in Hallettsville and why the special building had been built. John called Tress and Jim and they had just gotten the news. Everyone was excited about the killing of the leader of al-Qaida. The entire leadership had now been either captured or killed. The results might affect the operation in Chad because the terrorists were tied to al-Qaida. John decided to meet with everyone the first thing on Monday morning and see where things were. As far as any "chatter" about repercussions from any of the terrorist cells.

Monday morning everyone was gathered in the Intelligence operations area and waiting for Sandy and Tress to report on the "chatter". Sandy said "So far we have nothing concerning any plans to attack any US facilities that we can determine. The "chatter" is mainly about reprisals that should come but nothing solid. It looks as if the entire al-Qaida organization is in confusion and there is no leader coming forward. There will be a power struggle before anyone can take command".

Tress said "Our plan is still a Go as far as we know the cell we are targeting either does not have the word yet or could care less. Nothing has come out of their area about the killing of him, so we will proceed as we planned".

John and Jim agreed that the best way to continue was to strike as soon as possible. No one would suspect a strike this soon after the news of Bin Laden's death. The mission was now set for eight days. John was now waiting to see if Washington called to cancel the operation. The news was going crazy trying to get coverage of the operation in Pakistan. The news conference came on all TV stations at 11 AM from the White House and the President had the Joint Chiefs of Staff, the head of the CIA and the Secretary of Defense with him during the press conference. Of course, the stupid reporters asked dumb questions and most of them were not answered, but the mission was explained in enough detail that the press was somewhat satisfied. John laughed at the press. They were always asking stupid questions and when something was explained, normally the reporter had no idea what he or she had been told. It seemed to John that it had gotten worse over the years with the press and media in general. Tress and Sandy were going over any last minute, details on the operation. Don and Cindy had been monitoring the social media on the internet and had seen some postings from various cells about getting back at the US but nothing more than threats. Don had been able to get the latest email about the women hostages that had been sent to the Chad government. The terrorist's cell now was demanding $200 Million Dollars to release the women and the release of all the prisoners held by the Chad government. The deadline was in thirty days. John and Jim looked at the email and knew it was nothing more than a ruse. The terrorist group was already on line to sell the women on the black market. That was their plan and the sale would take place in ten days. Nothing had changed in the situation so Red Lion had only nine days to do the mission. The clock was ticking and ticking faster that John would have liked. The operators and the C-130 were set to depart the next day. Tress had communicated with Anderson on the container ship and Anderson was increasing the speed by almost double. It would use more fuel but that could be gotten in port when the ship arrived and was off loading the equipment and taking on the air crews. Time was now a very big factor.

Exxon had moved all personnel except the eight guards. These guards had been trained by Red Lion the year before. Everyone else was off the compound two days before the arrival of the operators, the C-130 and the rest of the aviation assets. The entire compound was open to Red Lion. The workers would return in three days so only the guards would have knowledge of the mission assets being at Exxon. The container ship docked and off loaded the equipment into trucks to be taken to the Exxon compound. The aviation assets boarded the ship and the ship now re-fueled, left the port. The other operators had gotten to the Exxon compound and were waiting for the equipment and the C-130 as well as the choppers to arrive. Tress was in constant contact with the team via SAT phone. The satellite had made three passes over the terrorist location and the buildings had been located. The buildings sat in a grouping of six in one line and four behind that line about thirty yards back. Each building was twenty yards apart. The buildings were made of mortar and had flat roofs. There was some electronic equipment located on the roof of one of the buildings which Tress figured was the headquarters. The hostages had not been seen in any of the aerial photos and there was no way to determine where they were being held. That was a problem the operators would have to figure out once they got on the ground. There were ten to twelve pickup trucks parked around the compound and five had machine guns mounted on the beds of the trucks. These were passed to the Cobra as targets to be taken out immediately. The road leading to the compound was dirt but very hard packed so the C-130 would use it as the landing area. Now things were almost ready for the operation to start. The C-130 touched down at the Exxon compound and the operators loaded the equipment and themselves on the plane. The choppers were there and ready. The jump was scheduled for 3 AM local time. The sun rose at 5 AM so hopefully by the time the sun was rising the operation would be in the final stages. The C-130 had two medics on board and the PA was on board one of the Black Hawks with another medic. It was almost time for the lift off and then in less than an hour the jump would signal the start of the operation. The entire Red Lion headquarters was waiting and watching the screens in the operations center. John was sitting and drinking another cup of coffee. He had no idea how many he had consumed so far but he needed to have the coffee. It was an old habit and he sure as Hell was not going to change now. The tension was thick, and everyone was worried. More than usual about this operation. There was just a feeling in the air.

The screen in the operations center showed the first operator exit the C-130. It was exactly 0300 hrs. 3 AM local time. John watched as the cameras on the operators showed pictures of the dark night. Only blackness was showing with a slight flicker of light from time to time. Tress got the word from the C-130 that all operators were out, and the equipment was now going to be dropped. The operators jumped from

20,000 feet, but the equipment would be dropped from 1700 feet as soon as the word was given that the raid had started. The Cobra was now two miles west of the target and the Black Hawks were right behind the Cobra.

Nelson was, as always, the commander of the ground operators and had split the operators into five groups of four men each. On the decent, Nelson had seen that there were two pickup trucks parked about fifty yards down each end of the compound on the side of the road. Nelson was sure these were the guards and early warning for the group. The operators were on the ground about one hundred yards from the compound and had not been seen. Nelson sent one team to eliminate each pickup truck as the first thing to be accomplished. The teams moved to the trucks and using silencers eliminated the guards on each truck. Then they returned to the main compound and prepared to attack. One team had gone to the buildings in the rear had discovered that two of these buildings had pad locks on the doors. There were no windows in these buildings and Nelson figured that was the holding area for the hostages. The operators silently removed the locks and prepared to enter the buildings. Nelson had two teams ready to attack the main headquarters building and another team set to attack the building to the left of the headquarters. Nelson called the Cobra and had the chopper start the run. Nelson then placed a strobe light on the headquarters building and waited for the Cobra strike.

The first missile went straight into the front door of the headquarters building and the explosion was huge. At the same time the operators entered the buildings where the hostages were held and secured the women. There was a great amount of screaming and confusion, but the operators got the situation handled and left two operators with the women as security, the others moved to the other two buildings and attacked the terrorists as they came running out. The main headquarters building was demolished by the missile strike, but Nelson still had operators go inside and make sure all the terrorists were dead. The other buildings had also been attacked and the fire fights were getting very heavy from the last building at the far end of the compound. Nelson marked that building and the Cobra made a missile attack firing two missiles into the building and destroying it. The operators continued to eliminate the terrorists as they tried to fight and in less than fifteen minutes every one of the terrorists were dead. As soon as Nelson got the confirmation he sent operators to retrieve the equipment that had been dropped and marked the road for the C-130 to land. The pickup trucks had been moved and were set on fire. The hostages were then all taken out of the building and checked by one of the operators that was paramedic trained. There were nine women that needed assistance and medical help. These women were placed on field stretchers that had been in the equipment bundle and were taken to the loading area. All the women were given water and taken to the loading area. The C-130 landed and taxied to a stop. The operators helped the women on board and six of the operators also boarded the aircraft. The total count of hostages relayed to Red Lion was sixty-three. The C-130 lifted off and headed north. The Black Hawks then landed and picked up all the remaining operators. Only one operator had been wounded and that wound was minor. The Black Hawks lifted off and headed back to the container ship. The Cobra then made the last run using the 20 MM cannon and the rest of the rockets to destroy the entire compound. The Cobra then headed back to the container ship. It was exactly 5 AM when the mission complete signal was received at Red Lion. John was very happy and thanked everyone for a job well done. John then sent a fax via secure line to Liz stating "MISSION ACCOMPLISHED. PLEASE PASS ON". John then left Red Lion along with Jim and went to get something to eat. Tress and Sandy were still monitoring the radio traffic from the operators, aircraft and the ship. In an hour and one half, John and Jim returned to the headquarters and Tress briefed them that all the choppers were back on the container ship and the ship was headed to the port to off load personnel. The wounded operator had been treated and was fine. In four hours the word was received that the C-130 had arrived in Israel and the hostages were turned over to the representatives of the Red Cross. The plane had off-loaded the operators and the medical personnel and was now in route back to the US. Then the bullshit began. John and everyone at Red Lion watched as the story unfolded on national TV.

The Secretary of State from the US, the Prime Minister of Israel, the Prime Minister of Chad, the same man that had been paid $5 Million Dollars, all held a press conference. The story was simple. With the help of the US intelligence agencies and the help of the Chad government, the Israelis had used a special commando unit to raid the terrorist base and free the Muslim women and return them to the Chad people by way of the International Red Cross. They were now being examined in hospitals in Israel and would soon be on their way back to their families. The Israelis did this rescue as a show of good faith to the Muslim community and as a humanitarian gesture. The world press was in a frenzy over the story. John and the rest of Red Lion just laughed and shook their heads. What a way to run a world. John made sure Sara sent the bill right away to the government. Total including bribe money $255 Million Dollars. Don had also located the terrorist's bank accounts and Cindy had emptied them. That total was $20 Million Dollars and had been placed after many re-routs into the Red Lion special account. John was very pleased, and Sara called John in two hours to say the bill had been paid. John called Bob and thanked him for his help. The day was over, and John was ready to go home and relax with Molly.

The next two weeks were busy for John. The operators and the aviation assets had all retuned to the Red Lion base and the container ship had been back in port and totally re-fitted with supplies and the necessary equipment needed. The supply people had re-ordered all the necessary equipment and had gotten the re-supply of ammunitions and explosives from Ft. Hood. All personnel had been given their bonus checks and were now on break for seven days. John had meetings with KBR and they had sent a team to Redman Beach to look at the airport project. John had a meeting with the representative of KBR and the bid was $2 Billion Dollars for the complete project. The estimated time was eighteen months to complete the entire project, but the runway would be done in ninety days. Then the taxi ways and the additional runway would be started. John was pleased and gave the go ahead. Dan went over the contract and it was exactly what Red Lion wanted. John signed the contract and KBR was to start on June 15th, one week away. John had called the Mayor and set up the necessary people to examine the project and issue the permits necessary. KBR was doing the paperwork for the FAA on behalf of the city. Harry was increasing the training at the Hallettsville facility and had now gotten some new clients from corporations that needed their people trained in special tactics and driving for personal protective details. The next 4 months were very quiet for Red Lion. Only the overseas operators on duty with KBR were really doing much. The headquarters was very slow, and nothing was going on that needed attention. John and Molly had spent two months in Redman Beach and had really become a part of the community. They had made a bunch of friends and had enjoyed having house parties and going to house parties as well as their time at the country club and of course at Ted's. Ray had decided to run for the Texas House of Representatives and was now preparing a campaign. John had no doubt he would win and offered to do what he could. Miles had also offered to assist in any way possible, so the entire family was now in the political business so to speak. In October, John received a call from Liz about a problem in the Sudan. It was another terrorist group that was out of control and making problems for shipping in the Red Sea after the ships passed through the Suez Cannel. The oil flow was of course one of the major concerns as well as the freighter and container ships. The Sudan government was not doing anything about the problem and it was getting larger with every passing day. Nineteen ships had been attacked and held for ransom and it seemed as if there was no end to the taking of vessels. The US Navy could not do anything without permission from Saudi, Egypt, Sudan and that was almost impossible to get. John had told Liz to send the information to Red Lion and it would be looked at. The information was received and given to Tress and Sandy to look at and to recommend a plan if any. Tress called John and they discussed the situation. Jim also was on the line and it was going to be another bad deal for Red Lion to do unless there was a lot of cooperation from many sources. John was planning on returning to Houston at the end of the week, so everything was on hold until he got back.

# CHAPTER 43

October was fast closing to the end and November was almost here. John had looked at the intelligence reports Tress and Sandy had gathered on the rebel group operating out of the Sudan and it seemed to John this was a small group out to steal not a political group trying to make a statement of any type. The best estimate was that the rebels numbered no more than twenty-five if that. The group used the same tactics that had been used by the pirates in other parts of the world. They would use a small fast boat to go alongside a ship and fix explosives to the side of the ship. Then they would radio the Captain and tell him to stop the ship or they would detonate the explosives. Once the ship was stopped the rebels would board and hold the crew captive until the money was paid. Jim had looked at the reports and he was convinced that the entire operation was a make shift affair and there was no actual backing from any terrorist group for these rebels. John faxed Liz and told her what Red Lion had come up with. John got a return fax in four hours asking if Red Lion could do the job. John asked Jim and Tress about it and after a great discussion everyone decided that the only way was to send the container ship as bait and see what the rebels would do. To send the container ship that far and back would cost a lot of money and if the rebels did not attack it would be a lost cause. John did not like the odds, so he told Liz that unless more information was gathered about the exact size and location of the rebels, Red Lion would pass on the mission, now. It took three days before Red Lion got a fax stating they needed to do the job. John knew exactly where the fax had originated, and he knew the President was not happy. John sent a fax back giving a dollar amount that would be required, and he got his answer in five minutes. The amount was approved. Red Lion was to be paid $500 Million Dollars. John called Jim, Tress and Sandy and explained the position Red Lion was in. The mission was a go, now all they had to do was figure out how to do it.

Tress could find a link to the rebel base in some "chatter" that had been going on for the past few weeks. The rebels were operating around the town of Suakin and probably used the port area to store the boats. Tress decided to send two operators to Sudan and have them gather the necessary intelligence for the operation. He contacted Nelson and two operators were picked for the mission. Tress was going to use the Diplomatic cover to send them in as special protection for the Embassy. That would get them through customs with their weapons and would also allow them to carry weapons on the flight over from the States and connecting flights. They would land and rent a vehicle then go to the Suakin area. The embassy of course would know nothing about this and Tress was sure the Sudan government would not even give it a second thought. The operators had everything ready and departed Houston the next day. Don started putting information on the internet about a container ship that had valuable items on it and would be traveling around the tip of Africa in route to Egypt through the Suez Cannel in the next month. These items were to be displayed at the Cairo Museum of History. The story was very believable, and the hope was the rebels would want to hijack the ship. Now Tress and Sandy waited for any sign the rebels had taken the bait.

The operators had been in Sudan for a week and were now ready to be extracted. They had the exact location of the rebel group and the size. They were also able to get information on where the group got information on which ship to stop. That was the best intelligence of all. Tress sent a private jet to pick up the operators. Going in he did not want to arouse suspicion by using a private jet but now he could care less about what the Sudan government thought. The jet arrived, and the operators had turned in the rental vehicle and were ready to leave. They cleared customs just as before using the Diplomatic passports and were on the way back. They arrived in eighteen hours back at Sugarland. One stop was made in South Florida for fuel. The operators came directly to operations and briefed Tress, Sandy, Jim and John. The whole operation was run by a man that was a ship broker in the city of Port Sudan. The man was called Bing and he ran the entire operation. The split was 50/50 but Bing always picked the targets and always tried to stay away from US Flag ships. He feared the US Government and did not want anything to do with a US Ship. Don had not put out the name or the registration of the container ship so now he could put out additional information. Tress decided to use the flag of Mexico because that was safe. No one would doubt that a Mexican container ship had gotten the contract for the shipment because of the price. Also, the rebels would not fear stopping a Mexican ship and knew the owners of the shipment would pay the ransom. Now the plan had to be created. Tress and Sandy went to work, and Nelson and Jim also went to work on how exactly the best way was to get the rebel base and to eliminate Bing. Don and Cindy were hard at work finding out everything they could on Bing and Don was working to find his banking. John sent a fax to Liz and said the plan was now in the works and he estimated a conclusion to the problem by the end of November.

The plan was now set. The container ship would leave Galveston with one Black Hawk on board and travel to South Africa to Port St. John's and refuel and take on the operators, chopper crew and the medic. Then the container ship would proceed up the coast toward the Red Sea and the Suez Cannel. The ship would follow the coast only a few miles off shore. During the night just before the ship came to the Sudan coast, the Black Hawk with six operators would be launched and land on the beach and wait. The six other operators would be on board the ship and wait for the rebels to board and then eliminate them. Once the rebels had been eliminated on the ship, the Black Hawk would then proceed to the rebel base and the operators would attack and eliminate the base totally. While this was in progress, Nelson and one operator would be in Port Sudan and eliminate Bing and anyone with him. Nelson and the operator would already be in Port Sudan two days prior to the ship entering the area. They would arrive by private jet. Don had found the banking and as always would empty the account as soon as he got confirmation from Nelson. The travel time for the container ship was 8 days to South Africa and then two days up to Sudan. Everyone approved the plan so the Black Hawk was put into a container and trucked to Galveston that day. It was loaded along with the equipment container that was also trucked to Galveston, and the ship left port at Midnight. The mechanics had ridden down in the truck and were on board. The rest of the operation was going to fly on commercial flights as usual. The flights were scheduled for six days from the ship leaving Galveston. Nelson and the other operator would fly by private jet the day the ship left Port St. John's. Don was busy getting more information on the internet under shipping news and under a special banner about the collection. The key was that the shipment was insured for over $800 Million Dollars. That would get Bing's attention and maybe others. It was a chance, but everyone was sure they would be alright what ever happened.

The ship was in the port at Port of St. John's and had re-fueled and was loading the operators, medic and the PA. It would depart in four hours. Nelson had arrived in Sudan and was now in place tracking Bing's movements. So far things were on schedule. The time for John had been spent doing some research on Houston housing. Molly and John had decided to buy a house in Houston and move from the apartment. They had been looking at areas and nothing had really stuck out as a great area to live. Neither one wanted a mansion, but just a nice house with a pool and maybe a few other things. They did not want to live way out, but the memorial area was the best area they had found so far. They were still spending the down days looking and waiting for the operation to get started. John had planned to be on site at the operations center when the ship entered the Sudan area. Tress did not have a satellite available for this, so it would be operator cameras only. Nelson had suggested putting an operator on the ground when the Black Hawk set down to see if the boat was still in the slip but that had been over ridden because of the chance the Black Hawk would be seen or heard that close to the rebel base. The Black Hawk would be unable to give any intelligence until it was in the air so only the ship's radar could be an early warning and most of the time the small boats used by the rebels were not detected. Anderson was aware of that fact, so he had purchased a special radar unit for scanning the water below the normal ship radar. It was installed right before the ship left Galveston.

The ship was now entering the Sudan waters off the coast. The Black Hawk had been launched an hour ago and was now sitting on the ground waiting the command to go. The radar was picking up a very small target coming out of the coast and heading for the ship. The sun was just coming up and the water was very calm. The radar operator watched as the small boat came closer and then one of the Navy crew spotted the boat on the port side. The boat pulled up and one of the rebels put an explosive charge on the side of the ship at the water line then the boat sped away and stopped about 300 yards from the ship. The radio crackled and a voice in Spanish said for the ship to stop or it would be blown up. Anderson had one of the crew that spoke Spanish ready and he talked complaining and then finally said he would stop the ship. The rebel told the ship that men would be coming on board and if they resisted the ship would be blown up by the men in the boat. Anderson told his man to acknowledge and he did.

The container ship slowed and finally stopped. four rebels climbed on board by using a rope with hooks to grab at one end that had been shot onto the deck. Each carried an AK-47 and had a pistol in their belts. While the rebels were climbing onto the ship, two operators had slipped over the starboard side and swam to the rebel boat undetected. Once the rebels were on the deck, the operators in the water grabbed the rebels in the boat and took them under the water. It was silent and over within ten seconds. The operators then removed the charge from the ship and placed it in the boat. They then climbed back up the latter onto the ship. The rebels were trying to round up the crew and Anderson was not really helping. Just as one of the rebels raised his pistol he was shot in the forehead by a sniper in the upper area of the container ship. As he hit the deck the three remaining rebels were shot. All died before they hit the deck. Anderson gave the signal to the radio operator and he sent the message to the Black Hawk.

The Black Hawk flew directly to the rebel base and in less than fifteen minutes set down in front of the building that had been shown to them at Red Lion headquarters. The operators jumped off the chopper and raced into the front door off the building firing their MP-5's and killing the nine men in the room instantly. The operators did a search for more rebels but found none. The explosive charges were set in the building, and set on the dock, and storage area outside the building. Another boat was tied up to the dock and the operators set a charge on it also. The charges were set on timers to explode in thirty minutes. The operators then loaded back on the Black Hawk and the chopper headed for the container ship. The entire raid was over in less than ten minutes.

While the raid on the rebel base was in progress, Nelson and his partner went into Bing's office. As the entered they saw three men sitting and Bing sitting behind his desk listening to a radio. Nelson shot Bing in the forehead then in the heart and then took out the man to Nelson's left. The other operator shot the first man to the right then the second. In less than 30 seconds all four men were dead. Nelson then down loaded Bing's computer onto a thumb drive. While Nelson was down loading the computer. The other operator searched the office. A safe was discovered and the operator placed a small charge on it and blew the door open. The safe had cash and a couple of notebooks inside so Nelson took everything and placed it in the brief case that was open on the desk. Nelson and the operator left the office and exited the building. They took a taxi back to the port area and got out. In about twenty minutes after changing clothes they left and headed for the train station to go back to the airport. The private jet was waiting, and Nelson and the operator boarded, and the flight took off headed back to Italy, then after re-fueling on to the US. The container ship was now headed back to South Africa and the members of the raid were going to fly back home commercial. All the equipment had been returned to the container and the Black Hawk had been re-packed for transport.

The word had been transmitted to Red Lion that the raid had been successful, and everyone was now in route back per the schedule. Tress told John the word had come so John sent a fax to Liz. Then he had Sara send the invoice to the special account. The payment was confirmed in two hours. $500 Million Dollars had been placed into the account. John laughed to himself thinking about what Congress would do if they ever found out about things. It was now time to start getting ready for the Christmas season. John and Molly had decided to do Christmas as usual at the ranch but then they were scheduling a private jet to take them to Orlando and a chopper to go to Redman Beach the day after Christmas. New Year's would be spent there.

# CHAPTER 44

Christmas was good the whole family was very happy, and Ray was really excited about his campaign. Miles and Linda were also looking forward to returning to Europe in the spring and seeing more countries. The children were going to come to Ray and Donna's during the trip and would be on spring break, so they could be with Ray's kids and enjoy the time. Linda's children were a boy seven and a girl nine. Ray had a boy six and a girl who was just turning five, so they were all still young enough to get along. John and Molly had really enjoyed Redman Beach at New Year's and knew that was the place for them. The airport was really looking good and KBR had told John the control tower and all the equipment should be done and in operation in forty-five days. Then the jets could fly directly into Redman Beach. No more Orlando. The President had officially committed to run for a second term and of course the Bin Laden thing had helped his image a lot. Also, the drawdown of troops was continuing and the war in Afghanistan was not as bad as it had been in the past year. John did not know if the President would win, but there was no real competition from the other party, so John guessed he would pull it off.

The Red Lion Board meeting and Stockholders meeting was held the first week in January and the corporation was in fantastic shape. The net worth was now over $745 Billion Dollars and John knew that the cash position was worth at least $650 Billion of that. Things were always working. The focus, for the coming year, was to increase our asset position by trying to buy a C-141 Star Lifter from the Air Force scrap yard. The planes were taken out of service and all the spare parts were put on them. Then they were sent to a field in Nevada to sit. The damn planes were probably in better condition after the parts had been installed than when they were flying. John had Jim call one of his Air Force contacts and see. Jim also had the C-130 crew see what they could find out since all of them were retired Air Force. The meeting was over, and John was back in his office thinking about the housing in Houston. He and Molly were going to spend the next week searching for that right house. The house search was now into February and John was getting very tired of seeing the same damn thing shown by real estate agents. Molly was almost crazy, and things were not getting any better. John and Molly were sitting at the bar in Molly's and she was patted on the back by a very tall good looking, man in his early 40's. She looked around and said "Jake Watson I will be damned. I thought you were dead or something".

Jake said, "After you broke my heart I was in hiding", and then he laughed.

Molly said "Jake this is my husband John. John this is Jake and I think he is just what we have been looking for". John shook hands and asked Jake to sit.

Molly said, "Jake are you still doing makeovers on houses?"

Jake said "Yes I have been in Dallas for the last year doing five makeovers and now I am back. You need a house?"

John said "God do we. In the worse way".

Jake said "OK then we need to get together. How about tomorrow?"

John said, "Great where do we meet?"

Jake said, "Right here say 10 AM". John and Molly both said, almost together, "You got a deal". The rest of the day was spent talking to Jake about what they had seen and what they really were interested in and about his business and him in general.

The next morning Jake was there with his foreman and John and Molly described exactly what they wanted and the area they were interested in living. Jake said "OK we will look at what may be available, and then get back to you. Give us about two days". John and Molly agreed, and Jake and his foreman left. John and Molly went back to the apartment and messed around the place doing nothing. It was nice to do nothing for a change. John and Molly decided to go to dinner and they wanted to stop by Molly's first and visit with some friends they had not seen in some time. It was 6 PM when they arrived at Molly's and the place was packed as usual. John found a seat at the bar and Molly put her purse behind the bar and started visiting around. About 7 PM John got a cell call. He answered and then he jumped up and ran for the patio. Molly watched then followed. John was yelling "Calm down Miles God damn calm down. Now tell me what happened". John listened and then said "OK call the police or sheriff or whoever the fuck is the law there. I will call Ray and I will be there as soon as the jet can get me there. Yes, I know you have a landing strip I have the coordinates, so I will come directly there. Just make damn sure someone is available to meet the plane and take me to the house". John hung up.

Molly said, "OH God what is wrong?"

John said, "The kids have been taken, that is all I know right now".

Molly said "Oh John I am so sorry. I am going with you".

John said, "Ok but I need to make some calls". John called Nancy, Tress, and Jim. They were now activating the recall plan for Red Lion. Then John called Ray and told him. Ray was going to get his plane and would be there as soon as he could. He would also call his buddy in the Texas Rangers. Molly went to the bar and yelled to Carol to get her cell phone. Carol handed the phone to Molly and Molly dialed a number. John heard her say "I need to speak to him now". In about a minute Molly said "Joey D I need your help. My niece and nephew have been taken. I do not have anything else right now, but you need to be by a phone until you hear from me. Get a fax that I can send you some information to and get it done now. I really need you to do this for me, Joey". She hung up.

John said, "Ok let's get out of here we have a jet to catch". John and Molly headed for the apartment, grabbed some clothes and their toilet articles and Molly's makeup and drove to the Red Lion field and waited for the jet to arrive. At 8 PM the jet taxied to a stop and John and Molly boarded. John gave the piolets the coordinates and the plane took off headed for Midland.

The flight took two hours and John and Molly were met by a man driving a SUV and taken to the house. Linda and Miles were both very shaken and the sheriff and three deputies were there in the house. The FBI was in route from Dallas and Ray was due to land in about thirty minutes. John went to Miles and found out what was happening. All anyone knew was that the children had been taken by two men and the housekeeper had been beaten and was now in the hospital. The men left a note that they would call about the money they wanted and to not call the police or they would kill the kids. No time for the call was given or anything else. The only description of the men was that they were big and Mexican and had black jackets on and wore head bands. John had a SAT phone and he called back to Red Lion. Jim was now the point of contact, so John explained what he knew. Jim was sending four operators out on the next jet. Tress came on line and told John that when he had any possible location to let him know and he would get the satellite directed to cover the location. Nelson was standing by with a team and would remain on standby for as long as necessary. Molly was trying to comfort Linda and she did not know how to help. How do you help when someone's children have been taken? That was always the question in a case like this.

The FBI arrived about two hours from the time John had arrived and started the questions and setting up a phone trace kit at the house. John saw that as stupid because now people used burn phones and those could not be traced. John called back to Red Lion and had Don and Cindy also start their magic on the phone and cell towers. The rest of the night there was no contact made from the people who had the children. At 6 AM the operators from Red Lion drove up to the house and John went out to speak to them. John asked them to check the entire area including back roads for any signs they may find and then to go into the town and see what they could learn. The operators left. At 8 AM Molly called Joey D again and told him about the Mexicans in black jackets and head bands. Joey D told Molly he would get back to her as soon as he had information.

At 1 PM a call came into the house. It was the person who claimed to have the children and the demand was for $25 Million Dollars in no bill larger than a twenty. The time for delivery was in two days and another call would be made to tell where to deliver. John asked Miles to ask for proof of life and if he did not get it no deal. Miles hesitated so John took the phone and said "I need proof of life or no fucking deal. Now listen and listen well! From now on I handle this, or no one does. Miles is my brother-in-law and I do his business. ".

The voice said, "I will call back". The phone went dead. John called the SAT phone and Don said he had the tower, but it was a burn phone so only the tower was good and that the signal could be bounced. John had Don give Tress the tower information. John then said "Miles I know you are worried so that is why I took the phone. I have been in this situation before and they are not my children. I know they are my nephew and nice but that is totally different. We are going to get then back. I promise that". Miles nodded and almost collapsed. Molly got him a drink and then Linda came in from the bedroom and sat down. John explained what was happening and she just sat and stared. The FBI Agent in charge wanted to talk to John outside so John walked out on the front porch with him. The agent started giving John Hell about the phone call and how he had acted with the caller. John stopped the agent and said "Look you have no fucking idea who I am or what you are into here. Call this number and ask them about me. I suggest you do it now agent". The agent took the card John handed him and moved away and called on his cell. The agent identified himself to the person who answered and told them he was on an active case and that a man named John Carter was here trying to run the show. After a brief few seconds the agent hung up and in less than five minutes his cell rang. He answered, and John heard the voice on the other end say "This is the Director. Now listen and listen very well! You are to do nothing but what John Carter tells you to do. Whatever he says is what will happen. You stay and follow those instructions. Son that is directly from the President. Do you understand?"

The agent said, "Yes Sir." The phone went dead and the agent put it back in his pocket and said, "Sir what do you want us to do?"

John said "Keep monitoring and keep gathering facts. I will tell you if we need anything else". The agent went back into the house. Jim had sent an urgent fax message to Liz explaining the situation and the person who answered the agent's phone call about John was Liz.

Ray arrived along with two Texas Rangers. John briefed Ray and the Rangers on what had happened so far and what was supposed to happen. John also explained that he was now speaking to the people who claimed to have the children, and this would continue. The Rangers agreed and said they were going to the hospital to interview the housekeeper. Cindy and an operator arrived about thirty minutes later and John had Cindy go to work on Miles security system. The system was very good and recorded everything. Six cameras covered the entire house and driveway leading to the house, but the discs had been taken by the kidnappers. Cindy started working and in about thirty minutes she had the complete footage back up for viewing. The FBI had wanted to send the hard drive to the lab in Washington because they did not have the skills to do what Cindy had done. Now there was video of the entire kidnapping and of the suspects. The video also showed the people leaving with the children. The key thing was the jackets they wore. They were motorcycle jackets and had a logo on the back. The logo was of the Los Diablos, a motorcycle gang known to the FBI, DEA, ATF, and to the Texas Rangers. The logo was down loaded by Cindy and printed. Copies were sent via email to Tress and a SAT phone picture of the logo was sent to the operators on the ground. Molly got a clear copy and called Joey D. She got the fax number he gave and immediately had the logo faxed to him. In about an hour one Ranger returned to the house and spoke to John, the FBI agent and Ray. The gang was known and was based in Las Cruces, New Mexico. This gang was a major player in drugs, weapons smuggling and human trafficking and had over 300 active members. John thanked the Ranger for the information and the Ranger told John that a complete file was in route from Austin and would be at the ranch in two hours. John called Tress and Sandy and when both came on the line, John said "OK this is the gang. It is called Los Diablos and is headquartered in Las Cruces New Mexico. I want everything there is on this bunch as soon as you can get it to me". Tress and Sandy acknowledged John and hung up. The two intelligence specialists went to work and in less than thirty minutes John received a fax of ten pages giving him everything he asked for. John read over the fax and then got Ray and Miles and went to a private area and briefed them. The gang was very unique in the fact that it was run by two brothers, who were in their 50's. Every member of the gang was a US citizen but was of Mexican heritage. Each member was therefore not illegal, so ICE had nothing to do with them unless they were caught at the border smuggling. The major players were the lieutenants who ran the gang. This gang was divided into cells that controlled certain areas of New Mexico and Texas. The gang was very ruthless and had killed many on both sides of the border. After John finished, Molly came in the room and said "Joey D has gotten information that the gang did in fact kidnap the children and here is what he is willing to do if you want it John. He will put out the word that a $5 Million Dollar reward is now offered for the location and the names of the people who took the children. This reward information will be sent out to every crime family in the US and given to all the members of each family". Molly then said, "I think it will really work, because these guys will be hunted by every criminal in the US for that kind of money".

John said "Tell Joey D thank you for me and to do it. I will personally make sure the money is paid but he knows that already. Thanks honey". Molly left and called Joey D. back and the reward was now active. It was approaching noon, so John went into the living room where the phone was set up for the FBI to trace and waited.

The phone call came at 12:15 PM and John answered. The caller told John that the money was to be delivered to Pecos Texas in forty-eight hours and then the children would be released. The money was to be placed in a parking rest area that was two miles west of Pecos and left. If the police, FBI or anyone that looked like authority was seen in the area the children would be killed. John then said "OK asshole now here is how this is going to work. First, I will be delivering the money. Second, I will have proof of life, namely the children will be there in plain sight for me to see before I think about giving you the money. Thirdly, you will have the children walk to me after I place the money on the ground. I will let you or a member of your gang come forward and check the money before you have the children walk to me. Once

I have the children then I leave, and you leave. That is it! Take it or fucking leave it. If you want the money this is how you will get it. Remember the children are no good to you dead and if in fact they are hurt in any way the deal is off. And just for your information why don't you check with your outlaw buddies and see exactly where you stand right now, then call me back. I believe you will be surprised to learn you are a totally wanted group by the major crime families in the country. How does $5 Million Dollars sound just for information on your ass?" The phone went dead. Don immediately called John and told him he had a location of the call. It was in Midland. John thanked Don and got the operators on the SAT phone and told them to search Midland for anyone wearing a jacket with the logo on it and capture them. The FBI was shocked and said nothing. The Rangers that were there smiled and said, "Sir, we feel you may have just gotten the children back. This gang is not afraid of law enforcement but they sure as Hell are of the Mob".

John smiled and said, "Yes I know and now they know". John went to the den and had a drink. Ray and Miles joined him, and Molly brought Linda in and gave her a drink, then poured herself one. Everyone waited.

At 3 PM John had a SAT phone call from the lead operator telling him that three members of the gang were now in custody of the team. They were being held in an old warehouse on the east side of Midland that Miles' company owned. John was given the address. John told the operator to hold them and start the process of obtaining information and he would be there after a while. At 5 PM a call came in and the caller wanted to speak to Miles. John told Miles to take the call and when Miles answered, the caller identified himself as the Sheriff of Pecos county and said "Sir, we have your children here at the Sheriff's department. They are not hurt and are only scared. The medics have already checked them out and have said they have no injuries, would you like to speak to them?"

Miles said, "Oh God yes, thank you". The children came on the line and Molly ran to get Linda. Miles talked to the children and then Linda talked to them. John asked to speak to the Sheriff and Linda handed John the phone. John told the Sheriff that they would be there in an hour and a half to get the children and thanked him. Then John said, "OK Linda, Miles come with me". John went out front and got into an SUV and Linda and Miles also got in. Two operators were in the vehicle and John told them to drive to the Black Hawk. John had sent for a Black Hawk and it had arrived in the early morning. It was fueled and ready to go. Miles, Linda, John and the operators climbed on the chopper and John gave the piolets the location to fly into. The chopper took off and headed for Pecos. The flight took a little over two hours, but the Black Hawk landed in the parking lot of the Sheriff's department and Miles and Linda rushed into the building. The children were sitting in a room watching TV and immediately ran to their mother and father. John met with the Sheriff and got a briefing on what had happened.

The Children had been left at a truck stop out of town about two miles and the owner had called the Sheriff. A bulletin was out for the children and so was an amber alert so immediately the Sheriff's department knew what was going on. A patrol car and an ambulance were dispatched to the truck stop and the children were taken into the custody of the Sheriff's department and brought to the office. The paramedics had examined the children and determined that they did not need medical attention, so they were left with the Sheriff. The only description about who had left the children was a brown van driven by a Mexican male. The van had stopped, and the children were taken out and sent into the truck stop. The van left immediately in a very big rush. John thanked the Sheriff and the deputies and got everyone back on the Black Hawk and the chopper lifted off and returned to the ranch in Midland.

Molly had received about three pages of information from Joey D. while John was gone. The information had a list of names. The heads of the biker gang were named Garcia, Faldo and Jose and they had ordered the kidnapping. The lieutenant that had done the actual job was named Carlos and the four men he used were also listed. The base for Carlos was in a small town just north of Midland but his area of operations covered everything all the way up to Amarillo Texas, including Lubbock and down to Odessa and over to the New Mexico line. Molly gave John the fax. John called Sara and had $6 Million Dollars immediately transferred to an account Joey D. had sent. Then he asked Molly to call Joey D. and tell him the children had been returned and the money was in his account and to thank him from everyone. The FBI and Rangers had left and so had the Sheriff Deputies so now things were almost back to normal. The children were alright physically but only time would tell about the mental situation. They were young and that was a plus, and the kidnappers had not actually hurt them in anyway. It had been a game of sorts because the time had been very short for the children to be away. John was deeply glad of that.

John left and went to the warehouse and met with his operators. The gang members had talked a lot and of course the team had Spanish speaking members, so nothing was missed. John now had the location of the base that Carlos used and the names of nine more members of his crew. The gang members were in bad shape after the interrogation by the operators. The operators had not treated the gang members easy and had to use a lot of physical punishment to get the information. John told the lead operator to make sure the gang members would not be a threat to anyone ever again and then John watched as each gang member was shot one time in the head. The bodies were loaded into a pickup and driven out into the brush. John returned to the ranch and spent time with the family. The operators and Cindy all went back on the Black Hawk the next morning and arrived at Red Lion around 1 PM. John had already given Tress and Jim the order to plan a mission to eliminate the entire biker gang. The plan was in the works.

# CHAPTER 45

ohn had decided to wait for at least three months before doing the mission to eliminate the biker gang. Tress had suggested that because he was concerned that the gang would be so afraid of the mob and of whoever they thought John was that they would be disbursed to locations not known and the mission would miss many of the members. John agreed so everything was on hold.

The container ship was now in the shipyard in New Orleans being re-fitted and having modification done. Anderson had designed a special movable deck that would allow for the landing area for the aircraft to be an additional 50 feet longer. The deck would be attached to the ship and could be moved forward to allow for the extra space. Also new electronic equipment was being installed and upgrades for all the computer and radar equipment were being done. The engines were also being overhauled to add additional speed to the ship with a new system. It was going to take about four months to do the work, so the naval crew would be in New Orleans for that time. Anderson would commute back and forth as necessary.

Barbara was now in the process of hiring new operators. Over twenty operators had retired or would in the next two months and John fully understood that. Age was a killer in the business Red Lion was in and most of these operators had been with the corporation from the start. They had made a lot of money and it was time to quit. Also, many of the overseas operators working the KBR mission were now not returning so voids were needing to be filled there. A total of seventy new people would be needed, in the next three months. The new operators would then need another two months of training before they could be used on missions. Harry was also winding down on the SWAT training. Most of the state SWAT teams had been done, but some cities and counties had not been able to spend the necessary money to have their people trained. The State was now trying to get funding to assist but that of course was a political deal and who knew when it would be done or even if it would be done.

Syria was in the middle of a civil war and Israel and the Palestine's were almost at war. Egypt had also had a government over-throw and things were really heating up in the Middle-East. The US was trying to stay out of the actual war, but pressure was mounting on the President to do something. John was sure nothing would be done until after the election, but no one ever knew what might happen so Red Lion was always preparing for a mission. Tress and Sandy were always looking at every area and planning the "what if" so they would be one step ahead if Red Lion got a call. Only minor missions for intelligence only were being conducted and these were two men missions that lasted at the most two weeks. A lot of these missions were for the DEA and ATF and were conducted in Mexico and other Central American countries. John had decided to wait until after the November elections to deal with the biker gang. This was going to be a totally different type of operation for Red Lion and John knew it would be all over the news. No one wanted that type of problem before the election. The federal government was going to be blamed for all the things that would happen, but, they would have no idea what was going on until someone, probably Liz put it all together. The President and especially the Attorney General would be having to answer a lot of questions, but because they would not have any idea, things would be alright.

Molly had been meeting with Jake and she needed John to be available to look at some houses on Tuesday. John and Molly were to meet Jake at Molly's and then go with him to see four locations he wanted to show. John cleared his schedule and told Nancy that only a life and death emergency would get him back to Red Lion. On Tuesday John and Molly went to see Jake's picks. The houses were all different, but Molly really liked the second house. John loved the location. The house sat on two almost three acers of land at the end of a street. The street dead ended into the front yard and the houses on the right side and left side were almost an acre away from the property John and Molly were looking at. The house had a nice entry hall, a living room and dining room off each other so a person could walk from the living room into the dining room. Behind the living room wall was a large den or great room. The damn room was 40 feet by 30 feet and the far wall was all glass that overlooked the patio and pool. The kitchen was off the dining room and went the length of the den. There was a hallway the led off the kitchen and the utility room was located there. Also, a door opened into a three- car attached garage. The den had a door on the end that led out onto the patio. The entrance to the den was to the left off the entry hall and then a hallway went to the right and off the hallway were four bedrooms all with baths. The last room was the master bedroom and it was very large. There was a guest half bath off the den where the utility room wall started. John liked the floor plan and so did Molly. Jake said the price was $1,900,000 and with the estimated remodeling that he and Molly had discussed another $700,000 would be added. John and Molly liked the house and especially the location. It was just off Memorial drive and Wilcrest drive and in one of the best sections of Houston. John and Molly told Jake to make the deal for the house and to have the architect start the drawings for the remodeling. Jake said things would be done in a week and he would let them know when to be available to sign the papers. John and Molly left and went back to Molly's bar and had a drink to celebrate. John looked at Molly and said "Lady a year ago we were living in an apartment and now look at us. We own two homes and four cars. What a way to live". Molly just started laughing. The next thing was to go to Redman Beach and see how the airport was progressing and to enjoy everything there. John knew KBR had all the radar and electronics in place and the tower was fully operational. Now small jets could land with ease. The other runway and taxi ways would be finished in three months. The hangers and terminal were almost done. John was looking forward to seeing the operation.

The jet landed in Redman Beach and taxied to a stop in front of the terminal building. John and Molly got off and watched as their luggage was taken off and placed in the taxi that was waiting. John told the piolets thanks and then he and Molly got into the taxi and headed for their house. When they arrived Louise, the housekeeper they had hired as a live in, met them and helped John bring in the luggage. The house was all ready for their visit and Molly and John went directly to the bedroom and changed clothes. Molly fixed a drink and they went out to the patio and sat and enjoyed the ocean view. That night John and Molly went to Ted's and had drinks and dinner and visited with friends. It was a great place for them both, after the last few months.

John and Molly were up about 8 AM and got ready to go see the airport. John drove, and Molly was watching all the activity. KBR had hired over 2000 local or semi-local people for the job and the economy was booming. Most of the items needed had been bought locally as John had originally requested even if it had cost a little more. The added cost was nothing compared to the good will it created by using the local businesses to furnish products. John met with the project manager of KBR and was given the tour. Molly was very impressed with the quality of the work in the terminal and the bar and dining room attached. The control tower was very up to date and John met the airport manager there. John liked the man right away and was very impressed with how he was on top of every detail. After the tour John, Molly, the KBR manager and Willis, the airport manager, sat and discussed the latest estimates of the completion schedule. The last things needed to be built were the hangers for Red Lion, the hangers that would be leased to individuals and the fire station. The parking garage was almost completed and so was the rest of the terminal. The roadway network was finished, and the large runway and taxi ways would be finished in thirty days. The fuel points had just been completed and the local fuel distributor was ready to take ownership of the facility. John had worked a deal so that the local fuel dealer would be allowed to own the refueling point because he had all the licenses needed to run the facility. The city would have to apply and then be granted the license and that was a real pain to get done in a timely manner. John and Molly finished the tour of the airport and the discussion with the KBR people and Willis and drove to the country club for lunch.

The Mayor was walking into the club when John and Molly arrived. John and Molly said hello and the Mayor returned the greeting. The three walked into the club and went to the bar and sat down. The Mayor told John that in the last month three airlines had approached the city requesting a contract to use the airport for service. The airlines were only going to use Redman Beach as a spur on flights at first but would have a gate and pay all the usual airport costs. Additionally, it looked as if there would be scheduled flights in and out every day from all three airlines. Only one flight per day from each but that would give three incoming and three outgoing flights, so the Mayor thought that would be enough. John and Molly agreed with him. The Mayor also told Molly and John that so far, the airport project had brought about $400 Million Dollars to the area. It was like a new era and people were excited beyond words about all of it. John was pleased and told the Mayor so. The Mayor finished his 2nd drink and headed out. John and Molly ordered another drink and had lunch. During lunch John and Molly discussed the house in Houston and by the time lunch was over they had decided that everything they wanted in Houston they already had plans, specifications, and all information on right here in Redman Beach. John called Jake and told him to put a hold on the fixtures, flooring, and all of that until he received the overnight package from John. Jake understood and said he would wait. Molly and John left the club and went back to the house and got out the plans, specs, and everything they had for the Redman Beach house and then John ran up to the FEDEX office and sent it to Jake. The next day Jake called to tell John he had the package and was passing it to the architect and would be ready in a week to sit down with John and Molly. John now scheduled the jet for the trip back to Texas, so they could leave on Sunday. Molly and John had four days left to enjoy the beach and the Redman Beach community.

On Monday John and Molly met Jake at the architect's office and went over all the plans and looked at the drawings. The house was going to be spectacular. John had decided he wanted a 20-foot-high rock wall, for the waterfall at the end of the pool and the architect made a quick sketch of the idea and John approved it. Molly also had wanted a sauna for use off the master bathroom so that was also added. Now everything was done, and Jake was now ready to start the process. Jake estimated six months for the work including the circular drive and the new landscaping. John told Jake to contact Don at Red Lion and he would tell Jake exactly what electrical lines, special video lines and all the satellite dish requirements to have put in and where. Things were now progressing, and John and Molly were set for a new adventure. The rest of the summer was normal for Red Lion and John and Molly spent quite a lot of time in Redman Beach. Jake had advised that the house in Houston would be finished by early October and wanted to make sure John and Molly would be in town then. John assured Jake they would and asked if he had a date. Jake said, "I am hoping for October 10th." John said, "October 10th it is then Jake".

# CHAPTER 46

t was now the end last week of September and John had a meeting with Jim, Nelson and Tress and Sandy in his office. Everyone was there, and John said "It is now time to start work on the plan for the Garcia boys. I have developed a very good plan and I want to run it by all of you to see how you feel. This is something totally different from what we normally do so things may seem funny at first, but I think this is the best way to handle these assholes". John then explained the plan. Four operators dressed in suits and ties and driving black SUV's just like the FBI does, would go to the house the Garcia brothers lived in. They would identify themselves as Federal Agents and present warrants for the arrest of both brothers. They would then cuff the brothers and place them in the SUV's, one brother in each vehicle. They would tell whoever was there that the brothers were being taken to Phoenix for processing and detention until they could be sent before a Federal Judge. The operators would then drive out of Las Cruces and head toward Phoenix. All of this would be done just at sunset. A Black Hawk would be waiting about thirty miles from Las Cruces and all but the operators driving would be loaded on the choppers and flown back to Red Lion headquarters. The SUVs would be taken north to Albuquerque where they had been rented and turned in. The operators would then board a private jet and return to Red Lion. The fake government plates would be removed, and the real plates put back on the vehicles prior to the turn in. Tress said, "Ok now why this plan rather than a straight attack and killing of the leaders?"

John said "I want the entire organization upset and wondering what is going on. Also, it will bring out the lawyers that work for these fucking guys and then we can also eliminate them. We will eliminate the sub command and many of the members but not until we have flushed out everyone we possible can that is connected. Don and Cindy will be monitoring all communications, and maybe if there is a leak or an informant in the government we will also locate that fucker. I just do not believe these guys have been able to not get caught without having someone in the inside".

Jim said "I think it will work like a charm. They will immediately have the lawyers go to Phoenix and sure as Hell the Feds will have no damn idea why they are there. Then the lawyers will start hollering conspiracy and everything else and shit will fly". Everyone agreed.

Nelson said "OK, Sir once we get them back here what is the plan?"

John said "Nelson you and your best interrogators will have them as long as you want to get every damn thing they have. Bank accounts, cross border connections, safe houses, locations of drugs and weapons and human traffic victims. Also, the entire breakdown of their organization. I do not want it made easy for them, but we need to keep them alive till we get it all".

Jim said "We are going to have to get a place to hold them and it has to be way out of the way. I will start on that today".

John said, "Any other questions?" No one had any so John thanked everyone and they left.

On October 10<sup>th</sup> John and Molly inspected the new house in Houston and signed the paperwork and took possession. John had already given Jake the total payment so now all that was left was to buy the furniture. Don had already installed the computers, video screens, fax, and the security cameras and alarms. John took Molly into the garage and handed her the keys to the red Mercedes parked on her spot. It was exactly like the car she had in Florida. John's was sitting next to Molly's. His was also exactly like his car in Florida. The next day Molly and some of her friends went shopping for furniture for the house. John had already purchased his for his office and it would be delivered that afternoon. By October the 14th the entire house was complete with furniture, dishes, everything. The movers had also moved the things from the apartment that were not put into storage. It was now time for Molly to have a party.

The party was set for Sunday afternoon from 2 PM until 8 PM and was an open house type affair. John had already met the neighbors that lived on the street when the construction was going on and he really liked them. There was a Senior Vice President of BP Oil Company, a Senior Inspector with the Houston Police Department, an Attorney, and a Doctor, actually a very high rated Heart Surgeon and that was the neighborhood. Only the Inspector had no children living at home, but John and Molly did not mind the children. They ranged in age from five to sixteen and so far, were very well behaved. John made sure all the neighbors were invited to the party. Parking was a problem because Molly was inviting about 200 people and almost all of them would come. John had already figured out the solution for the parking. There was a school one block, about ¼ of a mile west of his street and it had a huge parking lot. Because it was on Sunday John felt he could make a deal with the school to use the lot. John had Dan contact the HISD and worked out a deal to rent the parking lot from 12 noon until 12 midnight on Sunday. The rental would be $5000 which was what John had suggested to Dan to offer. John had also hired a valet parking company to park the cars as they arrived at the house. Houston off duty Police were hired to be the security and to direct traffic. Molly had hired a catering service and bartenders for the party. The party was a huge success and by the time everyone was gone, and everything was cleaned up it was 2 AM. John and Molly were exhausted but very happy. People had brought gifts and Molly had opened them and then had them placed into one of the bedrooms. Maria, the liv- in maid/housekeeper, had taken care of the gifts and had kept a record of each one for Molly. Maria had worked for Molly at the bar as the cleanup lady for years but when Molly offered the new position Maria was thrilled and immediately accepted. Maria had been the housekeeper at the apartment since John and Molly had lived together. John liked her and was glad she had taken the job.

November was now here, and the election was over, and The President had been reelected. Ray had also been elected so now John was ready to take care of the Garcia boys. A final briefing and instruction session was held, and everyone was ready. John wanted the mission to be two days before Thanksgiving, so it would be that much more problematic for the lawyers because the Federal system would be shut down for Thanksgiving and the day before a holiday nothing really gets done and the day after is about the same. Nothing gets done. The operators had been sent to Albuquerque and had the SUVs rented. The Black Hawk had flown to the designated spot and was waiting on the ground. Now all that was left was the taking of the brothers Garcia.

At 4:45 PM the SUVs drove into the front gate of the house that the Garcia brothers lived in. The operators had identified themselves to the guards and were let in as John had figured. The Garcia's did not want to start a fight with four Federal Agents holding a warrant. Nelson entered the residence followed by the other three operators dressed as FBI Agents and presented the warrants to the Garcia brothers. The warrants were perfect. Cindy had done an outstanding job and even had the official time clock stamp and the issuing Jude's signature in ink on the documents. The operators placed the brothers in hand cuffs and frisk them then led them to the SUVs. Faldo was placed in the first vehicle and Jose was placed in the second vehicle in the right front seat. Nelson told the man in the room that they were going to Phoenix and would be held until they could see the Judge and then walked out of the house and got in the rear of the first SUV. The brothers had said in Spanish to contact the attorneys and have them go to the Federal building in Phoenix. The SUVs pulled out of the drive and started out of town. The emergency lights that the operators had installed were on and working. It looked as real as real could be.

The vehicles were now about twenty miles out of the city and Nelson leaned forward and injected Faldo with a knock out shot. At the same time the operator behind Jose did the same. Both men were totally out in less than thirty seconds. It was now getting dark and the SUVs pulled onto a side road and went about a hundred yards and saw the Black Hawk sitting off the road on the right. The brothers and the operators, Nelson and another operator all loaded on the chopper and it took off. The emergency lights and plates had been removed. The SUVs now had the original plates on and were heading for Albuquerque. John received the report at Headquarters and was surprised that the SUVs had not been followed. The flight would take four hours and the Black Hawks would stop in Hallettsville to refuel. The SUVs would be in Albuquerque in two hours and the jet should be back in two hours after that. John knew that the attorneys would not even leave until a few hours after they were notified and by the time they got to Phoenix even if they flew the Black Hawks might be arriving back at Red Lion. No matter the Feds would not allow anyone into the building after it closed at 5 PM unless the FBI authorized it and why would they? The FBI had not arrested anyone named Garcia in Las Cruces. Tress and Sandy were trying to see if there was any "chatter" about the brothers but so far nothing. The charges specified on the warrants were for interstate attempted fraud more than $500,000 Dollars, and Racketeering. Both charges were

Class "A" Felony's. Any bond would have to be set by a Federal Judge. That is exactly why John had picked the charges.

The private jet landed, and the operators got off. The jet then took off and returned to the Hobby airport in Houston where it was based. The operators brought the emergency lights and government license plates to the storage and put them away. Then they went to change into their black fatigue uniforms. About an hour later the Black Hawk landed and the brothers were placed in a van and it headed out to the area Jim had gotten earlier. Nelson and the other operator also changed into black fatigues and then all four of the men got into a vehicle and left for the area where the brothers would be held. John and Jim got into another vehicle and had the operator/driver go to the location. The drive was about an hour and when they arrived they were out in the middle of nowhere. There was a brick building with an oil pump behind it sitting in the middle of a field about five miles down a dirt road. The turn off was marked by the sign that said Exxon Property No Trespassing. The view was about 300 yards in each direction of clear open field. John and Jim stopped next to the other vehicles that were parked and went inside. John looked around the building and saw two wire cages about six feet high and three feet wide. One of the Garcia men was in each cage and tied hand and foot and blind folded. The operators were in another section of the building that had been walled off and then John saw another section that had been made into a small interrogation room. There was a chair and one table in the room and another chair against the wall. John watched as Jim pointed to the cameras and mics that were placed around the area including the wire cages. In the back of the building John saw the electric shook units and the water board devices. There was also a table with various pliers and snips on it and another table with injection synergies and many bottles of various type drugs. John spoke to Nelson and was told that the very best interrogators would be working on the Garcia's. These men had done many interrogations in GITMO and other locations throughout the world. They were the best in the business. Nelson also said that always, a Spanish speaking operator would be in the area or in the room if necessary and that everything was being recorded so it could be studied by Sandy. John was pleased and asked to be notified as soon as there was any information that Nelson had been given a list of as needed for the next operation. Nelson said he would immediately notify Red Lion headquarters. John and Jim left, and Nelson and his group pulled Faldo out of the cage and took him into the small room and began the process.

# CHAPTER 47

John was at home and waiting for the arrival of the family. This year everyone was coming to Houston and John and Molly were hosting Thanksgiving. John had arranged for a limo to be at the air field when Ray's plane arrived. Ray was flying everyone down and he had gone to Midland and gotten Linda, Miles, and the kids and then he was in route to Sugarland. Ray flew his own Lear Jet and the plane could seat twelve, so there was plenty of room. At 4 PM the limo arrived, and everyone got out and went into the house. The luggage was taken in and put in the rooms by Maria and then Molly gave the grand tour. John went into the den and fixed himself a beer and waited for the tour to be over then he would get everyone a drink. Molly finished the tour and the children were outside playing in the yard. Maria was watching just in case as she always did. John got drinks for everyone and then they sat and talked. The family was just praising the house and could not stop saying how wonderful it was. John and Ray and Miles walked out on the patio and John said "I want this kept between us not even the girls should be told right now. We have the bastards that ordered the children taken Miles".

Miles said, "John what is this all about?"

John said "Well brother, you have a Hell of a lot to learn about your brother-in –law. We will see things on Friday so for now all you have to know is we now have the leaders. It will not be long before we know all of the fucker's names". Miles looked at Ray and Ray nodded. Miles said, "Ray you knew about this or at least about what John does?"

Ray said "Yes from the start but I could not say a damn thing. Sorry it was just how it had to be".

Miles shook his head and said, "Well I really do not care because he got the kids back and that is all that counts".

John said, "Amen to that brother". John changed the subject and they all talked about the house and the Redman Beach house. Maria brought the children in and they watched TV for a while and the adults had some more drinks and talked. Maria announced dinner about 7 PM and everyone went to the dining room table and sat down. Maria served the meal, and everyone had good conversation and ate. After dinner the adults went out to the patio and had after dinner drinks. The children watched TV and then at 10 PM they went to bed. The adults decided to sit in the hot tub and everyone had another drink and climbed in. About midnight everyone went to their rooms and to bed.

On Thanksgiving Day all the girls were up at 8 AM and in the kitchen working on the feast. It was a tradition and Molly loved it so did Linda and Donna. Maria had the day off and was planning on visiting some friends. She had left at 6 AM and would be back on Friday. The children were just getting up about 9 AM and Linda had breakfast ready for them. After they ate they watched the parades on TV and played outside for the rest of the morning. John, Ray and Miles were up and drinking coffee at the pool. Linda had also fixed some sweet rolls and had them ready for the men to eat while they had coffee. It was going to be a good day John thought. At noon the men watched a football game and had a drink. At 2 PM dinner was served so everyone went to the table and sat and ate. The food was wonderful and after dinner everyone was totally stuffed. The girls took a break then cleaned up the kitchen or at least got things put up and most of the dishes in the dishwasher. Maria was coming back on Friday and would do the real cleanup.

Friday John had reserved cars to take the girls and kids to the mall and other places Molly wanted to go and to take him, Miles and Ray out to Red Lion and then to Molly's bar. John, Miles, and Ray left the house and were driven to the Red Lion complex in Sugarland. The complex was closed as it always was over Thanksgiving, but the security guards were always on duty and the limo was stopped at the gate and John showed the Officer his ID and everyone in the vehicle showed ID and was logged into the compound. The limo stopped at the front and the three men got out. John showed Ray and Miles into the headquarters. John showed Miles everything and Ray also followed and saw the headquarters again. On the tour John explained exactly what Red Lion did to Miles. After the tour while Ray and Miles were looking around the operations center, John checked his secure messages and read the SITREP. About two hours had passed since the three men had arrived and John asked Miles if he had any questions. Miles said "John I had no idea any of this existed or was even real. I had heard many stories about covert type things, but I always figured they were wildly exaggerated and only the government could really do anything like this. WOW!"

John said, "Well Miles it really did start with the government, but it has now progressed into an international business and we are worth a Hell of a lot of money". Then John said, "OK shall we go get a drink and maybe something to eat?" Ray and Miles nodded, and all three men left the Red Lion headquarters and got into the limo and started for Molly's bar. Everyone was back at John's house by 4 PM and while the kids played outside and watched TV, the adults had a drink and about 6 PM started getting ready for dinner. John had made reservations at Eddie V's and the limo was going to take the adults there. Maria was fixing food for the children and would be watching them until the adults returned. The dinner at Eddie V's was fantastic as John and Molly hoped it would be and everyone enjoyed it. The group was back at the house and in bed by 12 midnight. The next day John and Molly followed the limo to the air field and told everyone good bye and Ray took off with all on board and headed back. John and Molly went back to the house and relaxed for a while.

On Wednesday before Thanksgiving the interrogators had made very little progress with the Garcia brothers. At 6 PM both brothers were stripped and put into the wire cages. One bottle of water and two corn tortillas were placed into the cage with each brother. The cages had been set with an electrical charge that would happen if the wire was touched. Of course, the brothers were not told that. Then extremely bright lights were turned on and the interrogators left the building. The only sound was the sucker rod of the oil pump behind the building. Operators had volunteered to take four hour shifts outside the building just to insure no one came on the property and so at 6 PM the first operator arrived and parked on the road about 100 yards from the building. The engine noise could not be heard inside the building and that was the point. The interrogators wanted total silence for the next forty-eight hours. Only the lights and the sound of the pump. The Garcia brothers of course touched the wire cages and were shocked with a charge equal to a stun gun set on the lowest setting. This would happen every time the cage was touched by them. The cell phones that the brothers had on them when they had been taken, had been given to Cindy and she had worked on them and gotten all the possible information recorded and then checked. There were many text messages that had been sent and received plus many phone numbers that were now calling the cell phones of the brothers and leaving messages. It was clear that the entire gang was trying to get in touch with the Garcia brothers. Each number was then traced to the tower that had been used and locations were plotted on a map. The map showed locations in Texas and New Mexico and Cindy was convinced that these were the locations closest to where the gang lieutenants operated from. Cindy passed this information on to Tress.

On Saturday the interrogators were back at work and each brother was taken into a room individually and the process started. The interrogators worked for eight hours on Saturday and then a thirty-minute break was given, and the process started all over again. The only food was the tortillas. One each time the interrogations stopped for the thirty-minute break and one bottle of water. The brothers were told that when the water was gone there would be no more until information was gotten. Various forms of techniques were used including electric shock and truth drugs. Also, water boarding was applied. On Sunday morning the Garcia brothers broke totally and told everything about the biker gang including names and locations of members, bank account locations, places where drugs were located and places where weapons and humans were being kept. They also told the names of the drug cartel people they worked with and the names of the arms dealers. Some information that surprised John was the names of government agents the Garcia brothers swore were on their payroll. By Sunday night both brothers were in very bad condition but of course no medical attention was given. The interrogators did give each brother some food in very small quantities and another bottle of water. All the information from the interrogation had been passed to Red Lion headquarters and was being analyzed by Sandy, Tress, Don and Cindy. The brothers were put back into the wire cages and left totally alone again.

On Monday, John received a fax on the secure line. The fax asked if John knew anything about the Garcia brothers. John sent a fax back which said "I have never lied to you Liz or to the President. I want to continue that record. So, I will ignore the fax that was sent so I can continue the record". John got a reply immediately which said "Understood". Now John was ready to plan the total elimination of the Los Diablos and he wanted it to be a very good elimination. John wanted to get as many of the gang as possible in one location so one raid would do the trick. John told Tress and Jim what he would like and both men went to work on a plan.

Sandy had now been able to gather information on what was happening in Phoenix at FBI headquarters there and at the Federal building. It was a mess. The attorneys both of Garcia's people had filed several motions with the Federal court to produce the brothers but of course the FBI did not have them, and Hell was on-going in the courts because no one believed the FBI including the Federal Judge. The CIA was also under the gun as was the DEA and ATF. Sandy had been able to get the exact names of the attorneys and passed that information on to Don who did a complete background search on them. Tress was busy compiling a list of things to be sent to the various agencies about the names of cartel contacts, locations of drugs, weapons and the humans that were being sold into prostitution by the biker gang. Tress wanted to have the different agencies do raids at the same time Red Lion did their raid but that was a problem. Tress and Jim talked to John and it was decided that John would talk to Liz. John called Liz and arranged for her to come to Houston for the meeting in five days. The Garcia brothers had told everything that they could to the interrogators and now were useless to John and Red Lion. The word was given to eliminate the brothers and it was done. Both bodies were removed from the building and disposed of. The building was then sanitized and left as it had been.

Liz arrived in Houston and John met her at the airport and drove her to the hotel he had arranged for her. When Liz walked into her suite she saw Tress, Jim, Sandy and Nelson all sitting around a table waiting for her and John. There were folders on the table labeled for FBI, CIA, DEA, ATF, and "Eyes Only" for the President. Liz said hello and sat where John had motioned. John then said "Liz I needed you here, so we can work out some things that should be done and in my opinion, must be done. I will need you to get the Boss involved so these things will happen exactly as scheduled. If after we finish, and you explain everything to the Boss, he does not want the agencies involved we will understand, but our part will go forward no matter what. It is totally personal with Red Lion and you know why".

Liz said, "John I know you had a very bad situation and seemingly you solved that, but what the fuck is all of this about?"

John said, "Just listen Liz, we will explain everything, and you probably need to write down most of this, so you do not get things confused". Sandy handed Liz a tablet and a pen. John said, "Tress will start". Tress explained in detail all the intelligence that had been gathered and which agency was considered involved. He also explained that a raid by officials needed to be done and had to be coordinated so every area was hit at the exact same time. That way no one could be warned and escape. After Tress finished, John said "Now Liz we have some major problems that need to be addressed now and dealt with immediately. Until we have completed the raids, these people need to be held with no communication to anyone. If we lose the court case so what, Red Lion can always take care of the situation, but these people must be taken out of the net immediately. I suggest they go to GITMO but that will be the Boss's call".

Liz said, "Damn John you sound like these people are terrorists or some dam thing".

John said "Worse, Traitors!"

Liz sat straight up in her chair and said, "Give me the names". Sandy handed Liz the list of names of the people on the Garcia's payroll. Liz looked at the list and said "John this is terrible. I will get this done immediately. God how does this happen?"

John said "Money. That is the deal. Money". The meeting had been going for over three hours and everyone was ready for a break. John suggested they all go down and have a drink and get something to eat and relax for a while before continuing the session. Everyone agreed, and the group left and went to the bar and got drinks and ordered food. After everyone had finished and had relaxed for a little bit the group returned to Liz's suite and finished the discussion. Liz told John she was going to leave as soon as the jet was ready and go straight to Washington. John agreed and took her back to Ellington AFB and watched her board the government jet. Sandy had taken care of the hotel and the rest of the Red Lion group was back at the headquarters.

Four days had passed since Liz had been briefed on the situation and still no word from Washington. John was getting frustrated and that was not a good thing. Christmas was approaching, and John knew all too well that Washington did not do a damn thing from December 15th to January 5th. John did not want to wait that long because the Garcia brothers had been missing for three weeks and the gang was starting to realize something was very wrong. John told Tress to get the raid set in three days regardless of the other agencies. Red Lion would eliminate the Los Diablos. Tress and Sandy had the operation plan ready the next morning and the briefing was set for 9 AM. At 4 PM John received a fax from Liz. The decision was made to have all the agencies involved wait until January to conduct a raid. They would coordinate with John then. John just laughed to himself and wondered how much money Red Lion would make because of the total government not being able to do a damn thing. John knew one thing for sure, Red Lion would be involved and that was a good thing.

The briefing on the raid was now going on and John was surprised at how simple the concept had been set up. Tress had decided that Don would send a text message using Faldo Garcia's cell phone to everyone on his phone that had been identified as a member of the biker gang. The message was to have all members go to their local headquarters and be ready to get a message via Skype. Then the raids would be done on each of the four locations at the same time. The operators would be in position a day in advance and would work their way to the exact location thirty minutes prior to the raid time. The timing was set for 9 PM, so the cover of darkness would aid the operators. Las Cruces was of course the biggest location and that was the only location that would receive a different text. The Cobra would be used against the Las Cruces location and Black Hawks against the other locations. The Black Hawks would be fitted with missile firing capabilities for this raid. Plans were set to use civilian air fields for all the aircraft, so Don and Cindy were working on hacking the computers at each field to authorize the landing and takeoff of the choppers. The operators were going to drive to each city and be prepared to start the raid at the exact same time at each city. Each team would consist of twenty-five operators and Nelson would be the overall operator in charge. The purpose was to inflect total elimination of everyone at each location and then set charges to explode the buildings that were being used as the headquarters. Nelson and one operator had a special mission and would be doing that as soon as the raids had been completed. They were to eliminate the attorneys Garcia had used. The attorneys were based in Las Cruces and had very expensive homes. Again, Don had a plan to get them in one location and it would work. The attorneys would receive a message from Jose to meet him at one of the attorney's house at 9:30 PM to get payment on their fees. The plan was now complete and was set for the 20th of December to be done.

# CHAPTER 48

The cities involved in the raids were spread out and in three different states, so no actual connection would be made immediately if any was ever made that the biker group had been targeted. Las Cruces in New Mexico and Phoenix in Arizona and Lubbock and El Paso were in Texas. All the operators were in place in each city and Nelson and his partner were set for the attorneys. The Cobra was set to land at the Las Cruces airport and the Black Hawks had clearance to land at Phoenix, Lubbock and El Paso. Each chopper would land and re-fuel then at the same time, the choppers would lift off and be gone. The clearances had been done under a special FAA code for military training and no one would question that. Don would erase the FAA authorizations exactly five minutes after the choppers had departed each airport. Midland at Miles' ranch was going to be used by the Lubbock and El Paso Black Hawks for refueling and Don was using another authorization sent to Albuquerque for the Cobra and the other Black Hawk. Then they would all fly to Hallettsville and again take on fuel for the return to Houston. Each operator team would drive back to the base in the vehicles they had used to get to their locations unless there was a problem. Then the operators would get back the best way they could and that was always the way the plan went.

Don had texted the messages and the operators reported seeing bikers arriving at each location. At exactly 9 PM the raids started. The Cobra made a pass over the Garcia house and fired rockets into the structure. The operators then attacked and eliminated any remaining members. The Black

Hawks also made the rocket runs on their targets and the operators did the same thing and eliminated everyone in the locations. Nelson and his partner entered the attorney's house and swiftly executed both attorneys. They were shot in the head. The operators used silenced weapons and were in and out in less than thirty seconds. No one in the house realized that the men had been killed. The total body count was over 200 dead. The exact number was not verified because of the explosions and fires. The operators suffered no casualties, and all were on their way out of the areas in less than twenty minutes from the time of the first rocket hitting the target. The choppers also were on their way back and everything worked perfectly, just as planned. In less than one hour it was over with and John and the rest of the Red Lion base were relieved. By December the 22$^{nd}$ all choppers and operators were back at Red Lion and the entire Red Lion operation was going to be closed for the next twelve days. John and Molly were planning on Christmas in Houston and then New Year's in Redman Beach. Jim and Latoya were coming to John and Molly's for Christmas dinner in the afternoon and would probably go with them to Redman Beach. Carol and Dan coming for Christmas dinner and John had invited Tress and Sandy to come. They were living together now so it was a family deal so to speak.

Christmas was very nice. Molly had ordered the entire dinner and it had been delivered the 24$^{th}$ and Maria had placed it in the kitchen ready to be served before she left for her holiday. Maria would not be back until January 3$^{rd}$ and that was fine with John and Molly. Molly and John had given Maria her Christmas bonus check of $10,000 and her presents Molly had picked so she was very happy. Maria went to her family's house for the Christmas holiday every year. John had arranged a private jet to fly her to Mexico City where they lived, and it would pick her up on the 3rd of January and bring her back. An operator had picked her up at the house and taken her to Red Lion to catch the jet. The guests showed up about noon and everyone was in a great mood. Molly and John fixed drinks and everyone sat and talked and relaxed. Molly, Carol, Sandy and Latoya were busy getting the food ready and about 2 PM everyone sat down to eat. The dinner went well, and everyone thought that Molly had done the right thing in having it catered. After the dinner was done, the women cleaned up the dishes and the kitchen and the men went out and had a drink and talked about the world situation, the upcoming year and other things. The women joined them, and everyone relaxed for a while. About 7 PM the guests left, and John and Molly got into the hot tub and enjoyed being alone.

John had planned to leave Houston on the 28th of December to go to Redman Beach and Jim and Latoya were to be at the airfield at 9 AM. John got a call about 6 AM from Liz. She was asking how in the Hell she was going to explain to all the agencies that the Los Diablos no longer existed. John said "Liz I told you if they could not move we would so tell them to get off their ass the next time and function. Happy New Year". Liz was not pleased but there was nothing she could do about things and she knew it.

Liz said, "When will you be available to speak to the agencies about the information we gave them?"

John said, "After the 5th of January". Liz said, "OK have a good New Year's". John hung up and laughed. He and Molly went to the airfield and met Jim and Latoya and they all climbed on the jet and headed for Florida. Louise had a car waiting for John and his group at the airport. The new airport was now completed, sand it was really first class. The car took the group to the house and Louise met them and got the luggage into the right rooms. Then Molly fixed everyone a drink and they all sat out on the patio and watched the ocean for a while. The house was just perfect as was expected. John excused himself and went to his office and turned on the computer, fax and the secure SAT phone and then returned to the patio. Nothing was going on and Jim had no calls, so things were alright. Everyone spent the next few days just enjoying Redman Beach at Ted's and walking around the boardwalk area and seeing things that were going on. They had dinner one night at the country club and one night at a new place about three miles out of town. New business was starting to move into the area and John was watching very carefully and hoping things would not really change much. The business was good but too much would take away the idea of the town. John and Jim discussed the C-141 idea, and both agreed it was something that Red Lion needed. Right now, there was no dependable way to get across the oceans in a fast way for Red Lion other than commercial flights and then the problem of the equipment always came into play. Jim decided that he would make the C-141 his main priority at the start of the year.

New Year's was different this year. John and Molly had been invited to the party at the country club, but they wanted to go to Ted's. John said, "Hell why not do both?" It was a done deal. The four left the house about 8 PM and went to the country club and mixed with the people there. Molly introduced Jim and Latoya to many people and John also was introducing Jim and Latoya around. At 10:30 PM John nodded to Molly and she got Latoya and Jim and they slid out to the parking lot and Molly had her car and John's car brought around. Jim and Latoya were using Molly's car because each car could only seat two people comfortably. John joined them in about two minutes and they all headed to Ted's for the real party. Ted's was very busy, but John found Ted and got a table. The band was good and at midnight everyone had a blast bringing in the New Year. The party went on until 4 AM then John suggested that the four of them go get something to eat. They drove to an all- night dinner and went inside and had a fantastic breakfast. After breakfast it was home and then into the hot tub for everyone. About 6 AM they all went to bed. John and Molly had a ball and so did Jim and Latoya. No one got up until sometime around 4 PM in the afternoon. The next day, Jim and John went to look at the airport in detail and especially at the Red Lion hangers and office. The hangers were exactly what John had asked for. There were three and two were large enough for the C-141 or the C-130 to fit into. The other hanger could house all three Black Hawks and the Cobra. The office area was also nice and in the rear of that building there was an area of about 10,000 square feet that was set up for storage of all the equipment and other items needed. The actual office was small but would do the job. It had a reception office area and 4 offices with two offices on each side of a hallway that opened into the storage area. John and Jim liked the set up and now all that was needed was for Don to get the computers and electronics installed. Jim said he would get with Don and have that done the first week of the year once everyone was back at work. John and Jim then discussed if they wanted a person to be at the office full time or if the office and hangers would be activated on an as needed basis. John did not want anyone really knowing what Red Lion was all about the way they would if a person was hired to be there all the time. Jim agreed so nothing would be done to activate the Florida base until necessary. If everything was in place activation would take minutes once the people arrived. John and Jim left and went to get the girls for lunch and some fun.

The next day, the jet arrived and all four of the group boarded and the jet took off to Houston. The vacation was officially over and the next day back to work. It was Jan 4th, 2013.

John was waiting at the house to see what the news was saying about Syria. Something had happened, and John did not get the report, the first time it was on. Molly was already getting ready to go to the bar and see how things were going. John heard the news. The Syrian government has used poison gas on its own people. Thousands have been killed and thousands more have been wounded in these attacks". John wondered what the President would do now and then thought nothing because the only real action would be to send ground troops into the country and that would be a declaration of war. Nothing was going to be done and the world knew it. Since the President had taken office the first time the reputation of the United States had fallen greatly and every day it fell more. Our allies did not believe the US would stand behind them when it was really needed, and the enemies no longer feared the US as they had before. This President was not doing well, and John knew it. The President's party still controlled the Senate, but the other party controlled the House and was causing major problems because nothing was being done about anything. The Mexican border was the biggest problem because it was allowing everything to come into the country un-stopped. Texas was really getting mad and so was Arizona and even California. The next problems in John's mind would be the damn border thing. Red Lion was damn sure staying out of that. KBR had completed all the work it was going to do in Iraq and now the Red Lion operators were being sent back to the states. The contract was over in March. Jim and Tress met with John and the three men discussed the idea of having Barbara interview the operators coming back from the KBR contract to see if any of these men would be suited for operators for Red Lion to replace the ones who were leaving. John was agreeable, and Tress and Jim thought it would be very good for everyone to keep some of the people already at Red Lion. The new operators when they were changed to that position would be sent to Hallettsville for a month to Harry, so he could train them in the style he had trained the original group. Jim told Barbara to get working on that immediately. The next item was the C-141. The plane was available, but it would have to be taken back to the manufacturer for a total inspection and possibly a refit. The cost was going to be $45 Million Dollars to buy the plane and probably another $10 Million to get it serviceable. The original cost had been $475 Million so it was a very good deal. John approved of the purchase. Barbara had also found a complete crew for the aircraft and a complete ground crew to maintain the plane. Jim told Barbara to contact the people and bring them on board as soon as possible. John was now ready for the annual Board meeting so that was set for the next Monday at 10 AM. Nancy put out the word to all concerned.

The Board meeting was ready to begin, and John called the meeting to order. All members were present as the roll was called so the meeting was now officially opened. John gave the opening remarks and talked about what had been accomplished during the past year and what was on the immediate future for the corporation. Barbara was invited to give the Human Resources presentation and she discussed the downsizing of the KBR operators and the movement of some of them to positions that were being vacated by the operators who were retiring. She also discussed the new aviation assets for the C-141 aircraft. Barbara finished and left the meeting room. John then had Jim give an over view of the status of all operations and equipment as well as any pending contracts. The last person to present was Sara with the financial report. She discussed the revenues and expenses for the past year and then gave the bottom line. The corporation had $670 Billion Dollars in assets including stocks, equipment, real estate, aviation, navel, vehicles and all other assets. The cash position was $560 Billion Dollars. Total worth of the corporation at market including the cash was $1.2 Trillion Dollars. John thanked Sara and then said "I would like to entertain the idea of paying a dividend on the stocks that each of us own. We are a closed corporation, so we need to vote the dividend to take money out other than our salaries. Based on the stock distribution we now have, I would suggest we pay a dividend of $200 Dollars per share to all stock holders".

Sara said, "John that would be over $200 Million Dollars can we actually cut our cash that low?"

John said, "Sara if we pay the money, we will still have $500 + Billion Dollars in the bank so yes in my opinion we can and should pay out the money".

John said, "Ok a motion is on the table do I hear a second?"

Jim said, "I second".

John said, "Motion seconded let us vote by show of hands, all in favor". Every member raised their hands. Then John said "Unanimous, motion carried".

John said, "Sara please prepare the payments according to our stock ledger".

Sara said "Yes Sir. I will have things ready tomorrow". John then asked for any other business and when no one said anything John made a motion to close and adjourn. The motion was seconded voted and passed. The meeting was ended. The stockholder's meeting was then started and only one statement was made by John and then the meeting was closed. The statement was: A $200 dollar per share dividend had been voted by the Board. John and Sara had a meeting in John's office after the Board meeting and discussed John's personal finances. Sara said, "John I have the figures here, so I will go over them with you". Sara handed John a piece of paper and then she said "Right now as of the 1st of the year, you have $420 Million Dollars in real estate, vehicles, and stocks. You have another $150 Million Dollars in oil revenues that were left to you by your grandmother and are paid each year. That changes with the price of oil yearly, but the $150 Million figure is pretty accurate. Your cash position is really the biggest portion of your wealth and is over $8 Billion Dollars and will increase by $102 Million when the dividend is paid. Now the special off-shore accounts have $4.6 Billion Dollars in them and they pay 28% per year interest. As you have told me, not counting the off-shore accounts you have a total financial worth of $ 12 Billion 570 Million in cash and other assets".

John said "Sara thank you very much. What is Molly's position looking like?"

Sara handed John another piece of paper and said "Molly has the bar worth $25 Million Dollars and then she of course owns half of the houses and her cars, but not taking that into consideration she has over $4 Million Dollars in Jewelry and her stocks are now worth $45 Million Dollars. With the new payments announced today she will receive and additional cash payment of $30 Million Dollars and that will bring her cash total to $100 Million Dollars. So, your wife is worth $183 Million Dollars by herself".

John said "Sara again thank you very much. David knows this I am sure so again thanks". Sara stood up and left and as she was leaving the office said, "You are very welcome Sir".

John decided to go to Molly's and give Molly the news. John walked in and saw Molly and Carol sitting and talking. The conversation seemed very intense, so John just sat at the bar and waited. After a few minutes Molly saw John and came over and kissed him and said "Damn you must be a mind reader. Carol and I were just talking about you and I was just getting ready to call you sweetheart".

John said, "OK what is going on with the two of you and what was that discussion all about?" Molly hollered at Carol and Carol came over to where John was sitting and said, "Hi John we were just talking about you".

John said "Yes dear Molly told me. So, what is going on?"

Molly said "Carol is coming to the house tonight and we need to talk. Can you call Dan and have Dan come too?"

John said, "Ok why?"

Molly said "We need his legal mind on this deal we have come up with. I will tell you all about it tonight, just call him please". John got his cell phone and called Dan and told him he was needed at John's house about 6 PM if he was free". Dan said, "Sure is something wrong, John?"

John said "I have no idea. Molly just wanted your brilliant legal mind".

Dan laughed and said, "OK see you at 6 PM". John then hung up his cell and put in back in his pocket and had another beer. He had no idea what was going to happen in about three hours, but it should be wild.

Dan was there at 6 PM and Molly and Carol had just gotten home. John had been home for about an hour. Dan came in the den and John got him a drink. Molly and Carol came in from the patio and said hello and then Molly got each of them another drink. Molly said "Dan we need you to help us out with a deal we want to do. Here is what Carol and I would like to have done if we can do it. We want to incorporate Molly's Bar and issue stock on the open market to investors".

Dan said, "Ok why?"

Molly said, "Well we feel it would be a very good thing and initially it would raise a lot of money for the bar, so I do not have to use my money and Carol does not have to use her money and we think people would love to own a bar".

John said, "Oh My God!"

Molly said, "You just listen, John".

Dan said, "Ok we sure as Hell can incorporate and how many shares do you want to offer?"

Molly said "1 Million".

Dan said "Holy shit. Well Ok I can do all of that so what will be the break down as to who will own what before we put shares up for sale and how much do you think you want to offer the shares for?"

Carol said "Dan, Molly and I each want to own 26% of the stock for a total combined of 51%. Then we offer the remaining 49% at $9 per share. Can we do that?"

Dan said, "Yes but I will need some facts about what the actual value of the business is worth and all that".

Molly said "Ok you will have that from the accountant. Carol will have him call you tomorrow and set up a time for him to meet with you".

Dan said, "Ladies it is a pleasure".

John said "I will be damned. This is something totally out of the blue. When did you two dream this deal up?"

Molly said, "John you are not the only business tycoon in this house". And started to laugh. Then everyone laughed, and Molly fixed everyone another drink. The night was very good, and everyone was having a great time. About 10 PM Dan said he was going to have to go and Carol said she was too

The next morning John and Molly were having coffee and discussing the financials Sara had given John.

# CHAPTER 49

John was now ready to stop doing as much as he had been doing because the Mexican bikers were done and everything else could be run by Jim and Tress. It was now almost the middle of February and Dan had done the corporation paperwork for Molly's Lounge and was just waiting for it to be returned. The C-141 was now owned by Red Lion and Barbara had hired all the personnel assets needed for the plane. KBR was totally out of Iraq and the original operators that had decided to retire were now officially out of the company. 30 of the operators that had been on the KBR mission had been moved into slots and were now operators for Red Lion teams. They were in training in Hallettsville. The total operators were now at 50 available for any operation. Nelson had also promoted five operators to team leader and broken down the teams so that five ten-man teams were now being used.

The C-141 crew had flown the aircraft to the factory and the re-fit was underway. Don had also gone to the factory to have some updated equipment installed and Jim had gone to coordinate with the factory for the special items Red Lion wanted installed on the aircraft. The plane was scheduled back completed in four weeks. The container ship was also completed ahead of schedule and had arrived back in Galveston. The new additions and specialty equipment had been installed and Anderson was delighted. The ship was now capable of making 50 knots and used less fuel. The new deck now allowed 6 choppers to land if required. The total computer system at Red Lion was now in the process of an upgrade. Also, all the TV monitors were being replaced. The supply tech had a total re-supply of all the equipment that was also up-graded, and some additional items had been ordered. Jim had also replaced all the vehicles and they had gotten back from the paint shop and were ready for use.

Dan wanted to meet with Molly and Carol on Friday night at Molly's, so John decided to go along just for the Hell of it. John and Molly arrived, and Dan was already there talking with Carol and John knew it was sure as Hell not about business. The four sat down and Dan said "OK Girls you are now officially a corporation and in business as such. Now we need to get a list of Officers, a Board of Directors and all that crap so tell me who is who".

Molly said "OK I am the President and CEO. Carol is the Executive Vice President. Hell, Dan why don't you be the Secretary and I have no idea who else we would want in the Officer positions".

Carol said, "I guess we need a formal Treasurer but who?"

Dan said, "Why not you, Carol?" Dan said, "You see Officers can hold other positions as long as they only hold two and no more so Carol you are the Treasurer".

Molly said "OK now for the Board. I guess we have duel Chairman because we both hold an equal share of stock is that Ok Dan?"

Dan said "No we want to have Board Members, then they elect a Chairman, so we know you and Carol, and I guess I will be on the board, but we really need a couple more. How about John?" Carol and Molly both nodded in agreement. The last member was going to be Latoya if she would take the position. Molly called Latoya and she accepted. Molly said, "OK how about having the Board of Directors meeting on Sunday at our house and then we can all have dinner and things". Everyone agreed so it was set.

Sunday at 1 PM the official first meeting of Molly's Bar Inc. was opened. The Officers were named, and the Board was named with the addition of Jim. He was now a Board Member and after a vote he was elected as Chairman. Jim accepted and now things were set to function. Dan announced that the official stock symbol would be MOLB and the IPO was set for April 10th and the opening asking price was $15 dollars per share. Jim and John would contact some brokers they knew and get them working on selling the stock. Carol and Molly were going to advertise at the bar, so things should look good on the 10th. After the meeting was done and all the documents were signed and so forth everyone had a few drinks and relaxed by the pool. Molly had called, and the food was due about 6 PM. She had it catered from the country club, so it was going to be a real deal. It was the first week of April and in four days the IPO would hit the market. When the food arrived, Maria took care of it and about 7 PM the group ate and then returned to the hot tub for after dinner drinks. Molly had decided everyone should stay the night, so it was settled. The next morning, Maria had breakfast and coffee as well as Bloody Mary's for everyone. Then about 10 AM everyone but John and Molly left.

John and Jim had talked to some broker friends and Dan had done an excellent job in having one firm he knew well be the lead agency for the IPO. Also, Molly and Carol had gotten the customers excited so on the 10th the stock took off. By noon the entire offering had been sold. The bar was now $18 Million Dollars richer after all the IPO shares were sold. During the selling the stock had reached a high of $36 dollars per share. Molly and Carol were very happy. Now they had plenty of money to do the renovations that were needed and to add things they wanted. Molly called Jake and he was hired to do the job. Jake decided to do the work in sections, so the bar would never be closed. Jake had bought 400 shares, so he was invested. The work started the next Monday.

John and Molly were having dinner at Eddie V's and enjoying the jazz group when John's cell phone rang. John looked at the caller ID and knew it was trouble instantly.

John said "Hello". The voice on the other end said, "John are you secure?"

John said, "No I am at dinner and on the cell and it is not a secure line".

Liz was on the other end and she said "John we need to talk to you ASAP so get somewhere we can call please. The Boss needs to speak to you".

John said "OK Liz it will be about thirty minutes so please have him understand. Should I call this number?"

Liz said, "Yes as soon as is humanly possible, John this is major". John hung up and told Molly he had to go, and she could stay if she wanted. Molly said No she would go with him. John got the check and headed home. He was back at the house and making the call in fifteen minutes. John listened, and the President came on the line. The President said "John we have a major problem in the Far East and it is going to be a total disaster if we cannot stop it within twenty-four hours. Can you do that?"

John said "Mr. President what the Hell is the problem? Then maybe I can but I have to have details before I can tell you anything".

The President said, "It is the entire BP Offshore oil complex that has been taken over by a group of terrorists and they are threatening to blow up the whole thing in twenty-four hours".

John said, "What do they want?"

The President said "That is the problem they have not made any demands and Hell we do not even know exactly who these bastards are. I have been on the phone with the Chairman of BP and he does not know anything. Hell no one knows anything".

John said "I see Sir. Have Liz fax everything we have on the situation and have BP send every detail of the oil field area as well as the number and location of the rigs, etc. to us. I will call you back, but we need a lot more time than twenty-four hours I do know that". The President said "Thanks" and hung up. John called Jim and Tress and had them do a total re-call of Red Lion. John then had a beer and waited for about thirty minutes then went to the office. Molly decided to drop by the bar and she headed that way when John left.

The fax was in the Red Lion office when John arrived, and Tress and Jim already had a copy and had read through it. John read the document and then went to Tress' office to discuss the situation. Sandy had pulled up the terrorist group and it was one on the list of possible targets Red Lion had complied months before. The group was unknown to most intelligence agencies worldwide and was very small in comparison to most of the radical Muslim groups in the Far East. John asked Tress what he thought about the twenty-four hours and Tress said "Sir, there is no way we can do anything in that time frame. We will need at least a week or more and then it will be pushing things. Hell, we do not really know where their base is or how many we are dealing with. I am sorry but that is reality".

John said, "I understand so what will we need?"

Tress and Sandy looked at the fax again and then Sandy said "Sir, we will need at least five days to even get people there and we really need the ship on this one so let me call Anderson and see how much time he needs to get there."

John said, "Alright do what you can and let me know immediately when you know something". John left and went back to his office. Jim was waiting. John sat down, and Jim said "I called the aircraft factory and we can have the C-141 in three days but not everything will be on it. They will need about an additional twenty-four hours to complete so if we can buy five days we can have it complete, but it will cost about double".

John said "OK I will see if we can buy that time. Thanks Jim". Jim left and headed toward Tress' office. John sent a fax to Liz and explained what was going to be needed and that he would have a complete time schedule in about two hours. The reply was "OK but Hurry". John knew there was panic at the White House. Sandy buzzed John and said Anderson needed nine days to get in position after he loaded. John then figured Red Lion would need ten days before they could do anything. The ship would have to port somewhere that the C-141 could land and off load the necessary personnel and equipment. John sent the fax to Liz stating how many days were required. In less than thirty minutes the reply came back. "Prepare and hold we need to get with BP and then we will advise". John thought "Ok then BP knows something. What the fuck is it?" John sat and had a coffee and waited for Washington. John received a call in two hours from Liz and she explained BP had just received a demand. The group wanted $500 Billion dollars, or they would blow up six rigs and two off shore holding platforms. The platforms held over eight million barrels of crude each so sixteen million barrels would be destroyed. The rigs were also a major loss if they were destroyed and there was absolutely no way to know how much oil would go into the sea. BP had already had a major problem off the coast of Louisiana in the years past. That was not completely settled as of now, so another problem would just about put BP out of business and send oil prices to unknown highs. The US could not let that happen nor could the rest of the world, but no government had the capability to move as fast as Red Lion did. Liz was trying to get BP to buy time and so far, it was working. The $500 Billion was a good thing because that money could not be raised quickly. Liz told John to proceed with the raid per the President. John went into Tress and Sandy and told them to get it working and do it in nineteen days. John sent a fax to Liz stating the Red Lion invoice would be $100 Billion. The answer was back in less than ten minutes. "OK GO. BP will pay. The White House guarantees that.

Jim had the complete helicopter assets sent by truck in four hours to Galveston. The equipment container was also sent. The container ship left Galveston at 5 AM the next morning headed out. Tress and Sandy were almost finished with the attack plan, but aerial photos were needed, so Tress re-directed three satellites to the target area and had them stay on station for six rotations. This would give Tress a complete picture of the area over a twenty-four-hour period. The C-141 would arrive in five days at Red Lion headquarters finished with all that was ordered. Nelson was in Tress' office going over the plan of attack. No one knew for sure if the rigs were already wired with explosives and that was a big problem. There was no way anyone could think of to find out without going to the rigs. Nelson had an idea and he and Tress discussed it. The basic idea was to send someone to the rig that was the biggest one or to the platform to negotiate about the employees and where to do the money exchange. It sounded silly, but if it was done right, it would look like BP was trying to do the right thing but just did not know what to do. If it worked, the operator who was sent could see if the rig he was on was rigged for explosives and then Tress and Nelson could assume the other rigs were also rigged. Nelson and Tress discussed the plan for a while. The location BP was in had some advantages because it was located between Sumatra, Java, and Kalimantan. These countries were small and most of them were friendly to the US government. They were also making one Hell of a lot of money doing business with BP Oil. Tress decided to contact BP and see where they were based for support of the drilling locations. He was told that the main headquarters was in Java, Jakarta to be exact and they would cooperate totally with Red Lion, giving the Red Lion any access that was needed. Now Tress had what he needed so Tress and Nelson formed a plan to send an operator out to the main platform. Nelson had just the man in mind, because he spoke the language used by the Terrorists and looked like an executive that would be with BP. Nelson briefed the operator on what was required, and they went over the questions to ask and the cover story. That afternoon the operator left Houston on a first-class commercial flight for Java. It would take twenty-four hours to get on the ground.

The container ship was going to use a port in Jakarta and the C-141 would also use the airport there. Cargo planes were flying in and out of the airport daily and ships were also using the port continuously. It was perfect for Red Lion. The operators were briefed on the mission. Tress and Sandy had decided to use the C-141 for a selective HALO drop and then the operators would use scuba gear to get to the rigs and platforms. The choppers would be in a holding pattern on the container ship with additional operators onboard and then they would fly directly to the rigs and platforms when the all clear was given that the explosives had been disarmed. Timing was going to be critical. The HALO drop would be for only sixteen operators, two per target. The main problem was the hostages being held. Each BP rig had thirty employees assigned and the platforms had forty employees on each one. A total of 160 employees, if none had been killed, would have to be taken off the rigs and platforms and the only way to do that was by using the Black Hawks or possibly boats that could be retained by BP. If the Black Hawks were used it would mean ten to twelve trips and with only three choppers, that would take a while. Tress and Sandy planned to use the choppers until they were told that BP could handle the evacuation of their personnel. John had been briefed by Jim on the operation and he was worried. It was going to be one Hell of a large-scale operation and John was worried about the timing. If one of the rigs did explode, not only would Red Lion operators be killed but so would the hostages. Also, the oil would flow.

Things were busy and tense at Red Lion. John had only run home for a few hours at a time and Tress and Sandy had not left the compound. Jim had only left once to get some clothes and Nelson had stayed since the re-call. The operation was now in the last days before launch and operators were double checking everything. A final briefing was set for 2 PM and the entire Red Lion staff would be in the briefing. Tress and Sandy had studied the satellite photos and the high-resolution images did show explosives on rigs. At least that was the assumption, but confirmation was still needed, and it had come through about twelve hours ago. The operator had been able to get on and off the platform and yes, all the rigs and platforms were wired with C-4. The probable trigger would be a cell phone for each rig and platform. Don was trying to figure out a way to block the cell transmissions but there were at least ten towers that could be used so it was going to be hard to block all of them. Sandy was still trying to locate the exact terrorist base and had it narrowed down to three locations. Don and Cindy decided to block all cell towers that any of the three locations could use. That was a real gamble, but the only one Red Lion had. The photos showed that each rig had six terrorists on them and the platforms each had ten to twelve on each of them. There were constant lookouts 24/7 so it would be impossible to use a chopper unless the explosives were eliminated. Then choppers could attack.

Tress started the briefing. The plan was to have the HALO teams jump from the C-141 at 25,000 feet and land in the water. They would then use the scuba gear to go to the rigs and platforms. Each team would move to the designated target and dispose of the explosives. Then on a set schedule, the Black Hawks would bring in operators and of load them on each rig and platform. The distance between the rigs was in Red Lion's favor and each platform was set at the far end of the field so one was on the east end and one was on the west end. About fifty miles separated the platforms. That was also in Red Lion's favor. The container ship was going to come within two miles of the oil field as soon as the choppers made their attack. The Cobra was going to be held on deck as a backup in case terrorists from the shore tried to approach any of the rigs or platforms. The radar on the container ship would detect that and then the Cobra would attack and destroy the boats. Once the operators were physically on their objectives, they would eliminate all terrorists as quickly as possible. As soon as the objectives were clear Red Lion would inform BP to launch the rescue boats or send in the Black Hawks. That decision would be known about a day before the attack. The distance from the field to the nearest shore was 100 miles so it was going to take a great deal of time if the Black Hawks had to be used for evacuation. At least one-hour flight time to go round-trip plus about twenty minutes on the ground and on the rigs loading and unloading. The most effective way to rescue the employees was by boat and John was now sure of that. The briefing was still going on, but John did not need to hear all of it. John went to his office and called Liz. John and Liz spoke, and Liz decided to have John speak directly with BP and gave John the number to her contact. John called the number and identified himself. In less than two minutes John was speaking to the BP Chairman and was telling him exactly what was needed. BP agreed and would have vessels available. John told the Chairman that BP would be contacted the next day and given exact instructions and they were to be followed exactly as they were set up. If BP deviated in any way Red Lion would stop the mission instantly. The Chairman said he understood and gave John his word everything would be done exactly as instructed. John then went back and told Tress the boats from BP were now available. Tress briefed based on that. The BP vessels were to remain four miles off the area of the rigs and platforms until they were called in. Then they would go to the designated rig or platform and remove the hostages. The Black Hawks would remain on station as security during this time fuel permitting. Once all the hostages were of the rigs, and the security personnel from BP that were to be on the rescue boats were in place, the operators would be picked up by the Black Hawks and returned to the container ship. Once all operators had been recovered and were back on the rescue ship, the container ship would head to port. The choppers would be placed back into the containers and the operators and air crews would be off loaded in port. The C-141 would then take everyone back to the US and to Texas and Sugarland. In the event of any of the operators being wounded they would be taken to the container ship for medical attention immediately by one of the Black Hawks and if necessary then transferred to the hospital via chopper. The container ship would re-fuel and return to Galveston as quickly as possible. All questions were answered, and the briefing was over at 3:30 PM. The next day was the launch of the C-140 with all personnel necessary on board.

John had gone home after the briefing and was in the hot tub when Molly came home from the bar. She immediately joined him, and they sat and relaxed. Sandy, Tress, Jim and Nelson had changed the plan after the briefing on Sandy's insistence. John was sent a fax he was reading when Molly climbed into the hot tub. The change had been to capture one or two of the terrorist and then take them to the container ship. The operator who had gone out to the platform as the BP executive would then along with two others, interrogate the prisoners to get the exact location of the terrorist's headquarters, while the container ship was in route back to port. If the information was not gained by the time the ship docked, the prisoners would be off loaded and taken to a safe house and the interrogation would continue. Once the location and any other information was gotten the prisoners would be eliminated. A new plan would then be devised to eliminate the entire group at a future time. The only problem with that was time. It would be much easier to do the job while the Red Lion assets were there. John called Tress, Jim and Sandy and instructed them to look at that idea. John was called in about two hours and told a new plan was now in effect to destroy the terrorists immediately. Jim would brief John the next day. John was now ready to spend time with Molly and be ready for the next day.

# CHAPTER 50

The C-141 was now on the final approach to the drop point and in twenty seconds the operators would jump. The Black Hawks were ready on deck to be launched along with the Cobra. The extension worked perfectly and now all the choppers were sitting ready for lift off at the same time. BP had the boats sitting about 4 miles away from the oil field and waiting for the call to go in. Don and Cindy were now jamming all the cell towers they had located so things were going as planned.

The first operators hit the water and immediately got rid of the parachutes and put on their scuba masks and activated the air tanks. Each team had landed within 200 yards of their objectives and had approached undetected. The operators climbed up the sides of the rigs and the platforms and started removing the explosives one at a time. The entire operation took forty-five minutes from start to finish. The all clear was transmitted by the operators on each objective and when all had been cleared, the Black Hawks lifted off followed by the Cobra. Two of the Black Hawks approached the platforms first and the operators exited the choppers. The guards opened fire and the gunner on the Black Hawk killed two guards with one burst of machine gun fire. The other guards were killed by the operators and then additional terrorists were killed in other areas of the platform. The third Black Hawk had deposited operators on the closest rig to the platforms and the operators had also come under gun fire from the terrorists on the rig. After three minutes of intense fire the terrorists were killed. This continued at each rig as the Black Hawks went from rig to rig. On the next to last rig, the operators from the

HALO drop had captured two of the terrorists before the fire fights started. The other terrorists were killed instantly by the operators from the Black Hawks. An hour after the initial all clear for the explosives was given the all clear for the objectives was broadcast and the BP boats started toward the rigs and platforms. The hostages had been released by the operators and some were wounded or in need of medical attention from beatings and other wounds. These would be treated when the BP boats reached the port. The two captured terrorists were tied with flex ties and taken on board one of the Black Hawks. Three of the Red Lion operators had received wounds and one was serious. The wounded were taken on board the Black Hawks and transported to the container ship. The prisoners had been taken to the ship and were now being interrogated below deck. The Black Hawks were ferrying the operators back from the rigs and platforms and at 5 AM the operation was completed. The boats had reached the rigs and platforms and the security personnel from BP had gone on the objectives and helped take the hostages off and get them on the boats. This was also completed by 6 AM. Red Lion got the mission completed message at headquarters and relayed it to BP executive offices in Houston and to Washington. One of the operators was taken to the hospital in Jakarta along with two operators to stand security. The other wounded operators had been treated by the medical staff on board the container ship and were now resting in the hospital section of the medical area. Red Lion was making the arrangements to get an air ambulance to Jakarta to bring the wounded operator back to the US. It was going to take twenty-four hours to get the flight there and twenty-four hours for the return trip to Houston's Medical Center.

The container ship was now waiting about eighteen miles off shore for the next phase of the operation to begin. The prisoners were giving very detailed information about the terrorist group and would be eliminated within the next two hours. Tress had received all the details via SAT phone and now along with Sandy had the exact location of the terrorist group headquarters. There were over fifty members that usually were at the camp. Tress and Sandy had the new plan completed and it was sent on the secure email to the ship. Nelson had the plan and was busy assigning operators to each Black Hawk and giving them the operation orders. The Cobra was re-fueled as were the Black Hawks and waiting the GO signal. The plan was very simple. The Black Hawks would transport all the operators on a direct assault of the terrorist camp. The camp consisted of four buildings that were all located in a small valley in the mountains about twenty miles outside Jakarta. There was only one road access and that was a winding road coming down the mountains to the valley floor. Tress had marked the location on a map that was dated 1959 so it was a real guess as to the actual accuracy of the information, but history had told Tress that in that part of the world nothing really changed much. The Cobra would fly cover and then make the final run firing rockets and using the 20 MM gun once the operators were clear. No prisoners were to be taken. The raid would take place in daylight and would be launched in two hours. The container ship would move to within one mile of the shore and launch the aircraft.

The time was set, and the container ship was in position. The aircraft were launched and headed the five miles to the target. In less than ten minutes the first Black Hawk set down and operators raced off and attacked the first building. Then the second chopper and then the third landed and in less than five minutes all operators were off and attacking all the buildings. The terrorists were taken by surprise and the entire raid was over in less than fifteen minutes. There were no terrorist survivors. A brief search of the buildings was conducted, and some information was taken. Then the operators were back on the Black Hawks and headed back to the ship. The Cobra made the first of five runs and after the last run there was nothing left of the buildings. The entire compound was in flames. The Cobra returned to the container ship and the ship headed out to sea. The choppers were stored back in the containers as was the equipment and weapons and the ship headed for port in Jakarta.

The container ship docked and the operators, air crews, medical staff and other members of the support group got off and headed to the airport. The C-141 was waiting and after the personnel were boarded the C-141 took off headed back to the US. There would be two stops for fuel in route. The air ambulance had arrived, and the operator was loaded, and the other operators were also on board. The plane took off and headed for the US. That plane would also make two stops for fuel before arriving in Houston. By midnight the container ship was fueled and departed the port in route to Galveston. The voyage would take eleven days. In twenty-two hours the C-141 touched down at Sugarland and the mission was officially over. The operators deplaned and went to do the debriefing then were on their way home. They were off for the next ten days. The C-141 crew were also on their way home and were off for the next ten days. Nelson came into the operations room and gave Tress two laptop computers and three note books. Tress called Don and Don came and got the laptops. Sandy took the note books. Nelson said "The body count at the compound was sixty-three. There was nothing left so maybe we can mark these assholes off the list".

Tress said, "I already did and thanks for a damn good mission".

Nelson said, "Any word on Michaels?"

Tress aid "Yes he is landing in about an hour and will be transported to Herman Memorial immediately. He was stable during the flight and breathing on his own. The doctors have already been advised and he is going straight to the operating room upon arrival".

Nelson said, "Thanks I will clean up some and head over there".

Tress said, "OK Jim is there so get with him". Nelson nodded and left the office.

In three weeks everything was back to normal. Michaels had been discharged from the hospital and was home recovering. The container ship was back in port in Galveston and all the operators were back to work at the compound. John had authorized a payment of $1 Million Dollars to everyone that had been on the mission and to everyone that had worked on the mission at the Red Lion compound. BP had deposited the $100 Billion Dollars into the Red Lion off shore special account and that was where the payment of bonus money came from. It was now starting the end of the year cycle and Red Lion was gearing up for time off unless of course something came up. Molly and Carol had completed all the renovations to the lounge and things were going well everywhere. John and Molly decided to head for Redman Beach for a few days or weeks however it worked out. They left on Sunday and were sitting at Ted's Sunday night listening to the new band he had and drinking their drinks and visiting with friends. Life was very good for them both. They stayed in Florida for a month before coming back to Texas. During the time at Redman Beach Molly and John really talked about the future and how things were going. It was nice to have Red Lion and John was very proud of everything he had done with the corporation, but he was ready to give it up and really give it up not just say he was. Molly had always enjoyed the bar, but she was also ready to not have the problems that always came up even if Carol was running the place 90% of the time. They both decided to leave Texas and move to Redman Beach on a permanent basis during the next year. November was the time for the move. It would give them both plenty of time to set everything in place and they would both still be stock holders in the respective corporations but no longer be active participants. They also decided to sell the Houston house and the cars there.

Houston was doing well, and things were very good, for almost everyone. Jobs were available, the housing market was doing well, business was booming. The holiday season was now in full swing and John and Molly had been invited to eight different parties all of which were top notch. They had also been invited to the White House for a special Christmas party. John and Molly were having a great time going to all the parties. Most of them were formal and Molly really liked that. John always enjoyed wearing a tux and he loved the way Molly looked when she was dressed to kill. The White House party was a very special one and only the President's closest friends and advisors were invited to that party. John and Molly were ready for the entire deal and looked forward to being in Washington again just for one night.

The trip to D.C. was alright and the jet landed, and the car was waiting. John and Molly were taken directly to the Army and Navy Hotel and checked into the suite and then went to the bar. It was 11 AM and the party was not until 7 PM so they had more than enough time to drink, eat and relax before having to start the dressing process. By 6 PM both John and Molly were dressed and ready, so they went down, and the car was waiting. They arrived at the White House at 6:30 PM and were sent right into the main ball room. The place was really decorated beautifully, and John went to the bar and got them a drink. People were mingling around, and John saw quite a few people he knew. Molly was right by John's side and enjoying all the chit chat that was going on. At 7 PM a receiving line was formed and then the President and First Lady came down the stairs. The band played the Presidential song, "Hail to the Chief", and then everyone went through the receiving line and then were escorted to their table. John and Molly were seated with Liz and her companion and three members of the Joint Chief's and their wives. There were about 100 people at the affair. The President made a toast and then wished everyone Happy Holidays. The dinner was very good and after dinner the band played, and everyone danced. John and Molly stayed for four hours then left and returned to the hotel. They had a drink in the bar then went up to the suite. Their flight back left at 9 AM and they were back in Houston by 1 PM. It had been a fun time and Molly really liked the experience. John had been to a few of these things when he was on active duty and he sure as Hell liked doing it as a civilian better.

It was now the 26th of December and John and Molly had just returned from Hallettsville and Christmas with Ray and Donna and their kids. Miles and Linda had stayed in Midland because Miles' mother was very near death and the trip would have been too much for her. Nancy had asked to speak in private with John so when he arrived at the office he had her come right into his office. Nancy sat down, and John said, "What is on your mind, my dear?"

Nancy said "John I am leaving Red Lion at the first of February. I am ready to quit work and spend some of the money you have made me plus I am just plain tired of working".

John said "Alright I truly understand that, and I will miss you terribly but please do not get out of touch with me and Molly. You know we consider you as part of the family".

Nancy said "Thank you John and I will stay in touch. I will still remain on the Board if you desire and of course I will remain a stock holder".

John said "I want you to remain on the board but not as an officer in the corporation. We will replace you as secretary, but you will still be on the board, is that alright with you?"

Nancy said, "Yes I would like that". Nancy got up and John rose and hugged her. Nancy left, and John called Jim into his office and told him the news. Jim and John talked and decided to have Jim's secretary move into the secretary of the corporation position. Also, John told Jim he was leaving in 2014 and wanted Jim to move into John's office and then Tress could move to Jim's office. Jim said "No when you leave we will totally remodel the entire office. Hell, John it needs it anyway and we need to really change some things around to be more efficient".

John said "I think that is great and if you want to start right away do it Jim. Hell, you are the fucking boss now". Jim laughed and left the office.

John called Sara into his office and they discussed the financial position of Red Lion. It was unbelievable the actual amount of cash the corporation had. John knew that was a real target for the Feds and for anyone who started snooping around so he asked Sara to find out exactly how many shares of stock were outstanding. John needed that information before January 15th the next Board meeting and Annual Stock holders meeting. Sara called that afternoon and said "John we have 900,000 outstanding shares and we have 100,000 we control in the company. What are you thinking about?"

John said, "OK now if we pay $1 Million Dollars per share as a dividend one time how much would we spend?"

Sara said "$90 Billion Dollars. Is that what you are considering doing?"

John said, "Yes it is. Hell, we made that and more on this last deal for BP and now it is time to pay the people benefits".

Sara said "OK but you already gave a bunch to the people involved so I am good with this new idea of making us all more money. Damn John I really like the way you think". Sara smiled and thought to herself "I love it here and I am going to be so damn rich it is not funny". The deal was set so John did have a real announcement to make at the stock holders meeting.

John called the Board meeting to order and a quorum was present. John made some opening remarks about the status of the corporation said, "KBR is now finished with our contract and does not have anything pending for us to do". Then John said "I am totally retiring this year and Molly and I are moving to Redman Beach on a permanent basis. Nancy is retiring in February, Anderson is leaving in March and so is Nelson. We are now losing many of the founders of this corporation and we are going to have to make the necessary adjustments. I have discussed this with Jim and with Tress and they are more than capable of running the corporation. In fact, the last mission was all their work. Now I feel things should be done to reward our stock holders mainly you people because you are the ones that own most of the stock. Only three people who are not present own stock and they will be in the next meeting. I have spoken to Sara and after we do what I am proposing we will still have over $500 Billion Dollars in cash available and over $70 Billion in assets, so we are not hurting as a corporation. In fact, we are probably if everything was known one of the richest if not the richest corporations in the United States. My proposal and I will make it in the form of a motion so legally we can vote it is simple. I want to declare a onetime dividend of $1 Million Dollars per share effective February 1st, 2014. It will be paid in cash to all stock holders, so each shareholder will get a million bucks for each share they own. Now I make the motion, do I have a second?"

Jim said "Second".

John said, "Any discussion?"

Tress said, "What will that do to our cash position again?"

Sara said, "After the cash payments of $90 Billion dollars which would be $1 Million per share for the 900,000 outstanding shares, we would still have $500 Billion in cash plus our other assets".

John said, "OK any other questions?" No one said anything, so John said "I call the vote. All in favor raise their hand. All opposed raise their hand. Motion carries unanimously". Then John turned the floor over to Jim and Jim made some remarks about how things were going and what was planned for the year including the renovation of the Red Lion headquarters and facilities. After Jim finished John made a motion to close the Board meeting and it was seconded and voted on and passed. After a brief time to let everyone freshen up and grab a drink or something the Stockholders meeting was opened. Nelson and Anderson along with Don and Cindy were now present so that meant Dan, Nancy, Sara, Sandy, Tress, Jim and John were the stock holders, and everyone was there, including Harry who had flown in from Hallettsville for the meetings. John gave some brief remarks for the record then announced that the Board had approved the one time, dividend of $1 Million Dollars per share to be paid on February 1st, 2014. No new business was brought up, so the meeting on motion was adjourned. The stock holders then went to the Lakeside Country Club and had lunch and drinks compliments of John Carter. Molly joined John at the club and each partner joined their partner there. Carol was with Dan, Sandy and Tress, Don and Cindy, Jim and Latoya, were together. Nelson had a very nice young lady join him and he introduced her to everyone as Beverly and said that they were now together. Keith was also there as a stock holder and he was typical Keith. He looked at every damn dime but that was needed. He was very pleased with the dividend. He was also very pleased with the way the quotes had been followed by management. John watched everyone as they talked and had a good time. He was very pleased with his decision to leave Red Lion as an active participant. He would remain as the Chairman of the Board. John owned 52% of the Red Lion stock or 490,000 shares. Today he just added $49 Billion Dollars to his wealth. It was a very good day. The lunch lasted until 3 PM then everyone went their separate ways. Tress and Sandy asked John and Molly if they could stop by the house so John said "Sure". Everyone would meet at 5 PM.

John and Molly were having a drink when Tress and Sandy arrived. John showed them into the den and fixed them a drink. They sat down, and John said, "OK what is on your mind, young man?"

Tress said, "Well we want to buy your house if you are going to sell it when you move to Florida".

John looked at Molly and then he said, "Ok now what do you want to give us for this wonderful mansion?" John could not keep from laughing and then Tress said "I was thinking about $5 Million for it as it stands. Of course, after you and Molly take what you are going to send to Florida".

John said, "Alright we can entertain that offer and we will sure as Hell get back to you". Molly then talked to Sandy for a little while and Tress and John walked through the house and John pointed out everything the house had in it and explained things to Tress. Molly and Sandy had also walked through the house and Molly had shown the things a woman wanted to see. Everyone was back in the den and Molly had gotten them another drink. Molly said "Hell John let's sell the house to them. I like them and why not? The price is fair, and we can have Dan do the paperwork. Is that alright with you?"

John said, "Yes, it is. Let's say April the 1st for the date to sign the papers. April Fool's Day seems right for this crowd". Everyone started to laugh. Then Molly called Maria into the den and said "Maria, these people are going to buy the house when John and I move. Now would you like to work for them under the same contract that you have with us?"

Maria said, "Yes Mrs. Molly I sure would".

Sandy said "Maria that is wonderful. I will be getting with you in the coming weeks and we can talk". Sandy had said it in Spanish and Maria was smiling all over. After another drink Tress and Sandy left. John and Molly went out to the hot tub and played around for a while then went to bed and made love.

The renovation at Molly's Bar was well underway. The renovation was also on-going at Red Lion. Jim and Tress had designed a completely new headquarters. The exterior was also being redone. A new fence system was going in and the same system would be constructed at the air field for the Red Line areas there. Two fences were being used. The exterior fence was ten feet high and surrounded the entire complex. Then twenty yards inside the exterior fence, a twenty- foot high fence was constructed covering the entire complex. Two gates were used one on each side of the main guard house at the entrance to the complex. The guard house was also redone or would be. Security was always a must at Red Lion and the guard house was manned 24/7 by two armed guards.

Molly was busy picking out what she wanted to take to Redman Beach from the house and a few things from Molly's bar. John had everything he was going to move ready and sitting in one of the spare bedrooms. The moving company was coming in three days to pack and crate the shipment and then deliver it to Red Lion at the air field complex. John was going to have the C-141 fly the crated shipment and Molly and himself to Redman Beach. This would give the crew of the C-141 a chance to look over the complex at Redman Beach and allow everything to be there when John and Molly arrived. Plus, John wanted the citizens of the town to know that from time to time, Red Lion aircraft would be coming in and out. The vehicles were going to be picked up the day after the flight by the car dealership and they would then deposit the money for the used cars into John's account. Everything was going to be packed and crated including clothes so only items that were of no sentimental value would be left for Tress and Sandy when they moved into the house. John had some boxes of things he had saved from his military days and some from Hallettsville. Molly had things she had saved throughout the years and between them there were only sixty boxes to be loaded not counting the clothes. John figured one large overseas crate would do the job. During the packing, John had taken a break and was watching the news on TV. The reporter was talking about the polls on the ranking of the President and on Congress. The approval rating or ranking of the President was down to 21% approval. The Congress was now at a historic low of 9% approval. The entire country was totally disgusted with both. The economy was not bouncing back even with unemployment at a low rate. People were not increasing their take home money and the banks were now in a position, after the terrible crash in 2008, of not loaning money for anything unless people had such a high credit rating it was almost impossible to have. The country was ready to explode, and it was not getting better. The mid-term elections were already heating up and things were really getting nasty on the campaign trail. The ads were totally negative and attack ads were almost all that were being run. Congress was having hearings on damn near everything and of courses nothing was ever accomplished other than a few Senators and Representatives got news coverage. John was very glad he was not involved with any of that. Ray was not having to run again, if he wanted to do so, until 2016. Then it would be another totally new deal. Molly came into the den and brought John a beer and sat down and sipped her drink and said, "I have now completed everything I need to have shipped, except my clothes of course".

John said, "Well Hell we will need another crate just for them, my dear".

Molly said, "Fuck you John Carter".

John said, "OK now?"

Molly smiled and said "Later my sweet man. Later". John laughed.

At 6 PM that night Dan, Carol, Tress and Sandy arrived and came into the den where John and Molly were waiting for them. Maria fixed everyone a drink and then Dan took out the paperwork and all the official signing was done. It was over in less than ten minutes and Tress and Sandy were now the new owners of the property. They would move in over the weekend. John and Molly were scheduled to leave on Thursday. After the paperwork had been done everyone went out to the patio and had more drinks and talked. Maria had dinner fixed so everyone had a bite of food that Maria had brought out to the patio and then about 9 PM they left. John and Molly hit the hot tub and enjoyed another drink then went to bed. The next day was busy for both John and Molly so they were up early and about their business. On Thursday the movers arrived at 7 AM right on schedule and by 9 AM the crates, both, were packed and loaded on the truck. John had given the movers directions to the air field and the C-141 crew was waiting to receive and load the crates. The flight was scheduled to depart at 1 PM. John and Molly said good bye to Maria and thanked her for her service. They also told her they would be returning to Houston from time to time and would always see her on their trips. It was emotional, but John and Molly finished and headed for Red Lion and then would be off to Redman Beach. John and Molly were due to be back to Houston on April 10th for a special party that Jim, Latoya, Tress and Sandy were giving so people could say farewell.

John and Molly were at the air field and boarded the C-141 at 12:30 PM. Molly had never been on a military plane and she was looking at everything. The crates were secured in the rear and John showed Molly around the plane before it took off. The flight was only 2 and ½ hours so it was not bad. The C-141 lifted off at 1 PM on the dot and headed east. Molly could go into the cockpit during the flight, and she was thrilled. The piolets explained everything to her and showed her how much of the controls worked and how the electronics worked. The plane was now on final approach to Redman Beach airport. Molly was sitting in a web seat and John was watching as she tensed as the plane touched down. The plane taxied to a stop in front of the Red Lion hanger and turned off the engines. John deplaned and opened the hanger using the door opener. John moved his car out by the aircraft and called the moving company. The truck was waiting in the airport parking lot and came directly to the hanger. The crew chief positioned the truck behind the plane and then opened the rear tail gate, so the crates could be unloaded and put on the flatbed truck. John and Molly thanked the crew and got into John's car and drove to their house. About an hour later the truck arrived and the movers unloaded the crates and brought all the boxes and all the boxes with clothes into the house. Louise was already putting the clothes away just as soon as they were inside. John thanked the movers and then he and Molly told Louise they were going to Ted's for a while. Louise was happy and continued to unpack the various boxes. John and Molly arrived at Ted's and went inside and were greeted by the group that was there. The C-141 crew was scheduled to fly back about 7 PM.

# Part Three

# CHAPTER 51

John and Molly spent the weekend getting settled into the house in Redman Beach. By Monday everything had been put up in the right places and it was now their home and looked like it. They were at Ted's for lunch and John saw Bob and motioned him to come to the table. Bob was a large man in his early 40's and weighed about 250 pounds. He stood six feet or maybe a little more and was tan and wind burned. Bob owned a 42-foot boat he leased out by the day for deep sea fishing trips. The boat was very nice and had room for twelve people to go comfortably on it. There was sleeping for six in three cabins and the boat had a full galley. Bob sat down, and John said, "Skipper I would like to make a deal with you about your boat".

Bob said, "OK John tell me what you would like".

John said "I want to be able to charter the boat and of course you and your crew damn near anytime I want so how do we work that out? I know you charter to people all the time, but how would I be able to be priority on the list?"

Bob said, "Well John how many days a week, month or whatever are we talking about?"

John said, "Hell I don't really know, but Molly and I want to go out probably twice a week to start and if we wanted to go to the Keys for a week or something like that could you do that?"

Bob said, "Sure I could but John that is damn costly".

John said "I know but what I guess I am thinking about is putting you on a retainer, so you get so much a month even if we do not go out. You could also charter on the days we are not going to use the vessel so can we figure out something like that?"

Bob said, "I am sure we can".

John ordered another round of drinks for Bob, Molly and himself and they continued to talk. Bob's normal charter was $500 per day so Molly said, "Bob would you be agreeable to being on call for us if we paid you $25,000 per month as a retainer?"

Bob said "Hell Molly you and John just retained a boat and crew. Sure, I would do that. Now how are we going to figure out if you want to go out and on what days?"

John said "I believe we would be able to give you a schedule by month, but it would be open to change if we wake up and want to go. How much time is required for you to be ready to leave?"

Bob said, "Well now, I will keep her ready 24/7 so let us say a two-hour notice, is that OK?"

John said "That is perfect. Now where do we put the money?" Bob gave John his banking information. Everyone had another round of drinks and Bob left. Molly and John left a little after Bob and went to the bank.

John and Molly met with the bank manager, a lady named Robin, and had money transferred into their accounts. John had $150 Million Dollars transferred into his account and Molly transferred $50 Million Dollars into her account. Robin was very happy and very taken a back knowing exactly how much money they now had in Redman Beach bank. Robin, of course, wondered how much money John and Molly had in total. All she knew was it must be one Hell of a lot and Robin did not want to ever make either one of these people upset. John also had Robin transfer $25,000 Dollars into Bob's bank account. John and Molly then left and went to the country club for a while. A lot of people were there, and John and Molly were happy to see them. John saw some of the people he knew and told them he was now living full time in Redman Beach and was really looking forward to that. Molly also saw some of the women she knew and told them she was now here full time. Everyone seemed to be very happy they were now back to stay. John and Molly left around 6 PM and went home. They got undressed and went into the hot tub and had drinks and relaxed for a while. The sun was setting over the water and it was fantastic.

The jet was waiting at 7 AM on Saturday the 10th of April and John and Molly boarded and were off to Houston. They had no idea what Jim, Latoya, Sandy and Tress had in mind but they both knew it was going to be something. The jet landed, and a limo was waiting. John and Molly were in the limo and it headed for the hotel Jim had arranged for them. It was now 12 noon and Jim and Tress were waiting in front to greet them as the limo pulled up. John and Molly got out and said hello to Jim and Tress and then all four went inside and John and Molly were shown to their suite. Jim and Tress went up with them and after the bags had been put in the suite, Jim said "Ok guys the car will pick you up at 5 PM and it is semi-formal tonight so dress in something you can have some fun in. We will see you then". The men then left, and John looked at Molly and she said, "What in the Hell are they up too, John?"

John said "Baby, I have no fucking idea, but you know it is going to be wild". John and Molly poured a drink and relaxed for a while. John turned on the TV and watched the news. Syria was still out of control and a new terrorist group was now very strong in Syria and taking over Iraq. It was called ISSL and was supposed to be 100 times worse than al-Qaida. John knew things were about to get very bad. Red Lion would stay the Hell out of this mess that was for sure.

John and Molly went to the lobby and the driver was waiting. They got into the limo and it headed downtown. John looked and had no earthly idea where they were going. The limo pulled to a stop at the Davis Center in downtown Houston. The center was used for many events and was large enough to easily accommodate about 20,000 people. John and

Molly got out and walked into the center. Jim, Tress, Sandy, Latoya, Dan, Carol and Don and Cindy were waiting in the front for them. After hugging and saying hello Jim led the way into the center. Molly stopped dead in her tracks. The place was decorated with balloons, streamers, and had special lights going. There were four bars set up and two buffet serving lines and over 500 tables with six chairs at each table. In the far end of the center there was a band stand /stage and the dance floor was huge. Music was being played by a band and people were dancing. There must have been 2500 people there and more were starting to come in. John smiled and looked at Jim and Tress. John and Molly were escorted to their table right in front of the stage and sat down. Instantly a waiter was there with a drink for them. The table they were sitting at was twice the size of the others and Jim, Latoya, Dan, Carol, Tress, Sandy, Don and Cindy were sitting at the table with John and Molly. Jim said, "I have invited about 4000 people to this thing so get off your ass and go mingle Sir".

John started to laugh and said "You people are just fucking crazy, but I have known that for years. God what a night this is going to be". John then got up along with Molly and they started making their way around.

Molly was looking toward the entrance when she saw Linda, Miles, Ray and Donna come in. Molly almost ran to them she walked so fast and hugged them and said, "My God you guys too?"

Linda and Donna both said almost at the same time, "Hell you know we would not miss this Sis". John then saw Ray and Miles and went to them to say hello. John had noticed that there were eight tables on the front row beside the table for John and Molly. These had name place cards on them. John was looking around and he saw everyone that worked for Red Lion was there including Harry and the instructors from Hallettsville. Anderson and his entire Naval Division were there, and it was great. Most of the Molly's group was there and so many of the people from KBR, EXXON, BP and Shell had come. John and Molly were working around to try to say hello to everyone, but it was impossible. John and Molly finally went back to their table and sat for a few minutes. About 6:30 PM John watched as some very important people started arriving. They came directly to John's table to say hello. The first group included the Mayor of Houston, the Police Chief, the County Judge, the Sheriff of Harris County, the Mayor of Sugarland and the Sheriff of Fort Bend County. Then both US Senators from Texas and four US Representatives came to the table. The last dignitary was the Governor of Texas and his wife. They came along with the Colonel of the Texas Rangers. John was truly surprised that all the dignitaries attended. The last person to come in was Liz. She came directly to John's table and said hello to him and Molly. The night was starting to be very special. John and Molly had their own waiter, so their drinks were always full. The party was in full swing and people were dancing and eating and of course drinking. John had made his way around to most of the tables and was now standing talking to the Senators and Representatives and the Governor. John had just finished talking with the Mayors and their people, so he hoped no one was offended but then he really did not give a damn at this point. John finished his visit and returned to the table. People were coming by and saying hello and wishing John and Molly luck in their new adventure. John and Molly danced some and had some food. The food was fantastic, and John knew it was a once in a lifetime thing he was experiencing. At 9 PM Jim got to the stage/bandstand and made some remarks about John and Molly and how much they both had done for Houston and for the entire community and how much they would be missed. Then the surprise of the night was sprung. Jim stepped off the stage and instantly the song "Whiskey River" started playing and the curtain opened, and Willie Nelson and his entire band was playing. The entire room broke into applause and Willie acknowledged it and the night went from great to wonderful. Willie played for over two hours and during that time he had Molly on stage to sing with him. It was a fantastic time. After Willie finished, the original band returned and played, and people started dancing again. Willie came over and sat with John and Molly for a while and talked with them. Willie thanked both John and Molly for the contribution they had made to his Farm Aid events and especially for this year's donation of $200 Million Dollars. He then left and about midnight people started leaving. They came by the table and said good bye to Molly and John. The congressional people all left at the same time as did the Mayors and their group and the Governor. It had been a wonderful thing that Red Lion had done for John and Molly. By 2 AM everyone was gone except the family and the people at John and Molly's table. Tress walked back from being out front and said "OK everyone get up and go to the limos. We have one more stop before this night is over". The entire group got up and went to the limos. The cars drove off and headed out toward the southwest part of town. About thirty minutes later, they pulled into the parking lot of Benjamin's Restaurant. It was the best place in Houston for breakfast. The group got out and went inside. Tress was met by the owner and the party was shown to a private room. The entire restaurant was empty except for the Red Lion party. The restaurant did not open until 8 AM. Everyone sat down at a long table and ordered a drink and then the breakfast was delivered. All the food was placed on a buffet table and it was help yourself. John said, "Damn Tress how in the Hell did you pull this off?"

Tress said "Damn Sir, you taught me how. I watched you for years do things and then it dawned on me. If you got the money, they have the time". The entire table broke into laughter. After the breakfast John and Molly said good bye to everyone and went back to the hotel. They were to fly out at 2 PM back to Redman Beach.

# CHAPTER 52

June was now here, and April and May had been great fun for John and Molly. They had gone out on Bob's boat twenty times and really enjoyed that. They also had gotten into the social life of Redman Beach and it was tourist season and that was always fun. John was sitting in the den and looking at the news reports on TV when the phone rang. John answered and said, "Hello Dan what is up?"

Dan was dead serious and said "John we have a fucking huge problem. You have a subpoena to testify in front of a Senate hearing. It is scheduled for June 6th in D.C. At the capitol. There is no way out, so you must be there. I can come with you and I think I should".

John said "Hell yes you should. What the fuck is this all about?"

Dan said, "From what I can find out it is about how Red Lion and you were paid for things done, or at least that is what these assholes want to try to find out".

John said "Jesus Christ. They need to pass laws not fuck with me. These no good, fuckers should be shot".

Dan said "John you need to stay calm and do not even think that out loud. There are ears everywhere, you know that".

John said "Yea I know Dan. Ok I will get with you on the 4th to figure out what we need to do. Let's meet in D.C. on the 4th. I will make the reservations and let you know. Thanks Dan".

Dan said "No Problem. See you on the 4th". John hung up and went directly for a beer. Molly was tanning, and John did not want to disturb her. Molly was finished in about thirty minutes and came in to the den and took one look at John and said, "Honey what is wrong?"

John said "The fucking Senate has a subpoena on me to testify in front of some God damned committee hearing. Dan says it is about the payments to Red Lion and to me when I was on active duty".

Molly said, "Oh Fuck".

John said "Yea". Molly went straight to the bar and fixed herself a drink. In two days they were to be in Washington to meet Dan.

On the morning of the 6th John and Dan walked into the hearing and John was sworn in. John and Dan sat at the table and looked at the six Senators who were sitting on the raised platform in front of them. Molly was sitting in the audience. John and Dan had discussed the event for two days and basically John was going to say nothing. That was it. As far as John knew everything was classified and he could not speak to anything. It might work, or it might not but if that did not work there was the 5th Amendment to rely on. The hearing was opened with remarks from the head of the committee a Senator from Kentucky named Phillips. He was a Republican and a conservative idiot, but he always raised Hell over things. His main goal was to destroy the government as people knew it. He had three other Senators on his side and the only two left, were Democrats and John was not real sure how they stood on anything. This Philips then said, "General Carter you have been called today to explain how you were funded for missions that were conducted by Red Lion and some of the missions you did when you were on active duty". John did not say a damn thing. John looked around and saw the news media was covering this whole thing on TV. Also, there were about thirty reporters sitting in the audience writing down every word this idiot was saying. Phillips said, "General how were you paid for the missions Red Lion did for the government in 2010?"

John said "We had a contract from Government Contracting to do security work and I guess they paid us. I do not know exactly which account it came from because you people have so damn many it is impossible to track".

Phillips got mad as Hell. Phillips said, "General what gives you the right to talk to me that way?"

John said "I am a US Citizen and believe it or not you work for me, you pompous ass. That is what gives me the right to talk to you any damn way I desire. Remember you wanted me here". There was laughter from the audience and Phillips slammed the gavel and hollered for silence. That brought more laughter.

Phillips then said "General what makes you so special? Is it because you wore a uniform or is it because you just think you are special? I would like to know that answer and I am sure the American people would as well".

John sat straight up in his chair and Dan knew what was coming but could not stop John. John said, "Senator did you ever wear a uniform of any branch of service of the US or any one?"

Phillips said, "General this is not about me".

John said "OK that is a firm NO so now first, you do not have the right to question me or any of the other 50 million veterans that did wear the uniform. Also, yes, I am damn special and if you knew anything about the law you would know that. That is if being from Kentucky you can read. Hell, Senator the Congress passed a law stating that if a company is 51% disabled veteran owned that company gets an automatic 15 % advantage on any government contract it bids. So yes, I am very damn special. And so is my company. Now next question".

Phillips was raging and could barely control himself. Some of the Senators on the committee were laughing and Philips got even madder. Then Phillips said, "General how much money are you worth?"

John said, "None of your damn business". Phillips lost it at that point. He screamed at John demanding that John answer his questions. John sat and looked at Phillips directly in his eyes. Another Senator asked a question. "General I would like to know about your involvement in the pirate attack that was conducted on the EXXON tanker in the Red Sea".

John said, "Senator I was not on that raid and anything I might know about that is classified and I believe it is classified beyond your clearance, so I cannot answer". Then Phillips said, "General I am sick and tired of your attitude and if you do not answer my questions I will hold you in contempt of this hearing".

John stretched and then said "First of all Senator, you cannot hold me in contempt. I can read. In fact, I have an idyllic memory and I know the damn law. And secondly, I do not have to answer any of your questions because I do know the 5th Amendment to the US Constitution. So, I now invoke that amendment. Now if there is nothing else you intend to ask that I may answer or want to answer I am finished here".

Phillips went wild. He screamed "You are finished when I say you are finished not until!"

John said "I guess you do not understand how these hearings actually work Senator or maybe you are just plain dumb. Either way yes, I am thru. Legally I appeared, I was sworn in and now I choose to leave and as an American citizen I have that right. I have not been charged with a crime and I cannot be held against my will. That too is the law of the land so good-bye gentlemen". John got up and he and Dan walked out of the hearing room. The news media went crazy. Reporters were jamming out of the room trying to get John to comment and John and Dan and Molly walked straight out of the capitol and hailed a taxi and returned to the hotel. They went to the bar and ordered a drink and sat and laughed until they were almost sick. All Hell was about to break loose on the evening news and John expected a call from the White House any minute. Reporters were trying to come in the bar and the hotel security was having a very hard time keeping them out. John saw that trouble was about to get deep, so he stood up and walked out into the lobby. About twenty reporters all with cameramen at hand started yelling questions. John stood still, and finally the reporters shut up. John said "Ladies and gentlemen and believe me when I say I use those terms loosely because you are anything but ladies and gentlemen, I have only one thing to say and here it is. Senator Phillips today tried to abuse his power as an elected official in every possible way. He had no agenda other than to try to gain information that is classified for National Security reasons and failing that he purposely tried to attack me personally. I feel he is a total disgrace to the institution of the Senate and to his State but especially to the people who elected him to serve their interests. He has forgotten the most important rule. The Senator is the servant of the people not them serving him. We fought a very hard war in 1775 to prove that point and we need to always remember that fact. Now if you as the news media have the guts to use this comment I will be truly shocked. That is the end of this interview and if you continue to harass me or anyone I am with I assure all of you I will file individual criminal charges on each of you and believe me they will hold up in a court of law. You are not protected by the 1st or any other Amendment for harassment charges". John then walked back into the bar and ordered another beer. The reporters left the hotel. Dan had received a phone call while John was with the media and Dan said "John we have to go back to the Senate tomorrow at 9 AM. There is no choice, so we go".

John said "Ok". Dan and Molly both looked at John and shook their heads. John, Molly and Dan had dinner that night and really enjoyed the time. No reporters were around and the discussion at the table was the evening news. All three had watched the TV news at the bar and it was something to see. Circus described it best. The lead story was "General spanks Senator". The reporters had shown most of the hearing and of course showed the exchange between Philips and John. Then they had legal analysis talking about the fact that John was 100 % correct in everything he had said to the Senators. The analysis even said John was absolutely correct when he left the hearing. Then of course the reporters tried to get interviews from Phillips, but he refused. The final blow to Phillips was the interview John gave in the lobby. The entire interview was shown just as it had been filmed. Social media. Facebook, Twitter and the like were going crazy. Everyone in the world it seemed was posting something about the day. John, Molly and Dan just sat at dinner and laughed at the situation.

The next morning John and Dan again walked into the Senate Hearing room. Molly took her seat again like the day before, and John stood and was again sworn in. At that time Dan rose and said, "Gentlemen General Carter would like to read a prepared statement to this hearing before any questions which is by law his right".

Phillips said, "You may proceed General". John moved the mic closer and started. John read his statement in a loud and clear voice. "Senators I am sure by now you have had your aids research what I said yesterday about the law and I am just as sure you realize I am 100% correct on what is required of me at these hearings. Now I can do this every day for as long as you desire, and the end result will be the exact same thing. I will either tell you I cannot answer because of National Security Classification or because I choose to invoke the 5th Amendment. Either way you will receive no answers to your questions and if you choose to try to do one damn thing about that I will file criminal charges against every member of this hearing for abuse of power by an elected official as well as filing civil charges for slander. I will also leave this hearing which is my right any damn time I decide to do so. That Senators ends my remarks". No one said a word. The media was shocked and was filming everything. Phillips said,

"Well General it seems you intend to not cooperate with us in any way is that your message?"

John said "No that is not what I said, but then again maybe you really are just not smart enough to understand anything that is said. I just do not know about that". Phillips was almost on the point of losing his temper again and John knew he had the man. John was asked about six questions and the reply was National Security or the 5th. After an hour John was dismissed and Dan, John and Molly walked out. This time John was going back to Redman Beach. Just as the three arrived at the hotel people were running into the bar and watching the TV. John and Dan and Molly went into the bar and saw what was happening. Four Las Vegas hotels had been bombed and the Las Vegas police station had been bombed. The death toll was already in the hundreds and rising by the minute. Thousands had been injured and the entire city was in a panic. John stood still and watched. In ten minutes John's cell phone rang and the caller ID showed Liz. John answered, and Liz said "Get your ass to the White House immediately. Jim and Tress are already in the air from Ellington and have been for thirty minutes. They are cleared directly to D.C. in a military jet and will be landing in two hours then brought straight here".

John said, "On my way". John hung up his cell and told Molly and Dan to go to the room or wait in the bar, he would contact them as soon as he could, he was going to the White House. John kissed Molly and ran out of the bar and hailed a taxi. He got in and said, "The White House now!" The taxi took off at a break neck speed.

# CHAPTER 53

ohn was now in the secure room at the White House. It was called the Situation Room and John had been in it a few times before. It was filled with people and John sat on the wall. The TV was on and the news was reporting the situation in Las Vegas. It looked very bad. Two hotels had collapsed, and one was half collapsed. The 4$^{th}$ one was engulfed in flames. The police station main headquarters was destroyed and burning out of control. People could be seen running from the hotel that was on fire and they were on fire. It was horrible and of course the networks were showing live feeds.

The President entered the room along with his Chief of Staff and Liz. Everyone sat back down, and the President said, "Do we know any more about these people?"

The FBI director said "Mr. President we have received this fax about twenty minutes ago from a group claiming to be responsible for this and claiming there are four more major targets that will be hit in ninety-six hours. They say they are "The National Revolutionary Army". I have copies of the document and our people have been working on it for the last twenty minutes".

The President looked at the head of the Joint Chiefs and said, "What about medical support?"

The General said "Sir, we have thirty units in route to Vegas. They include four field hospitals and the rest are medical combat field units with helicopters and paramedics. We have over 200 doctors in route as well".

The President said "Now what is the bottom line on this ninety-six-hour bullshit? Does anyone know anything as to targets or anything?" No one said a word. Then the President said, "OK Now how about troops and law enforcement?"

FBI spoke up and said "We have 140 agents in route including four forensic teams and the ATF has thirty agents in route. Everyone should be on the ground in four hours".

The Head of the Joint Chiefs said "Mr. President, 1500 Marines are now in route from California, and 200 have already landed. The entire compliment will be on the ground by 3 PM today. Also, we have sent a body recovery and identification team from Ft. Hood, TX and they are due to be there at 2 PM today".

The President said, "Does anyone have any idea who these people are and where they are located?"

The FBI director said, "We have some very limited knowledge of the group, but it never was anything more than some chat on the social networks and no we really do not know what we are dealing with right now, Mr. President".

The President said "OK then get to work and I need something concrete by 5 PM tonight. I have to go on TV to address the country at 7 PM and I need to be able to tell them something". The President got up and as he left the room he told John, "I need you to come with me now". John followed the President out of the room.

John saw Jim and Tress waiting outside the Oval Office as he and the President came down the hallway. The President went in and John followed as did Jim and Tress. Liz and the President's Chief of Staff also entered the room. The President sat behind his desk and motioned for everyone to sit. The President then said, "Ok here is what I want you to do. I need everything we can get on these guys and where the Hell they may be located. Then what are the targets in ninety-six-hours and some type of plan to stop them from carrying out whatever the Hell they are planning".

John said "Mr. President I think the targets are as follows: The Houston and probably Louisiana refineries and chemical plants, the EXXON, BP and Shell oil company buildings in Houston. The headquarters of the top 4 US banks and finally I feel these people are going to try to blow up an atomic power plant, I guess the one in California just because it serves the entire West Coast and that is where many of the computer companies are located".

The President said, "John how in the Hell did you come up with that?"

John said "Sir that is what I got from reading the fax they sent. It is just a guess but from what they say it makes sense".

The President said "Oh yes, I forgot you can read a million words a minute or something. Well Ok what else did you get from that fucking fax?"

John said "The paper is well written at least the first part is. That leads me to believe that the writer is educated and well educated at that. Then the paper talks about the large companies running the world and oil as an evil thing. Then it goes on about the banks running over the little people and killing people by taking their homes away. Then it says how computers have ruined the American life and that electricity is making everyone dependent on technology not using their hands to create and a bunch of other things. Mr. President, this is a combination of sane and totally out of the park ramblings. The demands are the worse part, the last page. Dissolve Congress and make a law that if anyone has ever held an office in the House or Senate they are disqualified from being elected. Next these people want a law effective immediately to stop all foreign aid, and make it a death penalty for the President or any member of Congress to start it up again. Next of course is to disband the Supreme Court. Then next is to deport all illegal people in the US within a month. Then the damn thing continues about putting two Army Divisions on the border from California to Texas, so they will do combat patrols 24/7 looking for drugs, illegals, and God knows what else. The last demand is the worse one in my opinion. That the "Nigger" President immediately quit. That Sir, is what I got out of the fax so far".

The President's Chief of Staff said "General I wonder why no demand for money was made in the fax. That seems strange to me".

Jim spoke and said "That is a problem for us too, because it shows that these people are either well-funded, which is what we believe, or they will start to rob to get money and banks will be the targets and they have no problem killing people. That is a real concern even if they are funded, because they have stated they hate banks". The discussion continued for over an hour. After everything was discussed and Red Lion was given the mission to stop the attacks if possible using any means necessary, the President said "Now I want all three of you back on active duty during this time. I feel it will be in our best interests to have that happen and I have already spoken to the Chiefs and the Secretary of Defense and here is what I have ordered. John, you will return at the rank of 4 Star General just like you had before. Jim, you will also be a 4 Star and Tress you will be promoted to a Major General, 2 Star. I also want Anderson to return as a 3 Star Admiral and re-call any other operators as needed, also at one rank higher, John. The orders are already at the Pentagon for you people and Anderson so just tell the Pentagon who else needs orders".

John said "Mr. President I need two things please. First, we need to meet with Major General Capp the commander of Special Operations Command and have him understand that we are running the operation. Second. I need someone, and I really do not care who it is, to explain to that fucking Senator Phillips that if he gets in our way in any fashion we will just plain eliminate him".

The President broke out into a laugh and then so did Liz and the Chief of Staff. The President said "I can help with General Capp, but damn John you cannot kill a sitting US Senator just because he pissed you off. Hell, I would have done that to about 90% of Congress already if that was the way it worked".

Tress said "Mr. President, yes we can. People have accidents every day and you would never have to know".

The President said "OK but please do nothing until he actually does something that is really a National Security threat. And that is an order Generals". Everyone nodded that they understood. Then the President said "Now Generals, you know what you have to do so do it. Keep Liz up to speed and she will get all information that comes into us to you immediately. Thank you all for doing this for your country and for me". The Generals stood and saluted and left the Oval Office. Everyone went back to John's hotel and went to the bar. John called Dan and Molly and had them join him in the bar. It was going to be one Hell of a job and would take everything Red Lion had to do it and probably more. All of them watched the President's address to the nation. It was a very somber address and at the end the President vowed to capture of the people responsible no matter how long it took to do it.

The next morning, Dan and Tress flew back to Texas and Jim, Molly and John flew to Redman Beach. Molly deplaned and went home, and John and Jim flew to Tampa to the Special Operations Command to meet with Major General Capp. Both Jim and John had their uniforms on and were in Class "A" dress. John loaned Jim a pair of General stars and when they arrived at Operations Command the shit was flying. General Capp was waiting, and the entire headquarters was busy as Hell with trying to find out who the National Revolutionary Army was and where the Hell they were located.

The meeting with General Capp was tense at first but John was able to get the man to relax and John then said "Capp we are here only because we need you and your guys to be an asset we may need down the road. I know you have your hands full in Afghanistan and with this new ISSL deal you are going to be stretched beyond anything anyone can imagine. Hell, I sat in your seat, so I know. Now Capp we need this from you. We need an estimate and a very accurate one, of how many teams you could give up with a twenty-four-hour notice. We also need a point of contact here at your headquarters, so Tress can interface with that person and instantly send and receive information. We are the lead on this goat fuck by order of the President, but I know just as you know it is going to require many things to be changed and for the first time since the Civil War US troops are going to have to fight US Citizens on US soil and it will be very messy. Red Lion will do our best to keep your people unidentified but on today's market you know the media is all over everything, so it may happen that Delta and SEALs are named as participants in things. Now Jim will be running the Red Lion part. I am going to be coordinating with Washington and other agencies but basically Jim will be running the show. Now Capp what are your questions of us?"

Capp said "General I have so damn many questions right now I will have to sort things out first, then I can tell you. I do understand what Red Lion will need and I have a good man ready to be the point of contact. I will have him give Tress a call immediately. As for my teams, I probably will have two Delta Teams and maybe three SEAL teams that you could use but we will have to crunch the numbers and give you an exact amount we can keep ready. Also, we do have airborne assets and some other assets we can pull from regular Army units if required. I can get you a Ranger Battalion anytime you need it from the rotation, so we can help in that way".

John stood up as did Jim, and thanked Capp and the two Generals left. The jet was waiting, and Jim took it back to Houston. John was given use of a Black Hawk and it took him to Redman Beach. John called Molly while he was in route and she was waiting at the airport when he landed. John and Molly drove home, and John changed clothes and then they went to Ted's for a bunch of drinks and some food. The TVs had news coverage of Las Vegas on and things were really a mess. The coverage was almost twenty-four-hours a day. John hated that. Everyone was talking about the attack and the President's speech. Most of the people in Ted's were in shock, so to speak, about the horrible attack and were asking the same questions, why? Some of the locals that knew John and Molly and asked John about it and he said "I don't know any more than you do. Just what I have seen on TV. It is a mess I know that". They seemed satisfied with that answer for now at least. John and Molly went home around 11 PM and got into the hot tub. John was very tired, and Molly was very worried. They just sat and tried to relax. About midnight they went to bed. The next morning John and Molly talked about what was going to happen and how much involvement John would have. John wanted to stay out of the day to day involvement, but Molly knew that was just a dream. John was going to be needed and needed badly on this and Molly wanted him to know it was alright with her. After they had talked for a good while John agreed he would be at the center of the operation because of how important it had become. John would go to Texas and Molly decided to stay in Redman Beach for a while for right now. John called to Red Lion and told them he was coming. Tress said "General, I will send an Air Force jet to get you. We cannot waste time on anything else. It will be there in three hours. See you in about five hours. Glad as Hell you are coming and so is Jim". John hung up and started packing his clothes and uniform. Molly drove him to the airport and in thirty minutes an Air Force jet, C-22, landed. John kissed Molly good bye and climbed aboard. The Jet taxied out and took off. In 2 and ½ hours John was at Ellington AFB in Houston and a car was waiting. John walked into Red Lion at 11 AM and headed to the new briefing room.

Don and Cindy were now ready to give Jim, Tress and John some idea of who these people were. Cindy had uncovered a site on the internet that was the home page for the National Revolutionary Army. It described the mission of the group and claimed to have over a million members in all fifty states. There was a lot of crap about making America sound again and all the problems America had because of the "Nigger" President and the corrupt Congress. Then the site attacked the Judges on the Supreme Court and then there was a section about the oil companies and banks being the people who ran the country and forced Congress and the President to make decisions in favor of them. There was also an attack page about the IRS and illegal immigration along the borders. The entire web site was a hate mongering site and white power was one of the biggest themes. The headquarters was not listed but Cindy had been able to find the nearest location that could be used by the group to update the site. Don was also tracking some emails that were from the organization. These emails went through many different servers and it took time to track the different locations. The best that Red Lion had so far was maybe in Colorado, some place about 200 miles from Denver. John and Jim and Tress were now trying to develop some sort of plan to locate the next targets. They were sitting in the operations center and the clock had just passed 2 PM. Sandy came into the room and said "My God. They have just blown up Bank America in Los Angeles at their headquarters and Wells Fargo at their headquarters in San Francisco. Both buildings have collapsed and are on fire".

John sat straight up in his chair. He said, "Sandy can you find any "chatter" about Citi Bank or J P Morgan Chase?"

Sandy said, "Yes there was some about forty-five minutes ago, but it was not specific, just the names, mentioned by someone from Kentucky who was talking to someone in Vermont about these banks".

John said, "Thanks keep on that and try to find an exact location of the callers". John went to Jim's office and called the White House. In five minutes the President was on the line. John said "Mr. President you have to give an order to evacuate the headquarters buildings of Citi Bank and J P Morgan Chase, both are in New York and it may already be too late. We believe the next bombs will be there. Also have the bomb squad and maybe military EOD go through each building and cover everything and they need to look at every possible place explosives can be put".

The President said, "Ok John do you have anything else?"

John said, "No Sir not now just that and I am positive that is the next targets to be hit". The President hung up and so did John. The TV coverage was now on every station and a split image was being used to show Wells Fargo and Bank America. It was terrible and getting worse by the minute. John was very afraid the President would now consider Martial Law and that would be exactly what these people wanted. It would bring out all the crazy people, not just this group. John had to make damn sure that did not happen.

Homeland Security had alerted the entire Houston ship channel area and all the Louisiana refineries and chemical plants to be on total alert for trouble. They had suggested to have people go through every inch of every plant looking for explosives. John was hoping this would happen. The attacks on the banks had been before the ninety-six- hours was up so John now believed there would be no more warning or anything else. It was total war and it was going to get very bad. John was watching the news reports and the stock markets had suspended trading at 4PM. The market had dropped 900 points in less than two hours. Things were in total disarray in the financial world. Washington was in a total panic mode and the President had not said a damn thing so far to the American people. John did not like that at all. The people were going to need strong leadership and it was not happening. John had called Ray and Miles, and both were very worried about the markets and everything else. No one was making any sense out of these attacks.

John got a fax that had been sent to Red Lion stating that explosives had been found at both bank locations. The explosives were very well set in shape charge form and over 200 were located at each building. Thermite grenades were also located at each location to cause fire after the explosions set them off. That was how the Vegas attack had taken place. The FBI was trying to find fingerprints on the devices or explosives. The trigger for the bombs had been cell phones, the disposable type, so they could not be traced. Don and Cindy had an idea, so John told them to go ahead. Don and Cindy figured that the cell phones had to be bought locally in Vegas, San Francisco, Los Angeles, and New York. If that was true and with the amount that were required, there had to be some type of record of that many phones being bought because no one store had enough on hand. Don and Cindy started tracking shipments of disposable phones. There were only ten manufacturers of disposable cell phones in the world and most of them were in China or Japan. Don and Cindy had hacked into every manufacturer and found one company that had shipped 15,000 phones to the US four months ago. The shipment went to Tennessee to a store in a town called Richardson. The population of the town was only 4500 people, so a red flag immediately went up. Don told Tress and Jim about the shipment. Cindy was now running all the information she could get on the store and the owner. The store owner was a man in is 50's who had ties to white supremacy groups in Tennessee and other southern states. He had been arrested six times for public demonstrations covering everything from gun ownership to abortion. His latest arrest was a demonstration about the Supreme Court and how it needed to be abolished. The demonstration became violent and arrests were made. Cindy now knew who had been arrested along with the store owner. Things were slowly coming together, but John knew that these people were not the leaders. Tress had gotten the word back from his contact with the FBI that the same cell phone manufacture had made the phones that were found in New York. That confirmed the tie to the group. Jim and Tress had a plan and called one of the operator team leaders into the operations center. Richardson was only thirty miles south of Memphis, so Tress wanted to send a team to capture the owner and bring him back to Texas to interrogate him. Jim said go so the team was set to leave on the C-130. Tress had filed a flight plan to have the plane land at Memphis as a cargo plane and stay on the ground for twenty-four-hours. A rental car was reserved for the operators and it was also waiting to be picked up in Memphis.

The operators waited until 9 AM, then three of them entered the store. One operator fired a dart into the store owner's chest and he instantly fell to the floor. Another operator put the closed sign on the front door and locked it. Then all the operators began an extensive search of the store. The store was a cell phone, computer repair, all type of gadget operation and the team leader decided to take every computer there. The SUV that had been rented was pulled to the rear door and computers were loaded into the rear of the vehicle. The other operators had now completed the search and had found some discs in file boxes and they were also loaded. Then the store owner was tied with flex ties and placed into the SUV and the operators headed back to Memphis. They arrived at the airport and pulled up to the C-130 and unloaded the computers and other items into the plane. Then they walked the owner onto the plane and one operator returned the SUV and then returned and boarded. The C-130 took off and in three hours was landing in Sugarland. The store owner was taken off and taken to a special area for interrogation. The computers and other items were taken to Don and Cindy.

Don and Cindy had a treasure chest in the computer of the store owner and in his personal laptop. After three hours all the information was now printed and given to Tress and Jim as well as to John. There were lists of email accounts, over 4000 of them, shipment records, emails that had been received and a complete listing of the officers of the National Revolutionary Army to include the mailing addresses and shipping addresses of each. Red Lion had just hit pay dirt. John was studying the emails and found one very interesting. It came from an account in Washington D.C. John immediately had Don and Cindy find out about the email account. Cindy came back to where John was sitting and said "Sir, this account is a government account highly restricted and it belong to the Senate system. I can probably get into it, but I will be breaking about fifty federal laws when I do it".

John smiled and said, "OK I think under the circumstances we are covered and if not, we will send you and Don on a very nice vacation to a country that has no extradition".

Cindy laughed and said, "Ok be back in a few". Cindy went back to her computer room and started hacking. By now a complete layout of where the phones had been shipped was available to Red Lion. Phones were shipped to LA, SF, Vegas, Houston, Baton Rouge, New York, Washington D.C., Chicago, and Atlanta. Jim and Tress accounted for the Vegas, SF, LA and New York phones but the other locations were still a mystery and that bothered them a lot. The emails were a great help and after analyzing them it was clear that the leader or at least the operational leader, was in Colorado, about 200 miles from Denver. The name of the town was Collins and it was in the mountains of the state very isolated and very hard to get into and out of. The town was small and the best guess for population was about 1200 and they were scattered over the whole area. It was a perfect place for a domestic terrorist group to be located.

The interrogation of the store owner was very productive. He gave information on all the leaders of each different group he had done business with and who the top man was. He also showed the interrogators the exact shipping information on where the phones had been sent. The information was verified by the shipping records and the owner knew he was facing so many federal charges he was never going to be out of prison if he did not get the death sentence. He wanted a deal, but nothing was offered at the time. Jim and Tress had decided that only regular interrogation techniques would be used at first on the owner because it was being recorded both video and sound. If these did not work the recordings would be stopped and other methods would be used. The regular methods had worked. In last attempt for a deal the owner said "I have one thing you want. I know the name of the founder and he still controls everything".

The lead interrogator said "OK the here is the deal we will offer. You will not be killed if you tell. Now if you do not tell we will then start the different type interrogation and I doubt you will live through that. Also, we must be able to verify what you say so make damn sure you have a way of proving what you tell us".

The owner said "The founder is Senator Phillips from Kentucky and I have a CD of him giving a speech to the assembly we have yearly. It is in my laptop in the rear behind the computer shield". The interrogator called Don and sure enough Cindy had already found the CD and was about to play it. Don called John, Jim and Tress and had they come to the computer room immediately. Cindy put the CD in and hit play. There big as life was Senator Phillips leading the pledge of allegiance and then giving the speech to the assembly of the National Revolutionary Army. He was calling for the over throw of the US Government using violence as the way to accomplish the mission and to kill as many of the opposition as possible. John was almost crazy when he saw it. Jim and Tress told Cindy to make about twenty copies and then let them know when they were ready. John was to have the first copy and Jim knew John would be on the first plane to DC and the White House. Jim ordered the interrogators to call Homeland Security and arrange a meeting for them to come get the owner and some of the evidence. Then Jim and Tress decided exactly what to give the Feds. Very little actually, because the longer Homeland had to work to get the information the longer Red Lion had to get the mission going. Tress called Homeland Security and spoke to his contact. The meeting was set for the next day. Tress had told his contact that Red Lion might have some useful information on one guy and that they were in the process of locating him to find out if it was solid. Jim and Tress were going to turn over the cell phone shipment records and the records from the manufacturer that the cell phones had been shipped to Tennessee. Then a few more things tying the owner to the terrorists. That would be enough to keep Homeland, the FBI and everyone else busy trying not to violate this asshole's rights and still get him to give up information. Tress also knew that the owner would say he had told Red Lion everything but of course that would be denied.

The next day Tress met with Homeland Security in Houston and turned over the store owner and all the evidence about the phones and the target lists to them. No questions were asked of Tress how he had gotten the owner or the information he had so it was a very short smooth hand off. Tress was back at Red Lion in one hour and then Jim, Tress and John sat down for a talk. John said "I am not going to D.C. with the disc. First, it was over ten years ago that this fucker did this speech and even with the latest records we have about the computer and cell phone use in the Senate, we really do not have enough to charge him and make it stick because he is a Senator. Now I think we need to have Cindy and Don put worms in everything in his office, on everyone he has on staff and of course on all his stuff including his family. We monitor it and gather what Intelligence we can. I am very concerned about Atlanta and I wonder why that was not listed on but one thing we have found. My best guess is the airport there, but we have no way to verify that. I am going back to Redman

Beach and I am going to look at that damn disc and try to find the head guy and if possible the bomb maker. Hell, they must be military, or at least used to be and maybe we can get lucky. Both of you also look at it and see if you can recognize anyone. If we hear anything from the "chatter" we can then plan on doing something. I have a feeling we will see more explosions in about two days so get ready". Jim and Tress both agreed that was the best course of action. John called the private jet and arranged for a flight that afternoon to Redman Beach. He called Molly to let her know he was headed home. She would be at the airport to meet him. John touched down in Florida at 7 PM and Molly was waiting. They drove straight to the house and in twenty minutes were naked in the hot tub sipping a drink. They stayed in the tub for an hour then went to bed and made love for most of the night.

The next day John was up about 7 AM and having coffee and studying the disc. He had it playing on the 60-inch TV and was stopping it almost every frame. He had been doing this since he got up and Molly came in at 9 AM and sat down and had coffee. They both watched, and John tried to identify any one he knew. John had explained to Molly about what had gone on in Houston and about the store owner. He also told her about the terrorists and that they were militia or a group like that in the beginning and played war in the woods on weekends. Then somehow, they had evolved to this group they were now and started blowing up innocent people for no reason other than to try to make a statement. Molly sat for a while and then she said, "John remember about five years ago at Christmas when we were in Hallettsville and you and Harry went and met with a guy about training some people in special tactics and even some to jump?"

John said, "Kind of why?"

Molly said, "Stop the CD and rewind it about twenty seconds". John did and when it started Molly let it go for five seconds and said "Stop". John did and looked at the screen.

The screen showed a shot of men standing in the audience and Molly pointed to one man and said, "John that is the guy you met with I know it is".

John looked and said "Yes you are right. God Damn we trained the fuckers sure as Hell". John immediately called the Hallettsville compound and spoke to Jackson who had replaced Harry as the man in charge. Jackson had been an instructor from the start, so he was totally familiar with things. John explained what he needed, and Jackson said he would check the records and get back immediately. John hung up and in an hour Jackson called. Jackson said "General, we sure as Hell did train the guys you asked about. They were supposed to be a group of reserve deputy sheriffs from some county in Colorado that needed training on special tactics and about fifteen wanted to go to jump training. The guy who signed the payment was named Jerry Oliver and he lives in a place called Collins Colorado. I have his mailing address and will text it to you".

John said, "Good job Jackson thanks". John got the text in two minutes. Now John had something to work with. John called Red Lion and got Cindy on the line. John gave her the time on the CD that showed Oliver's face and his full name. John wanted Cindy to do a complete check on him including military records and then send the information via fax to John. Cindy would also do facial recognition to make damn sure it was the right guy. About an hour later the fax went off and John watched as ten pages came through. John started reading.

Oliver was an ex-SEAL that had been dishonorably discharged from the military about eight years before. The charges were in the fax, but John now knew why the man was out of prison already. He had originally been charged with stealing over $1 Billion Dollars that had been sent to Iraq but after the investigation the only charge that would stick was lying under oath and AWOL. That got him a DD and one-year confinement. The money was never recovered so the records said. He was also involved with two special operators from a Delta team and they were both acquitted of the charges but left the military about the time Oliver was released from prison. Cindy had also gotten their records and one was a highly qualified explosives expert. John was now convinced he knew who had made the bombs and who was leading the group. The bomb maker lived in Atlanta so that was why a shipment had been sent there. John now was totally pissed and knew he had to absolutely destroy everyone connected to this group. John called and had Jim and Tress both on the line. John wanted them to devise a plan to take out the complex that Oliver used and if possible get the bomb maker there, so he could be taken out as well. Jim and Tress started to plan, and Sandy was now ready to start some "chatter" to get the bomb maker to Colorado. Sandy had a plan, but it had to be very slowly done. A little information leaked at a time until things were ready to explode. She figured two weeks and then she could drop the bomb shell. She started the first "chatter". Tress and Jim were working on the attack plan and Tress had directed a satellite to the location of Collins.

Sandy had picked up some "chatter" concerning a fishing trip that was not exactly right in her mind. Don had also gotten copies of emails sent to Houston, Galveston, and Iberia Louisiana all talking about a fishing trip. The trip was scheduled for a week from Friday and the boats were leaving the docks at 3 PM in the afternoon. That was very strange, so Red Lion started looking at any possible targets. They found 180 and it was very bad. There were 180 working off shore rigs in the Gulf of Mexico from Corpus to Louisiana and they were owned by twenty different companies. There were also nine large holding platforms spread out along the same coast area. John received the information and knew right away Red Lion did not have the ability to stop fishing type boats from attacking or planting charges on the targets. It would take the

US Navy and the Coast Guard and even then, some would probably get through. There were too many fishing boats in that part of the world to stop all of them and if pleasure craft was used, like John thought, it was impossible. John called Liz and told her what he thought was going to happen. Liz said she would be back to John in an hour. The country had not even begun to recover. It had only been ten days since Las Vegas and there were millions of people who could not get money from the two major banks in the US. The stock market was still in a mess and even though trading was going again the market was falling every day. Thousands had been killed and tens of thousands had been injured. Washington was not saying anything and that was fueling all type of speculation all over the world. America was in very deep trouble and the dollar was down about 50 % on the world markets. Something had to be done but no one seemed to know what. It was total disaster. John was also worried about his money position and he too had money in stocks and had felt the drop very badly. Molly had also felt the drop and the stock of Molly's Bar had suffered some but not as much because it was a very stable investment. Everyone drank and now even more. Red Lion was not an open stock, so it was fine. Ray and Miles did have some major problems and they had been affected badly with the markets crashing. Each one had lost millions of dollars and it was not getting better. Ray and Miles had decided to sell off all stocks as soon as possible and take whatever they could recover. The cattle and oil were still going to be good and when the time came the stocks could be bought back if necessary. They both had money in off shore accounts, John had made them do that, so they would survive for the immediate. John got a call from Anderson and Tress and Jim were both on the line. Anderson said "I have had my people doing some looking around Galveston and the other port areas here and they have discovered about thirty new pleasure boats that were not here two weeks ago. Also, these boats have been outfitted with extra fuel tanks on the decks and my people have seen night vision devices being placed on board the boats. It is not right for pleasure boats to be equipped that way. My men also have watched the people who are on these boats and they are not pleasure type people who enjoy going out for fun. Something is going on and I think it is the staging area for what Tress alerted me about with the rigs".

John said "Sounds right Andy. Keep then under surveillance. We will get back to you"

Tress said "Well we cannot take out that many boats in port and if they get out we will lose probably 30 % before we can take them out. Hell, I have no idea what to do".

Jim said, "I know we need to stop them before they leave but how is the fucking question".

John said, "We will let Liz and the President do that with the Coast Guard, Navy, and whoever else they pick. I will call Liz now and have her get with Andy".

Don came into Jim's office on Monday and sat down. Don was almost out of control he was so excited. Don said "God damn Jim we did it. We now know where all the fucking money is and exactly how it is sent out and to whom".

Jim said "I will be damned, Don great job. Tell me about this".

Don said "We looked at the store owner's bank records and at the records of this guy Oliver and bang it all came together. The store owner paid for the original shipment of cell phones by a bank transfer to China where the phones were made and shipped from. But his records show a deposit was wired into his account three days before he paid, and it was for the exact amount he paid out. The wire was from a bank in Denver, so we back traced the account and there it was. Oliver owned the account. Then we looked through the account and saw that every couple of months for the past four years, a transfer of cash had been received from an account in the Cayman Islands and these amounts were always under $9000 so the Feds would not be suspicious. Also, Oliver has four other accounts in banks in Denver and we know all of them. They have the same record of transfers to the accounts from the Cayman bank account but payments from these accounts have gone to many different accounts in all the states. Right now, Cindy is tracing each of these accounts and getting the names of the owners".

Jim said "Great job Don! Make sure we have everything in place to empty all of the accounts we identify so put one of your famous worms in as you and Cindy identify each one and we will watch these guys go fucking crazy". Don laughed as he left the office. The "chatter" was increasing between the various group leaders in each state and the headquarters in Colorado and Sandy was monitoring every word. The terrorists were trying to find out how the plans had been uncovered and who had done it. They were busy making sure the group had not been infiltrated by law enforcement or that one of the group had turned on them. That was going to take a while and Jim and Tress knew the time was approaching to do a massive raid and end this thing. Red Lion had most of the pieces of the group but not all and that was very troubling to John, Jim and Tress. Without the entire set up and the names of all the players it was not going to eliminate the group only slow it down for a while till others could step up. No to stop this thing everyone in any leadership position must be eliminated. No arrest and all of that, because they would never be found guilty the way the courts worked. They had to be taken out. Harry called John and wanted to discuss a plan to get everything that would be needed. John said, "Hell Harry why don't you come to Redman Beach for a few days and we can talk and probably go fishing?"

Harry said "I am on my way. See you in a day or so. I will call to let you know when I am arriving". John was happy. He really liked Harry and had not had much time with him because he had taken over the Hallettsville compound and that was how Harry wanted it. John got a call in two days from Harry and he would be landing in Redman Beach in an hour. It was 11 AM. John said he would meet Harry at the airport and Harry said," Alright. I have someone with me, so make damn sure General you do not bring that damn two seat car you always drive". John laughed and hung up. John had realized that his and Molly's cars were not good for anything but the two of them, so John had purchased a Cadillac SUV that he used to meet guests when they flew in and used to take them around the area. John and Molly had the SUV waiting at the airport when a private jet landed. It was a very nice jet and John knew right away Harry owned it just from looking at the plane. It had a decal of the 75th Rangers on the nose and the words "Rangers Lead the Way" painted under the decal. The plane taxied to a stop in front of the Red Lion hanger and Harry and a beautiful young lady got off. Molly ran forward and hugged and kissed Harry. John walked up and hugged Harry and shook hands. Harry said "Molly, John I want you to meet June. She and I are a couple and have been for about three years now". Molly extended her hand and shook hands with June and then John did the same.

John said, "Welcome to Redman Beach and we both hope you enjoy it as much as we do". The crew had loaded the bags into the SUV and Harry, June, Molly and John got into the vehicle and John headed for the house. The crew was going to service the plane then get a room until Harry needed them again.

When John got to the house Louise was waiting and took the bags to the guest room, then Molly fixed everyone a drink and they all went to the patio and sat down. June was a gorgeous woman in her early 30's and had long blond hair. She was about 5 feet 6 inches tall and weighed no more than 120 pounds. She had a figure that was extra special, and her breast had to be at least a 44 double D if they were an inch.

Her eyes were bright green and she was tanned all over from what John could see. She had on shorts very short and a halter top that showed her mid-section. Harry was wearing a Silk shirt opened at the collar and a pair of tan linen slacks and cowboy boots. Harry had to be in his mid-seventies, but he was totally fit. He had a tan as well and John knew he was in better shape than John had ever been in if the truth were known. Molly and June were talking, and Harry said, "Well General we have a fucking mess on our hands, don't we?"

John said "Yes we do, and it must be taken care of. Have you been brought up to speed on everything, Harry?"

Harry said "Yes Sir, every detail. That is why I am here. You are going to need me to get this fucking Senator and I know just what will do the trick".

John said "Ok then we need to discuss that but probably tomorrow on the boat. Now let's just have fun for the rest of the day and tonight".

Harry said, "Fun is what I live for now, Sir". June came over and got Harry's glass and then turned and said, "Does anyone want another drink?" Molly and John both nodded, so June got Molly's glass and headed to the bar. June was back with Harry's drink, a beer for John and Molly's drink then she made her own drink and sat down on the patio floor next to Harry. Harry moved his hand over June's shoulder and started gently rubbing it and rubbing her arm as he sipped his drink. June was very happy, and it showed. John said, "June tell us about June".

June took a sip of her drink and said "I am from Hallettsville originally, born and raised there. I spent a few years in Las Vegas but came back to Hallettsville just about the time Harry moved there. I met Harry at a local bar I was working in as the bartender/waitress and after a few times of him asking me to go to dinner I finally said yes and well, I have been with him ever since". John smiled and look at Harry.

John said "You, old bastard. No one ever knew a damn thing about this beautiful woman. We all thought you were just an old bachelor".

Harry said, "Well Sir, it was none of your fucking business, was it?"

John broke into a laugh and said, "No it was not".

Molly was laughing and said, "Hell Harry you never brought this gorgeous woman to any of our events why?"

June said "That was my choice, Molly. I was not comfortable being around so damn much money and with people who were so very important. Then Harry explained how you guys are and he also told me he was a Billionaire and I liked him so well here I am and now you will probably never get rid of me". John and Molly laughed and knew things would be great with June and Harry.

The four walked into Ted's and got a table on the patio. The waitress took the drink orders and when the drinks arrived, June said "Damn this is a great place. Molly you and John have it made from what I have seen so far".

Molly smiled and said, "Yes we really like it here and the town is really friendly and a great place to be". John saw Bob and went over and planned to have him take the boat out the next day, so all four of them could fish and just have fun. They would meet at 7 AM and leave and go down the coast for the day. John had told Bob that depending on how everyone felt they might spend the night along the coast so to prepare for about two or three days. Bob said "Ok John see you then. Anything special you will need on board?"

John said, "No the usual bar stock and food will do as far as I know".

Bob said "Great, see you in the morning". John went back to his table and all the group continued to talk and drink for the next few hours. About 6 PM John got everyone up and he drove them to the country club for dinner. The food was great and about 9 PM they all arrived back at the house. Molly and June immediately went to the hot tub. John and Harry followed. John had stopped long enough to fix everyone an after-dinner drink and for the next hours it was playing around in the hot tub and having a few more drinks. By midnight John and Molly were ready to go to bed and they left Harry and June in the tub and went to their bedroom and made fantastic love then went to sleep. Harry and June stayed in the tub for about an hour then went to bed. The next day the four were all on the boat at 7:20 AM and Bob headed out to sea.

John and Harry were sitting in the rear of the boat and Molly and June were sun bathing on the front. Harry said "Ok General here is my plan. We need to get into that Senator's house and take all his stuff from his computer and he probably has files and all type of stuff some where there. Hell, he probably has at least two computers and I know he has a safe. All these bastards do that. So, we can either do a home invasion when they are there and tie them up and go through the house or we can do a robbery when they are gone. Personally, I want to do it when they are gone for two reasons. First, we will be able to go through everything and then we can make it look like a robbery and secondly, we will not have to fuck with them at all. That is the safest way by far. The alarm system can be by-passed and then turned on as we leave so to speak so it will sound the alarm only too late. If we do a robbery thing we can take all the computers and shit like that and it will look like a bunch of druggies did the robbery. Even if he does know his stuff is gone, he will never connect the fact that it is anything more than a simple robbery. Hell, we can even have some of the stuff located a few days later if we want to go to that much trouble, but I think we can just ran-sack the house and we will be good".

John said "OK I like it, but how do we get them out at night. That is the time frame, three weeks and then in one week later we attack the Colorado compound".

Harry said "I have the plan for that too. This fucking guy is on the Armed Services Committee, the Intelligence Committee and the Appropriations Committee so he will go to any function that the military sponsors and invites him to. He is such a headline grabber he will be there especially if he knows the media will be covering the event. All we have to do is throw an event and I have a great one in mind". John was totally intrigued with what Harry was saying and he said "Ok CSM I follow so hold that thought till I get us a fresh drink".

John got up and went into the cabin and fixed the drinks. Molly and June were just getting out of the shower and putting on their swim suit bottoms. John went back up to the chairs, handed Harry his new drink and sat down. He said "OK CSM go on".

Harry said "I am going to present the bastard with an appreciation award from the retired Sergeant Majors Association at a dinner. That is how we get them out of the fucking house. It will work because I know the right people and we are going to pay for the dinner and all the things that go along with it. Hell, we only need about 100 people and in Washington we can get that in ten seconds if it is free. I will also have a friend at CNN cover the event and make damn sure he contacts the Senator to see that he will be attending. It is a perfect way to get the fucking bastard to be there without him having any idea we are behind it".

John said "Harry that is brilliant. How long will it take to put it together?"

Harry said, "I can get things arranged in a week and then on a Friday, we do the event".

John said, "I like it so now get with Tress and Jim and start the plan, well we will when we get back after today". John told Bob to just keep going slowly down the coast until he found a good spot to pull into so the four could enjoy some night life and dinner. Bob knew just the town and told John it was about two hours away. Molly and June had now joined the men at the rear of the boat and everyone was visiting and looking at the areas they were passing. In two hours Bob pulled into a marina and docked the boat. John, Molly, June and Harry followed Bob off the boat and along the marina until he went into a bar. It was a very nice place and was almost like Ted's. Bob said hello to the bartender and got a table for his passengers. Bob told John to use the boat for the night and Bob would be staying on shore and would see everyone at 8 AM so they could head back. John asked no questions and told Bob to enjoy. Bob left, and John and Molly looked around. The music was good, and John and Molly got up and danced a little. Harry and June also danced and then they all watched as people were coming and going. Bob had suggested a restaurant that was about six blocks away so after a few drinks, all four left and went to eat. They returned to the bar after dinner and listened to a new band and danced some more then went to the boat and retired for the night. The next morning Bob was right on time and the boat headed back to Redman Beach. Harry and June were going to fly to Houston as soon as they got back to Redman and could get packed and to the airport. Harry had spoken to Jim and Tress and they were waiting for him to get there to get things in motion.

# CHAPTER 54

Things were now set. John had contacted Liz and she had the President make a two-minute video congratulating the Senator on his award. It would be played during the program. The event was being held at one of the Washington Hotels in the main ballroom and Harry had thirty-six retired Sergeant Majors and their spouses or girlfriends, about twenty members of Congress and congressional aids, and even the Secretary of the Army coming. The Secretary was going to give a short speech after the award was presented by Harry. The award was a statue of a soldier made of bronze and had a plate with an inscription on it. Cocktails were at 6 PM for an hour then dinner and then the award would be presented. It was going to be a good amount of time, so the operators could do their job. Phillips lived in Maryland about thirty minutes from the hotel, so he had to leave by 5 PM to be there. The event would be running until at least 10 PM so that would give the operators five full hours to get everything out and stage the house. The operators had flown into an airport in Virginia and driven to Maryland in a rental van. They had stolen some local plates from Maryland and put them on the van and were waiting in a parking lot about two minutes from Phillips' house. The operators watched as Phillips chauffer driven car passed the parking lot in route to the hotel. It was 5:10 PM. The operators drove directly to the street, parked and two got out and disposed of the alarm and cameras covering the house. Then the garage door was opened, and the van pulled into the garage and the door was closed.

The operators went through the house and bagged computers, three of them, contents of the safe they found in the office, jewelry, and a lot of other items a burglar would take to include medications. They loaded all the TVs into the van and some of the sliver items in the china hutch. Nine guns were taken including rifles and four pistols and they even took some of the paintings off the walls. Then they totally ran-sacked the entire house breaking open cabinets and other items to make it look like it was not a professional job all the way. Don had covered the alarm by hacking the alarm company's computer. The operators had already cut the lines and they also cut the camera feeds. By 9 PM the operators had finished and were now driving to the airport they had used in Virginia. They had put the original plates back on the van and by 10 PM the jet was lifting off for Texas with everything on board and all the operators. The jet landed in Sugarland at 3 AM and everything was off loaded and taken into the operations center. The award event went off as planned and even though no one knew exactly who this organization was, everyone had a good time. Phillips was just beaming, and he was now on top of the world. Little did he know he only had about a month to be live, John was going to make sure of that. Harry had done the magic and now it was up to Tress and Jim to continue the effort.

Don and Cindy spent the entire day going through the computers and about 3 PM they came into Jim and Tress and said "We have the entire set up of the organization from top to lower management by name and location. Hell, we even have the email addresses of the fuckers". Jim and Tress looked over the information Don and Cindy had presented and were now convinced Red Lion had everything it would need to destroy this group. Jim faxed the information to John. Tress and Sandy then set about making the plan to attack. There were only eleven states involved with leaders. The entire set up was a copy of the National Guard set up for states.

Each state had a commander and then there were locations of units. Depending on the size of the state it varied as to how many sub-units were in each state. The Colorado Collins set up was the National Headquarters and all commands came from there to the state commanders who then passed the information on to the unit commanders. There was an overall leader in Washington D.C. and he was identified as Senator Phillips. He ran the show and gave the orders to Oliver. Phillips was not known but to a very few, only four people, as the leader. Oliver was always the person who gave orders and did the command work. The names were already being run by Cindy and information was being collected. By the next day, Red Lion had names, physical locations, bank account numbers, email addresses and everything of any use on over 5000 members of this group. Most of them were just want-to-be terrorists, but did participate in meetings and were available to do missions or so it was looking like. The main leaders and sub-leaders were the actual targets that needed to be destroyed. Sandy was monitoring "chatter" coming out of the headquarters in Colorado and so far over 500 individuals were located within five miles from the compound or on the compound. The "chatter" was especially troubling because anti-aircraft weapons were discussed, and Tress knew that meant Ground–to-Air Missiles. How many and exactly where were the questions that needed answering. Also, exactly what type of Missiles were these people using? Sandy figured they were shoulder held because there was no "chatter" about transport vehicles and if they were heavy missiles, transport would be required. Tress and Sandy were totally involved with planning the largest operation Red Lion had ever attempted and everything had to be done before September, so no snow would be in the Colorado Mountains to hamper the effort. It was also going to require use of at least three Delta or SEAL teams and that would be a John and Jim problem to coordinate. It was now the 5th of July and the holiday had been over for twenty-four hours and the country was slowly coming back to life. The whole country had been living in fear that another massive attack would happen on the 4th and nothing happened so now people were starting to relax, and the fucking news media was not crying wolf.

Phillips was of course very upset about the break-in at his residence and the police had offered nothing concrete except that they believed it was druggies because what had been taken. Also because of how the entire crime scene looked, the cops did not think it was the work of real professionals. Phillips had immediately contacted Oliver and told him about the break-in but neither man connected the robbery to anything other than bad luck. Even though the computers had been taken, Phillips assured Oliver that no one could break the codes on them even if they tried and that Phillips had back up files in his Senate office in a special safe. This conversation was of course heard by Red Lion and now things could go forward without fear Oliver would panic and try to change his location or anything like that. Phillips was the man in charge and the phone call really confirmed that. Cindy had made a copy of the call for the Red Lion headquarters to have in the file on Phillips. Now there was more concrete evidence Phillips was running the entire operation.

Tress and Sandy had the initial mission planned. The main attack would be on the Colorado compound and would take at least fifty operators. Red Lion would only have about twenty to use, so, Special Operations Command was going to have to be involved to get the job accomplished. John and Jim would have to speak with Capp and see what could be done. The eleven State commanders would be eliminated by Red Lion at the same exact time the raid on the compound would take place. Two operators per state would be used and only the state commanders would be eliminated now. All the other members of the state organizations names would be given to the FBI, for them to arrest or detain, whatever was decided. It would totally disrupt the organization either way, but killing every member would never be allowed and Red Lion knew that. It would be up to the Justice Department to do what they could do with the people and John and Jim both knew whatever the outcome, it would not be a pleasant experience and would take months. This way these people could be messed with totally for years probably before anything was resolved. John and Jim were to meet with General Capp the next morning. Jim would fly in from Texas and John would fly in from Redman Beach. Both would be in uniform and both were determined to get exactly what Tress wanted.

John and Jim both arrived at Tampa and were immediately taken to General Capp's office. The Generals then told the Special Operations Commander what was required, and Capp said "Very well. I can give you two each eight-man Delta Teams and one six-man SEAL team for this operation plus I can supply choppers for each team. Also do you need any other assistance we could provide?"

John and Jim said no not now, and told Capp where to have his people and when. They would initially go to Sugarland then deploy with the rest of Red Lion. John and Jim had lunch with Capp then both men left Tampa and returned to Texas and Redman Beach. Now it was up to Tress and Sandy and the rest of Red Lion to get the job done. The initial target date was July 30th only 11 days away.

Everyone involved in the mission was at Red Lion and the briefing started. Tress explained plan, and then Sandy went into detail on each individual target. Nelson was now back and had assisted in picking out the operators who would do the elimination of each state commander. The operators for this mission would leave Red Lion and Houston on commercial flights and use US Martial credentials so they could carry weapons and night vision on the aircrafts. They would arrive in the designated cities two days prior to the mission and do the necessary recon and be ready to go at the exact hour.

All would have SAT phone communications, so everything would go at the exact same time.

Tress then briefed the raid teams. There would be a total of six Black Hawks used and the Cobra would be used as cover and to do what was required. Each Black Hawk would have a team and each team would attack the compound from a different point. Ft. Carson was going to be the jump off point and the post commander had already been briefed by the Chief of Staff of the Army about the situation. All the assets would be going to Carson the day before the raid and would then leave from there. The raid was going to be a day light raid and the Black Hawks would drop from about 7500 feet straight down. The area was always over-flown by military aircraft, so things were not out of the normal. Any casualties would be flown directly back to Carson. If any prisoners were taken, and that was not likely, they too would be sent to Carson for Homeland Security to come get. After the raid was completed, the Black Hawks and the Cobra would return to Carson, refuel and then leave for Texas and Midland. They would refuel in Midland and then return to Sugarland. The Delta teams and SEAL team along with their choppers would fly directly from Midland back to Tampa and refuel along the way at per-designated points. The mission was going to be listed as a training mission for the active duty participants. All the operators were to give any computers, papers, or anything else to Nelson before they left the compound, so he could bring them back to Red Lion. After some questions and a lot of discussion on the estimated enemy force were answered, Tress then assigned the operators their targets. Photographs were distributed of Oliver and his top lieutenants and of various aerial shots that the satellite had taken over the past thirty-six hours. Because of the outlying buildings and the possible involvement of law enforcement from the county, one team was going to be used as a stand-by force to stop any reinforcements if they tried to arrive. Also, the Cobra was going to be on that mission. If the team was not needed as support to stop reinforcements, it would go on the attack of each outlying building or area as required until other operators could clear the compound and join in. Every building was to be attacked in the entire area before the mission was considered finished or complete. In the event of an aircraft problem, other Black Hawks would remove the crews and operators and the aircraft would be destroyed in place. The briefing ended and the entire unit including the special operations units were ready to deploy in three days to Ft. Carson. No one was to leave the Red Lion compound until then, so Jim and Tress had food catered in along with drinks.

John was now in Texas and had been for two days. He and Molly had flown in and were staying in the hotel that Jim had arranged for them. Molly had been spending most of her time at the bar and John was in and out of Red Lion and the bar. It was now the morning of the 30th and in less than three hours, the entire world would change. A change had been made to the mission and had already been accomplished. The change had come so the operators eliminating the state commanders could use the darkness and they had about five hours ago. All the state commanders were no longer a threat and had been eliminated. The operators had used simple methods and each commander had been shot directly in the head while in their bed. The wives or girlfriends with some of them had never heard the shot or been disturbed. The operators had been in and out of the residences in less than three minutes and were all now awaiting flights back to Houston from the various airports. Red Lion had been informed about five hours before that mission was completed, and no other actions had to be taken. Tress and Sandy had determined it would take until about 9 AM Colorado time for anyone to try to inform Oliver. Don and Cindy had already put all communications he could use out of service. The Collins compound had no communications by any means with the outside world. It would appear like an internet, phone tower or other normal problem was occurring, so the hope was no one would get worried for at least an hour or so. By then, it would be way too late to worry about things.

John was sitting along with Jim and Tress when Sandy came into the room and sat down. She said, "Phillips had tried to call Oliver about an hour ago and was still trying".

Jim said, "Can he get through?"

Sandy said "No way. He will think it is weather related".

John said, "Do we know if there is a land line connection to the compound?"

Sandy said "There was but it is not working now thanks to Don and Cindy frying the exchange in town. Hell no one has a phone as of 5 AM their time this morning and won't have one until it is repaired sometime this afternoon. That includes the sheriff's department. Radio is the only way and we cannot stop that". John smiled. Tress was listening to the radio/SAT phone and at 9 AM Colorado time the mission started.

The Black Hawks came swooping down on the compound and landed. The operators, Delta and the SEAL teams off loaded and started the attack. The firing was heavy and to everyone's surprise the defenders returned heavy fire on to the operators. As one of the Black Hawks started to lift off it was hit by a rocket fired from one of the outer buildings about fifty yards from the main headquarters building. The Black Hawk burst into flames and crashed to the ground. The Cobra had seen the missile fired and instantly came in on an attack run and fired two missiles into the building. The structure erupted into flames then exploded with enough force to demolish it. The Cobra then turned and fired two more missiles into the headquarters building and it too exploded in a tremendous explosion that leveled the building. Other operators were now attacking every building in the entire area and many were in flames. The crew of the downed Black Hawk had survived the crash but three were wounded and needed medical assistance. One Black Hawk came in and landed. The team on board assisted the wounded men on board and the chopper lifted off taking fire as it left. Then the Cobra made an attack run on the building that was firing on the Black Hawk and the 20 MM guns shredded the building. Operators were now inside every building on the compound and the firing was intense. Two more operators were hit and down. Then four more were hit and down. The Black Hawks were now firing their machine guns mounted on the struts at the building that was causing the most casualties to the operators. The guns were doing the job well and in a matter of seconds the firing was silenced.

John was watching Tress as he made a phone call to Ft. Carson. Tress had coordinated with Carson to have three medevac choppers on stand by and he was now giving orders to launch. The choppers were to go to a pre-designated, point five miles from the compound, and would be there in thirty minutes. The Black Hawks that had picked up the wounded operators had already taken them along with two Red Lion medics to the pickup point and were waiting on Carson to arrive. John was very proud of the planning that had been done. Jim now called to Carson and had an additional Cobra sent out. Sandy was watching the satellite screen and saw an SUV leaving the rear of the headquarters building of the compound. She recognized it as one that Oliver used and immediately alerted Nelson in the Black Hawk that was being used for support. Nelson had stayed on board that chopper to direct the attack and to insure no one escaped. The SUV was going down a small road headed away from the compound and was driving at a very high rate of speed. The Black Hawk with Nelson on board came in low and fired a burst from the door machine gun that stopped the SUV on the road. Immediately Nelson and three operators were out of the chopper and firing into the SUV. In a matter of one minute, Nelson pulled Oliver out of the front passenger side and threw him to the ground. He was dead. Nelson took a photo with his phone and then searched the body. Some papers and a cell phone were removed and then the body was left in the road and Nelson and the other operators re-boarded the Black Hawk and it lifted into the air. The SUV exploded about one minute later and flames engulfed the vehicle. Now the operators were in the process of mopping up and all resistance had stopped. All the buildings were in flames and most were destroyed and had exploded into pieces. One building was still standing and had not been hit. Nelson gave the operators on the ground orders to check the building and find out what was inside. The operators opened the large doors and found a cache of weapons and explosives. The operators reported over 5000 M-16 rifles, 900 9 MM automatic pistols, over 300 cases of 1-pound blocks of C-4 explosives and hundreds of thousands of rounds of ammunition were inside the building. Also, twenty shoulder fired anti-aircraft missiles were there. This was a huge problem that now was out of the hands of Red Lion. Tress told the operators to stand by and then he looked at John and said "General what are we going to do? We, sure as Hell, cannot blow up all of this, and holy shit we need to have ATF come, but then they will know all about us".

John said "Tell the Delta operators to stand guard until they hear from us. Then get Red Lion out and I mean everyone. Leave Delta and the SEALs there for now then tell them you will advise them to leave and when they get that command they are to get the Hell out immediately. Also tell them to eliminate anyone coming into the area of the building until they leave". Tress passed the word just as John had ordered. The Delta teams and SEALs took over the security of the building. John then called Liz and told her to get ATF on the line to him immediately. In five minutes John was talking to the head of ATF. John explained in detail exactly what was going on and what had been seized. ATF would have four agents immediately come by chopper from Denver and they would be there in one hour. John hung up and told Tress. Tress relayed the orders to the Delta commander and to the SEAL commander. They would leave in fifty minutes from the lift-off of the ATF agents which Sandy would know because she was monitoring the Denver air traffic control and would hear the ATF chopper come up on the net. John was concerned about the wounded operators and Jim was on the phone with Carson and the hospital there. The MEDEVAC's had picked up the wounded and were now just arriving at Carson. Because Jim was a 4 Star General he would be immediately informed as soon as the wounded had been evaluated. This was a certainty. The Red Lion operators and all but one of the Black Hawks were now in route to Texas. The one chopper that had been destroyed was still burning and Nelson had made damn sure of that. John was waiting until he was advised that his people were in Midland until he called Liz. Two hours had gone by and the word came in that the Red Lion group was on the ground in Midland. John went into Jim's office and called to Liz. John explained that the operation had gone off well and that Red Lion was sending a special fax with the names of every person connected to the National Revolutionary Army and their addresses and emails. He wanted this given to the Director of the FBI immediately and for the President to tell the director to pick up arrest of these assholes. No matter what came out it would take months before they would be out of jail and even if no convictions ever came of this, there would never be another group like this again. John also had Liz make damn sure the media was informed about what the FBI was doing as they did it. Liz said she would tell the President and that if the information was leaked in the right way the news would be all over this. John thanked her and hung up. John thought "now Phillips you are next and by God you are mine alone. I want to handle you personally".

John then went back to the operations center and was told the Delta and SEALs were in the air. John thanked everyone for a job well done and made sure Jim would let him know about the wounded. John then drove to Molly's Bar and had a few beers with Molly and Carol and Dan who was there. It was nice to see many old friends again and John and Molly spent the rest of the day at Molly's. Jim called and told John all the operators were in stable condition and would be transferred back to Houston in two days. That night John, Molly, Dan, Carol, Jim, Latoya, Tress and Sandy all went to dinner at Fleming's and John was very happy. The next day John and Molly flew back to Redman Beach. It was now August 1st.

# CHAPTER 55

The second week of September was the week to end all weeks. Tress and Sandy had put together a thirty-minute video briefing for John to present to the President and there were over 6000 documents of all types as the evidence used in the video. Don and Cindy had drained Senator Phillips' bank accounts leaving only a few thousand dollars, so he would not get suspicious when he paid bills or withdrew money. Also. the Red Lion operators had planted bugs and video cameras in the Senator's houses in Maryland and in Kentucky about three months ago. Everything was being recorded including phone calls, fax transmissions, computer emails everything. His Senate office had also been bugged the same way. John received the entire package on a Sunday afternoon delivered by an operator who had flown into Redman Beach and returned to Texas after delivering the package. John called Liz and set up an appointment with the President. John had asked that the Attorney General be at the meeting as well as the Director of the FBI and Liz agreed. The meeting was to be at 8 PM on Tuesday evening at the White House. John and Molly would fly to D.C. on Tuesday and spend the night.

John arrived at the White House with the package in hand at 7:45 PM and was shown to the waiting room outside the Oval Office. Liz was waiting, and they discussed briefly what was about to happen. At 8 PM the door to the Oval Office opened and John and Liz went inside. John was greeted by the President and then by the FBI director and the Attorney General. The Secretary of Homeland Security was also there, and John was greeted by her also. The Secretary was there at the invitation of the President. John said "Mr. President and Lady and Gentlemen I will get directly to the point. I have a Power Point presentation to present to all of you and in this box, is the proof you will need as evidence. During the presentation many of the items in evidence are referenced so please watch very closely and then I WILL GALDLY ANSWER YOUR QUESTIONS. Mr. President may I continue?"

The President said, "Yes John please proceed". John put the disc into the player and the screen of a 60-inch TV came to life. The first picture was of Senator Phillips addressing the National Revolutionary Army meeting ten years before. The presentation was narrated by Sandy. As the Power Point continued John watched all the people and saw the horror on their faces. The presentation outlined the entire structure of the rebels and showed every move that had been made. The next to last slide was the email conversation between Phillips and Oliver about the bombings of Las Vegas and the banks in LA and SF. It also addressed the oil rigs in the gulf and the platforms and the last words from Phillips were "This is a GO. Do IT Now!" Then the last slide showed the pictures of the leadership from top to the mid-level lieutenants from each state. All but Phillips were either marked as killed or in custody. When the Power Point was finished the room sat very quiet for about 5 minutes. The people in the room were staring at each other and shaking their heads. The President said "We have a fucking traitor here and we need to arrest him. Do we need a Federal Grand Jury indictment, or can we just go get the bastard?"

The Attorney General said "Mr. President it would be best if we had the indictment first. That way no slick lawyer can claim we did anything wrong in arresting the bastard".

The President said, "Then get the fucking indictment and get it now!"

The Attorney General said, "Yes Sir".

The FBI Director said "We will have to keep him under surveillance until we get the indictment. I can have that done".

John spoke up and said "Mr. Director, I would not do that if I were you. Phillips would know something right away and we do not know who he has here in Washington working for or with him. Hell, he already thinks he is above the fucking law, so he is not going to run at least not now. Once the indictment is out he probably will try to run but you can get him as soon as it comes out. I suggest you wait".

The Attorney General said "Yes that would be my thought. We wait until we have the paperwork then arrest him".

The Secretary of Homeland said, "How will my guys fit in on this?"

The President said "We need your people to make damn sure they have a case for domestic terrorism and that it is full proof. That is how". The discussion went on for another hour. John answered as many questions as he felt he could without giving away the Red Lion operating tactics. At the end of the session the Attorney General said, "I want to know how you got all of this in the first place John?"

John said "Sir, I am not going to tell you how. Just do your God damn job and get the indictment. It will hold up I can tell you that".

The Attorney General got red in the face and said "Well, Sir, if I find out that you or your corporation broke one law I will indict you. You can bet on that!"

The President said "OK Al (The Attorney General) you were not given access to anything that John does for that very reason. Now here is how it will go. If you do anything against John or any member of his corporation I will issue a full Presidential Pardon for all crimes that could have been committed for the last 20 years and any that might be committed for the next 100 years and the pardon will be done before the ink can get dried on the warrant. Do you understand me, AL?"

The Attorney General said, "Yes Mr. President".

The President then said "John is a retired 4 Star General in the US Army and a Congressional Medal of Honor winner. He is acting as a private citizen and he can damn near do what he wants because he is a patriot of the first order. Hell, Al, he does believe in the oath he took, "To defend against all enemies both foreign and domestic". Now is there anything else?"

Everyone shook their heads and John then said "Mr. President only one thing. I would like to be informed the minute the indictment is handed down if that is alright with you, Sir?"

The President said "Yes, it is John, and Al will personally call you with the news. Again, thank you John for all of this. I can never thank you enough". All the people in the room stood up, John saluted the President and said good bye to everyone else and left. Liz followed John to the elevator and said "John I will see to it that you have a copy of the Pardon. I think as time goes on it may be needed. You people really work differently that the rest of the world, so we never know".

John thanked Liz and left the White House. Molly was waiting in the suite and John and Molly went to the bar then the dining room after a few drinks, and ate dinner. It was past midnight when they got back to their suite. The flight back to Redman Beach was set for 10 AM. During the flight back, John and Molly discussed the meeting and John said "I know damn well that if the indictment comes it will be leaked. That is a sure thing with these people and I will bet that fucker Phillips will run. Hell, he knows if there is an indictment he is finished either way". Molly agreed.

It took until the 2nd week of October before the Federal Grand Jury returned the indictment. It was the largest indictment in history. 3400 counts including murder by terroristic act, treason, abuse of an elected office, attempted murder, fraud, larceny of government property and funds and other things. Each death was given a count of murder, so it was major and sure enough it was on the damn news before John even got the call. John got his call but by then Phillips was nowhere to be found. That is nowhere the FBI or Homeland could find him. Red Lion knew exactly where he had gone and where he was. Costa Rica. He was in a villa about two miles outside the town of Cahuita. Phillips was living the good life and John wondered how he had money to do that. Red Lion had missed something and now Don and Cindy were all about finding the funds. Tress and Sandy were listening to any "chatter" that was available from that area. John knew what had to be done and he was looking forward to doing it personally. Tress used his clearance to have a satellite pass over the villa five times and by then Tress had everything he needed. There were only a few guards, mainly local mercenaries and they were not equipped with anything but M-16 rifles and a few AK-47 rifles. They had pistols but nothing major. They were there to scare the locals as much as anything.

The mid-term elections were only three weeks away and it was looking very bad for the President's party. The country was tired of a "do nothing" Congress and a "do nothing" President. John agreed on both counts. It was going to be interesting to see how things would go. Phillips was on the ballot for the election and could be elected. That was so stupid, but that was how the system worked. His rival had been running ads about the indictment but who knew what would happen in Kentucky. John and Don were working on a theory. Phillips may have used his campaign money to finance his flight from justice. Also, John believed Phillips had a bank that contained part of the Iraq money that was stolen by Oliver. That bank was probably in Costa Rica. Don and Cindy were now hacking into every bank in the country. John and Molly were talking, and Molly said, "John has anyone looked to see if the money is under the wife's name?"

John said, "Yes and we did not find anything".

Molly said "Did you look under her maiden name? That is what I would use to hide money from the government. Hell no one would think about that". John reached over and kissed Molly and then called Don in Texas. John had Don and Cindy search for Phillip's wife's maiden name then check the banks. In less than an hour Don called back and said "Bingo we found it. $600 Million Dollars in the Bank of Costa in San Jose the capital of the country". John smiled and told Don to drain the fucking account immediately. Then John said, "Molly I think you deserve a finder's fee of 10% how about that?"

Molly said "Wow, have Don do it and thank you".

John had Don Transfer $60 Million Dollars to Molly's off shore account and put the same amount in his account. The rest was to be put into the Red Lion special account. John and Molly went to Ted's for the evening. During the evening Liz called and asked John if he knew where Phillips might be. John said he was working on it and would let her know if it could be confirmed. John had not lied and the only way to confirm, was to go to the villa. That was the next step.

Tress and Sandy were now finished with the initial plan to go after Phillips. There was an airport in Limon which was about forty-five miles from Cahuita and could handle the C-141. That was the place Red Lion would land the operators and the vehicles it would take along. There would be six operators, one medic and John on the plane along with two SUVs that had markings of a Mexican mining company that was familiar to the area. Tress had gotten that Intel and now he was coordinating with the airport authorities to make damn sure the C-141 could land without any problems. Don had already sent a fake flight plan and customs inspection to the airport and it had been approved with the exchange of money as was the case in Costa Rica. Money was an essential part of doing business there and everyone was on the take. One of the operators spoke perfect Spanish and he would do all the communicating with the towers and airport personnel. The plan was very simple. The C-141 would land and the operators, medic and John would get off and the SUVs would be taken off. The aircraft would remain at the airport for 24 to 48 hours depending on what John decided. The SUVs would then transport the operators, medic and John to Cahuita and then to the villa. The actual attack would be conducted at night about 11 PM and would be a straight forward attack on the guards by operators that had moved overland to the villa. After the villa and Phillips were secure John and the Medic would then drive the SUVs into the villa and start with Phillips. No guards were to be left alive. Don would jam all cell phone and any other communications five minutes before the attack. After John was finished with Phillips, the entire group would return by SUV to the airport, load up on the C-141 and return to Sugarland. The entire mission would take no more than 36 hours. John was briefed via SAT/video phone and approved the mission. The C-141 would pick him up at Redman Beach and top off the fuel then fly directly to Costa Rica. The mission was set for the next day. John would be picked up at 6 AM.

At 6 AM John was waiting for the C-141 to land from its final approach to Redman Beach airport. The plane taxied to a stop in front of the Red Lion hanger and John boarded. The C-141 then taxied to the fuel point, topped off the tanks and headed to the runway. The C-141 took off at 7:30 AM headed directly to the Limon airport. The Mission was on.

# CHAPTER 56

The C-141 had landed without incident and taxied to the designated location given it by the tower. The SUVs were off loaded, and the operators, medic and John got off the plane and into the SUVs and were out of the airport headed toward Cahuita within an hour. It had started to rain like it always did in that part of the world but that was good for this mission. Rain would make the guards look for shelter and not be alert. The drive took two hours in the rain an on the very bad roads. The SUVs pulled up about fifty yards from the entrance road going to the villa and the operators got out and headed overland toward the villa. The rain was now only slight, and the entire area was dark except for the lights in the villa. One operator was going to cut the power just before entering the villa. Each operator, John and the medic had on black fatigues, body armor, helmets with night vision devices, radios and SAT/phone communications. They all carried MP-5s with 400 rounds of ammunition and a 9 MM pistol with silencer and 100 rounds for it. The operators also had one flash bang grenade and one HE grenade on them plus flex ties and tape. Each man had a flashlight as well as two glow sticks. The medic had only the MP-5 and pistol but carried a medical bag with various drugs that might be needed in the interrogation. The medic also had emergency medical supplies in the event of wounded operators. John was carrying an MP-5 and a pistol. He had special rounds for his pistol that he would use on Phillips.

The operators were now in the villa court yard and saw two guards sitting under an overhanging roof for protection against the rain. The guards were eliminated instantly with a pistol shot to the head on both. No sound was detected. The operator then cut the power and the entire villa was dark. Because of the rain John was hoping everyone would just assume it was a power failure and not investigate very closely. The operators went into the main house and immediately encountered two guards sitting in the first room to the right off the entryway. The operators eliminated the guards instantly and then searched the lower floors for additional guards. The floor was clear. The operators on the outside had also made a search of the entire area and found no additional guards. John was monitoring the communications and he figured Phillips had only hired four guards. John and the medic started the SUVs down the drive and went into the court yard. The operators had gone upstairs and searched every room but the master bedroom. Nothing was found as far as personnel, so they went into the bedroom. Phillips and his wife were in bed and sleeping. Two operators grabbed Phillips and immediately tied his hands and feet with flex ties. He was screaming so one of the operators put tape on his mouth. The other operators had grabbed the wife and tied her hands and feet with flex ties. They also taped her mouth. The lead operator sent the message to John and to the operator at the electric box. John entered the villa just as the lights came back on. John walked into the living room and saw Phillips tied to a chair in the middle of the room. The operators had brought him down stairs and were waiting for John. Phillips wife was still in the bed and that was where she would stay for now. John walked to the front of Phillips and removed his helmet and night vision device and looked directly into Phillips eyes. There was pure terror in Phillips eyes and on his face. John ripped the tape off Phillips mouth and immediately Phillips said "Are you crazy? I am a sitting United States Senator. You must be crazy to think you can get away with this".

John said "Fuck you. I am a 4 Star General in the United States Army and we kill traitors. Here is how this is going to go. You can answer my questions and I will kill you instantly or you can fuck with me and I will make your death very painful. In fact, I brought along a medic to keep you alive, so it will be doubly painful if you do not cooperate. Now do you understand that Senator?"

Phillips started to say something, and John pulled out his 9 MM and fired one round through Phillips right foot. Phillips screamed in pain. John then put his foot on Phillips foot and pressed down. Again, Phillips screamed in pain.

While John was interrogating Phillips, all but one operator was searching the villa. John had instructed them to take all jewelry, money, electronic devices, anything that could be turned into cash. John also had the operators remove every piece of clothing in the villa for both the male and female. The dead guards were also stripped, and all the shoes were taken from the guards and the villa. By the time the operators were finished there was nothing of any value to anyone left in the villa. Everything was loaded into bags and they were put into the SUVs. Some papers were found and both computers were taken as well as three cell phones. A safe was also found in the study and the operators blew it open. Inside was cash in five different country currencies and more papers and a note book containing records of payments to individuals by name and the date the payments were made. The operators gave John the notebook and put the cash into a separate bag for transport.

John was now asking Phillips questions about who else he had involved in this plot and Phillips was refusing to answer. John shot Phillips in the left knee and watched him scream and wither in pain. The medic had bandaged the foot and now told John Phillips was going into shock. John nodded, and the medic started an IV, so fluids would run and stop the shock. John had special bullets in this magazine only. They were small load and did not due a great deal of damage when they hit the target but because of how they had been made hurt far more than a standard round would. The pain was very bad, and John knew Phillips could not take much more. John asked again and again Phillips refused to answer so John shot Phillips in the right elbow. Phillips screamed horribly and when John again asked the question Phillips said "OK I will tell you what you want to know. No more please." John had one of the operators start to record Phillips with a video camera and sound. Phillips talked and answered all of John's questions and John kept going over them again and again. Finally, John was satisfied he had all he was going to get from Phillips. John removed the special magazine and inserted a standard magazine and fired one shot directly into Phillips right between his eyes. Then John moved to Phillips rear and fired a round into Phillips head at the base of his neck. Those shots were not recorded. The medic confirmed Phillips was dead and removed all the medical supplies used and the IV. John went upstairs and looked at the wife. John said "I am going to let you live. You have only the nightgown you have on and nothing else. When you do get free, you will have nothing to sell, no cash and no way to get out of this country. I hope you rot in Hell". John turned and walked out and down the stairs. The operators, medic and John got into the SUVs and headed back to the airport. It had stopped raining. When the SUVs reached the airport, they drove directly onto the C-141 and were secured. The operators and medic got out and changed into the original clothing they had worn down on the flight. John also changed and in an hour the C-141 was airborne and headed back to Texas. John was on the SAT phone with Tress and gave the mission accomplished key word. Then John called Molly and told her he would be back in two days. Molly said "OK why don't I come to Houston to see Carol and we can spend a little time there. I know better than to think this is really over, John".

John agreed, and Molly called the jet to get her out at 11 AM headed to Houston.

The C-141 touched down in Sugarland and everything was off loaded. Now John had to get the video processed by Tress and Sandy and then he could begin the next and final phase. The cash was taken to Sara and she figured it out to be about $3 Million Dollars total. It was Euros, Mexican Pesos, Saudi Riyals, and Canadian Dollars as well as US Dollars. Sara told John and John was puzzled about the currency and why Phillips had that particular type. John understood the US and the Euros but Saudi and Canadian. That was puzzling. Sandy was now trying to track any "chatter" about Phillips and none was up coming. Nothing was coming up about his wife either. All Sandy was hearing was that the FBI was still looking for Phillips. John and Jim sat in Jim's office and John handed the notebook to Jim. Jim looked through it and then said, "My God John do you realize what all of this means?"

John said "No not really Jim. I have just briefly glanced at the book. I think you and the gang should really examine it and find out exactly how deep this damn thing goes. It is much worse than we expected I am sure".

Jim said, "Hell yes, it is. Just from some of the names I see this is going to be a real nightmare. Hell, there are two Senators and six Congressmen I instantly recognized in this book plus probably many DOD and other government agency employees. Shit John what is going on?"

John said "Jim I have no fucking idea. Guess we will have to find out. Before we tell anyone, we need to have all the facts and that will take a while I am sure". Jim agreed, and Jim got up and went to find Tress. John went to take a very hot shower, shave and get dressed for Molly's. It was now 3 PM and Molly should be landing or probably already there. John was ready in thirty minutes and an operator drove him to Molly's bar. He walked inside and saw Molly and Carol talking. Molly saw John and ran to him and hugged and kissed him. Carol handed John a cold beer and John sat at the bar and drank it in four gulps, then had another one. Molly said, "How was it?"

John said "Honey I am too fucking old for this anymore. Thank God! I did not have to jump in. It was fine, and we did the job. Phillips is no longer a threat to our way of life and neither is his wife. She is broke, has absolutely nothing but the nightgown on her back and is stuck in Costa Rica. That is justice my dearest". Molly started laughing. It was perfect in her mind.

John and Molly were now back at Redman Beach. They had stayed for a couple of days in Houston and had enjoyed being with everyone, but now they were back and enjoying the sea shore. Red Lion was examining the papers, the notebook and the computers and cell phones that had been brought back. Cindy had the names of everyone in the notebook and was now pulling everything available on each one. There were over 200 names in that damn book. Phillips must have not trusted anyone including his own wife. These records were going to blow Washington and the DOD up. Also, some defense contractors and suppliers would be ruined. It was going to get very messy in a very quick time.

The mid-term elections were now a week away and everyone was predicting that the President's party would take a pounding and that the Senate would go to the Republicans. Phillips was a Republican, so he was out of course and that would mean a Democrat would be the winner unless Phillips won. Then the Governor would appoint the new Senator until a special election was done. The President had not been involved in many of his people's campaigns because his approval record was so bad. He was now 21% approval and it was falling daily. John knew things were going to really change and he wondered how this would affect Red Lion. No matter which way it went, Red Lion could survive but the question was, did it want to survive? John knew that was going to have to be discussed by the board and stockholders. Red Lion now had 700 employees worldwide and many of them needed to stay working. Then the amount of equipment was another thing that needed to be looked at very closely.

# CHAPTER 57

November was half way finished and Thanksgiving was almost upon John and Molly. They had been invited to Hallettsville and to Midland and back to Houston to Tress and Sandy's for the day but neither one of them had really decided what to do. The President had gone on a trip overseas and Liz was with him, so John was not in any hurry to start anything about the new information Red Lion had. Tress, Sandy, Don and Cindy had uncovered so much shit that it could be so bad only the President could control things and he might not be able to do that after all. John and Jim and Tress decided to sit on everything for a while. They needed to have a "one on one" with the President before anything was released to anyone.

Molly was ready to get things going for a boat trip to the Keys. She and Bob had decided one night at Ted's that it would be great to just go down for a few days and look things over. John was ready, and he really liked the idea. The weather was supposed to be good for the next week, so Monday morning John and Molly were on the boat and Bob headed out and down the coast toward the Keys. It was going to take about two days or more to get there but there were plenty of places along the way to stay the night or even sleep on the boat if they wanted. The ride was good and the views of the different places along the shoreline were fantastic.

John and Molly spent most of the time talking about where they wanted to go with their life. They were both getting older, not ancient, but older and they had more than enough money to do anything they wanted. They both knew they would need something to challenge them and could not just quit and do nothing, but what to do was the major question. As the miles and time went by they were no closer to a decision than they had been before the trip. The first night was spent in Ft. Lauderdale and John and Molly enjoyed a very good dinner and some good nightlife. They got back to the boat around midnight and sat on the deck and had a few drinks and watched the people moving around the marina and the area until 2 AM then went to bed. Bob was sleeping on shore and would be back to the boat around 9 AM. Bob was right on time and the boat pulled out of the marina heading south at 9:20 AM. The day went by fast and Bob had taken the boat out further because of Miami so John and Molly had done some fishing. They had caught some fish, but let them go. It had been fun fishing and Molly always enjoyed doing that. John was not quite as fond of it as Molly, but he had fun watching her. The next stop was Key Largo and then down all the way to Key West. The boat pulled into Key Largo and docked at a private marina Bob knew about. John and Molly got off and wondered around town going to different bars and looking at everything. Neither of them had ever been to the Keys and they were having a lot of fun. The weather had been great, and it was just a blessing to be warm. The whole country was in a major cold spell with freezing temps all the way to the Gulf coast in Louisiana and Mississippi and Alabama. Texas was also freezing, and John was damn glad he was not in cold weather. He hated the cold and it made him hurt all over. Ever since Viet Nam the cold had really hurt John in the shoulders, and back especially. Molly did not like cold one little bit. In fact, she hated it when it was below 75 degrees. Molly liked to be able to wear sandals and summer things year-round, so that was another reason they had moved to Redman Beach. John and Molly spent two days in Key Largo and really enjoyed everything. Then it was off to Key West.

Key West was not what John or Molly had thought it would be. It had become totally commercial and neither one of them really liked it. They went to dinner in a good restaurant and then saw some of the nightlife and were not very impressed. Bob had told them things had really changed over the last five years and Bob did not like Key West at all. John and Molly saw why and so the next morning the boat left and headed back up the coast. About noon, Bob pulled the boat into a cove off and island named Monroe. John looked at the charts and did not see the island as a major stop. Bob said, "Now my friends, this is what you really want to do". Bob pointed to a small stream that was coming from what looked like a jungle. Bob said, "John follow that stream about 200 yards and then you will see what I love about this place". John and Molly got off the boat and were standing in about 2 feet of water. They walked toward the beach then on down the trail beside the stream. John had noticed that they had been walking uphill since they left the beach and he calculated that it was about 200 feet higher were they were than the beach. The trail bent around slightly and after another fifty yards John and Molly stopped dead and looked. There was a pool of water about 300 yards wide and 200 yards long and a waterfall was at one end of the pool. The water was rushing down and it was beautiful. John walked to the edge of the pool and felt the water. It was warm and almost hot. The water was crystal clear and John could see the bottom of the pool. He estimated the depth as thirty feet. There were all types of flowers and plants growing around the pool and Molly was just thrilled. John and Molly both got into the water and swam around for a few minutes. John and Molly were swimming and not really paying any attention to the trail or anything. About 5 PM John and Molly packed up and started back down the trail toward the boat. Bob headed the boat out of the cove and started north up the coast. The sun was setting, and the view was wonderful. About 8 PM Bob pulled the boat into the marina at Key Largo for the night. John and Molly stayed on the boat and Bob again went on shore for the night. The next morning Bob headed the boat straight north and by 11 PM all three were back at Redman Beach in front of Ted's. John and Molly got off the boat and went in to Ted's for a drink. Bob said good bye and left. Molly and John stayed at Ted's until 2 AM then went home. The trip was wonderful and they both had needed it very much.

John and Molly had decided to spend Thanksgiving in Houston and to accept Tress and Sandy's invitation. John arranged for a jet to pick Molly and him up on Wednesday morning and fly to Sugarland, and then Tress could take them to the house. The jet arrived in Sugarland about 2 PM and Tress and Sandy were waiting. Everyone loaded into an SUV Tress had at the air field and went to the house. John and Molly were glad that Tress and Sandy had bought the house and Sandy showed Molly all the renovations she had made. Tress and John went to the den and had a drink and talked. Molly and Sandy came in and joined them and they all talked about how things were going. Around 7 PM all the group went to Molly's bar for the night. It was a very good time and John and Molly saw many of their friends and visited with many people. Molly and Carol also visited some, but Molly wanted to wait until the next day to really talk with Carol. She and Dan would be at Tress and Sandy's for the dinner, so Molly would talk to her then. About midnight everyone went back to Tress and Sandy's and went to bed.

Thanksgiving Day was quite the production at Tress and Sandy's. The guests were scheduled to arrive at noon. The actual dinner was not until 6 PM but of course everyone would have drinks and be able to visit and do pretty much what they wanted in the afternoon. The TV was set to the Football game so if someone wanted to watch they could. The caterers arrived about 9 AM with the food, which Sandy had ordered. Turkey, ham, roast beef, and about seven side dishes as well as four complete trays of various desserts. Sandy had also ordered trays of finger food, so the guests could snack all afternoon. Maria was there and another Mexican girl, named Lucy. John and Molly were very glad to see Maria and she told them that she had not gone to her usual spot because they were coming, and she wanted to see John and Molly. That was a very nice thing for John and Molly and they spent time talking with Maria. Lucy was now living in the house and the two maids/housekeepers had everything running smoothly.

By 1 PM Dan, Carol, Jim, Latoya, Don, Cindy, Nancy and Sara had all arrived. Everyone was having a drink and visiting. The men had all gone to the patio and were discussing Red Lion business and the women were sitting in the den and talking about many things. Molly and Carol had decided to speak in private after dinner. Tress and Jim were telling John about the new facts they had found and that they were ready to meet the President whenever John felt the time was right. Don told John that Red Lion had the entire group now identified and even their bank accounts, investments and anything of value was known. There were two Senators and four Congressmen involved plus eight DOD, mainly Army, people involved and three people from the rifle manufacturer. John listened, and Tress explained how the deal worked. DOD would order weapons, M-16 rifles, 9 MM pistols, hand held surface to air missiles, LAW rocket launchers, and other items as usual. These orders would go to the manufacturers and be shipped out. All the paperwork at the manufacturers would show that the shipments went to various Military depots just as always. The invoices would be sent to the payment office of DOD and would be paid according to the receiving documents on hand. On the surface things looked normal. What was happening was entirely different. 1/3 of the order would be shipped directly to the terrorists in Colorado. The paperwork would not reflect that and when the shipments arrived at the depots, they would be received just as if the entire order had been shipped. Over time, the Colorado group had stock piled whatever they wanted and that was what Red Lion had found. The system was full proof, if no one checked into anything, and with all government operations no one ever did. The paperwork was right so payment was always made. The inventories in the depots were right because they had been changed. There was never a missing amount, because the paperwork always was changed. Red Lion now had copies of all the original orders, the fake shipping documents, the fake inventory documents, the shipping documents from the 1/3 that had gone to Colorado and the fake invoices that were sent to DOD. They also had copies of bank transfers to everyone involved in the operation. That included the politicians and the amounts they had received to make things happen by not doing the over site or by making sure certain manufacturers were given the DOD contracts. This was bigger than John had ever imagined, and John knew the President would go crazy. Now all Red Lion had to do was get the information to the right people and maybe things would work the way that they should. The FBI would be the lead agency on this, but Army CID would also be very involved. The ATF would probably want to also be involved so John could see a battle for "turf" building. Why the God damned government could not function without having to be "one up" on the other branches or agencies was beyond John to figure out. It always worked that way, and no one was punished. The discussion ended, and the guys started watching the football game.

Dinner was fantastic and after it was over Molly and Carol met in John's old office, which now Tress used and had gladly given Molly permission to use. Molly said "Carol I am thinking very seriously about giving up Molly's all together. I think it would be the best move for me and for you, business wise. I am now in Redman Beach and I have no idea what is happening on a day to day basis and really don't care that much anymore. You have done an excellent job and you and

Dan seem to be running things as well as they can run. Now, sweetheart, I want you to buy me out totally".

Carol sat for a moment and then she said "Molly we have been friends for a long time. I hope this is not about anything I have done. I really do not know what I could have done so please tell me."

Molly said "Carol it has nothing to do with you and me. We are friends and always will be. I just do not want to be involved with Molly's because I am living in Florida and I do not think it is fair to you, me or anyone for me to still be an officer of the corporation. It has nothing to do with you and me. I promise".

Carol said, "Ok well how much, do you think I should pay you for the part you have?"

Molly said "That my dear is up to you and Dan. I know you will be right with me so talk to him and let me know. Hell, have him fix up any paperwork we will need".

Carol and Molly hugged each other and came into the den and joined everyone else. About 10 PM everyone started to leave, and John and Molly got into the hot tub with Tress and Sandy. They had drinks and relaxed. The next day was going to be a very slow day and John and Tress were going to do nothing. Molly and Sandy were thinking about doing a manicure and pedicure. Nothing was planned before 11 AM.

Friday had been a great day for John and Tress and for Molly and Sandy. Jim and Latoya had a party planned for Friday night at Eddie V's and of course the entire Thanksgiving crowd plus about twenty people from Molly's were invited. The party was at 7 PM with an open bar then dinner and then everyone would stay and listen to the Jazz combo until all hours. It was Jim and Latoya's Holiday party because they were going to Europe for Christmas and New Year's this year. John and Molly were dressed and waiting for Tress and Sandy to finish and then they all would go in a hired car to Eddie V's. Molly had fixed both John and herself a drink and they were enjoying sitting on the patio and drinking and remembering when they had first bought the house. Things had really changed for them in so many ways but had remained the same in so many ways. Molly was happy with her decision to leave the bar and John was now thinking about doing the same thing at Red Lion. Just as soon as this deal with the remaining rebels was over with John was through. Tress and Sandy came out and John and Molly got up and all of them went out to the car and got in. The driver headed to Eddie V's.

The party was going well, and John and Molly were really enjoying talking to many of the people from Molly's that they had not seen in a while. The dinner was great as always and just as it was finishing Tress got a call on his cell phone. Tress was sitting next to John and John watched as Tress looked at the caller ID then said, "This is Tress". John could hear the person on the other end say "Sir, hate to bother you, but doesn't the General live in a place called Redman Beach in Florida?"

Tress said, "Yes why?"

The voice said, "We are monitoring traffic like we always do but all Hell is breaking lose there and we wondered if it could involve the General?"

Tress said, "God damn it what is breaking loose, Phil?"

Phil said "Sir, something about a bank robbery, a mall shooting and robbery, some other robberies all over the town and something about a club being robbed. Anyway, the reports are fucked up but the best we can gather is five law enforcement officers have been killed or wounded and over sixty civilians have been hurt and some have been killed. We just figured we should tell you right away".

Tress said "Thanks Phil and stay on this. I need to know everything about this as soon as we can. Call me as soon as you know any more". Tress put the cell phone down and looked at John. John said, "Tress what is going on?"

Tress said "General something bad has happened in Redman Beach and we do not have many details. A bunch of robberies and law enforcement killed and wounded, and a bunch of civilians hurt and possibly killed. That is all we know. The FBI and State Police are on the way and it looks very bad".

John said, "Oh My God No". Molly heard John and said, "John what is it?"

John said "Redman Beach. Major trouble very bad". Molly sat and started to cry. Carol held Molly and then everyone at the party saw what was happening and questions started being asked. Jim said "Ok people we have just been informed of a situation and now I must ask everyone not with Red Lion to allow us to leave and please continue to enjoy the rest of the night. We will let you know what is happening when we know. Thank you for coming". All the Red Lion personnel got up and headed for the front door. Carol was still holding Molly and trying to comfort her. The limo was waiting, and Tress told the driver to go to the Red Lion headquarters and gave him the directions. Jim and Latoya were right behind the limo and Dan and Carol, Don and Cindy were following Jim's car. On the way to the headquarters, Tress was on his cell talking to Phil again. When everyone arrived at Red Lion the security guards had the gate open and directed them in to the parking lot in front of the building. After everyone was out the limo left. Inside things were moving fast. Tress had instituted a watch program about a year before. There were two people who listened to radio traffic and watched TV news 24 hours a day and recorded anything that may be of value to Red Lion. They especially watched for any coverage of any operation Red Lion had on-going or was planning. John had remarked how brilliant that idea was and now John was sure of it. If these operators had not been monitoring things no one would have ever connected Redman Beach to anything until maybe the national news covered a two-minute story. John started calling people in Redman Beach and his first call was to Ted. The phone went straight to voice mail. John tried about eight other contacts and every time straight to voice mail. Finally, John called Willis and got an answer.

Willis was very upset, and John finally got him to calm down and tell John what was happening. John put the phone on speaker, so everyone could hear and then said, "OK Willis what the fuck happened?"

Willis said "John it is horrible. About 4 PM four guys robbed the Redman Beach First National Bank. They stormed in and started firing automatic weapons and ordered everyone to the ground. They killed the guard right away then shot some of the customers for no fucking reason. The robbery was over in less than five minutes. Then about 4:30 PM a group, maybe the same guys but we do not know went into the mall and started shooting. They killed two of the off-duty police officers doing security and robbed eighteen stores. Many people were hurt, and we have no count on how many were killed. Just mass wounded. Then about 6 PM a group of about ten started down the beach front robbing all the bars and restaurants. Ted was shot, and I do not know how badly, and many people were also shot or hurt. At the same time, a group of six entered the country club and robbed the charity event that was going on. You know that big charity thing they do every year. Well the Sheriff and the Police Chief were killed and so was the Mayor and two city council members. Many people were hurt and some of the club employees were also killed. The police and sheriff deputies tried to stop the country club robbers, but a huge gun fight erupted around the airport and three deputies and two police officers were killed. One of the robbers was also killed but all the robbers had automatic weapons and our cops did not have a chance. Right now, I have medical people in bound and the FBI and State police are in bound. The Governor is thinking of sending the National Guard. We do not have enough medical staff at the hospital to handle this John and I have no idea what is going to happen. It is so very terrible. And to top it off the fucking news people are already coming in".

John said "OK Willis I will be there in about five hours. Make damn sure the C-141 and the C-130 can land. Get someone to open the Red Lion gates when I call you. I will also need as many SUVs as you can get rounded up. Call the dealership and tell them I want the fucking vehicles and to have them at the airfield. Make sure we have at least twelve. I will see you as soon as we can get there. It will be alright, Willis. I will make sure of that". John hung up. Sandy had already sent out the Red Lion recall order to everyone and now it was a waiting game until the personnel started arriving. Molly looked at John and said "Why John? Why our town? Is it because of us?"

John said "No Honey if it was us, they would have made damn sure we were there. No, it is just the way things are today. We did not cause this, but we damn sure are going to finish it".

# CHAPTER 58

The C-141 was on final approach to Redman Beach airport and John had talked to Willis and the Red Lion area was open. The C-130 was about an hour behind the C-141. On board John's aircraft were Tress, Sandy, Jim and Norman, the new operator commander. The C-130 had all the Red Lion medical personnel and about three tons of medical supplies. The aircraft landed and taxied to a stop in front of the Red Lion hanger. The ramp opened, and everyone got off. Molly took John's car and headed to the house. The rest of the Red Lion group went into the hanger and started the startup operations on the equipment. John had made sure there was a complete operations center at Redman Beach when he had built the complex. The center was not as large as the main Red Lion Headquarters, but it had most of the equipment that would be needed. Jim and Tress were busy getting things running and Norman was doing a quick walk thru to see what was available. Sandy was now on the SAT/phone with NIS and trying to get information on what they had been able to retrieve from their tapes. John got into one of the SUVs and headed to the hospital. Now was when he really wanted to have the President on board so on the way John placed a call to Liz. She answered on the first ring. "John are you or Molly involved and are you alright?"

John said "Liz we were in Houston and I just landed. I need the Boss to clear the way with the FBI on this one for me and my people. Can you make that happen?"

Liz said "John he gave that order to the Director three hours ago. We were just waiting to hear from you. Now what do you need us to send or do?"

John said "I do not have all the SITREPS, so it will be at least two hours before I can tell you specifics. I do know they need medical personnel and they need them now".

Liz said "Ft. Benning and Ft. Stewart have people in route. I will also get some civilians to the area as soon as we can do it. What about Air Evac?"

John said "I am about at the hospital now. I will let you know. Thanks Liz". John hung up and parked in front of the hospital. It was a mess. People were everywhere and of course no law enforcement was around. John knew this was going to be very bad.

John went into the hospital and was immediately stopped by a State Trooper. John had picked up his US Marshal ID and now showed the trooper and was allowed access to the entire hospital. John went to the administrator's office and saw David, the hospital administrator, who John knew. David was still wearing his tux and John knew David had been at the country club when all Hell broke loose. David had a total look of relief on his face when he saw John and said "God I am glad you are here. Do you know what happened?"

John said "Some of it. Now what do we need as far as medical?"

David said "We need doctors, nurses, supplies, Hell John everything. It is a total disaster and I have no idea exactly how many are dead or wounded. I just cannot get a good count".

John said "OK David. Now we have medics that are just landing, and the military is sending people from 2 forts. I will get some of my people to try to get an exact count of the dead. Where are they being taken?"

David said "To the high school gym for now. That was the only place we had enough room".

John said "I will get on that. Now David you need to get cleaned up and some food and maybe a little rest. Just a few hours. If not, you are going to collapse".

David nodded and John left. John went directly to the high school. On the way to the high school, John called Norman and had him meet John there. John also called Tress and told him to send all the medical team directly to the hospital and to see David, just as soon as they landed. John knew that the medics would be great with the injuries because they were combat trained and this sure as Hell was a combat zone.

John and Norman entered the high school gym and looked at the bodies on the floor. John quickly counted thirty-eight and then he saw one over to the side and three on the other side. The three were children. John saw the FBI and went straight to the agent and showed John's ID and the agent acknowledged it and said, "General we have a total mess and I have no idea who did this or anything about why other than greed".

John said, "I fully understand Agent, and we will work together to solve this fucking thing I can tell you that".

The agent said "I have been briefed about you Sir and so have all the agents. The Director was very plain about us giving you everything you need. Just let me know how we can help?"

John said "Thanks but for now you guys do what you do. I think you are the best, so I feel you can do whatever it takes."

John then walked to the body separated from the rest and removed the sheet. John looked down and saw a black man in his 20's. He had been shot in the chest and in his left leg and arm. John pulled out his cell phone and took photos of the face, arm with a tattoo and of the man's neck and another tattoo. John then emailed these back to Red Lion and Don and Cindy. Next John saw that ten bodies had badges on the sheets and he knew they were law enforcement. The count was staggering because over 75% of the law enforcement in the city and county was now dead. All the leaders were gone and that was of course a real problem. John started looking at the tags on the sheets and saw the name of the Mayor and of the city council members. One male and one female, both of whom John liked. The total count in the high school was forty-two including the one robber. John was sick. This was not going to be good for the town and John knew it. The city had two funeral homes and all the personnel from both were in the high school. The coroner was of course a funeral director and he was there doing his paperwork. John saw the overwhelmed look on everyone and knew that help must get here quickly. Norman had taken prints off the suspect's right and left hands and of course so had the FBI, but Norman wanted Red Lion to have as much info as possible to work with. He had sent the prints via e-mail back to Cindy and she was working on identifying this guy.

Now the medical personnel were arriving. The Red Lion personnel had already been at the hospital for about three hours and the Army people were now starting to arrive. Things were getting better. John got a call from Willis and was told a plane from FEDEX was in bound and would be at the airport in twenty minutes. Trucks and people would be needed to off load the plane and Molly had asked Willis to tell John. John had no fucking idea what was going on, so he called Molly. Molly answered and said "John I am with Cindy, you know Dr. Ben's wife, and we called and had a complete plane of the medical supplies we need sent from Miami. Now we need people to unload it and get them to the hospital. I just paid for all of this and told them if it was not here in four hours I would personally have their ass. Guess they did not want to fuck with me".

John started laughing and said, "Ok I will call Bob and see what we can do".

John called Bob and he answered on the first ring. Bob was overjoyed to hear John's voice and after John explained the situation, Bob said "Hell yes I can have at least six trucks and a dozen people at the air field in about thirty minutes".

John thanked Bob and now John needed to see how things were with Ted. John drove back to the hospital and found Ted's room and went in. Ted was sitting in a chair staring out the window and when John walked in Ted said, "Damn I am so glad to see you my friend".

John said, "How are you Ted and what the fuck happened?" Ted told John the whole story of how the guys had come in the bar and started shooting up the place and then taking the money from the registers and stealing cell phones and cash from the customers as well as wallets and purses. Ted had been shot because he was behind the bar standing by one of the registers. Ted was hit by a shot gun in his right side and right arm but luckily, he had not been hurt very badly. He was due to be released that afternoon to go home. Then Ted said "John remember when you told me about the surveillance system that sent the feed via WIFY to another location so nothing was in the bar? Well I had that system put in about three weeks ago and all the feeds go to my house. I think I got them on camera and I think it shows a lot. I need to get home and check".

John said, "OK Ted let me find out when you can leave, and I will take you home and we can check the feed".

Ted said, "They looked for the disc players but could not find them so the shot up all the cameras, but it was too late then". John went to find a doctor and get Ted released. John was back in about twenty minutes and John helped Ted dress and took him home. John and Ted opened a beer and Ted played the tape feed. Ted was right. The pictures were clear, and they showed the faces and even some of the tattoos that these punks had. John asked Ted if John could take the tape and Ted said "Sure". John finished his beer and made damn sure Ted was resting, then left and headed to the airport and to the hanger.

John gave the tape to Tress and Tress immediately had it on the way via SAT/transmission to Don and Cindy at Red

Lion Headquarters. Tress and Sandy had decided to go back to Texas and John agreed. More could be done there for the planning and identification than in Florida and John told them to take the C-141 and head back. John also told Tress that these people needed to be found and stopped and that was the only priority for Red Lion as of now. Tress agreed, and Jim had also decided to go back to Texas. John and Jim discussed the C-130 and now that the Army was on site they decided to send it back as well. Jim would ride on the C-141 with Tress and Sandy because it was faster.

John had seen Bob and his people when John had come back to the airport and they had almost finished unloading the FEDEX plane. The supplies were now heading for the hospital. The State Police had taken over all law enforcement functions for the county and city and things were slowly coming back to normal. There was a lot of damage to businesses and especially to the beach bars and restaurants. These guys had torn up these places for no reason. John was trying to figure out why they had been so damn destructive and wondered if it was something to keep the police from finding out details of the robberies. No matter, John now had the tape from Ted's and in a few hours, John was sure many things would be known. John's cell phone rang, and it was Liz. She said, "John do you have any clue as to who these people are?"

John said "Liz we have a lead but so does the FBI. The guy who was killed had a tattoo on his arm and neck and we are trying to find out about that. The FBI might have that tattoo on file in their system".

Liz said "Ok John the Boss wanted to know. He may go on TV, but I think it would be better if the Governor did the news conference, so we will see. Please let me know as soon as anything breaks. I will call the FBI".

Liz hung up and John smiled. John knew damn well the FBI still did not know a fucking thing and with their system it would take about a week before they could identify the tattoo if they even could do it. John headed for the house and Molly. It had been one Hell of a day.

When John arrived at the house, he saw four cars parked in front. John went in and Molly was sitting in the den with four women and they were talking and making a list of things. John said hello and they said hello to him and Molly said, "Honey get a beer and come join us". John started to head for the bar, but Louise already had a beer in her hand and gave it to John. John sat down and said, "OK what is going on?" The women were all friends and their husbands were either doctors or businessmen that owned the mall. Molly and the women were in the process of planning for the funerals of the people who had been killed. Molly had decided that the five of them would pay the costs because most of the people did not have much money and under the circumstances it was what Molly wanted to do. John was very proud of his wife and of the women and told them so. Things were in such a mess it was going to be at least a week before any funeral could be done and now where to keep the bodies was the problem. The county morgue only had room for six bodies so after that the funeral homes could embalm them but that too was a problem because they had to be kept cold even then for that amount of time. Moving them out of the county would be another problem because then where could they be taken and who would accept that responsibility. The hospital could only keep four for a short period of time. There set up was only temporary and usually the funeral home was there in a few hours to remove the remains. John said, "Ok we can solve this, but it may be bad for the families if we let them know how".

The women looked at John and he continued "In war we use refrigerated trucks to hold bodies until they could be transported to the local funeral homes, so we could do that now. The only thing is the families and how they will feel about using a truck to keep the remains".

The women sat for a minute and then one said, "Do we really have a choice, John?"

John said, "I do not see one right now". Just then the doorbell rang, and Louise answered. John got up and walked to the entrance way and saw a lady about 75 years old dressed in a very smart business suit. The lady was asking to speak to Molly and Louise had her come in. John looked out and saw a black Lincoln Town Car waiting in the front. John walked forward and said, "Hello I am John Carter, Molly's husband, may I help you?"

The lady said "Yes General Carter, I am Mary Davidson and I need to speak to Molly about the funeral problem. I have the solution".

John showed Mary in and asked if she would like a drink. Mary said, "Crown Royal with a small splash of water please". Louise went to fix the drink and John introduced Molly and the other women to Mary. Mary knew three of the women and she took a chair facing Molly. Mary got her drink and said "Now we have a major problem and I want to help. We have so many dead and no place to keep them until everything is done so I want to use our Ice Cream plant. I know that may sound awful, but my employees can make things as nice and respectful as possible and we really do not have a choice".

John was shocked, but Molly said "Mary that is wonderful. Thank you and yes we do need you to help us".

Mary said "Molly just call this number and James will take care of everything. Now how do we want to do the funerals? I think we should find out if any of the victims must be sent away or if all are going to be buried here locally as a first step. Then the children must be first for the parent's sake don't you think?"

Molly agreed and so did the other women. John excused himself and went to his office and called Red Lion. John thought, "ice cream factory is a Hell of a lot better than a fucking truck". Don came on the line and John said, "Where are we on identification?"

Don said "We know all of the people we have pictures of and where they come from. I am just now getting everything in print and sending it to your email. Do we tell anyone else or do we wait?"

John said, "We wait and thanks". John hung up and in about thirty seconds the email popped up on John's computer. John opened the email and started reading. He now knew where some of these people came from and it was Georgia. Right outside of Atlanta. John had Louise bring him another beer and he started reading the bio sheets on each person that had been identified. John knew the FBI was still trying to identify the only person of this gang that had been killed and Hell Don and Cindy used the FBI systems. John just thought "Shit no wonder nothing gets done for years and then no convictions because of the bullshit courts and the rules". John continued to read and the more he did the madder he got.

A week had now passed since the attack on the town and some of the funerals were taking place. Only eight bodies had been shipped away so now things were going to be bad every day until all the rest had been buried. Thirty-three bodies had to be buried and so far, only three had been done. They were the children and it was a very bad time. The law enforcement officers were all going to have the funerals on the same day in the same place, the high school gym. The procession to the cemetery would then be done and then each officer would be buried in his plot one at a time. It was going to be a very long day, but the families had agreed because so many officers from so many districts were going to be coming. It was estimated that over 3000 would be attending and the motorcade would be for miles. The Governor and all the State officials would also be there. The way things were going it would take a month to finish the funerals and the city was having a very hard time with that as were the families of the dead. The funeral homes were trying to schedule three services each a day for a total of six bodies each day and that was a great help. Molly and her women had told each funeral home to do what was necessary and to send the bills to a special account that was set up for just that purpose. No family would spend a dime for the service.

John was still trying to figure out why this gang from Georgia had picked Redman Beach to do this. Cindy came up with the answer. About nine months before three of the gang had been put in jail at Redman Beach for ninety days because of a drunk driving and possession charge. One had the DWI and the other two had been in possession of drugs so all three were given ninety days in jail. During that time, they had worked on various prisoner projects such as street cleaning and trash pickup and had seen the city and how much wealth it had. They also had a revenge motive, so it was a target. Cindy had researched the city and county records and discovered this was the only tie to Redman Beach that made any sense. John agreed and now he wanted the leaders of this gang and wanted them badly. John called Red Lion and talked to Tress and Jim and explained what John wanted. Tress said, "We have four operators on the ground in Atlanta and we are gathering Intel on the gang as we speak, Sir".

John said "I figured that, but I just needed to hear it. Ok let me know as soon as we have a plan".

Tress said, "Of course Sir".

Jim then said, "John are we going to give the Feds any of this before we do things?"

John said "I don't know Jim. What do you think?"

Jim said "Well, it is close to home and they will sure as Hell know we did the deed if we do not let them in on it. I have an idea and Tress and I will work it then we will let you know is that alright?"

John said "Hell Jim you guys are the boss so Hell yes. Do what you think is best for the corporation. I just want it done as soon as possible and you both know why".

Jim and Tress said, "Yes Sir we totally understand, and it will be quick". John hung up and walked into the den and got a beer and sat down. Molly came in and sat with him and sipped her drink. By December the 12th all the funerals were finished, and the city was trying to get ready for Christmas. It was very hard. The remaining city council members wanted to have an election in January to elect a new Mayor and to fill the two seats on the council. The city administrator was taking applications for a new Police Chief and the Chief Deputy was running the Sheriff's department until an election could be held. It looked like the city and county election would be held together at the end of January to save money and to give time for candidates to do some campaigning. John and Molly had talked and because of what had happened they were staying in Redman Beach for Christmas and New Year's this year. Jim had canceled his plans for Europe, but John made him go. Nothing was going to happen in the next three weeks, so Jim finally relented, and he and Latoya left for Europe. John and Molly were not really looking forward to Christmas or New Year's, but they knew it would come anyway.

# CHAPTER 59

Christmas had been alright for John and Molly and Ted's was open and Ted was there for about six hours each day. On Tuesday John was invited to the country club for a lunch with many business leaders, four doctors, David the hospital administrator, some of the attorneys in town and several other people including Willis. John arrived and went in and had a drink and walked around and visited with the people there. Then everyone sat down, and lunch was served. Ted had come, and he rose and said, "John we wanted you here today because the Governor has approved the special election in January and all of us want you to run for Mayor".

John sat and did not say a word. Finally. John stood up and said, "I have no idea how to be a Mayor or even what a Mayor does except ride in the yearly parade so why me?"

Mike, one of the town's business leaders said "John you were a General in the Army and you were the CEO and Chairman of a multi- Billion Dollar corporation. You have done a lot for this city and you are more qualified than anyone we can think of. And the best reason is we all like and respect you".

John still was almost speechless. Finally, John said "I want to think about this and talk to Molly. I will let you guys know tomorrow is that alright?"

Mike said, "Of course but damn it John we really want you and to be very honest we need you to lead this city". John and the others got up and John after visiting with just a few of the men left and drove straight home. He walked in and Molly said "John what is wrong? You look like you just saw a ghost or something".

John said "I need a drink and I do not mean a beer. Scotch will do the trick" and he went to the bar and poured the scotch. Molly looked at him and shook her head. John sat down and said "These people want me for Mayor. What do you think about that?"

Molly said "I think it is great. Hell, John you already run the fucking city so why not make if official. Hell yes. I can be a Mayor's wife. I was a General's wife, so this should be a cake walk". John started laughing. The next day John called Mike and told him it was a GO.

John and Molly were up and sitting in the den at 8 AM drinking coffee. John had the SAT/communications on and was waiting. Tress had picked New Year's Day because the idiots had made it easy for Red Lion. The operators in Atlanta had passed the word that Maximilian was having all his Captains and some other gang members over to his house for a New Year's party and they would stay there until sometime during the day on New Year's. This meant that the operators would only have to go to one place to get everyone of the leaders. The gang members involved in Redman Beach were going to be at another location so all of them could be taken at the same time. The Intel was the key that made Red Lion the best in the world and John was very proud of that fact. The raids would go off at 9 AM on the dot in both locations. The operators all 40 of them had arrived at Atlanta at 2 AM and the C-141 had taxied to the commercial part of the airport and off loaded the men. Vans had been rented via computer and were waiting in the lot, so the operators got the equipment and were on their too the locations. The operators were broken down into twenty-man teams for this raid and each team was in place by 8 AM waiting for the GO command from Tress. At 9 AM exactly, local time, the command was given over the SAT communications and the raid was on. John listened and could now watch the camera feeds from the operator's cameras. The screen was split into two sections and each location was shown. Molly watched closely as the operators entered each building and realized she was watching an operation live for the very first time.

The team going after Maximilian and the Captains were now in the residence and had taken out five gang members that were in the living room. The operators had silencers on the pistols and the MP-5's so no sound was made. The team spread out throughout the house and each room was checked. The Captains were located and one by one given a shot and were out cold in a matter of seconds. Maximilian was in the back bedroom and two women were in bed with him. The operators entered the room and the women started to scream and jump from the bed, before they were shot. Maximilian tried to grab a weapon, but an operator hit him in the face with the butt of the MP-5 and another operator injected him with the drug and Maximilian was out cold in less than fifteen seconds. The operators carried the Captains and Maximilian out to the vans and loaded them inside and headed back to the airport.

The raid on the gang location of the suspects from Redman Beach went almost as well. The operators had entered the residence but there were two floors in the house, so it took longer to search and find the right people. The place was crowded and some of the people were awake. There was an initial confusion from the gang members then some tried to grab weapons. The operators shot anyone moving and then started finding the suspects they came for. Each suspect was given and injection and then carried out to the vans and loaded. The gang residence had required the operators to kill many more gang members that had been planned for, but it really made no difference. The Atlanta police would work that case and how they figured it was their business. Even if the vans were seen by people, they were already covered as who had rented them. The vans were also now in route to the airport and at 11:45 AM the C-141 was cleared to take off. All the operators and the prisoners were on board and the aircraft headed to Redman Beach. The prisoners had been tied hand and foot with flex ties and their mouths and eyes were taped with duct tape. They were laying on the floor of the aircraft. John was given the signal to call the State Police and he made the call. When the C-141 landed and then taxied to a stop in front of the Red Lion hanger at Redman Beach, eight State Police cars were waiting. The gang member suspects were delivered to the officers and loaded into their cars and taken away. The C-141 then took off and headed out over the water for about 100 miles. When the C-141 reached the 100- mile mark, it was at 25,000 feet and it started a decent to the water. When the aircraft was 2000 feet over the ocean the tail ramp was opened, and the operators pushed the Captains and Maximilian out still tied hand and foot and taped just as they had been on the flight. The ramp was closed, and the aircraft climbed to 25,000 feet and headed to Texas. John was given the word about the Captains and Maximilian and he was satisfied.

When the C-141 landed at Red Lion headquarters the operators got off and one of them took a bag with cell phones and the computer that had been taken from Maximilian's house, to Don and Cindy. They immediately went to work on the items. Don had used a throw away cell phone to call CNN and four other news media networks and tell them about the State Police capture of the Redman Beach suspects. John was now watching the news and just as everyone counted on, it was a complete circus. The FBI was now at the State Police Headquarters where the suspects had been taken and they and the State Police were talking to the media. It was almost 10 PM in Florida and things were hopping on all the network news feeds. Special cut on regular programs were happening and reporters from every news outfit imaginable were headed to the location of the suspects. John knew it had been a total success and so did Washington. Don and Cindy had already discovered the banking for the gang and had drained the account of a little over $6 Million Dollars. The cell phones were not very helpful other than having numbers of the additional gang members, so Don sent that info to the FBI via an email to a special agent he always used. New Year's Day was about over, and Red Lion had done the job. Now everyone went home and relaxed until the next day. John and Molly were very happy that Redman Beach would know that these people who had done such a horrible thing to the community were now in jail and would be charged and the death penalty would be asked for. John figured it would be given.

It was now officially 2015 and the new Congress and Senate would be taking office any day. John was also having to concentrate on his run for office. He was the only candidate on the ballot so far, but the ballots did not close until Jan 10[th,] so someone could decide to run. Molly had already gotten a group together and the election posters were ready to pick up in the afternoon. Molly was going to put them up everywhere in town and she had ordered 3000 of them. John was marveling at how Molly had jumped into this damn election and he was thankful he would not have to go through debates and all that crap. Mainly John was waiting to have the damn thing done and then he would try to learn what he was supposed to do as Mayor. Everyone in town knew John would win or so they said. The charges on the suspects were wide ranging and so far, forty-three counts of first degree murder and ten of those had law enforcement enhancement along with them, had been filed. Also, robbery and criminal action charges were filed for twenty counts on each suspect. It was now time for the FBI and they announced charges of bank robbery in the first degree and four other federal charges on each suspect that had robbed the bank. The interrogations had produced many things, and each suspect was talking trying to get a deal. Most of the suspects were saying the

Captains or Maximilian had ordered the raid but no matter how hard the news media looked they could not locate any Captains or this person who was called Maximilian. By now, people thought the suspects were making things up.

John and Molly were having lunch at the country club and one of Molly's friends stopped by the table and said "John we would like to thank you for getting those bastards. We really did not think they would ever get caught".

John said, "I really had nothing to do with it".

The friend said "Well then why did so many State Police cars meet that big plane of yours and take people off? Oh well it really does not matter because they are going to fry any way. But thank you all the same". The friend left, and Molly started laughing. John said "I will be damned. Nothing in this town is secret is it my dear?"

Molly said, "Not one damn thing". They both laughed and ordered another drink. Mike came to the table and said "Hello! How are you guys doing?"

John said "Good, Mike and you?"

Mike said, "I am great, and the campaign is really in high gear, John".

John said, "Well Mike, no one has signed up to run against me yet so now what do we do?"

Mike said "I think we should have a meet and greet the candidate. You and Molly can be at the Mall on Saturday morning and just shake hands with people and visit with them and really let them see who you are. Is that alright with you guys?"

Molly said, "Sure so what time and exactly where at the mall do you want us, Mike?"

Mike said "I would think about 11 AM and why not at the main entrance inside. We will set up a table and have some people there to pass out stickers and things like that". John and Molly agreed, and Mike left. Other friends came by the table and said hello and thanked John and Molly for taking care of the people who raided the town. John and Molly left after about 3 hours and went to Ted's and sat outside and talked. Some people there also came by and thanked John for taking care of the problem with the suspects and getting them arrested.

On Saturday, John and Molly were at the Mall and John was shaking hands and visiting with people about his campaign. Molly was also talking to people and making sure everyone was ready to vote. The day went very well and about 4 PM John and Molly decided to leave and go to Ted's. The election was on Tuesday and John knew it would go well. The news media had been covering the election only because they had been in town covering the story of the raid. John had not given them any interviews and put out a statement stating he would not speak with the national news about the local election and that was that. Of course, the news people were pissed off, but John did not care, and the media knew they could go no further in their quest to make the election a national story. Ted was also on the ballot for a City Council position and so was Wayne, one of the local doctors. No one else was running. The Sheriff's position was also a non-contested race and the Chief Deputy, Jim Yarbrough, was the only person on the ballot. John liked Jim and knew things would be very good when he was officially the Sheriff. John and Jim Y had talked some about a vision John had for the county and John was sure when the election was over they would be able to really get things done. The new quest for a Police Chief was also coming along and John had asked that nothing be done until after the election. John by law, was supposed to hire the Police Chief, Fire Chief and so John wanted to wait until he was the Mayor. The City Administrator position was also open because the present administrator had resigned effective January 15th for a much better position in another city. John was now going to have to look very hard to fill that job with the exact fit. John and

Molly were enjoying Ted's as they always did. Many people were coming and going as usual and John was talking with various people about the election and about the town. Molly was speaking to Judy, one of the women that was helping with the campaign and Judy said "Molly when this is over, I would like you to consider coming by the office and looking at some things I have done to present to the City Council. I really think you would be a great help with making sure it was presented the right way".

Molly said "I would love to do that, Judy. Is that the new beach front park and recreation area you have been talking about?"

Judy said, "Yes, it is. We even have some drawings and other things to present".

Molly said "OK. Then when all of this is done, call me and we will make a date". Judy thanked Molly and went to do other things.

On Tuesday the polls opened at 7 AM and John and Molly voted about 9 AM. Then they went back to the house and relaxed in the hot tub and pool. At 7:30 PM it was official. John was now the Mayor-elect and Ted, Wayne and Jim Y had also won. Over 17,000 had voted and John was very happy about that. Usually when the elections are uncontested people stay home, but this was a true show of support by the town and county. The ceremony to swear everyone into office would be on Friday at 9 AM at the county court house. Then John and Molly had a very large party planned for the entire town and county at the country club. The party was to start at 2 PM and go until probably midnight. It would be an open house again, that was the best way for people to get to come because of work schedules and other things. John figured about 5000 people would drop by and that was fine. The phone rang at 8:30 PM and Louise handed the phone to John and said, "Mr. John, it is the President for you." John said, "This is John Carter".

The President said "Congratulations Mr. Mayor. You are a politician now by God!"

John said "Thank you Sir. I guess I am at that".

Then the President said "John we need to discuss some things, so I will have Liz contact you. We have this nasty unfinished business to take care of and I want it done as soon as we can".

John said, "Anytime you call Mr. President, I will be there".

The President said, "I know that John and Thank you". The President hung up. John hung up and looked at Molly. Molly said "That was nice of him. Now what does he want?"

John said, "To finish this fucking thing with the National Revolutionary Army".

Molly said, "Hell so do I".

The party was again a sensation and the entire town was happy even to be invited. John was right. About 4000 people came by during the day and night. All the new elected officials were there, and things were really going well. The election had now allowed the town and the county to feel like a new start was going to happen and people had energy and seemed to be looking forward to things again. John spent a lot of time talking with Jim Y about the law enforcement situation and other things concerning how things might be changed. Jim was very receptive to John's ideas and wanted to get together as soon as possible to explore them. John also talked to the council members, the new and the two old members and they also liked what they heard. The wheels were now rolling for the type changes John wanted to introduce and most of the people were on board. It would be now a case of speaking to the two County Commissioners and the County Mayor to present the plan to them. John knew that would be a little tricky, but with the right presentation, it would be easy to get an agreement. The County Commissioners and the County Mayor were of course at the party and John visited with them and gave them a quick review of what John had in mind. The commissioners and the County Mayor seemed to be receptive and told John to schedule time at the next commission meeting. On Monday, John had a call from Liz. John, Jim and Tress would to come to the White House on Wednesday at 6 PM to meet with the President. John informed Tress and Jim and they were going to fly to Redman Beach and pick John up then go on to D.C. John made reservations at the Army and Navy Hotel.

# CHAPTER 60

At 6 PM John, Jim, and Tress entered the Oval Office. They all saluted the President and observed the men in the room. The Secretaries of Homeland Security, Defense, and State were all there. The Directors of the FBI, CIA, NSA, NIS and ATF were there. The President's Chief of Staff and Liz and the Attorney General were also there. The President said, "We will be meeting in the Cabinet Room for this so why don't we go there and get this done?" Everyone followed the President to the Cabinet Room.

As John went into the Cabinet Room, he saw the Army Chief of Staff, the head of the Joint Chiefs, the general in charge of CID and three other men at the table. Everyone sat, and the President said, "John now what do you have?"

John said "Mr. President and lady and gentlemen we have absolute proof that this National Revolutionary Army is much bigger than Senator Phillips. In fact, it is bigger than anyone could ever dream of. We have prepared slides, and other things to present as well as we have brought all the documents we have discovered in hard copy. I will now let Tress present the Red Lion evidence. The things we have gathered were gathered as civilians and are not subject to chain of custody requirements until we turn them over. Also, we as civilians, are not bound by Miranda or any other things that law enforcement is, and we can and did use whatever was necessary to gain information. It is not pretty but the results speak for themselves".

Tress stood up and walked to the DVD and put in the disc and started it playing.

The disc showed the way things had been done and Tress explained each step in the process as he showed the different slides. Everyone in the room sat stone-faced and watched the screen. The last part of the slide show was the confession from Phillips naming everyone involved and stating that he was in fact, the head of the organization. When the disc finished a hush came over the entire room. John said "That is the story Mr. President and that is what we have. I see two ways to handle this. The first is to let the various agencies, FBI, CID, GAO, and the Attorney General take this and get arrest warrants and go to the legal process. That will of course take years and probably will result in very little punishment because the news media will be totally involved, and your administration will be held accountable for letting this get so out of hand. It has been going on since before you were first elected President, however, no one will give a damn. You will be blamed by the public and especially by the Congress. The 2nd way to handle this is to turn everything over to Red Lion and let them do what they do. It will not be pretty, and it will not be public, but it will eliminate the entire issue once and for all. Once that is done, then investigations and all of that can be conducted on the way things were done and changes can be made to insure this cannot ever happen again. Mr. President it is your decision to make".

The discussions then began, and John sat back and watched each person as opinions were given. Most of the military were in favor of letting Red Lion handle the situation. The Attorney General had a real problem with how the evidence that was presented had been gathered and did not think it would be admissible in court because of the torture. The Secretary of Homeland wanted to let law enforcement doe their job, and arrest everyone involved and then bring them to trial. The Secretary said "We will show the nation that this administration did identify and arrest the persons responsible for these horrible crimes. They were brought to justice under the laws of the land without any favoritism as to the positions held".

John almost laughed out loud when that was said. Finally, the President said "I am going to need some time to consider what the best option is for this and I do not want anyone to do anything until I give the word. Is that understood?" Everyone nodded in understanding. The President then rose and walked out of the room. Liz and the Chief of Staff followed. Everyone else was standing and then each person slowly left the room. John, Jim and Tress left and took all the documents they had brought with them. Liz came out to the hallway and said, "John the Boss wants to see you alone, now". John followed Liz into the Oval Office and as the President motioned to a chair, John sat down. It was John and the President one on one.

The President said, "John I want a drink and I think you do also?"

John said, "Sir that would be the best offer I have had in the past four hours, please". The President pressed the buzzer and instantly a butler appeared, and the President told him to get the drinks. The butler returned in minutes and handed the President his drink then handed a beer to John and then left the room. The President took a long drink out of his glass and said "John we cannot kill two US Senators and four members of the House and keep it quiet. It was hard enough to keep Phillips' death and disappearance quiet and we used National Security for that, but it still is a problem with the news media asking questions. They would go crazy if that many elected officials disappeared. Do you have any other plan?"

John said "Mr. President there is another way but in the end, they are going to have to be eliminated. We can do it over time, but only killing them will save you. Mr. President, going all the way back to Washington every President with very few exceptions has had people like me. When the former President first asked me to do what I do he realized that there are many times when only what I do can accomplish the mission. My priority is to this country. My second is to the President. I have and always will be a patriot. I do not agree with 90% of the things that are happening right now in this country and I do not think the Congress is worth a damn. You have not done what I thought you would do and that of course upsets me a lot, but I also know I probably do not know the entire situation on many things. Right now, we have a huge problem and if it is not taken care of, it will bring this country down and there may be no getting back up, at least as we know it".

The President took another long drink and said, "OK John I can respect what you said but how do we stop this?"

John finished his beer and reached into his coat pocket and pulled out a folded piece of paper and handed it to the President. John said "Mr. President this is how. We have the plan and we can start it immediately. As you can see, there are eight DOD employees, six US Army active duty and two DOD civilians. The first move is to have CID arrest the military members and the FBI arrest the civilians. The charges will be unlawful use of government equipment, making false statements, and at least a dozen more charges the Attorney General and the Head of JAG can come up with. Make it public as Hell and have every news agency in on it immediately with a "leak" from the White House and the Pentagon. That way it will look like the administration is wide open and not covering up a damn thing. Once the arrests have been made, then let the interrogators work on these people. If they lawyer up, so fucking what. The investigation goes on and believe me, someone will try to cut a deal instead of spending the next sixty years in a federal pen".

The President said, "OK then what about the Senators and Congressmen?"

John said "That Sir, is what Red Lion does. They have terrible accidents over a period of about nine months. We will have one, you pick, commit suicide. Then when things are investigated, information will come out about the involvement in this rebel group. That way, you are totally covered and so is everyone else. You get good press for fighting crime in the government and so does the FBI, and anyone else involved".

The President rang the buzzer and ordered another drink for John and himself. When the drinks had been delivered, the President said, "John I know you hated Phillips but was it absolutely necessary to do what it showed on the screen?"

John said "Probably not, but we got the information a Hell of a lot faster and he deserved that and more. Mr. President he was a fucking traitor to this country, to you, and to the people he was supposed to represent. His entire life he was out for what he could get and only that. Yes, I hated him, and I am damn glad he got almost everything that was coming to him. I just wish it could have lasted longer and been more painful. Does that answer your question, Mr. President?"

The President said, "John remind me to never piss you off", and started to laugh. After the drink was finished, John said good bye to the President and left the office. He would be contacted the next few days by the Army and the FBI at his house in Redman Beach. John got Jim and Tress and the three men went back to the hotel and sat in the bar. It had been one Hell of a day. After a few drinks, the three men went into the dining room and had dinner. They were in bed by midnight and up at 5 AM to go to the airport and catch the jet back to Redman Beach and then it would go on to Texas. John would advise Jim and Tress when he was told what was going to happen with the Army and the FBI.

John and Molly had discussed the trip and Molly was very glad John was letting Tress and Jim do all the work. John was now in his office at City Hall learning how to be a Mayor. John had read all the things the Mayor was to do at City Council meeting and the other duties and, John had very little to do except just be there. He would open the meeting and present the agenda, then as things were discussed John would call for votes after motions were made and seconded. The only time John voted was to break a tie. John could not put things forward, a council member had to do that, so that was John's job at the meetings. John did have the hiring and appointing power for certain city positions and he also had to submit a yearly budget. Other than those requirements, John really had nothing to do. The position of City Manager was the power in the city. Whoever was in that job really ran the city on a day to day basis. John was going to have to appoint someone to that job and then the City Council hired that person by contract. John was buzzed by Laney, his secretary. Laney had been with the city in that position for fifteen years and was very efficient. Laney told John he had two men from Washington there to see him. John had them come into his office and stood to meet the men. Brad was the Special Agent from the Army CID and Jerry was the Special Agent from the FBI and John had met both men before. John shook hands and had the men sit down across from John's desk. Brad said "General, I have been briefed by the Army Chief of Staff and now all we need is the records on the military personnel involved in this".

Jerry said, "General I was briefed by the Director and I need the civilians and the names of the people at the weapons companies".

John said "OK I will give you the phone number for my man at Red Lion and have you call him. Then I suggest you head for Texas. I will wait until you are ready to do the arrest and then we will do our thing. Let us know so we can then get a timetable going. From now on you will be working directly with the Red Lion headquarters, and remember all the people you will be working with are Generals also." John gave Brad the phone number and the men shook hands and left John's office. John called Tress and Jim and gave them a "heads up".

John called Jim Y and had him meet John at the country club. Jim Y was now the Sheriff and John wanted to discuss a few things that were on John's mind. The men met and had a drink then John said, "Well Jim is it any different now that you are elected rather than being appointed?"

Jim Y smiled and said "Yes John. Now they cannot fire me as easily. Nothing else has really changed so far. Now what is this all about?"

John said "Jim I need to present a few things to you and see if you agree or if you even want to do them. As you know, my police department is almost non-existent, and we now only have four officers able to do road work. I have four more that will be coming back over the next six months, but they are a question mark due to the injuries they suffered. I have no Police Chief and we need to make some major changes in the way we do business in the department. I would like to do away with the Redman Beach Police Department and have you and your force take over all the law enforcement for the city and the county. That would also include the jail. Hell, we only have two cells, so we really do not have a jail, only holding cells. What do you think about that?"

Jim Y looked at John and took a long sip of his drink. Jim Y said, "John I could do it, but it would cost a fucking fortune and the county does not have that type of funds".

John said "I know that, but I can solve that as well. Right now, the city has a police dispatcher and a jailer who do little so what if they went to work for your department and the city paid their salaries. The same would be done with the officers and we would also pay for all inmates that were in on city charges. In other words, if it was not a state charge we pay the county for the cell. City charges would also be enforced by your Deputies. Then I also have an idea to run by you about the jail".

Jim Y said "Hell John this may work like a charm. What about the jail?"

John said "We need to build a jail that has 100 beds that can be used at all times not counting the thirty you have now. It will cost about $21 Million Dollars, but then we rent the fucking beds to the Government at $150 dollars a day per bed, on a contract. See Jim, the Feds pay on contract 365 days a year just to have the beds available and because Orlando is where the Federal court is, we qualify. No other county can offer that because they do not have the beds. It is a total win situation for the department and the revenue is $5,475,000 Dollars per year. Not bad!"

Jim Y sat for a minute and said, "OK John how the Hell do I get $21 Million Dollars?"

John said "The County borrows it from me. Simple".

Jim Y told John he liked the idea, but it would be a hard cell to the commissioners Jim Y believed. John and Jim Y talked a little more and decided to have a meeting with the commissioners in the next few days. John was going to have them for lunch at the country club. He was also going to have the city council there as well.

# CHAPTER 61

Tress and Jim had the meeting with Brad and Jerry and gave them all the information that they needed to make the arrests. John and Molly were watching the TV news and sitting in the hot tub having a drink when the arrests were announced. John watched as the military members were walked out of various locations then the next images were the civilians at the Pentagon being arrested by FBI agents. The last images were the employees of the arms companies being arrested by FBI agents and ATF agents. The "leak" been perfect and now the news was buzzing. The Attorney General had made a live statement and so did the Army Chief of Staff. Things were going well and just as John had told the President they would. Tress had one of the Congressmen set for a very bad car wreck the next day. It would never be connected to the arrests, because Phillips was still the only person in the Senate or Congress that had been identified as being in the rebel camp. John was very pleased, and he and Molly got dressed and headed to Ted's for the night. The next morning the automobile accident was only a brief headline on the morning news. The Congressman had lost control of his car and gone off a bridge into a river and had been tragically killed. No drugs or alcohol had been detected. The death was ruled as accidental. Don had drained almost all the bank accounts the man had, and now Red Lion had an additional $7 Million Dollars in the special fund. Enough had been left so no one would question anything about the accident.

The people that had been arrested were talking to the interrogators and telling everything they knew. It was just confirming what Red Lion already had discovered and nothing new came out. The charges were very harsh and only a miracle would save any of them and that would be the Presidential Pardon. It was not going to happen. Bail was set at $10 Million Dollars on all the civilians and the military were put in per-trail confinement. The military personnel were looking at thirty years at hard labor plus a Dishonorable Discharge and loss of all benefits. Reduction to Private. No Matter how hard they talked CID was not listening too much they had to say. Tress and Jim had now planned the other eliminations and were just waiting for the timetable to come around. One would be a mugging in downtown D.C., another car accident, only away from D.C. and then a couple of heart attacks. Finally, one would be a suicide. That would be the final key which would tell all. Then it would be over. That was the plan so now Red Lion waited. All of this was going to happen in eight months. Don and Cindy had already sent enough email messages or at least had them timed and dated to be released and all the bank accounts were going to be partially drained leaving only a small amount of money so no suspicion would be raised. John was glad it was almost over.

Red Lion needed to have a Board and Stockholders meeting and John was thinking the first of March or in that week anyway. Everyone was informed, and the meetings were scheduled for March 5th at Red Lion Headquarters. John and Molly were going to fly over on the 3rd and spend a few days in Houston. John had a lot to do during the last weeks of February at Redman Beach and it started with a lunch with the city council and the commissioners. The Sheriff was there along with the city engineer and city attorney. The lunch was at the country club in the private dining room. John had a bar set up and of course everyone had a drink before lunch. The lunch was served, and John waited until almost everyone was finished then he said "I wanted to have all of you here today to discuss a few things about the coming year and some of the visions I personally have. I am not trying to offend anyone so please do not think I am trying to cram anything down your throats, but I just wanted to put out some ideas and see how the leaders of the city and county feel about them". Everyone listened as John put out his ideas for the city police and the county sheriff and for the extra things he had not discussed with Jim. One of the things was to hire a professional grant writer for the city and county so each could apply for the Billions of dollars that were available to cities and counties in Grants. John proposed that the salary be split between the city and county and that the person work in an office apart from the city or county. Then John placed the major bomb on the table. John wanted to build a desalination plant for the city and county to have fresh water in an unlimited supply. John also wanted to hire a person to promote the county and city to businesses and other enterprises such as retirement communities and things of that nature. When John was finished, the discussions started. Most of the members of the city and the county that were at the table were almost in shock. Many liked the ideas of the police department going to the Sheriff and they liked the idea of the revenue the new jail would bring into the county, but money was the hold up. The city engineer was very happy with the idea of the water plant but again money was the hold up. After all the discussions had almost run their course, John said "I also have one more item, to put forward, but the city and county attorney who as it turns out are one and the same, must approve this. I will loan either the city or the county as much money as is necessary to do all the projects I described. My interest rate will be prime rate less 2 % and the loans can go for 30 years. Payback can be with Tax breaks to me or one of my businesses or I can be repaid with cash. That would be a decision of the city council or the county commission or both. One can pay one way the other can pay another way or both can pay the same. I do not care".

Tommy the attorney said "John the offer is overwhelming, but it is not legal under Florida law. A city cannot take out a loan without a bond issue on the ballot of more than ½ of the yearly operating budget and either can a county so as good of a deal as this is, we cannot do it. I am sorry".

John said, "Ok then if I had a foundation and the city and county applied for a grant could I just give then money as a grant and they could accept it?"

Tommy said, "Yes under certain circumstances and I will have to research that and get back with you".

John said, "I understand".

Then Tommy said "The law enforcement thing can be done by a vote of city council and a vote by the commissioners. That is an easy thing to do. Now the water plant of course is going to be hard because of the federal regulations and all that crap and I suggest it be a private venture then why not do what you did with the airport?"

John said "OK I can sure as Hell do that. I can also build the fucking jail if it takes that to get things started". The entire table broke into laughter. The lunch was over, and everyone left and headed back to do what they do. John was set for the first City Council meeting which was the next night at 7 PM.

John opened the council meeting according to the rules he had memorized. There was an audience of over 200 hundred people and John was nervous as Hell. John made the call that all council members and the Mayor were present, and that new business was now on the floor. Michelle, one of the surviving council members, made a motion that the city immediately hire a city administrator. The motion was seconded, and the vote was 4 to 0 in favor. Then Ted made a motion that the police department be dissolved and that the Cobb County Sheriff's department immediately start doing all law enforcement for the city. The motion was then opened for discussion and citizens started to ask questions from the floor. John listened and after a few questions had been asked said "I would like to explain the motion so there is a very clear understanding by the council members but especially the citizens here and throughout Redman Beach".

John then stood up and said "This motion comes with a very heavy heart and as we all know the events of the past few months have left our police department almost non-existent. We only have four officers capable of doing police patrol and that is in no way a realistic way for the city to operate. Four of our officers are still on sick leave from injuries they received during the horrible raid on our city and we lost five other officers including our Police Chief. I have discussed our situation with Sheriff Jim Y and if we pass the motion, we will be doing three things. The first will be that all calls for Law Enforcement will be answered immediately within bounds of the call. Secondly our existing police personnel, officers, jailer and dispatchers will have a permanent job and at higher pay. The dispatchers will go to either the Sheriff's office or to the 911 dispatch center. The jailer will go to work in the Cobb County jail and our patrol officers will become deputy Sheriffs and be working road duty. The officers that are now on sick leave due to injuries will go to the Sheriff's Department like the other Redman Beach officers when they return, or they will be given the option to be medically retired with full benefits and pension. By doing this motion we as a city will not only have law enforcement coverage, but we will save about $1 Million Dollars per year in the city budget. I truly believe this is the very best move for our city".

A few of the people in the audience ask a few more questions about what would be done with the police department building and things like that and then John called for a second and a vote. The vote was again 4 in favor 0 opposed so the motion passed. The rest of the meeting was a discussion of various things concerning the city and under old business some ordinances were passed. The meeting was adjourned about 9 PM. John and Molly went to Ted's and Ted followed. The other council members also came to Ted's and so did Tommy the city attorney.

Two days after the city council meeting John and Molly were spending a nice afternoon in the hot tub when Tress called. John answered and then said, "Molly turn on the TV". Molly turned the TV on and the news bulletin was talking about a member of the House of Representatives that had a heart attack and died in the House dining room about thirty minutes before. It was one of the house members on the list. Molly said "Damn John how in the Hell did Red Lion pull that off? There must have been 200 people in that damn dining room".

John said "I have no idea. Guess Tress and Jim knew something I don't". The news was still covering the tragedy and of course the White House sent their condolences. The House was on recess for the rest of the day. Now there were only five left. John and Molly spent the day lounging in the hot tub and the sauna and in the pool.

John was very busy the next day at his office, with doing the hiring process which was totally a different animal for him. All his career, John had people to do things like he was now doing. He had looked at about twenty resumes of various people applying for the city administrator job and nothing jumped out at him. Most of the applications showed that the people were technically qualified for the position, but John was not very impressed. Laney buzzed John and said "Sir, there is a young lady here to see you about the city administrator position".

John said, "Did I have an appointment?"

Laney said, "No Sir, she just walked into the office and asked to see you".

John said, "OK send her in please". John got up and walked to the office door and saw a young woman in her mid-thirties walking toward him. She was about 6 feet tall in heels and weighed no more than 130 pounds. Her hair was light brown with reddish highlights and shoulder length. She had an amazing figure. John said, "Hello I am Mayor Carter and you are?"

The young woman said, "Mr. Mayor I am Stephanie Ball and I am here to get hired as the City Administrator".

John said, "Well Ms. Ball please come in and have a chair". Stephanie went into the office and sat in a chair facing John's desk. John sat behind the desk and said, "OK tell me about yourself, please".

Stephanie started telling John all about Stephanie. Stephanie was 38 years old and had graduated from Florida State University when she was 21, with a degree in Mechanical Engineering and a minor in Oceanography. She had then gone into the US Army and was assigned to the Corps of Engineers and spent one tour in Iraq and one year in the UAE. She spoke Arabic, Spanish and Vietnamese. Stephanie had gotten out of the Army after six years at the rank of Captain and went to work for an engineering firm in Houston Texas. She had left the firm about one year ago and had moved back to Florida and was now living in Redman Beach. Her present job was as a bartender at one of the beach restaurants, but she was now ready to get back to work in something solid. Stephanie was single and wanted the job. John was damned impressed.

John said, "I understand the Spanish and now that you told me about your military service I can see the Arabic, but why Vietnamese?"

Stephanie said "Well Sir, on today's market, most if not all of the nail shops and many of the beauty shops are owned by Vietnamese so I wanted to know what the Hell they were talking about. Also in this job, it will be a great asset to be able to know what they are saying when we do business with them".

John said "That my dear is a great point. Now what do you know about running a city?"

Stephanie said "Not much, Sir, but I do know how to run an Engineer Company in combat and in a peacetime setting. Also, I know that the city depends on small business and that people want good streets, garbage pickup, police and fire protection and above all else, they want to feel the city cares about them. I can learn all the other things and even create some things of my own if given the chance".

John said, "Sit right here for a minute". John got up and left the office and went to get Laney, so he could get an application for city employment. John was back in about five minutes and said "Stephanie, May I call you that?"

She nodded, and John continued "I want you to fill out this application and when you get through give it to Laney at the desk and I will be waiting in the front lobby". John walked out of his office and called Molly. John wanted Molly to meet him and Stephanie at the country club for lunch. When she had completed the application form and attached her resume to it, Stephanie walked out, and John and Stephanie got into John's car and headed for the country club.

Molly was sitting at a table when John and Stephanie walked in. John introduced Stephanie to Molly and then sat down next from Molly. Stephanie sat across from Molly. The waiter arrived, and John ordered a beer, Molly had a Vodka and soda and Stephanie had a glass of white wine. Molly started asking questions and she and Stephanie talked for a few minutes. John listened to everything that was being said and was even more impressed with Stephanie. The lunch took over two hours and when they finished, Molly said "Steph I think you will be a very good asset to the city".

John said "I do also. Now why don't we go back and get you in-processed young lady?"

Stephanie stood up and hugged Molly and then John leaned over and kissed Molly and said "See you at home later. Have a good day sweetheart".

Molly said "Thank you. Love you too and I plan on it". John and Stephanie left, and Molly had another drink and moved to the bar to talk to some of the women that had come into the club.

John showed Stephanie around the city hall complex and showed her the office she would have. It was next to John's and Laney would serve as secretary to both John and Stephanie. John was not in the office but maybe two times a week, but Steph would be there every day for at least eight hours a day and sometimes on Saturday and Sunday depending on what was happening. Laney took Steph and started her in-processing. John had a meeting with one of the business leaders in town and Kyle was waiting when John came back to his office. John showed Kyle into the office and motioned to a chair. Kyle sat, and the meeting was on. Kyle took out some plans and drawings and showed John the concept for a new development along the beach. Kyle and his group had bought three and ½ miles of beach front property that extended back from the beach two miles. This property was located across the main highway from the country club and Kyle wanted to develop the property into a housing development including high dollar single homes, condos and some apartments. The total housing would exceed 1500 units including the condos and apartments. The land was outside the city limits and that was the problem for the investors. No city services. That was what Kyle wanted to discuss with John. How could the city provide services such as water, sewer, trash, electricity, and street repair as well as fire and police if the city did not annex the development? The answer was simple. The city could not! John listened to Kyle and after Kyle finished, John said "Then what you are asking me to do is annex the entire property including the areas on either side which would be about two miles each direction and two miles out from the water?"

Kyle said, "John that is exactly what we need."

John said "OK then get a complete plan ready and meet with Stephanie, our city administrator and we can schedule you for a council meeting. When do you want to start this?"

Kyle said "Yesterday, but as soon as possible".

John showed Kyle out and Laney made the appointment for the next day with Stephanie. It had been quite a day for the new Mayor and he was ready to go home and see Molly. John left and drove directly to the house. Molly was in the hot tub totally nude and sipping on a drink. John joined her and had a beer. They talked about the day and played around with each other then went to the bedroom and made love.

# CHAPTER 62

The last week of February was getting crazy in a hurry for John. The Red Lion board and stockholders meeting was scheduled for March 6th and the city council meeting was now set for March 8th. John was sitting at the desk at home when his cell phone rang. John answered and the voice on the line said "John this is Capp. I would like to come to see you and bring along a few other guys if you can spare us some time."

John said "Hell Capp what have you gotten into now? Sure, I can spare time, Hell I am retired, don't you remember?"

Capp said "Yes retired my ass. We would like to meet with you tomorrow say 10 AM. Is that alright?"

John said, "OK I assume you are coming to Redman Beach is that right?"

Capp said "Yes and we will need someplace very private and secure. There will be six of us and you know everyone".

John said "Ok look forward to seeing you at 10 AM. When you get to the airport have your guys get directions to the country club. We will meet there. It is just what you are asking for". Capp said good bye and John put the cell back in his pocket. John was now very intrigued. About an hour later his phone rang again and this time it was Dan. Dan had all the paperwork ready for the foundation and wanted to come to Redman Beach to have John and Molly sign the necessary papers. John said the next day after 6 PM was great and Dan said he and Carol would be there. John would arrange for them to be picked up at the airport and brought to the house.

The next morning John was up and dressed and at the country club at 9 AM. John arranged a private room and lunch as well as a bar in the meeting room. At 9:45 AM the men arrived and were shown into the meeting room. John was standing at the bar and was dressed in a pair of tan slacks and a yellow silk shirt opened at the collar. He was wearing sandals. The men came in dressed in suits and ties and John knew every single one. John was entertaining six General Officers, well five four-star Generals and one four-star Admiral. John greeted the men and all of them made themselves a drink. Then they all sat at the large table and General Capp said "John we want to buy Red Lion. Everything you have, equipment, aircraft, that damn ship, and all the equipment currently in your base and the buildings and the fucking airport. The training facility we do not need, nor do we want anything here at Redman Beach. Houston or as you say Sugarland is what we are interested in".

John said "Oh My God. Why?"

Capp said "We are ready to retire from the military and we know what you have been doing and how damn much money you have made, and we want to buy the damn business. It is that simple".

John said "Hell I need another beer. Boys drink up because I am about to tell you how damn much money you will need".

John got his beer and the rest of the men got fresh drinks. John said, "Off the top of my head you gentlemen are looking at needing $900 Billion Dollars to buy Red Lion as it sits right now". There was not a bit of hesitation reflected on any of the faces looking at John.

Capp said, "And exactly what does that buy General?"

John smiled and said "The buildings in Sugarland, all the choppers, three Black Hawks and one Cobra, the C-141, the C-130, and the container ship. Then we add in thirty SUV's and then we start with the computer, SAT/phones equipment, munitions, weapons, and then we talk about medical and mechanical equipment and supplies, and the most important thing is the name Red Lion. That gentlemen, is what you will be buying. No cash or anything like that. Just Red Lion as it is".

Capp said, "Ok now would you be willing to speak to Washington about this on our behalf?"

John said "Sure I can do that. But I can have an exact figure for you after March 5th and it may be a little lower. When do you want to do this, if the board wants to sell?"

Capp said, "We are looking at April 1st, April Fool's Day".

John said "That sure as Hell fits. I will let you know what is decided at the board meeting. Now as far as our employees are concerned, you will have to make that deal individually. They do not come with the package".

All the officers at the table agreed and John said "Well Gentlemen let us go eat some lunch and have another drink. This is quite a day so far". John lead the way to the bar and buffet and everyone fixed a plate and got a drink. John watched as each man ate and ran them through his mind. Capp was the head of special operations. Henry was the head of Army Intelligence. Davidson was the head of Army logistics. Ben was the Chief of Staff of the Army. Dawson was the overall commander of Compact which included all forces in Europe, The Middle-East, Africa, and the lower Far East. And then Biggs was the Naval Commander for all the fleet. Quite an impressive bunch of military men. John and Capp were talking, and John said, "Capp where in the fuck do you think you can get the type of money we are talking about?"

Capp said, "Hell John we already have over that and can get as much as we need".

John looked and said, "I do not want to know where, do I?"

Capp said "John you already know. Just think about it for a minute or two and it will make perfect sense to you". John sat back and thought. There were only 200 four-star military men in the United States Military either still on active duty or retired. All the men in this group had been under-studies for a four-star doing their carrier and John knew where each

General who had retired was now. They had all gone into private work for major firms. Of course. These firms were the largest firms in the fucking world and they wanted their own "hit" teams. How better to do it than buy Red Lion. Hell, John had probably done work for most of the corporations. Very smart. John liked the idea and wondered how Washington was going to react. Then John realized that three former Presidents and the current President, as soon as he was out of office, controlled most of the corporations John was thinking about. Pure genius. The lunch was winding to a close and Capp thanked John and the Generals and Admiral left. John would call Capp with the exact dollar amount after the board meeting if it was a go. John left the country club and drove to Ted's to meet Molly. John took Molly out on the patio and told her about the meeting. Molly said "Holy Shit John. Does this mean what I think it means?"

John said, "Yes my dear it does". They went back inside and visited around the bar with friends. Carol and Dan were due in about three hours.

Dan and Carol arrived at John and Molly's house and Louise placed their luggage in the guest bedroom. Carol immediately put on a two-piece swim suit and went to join Molly in the pool. Dan and John went to John's office and went over the paperwork on the foundation. It was ready for signature and Dan had deposited $300 Billion Dollars in the bank account for the foundation. The entire foundation would be based in Florida at Redman Beach and now all that was needed was a staff and a location. The bank had been more than ready to handle the deposit and was fast becoming one of the richest banks in the United States. With the foundation money and John and Molly's personal money that bank had over $800 Billion Dollars on deposit just for them. Of course, they both still had the off-shore accounts and that would continue. Dan and John finished their business and Dan packed the papers away then both men changed into swim suits and joined Molly and Carol. By now both women were and sitting in the hot tub. John and Dan sat in the hot tub sipping their drinks. John said, "Dan we have a buyer for Red Lion".

Dan said "What?"

John said "Yes a real buyer. That will be what the board meeting will be about next week. What do you think about that?"

Dan took a long sip of his drink and said "John to be honest I think it is time for all of us to get the Hell out of this business. We have been doing this for a long time and so far, we have only lost a couple of people. I always fear one day that will change and change in a very big way".

John said "I know exactly how you feel and that is the main reason I think we should take the offer. They are offering $900 Billion Dollars for everything. Now our people will have to negotiate their own contracts, but I would like to give everyone who works for us $2 Million Dollars as a bonus. How many employees do we have just off the top of your head?"

Dan thought for a moment and said, "John I would say 400 actual employees not counting the board or stock holders".

John said "OK then we are looking at $800 Million Dollars. We can damn sure do that". John and Dan discussed a few things when the girls left them alone which was not often. About 9 PM they all decided to go to Ted's and have a bite to eat and do some dancing and more drinking. It was a good night and by 2 AM they were all home and in bed. The next morning John and Dan went over a few details and then Dan and Carol left for the airport and took the jet back to Texas. John called Sara and Kevin and explained what he needed done by the board meeting. They both assured John it would be sitting on his desk at Red Lion on the morning of the meeting.

The Board meeting was quiet as John stood and announced the proposed offer to buy Red Lion. After a minute or two, Jim said "I am totally agreeable to selling". Tress said

"I agree with selling. We need to get out of this business while we can before we have a real problem". The rest of the Board agreed and after a vote the motion was passed with no dissenting votes. John then said, "OK Sara and Kevin what is our financial picture as to cash and include the off-shore accounts?" Sara said "We currently have $800 Billion Dollars in cash. That includes everything". John said "I see it this way. We will need $800 Million Dollars to give every employee a check for $2 Million Dollars as a going away bonus. That will leave $790 + Billion Dollars plus the $900 Billion for the sale for a total of $1 Trillion, 690 Billion Dollars to be split up as follows: Every stock holder will receive $900,000 Dollars per share. That will total $900 Billion Dollars. The balance of money will be put into the Hallettsville Training account as a good faith jester from Red Lion, so they can continue to operate if they wish. John watched the faces of everyone at the table and saw smiles come on all of them. Then John said "I want to thank each of you for everything you have done since we started this little venture. I am very glad you are Billionaires many times over. Never ever get out of touch with each other and especially with me and Molly. I plan to have every employee at a function in two days at the Houston Country Club. Then we will pass out the checks. Again, thank you all".

The stock break-down was then announced by Sara. John owned 51% or 510,000 shares. Jim, Tress and Harry owned 10% each or 100,000 shares each. Dan owned 5% which was 50,000 shares. Anderson and Nelson owned 3% each or 30,000 shares each. Sandy was a 2% holder with 20,000 shares. Then Molly, Nancy, Sara, Don, Cindy and Kevin all held 1% stock each or 10,000 shares each.

John closed the board/stock holders meeting and everyone moved around talking about many things. John left the meeting room and walked around the headquarters remembering how it all started. Tress joined John and they talked about the mission still left undone. John was worried that the new people would not complete that mission because they did not know the facts and John was not cleared to tell them. Tress said, "General I have an idea, but it may be a problem for you at Redman Beach".

John said, "Ok tell me". Tress outlined how the hanger at Redman Beach could be used by selected operators to stage from and all the targets could be eliminated. They would have to be done at a faster pace, but it could be done with no problems from Florida. John said, "Do it General". Tress smiled and saluted John. John went to Jim's office and called Capp. John said "Capp you just bought a corporation. The price is $900 Billion Dollars and here is the routing and account number. How long before you can send the money?"

Capp said, "In two hours my friend".

John said, "Fine and Dan will be in Tampa in five days with the papers".

Capp said, "John thank you for this".

John said "Capp I hope you realize what you are getting into and best of luck. Now I am going to tell all our people you will be interviewing starting April 2$^{nd}$ is that a good date?"

Capp said, "Yes John that is perfect". John hung up and told Sara to expect the funds in two hours in the account Red Lion used for transfers. Then John walked to Don and Cindy's office and spoke to them. John made damn sure they could remove all traces of the banking Red Lion did. They told John it could be done as soon as they were told. John then left Red Lion and went to meet Molly at the bar. Molly had gone there as soon as the board meeting was over.

The day of the event at the Houston Country Club, John had the instructors from Hallettsville come to the bar early. John got them a drink and then they all sat at a table and John said "Well it is my understanding you four want to continue to run the training center. Is that correct?"

Watson, the head instructor, said "General we would like to do that, but we do not know if we can actually finance the operation. We will have to look at things really hard but yes if we can possibly do it then we want it".

John said "OK" and handed Watson and envelope. Watson opened the envelope and almost had a stroke. There was a check made out to the training center for $500 Billion Dollars.

John said "Now guys you can do what the Hell you want with the place. Make damn sure you pay Ray his yearly lease payments, OK?" The instructors thanked John over and over.

John was standing on the platform that had been erected in the front of the room. 400 employees were sitting in chairs in front of him. The wives and girlfriends or husbands and boyfriends were not to arrive until an hour later and if they were already there as many were they were in the other ball room having drinks and talking. John started his speech and every eye was on him. John said "It has come time for all of us to look at the future and Red Lion was sold to another group yesterday. Now, if any of you want to continue with the company, and believe me when I say this, the new owners want you to stay. Paper work will be done on April 2nd at the Red Lion Headquarters. I am so damn proud of all of you and I have been honored to know each of you. It is rare in life when people like us can come together and really make a difference in the world, but we did just that. We have eliminated so damn many bad guys it is unbelievable to anyone but us. No one could or should talk about what we did and still do and for that reason I am especially thankful that we never had a security breach in all the years we were conducting operations. I knew many of you when we all were on active duty and since then I have known the newest arrivals. We have lost operators and that will haunt me to my last day, but we were damn lucky in the fact that our losses were small compared to the danger we were operating in. I will always be proud I was a part of Red Lion and I hope every one of you do well, as you continue through life. Now you may have wondered why you had to sit in a certain seat. If you look under the chair you will find the answer".

The employees reached under their chairs and got the envelopes that were taped to each chair. John said "Now Red Lion open these and enjoy your life. This is a simple thank you from your Board of Directors. Let's party". The employees opened the envelopes and started screaming. It was damn near too much for some of them. By the time they had opened all the envelopes the group was in a complete frenzy. John led the way into the main ball room and the band started playing dance music. The drinks flowed, and the food was set up buffet style. Employees were eagerly showing their better halves what was in the envelopes. The party was in high swing and John and Molly loved it. John had called all the city council members and had postponed the city council meeting for three weeks. They had all agreed and now John and Molly were free to stay in Houston for a few days.

The three days after the gathering at the club, John and Tress met with a group of twelve operators and Tress briefed the new plan for eliminating the remaining Senator and the remaining Congressmen. The operators were ready to go on the mission. Tress had the C-141 loaded with two special SUVs and the necessary weapons and gear and had it ready to fly to Redman Beach on Friday. John and Molly would fly on a private jet the same day and would be there when the C-141 landed. John left the operations center and went back to the hotel and he and Molly drove to Galveston for the rest of the day and that night. They had a wonderful time and were sorry to leave the next morning. John and Molly got back to Houston and went to see Carol and friends at Molly's. John found Mike and talked to him about doing some projects in Redman Beach. KBR was never slow but now that they were no longer in the Middle-East, things had slowed a bit, so Mike was sure that would be no problem for KBR. John told Mike he would have the project manager for the city call in about a week. Mike was ready and then the men talked about many things and had a few drinks. Molly and John left Molly's and had dinner at Eddie V's and then went to the hotel. The next morning, they flew back to Redman Beach and home.

# CHAPTER 63

The C-141 had landed and the SUVs and four crates had been off loaded and were now inside the hanger. The operators had removed the Red Lion signs and there was nothing to tell the outside world what the hanger was or who it belonged to. John and Molly had made reservations for the operators and the air crews at the hotel in Redman Beach and John had invited all the group to Ted's for the night. Ted's was hopping when John and his group arrived, and everyone spread out and did their thing. The next day Tress called the operators and gave them the mission orders. The operators left Redman Beach in the SUVs and headed to Washington D.C. John was now back in the Mayor business and in city hall preparing for the city council meeting. Stephanie was at work and had already met with every department head. She had also done research on every department and had looked over the budget of each department. She was now ready to make some changes in how business was done in Redman Beach. Stephanie set up a meeting with the chamber of commerce and went over a list of things that were needed in Redman Beach. First on the list was industrial expansion and that was the main priority for the next year. Second was to keep the beach area a tourist attraction and exactly like it was. No changes would be authorized by the city. Third was to improve the chamber's participation in all events the city had no matter what they were. It was vital that the chamber took the lead in planning events and doing the coordination for them. After the meeting the entire chamber was now on Stephanie's side and were ready to work her ideas.

Tress and Sandy arrived the next day and would stay with John and Molly. Tress was at the hanger and in less than two hours the SAT/phone communications were up and working. Sandy had gotten a computer set up and was now ready to go online and work with Don and Cindy. They had moved their equipment from Red Lion to their house in Houston and were now back on line. John had a SAT/phone in his office at the house and he could follow the operator traffic when he wanted to do so. John was very careful not to take the SAT/phone to the city offices or have it on him at any time. That would bring too many questions into play. There was a lot going on and John was involved in all of it. John was trying to concentrate on the city council meeting and he was finding things hard because he really wanted to follow the operator's progress in D.C. Finally, Tress told John to relax and as soon as the operations started Tress would advise. John was good with that.

The next day John received a call from Tress on the secure line. Tress told John the first operation was now in progress and in about an hour the news should be picking up the story. John turned on the TV and waited for the bulletin to come on. CNN was the first to report that a Congressman from Alabama had been killed in a small plane crash just outside Washington D.C. The plane had crashed just after takeoff and was in route to Alabama. There were no reported survivors. Emergency units and the NTSB were on the way to the location which was in a very heavy wooded area along the Potomac River. More was to follow. John turned off the TV and counted to himself. And now there were four. Molly came in and said, "Was that what I think?"

John said, "Yes it was my dear".

Molly said "Good".

During the next twenty days, things sped up with the operators and their missions. John had been waiting for Washington to call but so far nothing and John was glad.

Two additional members of Congress had been eliminated. One had died in a street mugging in Georgetown and the other had died in a house fire in Arlington. There was only a Senator left on the list. Don had been busy on emails and the trail was easy to find but hard to follow. Threats had been sent to the Senator, at his office and at his home. The FBI was of course looking at these threats, and they believed them. The Senator was given special security and so was his family. It had been on the news and John could not figure out what the Hell Tress was doing. Things were moving along, and John knew Tress was up to something but what?

Jim called John and said "Our boy is going to Memphis just like Sandy predicted and will be there Saturday and stay until Monday. Saturday is a big fund raiser, then the Senator will go to Tunica for the day and night Sunday. He has also told the FBI that for his own security he will furnish his own people. It was hot and heavy, but he won that fight. The FBI will of course still have two agents with him, but they will only be in the background. Tress has the plan and God damn John it is like something out of the fucking movies. I would send it to you, but I do not know if we are that secure. What do you think?"

John said "Hell Jim we are more secure than the fucking White House or any other government agency. I think we will be ok. Send it in code and then I can decode it with the system".

Jim said "You got it. Should be to you in ten minutes. Make damn sure you have a beer when you read it". Jim hung up. About eleven minutes later the secure fax started. John watched as six pages came over the fax. When the fax stopped, John took the pages and placed them into the decoding machine and hit start. In less than two minutes the new pages appeared in plain English. John took them and went to the patio and opened a beer and started reading.

Jim had been right, this was like a damn movie. The plan was actually very simple, but it had to be done so damn coordinated it became a system of exact timing. Sandy had studied the Senator from Tennessee and he had a major flaw. He could not stay away from women and he always had them on the road with him. Usually an aid got a prostitute for him in whatever city he was in, so Sandy had this deal set. Sandy knew a very good hooker that worked in Tunica and was very high priced so of course Sandy made a deal. Sandy arranged for the girl to get with the Senator just as soon as he hit town. He would stay at the Horseshoe Casino hotel and that was the first step in the plan. Don had arranged the suite suing a donor as the person who had given the hotel suite for the Senator. Don had also arranged for the FBI to be in a room, three doors from the Senator, and for the Senator's security to be two doors away in a room. The security for the Senator consisted of four private guards, Sandy believed were members of the Rebels that stood guard in twelve-hour shifts. When the Senator was in his room the guards sat in a chair on either side of the door. Surveillance showed that they never actually entered the suite to check it, they just made sure the Senator was inside then sat down. Don had been able to pull tapes from one of the Horseshoe hotel's cameras and Sandy and Tress watched how these private guards acted. John was reading and was shaking his head as he read more.

The plan was for two operators to enter the Senator's suite and remain there until the Senator and the hooker came into the room. Cindy would open the door for the operators with her computer using the passkey of housekeeping. When the Senator and the girl had gotten into bed and were doing whatever they would do, the operators would move in and use a special spray that was colorless and odorless. The spray worked in about thirty seconds and the person sprayed would just go to sleep. The effects lasted for about two hours and when the person woke up there was no lingering effect. They just woke up. Once the Senator and the girl were asleep the operators would remove the Senator from the bed and hang him by a belt in the bathroom. Because he would be alive when the hanging was done, it would look like he had done it to himself. Only alcohol and anything else he had used would be in his blood and there would be no needle marks or bruises to betray the suicide when the coroner and medical examiner did the autopsy. The girl would of course look for the Senator and probably find him in the bathroom because she would go in to use it when she woke up. That would be when she would discover the body hanging and what she did then was on her. While the operators were in the room working on the Senator, just after the Senator and the girl had entered the room, two operators dressed as FBI agents would approach the guards outside and spray them. The guards would be sleeping in the chairs and an all clear would be given the room operators and out they would come. Don would erase the hotel security tape, scramble, the camera about five minutes before the Senator and the girl arrived in the hallway and then let it stay scrambled until someone in the IT department of the hotel fixed it. Because the security tape had not been erased just the camera scrambled, no one would suspect a damn thing other than equipment failure on that camera. Because the other cameras on the floor did not show the Senator's room, they would be left alone. Inside the Senator's room a laptop he used would have a complete confession to a certain point, on it showing the Senator's involvement with the Rebel group and his worry that he was going to be found out and arrested. Don and Cindy had planted that about six days before and would activate it when they received the signal from the operators. John finished reading and was damned impressed. Now it just had to work.

Sunday John and Molly were relaxing at the hot tub and having a drink. John had the TV on and it was on CNN. A news bulletin flashed on the screen and John turned up the sound. "Senator Jefferson from Tennessee had just been found dead at a casino in Tunica. First indications were suicide. More to follow". John broke out laughing. John said "I will be damned. They did it. Sure, as Hell they did it".

Molly said, "John what are you talking about?"

John said, "Honey our guys got the bastard and it worked just like it was supposed to".

Molly said, "I had no idea they were still doing that".

John said, "This was the last of the Rebel deal and now we are finished".

Molly said, "I will believe that when I see it, John". She started to laugh, and John did too.

Tress called on the secure line and told John what had, happened. Tress said "General the plan went perfectly. The operators in the room had both the Senator and the girl out in five minutes after they arrived. Then the Operators took the asshole into the bathroom and hung him by his belt and he died by choking to death. The girl woke up and sure as Hell went into the bathroom and started screaming. Her screams were so fucking loud, the FBI agents as well as the private security people broke into the room and found her naked standing in the middle of the room screaming. Then they found the Senator hanging in the bathroom. They also found his laptop sitting on the desk and it was on. Then of course all Hell broke loose. The EMTs were called as was Washington and more agents were sent to secure the scene. The girl was taken into custody by the FBI and the hotel security was told to deliver the tapes. The hotel also gave the FBI tapes of the Senator and the girl from the time they entered the casino until the entered the Senators floor that night. From what we can learn so far it looks like the FBI is the lead on this because of the Senator and the local cops do not really have the talent to investigate this. Our operators are already back in Texas. Now we have drained all accounts the Senator had, and the only question is where in the Hell does Don put the money now that we are no longer Red Lion?"

John said, "Have him transfer it to the foundation bank account and how much are we talking about?"

Tress said "$19 Million Dollars, General".

John said "OK then here is what we do. Everyone on this mission from start to finish including the aircrews and all the operators, you, Sandy, Don and Cindy will split up $12 Million Dollars equally. The other $7 Million Dollars will go into the foundation. How does that sound?"

Tress said, "If that is what you desire it will happen, Sir".

John said, "That is what I want, and thanks to all for a good job". John hung up. Now it was officially over. Red Lion was not his problem any longer.

On Friday Capp called John and asked if John would be able to go to Washington D.C. to the White House with Capp the next morning. John agreed, and Capp said a plane would be at Redman Beach at 9 AM to pick John up and John should be back about 6 PM. John hung up and told Molly. Molly was worried, but John assured her it was just to introduce Capp to the President and to make damn sure everyone knew Red Lion was no longer in business. One of the conditions of the sale was the name change. The new company would be United Security Associates, Inc. John got ready and then Molly and John went to Ted's for a while.

The military Jet landed, and John got on board. Capp was sitting along with General Ben and John took a seat across from them. The plane took off and headed north to Washington. John said "Capp I have a question for you. It is none of my business but why are you doing the point work on all of this when other Generals are senior or at least maybe better known to the White House, like Ben?"

Capp said "Well John that is exactly why. I am an unknown on almost every circle, so no one pays a damn bit of attention to me when I go someplace or do something. It is a perfect cover and it was the same one you had for many years".

John said "Yes it was, and it makes sense now that I look at it. Ok". The men talked and then the plane was on final approach to Andrews Air Force Base in D. C. As soon as the plane stopped the men got off and into a staff car and headed to the White House. The Generals were in full uniform and John was in a suit and tie.

The car stopped in front of the north doors and a Marine guard opened the doors and saluted the officers as the exited the vehicle and walked into the White House. John thought "God how many times have I come to this building over the past years?" John walked on, and an usher directed the men to a small dining room off the East Room. The table was round, and five places were set with the Presidential China. Exactly two minutes after the Generals and John were in the room the President came in followed by Liz. John and both Generals came to the position of attention and saluted the President. The President returned the salute and said, "Please sit gentlemen and I am glad you are here". Everyone sat.

The President said "Would you like a drink, I am sure as Hell going to have at least one. It is Saturday, my day off or so it is said". Everyone ordered, and the butler left and returned in and matter of minutes with the drinks then left the room. The President said, "OK John, Liz said this meeting was important and you had a very special announcement for me so what is all this about, General?"

John said "Mr. President I sold or rather the corporation sold Red Lion and we are no longer in business. That is the announcement".

The President said "Well then these Generals must be the new owners or whatever. Is that right?"

John said "Yes Sir these men represent part of the group that bought the corporation. I believe they could fill you in on all of that much better than I can".

The President said, "Very well Generals tell me all about this new deal you want me to agree with".

The two men began to brief the President and about half way thru the President ordered another round of drinks. The briefing was very detailed and took about forty-five minutes to complete. The President then ordered lunch to be served and after it arrived, and everyone was eating he turned to John and said "John are you good with this. I mean really good with it?"

John said "Mr. President if I may be your advisor on this, I am very good with this. In fact, I think it will be better than it was for a few reasons. First, all the original Red Lion were active duty military and that was breaking, the law when and if things had to be done and Congress did not get informed. Sure, you had executive powers as did the former President but Hell that as we all know can be a bitch if Congress gets a burr up their ass and presses the issue. Now no one is active duty and this new company was not even in business when any of these men were on active duty. It does not start until 5 April of this year and all military personnel will retire effective April 1st. Secondly, it is going to be a smaller company with less exposure than Red Lion was. Hell Sir, we damn near got out of hand with everything we were doing and that can be dangerous. I feel these men can and will be as good if not better at handling the situations that arise".

The President said "Alright then we go forward. What has to be done?"

John said "Mr. President and Liz here is what must happen on April 1st and not before or afterwards. 1. The contract that is open must be changed to reflect the new name of the company. 2. All email addresses and fax numbers must be changed. All secure phone lines must be changed. 3. The clearance for Tress to move the satellites at his will must be given to the person these men designate. 4. The agreements with all the military installations must be changed to reflect the new name and new contacts at all agencies must be changed or established so these men have them and Red Lion no longer does. After that, it is play it by ear until everyone is comfortable".

The President said "I understand so Liz please make that happen and as John said not before April 1st. Now John do we owe you any money from your last mission?"

John smiled and said, "Mr. President let us say that one was on Red Lion if that is alright?"

The President smiled back and said "Yes you can and thanks. The suicide was a stroke of genius and how in the Hell you pulled that off is beyond me. I want to keep it that way also".

John said, "My pleasure, Mr. President". The lunch was now about finished, and the President had instructed Liz to get with Capp and start things in motion the next day. There were only four days left until April 1st. The President got up and so did everyone else. John and both Generals saluted the President and he walked out of the dining room. Liz led the men out and said good bye. The staff car was waiting, and the three men got inside, and the car headed back to Andrews. John was back at Redman Beach at 5:30 PM. He said good bye to Capp and Ben and drove to the house. Molly was waiting, and they had a drink and John filled Molly in on the day he had. Before John had talked with Molly John had called Tress and told him to use the satellites to fly over Redman Beach as much as possible and take pictures of everything in the city and all of Cobb County in every resolution available. Then when that was completed send the pictures to John via the SAT/phone video communications. John had also called Don and made sure he would bring a copy that could down loaded into the Sheriff's Department computer system of the facial recognition-program's, and any other programs that Don and Cindy thought may be useful be of use.

# CHAPTER 64

pril was a great month for John and Molly. The city council had approved Lyle's plans for his beach front development and a few other changes had been approved. One major ordinance had been voted in that would be a tremendous help to the city. Stephanie had proposed a new ordinance for the issuing of building permits by the city. The new ordinance stated that all projects costing over $2 Million Dollars had to have two things accompany the permit request. One was an estimated completion date. The second requirement was a surety bond for 50% of the project cost with the bond made payable to the city in case of default. The ordinance listed default as abandoning the project by not having work on-going for more than one week (weather conditions excepted), and not completing the project within ninety days of the date registered. To keep from the ninety-day violation an affidavit must be notarized and submitted stating that unusual circumstances had occurred, and these circumstances had to be explained in the document. The council also approved the grant writer to send grant request to forty-five different agencies including John's foundation requesting grants for specific city needs. Finally, the council approved the idea of constructing the water salivation plant and ask the grant writer to do a request for the money.

John and Molly had discussed the foundation and John wanted Moly to run the thing. Now her job was not going to be an 8 a.m. to 5 p.m. deal, but she would be the boss. Molly was very happy with that and jumped into the job with both feet. The only office type building in Redman Beach was the bank building a five story older building that was downtown.

The bank used three floors and one floor was used by five lawyers who had offices there. The top floor was open, and Molly rented it. It took only four days for her contractors to totally re-do the floor and create what she wanted. Then Molly pulled her best punch. She hired the senior vice president of the bank to be the head administrator of the foundation. The president of the bank was quite upset at first until he realized that if he said or did anything Molly and John would move every cent out of his bank and go to another bank. He calmed down instantly. The new administrator was named Patty and she was a house of fire. She and Molly were now interviewing people for positions at the foundation and Molly insisted on only local people be hired. By April 15th eight new employees were now working for the foundation and Molly was happy. All the new people had been looking for work and now they had a job. Patty was now doing training every day for each employee and things were starting to come together.

Tress had sent the photos to John and they showed in detail exactly what was what in Cobb County and in Redman Beach. John went to the county courthouse and spoke with the collector and got the property owners names on about forty pieces of land. Then John got the city zoning for about twenty pieces of land inside the city. The county had no zoning restrictions. John looked at the aerial photos and saw that only one US highway ran through Redman Beach and only three paved county roads did as well. There were many streets but only the highway and county roads were in and out access. The interstate highway was twenty-two miles west of the town and ran right through the county. The county was thirty miles more of undeveloped land on the western side of the interstate. There were some small farms and ranches but not many and only a few of them. Cobb County was fifty-eight miles long and seventy-nine miles wide. John called Miles and asked if he and Linda could come to Redman Beach for the weekend, so John and Miles could talk about some projects and so Miles and Linda could see how John and Molly were now living. Miles said "John that is great and yes we can! In fact, why don't we come in on Thursday evening so then we can spend Friday and if necessary Saturday doing business and Sunday having some family time with you guys?"

John said "That would be great. Call me when you are about thirty minutes away and we will meet you. Do you want me to make reservations for the crew?"

Miles said, "Yes please".

John said "Done. See you on Thursday". John called Molly and told her about Miles and Linda coming in. John knew Miles was just what John needed to make his plans work. Miles had oil and cattle and that had been the main family business and still was. Miles also had an oil field supply company with twenty locations in Texas, Louisiana, Oklahoma, and New Mexico. Miles was also the head of a group that did land development and they had done projects in Houston, Dallas, San Antonio, Tulsa, Oklahoma City and Denver. Miles was in his own right a Billionaire. John knew Miles would be perfect for this and was very excited they were going to talk.

John and Molly were sitting on the apron of the airport in the Cadillac Escalade waiting for the plane to land. Both were excited and somewhat nervous. The plane landed and taxied to a stop in front of the SUV and Miles and Linda got off and headed to the vehicle. Molly jumped out and grabbed Linda and hugged and kissed her. Then Molly did the same thing to Miles. John hugged and kissed Linda and shook hands with Miles then hugged Miles. The air crew had put the bags into the rear of the SUV and everyone got in and John headed for the house. Molly was pointing out things as John drove. Louise was waiting and got the bags in and into the guest room. Molly fixed everyone a drink and then gave the grand tour. After the tour of the house, they all sat on the patio and visited. Louise had prepared some snacks and brought them out. The rest of the night was catch-up time for everyone about what was happening in all their lives.

Friday everyone was up and having breakfast at 8 AM. John and Miles were going to be looking at many things and Molly and Linda were going to go all over the town seeing everything there was to see and shopping and having a great time. John and Miles finished breakfast and went to John's office and sat and talked. John said "Miles I think this can be a gold mine for your investment group and it can be the greatest thing this part of the world has ever seen. I have the aerial photos of the entire county and of course the city and I have circled some areas I want to show you. I think we can build an industrial park and at least one or two major shopping areas. Then we can create at least three sub-divisions with houses ranging from $80,000 up to $100,000 plus parks and all the things we need. Schools, fire stations, police sub-stations and anything else you can do. I have the financial backing, but I would like you and your people to also be involved. Actually, I want you to run the whole deal."

Miles said "God damn John this is overwhelming. Shit you are talking about building a whole fucking city. Do you realize how much fucking money we will be talking about not to mention the upgrades in utilities, sewers, streets, water and other things?"

John said, "Miles I know it sounds like a lot, but we have a plan to get a bunch of the money from grants and then we will be selling properties and leasing out other properties so can it be done?"

Miles said, "It can be done, but WOW!"

John said, "Ok then let's go look at my city". John and Miles went out and got into John's car and started driving around Redman Beach. John pointed out certain areas and answered Miles' questions for the next two hours. John pulled into city hall after two hours and they went in and to John's office. John showed Miles the basic outline of Redman Beach and said "Miles I want to keep the city exactly how it is. No expansion other than one office building and a new medical building. We can add onto the hospital but most of the new projects need to be in the county".

Miles said "I see what you are trying to do John and I agree. Keep the basic city as a tourist resort and very quaint but enlarge the county with population and industry. Not a bad plan at all. It makes sense now that I see the layout. I have some vital questions I need to know answers to, before I can even get going on this so who is your smart guy?"

John said, "Let me get her for you". John walked out and returned with Stephanie. John introduced Miles and Steph sat down and Miles started asking questions. Steph was busy taking notes. John had listened to Miles and he was very impressed at the questions that were asked. Miles knew his business and John was sure when things were all said and done, a project would happen. Miles was finished with his questions and Steph said "Miles, I will have your answers by this afternoon. Do I call John or you?"

John said "I will do you one better Steph. Meet us at Ted's and give Miles the answers then join us for the night if you wish. You can also bring a guest".

Steph said "You boys have a date. See you then". Steph left, and Miles looked at John and said, "Where in the Hell did you find her?"

John said "It is a long story. She just walked in and said, "I want the job and I am damn good". She is, and she got the job." John and Miles left city hall and went by the Sheriff's department then out to the country club and met Molly and Linda for lunch. The girls had a great day so far and Molly was very excited because Linda had given her many ideas to think about. During lunch everyone talked about Redman Beach and how much they liked it.

John, Molly, Linda and Miles were sitting on the patio at Ted's when Steph came out and joined them. John introduced

Linda and then Steph handed Miles a sheet of paper with all the answers to each of his questions type written on it. Miles said "Thank you very much. Damn this is efficiency to the max, John".

John said, "I told you that". Step ordered a drink and looked around a little. John was wondering who she was looking for when Jim Y, the Sheriff came over. John said, "I did not do it". Everyone laughed.

Jim said "Oh yes you did John. Why in the Hell do you think I wear this star?" The laughter got heavier. Jim Y leaned down and kissed Steph and sat down. John introduced Miles and Linda. John now knew why Steph was in Redman Beach. Jim Y ordered a beer and made sure everyone had a round. The group talked and then the band started, and the dancing began. Jim and Miles talked a lot between the times when they were not dancing and by the end of the night Jim Y and Miles had developed a good friendship. John was very pleased. Molly really liked Steph and so did Linda. They had been talking as the night went along and John was glad Molly and Steph were getting along so well. John had spent some time talking with Ted and was very impressed with the way Ted had started leading the city council. John had made Ted Mayor-Pro-Temp so when John could not be at an official function Ted was the acting Mayor. Ted was liking the new way the city was headed. His business was improving and so was the business at the other beach front places. The tourists were coming again and more than ever it seemed like were here. Steph knew that her involvement with the Chamber of Commerce had been a great help in getting that done. Now Steph was on the track of industry to come to town. John and his group left and went to the house. The girls decided to take a quick swim, so John and Miles joined them in the pool

The next morning John had everyone, up and out to the airport by 9 AM. The helicopter landed at 9:20 AM and they all climbed on board and the piolet took off. John had the head set on and directed the piolet. The chopper started flying over the city and Miles was watching very closely and making notes on a pad he had brought along. Then when the chopper left the city limits it flew straight down the coast to the county line and turned west and followed the county line until it ended. Then the chopper turned back to the south and followed the county line until it ended. The last leg was back to the city limits following the coast line and the county line. Then John directed the piolet to fly back over some of the areas Miles had asked about. The ride was about two hours and when the chopper landed back at the airport John thanked the piolet and everyone got off and into the SUV and headed to the country club. The party arrived at the club and went to the bar and had a drink and discussed the flight. Linda was thrilled with what she had seen, and Molly was taken aback. Molly had never really seen the entire area and she was thinking of so many different ideas she almost exploded. John had been especially watching the railroad tracks and how they were in the county and exactly how many tracks there were. Miles had made extensive notes including the railroad and the surface roads. Also, Miles had looked over the port area and made notes about that. The port was only for small craft and mainly for charter fishing boats. There was of course enough land to build a port but that was not a reasonable thing with Orlando only seventy-eight miles away by rail and ninety miles by Interstate highway. It was now approaching 2 PM and John told everyone to finish the drinks and get ready to leave. They loaded back into the SUV and John drove to the dock area. Bob had the boat ready and the group got on board and Bob headed out and down the coast. Miles and Linda were in heaven and Molly was very happy John had done this. Molly fixed everyone a drink and then she and Linda went forward and laid on the deck and sunned for a while. Both men sat and drank and relaxed. The boat ride lasted until sunset and as the sun was going down Linda,

Molly, John and Miles watched as the beauty was almost overwhelming. Bob got back to the dock shortly after sunset and everyone got off and headed to the SUV then home. They all took showers fixed their makeup as needed dressed in nice clothes and went out for dinner at the sea food restaurant on the beach front. The next morning Miles and Linda said good bye at the airport and got on the jet and headed back to Texas. Miles had told John he would be in touch in about a week. John and Molly went home and relaxed for the rest of the day doing nothing but hot tub, pool and sauna.

May was now here, and John had a reply from Miles. Miles was going to not only do a housing development of 4500 homes, but wanted to build a factory to produce oil field equipment. He also had four other parties interested in putting in factories and two people who wanted to put in shopping centers and some other business in Cobb County. John was thrilled but now the real work started. Permits from the EPA and about six other government agencies would be required and that meant time and John did not want to wait six years for some fucking approval to come in because a God damned bug might be hurt. John was now ready to call in favors he had built up over the years from Washington. John called Miles and told him that John would need a complete description of every project as soon as possible. The main things would be the environmental impact if any and any other thing that Washington would have to approve. Miles understood and told John in one week he would have everything. John was ready to get things done and needed to speak with some local people about an idea that was starting to develop in John's brain. John called the people he wanted to meet with and had them all come to the country club the next day for a working lunch. They all agreed and would be there at 10 AM.

The guests for the lunch started arriving at the country club about 9:50 AM and John greeted each person and showed them into the large meeting room. A bar was set up in the corner and a buffet table was against one wall. John had arranged for a large round table that would seat twenty people to be placed in the middle of the room so as people arrived, John had them get a drink if they wished and then pick out a seat at the table. By 10:10 AM everyone had arrived. John was pleased. All the Redman Beach city council was there. All the Cobb County commissioners were there. The Sheriff, the city and county attorney were there, Stephanie, and Mason, the bank president, and Kyle the local developer were also there. John now was set to open a very large can of worms.

John stood up and said "I would like to thank all of you for being here today. What I am about to propose is a very radical idea and I am sure some of you will immediately resist it. Before that is done, I would ask that you all listen with open minds and with the knowledge that as things progress in life, things must change". John watched each person and noticed that no one was even nervous. John continued "In the next sixty days, Cobb County is going to receive requests for over $100 Billion Dollars in new construction. This is of course going to affect all of us. I know who is doing this because I asked them to come and do it. There will be requests for permits to build housing developments for 4500 homes, permits for hotels and motels, shopping centers, strip mall locations. Then there is going to be people asking for permits to construct a major factory and some smaller manufacturing plants. Also, there is a damn good possibility a permit request will be asked for a specialized port to be built. Now Ladies and Gentlemen, Cobb County will soon be asked to move into the 21th Century in a very big way. I know all the principals involved and the only demands I put on them are as follows: 1. They will not be allowed to do any building inside the Redman Beach city limits. 2. They must use local supply sources to purchase all materials required in the building process. 3. Whenever possible local workers or firms will be hired to do the work. Basically, it will be just as it was when we expanded the airport. It is estimated that over $90 Billion Dollars will be spent locally by the time all of this is finished. Additionally, another $80 Billion Dollars will be spent for projects in water, electrical and other infrastructure improvements. Now you all have the big picture of what will be asked of the county and in only two instances the city".

John paused and went to get another beer. Some of the guests also refilled their drinks. Everyone was back in their seats and John said "Now here is my proposal and it is in a few different parts so please listen carefully. After I finish, we can then discuss things but please let me present everything to you first. I understand that you, Warren, are going to retire as Mayor of the County in July. Is that correct, Warren? "

Warren said, "Yes John my wife and I are moving to Mississippi to be with our daughter".

John said "Alright. I would like you to appoint me as the Interim County Mayor which you can do. I will run for the office in the 2016 election and there is no need to spend the dollars on a special election if the commissioners approve the appointment. Now the next phase is that Ted is now the Mayor-Pro-Temp and he would just stay in that position until the election. Whoever runs for Mayor will run and things will be just as they always have been for any election. I will continue to coordinate with the city council and that will not change. In fact, if there is anything the County wants to do that might affect the City, we will present it before we do it. I will give that guarantee". There was some murmuring, and a few people were moving in their seats after John had said what he said. John continued" If in fact all of the business comes to Cobb County and I know damn well it is, we will have a huge problem with utilities. The county has none so here we have a problem, but I think this proposal is the solution. I would propose that Cobb County buy the water distribution system, the sewer plant and system and the electrical generating system complete, from the City of

Redman Beach. By doing this, then a utility commission can be formed at the county level and service can be given to everyone in the county. Presently only a rural electric cooperative is set up for service to County residents and that coop buys the service from Redman Beach. It would actually lower the costs to citizens of the county who are now on the system". John again paused while people absorbed what he had just said.

John went on "Now because of the restrictions I have placed on the new building, I feel we need to do one major thing. The City of Redman Beach needs to annex an area that will make the city limits five miles farther out into the county than they are now. If we go from the present city limits and make a large U-shaped annexation, we will create a five-mile buffer zone between any potential industrial complex and the city. If you would please look at the map that is on the screen, you will see that there are only three structures in the area I am referring to. Now to make it a deal and not a deal breaker, the city will agree to not levy a city tax on any of the new annexed property for five years. That way the owners will not have to pay city and county taxes just continue to pay the county taxes until the five years is up. The new area annexed will become a "Green" area with walking trails, parks, and things that will not impact the area with buildings or anything that will distract from the open area. And now, the last part of my proposal is about people. As all of you know I was a military officer for many years and had the pleasure to command some of the finest troops in the entire world. It is with that thought in mind that I offer this last part. I would like to ensure that every city employee involved in any transition from city to county retain the pension fund they have now exactly as it is and is automatically given the county benefits of pension and complete medical coverage for them and their families. Also, the years of service to the city would be transferred to years of service to the county.

It would be exactly like it was for the police force when the Sheriff took over that mission. The fire department and EMS would also become county operated and of course the same would be given that service". John then looked around the table and into everyone's eyes before he continued.

"My wife, Molly, and I, as most of you know, have a vast wealth and we are in all reality probably in the top five richest people in the United States. I say that only to let you know that we have a foundation and legally we can and will give grants to make damn sure the city and county can do what they need to do. We love this place and we intend to make it not only our home but our mission to have everyone enjoy a very good life. I have been talking for a long time. Now everyone get a fresh drink if you like, and enjoy the food. I will be very happy to talk one on one to any of you if you would like and we can discuss anything you like for the rest of the day here. I am open. Again, thank you for coming".

John then walked to the bar and opened a beer. The rest of the people at the table got up and either got a drink or food. The conservations started among the group. John was walking around and speaking with various people and listening to some concerns but mainly he was hearing good reactions to his proposal. By 3 PM everyone was gone, and John left and headed home. It had been a damn good day. Now John would wait to see the reaction.

John did not have to wait long. John and Molly were sitting on the beach enjoying the night and listening to the waves slap the shore. The night was clear, and stars were out, and the moon was just rising over the water. It was a wonderful sight and Molly was very happy. She was going to Washington D.C. the next day to meet with the DAV officials and then the Wounded Warrior Project officials to discuss some things she wanted from them. At the first of January, John and Molly, Jim and Latoya and Tress and Sandy had each given $100 Million Dollars to each organization as a donation.

It was what all of them had wanted to do and it was of course the largest donation in history that these groups had ever gotten. Now Molly wanted to use the foundation to do more good. John had just started toward the patio to get new drinks for each of them when his cell phone rang. John said "Hello". The voice on the other end was Warren and he said "John you are now the new Interim County Mayor. The commissioners voted you into that position about an hour ago in a special meeting. If you will come by the courthouse tomorrow, the District Judge will swear you in. Just call me and we can set a time. Congratulations".

John said "Thank you Warren. I really appreciate this". Warren hung up and so did John. He got the drinks and returned to the beach and told Molly the news. She was thrilled. Now John needed to call a special city council meeting to announce his resignation as Mayor. He would do that tomorrow after he was sworn in. John and Molly stayed on the beach for another hour then went back inside and to bed.

John had taken Molly and Patty to the airport and the private jet had taken off with them on board and was headed to D.C. John had arranged for them to stay at the Hilton in a suite for the night and had reservations for them at the Capitol Grill for dinner. John was now on his way to the courthouse and would be sworn in at 10 AM. The ceremony took all of ten minutes and the commissioners and Warren were there. John was now officially the new Mayor of Cobb County and the leader of the commission. John looked at his new office and told Warren to take as much time as he wanted before he left. Warren said "John I will have this cleared out by the first of the week. I will call you to let you know exactly when I get this crap out".

John laughed, and the men shook hands and John left to go to city hall. John arrived at city hall and had Stephanie come to his office. When she was sitting down, John said "Well we have to do some real arranging and we will need costs on things and then I need to meet with the entire city staff and all workers that we pay. I need this done in the next two weeks so what do you need from me to get started?"

Steph said "I need to know who will be left as city employees and exactly what I should value the equipment and plants at so the county will be able to buy all of this. Then Sir, what in the Hell am I supposed to do as city administrator with nothing to administer?" John laughed and said, "Oh My dear you are going to run the fucking county, did I not tell you that?"

Steph said "No damn you that must have skipped your mind. Maybe on purpose?"

John laughed again and said "I always knew you would come along especially now that things are going to be really exciting. I will get with you later. How about you and Jim Y coming over for dinner when Molly gets back?"

Steph said, "I would like that, just tell me when to have that man of mine there".

John said "I will. Now get me the figures and low ball the equipment as much as possible. It must look as if the county paid something, so no one will scream, but we do not need to rape the county either. After all it is now all for one". Steph got up and headed back to her office. John then called Laney and had her come in and sit. John then explained the entire situation to Laney and after he finished, he said "So now here is my proposal to you. I would like you to remain here at the city with a 25% raise in pay. You will be the city secretary and the city administrator. It will be slow most of the time I am sure, but it is necessary just the same. When things get shaken out there will be only a few actual city employees left so I think you should have no problems in running things".

Laney said "Sir, that sounds like a good thing for me and the city. Yes, I will stay and take over whatever I need to, and thank you".

John said, "Laney it is my pleasure, thank you". Laney left John's office and John called the bank and spoke to Fred the bank president and majority stock holder. John and Fred would meet for lunch at 1 PM at the country club.

John saw Fred when he entered and waved him to come into the bar. The men shook hands and John ordered a drink for both men then they sat at a table and started talking. Fred's family had founded the Redman Beach National Bank about eighty years ago and Fred had grown up groomed to take over the bank. Fred was an old school banker in his early 50's and of course very conservative as many bankers in his time were. Fred did not believe in taking any risk if he could help it. When John and Molly arrived in Redman Beach the bank had about $75 Million Dollars in net worth not counting the building. Now after John and Molly had started using the bank for many things, the bank had over $900 Billion Dollars in net worth. Fred was very aware of that fact and did not want John to ever leave his bank. John explained how things were going and asked what Fred had thought about the meeting John had with all the people. Fred was very frank and said "John I know how you are and that you are always thinking far ahead, but it scares me a little. I have never been in a position like I am now, and I really do not know what I should think. I like the idea of all the business coming in to the area, but it will also mean other banks will start to come in as well and that could hurt us. That is one of my concerns. Another is will we become too big and have all the problems the large cities do? That only time will tell I suppose but it is a worry".

John said "Well Fred you have a right to worry about some of this, but I will assure you there will be no fucking crime. I mean none that is important. The petty shit will always be with us because people are generally stupid, but nothing major. Now other banks coming in. Sure, they will but they do not know the people and the county and city will not leave you. When the new things start then you need to get off your ass as a banker and go get the business. Hell, you can offer everything in the world to these new people and they sure as Hell will need a bank for payrolls and to use to buy products they need. Also, when the homes are ready someone will have to do the loans and that my friend should be you. Your problem is that as the type of banker you are if you do not change you will lose that business".

Fred ordered another drink and John joined him. When the drinks arrived, Fred said "John I am sure you are right, but I have a board and stock holders to satisfy and I have employees that depend on the bank to stay strong and remain open".

John said "Fuck that Fred. You are a greedy little fucker that wants to squeeze every fucking dime out of everyone and we both know that. I do not blame you. Banks have been doing that for years and always do. I am telling you in front if you do not consider what I say then no matter how much you want to be involved with the loans you have no fucking chance. I know that the people who are building the homes and have financing ready for buyers and if you will work with me, I should be able to get you at least half of that business".

Fred said, "John how in the Hell can you guarantee that?"

John said "I know the backers and I have the influence. But it must be on my terms, and mine only. If you are agreeable to that then we can do big business. If not, then kiss your chance good bye and maybe part of our deposits as well. I am not threatening you, but it is just a fact that I state".

Fred said "John that is bullshit. You are out right threatening me and the damn bank and we both know it. So, what do you want us to do?"

John said "I want you to make loans to buyers of these houses based on them not the fucking credit score and I want the interest rate to be lower than the average in this state. Now fuck the past records and all that you people use. I want every possible consideration given to people applying and here is how you really win. No fucking closing costs. We both know those are the hidden way the bank makes make tremendous amounts of money and there is no reason in Hell for it".

Fred said, "Damn John you really hate banks and bankers, don't you?"

John said "Not all bankers but damn near all banks. You Fred are my exception. Hell, I really like you. That is why I am having this meeting with you. See things are not all bad". Fred laughed and so did John. They had another drink and ordered lunch. By the time lunch was finished and the men were ready to leave Fred had guaranteed John the bank would change the lending requirements and would also go after the commercial accounts in a very big way.

Molly's plane landed, and John picked her up. Patty was being picked up by a friend, so John and Moly went home. Molly was bubbling and wanted to tell John all about her meetings. Molly changed into shorts and a halter top and joined John on the patio. John had fixed them drinks and Molly started telling John about the trip. Molly said "The DAV was very cooperative, and they are going to send us applications from their people, so we can screen them and see if we can help with college and vocational training. Also, with their children's educations. The Wounded Warriors were even better. We got about twenty applications for people who live in Florida, and many of them could be hired by the foundation. I think that in the long run we will be able to really make a difference John".

John said "Honey that is wonderful. I know you are very pleased and you should be. Maybe we can really get some good people hired and then we can expand what you will be able to do".

Molly said, "That is my hope". John kissed her, and she kissed him back. John then told her about the new deals he was working with the bank and about his plan for the city workers and the new annexation. Molly loved the fact that the city would have a buffer zone so to speak and would remain as it was. Things were rapidly moving along, and John was ready.

# CHAPTER 65

The city council meeting had gone very well, and everything had been approved just as John had wanted. Now the county would be taking over all city services and equipment. The price for all of this was $30 Million Dollars and the county would pay the city over a ten-year period. The city hall would be divided into two sections. The city offices of which there were only four, would be on one end along with the city council chamber and the rest of the building would now be county offices. Actually no one or almost no one was moving. All the city service areas would now have the signs changed to county and remain in the same locations. The city hall and the county courthouse and offices were only one-half block from each other so that was an easy decision. The equipment would be re-painted to show Cobb County Fire, EMS, Trash, Water, Sewer, Electric, Gas, and all of that. The municipal Judge would use a court room in the County Court house when municipal court was held. The court staff for the city would remain in city hall as well as the cashier for the city. Also, the secretary and Mayor would remain at city hall along with the city council offices. Everything else would now be county.

Because of the new situation, John had suggested, and the city council and commissioners approved the fact that everyone who had inspected city business would continue to be responsible for that part of the new county arrangement but would also do county business as needed. New employees would be needed in all departments and the ads for employment had already been put out. John had arranged for a meeting to be held for all city employees and it was mandatory. On duty fire and EMS would bring their vehicles and in the event they received a call would leave from the meeting. The only location that could hold all the city workers was the high school and John had worked a deal to use the auditorium on a Saturday morning at 10 AM. The workers were told to be there, and John had Steph get a packet ready for all employees outlining every change and giving them information. John would address the employees and cover the information in the packet but in a much more personal way that just handing them a packet. The meeting was scheduled for June 29th and the new effective date for everyone was July 1st.

John was on the platform and the mic was ready as was John. The auditorium was almost full. Over 200 city employees were there. The packets had been passed out as the employees came into the building, so they had already look through them but not studied the information.

John said "Good morning. I am John Carter as most of you know and I am the Mayor of Redman Beach or at least I was until a week ago. Now I am the Mayor of Cobb County and Ted is the Mayor-Pro-Temp of the city and will be running things until the next election in 2016. I have asked you to be here to explain how the new setup is going to affect you and to tell you all about it. First, I want everyone to know no one is going to be released or fired or any of that crap that has already been going around town. In fact, everyone is getting a raise in pay of 20%. Now that we have that out of the way, I will explain exactly what is happening and how it will affect every one of you".

John explained in total detail exactly what was happening and all about the technical transfer from city to county. He also covered the pension, medical, leave, all the personal things that affect workers. John then explained how the new sections would work and that basically everyone would stay exactly where they were as to locations with only three or four exceptions and that those affected would be told individually after the meeting. John was good at explaining the situation and why the change. He talked about the new businesses that were coming and about the new buildings that the county would be doing including the jail, and the water desalinization plant that was coming. Also, that a new high rise eight story office building was going to be built and an expansion to the hospital was coming. John explained about the new sewer plants, electrical stations, water pumping stations, gas supply stations and all the things needed for the new developments and plants. John also explained the annexation, so the city would have a buffer around it against being changed by the new expansions. John was on the platform for a solid hour. When he finished, he told the workers that it was now a time for them to realize the dreams they had and to start a new phase in their lives. When John started to leave the entire auditorium stood up and applauded him as he went off stage. As luck had it, the fire and EMS had no calls during the meeting. By the time John had gotten to the front of the building, more than 180 employees had shaken his hand and thanked him. John got in his car and headed home. Molly was sitting beside him and was very proud of John.

July 1st things went off like they should and now everyone was a county employee except six people. The paint jobs were completed by the local body shop and everything looked new and fresh. The sign company had installed all the signage and now the entire county was new and ready to operate. John and Molly were sitting in the hot tub and the phone rang. Louise came out with the phone and handed it to Molly and she said "Hello". Latoya was on the phone and John watched as Molly nodded her head. Then Molly said "Of course, and what time will you be here?" Molly nodded again and said "Ok baby, see you then. We will meet the plane". Molly told John that Jim and Latoya would be there tomorrow about 10 AM and were staying until July 6th.

John said "That is great. Did she say why or just because?"

Molly said, "She said they had something to tell us". John smiled.

The jet landed at 9:55 AM and taxied to a stop in front of the SUV. Jim and Latoya got out and the crew placed the luggage in the rear of the SUV. After hugs and kisses everyone was in the SUV and John drove to the house. Louise got the luggage into the guest room and Molly fixed drinks for everyone. Latoya and Jim took the drink and excused themselves to go change. In ten minutes they were both back in very comfortable clothes. Jim was wearing a pair of shorts and a knitted shirt and Latoya had on shorts and a halter top. Everyone sat on the patio and Jim said "Ok now hear this! We got married last week in Vegas."

John and Molly both smiled and congratulated them. Then Latoya said "We wanted to come here to tell you good bye for now. We are leaving on the 7th from Miami and going to France for our new home".

John said "What?"

Molly said, "What are you talking about your new home?"

Jim said, "Well guys we bought a villa in the south of France and we are now moving there to live".

John said "I will be damned you fucking-old fox. Both of you". Everyone started laughing and Molly got more drinks. Latoya helped. The girls decided to go down to the beach and John and Jim told them they would join them in a little while. The girls headed down to the beach and Jim and John talked about everything that had happened over the past three months. John told Jim about the city county deal and about the deal he had with Miles. Jim listened and after John had finished explaining everything, Jim said "Damn John don't you ever get tired of all of this? Shit you are like a fucking motor boat running on all cylinders all the damn time".

John laughed and said, "Hell Jim you wait until you have nothing to do and then tell me how fucking great retirement is".

Jim shook his head. Then Jim got very serious. Jim said "John I have no way to thank you for everything you have done for me. If it was not for you none of this would have happened and I would probably be an old retired Colonel still thinking about what used to be. Thanks, is all I know to say".

John said "Jim you are welcome, but believe me, everything you have you worked for and damn sure deserve. Hell, we got lucky beyond anyone's dreams at the right place and right time. Never again will that happen or at least not in our lifetime. It was just an amazing opportunity and we all made the best of it".

Jim said "I suppose you are right but thanks all the same. I will owe you until I die". John got up and got them another drink. Then they walked to the beach and sat with the girls. About 5 PM everyone went back to the house and showered and got ready to go out for the night.

The visit with Jim and Latoya had been fun. One day, Bob had taken them out fishing and they caught fish. Then John had driven them around the county and showed them where everything was planned to be built. Molly had taken Latoya to the foundation and showed her around and then they had gone shopping and sightseeing on the beach front. The 4th of July fireworks had again been quite a show and John had again furnished all the fireworks and paid for the people from Orlando to come up and do the show. John liked to do that for the town and would do it every year. Jim Y and Stephanie had joined the group for the fireworks and time at Ted's on the fourth. John still needed to talk with Steph, but she understood so she told John that there was no real hurry. Nothing was really pending that she could not handle so relax and enjoy his company. John appreciated that. The morning for Jim and Latoya to leave was now here and John and Moly took them to the airport and they all said good bye. Jim and Latoya boarded the jet and it took off. John and Molly drove back home and were both feeling a little sad. Harry had been the first of the original group to go away and now Jim and Latoya. Who would be next was anyone's guess. John and Molly got home, and another shot happened. Louise asked to speak to them so of course they sat and listened. Louise said "I am going to have to quit here. I am so sorry, but I need to go back to New Orleans for my daughter and her kids. She is very ill, and I just have to be there".

John said "Louise I did not know you even had a daughter or grandkids. Why didn't you tell us about them?"

Louise said "Mr. C I am a very private person and things were never good with me and my daughter. I was not allowed to even see her or the kids when her husband was there, so I just did not try any more. I am sorry but now he is dead, and she is very sick, and I need to be there".

John got up and put his arm around Louise and said "It will be Ok I promise and yes we understand. Now you calm down and after a bit we need to talk about how we can help".

Louise said, "Thank you" and went toward her room. Molly was almost in shock. John got her a drink and made a drink for himself. Beer would not get it right now.

The next morning John called the hospital at 8 AM and had them get Dr. J the Chief of Staff to call John immediately. At 8:15 AM Dr. J called, and John explained the situation and asked if J could get in touch with doctors in New Orleans and find out where to take the daughter. Dr. J said "John I will call but it may take a few hours.

John and Molly were back home at Redman Beach. It had been five days since they had gone to New Orleans. A lot had been accomplished in the five days. Molly had taken Louise and the children shopping and bought new clothes for all of them. Then Louise and Molly had gone to a furniture store and bought furniture including appliances for the new apartment John had leased. Louise now had everything she would need to have a household. Molly had also gotten Louise a cell phone and it was paid a year in advance. John had been doing his business as well. He had leased a four-bedroom apartment in one of the better sections of New Orleans and paid the entire year in advance. John had all the utilities turned on and in Louise's name as well as getting her set for TV and internet. John had taken Louise to the bank, the one Fred had already spoken to, and set up her account with the $500,000 cashier's check. Louise was also given a credit card with a $50,000 limit and a debit card. The last thing John did was arrange for a car service to be available to Louise whenever she needed it. All those bills would go directly to John. The final thing John and Molly did before they left New Orleans, was to talk to the medical staff and find out what the situation was. It was good news, because Louise's daughter had been moved out of ICU and was in a private room and starting to respond to treatments in a very positive way. The medical staff said it would be at least a month before the daughter could go home but they were confident she would make a full recovery. All in all, it was a good ending to a very bad situation. Now John and Molly had to hire some staff.

John was now back at work in the courthouse in his new position. He had moved Stephanie over to the county as the County Administrator and she had a small staff of three people working for her. Molly was at the foundation and busy making sure things were running smoothly. July was almost over. and Miles had sent all the required paperwork and studies to Stephanie and the permits for his projects were in the process of being issued. The tentative start date was September 1st and the first four projects were new hotels. John and Miles had realized that Redman Beach did not have enough hotel rooms available to have a construction project as large as the one that would be on-going, so the hotels were the first-priority. John also had the owner of the RV Park in a meeting and it was decided that small trailers would be an asset because the workers could rent these and stay in them during the construction. Mason, the RV Park owner could furnish 150 trailers in thirty days. John agreed that he would personally back Mason as to the financial situation in getting these trailers delivered. Mason would be the one paying for them, but to get the manufacturer to send them, John would be a guarantee for the money. The next thing John had to do was meet with Mike and KBR and they were due in on Wednesday. Jim Y came to John's office and wanted to discuss the jail situation, so John had him come in and sit. Jim said, "John I think we can be ready to start the jail project by September 1st and I have the plans ready".

John said "Ok Jim we have KBR coming on Wednesday, so I will let you know what time and where. Probably the country club".

Jim said, "Good I will wait to hear from you". Jim left, and John looked at what was on the table. It was massive.

Molly was at home and John came in about 3 PM. Molly said, "John I have someone coming at 5 PM and I want you to interview him for the House position".

John said "OK but did I hear you right? A him?"

Molly laughed and said, "Yes my dear a male". John got a beer and fixed Molly a glass of wine. At 5 PM on the dot the doorbell rang, and John answered the door. A man about 5 feet 10 inches and weighing about 170 pounds was standing at the door. John looked at him and saw he was blond and had blue eyes. He was dressed in a suit and tie and his shoes were almost spit shined they were so polished. The man said "Sir, I am Justin Miller. He stuck his hand out and John shook hands and invited Justin into the house. Molly said "Justin I am so glad you came. Can I get you a drink or something?"

Justin said, "No thanks Ma'am". John had Justin sit and then John said "Well, young man, tell me everything there is to know about Justin Miller".

Justin said "Sir, I am 42 years of age and single. I have a degree from Cameron Technical Institute in Physical Therapy and Physical Massage and hold both licenses in the State of

Florida, Texas, and Nevada. I also have a degree in Restaurant Management from the Culinary School of America and I have a degree from the Cordon Bleu Institute in Paris, France. I speak, read, and write, English, French, Spanish, Italian and German. I hold a Concealed Carry License in Florida, Texas and Nevada. And the last thing you should know about me is I am Gay".

John said "Well that is very damn impressive, and I am very glad you were forth coming about being Gay. You see Justin, I could care fucking less about that and I feel that is never a problem so long as you take care of yourself and from what I see you have and do. Now why do you want to work for us?"

Justin said "Sir, I have worked as a therapist and as a chef and it was alright, but I have also worked two years as a House Manager for a client that passed away two months ago. I found that being a House Manager and doing the work required was very satisfying and I think that is my calling. I have done some research on you and Mrs. Carter and although it did not really tell me much, I feel I can and would be very good for you in the position".

John said "I think so too. Now tell me about what you will require as a salary, time off, and all of that?"

Justin said "I am looking to make something around $50,000 per year, with living arrangements. I was making that at my last position so yes. $50,000 would be the right amount".

John said "I think we will look at a salary of $100,000 per year, and of course you live here. Also, we will cover your medical insurance. Now, I will need to do a complete background check on you and believe me when I tell you this it will be complete. I need your full name, and aliases, your SSN, your date of birth and place of birth. Also, a list of every job you have had since you were 18 years old. So, how soon can I have that information?"

Justin said "Tomorrow morning I will have the complete information. Where do I send it?"

John said "Just drop it by the courthouse. I will get it then. The check will be done by tomorrow night so make sure we have your contact number".

Justin said, "Very good Sir".

Justin looked at Molly and she said "Justin I think we are going to make a good team all three of us. Thank you for contacting me".

Justin stood up and shook hands with Molly and with John and left. John looked at Molly and said "Baby, you sure know how to pick them. If this guy checks out and I am sure he will, we have probably found a diamond".

Molly smiled and said, "Yes we have, and I love it".

The next morning John arrived at the court house at 9 AM and the package from Justin was waiting for him. Stephanie had gotten it at 7:30 AM just after she arrived. John took the package and went to his office and read the information in it. There was one page that immediately caught John's attention. It was a police report of a shooting in Nevada that Justin had been involved with. The report was not very detailed, but John liked the fact that it was in the packet. John called to Houston and got Don on the line. John told Don what he needed, and Don said to scan the packet and email it to a number he gave John. John thanked Don, hung up and did what he needed to do. In three hours, Don called John and said "John I am sending a report on this Justin guy and I think you are going to be very pleased. Hell, where did you find him?"

John said, "I didn't Molly did".

Don said "Oh and by the way, we will be coming by to visit in about three weeks if that would be good. We are moving so we wanted to see you and Molly".

John said, "Hell yes, that is fine, but where are you guys moving?"

Don said "Tennessee. I will tell you all about it when we see you". Don hung up and John waited about five minutes and then the email came up on the computer. John printed the email and started reading.

Justin had an outstanding work record and had never been in any trouble before 2010. Then he was involved in a major gun battle in Las Vegas when three men tried to rob him after he closed the restaurant, he was the head chef. The police report detailed the event and it seemed that Justin had left the restaurant at 3 AM and was going to the night deposit as he always did. When he was in the parking lot of the restaurant three Mexican males jumped him and demanded the cash bag. They were armed and shot Justin in the side. Justin then pulled out his pistol and killed all three with only three shots. Justin was in the hospital for two weeks recovering. He left Vegas as soon as he was out of the hospital. His last job had been for a Billionaire that lived in Orlando and had died of cancer. John was satisfied and called Justin and told Justin to come to the house at 4 PM that afternoon. John called Molly and told her he was hiring Justin and that Justin would be at the house at 4 PM. John then did some work as the County Mayor and at 2 PM left the court house and drove to the bank and met with Fred. John got another debit card for the new household account and put Justin's name on the account as a user. Then John stopped by ACE hardware and had keys made for the house and for the SUV. Then John went home. Molly was waiting, and they had a drink and waited for Justin to arrive. Molly was thrilled, and John was very happy she was, and that Justin had worked out so well on his check.

Justin arrived as scheduled and John had him come in and then Molly, John and Justin sat on the patio and talked. Justin was wearing his black suit, with vest and a white shirt and black tie. John said, "Justin you can of course wear other clothes, we are really not that formal".

Justin said "Sir, I would prefer to wear this and I do remove my coat and work much of the time in just my vest. Will that be alright?"

John said, "Justin whatever you want is fine".

Justin was sipping on a drink and he said "Now Sir, what do I call you? You have so many titles. Is it General, Mayor or Mr. Carter?"

John said, "Well what would you like to call me?"

Justin said, "I would like to address you as Mr. C and your wife as Mrs. C if that is alright?"

Molly said, "Then we are Mr. and Mrs. C from now on".

Justin said, "Very good ma'am".

John then said "OK now Justin we spend a lot of time here and in the hot tub and pool and most of the time we are naked so do not get flustered if you see that. Just do what you do, and we could care less. Also, here is your keys to the house and the SUV. I want you to use the SUV when you go places for the house and to be our driver when necessary. Do you have a vehicle, I have never seen one?"

Justin said "No Mr. C I do not. I use taxi services so now I will use the SUV except when I am on my time".

John said, "Yes now tell me what you want as off time".

Justin said "For now Mr. C I do not require any set days. I would like to just give you plenty of advanced notice if I need time off. Will that work?"

John said, "Yes it will". John then handed Justin the debit card and an envelope.

Justin said, "I assume this is the household account I will use for all business but the envelope?"

John said, "Open it". Justin opened the envelope and removed a check. The check was in the amount of $8,334 Dollars and was made out to Justin. Justin looked puzzled and John said "That is your first month's wages young man. Now lets us walk".

John got up and Justin followed, and John showed Justin everything in the house, garage and Justin's suite. After the tour, Justin removed his coat and said, "May I fix either of you another drink?"

Molly said, "Yes you can". John nodded. Justin prepared the drinks. After a few hours, Justin said "If it is alright, I would like to go get my things and move in tonight."

John said "Justin that is a great idea, take the SUV and get what you need. We will see you later. We are going to Ted's for a while". Justin grabbed his coat and left. John and Molly went to Ted's.

Wednesday Mike and six men from KBR arrived and John met them, and they all went to the country club. Stephanie was already there and had a room set up. The county engineer and department heads from water and electric were there and so was Jim with the Chief Deputy of the Sheriff's Department. Everyone went into the room and sat at a huge table. John introduced the people and then said "We are here to start our projects. We have three major projects that KBR will do and one minor well at least it is the smaller one. I know how KBR works so that is why they have the jobs. One of the projects is my personal project but the rest are either the County's or the hospital's, so we will leave mine for last. Mike, how do you want to start this?"

Mike said "John let us start with the jail. That is going to be the most intensive one for us to do and we will try to work it on a 24/7 basis depending on weather of course. The other projects will be the same as for the 24/7 work. The water desalination plant will be the easiest because 90% of it will be per-fabricated in Houston and sent by barge to Redman Beach".

Mike continued to explain all the work each project at a time. The KBR contract was for the Jail, the hospital 700 bed expansion and a new clinic plus an expansion of the parking garage to hold an additional 300 vehicles, the desalination plant and holding tank of five million gallons and then John's office building, an eight-story building with a garage that would hold 500 vehicles. The total price for all of this was $5 Billion Dollars and $750 Million of that was John's expense.

Mike was finished and then the KBR people talked with the water and electrical people from the county and with the Chief Deputy about some of the immediate details. All the construction was to start on September 1st.

John, Mike, Jim Y, and Stephanie left the room while the engineers and project managers and department heads talked about the construction and went to the bar and ordered drinks. They sat at a table and Mike said "John my only concern on all of this is the fucking EPA permits and approvals. They usually take years and if we start some of the projects we can be fined if they do not approve our requests".

John looked at Steph. Stephanie said "Oh they are all sitting in my office approved and the licenses have been issued. Sorry I forgot to tell you, Mike".

Mike looked at John and said "John I have no God damned idea how you did that, and I really do not want to know. We will now have no problems".

John thought "Hell I pulled every favor in the world, but Liz came through like I knew she would. When the President says approve it now, usually the people do what he says and that is exactly what had happened". Jim asked Mike about the jail and how it would be connected to the present jail?

Mike said "Jim that will be the very last thing we will do. The exterior wall that is in place now will be opened after the new jail is completed so all cells will connect. It is the easiest part of the entire project". Jim was satisfied. The meeting in the main room was now about finished and everyone had the contact numbers, emails, fax numbers and everything else that was needed so John moved everyone into the dining room and had lunch delivered. By 4 PM KBR was back at the airport ready to leave for Houston and everyone else was either back at their offices or on the way home. John was heading home and ready to relax in the hot tub.

# CHAPTER 66

Don and Cindy arrived in Redman Beach on Friday morning about 10 AM. Don called John and John drove to the intersection where Don had stopped and led the way back to the house. Don and Cindy were driving a huge van and of course looked like something out of the 60's hippie era. Don parked in front of the house and Justin came out and got the luggage inside and into the guest room. Molly ran out and hugged and kissed Cindy then Don and John watched as the three of them went inside. John parked his car in the garage and joined the gang in the den. Justin came in and asked about drinks and of course everyone was ready for a drink. Don and Cindy were Margarita drinkers and Justin showed his talent by making a perfect one. Molly had her usual Vodka and club soda and John his beer. They all moved to the patio and sat and talked for a while. By the time Justin was bringing the $3^{rd}$ round of drinks, Molly and Cindy were sitting in the hot tub. As soon as John and Don got their drinks they joined the girls in the hot tub and continued to talk. Don and Cindy had bought a fucking mountain in Tennessee about three years before and were now moving there. Don explained to John that the new people had offered a job to each of them, but Don and Cindy did not like Capp or any of the new bosses, so they had declined the offer. Don talked about the situation and that USA would never make it the way Red Lion had done because there were too many controls on them from Washington. John had figured that might happen and he had warned Capp about that very thing. Cindy said "We now own this mountain, well we actually own most of the mountain and it is perfect. It is half way between Nashville and Louisville. The name of the town is Cook, and it has a population of 4000. We have bought an internet company there, but we did it, so we can do our thing anytime we want. The mountain is two miles out of town and goes up 1800 feet. There is nothing on it but us. We own 80,000 acers and we have two towers for cell phones and other communications on the mountain we rent to service providers. Don has installed five dish locations and we are using wind power for everything. We built four windmills to supply power to our place and of course drilled a well. We also put in a small but totally modern sewer/waste treatment plant. The house was completed a month ago, so we are on our way".

Molly said, "Well you two now have exactly what you want out of life don't you?"

Cindy said "Yes we do, and it is beautiful there. We want you and John to come visit".

Molly said, "That sounds like a plan".

At 5 PM all four of them were ready to go to Ted's and meet Jim Y and Steph. They arrived and saw Jim and Steph and sat down at the table they had. John introduced everyone and then ordered drinks and some food. Don and Cindy had a great time at Ted's as did Jim and Steph visiting with Don and Cindy and learning something about them. John and Molly listened to the conversation and went around visiting with people there at Ted's. The night was fun and about midnight John, Molly, Don and Cindy said good night to all and went back to the house. Don and John were going to meet Jim at the Sheriff's Department at 9 AM the next day so Don could install some special programs for Jim.

The installation went well and now Cobb County Sheriff's Department had software that only a very few people in the entire United States had. John was very glad because now, anything that was needed could be done locally without having to depend on the FBI or NSA or any agency in the government. The key thing was to make damn sure it remained a secret and Jim had that covered. Don had also upgraded the in-car computers for the Sheriff and Fire departments and now all calls could be sent with a map to the location. This was also in each of the EMS vehicles. This system could also be used by the county utility departments as well. Don and Cindy had also upgraded all the 911 operator's computers and the entire system. It took most of the day to get things right but by 3 PM everything was up and working perfectly. Don, Cindy and John left and returned to the house. Molly was in the kitchen with Justin and he was preparing the meal for the night. It was a special one he and Molly had decided to do rather than going out. Don and Cindy were leaving early the next morning so staying home was the best plan. When everyone had returned to the house, Molly got them drinks and they all went to the beach and sat and talked about the many adventures they had all had and what was next in their lives. Justin called everyone to dinner at 7 PM and it was spectacular. After dinner they all got into the hot tub and enjoyed after dinner drinks. Everyone was in bed by 10 PM and the next morning John and Molly said good bye to Don and Cindy at 8 AM. Don and Cindy drove out and headed for Tennessee. They would call and give John and Molly the contact numbers, emails and all of that when things were set up at the mountain. It had been a great weekend for everyone.

The next few weeks were busy for John and Molly. Molly had started a division of the foundation that promoted single women or women who had had problems in their marriages and were now single mothers or had never been married and had children to care for to start their own businesses. The foundation had staff that could guide the women in business plans, financing and other aspects of the business world and then the foundation would give a grant as startup money so these women could follow through. So far, twenty new businesses had been started in the area, which included Cobb

County and the three Counties that adjoined Cobb. Molly was happy with this new area and knew this would do some good. The foundation already had a division that helped men and anyone, but this was the only place single women could apply without having to show vast experience and other things normally required by banks or other organizations.

During the next three months, many things were working in the Redman Beach/Cobb County area. KBR had arrived and started on the jail, John's office building and the water plant. Miles had started his sub-divisions, hotels, strip malls and the factory. five additional companies had requested permits to start manufacturing plants in the county and the foundation was growing at a very fast rate. Over $500 Million Dollars had been donated to the foundation so far that year and it was now doing many things. John had met a new person by the name of Tim Davis and John had hired Tim and his firm to be John and Molly's CPA and the foundation's CPA. Additionally, Tim had a firm that dealt in stocks and bonds, so John had retained Tim for that function as well. Tim was in his mid-forties and had a very good background. Tim had done four years in the US Army and was familiar with military procedures. When John had first met with Tim it was a very intense meeting and Tim was, as he told John, "Totally astounded" at what John had told him about John and Molly's finances and the finances of the foundation. Tim was very sure he could keep everything secret as John had insisted and John believed that. The two men really hit it off and John now had his new financial advisor and accountant.

The Governor and State Senator plus the State Representative for the area had visited twice during the past three months and each time John had been very gracious and showed them all that was happening. The news media had always been along and now the national coverage was beginning to be a pain in John's ass. The last thing John needed or wanted was for a bunch of reporters to be asking questions and trying to make a huge story out of the new things going on. John talked to Jim Y and neither man could legally come up with a way to stop the media. The last resort was to give them total access to everything and that is exactly what John and Jim Y did. No having to register in the County office, no being escorted by deputies, nothing. The media could come and go as they pleased and in a matter of thirty days all stories were gone. It was just too easy for the media and if they had access there was no real story that would bring in the headlines, so problem solved. John was amazed at how fucking stupid the media really was. They still had a few reporters around doing human interest pieces, but even those were not gaining any real foothold nationally, so it became a simple situation of occasionally a story came out about something, but the story only helped the community. John was no longer mentioned in most of the stories and that was fine with him. The new construction on the hospital was now in full gear. John was especially interested in that and that is where the news media were given most of the information. John had also been asked to become a board member of the country club and he said yes to the invitation. Now that John was a board member, Tim had an idea. Tim wanted John to buy the country club. There were two main reasons. First the country club needed improvements and had no money to work with. Second was the fact that if John bought the club he would get a seven- year tax break because it was a natural item and it took longer than the three years to show a profit. The tax laws said seven years was allowed for things where nature was involved. John made the proposal to the board and the last of November, John bought the country club for $30 Million Dollars. New renovations would start in January and would cost about $40 Million Dollars.

Christmas that year would be in Midland at Miles and Linda's and John and Molly would attend. It would be nice to be with family and John knew Molly always liked to be around Linda and Donna. Ray was now going to run for State Senator and Miles was going to back him in the race. John would of course donate to the campaign and do what he could for his brother, but John was not able to do much now that he was in Florida. It was not going to be as easy for Ray as the other elections had been, but John had confidence Ray would win. The family was all together, and Christmas was a great success for everyone. John and Molly spent three days in Midland and then returned home for the New Year's celebration. John again was doing the fireworks thing and now it was becoming a tradition. The house next to John and Molly's on the north side had been for sale for two months. The doctor who owned it had bought a new place in Kyle's new sub-division and now on one lived in it. That was going to change, and John found out why three days before New Year's Eve. Dan called John and said "Carol and I are coming to Redman Beach tomorrow and have something to tell you and Molly. Can we stay a day or two with you if you are going to be in town?"

John said, "Of course and what is this news you have?"

Dan said "You will have to wait until we arrive. See you tomorrow. I will call you when we are about an hour out so if you do not mind, you can get us at the airport".

John said "You got it. I will tell Molly". John called Molly at the foundation and told her the news. Molly was thrilled.

Dan and Carol got off the private jet and Molly and John were waiting. After the bags were loaded and Molly had hugged and kissed everyone John headed the SUV toward the house. Justin was waiting and got the luggage in and fixed everyone a drink. They all sat on the patio and Dan said, "Well I guess we are your new neighbors".

John said "What! You have to be kidding me".

Dan said "NO we bought the house last week and we will close on it tomorrow at 10 AM. At the real estate office".

Molly was thrilled and hugged Carol again and again. That night everyone went to Ted's and John introduced Dan and Carol to many people including Ted and Jim and Steph. The next morning Dan and Carol went with Molly and John to the real estate office and signed the final papers and got the keys. Then all four went back and looked through the house. After the tour of the house, they all returned to John and Molly's house and got into the hot tub and pool and talked about this new life Dan and Carol were starting. Dan had passed the Florida Bar three months earlier and Carol had sold her stock in Molly's or at least most of it. Carol was now like Molly, a board member but only owned about 2% of the actual stock in the bar. Their furniture or at least what they had shipped should arrive the 2nd week of January. They had planned to buy all new things for the house and would also buy new cars. Dan asked John about a banker and John told Dan he would introduce him to Fred right after New Year's. John would also take them to the car dealership and the furniture store, so they could get all of that done. Dan also wanted to know of a good contractor and John said he would call Mike. Carol and Molly were talking about maids and all of that and Molly called Justin in and said, "Justin do you know of a person who could be Carol and Dan's Justin?"

Justin laughed and said Mrs. C. I have a person in mind so let me call him. Right now, he is in Orlando, but I think he would move. I will see and get back with you".

Molly said, "Thank you".

New Year's was again a total success and of course everyone had a great time. John had introduced Bob to Dan and Carol and immediately Dan started negotiations with Bob about the boat. Bob explained to Dan that John always no matter what had first call for the boat, but Bob would be open to Dan at any time John did not need the boat. Dan was satisfied with that arrangement, so another deal was made with Bob for the boat. Dan had met quite a few of the local people and he was now in the elite of the community. Carol had also met Molly's friends and she liked all of them and they like her. Carol had been invited to join some of the organizations the women were in and readily accepted. New Year's Day was spent lounging by the hot tub and pool. Some of the day was spent on the beach and that night John and Dan cooked steaks out on the grill for all. Justin had taken some time off and would return on the 3rd. The four people, had a very good time just playing in the hot tub, pool and in the house.

On the 2nd John and Dan went to the bank and John introduced Dan to Fred. Fred was almost overwhelmed when he found out how much money Dan wanted to put in his bank, but recovered fast and got things done in record time. Fred said "In 24 hours everything will be in place, but do what you need to do in the meantime, things will be covered. Now do you need any cash, Dan?"

Dan said "No Fred I have a few thousand and that should take care of things until everything is in place. I also have my credit cards, so I am fine". John and Dan left the bank and went to meet with Tim. Dan immediately liked Tim and they hit it off in grand style. The meeting with Tim lasted an hour and a half and when it was finished, Tim was now Dan and Carol's personal CPA and their financial advisor and broker. Just as he was John and Molly's. The last step for the day was to meet Molly and Carol at the car dealership. They all arrived, and Carol and Dan picked out cars. The vehicles would be delivered to John's house the next day. John and Dan were now set up to talk about what Dan was going to do. The girls left the dealership and went shopping and walking along the beach area stores and businesses. John and Dan headed for the country club and had a drink in the bar and discussed Dan's plans. Dan explained to John that he was not interested in having a private practice in any way. Dan had only gotten his Florida license because he wanted to always be licensed in the state he resided in. Dan explained to John that he wanted to continue to serve as John and Molly's attorney. John said, "I fully understand that, but would you be willing to be the foundation's legal person?"

Dan said "Of course. That is without saying".

John said, "OK now we need to get with Tim and find out what we need to do as a retainer for the foundation and for us personally".

Dan said "I understand, but I already have that handled. Whatever you pay me from the foundation and from your individual accounts I am going to donate that money to the foundation. Hell John, Carol and I cannot make more money that we do and not pay it all to the fucking government. That way we are not showing any income, and everyone wins".

John smiled and said "Thanks Dan. That will be a fantastic thing for the foundation". John and Dan had another drink and then left and went back to the house. Molly and Carol were there when they arrived. The next day Molly and Carol went to the furniture store and bought what Carol wanted. Dan and John met with Mike the contractor and Dan explained what was required. Mike said he could get it done in thirty days. Dan told him to start immediately. Justin had returned and told Carol he had found a person to interview for the job. The interview was done the next day and Dan and Carol both liked him. Jerry was a carbon copy of Justin and about the same age. He was also gay. Dan and Carol hired him immediately and he was to move in in three days.

# CHAPTER 67

January was now gone, and it was almost February the 14th, Valentine's Day. Dan and Carol's house was finished, and they were in and doing well. Molly was spending time at the foundation and Carol was also getting involved. Molly had also gotten some other business going through the foundation and they were all doing well. The construction was moving at a very good rate and the country club renovation and the building of the additional course was underway. John was now doing very little in the way of the commissioners and things in the city were going along without any problems.

John had gotten a call from Tress the day before and he was going to run for Mayor of Houston Texas. John knew this was going to be quite a deal and told Tress anything John could do he would. Tress thanked John and said "John if you can call some of your contacts here and see if they can support me it would be a great help. I am going to spend a bunch of money on this, but then thanks to you I have it to spend".

John said "Hell I can donate, I need it for taxes anyway. I will send you a check. Now who is your major competition?"

Tress said, "A couple of lawyers, some civic leaders and of course the black and Mexican candidates they always run".

John said "OK I have an idea. Run on your military record. I will make a call or two and see if we can get an election-specialists down there".

Tress said "That would be great, Thanks General. You never let me down". John hung up and put in a call to Liz. She called back, and John and Liz discussed Tress's situation and Liz said she would call Tress and get the ball rolling. John thanked her and hung up.

John was sitting at his desk in the court house and going over the notes for the commissioner's meeting. It was in an hour and nothing big was on the docket. The phone rand and John said "Hello". It was Tress. Tress said "I want to thank you again Sir. The election specialist has arrived, and we are going to do the campaign planning this afternoon. She will be here all the way and she was on the President's campaign both times. She is very good, from what everyone tells me. Thank you again".

John said, "Your welcome and good luck". John hung up and walked toward the commission room. The commissioners were there as were the county attorney, and Steph. John sat down at his position and called the meeting to order. There were only four items to discuss and they were mainly about the construction. The county engineer presented the updates and gave an estimate of the time for completion of certain phases. Next was the Sheriff and Jim Y presented his request for additional officers. He wanted to hire twenty new officers and the commissioners approved that request by voice vote. The next item was a request by a civic organization to use the county fairgrounds for an event. The event was a fund-raising event for the Star of Hope Mission and the request was approved subject to the contract that was always done being signed and a bond posted. The final item was the extension of the filing deadline. A request had been submitted to extend the filing deadline for county offices by sixty days. This was voted down by all commissioners. John then closed the meeting.

For the next eight months John and Molly enjoyed life as beach residents. Bob took the boat out many times with Dan, Carol, Molly and John on board and each time everyone had a very good time. At night Ted's was always a popular place to go. John was doing some campaigning and so there was no doubt he would be elected. One person had signed up to run against him, but it was not even a real challenge. John did not take it lightly and did do campaigning and bought TV ads and radio ads. John also ran full page ads in the local newspaper and sent out mailings to all residents of the county. The national campaign was a total mess, and no one knew who would come out the winner in any of the races. The American public were very tired of all politicians and especially the Congress. The Presidential race was between two people who no one really liked but they were the only ones running so it would now be a best of the worse-case vote. Ray was doing well in his race for the State Senate and was twenty-eight points up in the polls. Tress was also ahead in his race.

The elections were on and the polls were open. John and Molly voted early, and John made a couple of stops around the polling places and campaigned as he could. All the county races were sounding like everyone was winning that John hoped for. The national races were another thing all together. John had decided to have his watch party at Ted's because Ted was also on the ballot running for Mayor. Almost all the county people were running, and they were all at Ted's. The results were now coming in and it looked very good for all the people John wanted in. By 8 PM the results were 95 % counted and John, Jim Y, all the commissioners, Ted, the other city council members, the District Judge and the associate judges had all won. Now everyone waited to see the National out comes. John had called Ray and Tress and so far, both had a commanding lead.

The night was now almost over, and it was 4 AM and still no results for the Presidential election. Many of the Senate races were over and twenty-four Senators had lost bids for re-election. Only six Senators had remained in office. The house vote was historic. 75% of the house had been replaced by the voters. It was the largest replacement of incumbents in the history of the United States. Twenty-Seven Governors had also been replaced by new people. About 6 AM the news media finally declared a winner in the Presidential election. The new president-elect was from the opposite party the current President was in and from the makeup of the new Congress his party would control both the House and Senate. The next day John had word that Tress and Ray had both won and now in January John, Ray and Tress would be sworn in for four-year terms, and then we would see how things would go then. John and Molly were sitting in the hot tub when Carol and Dan came over. They joined John and Molly and all of them had drinks and relaxed. The day slipped away and about 11 PM Dan and Carol left and went home. John and Molly went to bed. Molly was sleeping, and John was thinking about everything. Things had really changed since John had been in the military and now they were even stranger. John thought about how of the original five couples that had been involved with Red Lion an unusual bond had developed between them. Over the many years, each couple had always enjoyed being naked in almost any environment, but the funny thing was no matter what no one did anything of a sexual nature with anyone other than their partner. It was always with their partners. There was never any suggestion or an attempt to swap partners or even have a three some or anything like that. If the girls wanted to do something with each other, that seemed to be a very acceptable thing and on many occasions, they had but never had anyone had a relationship of any type with another person's partner. John knew that would be very hard for anyone to believe. John liked it that way and he was very glad that was the way things were. John drifted off to sleep.

# CHAPTER 68

The next three years had gone very fast it seemed to John. The construction was 99% complete on all the projects that had originally been started. The Jail, hospital, John's office building, the golf courses and the country club and three of the four manufacturing plants were completed. The water desalination plant was completed and on line. The mall was going to be completed totally in two months. Of course, there was other construction on-going, but the major projects had been completed. The jail contract with the Federal Government was signed and it was for a period of five years. Jim Y was very pleased and had been able to hire three more jailers. The foundation had moved to John's office building and now occupied three floors. Other offices had been leased and the building was 95% full. The top floor had been built as a restaurant and Justin had his friend/significant other lease the restaurant and create a first-class dining place for Redman Beach. The bank had grown very large and now had four branches open in the county. The bank building was now used by the bank except for one floor that was still occupied by a law firm and a contractor/architect. Miles' housing development was almost sold out and people had moved into the county because of the jobs available. The county was now over 250,000 in population and growing every month. The average income was $92,000 per year. The country club had expanded the membership and now had 2400 members. Life was great in Cobb County and fantastic in Redman Beach.

John was contacted by a representative of the President and asked if he could meet with the President before John went back. John agreed to the meeting and called Dan to come to D.C. immediately. John set the meeting for Monday. Dan and Carol arrived Sunday afternoon and all four met in the hotel bar and had drinks and John explained to Dan what was going on or what he thought was going on. Molly and Carol decided to do some sightseeing Monday, while the men were at the White House. The meeting was at 10 AM. John had learned that the new owners of the old Red Lion had not only moved the new company to Arizona but had sold the container ship, the C-141 and now had only twenty operators and very little internal staff. The piolets for the C-130 and the helicopters were still there, as was the ground crew for the maintenance but the medical personnel and most of the logistical personnel were no longer employed. John and Dan were scheduled to meet with Martin Savage, an old and dear friend of John's the day before meeting the President. Martin had been in Washington D.C. for over 50 years and knew everything about everything that happened in every administration as well as almost everything that happened in the United States concerning the people who had the money and control of government. The circle was extremely small, and John had purposely never gotten involved with the "Golden 20" as they were called. John and Dan arrived at Martin's residence at 5 PM and his butler showed them into the den where Martin was sitting. After the introductions and hellos were done, the butler got John and Dan a drink and then Martin said, "John how can I be of help to you?"

John said "Sir, tell me about the company that bought Red Lion and why they are downsizing it?"

Martin said "The people who bought your company were not who you thought and were in fact not acting for the good of the country. John, you had built up an organization that was feared by every country in the world and by the "Golden 20" especially. You had no idea how fucking powerful you were. Even more powerful than the God damned President.

That my boy scared the shit out of everyone, so they knew killing you was out of the question because your people would track them down no matter and because your people could and did run the company as efficiently as you did. You made damn sure of that. The only thing to do was buy you out and that is exactly what they did. Take away all threats. Let you think it was Ex-Presidents and retired Generals but you now see it was and is not". John and Dan sat and listened to Martin as he explained the entire plan. Martin spent three hours telling John and Dan how the new group was going to be used and John did not like it one damn bit. Dan also saw many problems that would arise, and he also knew with the right control these people would run the world and no one could stop them. Martin said "John that is why the new President needs to speak with you. He needs to know how to stop this group and not let it get out that there ever was a Red Lion or anything like it. I sure as Hell do not have the answers to tell the President, I just hope you do".

John said "Sir, I have the answers, but the question is will the President like how I will present them and then, will he follow the course of action I recommend?"

Martin said, "That I do not know". John and Dan thanked Martin and said good bye and returned to the hotel and took the girls to dinner. During dinner Dan and John discussed the next day and how John was going to approach the meeting. Molly and Carol both listened and made some very good suggestions.

At 9 AM the car was waiting in front of John's hotel and John and Dan got in and the driver headed to the White House. John was wearing a dark blue business suit and a white French cuff dress shirt. The cuff links were gold and had the emblem of Special Operations on them. John had a lapel pin showing he was the recipient of The Congressional Medal of Honor. The only ID John ever used in Washington D.C. was his Military ID showing that he was a retired Four

Star General officer. Dan was dressed in a dark gray suit with matching vest and white shirt also French cuffed. Dan had a red tie and the cuff links were gold and had his initials on them. Each man had on black highly shines shoes. The car stopped, and John produced his ID as did Dan and the guard passed them through the gate and on to the north door of the White House. The Marine guard opened the door of the car on John's side and when John got out the guard came to attention and saluted John. John returned the salute and waited as Dan came along side and joined John. The men then entered the north doors and an usher lead them to the elevator. When the elevator doors opened John and Dan were in the waiting area for the Oval Office. John had been there many times over the years. In three minutes the door to the Oval Office opened and a lady said "Gentlemen, the President can see you now. Please go in". John and Dan walked into the Oval Office.

The President was standing in the front of the room and said, "Good morning General". John saluted the President and said "Good morning Mr. President. You remember Dan my council?"

The President said "Yes nice to see you again Dan. Now please sit and let us talk". John and Dan sat in the Queen Ann chairs and the President went behind his desk and sat down. There were six men in the room beside the President and the President introduced each man. The Secretaries of State, Defense, Homeland Security and the Army were all sitting together in chairs. To their right was the Attorney General and to his right was the head of the Joint Chiefs of Staff. John made a mental note that the CIA, FBI, NSA, or ATF were not there. After the introductions the President said "General Carter we have a very serious problem and would like your help with it. Actually, I would like your help".

John said "Mr. President I will be more than happy to try to assist. What is the problem, Sir?"

The President said "Jack, tell General Carter what our problem is".

The Secretary of Homeland Security said "We are very concerned with the people who bought Red Lion, they call themselves USA. Our problem is that they are not asking Washington for anything before they act. In fact, they have been acting in direct conflict to many of the President's policies and so far, they refuse to even meet with us and discuss what their role should be".

John said "I would like to speak very frankly and if I do so, I am going to say things that will offend you Mr. President and probably everyone in this room. If I cannot speak plainly then I see no need to continue this conversation, with all due respect".

The President said "John I know your reputation and please tell us exactly what is on your mind. Hopefully we have thick skins".

John looked around the room and took a deep breath. John said "Mr. President your problems is very simple. First you have no fucking policy on anything. No foreign, no domestic nothing. This administration jumps from one God damned thing to another and nothing gets resolved or fixed. You have stopped doing what must be done, well actually you never started. The entire world looks at the United States as being weak and knows nothing will ever happen but maybe a sanction or two may be put in place that does not mean a fucking thing to most of the people who we have problems with. Yes, this new group acts without your authority and approval because they can. They are owned and financed by the "Golden 20" and these people will do anything necessary to keep their way of life. Hell, if they were not who they are, we would be looking at them as potential terrorists. Home-grown and all".

Not one person moved or said a damn thing. John looked at the President and he was not very happy. John said "Now

Mr. President when Red Lion was first formed or when I was first asked by the President, then in office, to form a team to do what was necessary to protect the country and to make damn sure nothing ever got back to the President, I believed in one simple thing. My Oath. That Oath said "I do solemnly swear that I will support and defend the Constitution of the United States against all enemies, foreign and domestic, that I will bear true faith and allegiance to the same, that I take this oath freely, and that I will well and fully discharge my duties of the office upon I am about to enter. So, help me God". Mr. President that is the same oath you and everyone in this room took. I did then and do now firmly believe in that oath. I took on the job I was asked to do and believe me Sir, we made a bunch of mistakes along the way. We became way too big and because of that we were looked at by many people as a threat, the former President when he took over damn sure thought of us as a threat and he forced us to become a civilian firm and was still not sure he needed us until things went so God damn bad he had no other choice. He too had no fucking policy for anything and that is why the country is in the shape it is in today. Mr. President when you won the election it was put out by your camp that Red Lion type companies would be no longer needed. If that was true or not I do not know, and I do not care. Because of your way of doing business, I knew it would be only a matter of time before you would phase out Red Lion or the new company that bought us. That is why we sold out and disbanded".

The President said "General you are right about how I feel business should be conducted for this country. But the world is not ready to accept my ways or even accept anything but war and chaos. As I remember you also worked for the "Golden 20" on more than one occasion".

John said "Yes Sir, we did, and we had the blessing of the former President every time. He used what we did to make deals that helped the country and helped create many things only certain people could make happen. In the long run what we did was to stop terror in many parts of the world to include inside the United States. That is the point you and the men in this room do not understand or accept. Being right and doing the right things is one thing but when the time comes, you turn your back and call for guys like me to get the fucking job done no matter what it takes. So far you and your people refuse to accept that little detail and that is why you are in the bind you are now".

The President said "OK General. You have made your fucking point. You do not like me or my administration and how we are running the country. Fine. But now can you tell us how to fix this problem or is this just another big talk no action deal?"

Dan said "Mr. President if I may. There are two immediate fixes to the problem and both are legal as Hell. First you have the power to re-call all the Generals to active duty. That is in the contract when they accept a Flag position. So, do it. If they refuse, then General, (Dan pointed to the Head of the Joint Chiefs), you charge them with AWOL under the UCMJ. Send them the re-call orders and give them a report date. If they do not report charge them and have CID arrest them. Also, if they do not report stop the retirement, which should be stopped when the orders are published"

The Head of the Joint Chiefs said, "What the Hell do we do with them when they arrive at the Pentagon?"

Dan said "Now Mr. Secretary of Defense this is when you come in to play. They will be assigned to you as Special Advisors. Yes, give them aids, secretaries, offices all the things Officers of their rank should have. Then Mr. Secretary, make sure they have nothing but bullshit to review, but, have them brief you once a week. It will not take these Officers but about four days to figure out that everyone knows exactly what they were doing and planning. The "Golden 20" will get the message loud and clear and no one will have to say a damn thing".

Dan then continued "Then the second thing you Mr. President, need to do is get with your predecessors explain the situation to them and get the Presidential Executive Orders that ran Red Lion and even before including all the contracts and special slush funds. Then cancel all of them immediately. Believe me Sir, the former Presidents do have copies of the orders. All Presidents keep things like that for their memoirs".

The President looked at the Secretary of Defense, the Head of the Joint Chiefs and then at John. The President said, "I understand that but now how do we get a group together to work for us like you did John?"

John said "Now Mr. President you issue an Executive Order of your own for whatever you want. Remember the team must have funding and Congress can never know about that. Also, it must have access to everything it needs whenever it needs it. I would suggest that three things happen. Number one, the team be no more than twenty operators. Keep them military no matter what. That was our mistake. Secondly, use the authority you have, to promote each member at least three pay grades above what they are now. Promote both Officers and Non-commissioned Officers. The team should be made up of Delta Force personnel and SEAL personnel. And the third and most important part is to make damn sure each member of the team understands that they do not have to follow the law if it is necessary to do something for the mission. That part the Attorney General will just have to live with. Mr. President the men you finally get will be the best of the best and they will believe in the Oath just as I do. Also, they will believe in protection of the institution of the Presidency and making damn sure nothing can track back to you".

John then said "The last thing I offer is that you Mr. President need to set up one person and only one person to be the go between for the new team and you. Make damn sure the person you choose is not in your inter-circle spotlight but is totally 1000% committed to you and your ways. This is an absolute must or things will leak. They always do in Washington".

The President said "John and Dan thank you for coming and for stating your true opinions and giving us your expert help. I am sure I will need to speak with you again". John and Dan rose, and John saluted the President and the men left the Oval Office. The meeting had gone on for over one hour and John and Dan both thought it had been more. John and Dan went down to the car and got in and headed to the hotel. Both men were drained and exhausted. When they arrived at the hotel they went to their suites and changed clothes and met at the bar for a drink. Then they had a few more drinks and discussed the meeting. John and Dan went to the sauna then to the steam room and then hit the cold plunge. They returned to the suites and the girls had gotten back from their day on Washington. Everyone dressed and went to dinner at the Capitol Grill then enjoyed the night life in Georgetown. They were back at the hotel by 2 AM. The plane back to Redman Beach was scheduled at 11 AM.

# CHAPTER 69

John and Molly had been back at Redman Beach for two months and things had been going smoothly. The foundation was doing great things and Carol had become a very great help to Molly with much of the foundation work. John had turned over all the old Red Lion facilities at the airport to the Cobb County Sheriff's Department, who now had two helicopters, and to the State Police for use when they needed it. The hospital now had an Air Evac helicopter that flew from the hospital pad and used part of the old Red Lion area for mechanical work along with the sheriff's department people. John was now ready to totally retire and enjoy life. He was still the Mayor and head of the commission but that was a very simple job now. Allan Marine had come in and requested a permit to build a barge terminal and that had been approved. Construction was well underway, and the railroad was now going to run spurs to all the factories and to the terminal.

John had gotten word that all the Generals had been re-called to active duty and that USA was now bankrupt and out of business. The "Golden 20" were going crazy and that was not a good thing for the President, but he was handling it well and he had clamped down on a lot of things they tried to do so they were now having to go along with him despite the problems.

On Monday in April, John received a call from the US Army Chief of Staff and was asked if he would go to Ft. Bragg and meet with the new commander of the Special Operations Team that now was the President's new deal. John agreed, and Tampa sent a Black Hawk to pick John up on Tuesday morning. On Tuesday John boarded the Black Hawk and in 2 hours he was landing at Pope AFB at Ft. Bragg. A staff car was waiting, and John was driven to the Delta Operations compound.

John walked to the entrance gate and showed the MP on duty his ID. The MP immediately saluted John and showed him into the compound. John was wearing tan linen slacks and a yellow silk shirt open at the collar. He had on brown suede shoes and was carrying a brown suede sport coat over his arm. A tall man about 6 feet 3 inches wearing a battle dress uniform came toward John and saluted and said "General I am Command Sergeant Major Hollis. The General is expecting you Sir, please follow me". John had returned the salute and followed the CSM into the building and into the Commanding General's office. John saw a man of 6 foot and slender build get from behind the desk and salute. Then the two-star general said, "General welcome to our little team".

John said, "Nice to be here, and what is your first name, General?"

The Major General said, "Bob Sir".

John said, "OK Bob let's talk about what you have here and how I may be of help". The men sat and talked about the new unit that was now formed. Bob explained that the unit was made up of twenty-two actual operators. The teams were broken down into eleven-man groups with a full Colonel as the head of each eleven-man team. Then a Sergeant Major was leader of each of the five-man teams when it was necessary. The rest of the operators were Master Sergeants or Sergeant First Class in rank. Then Bob said "General we also have a special asset well actually two of them. We have two female operators. These ladies are Warrant Officers and are specialists in intelligence gathering. They are fully trained as operators and have been through all the training that the male operators have done so they can function on any mission. The inside group consisted of two Intelligence officers in the grade of Lieutenant Colonels. Then there is a Master Sergeant that does the computer and cell phone work". The CSM John had met earlier was the operations control for the entire unit. Bob then explained that all logistical support would come from Bragg and air support would come from Pope AFB. John said "Bob sounds like you have things well in hand. Now tell me about your people".

Bob said "General all of them and I mean all have done combat tours at least two. All are US Army and either Delta or SF. My Intelligence people were with the Ranger Battalions as S-2 Officers. The female operators came to us from the CIA and I personally picked them. They had been on loan from the Army to the CIA so recalling them was a very simple process. They are experienced and speak our languages".

John said "I am very impressed so far, Bob. The females are probably going to be one of the best assets you will have if and only if they have no moral hang-ups. I feel you will use them in many areas as things progress".

Bob said "Now General I would like you to address the entire unit and please tell it like it is. Would you please do that for us?"

John said "Of course, but Bob if I really tell it like it is, you may just lose some folks".

Bob said "General, I am willing to take that chance". Bob called the CSM and had him notify every member of the unit to come to the briefing room immediately. The CSM also brought coffee in for both Generals.

The Generals sat and finished their coffee and then Bob lead the way to the briefing room. John entered and stood by the door as Bob walked onto the slightly raised platform in front of the room. All personnel were standing, and Bob said "Good day, we have a very special guest with us today and he is going to speak to you. General". Bob pointed his hand and arm in John's direction and John walked to the platform. John said, "Please take seats". Everyone sat. John said "I am here to day to speak with you about what you will do and many other things. My name is General John Carter. I am now retired, but I was the Commander of Special Operations Command for some time and then I was the founder of the first unit like this in the US Army. Then I opened a corporation called Red Lion and expanded what units like yours do about 1000%. Some of you may have heard of Red Lion and even me". The unit was quiet and listened to every word that John spoke.

"I want to talk to you about what you will be expected to do and what you will have to do to survive in this job you have chosen. The basic job is that of a professional Killer. That is the long and short of it. You are not required to take prisoners unless that is your mission. There are no innocent people ever. When you are given a mission and a target that is the only damn thing that matters. The Mission! No matter what it takes get the Mission done. You will be working against enemies both foreign and domestic, just as it says in the Oath each of you took. Today this country has damn near as many enemies inside it as it does outside. The FBI, CIA, NSA, NIS, ATF and Homeland Security will not be your friends or allies in the long term. Use them like they are informants and never under any circumstances tell them a God damn thing about yourself, the unit or any mission you are on or ever have been on. You will work directly for the President of the United States, but no one will ever know that. You cannot tell your wife, girlfriend, boyfriend, or your mother or father what you do for your country. Secret is the word you will live by for the rest of your lives and it even goes higher than that. It is only known by three people in the government that this unit even exists and that is probably three too many but of course some things must be known. Now, I suggest that if you have morals you get fucking rid of them. There is absolutely no place in this unit for morality. What I mean by that is you as operators will use everything that is available to you to get the mission done. If it means having sex with someone then do it. If it means finding out the deepest secretes on people do it. The key to winning is that you are better than you enemy. An example of that is this. One person is the target to be eliminated. However, when you arrive there are four others in the house, room, whatever so you must be able to eliminate everyone no matter gender, age or anything else. Then and only then are you a Complete Operative".

"Now the last thing I would like to discuss with you is each other. The bond you must make will be stronger than any bond you have ever made with anyone in your life. There are twenty-eight of you in this unit and as of now you must think of each person as your brother or sister, wife or lover. This must be the most important person in your life and looking out for their safety is vital to success. The only people who you can count on are in this room. If you all do that you will be the best damn unit in the fucking world. I also hope you as the days and months go forward remember the words you heard here. The ways that were used when this type of unit was first started are just as important today as they were then. No matter what is said or what people think, you and your type of unit are vital to the United States remaining free and a world power and leader. Presidents, Generals, and especially politicians come and go, and policies change with the flow, but always it comes back to this type of unit to do what no other can. I wish all of you good luck and good hunting". The unit immediately stood up and the entire unit came to the position of attention and saluted John. John returned the salute and exited the platform. John walked out of the room and Bob followed. As John was walking down the hallway he heard the CSM give the command. "Unit dismissed!" John followed Bob to Bob's office. A Colonel took John to the airfield and John flew back to Redman Beach on the Black Hawk.

# CHAPTER 70

The summer had gone by quickly or at least John thought so. It was the start of September and Labor Day was in two days. John and Molly had spent a lot of time together and it was wonderful. They had walked on the beach, picnicked in a special section of the beach about four miles away from anyone or anything and acted like they were twenty again. They had also been very interested in watching the TV news reports of the problems in the Middle-East and in Israel. Major fighting had again erupted between Israel and the Palestinians and it was not going to end quickly. Fighting had increased in Afghanistan and it was coming on twenty years US Troops had been fighting there. Iraq was also in a mess and fighting was heavy there as well. The US had sent troops back but as advisors only. John knew better, but the administration could not admit that these "advisors" were Delta, Special Forces, SEALs and even some standard infantry combat troops. The new terrorist group had increased and now they were an army with over 400,000 followers fighting in three countries. The Russians had also been causing problems in the Ukraine and that too had been going on for at least four years. Other spots were also seeing an increase in terror activity. At home, the race issues were as bad as they had been before the 1964 Civil Rights Act. In a period of twenty-three days young black men had been shot and killed by white men, six of them being police officers and all the men killed had been unarmed. No charges were ever filed and that sent the entire nation into a frenzy. There had been marches, looting of areas, burning of buildings, stores, police cars, and even schools in nine cities so things were very tense. Many people were calling for a revolution and to have the country taken over and the politicians immediately removed or worse. John was very glad Redman Beach and Cobb County had no such problems. In fact, the race relations were better than they had ever been. The Sheriff's department had 28 % of their officers from the black community and 5% from the Latino community. The fire department had about the same mix.

Labor Day had been very good and of course a parade was held. John and Molly had watched from the foundation windows and had really enjoyed the scene. John was putting the finishing touches on the Golf Tournament and it was already being worked on at the country club. Molly had completed another phase of hiring and placement and the foundation was again creating opportunities for many low income or unemployed people in the county and throughout the country. Things were good, and John and Molly liked the situation a lot. On Friday Molly asked John if it was alright if she invited some people over on Saturday afternoon and then had a dinner party. John agreed so Molly got with Justin and things started happening. The invitation was given to Dan and Carol, Jim Y and Steph, Ted and his girlfriend, Kathy and Bill her husband, Lucy and her husband Ed. All the people were friends of Molly and John and they all said yes when they were asked. The event was to start at 2 PM and continue through the night. John had no idea what was going to happen but that was always the fun of Molly doing things. Justin and his friend would be serving and cooking.

By 2:30 PM on Saturday everyone had arrived, and the guests were having drinks and lounging in the pool or hot tub. John and Dan were sitting on the patio watching the events play out. By 4 PM hot of the group had taken off their swim attire and were totally naked and still enjoying the hot tub and the pool. A few couples had gone down to the beach and were enjoying the water. They were also naked. It was exactly what John had figured would happen because all these people loved to be naked and have fun. John and Dan decided to join in and they removed their clothes and sat in the hot tub and relaxed and sipped their drinks. It still amazed John that no one ever had any sexual contact with anyone other than their partner. No matter how much people drank or smoked in certain circumstances, it never happened and as a result no one ever got mad or angry. John knew no one would believe that many adults, and basically good-looking people could run around naked and only have sexual contact with their partners. At 7 PM everyone was now coming out of the pool and hot tub and up from the beach and starting to get dressed for dinner. Justin had arranged for people to use the guest rooms and his apartment for changing and showering. Dan and Carol had also invited a few to use their house. By 8 PM everyone was changed and back at John and Molly's and enjoying a cocktail. Dinner was to be served at 9 PM.

The guests were now all sitting at the table and Justin was serving the first course. The first course was a sea food delight with shrimp, crab, lobster and oysters. It also had some sliced cheese of three types. Justin poured the wine he had selected to go with the course and everyone started to enjoy the food and drink. The second course was a Cesar Salad made at the table and Justin showed off with his skill. The guests loved it and enjoyed the salad. The entrée was spectacular. It was a special cut filet broiled and a lobster tail served with a sea food cream sauce containing sea scallops, shrimp, crab meat, and lobster on top. Mushrooms accompanied the entrée as well as asparagus and twice backed potatoes loaded. Fresh bread was also served with each course. The sauces for the steaks was also special and had a tremendous flavor. It was a mixture of Brandy and goose pate and had a lot of real butter in it. The entire meal was not on the diet charts. Everyone was enjoying the food and wine, Justin had again picked another wine to go with the entrée, so more wine was flowing, and the conversations were good. By 11 PM everyone had finished, and Justin had cleared the dishes from the table and brought out expresso coffee and a small B&B liquor for all. The crowning glory was the home-made Cheesecake topped with fresh strawberries in a special sauce. Justin had just completed serving when the house telephone rand. Justin went to answer it. In a matter of two minutes Justin came back into the dining room and walked to John. Justin leaned down and whispered to John," Mister C, you have to take this call immediately Sir". John looked at Justin puzzled and then Justin said, "Immediately Sir". John got up and excused himself and walked toward his office.

John saw the secure phone laying on the desk and picked it up and said, "This is John Carter". The voice on the other end of the line said, "General Carter please hold for the President of the United States".

In less than ten seconds the President was on the line and said "General what I am about to tell you is so very terrible it is hard to say. One hour ago, Telavi Israel was hit dead center by a nuclear missile. Also, the port of Hypha was hit by another nuclear missile. The reports of dead are in the tens of thousands and the wounded are greater than that. They are in the hundreds of thousands. Most of the Israeli government is either dead or wounded. The city is in total chaos and the port is on fire. Now General, I know that on Monday if not before the Congress will declare War. It looks like the missiles were fired by the ISSL terror group but so far, we do not have exact intelligence, and no one has claimed responsibility. It could have been the Hamas, but we are not sure, and the last idea is the Iran had in fact bought weapons from the Russians. Everyone is of course working every source they have but as of now all we have is two massive explosions that are nuclear. John, I do not know exactly what if anything you will be asked to do but I want to know if I can count on you if your country needs you once again?"

John said "Mr. President I shall remain at your disposal. Please keep me or have someone keep me informed. Thank you for advising me Sir. God be with you, Mr. President". The phone went dead and John hung up.

John walked back into the dining room and people were laughing and talking. Molly looked at John and said "Honey what the Hell is happening? You look white as a ghost. Who was on the phone at this hour?"

John sat down and told Justin to get him a Brandy and some coffee. By now everyone was looking at John and no one was talking. Justin returned with the Brandy and coffee and John said, "Thanks and go turn the TV on CNN". Justin left the room. John took a long drink of the Brandy and said "Ladies and gentlemen, my friends all Hell has just broken out and by Monday if not sooner the United States of America will be at WAR! That was the President on the phone. Two nuclear missiles have been fired into Israel about two hours ago. One hit dead center in Telavi and the second one hit the port of Hypha. Hundreds of thousands are dead and at least that many wounded. Radiation is all over the country as the winds blow. So far no one has claimed responsibility. That my friends are where we now stand. I suggest we all move into the den and check the news coverage for a while. Justin will get you drinks or whatever you would like".

The entire crowd was silent and almost in shock. Then everyone moved into the den and Justin brought out glasses and the Brandy and left the bottle, so people could pour as they desired. Justin then went into the kitchen and he and his friend watched the TV there and started the clean-up process.

Dan asked John if John was going to be involved again. John said "Right now I do not know. Things are moving very fast and all I do know is hundreds of troops are preparing to head for Israel. I am sure the British and other countries are doing the same so now we wait".

Molly had snuggled up to John on the couch and was holding him very tightly. She was very upset. In an hour everyone had gone, and John and Molly moved into the hot tub and both were naked and sipping on Brandy. Molly said, "John what does this mean?"

John said "Sweetheart I do not know, only time will tell. I do know this. Things are very bad and are going to get one Hell of a lot worse I am afraid" ……………